Green Mountain Breakdown

By

Robert A. Pittman

The author is a former member of the Vermont House of Representatives. The inspiration for the hero of the novel, Bill Parker, is still serving in the House, although under another name. This book looks at Vermont's present political climate and suggests that from a legislature that borders on the far left can come the breeding ground for unexpected consequences for every Vermonter.

ISBN 0-7414-2790-7

Published by:

INFINITY
PUBLISHING.COM

1094 New DeHaven Street, Suite 100
West Conshohocken, PA 19428-2713
Info@buybooksontheweb.com
www.buybooksontheweb.com
Toll-free (877) BUY BOOK
Local Phone (610) 941-9999
Fax (610) 941-9959

Printed in the United States of America

Printed on Recycled Paper

Published October 2005

This is the third Bill Parker novel
set in Vermont by Robert A. Pittman.

Others are:

The Legislative Body

Still Waters

§

This was a great small-stream trout fishery. But you had to know the water. And you had to appreciate everything about this little gem of a trickle coming from somewhere in the hills and emptying into the big river. And the fisherman standing on the edge of this magical little stream was a champion appreciator, never more so than this evening. The beginning of a rising moon was in evidence, the flying bugs had stayed home, and all was right with the world of fishing for this fisherman who was stalking his prey. He was always very happy on the water. If anyone at that moment had told this fisherman that tonight was the last calm and untroubled evening for him for the next several weeks, and perhaps forever, he would have looked around, completely surprised, to see if it was actually he who was being addressed.

And it would have been.

§

1

It was getting on toward evening when Bill Parker, former member of the Vermont House of Representatives, presently holding the titles of President, CEO, Treasurer, and Clerk of the Bill Parker Insurance Agency of Bridgeton, Vermont, intently squinted at the slowly flowing water coming down toward him. He was waiting for his arch enemy to show himself, and being still and quiet was essential. While doing nothing but waiting with a total intensity that would be seen as impressive by any onlooker, Parker's thoughts automatically slid over to all kinds of different subjects, even, God forbid, his little insurance empire. Probably I'm thinking about it, he thought, because of my guilty feelings of neglect of my small but active business.

His Secretary and partner, Mrs. Irene Doughton, without fanfare or a public announcement of any kind, actually ran the agency - and Parker knew it. But he still had the titles, and that both pleased him and, at the same time, because Parker was an honest man, made him feel slightly inadequate.

Parker was a graduate of the University of Vermont at a time when that meant something. He was a farmer's son before that and, most important to Parker, a semi-expert dry fly fisherman who had just decided to change the fly he was using to defeat his targeted opponent.

This was no small project. He was crouching behind a large boulder on the edge of the Chateaugay, a small trout stream that ran down through the center of Bridgewater Center and dumped into the Ottauquechee River, just west of Woodstock. He had been in this painful and numbing position for 35 minutes, watching a nice native trout eat its dinner by sipping aquatic life from the top of the water at two-minute intervals, regular as rain.

Of course, every nice trout was a brook trout to Bill Parker when the fish was still in the water. Most of the time they turned out to be rainbows or browns - nice fish, but not the legendary brookies. He was therefore mildly disappointed on most occasions, but he was very certain this time.

Addie, his tolerant wife, when she heard about her husband's frustrated fishing hopes for native trout, remarked that it was just like the baldheaded kid who kept trying to kick a football held by a bratty little girl who kept snatching it away at the critical moment. Parker was not pleased to hear that slant on something as important to him as was wading around in cold water.

As Parker was tying on the fly, he again noticed the car. It was moving along on the streamside road, which was about eight feet higher than the water in which he was presently freezing the lower half of his body. He noticed the car because it was moving more slowly than the road could handle, and this was its fourth trip along this road, constituting a rush hour for Bridgewater Center. It also had what sounded like a bad valve, and it made a distinctive sound to the trained ear of Parker, who owned an ancient pickup truck. A bad valve positively shouted at him when he heard it. This bad valve was looking for something, or somebody, he decided. If they want me, thought Parker, they'll have to wait. I have an appointment with a nice native trout.

Parker stood up, slowly and silently, creaking here and there, and watched for the slight disturbance of the water surface where this trout was feeding. Darkness was moving in around Parker, seeming to drift in through the trees on the edge of the stream like a grayish fog, and whispering to Parker that he was almost out of time. He quickly began to strip line from his reel in preparation for what he knew would be the finest cast of his life over this 35-foot stretch of water. The fly, Parker knew without doubt, would be exactly what this native was looking for - except for the hook, of course.

And the cast was pretty decent, too, he knew, as the line snaked out, uncoiled and settled gently on the slowly moving water and the ten-foot leader loosely deposited the fly right where the trout had been feeding. Parker could just see his lure in the thickening light when he also noticed, about five feet away, the telltale dimple of a feeding trout that had changed its supper table location solely in order to frustrate Parker.

Well, thought Parker, grinning inwardly, this guy sure succeeded in avoiding my obvious skills with a fly rod. Another time, he thought, without any frustration. There was a lot more to brook fishing than catching fish, he knew. He coiled up his line as it drifted back to him. He'd had a great two hours on this little stream. The time included seeing two deer, a flock of turkeys, and four small, but legal, rainbows he was taking home. Addie would be delighted.

As Parker climbed up from this placid and beautiful little brook onto the road, he remembered the time, a year or so ago, when his friend, Marvin Bailey from Bridgeton, thundered into his office one Saturday morning after being attacked, as he put it, by a bear and her cubs on this little stream. It turned out that both the bear and Marvin ran away from each other, and never saw each other again. Parker still chuckled when he thought of that wildly loud and humorous episode as described by Marvin.

Parker slogged along the road, boots flapping, to the bridge he would cross to his truck, which he had parked in the tree line along the brook, thinking good thoughts and of good deeds he would perform for Addie. Maybe she would even clean the fish, although that was doubtful.

As he neared the bridge he could see a glint of chrome from his pickup through the line of trees along the stream. Good, he thought. Nobody had stolen it. Addie had once said that his truck would only be stolen by some museum director from down country on vacation in Vermont. It was at that moment, he thought, as he trudged along, that he knew that Addie would never understand the ownership loyalties demanded of the owner of a pickup. Her loss, he mused.

As he reached the end of the bridge, he saw a second car, engine idling, parked beside his truck. He knew by the click, click, click sound that it was the bad valve looking for him.

He walked across the bridge, looking at the car, trying to see inside. He reasoned that if an ambush was planned, keeping their engine idling was not too smart. So, no ambush, but Parker was still wary.

William Parker had become the most wary citizen in Vermont since his escapades with two nuthouse killers in Vermont during the past three years. He wanted to say that things were safer in the Statehouse when he was in the Legislature until he remembered he had "taken a bullet for freedom", as Doc Malcom described it, "from a demented woman with a rifle". A great exaggeration, Parker decided. After all, what did a psychiatrist know about the mind. They were all crazy themselves.

He reached his truck, walking along the passenger side of the strange car to the truck's driver's door. Since he didn't know who it was, he proceeded with care, and keeping clear of unknown people in unknown cars in remote areas was exhibiting that sort of care. This care, or caution, or probably fear, Parker would say, was based on his experiences of the last three years. He had, during that time, been shot, been threatened, been damned near burned to death, had caused the death a man in the dome of the state's capital, and had been a party to the death of another man in northern Vermont. And maniacs and boobies, or "psychologically unprepared" people, which is what the Mental Health monopoly in Vermont might call them, had been the culprits in all of these occurrences.

He noticed that the vehicle carried a decal of a Burlington car dealer on its rear bumper. There certainly weren't that many of those identifying vehicle marks in these parts. As far north as most of these settlers went was to Bethel when they wanted to buy a vehicle, and that was a trip avoided whenever possible.

There was no sign of activity inside the visitor's car.

Parker casually sat down on the running board of his truck, his every sense humming under the surface, and removed his waders, taking his time, every once in a while shooting a glance into the visiting vehicle. He was trying to give off the aura of coolness under fire, of not being anything but in control. He knew he wasn't too good at that sort of thing, but it seemed appropriate at the moment. It was too dark to really see the driver with certainty, but Parker thought it was a woman.

He stood up, pulling off his fishing vest, tossing it and his grubby hat into the space behind the seat, stretched, and then leaned over and tapped on the window of the mystery vehicle.

The window slid down and he heard a familiar voice from his legislative days. "Hello, Mr. Parker. Remember me?"

He thought he did. And then he knew who it was. It was Jan Evlin, the writer from the Chittenden Free Progressive daily paper. His first clue to her identity was a very slight lisp in her speech, almost unnoticeable. It certainly wasn't unattractive, and it didn't inhibit her from speaking out. It was just something he noticed. One of Parker's legislative friends was George Shaver from the Northeast Kingdom, and he had called her the "reporterette". She was about the only woman in Montpelier, having been identified in this way, who didn't believe that George had assaulted her feminine dignity to the extent that she would sic the Governor's Commission on Women on him and, if that didn't work, sue him, using any number of hungry lawyers in Vermont for the purpose.

It was this woman who was willing to risk her career to report the truth about Parker's discoveries of the corruption of Vermont's legislative direction of the past thirty years. It was this woman who took on the high priests of Vermont's extraordinarily leftist news media, including Dieter Paine, Morton Draft of VTEliteTV, Donald Flake of some news "service" or other, and the list of interesting characters that populate National Public Radio, and Vermont Public Radio, too. And with the ProgDems' daily newsletter, the Mid-Vermont Bugle, thrown into the mix, it was a dangerous place for the responsible printed or spoken word to venture. Pravda, Parker thought, if it was still in its old business, would have been in about third place in a "distort the news" contest if a competition on this subject were held in Vermont. Vermont needs about eight more "reporterettes" just like Jan, he thought, to go into the trenches against these old and ignorant leftists.

Parker leaned down to the open window. "Jan, of course I remember you. It's nice to see you again. It's been awhile. But what in the world are you doing out here? And how did you even know I was here?"

"I called Addie, Mr. Parker, from a pay phone." Parker noticed, without even thinking about it, that she was careful to tell him that she had called from an outside line. He couldn't figure out why. "She described where you'd be. Quite a lady, Mr. Parker. She never asked a question of me."

"What I meant, Jan," Parker said, "was that you know where I live, and you've met Addie. You could have waited for me at my home and we could have talked in comfort in my kitchen."

Jan said nothing in answer to Parker. In fact, she may as well not have heard him at all.

She said, "Mr. Parker, what I've got to tell you must, really must, remain between the two of us. I can't be seen with you, and you can't be seen with me. You will learn why if you're willing to talk to me. And then, of course, you'll have to believe what I say."

Parker studied her for a few seconds. Then, as if making up his mind about something, said, "Follow me, Jan," and clambered up into his truck, started up and drove across the bridge, unwilling to listen to any argument from Jan, and back into civilization, followed by the sound of a bad valve.

2

Parker headed back toward Woodstock on Route 4, and then abruptly pulled in to a hamburger and ice cream stand that is a favorite of the tourists and locals together. The former enjoy it because it's a quaint thing to do, and the latter because it's a place to go with kids while the parents regain their sanity. It was also a place where Parker and Jan could talk, either in a vehicle or at an outside table on the river's edge and, Parker hoped, hide out in plain sight. Parker thought about that "hide out" business, and wondered what it was that he was "hiding out" from, other than trout. Oh well, he thought. If it's important to Jan, then it's important to me.

This dispenser-of-calories emporium was located not far from the local weekly newspaper, The Green Mountain Criterion. This paper is seemingly an extension of the Mid-Vermont Bugle and its empty editorial policy in support of any candidate who wants increases in the size of government programs of any type, while ignoring the failures of the same sorts of programs already in place. Parker could never understand these people. Unless, he thought, their educations had consisted of indoctrination, rather than ways in how to think, by instructors who themselves had been poorly educated at some august, and expensive, education factory with a fancy name.

Parker wheeled in to an out-of-the-way space and watched Jan Evlin roll tentatively in beside him. He got out of his truck and walked over to her. "Jan," he said, "let me get something for us. Are you hungry? I certainly am." He glanced at her and then he took the time to look at her more closely. "I think you're hungry, and need food and coffee right away. I also think you're exhausted. Food first. Then we'll talk. What'll it be?"

Jan gestured with her hand to indicate that she wanted nothing. Parker said, "Refusing food, such as it is, Jan, is not one of your options. Cheeseburgers, coleslaw, fries, and coffee okay? That probably exhausts their menu anyway."

She nodded, a slight smile on her face, and Parker turned and went to the counter before she could say anything more.

The food line was long and the wait for his order, once Parker had given it, seemed interminable. He was finally the recipient of a hastily packaged order, but it had been twenty minutes before he finally got back to the car.

Jan was deeply asleep, snoring with a soft and muffled buzz. Parker decided that she must need both sleep and food, but food had to come first because he had gone out and gotten it and he was hungry. Callous of me, he thought.

He tapped on the window and, receiving no response, thumped on it with authority. Jan came up from sleep almost like a fighter getting up after a ten count. "Mr. Parker?" she asked groggily.

"The one and only," Parker answered. "unlock the doors and let's eat."

Parker plopped into the passenger seat and deposited the bag of burgers on the space between them. Jan seemed to decide that she needed food after all and, along with Parker, started opening the various packages of great tasting goodies.

She had taken two large un-ladylike bites of her cheese-burger before she said anything to Parker. "I hope, Mr. Parker, that you don't think I'm silly for coming all the way down here tonight. I also want to personally express my regrets in the accident that resulted in the death of your great friend, Dick Obrist."

Parker thanked her for her sentiments, noticing that her knowledge of Dick's death was limited to describing it as an accident. And that's fine with me, thought Parker. The Dick Obrist death is a closed book, and the murderer is dead. Nothing else needs to be remembered.

"No, I don't at all, Jan, but you must admit that it's a long drive for you to come here to see me when we could have met closer to your hometown, or at least in Montpelier, which I still visit once a month or so."

"That's why I'm here, Mr. Parker. That's why I said that no one must know that we have met and talked. We couldn't have met up there. Both of us are very well known up there. But down here, with you in those ridiculous fishing clothes, I have safe haven, I believe. And I'm scared, Mr. Parker."

3

Parker looked at her and could see that her face, in the dull illumination of the outside light streaming in from the busy hamburger stand, had the look of the hunted. Her eyes were hollow, and carried dark rings around them. And she had definitely lost weight. Whatever it was that had caused this change in her, he thought, she must think it's very real, and it was confirmed by the trouble she took to find me.

"Tell me, Jan," Parker said, keeping his voice as calm as he could, "what did you say to Addie when you called her? Did you hint at being afraid, or concerned, or upset? Do you think that Addie is wondering about your call, or did you tell her something that would not start bells ringing in her mind?"

"No, Mr. Parker, I'm certain that Addie has no idea of the reason for my call. I simply said I needed you to fill in some details on a major feature story I'm writing for the paper. And you were the only person who could put this detail into a perspective that would fit what I'm writing about. And I said this in a way that indicated only the professional interest of a reporter with a deadline to meet."

Parker nodded, thinking to himself, "This woman doesn't know my wife at all. Addie has an almost Sherlock Holmes way of dissecting information and the nuances in its delivery and then knowing what was really said without hearing any of the necessary words".

At the beginning of his marriage, when Parker discovered this talent of his wife, it scared the hell out of him. He eventually got used to it, and then became glad that she was that smart. He never admitted that to a living soul. And he certainly had never told Addie that he had discovered this secret weapon of hers.

"Well, then, Jan, let's hear your problem, although I don't know what I can do about it. I'm older now than when we first met, you know."

Jan looked at Parker with a slight hint of a smile on her face. "You'll do, Mr. Parker, you'll do."

Parker settled back in the passenger seat, watched Jan, and waited.

Suddenly, Jan blurted out, "What do you know about the non-profit industry in Vermont, Mr. Parker? For example, The VNRCAUC - the Vermont New Relativism Council Against Uncontrolled Commerce? Or other non-profits, like the Continuing Tradition Trust for the Victims of Capitalism, or even state programs, funded by taxpayer money, such as GAGS, the Global Association for Geopolitical Solutions?"

This was the last subject that Parker expected to hear about. He remembered the occasions when he, and others in the House, asked for specific information from these public and non-profit institutions and he had always felt that they were never forthcoming. It was almost as if they had something to hide from scrutiny so they danced around the questions.

After a brief pause to collect his thoughts, Parker said, "I know almost nothing, Jan. I've heard of them, of course, and I know that some of them are not what they seem. Is this what we're going to be talking about?"

Jan glanced at Parker, and then said, "Mr. Parker, what I'm going to talk about is the very profitable non-profits in Vermont. And the Trusts, initially set up by innocent people long dead, operated by present-day types of people who don't give a damn about anybody but themselves, and turning Vermont into a third-world state, allowing only the very rich to live here, governed by their people through their political action committees. That's what we'll be talking about." That got Parker's attention. The general thrust of what she said was all too familiar to him. What now, he wondered?

Parker remained silent, watching Jan seem to visibly prepare herself to unload information kept under wraps for too long.

"About two months ago, Mr. Parker, I got a call from my editor to come to a meeting in his office. You may know him. His name is Hal Birdsall."

"I certainly do know him, Jan. He was, in hindsight, and as far as I could tell, the only person in the Vermont media who believed what I was saying on the day I was used for target practice on the House floor. His paper didn't like me very much, however."

"He's a good person, Mr. Parker. A very good person." Jan was quiet for a second or two, and then suddenly started talking again. “Well” she said, “to continue. I thought, for some reason, that there probably would be a dozen people at this meeting, like all the other meetings I’d attended in that building. The purpose of this meeting was a mystery, of course, but even that was explainable, I told myself, and never gave it another thought.” Parker was watching Jan as she spoke, and could see that she was warming to her subject, and silence on his part was the flame that would keep this dish cooking.

“Imagine my surprise,” she continued, “when I arrived and there was nobody else there. And then my editor told me that nobody else had been invited, either. I wasn’t at all uneasy, but meetings alone with your editor, and I a lowly reporter, just didn’t happen. Maybe to other reporters, but not to me. I knew this man quite well – he was a friend of my parents - and he acted, I thought, well, odd. To be honest, I thought he was going to fire me for some reason or other.”

Jan suddenly said, “Oh, and one other thing, Mr. Parker. I had entered his office through a back door, probably built to allow him an escape hatch for use once in a while. Like the Governor’s office in the Statehouse, you know. In all other meetings in his office people attending came in through the door from the more formal main entry, past his secretary. But this time, he required me to come in through this escape hatch.”

Parker thought about that point, but it had no significance for him. “Was there something that happened at the paper that was worrying to him? I mean, something that you had heard rumors about, but wouldn’t alarm you as a ‘lowly reporter’? Anything like that?”

“Don’t you mean a ‘reporterette’, as Representative Shaver calls me? And yes, he still does call me that, Mr. Parker.”

This little remembrance from the past had caused Jan to try a little joke. Parker noticed this and hoped that talking to somebody like him about her problem would help her to relax.

“There was one possible concern for my editor, other than the fact that his office was awfully cold that day, and he complained bitterly about it to somebody. When he spoke that way I thought he might be under some strain about something.” Jan thought about what she had just said. “Well, that doesn’t really mean anything, does it? It just popped into my head as part of an answer to your question.”

Parker wondered where this was all going and was about to ask Jan what possible help he could be. "There *was,* however, one other thing, Mr. Parker," she said, after a few seconds of studied thought. "I can't say, of course, that this occurrence was bothering him enough to cause him to act irrationally. But, here it is, for what it's worth. A few months before my meeting, Mr. Parker," Jan said, "his brother had been killed in a hunting accident in the Northeast Kingdom. Losing your brother would be enough to upset anybody, but wouldn't reach as far down the line to somebody at my level. We all felt sorry for him, of course, but our work just went on. After all, it seems that somebody gets killed during hunting season every year or so, doesn't it?"

Parker said, "That's why I remember him, Jan. I read about somebody named Birdsall, and when you said his name, I remember reading about a hunter being killed up there in the Kingdom. It's a rather uncommon name, and that's why I remembered it."

Jan nodded, and took a sip from her coffee. She also finished off the last of the fries, which Parker had reserved for himself. "Thanks for the feast, Mr. Parker. It hit the spot."

"At your service, Ma'am," he said.

"Then my editor said something that surprised me," Jan said. "He told me he'd had his eye on me for two years - ever since I sent in my stories about you and what you had found going on in Vermont, and got shot while doing it. He thought that what I had turned in was 'brilliant'. Honestly, Mr. Parker, he said that."

"That shouldn't be a surprise, Jan. Those articles you wrote *were* brilliant. You became a real reporter during those wild days. And you created massive envy in the rest of the communications world, too. Specifically, I was thinking about Morton Draft of VTEliteTV, and Dieter Paine, columnist for that weedy little paper in Burlington that, along with the Mid-Vermont Bugle, is the daily and weekly newsletter of the ProgDems in Vermont. They were in a real tizzy, weren't they? It was beautiful to see. And they have a new starlet up there now, don't they? Gracie Taller is her name, I think, and she's just as hard-left, and ignorant, as that other reporterette who works for the Bugle – what's her name? Suzy Smatter, or something like that. Where the hell do they find these people? Well, sorry, I changed course for a second. Keep talking, please, Jan."

"Mr. Parker," Jan said, looking at Parker with warmth, "you gave me all the information, the time line, and the incredible detail of the night you spent in the capital dome with a madman. You also gave me a copy of the police recording of that night. All I had to do was assemble it into a series of articles and send it to my editor. I know who I have to thank for any plaudits I received."

"Jan, you organized all of it. I couldn't have possibly done that. And I knew I could trust you to do a proper job with that material. I don't say that lightly. In that Burlington swamp you work in, there are no others who could, or more importantly, would have been brave enough, or independent enough, to do what you did."

Jan was pleased at this, and it showed in her face, which was more relaxed by far than it was when they had met earlier in the evening.

"Well, Mr. Parker," she said, "I was at a meeting to receive an assignment, and it was an assignment about which I was not to reveal that it came from the paper. Just that it was a long-term project that I would be doing that would be a feature someday. All on my own, you see."

Parker was astounded. "You mean that the paper was not to be involved or connected to your work? Isn't that strange? Is that usual in your business?"

"It most certainly is not normal, Mr. Parker. In my experience, assignments were something that your paper wanted researched. We didn't blab about them because other reporters wouldn't care anyway. However, we would talk about an assignment if someone else might have some information on the subject. I suppose that I shouldn't rule out secret assignments, if that's what we want to call this, but I never heard about one, and believe me, Mr. Parker, a newsroom is filled with all kinds of gossip, mixed in with the rare fact or two. I've learned that after a while everything comes out. But no secret assignments ever surfaced. And why would the paper disassociate itself from the work one of its reporters was doing?"

"But you had a secret assignment handed to you, didn't you - if you would take it?" Parker said this in a quiet way, hoping to quiet her down from her sudden spurt of excitement.

"Yes, Mr. Parker, I did, and I accepted it, too. It seemed, at the time, a lark. I already knew something about the topic. I admired the non-profits for their work, and their unselfish direction, as represented by their mission statements. And I had many friends who worked for non-profits. And many volunteers, too, are my friends."

Jan seemed to drift away for a few seconds at that point, as if trying to line up in her mind the order of things that she would say, before she plunged into the part of her story that would determine whether Parker would help her.

"However, Mr. Parker, as I got deeper into the subject in that first week of working on the story, I became concerned. My ideas and notions of the role of the non-profit organizations in Vermont were changing. I seemed to be sliding into some sort of a murkiness that blurred them in my mind, and their reasons for existing, too – at least that's what my imagination told me anyway. I even told myself that I was being completely silly. Probably too much on my mind, I thought. But then, today, something happened that made me leave the newsroom and come all the way down here to find you, fishing in the dark on a remote trout stream. I want something from you, Mr. Parker, but I'm not sure I know what it is yet. I know that that sounds strange, but it's true." Jan was staring straight ahead as she talked, her voice feathery and light, faltering despite the effort she was making to communicate her anxiety to Parker.

"Jan, I'm not sure what you want either. And then I'm not sure what I can do, even when you tell me what's upsetting you. I've been away from your world in Montpelier for three years, you know. Tell me what it's all about. And why you came to me, when others up your way would no doubt be more knowledgeable, just as discreet, and therefore more suitable." Parker patted her shoulder as he spoke, much the way he'd pat one of his dogs in a thunderstorm.

Jan looked directly and steadily at Parker for the first time that evening. "You really don't know, do you, Mr. Parker? You have no idea why I've come to you and no one else?"

"That's right, Jan." Parker was puzzled by this turn in the conversation.

"For the same reason, Mr. Parker, that all of the reasonable people I know in the Legislature would come to you for quiet help if they needed it – on any subject. You see, you are remembered."

Parker tried to say something to that comment, but Jan just plowed right on. "You have a reputation in Montpelier, Mr.

Parker, for being a very stubborn man in all things, especially when you are on the track of something. And you are unafraid."

Parker was struck dumb. Her words conjured up in his mind the image of an old, mangy hound dog, sniffing along, and bumping into things. Walt Disney had it right in Lady and the Tramp.

"That's why I'm here, Mr. Parker. I need help of the kind that I know can't be supplied by anyone else. And don't forget that I know you very well because of the information that you and Mr. Obrist supplied only to me three years ago. I trust you, Mr. Parker. I won't say that about anyone I have ever known, including my own kids. They'll tell a secret first, and then get on to the hum-drum stuff later."

"Jan, listen to me. I was afraid almost to immobility all through that situation when Kerm Mayes was murdered in the Statehouse. I admit that freely. I think I can keep a secret, but I'm no great brain. And I am getting older. Don't put me on a pedestal. I definitely don't deserve it."

Jan looked at Parker with a slight smile. "All of what you just said, Mr. Parker, makes me glad that I made the drive down here tonight. There are so many people who try to give the impression that they are brave, thoughtful, smart, and loyal. Only a few might meet those standards. You do, and your denial of those attributes, when you have proven otherwise under real pressure, make you a rare one. You wouldn't know how to let a person down."

"For goodness sake, Jan, enough," pleaded Parker. "Give me the story that has affected you so much – and made you afraid, if I'm any judge."

Jan hesitated, took a deep breath, and said, "I had a death threat, Mr. Parker. A real one. Just this afternoon."

Parker visibly started when he heard this. "A death threat, Jan? How do you know? When did it happen? What form did it take?" Parker knew that she was extremely upset at this point, and he also knew from experience that it becomes very easy to misread any external signals when that sort of pressure exists.

"I'll be glad to tell you, Mr. Parker. But let me get to it in my own way. All right?" Parker nodded, still watching Jan closely. He could see that this was a very upset woman. Just give her the space to tell her story to me, he thought. The story will be clearer, and she'll be better for it.

“My doubts started within a day after I started working on the story,” Jan said. “I had just gotten through talking with a classmate of mine from high school, who works for one of the non-profits in Chittenden County. She’s one of the people that I knew was close to the subject of non-profits, and I still hesitated to contact her for fear that she would innocently say something to someone who would think that I was working on a story about them for the paper, and Mr. Birdsall wanted this all kept quiet. You can see the difficulty, I’m sure.” Parker affirmed that he understood.

“What I found out, however,” she continued, “was that she was having real doubts about her employer and, surprisingly, she came to me. As I think about it now, it was actually funny, in a way, because we both sort of danced around the subject, I more carefully than she, in and out, back and forth. I suddenly realized that she wanted to talk with me about the non-profit industry in Vermont, and her employer in particular, but was afraid to say anything because she didn’t know how I’d take it. It seemed that this was a decision she made on-the-spot – you know – not premeditated.”

Jan cocked her head at Parker at this point, and said, “By the way, Mr. Parker,” in a tone of determination that he hadn’t heard before, “did you know that there are, at the present time, 592 non-profit organizations in Chittenden County alone?”

“What?” yelped Parker. “That can’t be true. There aren’t that many causes in the world to support them all. Just in Chittenden County? I’d be almost as surprised if you told me that there are 59. But 592 is unbelievable.”

“You can believe it, Mr. Parker. I’m in a way of being an expert on this subject. And did you know that the non-profit industry in Vermont is the largest employer in the state? In second place is the state government. WBM, the electronics plant in Chittenden County has dropped to third place.”

“My God almighty,” wheezed Parker. “And these non-profits can all raise money from outside sources?”

“You bet, Mr. Parker. ”

Parker felt his anger fizzing in his mind. “Well, Jan,” he said tightly, “what’s coming next?”

“First of all, Mr. Parker, I’m using no names. Okay?” Parker nodded firmly.

"Our conversation took place on Church Street in Burlington, Mr. Parker, in one of those sidewalk cafes. I remember it was chilly, and I suggested we go inside, but she wanted to stay out there. There was only one other person out there, about two tables away. My friend told me that it was too crowded inside and would make it difficult for two old friends to talk. I remember that that reason seemed somewhat lame because we saw each other at least every month at school board meetings, but I let it pass, of course." Jan lowered her voice as if to keep secret what she was saying in this closed space.

"Then she told me that her employer, the Truth, Prosperity, and Sharing Coalition of Northern Vermont, was only a political action machine for the ProgDems, and that all of their 200 employees and many of the thousand volunteers in the northern half of Vermont were candidate recruiters and campaign workers for the hard political left up there."

Parker had suspected that something was off base about many of the Vermont non-profits. He just didn't know what. Addie had done a lot of volunteer work for non-profits near Bridgeton, and had gone to many meetings around the state as a representative of those organizations in the Bridgeton area. She had stopped that activity all at once about three years earlier. Parker hadn't thought to ask her why.

He had made a couple of forays into the inner workings of some of the big ones himself but never got anywhere. He learned, however, that the non-profit industry as a whole didn't like him too much. He never knew why.

"She also told me that most of the money they bring in has nothing to do with the social commitment they advanced in their mission statement," Jan said. "No one ever asks them to report their revenue and how it's spent – or at least no one ever audits them and their reports. They have to report their activity information annually, of course, in order to maintain their tax-exempt status - and they do, but these statements to the IRS don't match what's going on. In fact, she told me that some financial expenditures are not even explained. She has heard some people laugh at what they are using the money for. She said that she knew for certain that thousands of dollars are being laundered and put into political campaigns. Can you imagine that, Mr. Parker?" Parker had no trouble at all in imagining that.

“And another thing that shocked her, Mr. Parker, was that they have on the payroll people who my friend had never seen. It was hard to find, but she was lucky. She found out, without really meaning to, that they were members of the Vermont House and Senate. This allowed people who supported their very far-left point-of-view to have no real financial worries while running for public office. I don’t remember them mentioning this fact when campaigning.” Jan was showing anger, her face reddening.

“And since she isn’t allowed to have copies of these tax status reports in her files,” said Jan, her voice tight, “the references to it are only in the form of her statements. So she says nothing.”

So that’s how it was worked, thought Parker. He was surprised that this candidate financing from a non-profit was so simple. But if no one was checking the annual reports with a suspicious thought in mind, then no one would know about this under-the-table support.

And many of these far-left non-profits had such pleasant and upstanding names, too. Sort of a tribute to apple pie, motherhood, and the flag, all the while maneuvering Vermont’s taxpayers into the impossible position of facing runaway taxation in support of legislation that none of the taxpayers would have ever wanted.

Beautiful.

And if true, and it certainly sounded believable to Parker, then there was no way out for any of us, he thought. Vermont voters elected these pied pipers of ignorance. When this racket is exposed, if it ever is, Vermont will have fallen back too far to retrieve without major surgery. And the people who could do this difficult job were leaving the state. And the other non-profits would use their media friends to trash the reformers. Everything is in place, Parker realized, for them to do whatever they wanted with other people’s money.

Jan intruded on his thoughts by saying, “She just blurted this all out, Mr. Parker. I told her to quiet down and tell me how she knew this.” Jan was almost angry as she talked to Parker, and he knew that she was deeply affected by what she had learned and what she was relating to him.

“How *did* she know all this, Jan?” asked Parker, prompting Jan to continue.

“She is an assistant accountant, Mr. Parker. She has seen many of the IRS statements they file, and has assembled many of the reports for the information regarding their contributions. She realized that less than half of their income was spent in support of their mission statement. So, she came to me, and she was not comfortable doing so, I can tell you that."

"Jan, why did she choose you to listen to this story? It seems to me that it was too important to her, personally, to risk her job to have just anybody listen to what she had to say. Maybe not, but that's one of my reactions, anyway."

Jan looked at Parker with satisfaction on her face. "Another reason why I'm glad I came down here, Mr. Parker, is that practical and skeptical mind of yours. And what you asked just now is another factor in the equation that has made me nervous about this whole thing. You see, my friend also said that she was telling me this because her employer had written a note to the Treasurer of the non-profit. The note said that they thought I was working on a major article on their industry for the Free Progressive newspaper. The Treasurer simply thought that my friend should see it, too. That's why she came to me."

Parker looked up at that. "How is this possible?" he gulped. "I'm assuming that you told no one what your assignment was, and I'm sure that Mr. Birdsall wouldn't have told anyone after taking all those precautions to keep things quiet about your assignment. True?"

"Very true, Mr. Parker."

"Did you ever have the impression that you were being followed, Jan? I know that that sounds very melodramatic, but it's a logical question."

"Not at all, Mr. Parker. Maybe I have been followed, but I don't think so. I can't imagine anybody following me. I'm just not important to anyone except my husband. I've never wanted to stand out in any way. I think I'm a good reporter, but I don't want any awards for it. I just like being at the Statehouse and writing good stories. No, Mr. Parker, my work life hasn't changed – until today."

"How do you account for this knowledge being out there?" asked Parker. "And not just in a select, small, group of people, either, I think, but possibly out there as general information. And that's because your friend knows about it and she isn't in any select group. Was it a mistake for her to hear about it?"

"I can't account for it, unless my editor let the cat out of the bag without meaning to. And I can't see that happening. He was so serious. I remember at the time that it seemed almost a personal thing with him."

"Let's go back to that meeting of yours with your editor. Were you convinced that he not only wanted the subject of your meeting kept private, but took extraordinary precautions to insure that it stayed just between the two of you?"

Parker could almost see the gears turning in Jan's mind, processing the remembrances of that day two months ago. After a few seconds, Jan turned to Parker. "Nothing special, Mr. Parker. All I remember is that he closed the door, and told his secretary that he was not to be disturbed. I thought we'd end up talking in hushed voices, too, but we talked in normal tones, although I don't know why I remembered that either. It just popped into my mind."

Parker nodded. "Well, Jan, we're at the point now where you believe you've been threatened. We've stayed away from that, haven't we? Tell me how you got that threat. And tell me if, after all we've talked about, you still believe you received a threat."

"That's just it, Mr. Parker," Jan said, as she twisted around in her seat to face him. "With all this talk, I wondered if my threat would diminish because I would find that I was looking at things in the wrong way. But no, I still know it was a threat."

"What happened, Jan?" asked Parker.

"It was very simple, really, Mr. Parker," she said. "Shortly after I met with her I had a message on my answering machine. It surprised me because she had never called me at work before. Her message was not difficult to understand, Mr. Parker. However, it was preceded by her telling me that she had been fired, just that afternoon, from her job of fourteen years with the Truth, Prosperity, and Sharing Coalition of Northern Vermont. The reason she was given was that she had become a 'risk', as they put it, to the mission of their coalition."

"A *risk*, Jan?" How could anybody in her position be a risk to their Coalition?"

"She told me that there was never any detail given. She just couldn't work there anymore. That was the formal statement and when she asked for the particulars of this charge, she was told that it had been determined by the leaders of the Sharing Coalition that she was a risk and that she presented to all the non-profits in Vermont the same risk. She also told me it would be useless for her to sue them over this."

Parker was angry. “Jan, there has to be more than this. And there has to be a remedy in law for these kinds of terminations. Wherever I’ve ever worked, and whatever companies I’ve worked with in my insurance business, they all had a set procedure for the employee prior to termination. A kind of ‘steps-along-the-way’ process, in which a person would be advised of behavior that had to change or specific improvements in their work. The company would discuss what he or she was doing, and then they’d help the employee to correct this behavior. No responsible company wants to have even a hint of unfair behavior toward its employees. And they don’t want to lose employees who have potential. They know that they can’t stay in business with a burden like the issue of unfairness weighing them down.”

Jan raised her hand slightly and said, “There’s more, Mr. Parker. When she was escorted to her office to pack up her personal things, the woman who had been given the job of this escort service was known to her. In fact, she was married to a cousin of my friend. While they were in Jan’s office, this woman said that she saw the note on the desk of the President of the Sharing Coalition that demanded my friend’s termination. In fact, she was able to read it quickly. She was angry about all this. She told my friend that the president of the coalition said she didn’t know where it came from. Then the president threw the note in her wastebasket prior to shredding at the end of the day. When the president went out to her secretary to tell her what had been done, my friend’s ally took it out of the basket and shoved it in her pocket. Here it is, Mr. Parker. I received it in the mail this morning. It’s a little beaten up and soiled you’ll notice. It also contains the threat to me, I believe.”

With that, Jan opened her cavernous leather handbag, which was more like a small suitcase with a rose imprinted on its broad side, than the normal definition of “handbag”. It had an interesting pin attached to the wide strap of the handbag. It was the size of a silver dollar and it read “Syria, Go Home”. Jan was ahead of her time, Parker thought.

The envelope Jan had received was inside a small plastic bag. Parker extracted the envelope and removed a piece of folded notepaper. He opened it and read.

Dear Ms. Carnovan-Bloom,

It has come to my attention that Ms. Margaret Phillips, Treasurer Assistant of your organization, The Truth, Prosperity, and Sharing Coalition of Northern

Vermont, has become a risk to the united efforts of the non-profit industry in Vermont. She must be terminated from your employment immediately. She is to be told nothing of detail except that she is a "risk" to our programs.

She is known to be involved in an investigation, along with a reporter from the Chittenden Free Progressive, of our industry of non-profit, public-good organizations in the state of Vermont. This investigation will stop immediately, on my orders. I know how to accomplish this.

I expect you to carry out your task with no delay regarding the termination of Ms. Phillips. There are other organizations that will be irreparably harmed if this task is delayed.

This is a most important undertaking. If she is any trouble, let me know without delay. We have other means of correction in the instances of potential problems.

Z

Parker read it again, and then a third time. The handwriting was neat and precise. "You believe that this is a threat to you, Jan?" he asked.

"Yes, I do, Mr. Parker." She was showing signs of the nervousness of earlier in the evening. "I really do."

"Any idea who 'Z' is, Jan? It sounds like the Zorro that scared me when I was a little kid, sitting in a movie theater in the dark."

"No idea, Mr. Parker. Strange doings, don't you agree?"

Parker nodded and pretended to study the note while he thought about Jan's reaction to it. This note could be anything, he thought. If you were nervous and scared, it could be taken as a direct threat. If Jan's unsettled imagination was not part of this equation, then this note might be seen as the ravings of a person who actually thought he or she had the power to do anything they wanted. Parker, however, was concerned. He had never seen a note like this, and he could see why Jan's reaction to it was as visceral as it seemed.

"I need time to think about this, Jan," Parker said. "And, by the way, what's your friend going to do for work now that she no longer is employed by the Truth, Prosperity, and Sharing Coalition of Northern Vermont? I may want to talk to her. Also, that title is a load of crap if I ever heard it. Pardon my language, Jan. I knew about them, and plenty of others, when I was in the House, and there were jokes about them being the front line shock troops for everyone and everything way left of center. But to return to my question, what's your friend going to do?"

The answer from Jan made him sit up a little straighter in the car seat.

"She's leaving Vermont, Mr. Parker. She's very much bothered by the whole tone of her dismissal, the direction of the non-profit groups in Vermont and, as she calls it, the 'sweet-sour smell of corruption'. A little flowery, I think, but she meant it, I'm sure."

"Jan," said Parker carefully, "You'll have to let me think about this for a few days." She eyed Parker in a way that said "you really don't take this seriously, do you?" And it seemed to Parker that Jan Evlin had taken on the look of someone who suddenly finds out that all her work that day was for nothing. And Parker didn't want to leave things that way.

"You see, Jan, I have to determine who I can talk to about this without raising any red flags. If the word is out on the street that you are working on this story, it won't do you or me any good. And if I do something clumsy while I'm thrashing around on this problem of yours, it will spoil any of your efforts to write the story. Also, I'd like to keep this note for a while," he said, as he slipped the notepaper back into the envelope and put both back into the plastic bag. "That okay with you?"

"Of course, Mr. Parker. Does that mean that you'll help me?"

"Yes, it does, Jan. I just want to figure out what I should do to get started. You understand that, don't you? And something else. I want to talk this over with my wife. She always has insights that I don't get anywhere close to."

She nodded, and placed a hand on Parker's forearm and squeezed. "Thanks, Mr. Parker. You're everything I thought you were."

An embarrassed Parker hurriedly said, "God, I hope not, Jan." Then he said, "I'll be in touch before the end of next week. Is that okay?"

"Perfect, Mr. Parker. I do feel better already."

4

As Parker drove out of the parking area of the outdoor restaurant, he felt a mood descending on him that reminded him of the chase, the previous year, of the killer of the Speaker of the Vermont House, Dick Obrist. It wasn't necessarily a feeling of frantic and persistent worry that accompanied that terrible time of his life, when both he and Addie were in danger, along with many of their friends. It was more of the same feeling he had when, two years before, he not only uncovered the killer of his friend and fellow House member, Kermit Mayes, but found corruption of Vermont's political and social structures that still haunted him to this day. There were people who would not speak to him, even now, because of what he discovered.

His reaction to Jan Evlin's story was similar to the feeling he had during those early days of his involvement in the death of Mayes – an innocence that turned into shock when he found out the truth, then fear, and then the threats, injury, and lies that invaded his life.

The suspicions brought to him today by Jan Evlin had that same texture of innocence – except that now he found himself ready only to be surprised, rather than shocked by the unexpected. If he decided to become involved with Jan's suspicions, he wondered what he would discover at the end of it all. What's out there that I don't know now, but will find out about? Is Jan even correct? Is there something in the non-profit world, and the other public foundations of that same world, with all their high-minded pronouncements, their "Mission Statements", their soft-edged fundraising letters of compassion and concern, and their well-dressed and articulate spokespersons, that isn't real?

Well, maybe he'd find out. Maybe there's nothing but smoke. At least this would only take some quiet digging. No danger to life, limb, and family on this trek. And I can be a help to a friend to whom I really do owe a favor, Parker reasoned. Jan was obviously overreacting to what she learned as she plugged along in her quiet quest for information. It happens to all of us at one time or another, he thought, no matter what we do for a living. He took comfort in this pleasurable picture he had established in his imagination. It provided him with a certain consolation as he rumbled along, southbound on Route 155, heading for Bridgeton and hearth and home.

5

As Parker pulled up the long driveway into his front yard his headlights swept onto and past the big SUV with the Colorado plates parked in his spot. That was all right with Parker. This was the vehicle owned by Kate and Duane Emery of Rifle, Colorado. Parker knew that they would be arriving some time during the day, depending on how steadily they wanted to travel. And Parker knew that once Duane decided on something, it happened, regardless of the obstacles.

Kate was the unofficial adopted daughter of the Parkers. Dick Obrist, the Vermont Speaker of the House, was her father. Dick had been a very close friend of the Parkers, and his death, a year ago, left behind one living relative. It was his daughter Kate. Parker discovered that Dick had been murdered, and he had set out to find the killer, whose next target was Kate. Bill and Addie saved her from the killer, and Kate became part of their family.

Kate's husband, Duane, was a Montpelier police officer, turned lawyer, who met Kate during those days of fear, turmoil, and danger. At the end of it all, and after Duane had struggled with a misguided sense of honor, set right by Parker, they decided to get married. Or as Parker's father would have put it, they decided that it "got too cold in the barn and too warm in public, so marriage was the only choice they had left." Parker's wife Addie disliked that casual way of putting it. She felt it didn't show proper respect for the important institution of courting. Her husband couldn't see the difference.

After the wedding, they moved out to the western slope of Colorado where Duane had started his law practice.

Parker thumped up onto the porch, dropping smelly fishing vest, boots, and hat as he went. He hadn't reached the door when Kate stepped out through the door with her arms outspread and a huge smile on her face. A hug and an embrace reminded Parker that Kate was pregnant and was getting "as big as a load of hay," as his mother used to say.

When they walked into the immense kitchen he was greeted by Duane. Parker shook hands with him, patted him on the shoulder, and then gave Addie a hug and told her that he had had some good luck on the stream.

"And did your friend from the newspaper find you all right?" she quietly asked.

"Yes, she did," Parker answered. "She talked about some real interesting things, some of which I guess I knew, or suspected pretty strongly when I was in the House, and other parts of her tale that surprised me. We'll have to talk about all that, Addie. You may have knowledge about some of it that you don't even know you have."

"This sounds like a new chapter in the saga 'Bill Parker Rides Again', written by the Hoot Gibson of Bridgeton," said Kate. "You'll have to tell us about it, Mr. Parker."

Duane groaned softly and shook his head. "How do you get into these scrapes, Bill, where someone else has to dig you out? Right off the top of my head, I know of two bad situations for you in just the last three years."

"Now Duane," said Parker. "I've never been in enough danger to require the services of another person. It just seemed like it to inexperienced young people at the time. In any event, this subject has to do with all of the non-profit organizations in Vermont, along with the foundations and other groups that have a mission of social good. Very benign stuff, as you can see."

"I heard it said, Bill, when I was a cop, that the quieter and gentler something seems, the rougher and more dangerous it can be. Just bear that in mind, please."

Parker couldn't see the reason for the soft-edged warning. He knew he wouldn't lose more than a day or two trying to help Jan.

6

After dinner, while Kate and Duane sat on the couch in front of the fireplace, Addie and Parker finished up the dishes.

"Tell me, Willie, what did the reporter have on her mind? She sounded very worried about something. I almost had the feeling that she didn't want anybody to even know she was calling our number."

"You know something, sweetie?" he answered. "I think she's been too close to something she's working on, and lost some perspective along the way. She believes that she's been threatened by someone or something and she decided that she had to get to somebody. And that somebody happened to be me."

Addie cocked an eye at Parker. "Why you, Willie?" she asked. "There's got to be somebody else up her way that can be of more help than you can." Parker knew that this question meant a great deal to Addie. She, along with Kate, had come very close to losing her life in Parker's last escapade. A year had gone by and Parker knew that the lingering shock of that experience hadn't left her, and probably never would.

"That's exactly what I told her, Addie. She gave me some story about why she drove all the way down here, at night, too, I'll remind you, called our house from a pay phone that she made certain I knew about, and then tracked me up that road along the Chateaugay and waited for me. The whole thing seems to be an effort by Jan to show me that we couldn't be traced to her. Based on that, alone, I think she's really spooked."

"Willie, that sounds like she had a very good reason to come down here."

"If she did, she didn't convince me," Parker stated, with too much certainty. Addie glanced sharply at him. Fooling Addie was always difficult, if not impossible, for Parker.

"What did you tell her, Willie?" Her voice held a tightness that wasn't there when he had first arrived home.

"I said I'd think about it, and get back to her later - by the end of next week."

Addie smiled. "Why didn't you tell her that very thing when she was talking to you about her fears, Willie? You must have had your doubts formed in your mind."

Parker stood beside Addie for a few seconds, absently wiping a dinner plate for much longer than was necessary. "I couldn't do that, Addie. You see, I feel I owe her a favor somehow, and I just couldn't shut her off. She deserves better."

"What favor, Willie? Your political life has been over for three years, for goodness sake." Addie didn't want her husband to get back into any more entanglements that might involve any sort of danger, even if no danger was possible. "These past three years have been rough for us, you know. And for Kate and Duane, too, remember."

How could Parker forget the past three years? He had almost lost his wife and Kate. In fact, he'd almost lost everything he owned, including his life.

At the sound of her name, Kate looked up from the couch. "What are you two talking about that includes me?"

"We were talking about you both. About how good you both look. Living in Colorado agrees with you," Parker answered with a smile.

"No you weren't," said Kate, "but we'll let it go for now. Ellen Franklin sends her regards to you both. She hopes you'll get out our way soon."

"You tell her we'll be out when our grandchild is born," said Addie.

Ellen Franklin, of Rifle, Colorado, was a young teacher in the Vermont high school Kate had attended, and she and Kate became fast friends. When Kate left home for good, she went to Ellen and Ellen took her in. Then Ellen helped Kate with the rest of her education, and generally gave Kate the time to put her life back together.

Kate climbed up and out of the grasp of the old couch, with help from her husband, and went over to Addie and hugged her. The word "grandchild" had meant more to her than anything else could have.

"How is Ellen, Kate? Is she still teaching out there? Is there any young man following her around who she has to fend off every now and then?"

"Willie, for God's sake," snapped Addie. "Show a little respect and regard for a terrific young woman."

"I just did, Addie," he answered. "She's a great looking, intelligent young woman and she needs to discover that a man finds her so, and wants to haul her off to his cave."

By this time both Kate and Duane were laughing. "All right, all right, you win," Addie said, with a certain sternness in her attitude. Parker kept a straight face. This could be dangerous ground. Addie didn't have many hang-ups, but playing fast and loose with relationships required respect, admiration, and a certain sanctity, as far as she was concerned. Her husband crossed that line occasionally with his less-than-respectful choice of words in describing these relationships.

"She's fine, Addie," said Kate, through a chuckle. "And, as a matter of fact, there is a young man who appears out of nowhere to open a door for her or invite her to have coffee, or even out to dinner once in a while. Max was a problem, for a while, but even he has mellowed toward this guy."

Parker didn't believe that for a second. Max was Ellen's cross-breed dog, and the word "dog" didn't adequately describe him. "Mastiff" came close, except a mastiff didn't appear dangerous when it was asleep. Max, however, took on another dimension when he should have been sleeping. He never even tried to sleep when Parker was there. He just stared at Parker, the object of his distaste and contempt, until that object moved away. Ellen Franklin was very safe with Max around. Parker was a little miffed that this guy he didn't even know was able to win Max's tolerance, for surely it couldn't be any more than that.

7

"Tell me, Willie," Addie said, "what did our Ms. Evlin have to say that was so important? She certainly didn't have any deadline to meet, did she? And she sounded wrung out, too. She must have wanted you to do something for her that she couldn't do herself. And it must have been very important or she would never have felt the need to drive down here at night just to see you. Was what she needed done, dangerous, Willie?"

Parker knew he wouldn't have to explain much to Addie. She had it all sorted out and wrapped up better than he did, and he was the one who heard it all firsthand. However, Parker had long ago gotten over any twinge of resentment that his wife's mind allowed her to play mental chess while he played checkers.

"Absolutely not, Sweetie. I'm through with candidates for the booby hatch who like to kill people. Just a simple matter of some research. And I told her I'd consider helping if I felt she really needed it. I also hinted that I'm very busy, and time might be a problem."

"What?" cried Addie. "These past few months you've been in slow motion, and enjoying it, I think. Irene runs your office, and does it very well."

"I've been resting and healing," Parker answered, with some amount of huffiness. "This young lady and her husband," he said, and gestured toward Kate and Duane, "got me into trouble last year. So, I've been catching up with my life."

Addie just gazed at him in wonder.

"What did she want, Mr. Parker?" asked Duane. "Let us in on it."

"It's not anything out of the ordinary, Duane. She's been doing the research for a story on the non-profit industry in Vermont. That includes all the tax-exempt foundations, trusts, and other tax evaders we have in this state."

"Tax evaders, Mr. Parker? What does that mean to us simple country lawyers from the flyover zone of our great country?" asked Duane.

"It means, my boy, that all these very profitable non-profits can accept contributions, with the donations representing a tax write-off for the giver, and the recipient doesn't have to pay tax to the Feds on it – which means that the state of Vermont can't receive taxes from their fund balances either."

"Oh, that's right," Duane said. "Vermont just uses the information from a person's federal income tax to determine what they owe to the state. Well," said Duane, "these organizations do good work in the community, don't they? At least I assume they do, so why tax them?"

"Well that's a good argument for not taxing them, I admit," said Parker. "But my reporter friend, who used to be a big supporter of non-profits, seemed to find her confidence in these groups diminishing as she investigated them. In fact, I think she thought that the majority of those she's checked so far were not doing what everybody assumed they were doing, as represented in their mission statements."

"That's pretty rough, Willie," said Addie. "So, what does she want from you, and why?"

Parker had been thinking about answers to those questions from the time he had left Jan in the parking lot of the hamburger stand. And he wasn't sure that he knew the answer to either of them. But, he took a stab at it.

"She told me that she knew she needed something from me," said Parker. "Then she proceeded to tell me that she didn't know what it was. Being a bear of little brain, I didn't know what the hell she was talking about."

"Then why did she come to you at this particular time?" Addie asked. Aha, thought Parker. Another of Addie's intuitive guesses turned into a question that pushed Parker right into a corner.

"She believed that she had received a death threat," said Parker, simply, "and brought something that she thought was evidence of it."

Addie looked at him. "And what was your considered opinion, Willie?" she asked, concealing the steely edge to her voice from all except Parker.

"I think it's very possible that she received a death threat, Addie, although I didn't tell her that."

Parker could feel the actual heat from Addie's glare without even looking at her. He knew he had to say what he did because

Addie would have figured it out anyway in the next few minutes, and she'd then wonder why he'd held it back in the first place. That would have been more trouble than just spilling it out.

"So, no danger, eh, Sam Spade?" Addie said quietly.

Kate walked over to Parker, put her arm around his waist, and said, "Mr. Parker, or should I call you Don Quixote, as Addie has in the past, I think. You've become a well-known force over the past three years as an honest and tenacious helper of people. In fact, stubborn is probably the right word to describe you. I'll bet that's why she came down here tonight."

"That's pretty much it, Kate," Parker said. "It has nothing to do with my stubbornness and whatever else you said. She simply didn't feel comfortable talking to anybody else. I think I gleaned out of what she said that a person from up her way might be tied in to the very thing that she was looking into."

"But, why you, specifically, Willie?" asked Addie. "There are still a dozen people she could have gone to, including a lawyer. And lawyers," she said, turning toward Duane, "are sworn to keep their clients' secrets to themselves, aren't they, Duane?"

Duane nodded, and then said, "However, Mrs. Parker, some lawyers have more difficulty than others in separating the knowledge of one set of facts, presented in one situation, from another set of facts they receive from another client, if the two pieces of information touch one another in any way at all. And sometimes information can suddenly confront an attorney when he least expects it. Just no way to avoid it, I've found. And sometimes this knowledge can color what they do in another case, both for their clients and, sometimes, against their clients. Depending on what the information is, and how serious Ms. Evlin thinks it is, will determine if any danger exists to anybody."

"She said she trusted me because she knew me from the days in Montpelier, and also that I lived a ways away from Montpelier. That seemed to be a big advantage in favor of me, too. In addition, she thought I approved of her work in reporting all the bad stuff against me that was flying around two years ago. Which I did, by the way."

"Including bullets and bombs, Willie," whispered Addie. "You got shot during those days. Remember?"

"There is that, too," said Parker. "Anyway, she came here, she told me her story, and I told her I'd get back to her later on this week."

"Do you have the evidence with you, Bill? If so, can I see it?" asked Duane.

Parker reached into his inside pocket and produced the plastic bag containing the envelope Jan had given to him.

Duane took the plastic bag by one corner, dropped it on his lap, and opened it using a table knife and a fork, and extracted the envelope and its piece of notepaper. He looked at Parker and grinned. "Once a cop, et cetera, eh, Bill?"

When the note was removed and opened, Parker noted that Duane looked at the back of the paper first, holding it up to the light by the edges, and then studying the paper from a series of angles. Then he turned it over and read the written words. He studied them for a long time, then held this side of the note up to the light, following the same routine he had used for the back. Then he looked the envelope over closely, rubbing it with his fingertips, then holding it to his nose. Parker couldn't determine what the hell he was looking for.

After several minutes, Duane leaned back into the couch and rested his head on the back, eyes closed. Then he started to speak. "I agree with you, Bill. This is a death threat, although I couldn't prove it in court." Parker knew that this young man was very perceptive and bright, because he had seen him in action when it really counted. He decided that listening carefully would be a good move.

"First, the quality of the paper is first-rate. It's heavy bond and of a rare size, used, I'll guess, to make his or her communications 'sit-up-and-take-notice' demands on the recipients. Therefore, it's not in common use, and is not usually carried by any stores that sell quality stationery. I know something about this subject because I had a client back home in Colorado who had to trace a certain type of notepaper regarding a patent infringement. I learned more about paper, stationery, and writing implements than I ever thought I needed to know." Then he grinned at Parker. "Justice works in strange ways, Mr. Parker, doesn't it?" Then, with a suddenly sober look, he said, "and there is something else. The top two inches, or so, I believe, have been cut off this particular piece of notepaper, probably to disguise the heading."

Parker blinked, and then thought about the wonder of it all, that anyone would have the knowledge to notice something that could have been so easily missed by even a careful investigation. By an amateur like me, for example, he thought.

“Fascinating, Duane, just fascinating,” exclaimed Parker. “But, what the hell does all that paper stuff mean to the unwashed citizen like me?”

Duane smiled at Parker, and said, “Maybe nothing. Maybe I was just showing off for the great unwashed, as you put it. Maybe, though, just maybe, you’ll find yourself a little further along this bumpy road of questions than you were before I turned my great mind and knowledge loose on it.”

Parker was properly contrite, to the point where Kate came over to him and hugged him and said, “Mr. Parker, don’t pay any attention to him. He *is* showing off a little, but hear him out. He’s really quite good at this deduction business using just scraps of information. Go ahead, Duane. Impress us.”

“Well, folks,” Duane said, “here we go, for what it’s worth. The writer is a person who has been in Vermont for a few years. At least, he didn’t just arrive. Why do I say that? Nobody threatens anybody with ‘other means of correction’ in this small state without knowing how to do just that. And you’ve got to have been here awhile to know what the buttons are that have to be pushed. Don’t forget, Bill, a statement like that isn’t just thrown out there. He or she knew exactly what they were saying. Also, the writer of this note is known to the head of the ‘Truth, Prosperity, and whatever the hell the rest of it is Coalition’, and the writer knew that that statement would have the desired effect on the head of this Coalition.”

Parker hoped that this exercise would lead somewhere useful. “Keep going, Duane. You’ve got my attention.”

“I’ll guess,” said Duane, “that the writer came here from outside the United States. It’s only a guess, but the phrasing is not of a native-born person. ‘Treasurer Assistant’ for example smacks of Canada, for example, or even western Europe – France, for instance, or Germany, but not Britain. Just the way the order to fire this Phillips person was written in the note gave off the aura of arrogance, and a sort of mild brutality, if that’s the right word – and I think it may be.”

Parker was now listening closely, and saw what could be called “the pattern” that was emerging - a pattern of a central, and possibly unhealthy, direction of the non-profit industry, or at least a part of it, with a purpose that had yet to be determined.

“In addition, the writer of this note mentions ‘other organizations’. What are they? Of course I don’t know. However, these 'other organizations', I believe, have a similarity of goals with the non-profits. In fact, they would have difficulty in working together without some sort of solid understanding of what they do."

The room was silent as Duane continued his analysis, oblivious of his surroundings.

"Lastly, from the way the note was written, the writer used the word 'investigation' instead of 'researching a story'. 'Investigation' sounds so much more threatening than 'researching a story'. That caught my attention. This writer – 'Z', is it? – wanted to put the fear of God into the leader of this Coalition, even if this leader didn't know what in the world 'Z' was talking about. But Ms. Evlin knew, didn't she? And got scared, didn't she? So she came running to you, Bill." Parker hadn't looked at the whole situation as Duane just had.

"You see, Bill," Duane continued, "that one thing alone convinced me that the implied threat, the reality of which you were trying to downplay as you thought about this note - and couldn't do it, of course - allowed me to agree with her, and have no doubts in doing so."

Parker squirmed uncomfortably in his wooden kitchen chair. Duane was exactly correct, of course, and Parker was somewhat unsettled when he admitted it to himself. "You're painting quite a picture of this person, Duane. Sort of like 'Z' is a spider in the middle of his or her web, and waiting for something that bumps into the web and causes a disturbance in the non-profit world. So 'Z' rushes out to see what's going on and takes care of the problem quickly."

"Very good, Bill. A good way of looking at it. Unnecessarily graphic, for sure, but I like it. Want to hear any more?"

"You mean there's more from this crumpled piece of paper, Duane?"

"A little bit more. And I'm just making some speculative guesses, but they might become important during your travels and the 'thrashing around' that you do. Don't forget, Bill. I've seen you operate."

Addie sat up in her chair and was about to say something when Kate jumped in ahead of her. "No thrashing around this time. Right, Mr. Parker?"

Parker just grunted something unintelligible and gestured for Duane to go on.

"I mentioned that the notepaper was of very high quality. The envelope, too, come to that. What I learned from the patent case I handled in Colorado is that extraordinarily expensive notepaper like this is almost always an expression of ego. I don't know how this helps, but you should know this, because I think it will be one of the major identifiers of the person who wrote this note. However, cutting off the top of the stationery tells me that 'Z' didn't want to have this communication traced back to him – or her. You'll notice that the postmark is out of the Montpelier post office, but it doubtless came from somewhere else. Probably north of Montpelier, but not in Chittenden County."

"Now, how do you figure that?" asked Parker.

"This is just a guess, Bill, but look at the envelope. It's dusty, rather than dirty, isn't it? That dusty condition isn't something that would be on the envelope if the note had been written in Montpelier. Remember, I worked as a cop up there. Anything such as a letter or a note like this was considered as 'dirty' in Montpelier when it was muddy, greasy, water-stained, or stomped on. But this envelope is *dusty.* Notice that? The envelope isn't Montpelier-dirty. It's *dusty*. And it has an odor that's distinctive. Take a whiff. Do you think it has an odor? If so, what do you think it is?"

Parker handled the envelope gingerly, as opposed to the cavalier method he had used before Duane started teaching him how to look at common items and find uncommon things.

The faint smell was overwhelming to him. It wouldn't be noticed by a lifelong city dweller. But it would bring back instant memories to an ex-farmer, no matter how long he'd been away from that home place and its acres of plowed and cultivated land, fertilized with nature's best. It was a cornfield, or something like it, mixed into a cow barn potion. It was hay, it was silage, it was home, it was spring mud, it was fertilizer made the old-fashioned way, and there was no mistaking it. All of these smells were suggested to him when he had lifted this small envelope to his nose. Probably most people wouldn't believe that the smell of a farm would permeate everything within its grasp. However, it certainly does. "This envelope has come from a farm, hasn't it? I find it unmistakable, Duane." Parker remained silent, almost seeming to be in another world for a time.

Then he said, in a quiet voice, "All this is extremely thin, you know. I can't think of one lawyer who would bring this up in court. He'd never hear the end of it."

"That's what I thought, too. Not very solid evidence, I know, but I know that that envelope, and probably the notepaper, high class as it is, came from a farm. Or maybe a fertilizer plant."

"No," said Parker, quickly. "I've been in a fertilizer plant; a good many of them, in fact. When I got a whiff of that envelope, I never thought about a fertilizer plant. Never entered my mind. What I did think of, right off, was a farm. Or a pickup truck, brought up and worn out on a farm," said Parker, quietly. "I'm not a farmer anymore, as you know. Haven't been a farmer in more years than I care to count. But I still have all the bad habits of farmers and their use of their personal vehicles. How does this tie in with what we're talking about? It ties in this way, Duane." Parker leaned against the kitchen counter, folding his arms across his chest.

"Are we about to receive the blessings of another Willie Parker story about life on the farm?" asked Addie.

"You bet, sweetie, and listen closely. You'll learn something, although you were brought up on a farm, too. Maybe your life skills from growing up on a farm didn't include stories. This will be good for you."

Addie sighed, got comfortable, and said, "Is this a story that will bring knowledge to all of us, Willie, not just me? For example, will Kate be edified and charmed by it? She wasn't brought up on a farm, you'll remember. Duane, I think you were, so this story has to satisfy both ends of the spectrum. Go to it, Willie."

"Am I going to be constantly interrupted by a member of this audience, or can I proceed? This is serious, you know. Thank you," said Parker, not waiting for an answer.

"I remember when my father bought a winter scarf for my mother for Christmas. I was a junior or senior in high school at the time, I guess. He bought it in August or something like that. Didn't dare to bring it in the house because my mother was a shaker and pincher of what looked like potential Christmas gifts. So he threw the scarf behind the seat of his truck and promptly forgot about it. The scarf was in a bag but it wasn't sealed or anything. And I know that little detail because right in the middle of opening gifts on Christmas morning, he remembered the scarf.

He took me aside and whispered to me to go find the gift, sneak it in the house and slip upstairs and wrap it. Then I was to bring it back to the Christmas tree and set it down without my mother seeing me do it. Well, I was willing to do what my pa wanted, of course, but I knew that I'd never be able to get this whole thing past my mother. It seemed to me that she always knew what was going on, even when she was in another room."

Parker was into his story, and didn't notice the smiles as his family settled back into their chairs, allowing Parker to tell them another tale about his life on the family farm.

"I told him I'd do my best. I found the scarf in the truck and put it inside my shirt and walked back into the house and upstairs. When I reached into that bag and took out the scarf, I really thought that I was back in the cow barn. I probably wouldn't have noticed it if I actually was in the barn. But in the spare room upstairs where we wrapped the presents, it hit me right over the head when I took hold of that scarf. It was then when I wondered if everything I owned smelled like that. This could be a crisis, I remembered thinking. And, I wondered, as any young man would, if this crisis was real, how was I ever going to get a girl to look at me twice? Unless she was a farm-reared girl, and that was unlikely at the University of Vermont because fifty-five percent of the students were from the city. Concealing my background from a city girl suddenly became a real problem, unless I bought a whole new wardrobe, and who had money for that?"

Parker looked around at the faces of his family. "The moral of this story, my friends? If you've been brought up on a farm, buy a second suit of clothes immediately, and nobody will ever know. Well," he hesitated, and then continued, "the young woman still might know, but you will have done your best to conceal your dirty little secret so you'll feel better, anyway, as you go down in flames." Parker shifted his gaze around the room. "End of story, folks. So, Duane, it's nice to know about the odor, but we can't make any use of the knowledge, can we?"

"Correct. I don't know who we can tell this stuff to. I don't know why you'd have to, unless your 'thrashing around' came too close to 'Z'. Also, 'Z' would have had to do something really bad to make us want to talk about it."

"So, Duane, what are we left with here? What sort of person is 'Z'?"

"Bill, I think this person is a little strange. Not born American, a decent education, judging by the well-written note, although whether or not he or she actually knows anything is uncertain. Used to having his or her own way, I think, and a messy person in some ways, based on the poor handwriting and the ink blotches – you noticed that, I hope." Parker nodded. "And they were keeping this high cost notepaper in a truck, or at least on a farm somewhere for a time. And, finally, I believe that this person isn't one of the crowd when it comes to modern methods of communication. At least he or she isn't when sending out their little threats of intimidation, like this." He waved the note in the air. "I think that this person generally doesn't like things too modern. And this person definitely has something to hide. That's all I have for you, Bill. And you may think that this is pretty flimsy material, but I'm comfortable with it. And I don't think I'm too far off. Let me know what, if anything, you find out. I'd be interested."

Addie piped up at this point. Parker believed that her quick mind no doubt absorbed every item of Duane's remarkable performance. And she still had a question. Parker had none of his own. "I stayed with you pretty well, Duane, until this last bit. Why do you say that this person has something to hide? What tells you that?"

"Because this contact was made by snail mail, and was carried to Montpelier and dropped in to the Post Office there. Very difficult, if not impossible, to trace, you see. E-mail would be the fastest way to get this message out to the head of this Coalition, but e-mails can end up anywhere, and this person couldn't afford that. So, he or she takes the safe way with the US postal service, and signs it with the warm and affectionate 'Z'. However, if this situation is at all sinister, it was the unsafe thing to do, because someone – us – has the original note, and we've done a bit of tracing. That note in our hands was a mistake made, and we've benefited."

"Well," said Parker, "we've benefited a little if we have a spooky situation to deal with. We probably don't, and all of this can be explained very simply."

"Really, Willie? Just how do you explain it?"

"Just an overactive imagination on the part of Jan Evlin, and overactive criminal minds on our part."

"You didn't believe that earlier this evening, did you? Why have you changed your mind? Or have you just said you've changed your mind to calm me down? Fess up, pard."

Parker just smiled slightly, walked over to Addie and kissed her on the forehead. "You're too much for me, kiddo."

Addie looked at Parker with affection and exasperation, the combination of which made Parker a little uneasy. "We'll talk about it tomorrow morning. I'd like to think about this whole thing for a while."

8

Parker ambled down to the breakfast table the next morning, having shaved, showered, shined, and discovered, once again, that nothing he did would improve what he saw in the mirror. He was an hour behind his normal schedule because of the activity of the day before, and he felt as if he was about a quart low.

Addie, Kate, and Duane were all up and looking perky. Parker plopped down in a chair at the table, and Addie set a cup of tea down in front of him as he did so. Right after that, she set down eggs, toast, and bacon, as if she knew he was coming to the table by use of some mystical set of powers known only to herself.

"Try this medication, Willie. You look a little drawn this morning."

"For that kind of service you'll receive a tip larger than usual, my dear," he said.

Addie smiled and touched his shoulder as she turned away, saying, "If I made as much noise getting ready for the day as you do, you'd be able to time breakfast for me, too. You should hear yourself thump around upstairs while doing the simple chores of getting up, cleaning up, and coming down to breakfast. If you had any consideration for me, you'd be hard at work trying to be quiet in the morning. Although knowing you as I do, I've given up hope for success on your home schooling in this area."

"Well, ladies and gentleman," said Parker, ignoring what he considered to be these disrespectful comments from his wife, "any further thoughts about last night's conversation? Anything brilliant bubble up to the surface that changed your opinion of anything we heard? Speak up, or forever etc., etc."

Kate slid over next to Parker, kissed him on the cheek, and said, "Good morning, Mr. Parker. Nice to see you looking so crisp. And yes, I will start off by saying that your reporter friend has a problem. Is it as big as she thinks? Probably not, and I don't think her life is in danger, but there could be a person out there, working in this non-profit industry, as you call it, who likes to upset people because it gives him a feeling of power."

Addie looked steadily at Parker, and he knew what she was thinking about. In some way, this person they had become aware of yesterday, who sends little notes to undesirable people, was something like the person who threatened Kate more than a year ago. Parker was certain that Kate could see the similarity in the two situations as well as the rest of them could. But Kate was a strong and intelligent young lady. Those terrible days when she was in danger were only a memory now, and did not affect her to the point where she couldn't discuss them or even allude to them in an oblique way. They happened. She survived. Life went on.

Good things happened during that time, too. Kate met Duane, who was a policeman in the Montpelier Police Department. His boss, Supervisor Peter Morgan, knew how bright, resourceful, and brave this young man was. Losing Duane to law school and a career in law was a disappointment to Morgan because he felt about lawyers the way a cow cares about too many flies. And here they were; Kate pregnant, Duane trying to build up his practice in Rifle, Colorado, and still taking the time off to come back east and see Kate's adopted parents.

Duane straightened up after listening to Kate's assessment of things and frowned, but said nothing.

Addie said, "What do you think, Willie? Will you go any further on this?"

Parker munched silently on his toast. Then he looked up and said, "Yes, I will, Addie. I will give this a very good checkup. Very quietly, too, you can bet. We'll see how that goes, then we'll decide if we need to go any further." Addie's face didn't change its expression. She simply nodded and started clearing the table.

Parker went back to his morning paper. It was the Brattleboro Opposition, the daily Progressive Party newsletter to which most people in Windham County subscribed. It was just like the Mid-Vermont Bugle. As Parker had become more politically sophisticated regarding what he read, he found that these left wing papers revealed as much about themselves by what they didn't print as by what they did. Any article that made the collectivist point of view out to be the philosophy of crackpots was not printed. The article would appear in the Eagle Banner, a New Hampshire paper, trying to be a balanced paper, and not making it yet, that was making inroads into Vermont. The same article would make it into some of the weekly papers, too, but not the Vermont daily papers in bed with the Vermont left.

Parker's daily routine included the Opposition, to see how Socialism was doing this morning, and then a half hour with Fox News on TV. The contrast between the two regarding national news sometimes made him feel that each news source lived in different countries.

The Mid-Vermont Bugle was worst, if that could be believed. It was famous for its shift from liberalism, which was generally tolerated by reasonable people, to the new task of indoctrination of its readers in a hard left political doctrine located somewhere out on the fringe. It had gotten so frantic that it had even printed letters that criticized earlier letters to the editor – which is their right, of course – except that they had refused to print the initial letter that was being criticized. The paper had become a joke. There was even a web site entitled "DefytheBugle.com." There was a bumper sticker with that emblazoned on it. And apparently, thought Parker, the Bugle wondered why there was so much resistance to the paper out there.

Parker knew that it was merely a tentacle of the New York Times, printing the columns and occasionally the editorials from the Times, to further the periodic training of Vermont's rural bumpkins.

One of their columnists, a woman named Cloud, was so shrill in defending anything coming from the left that the columns she wrote were impossible for Parker to read and understand. It was as though she had a method of dumping words onto a piece of paper and hoping that they would arrange themselves in some kind of order. The Times would then print her stuff as long as the spelling was reasonably correct. Parker had decided, some time ago, that at some point in her column, she would lose track of her main point, not realize it, and slog on to the end. She succeeded in making his head ache.

Another New York Times sort of writer was a guy named Slugg, who, Parker thought, was, or might still be, a professor of economics at Yale or Princeton, or one of those Ivy League schools. Parker felt sorry for those students who came in contact with him. He was certain that they came out of his classes a lot dumber than they were when they first went in.

The Ivy League schools, Parker thought, had been wonderful until about twenty-five years ago. Today, they could be objectively viewed as having failed to consistently meet the standards for which they were known. Parker had been told by graduates of these schools, who now had their own children to consider when selecting a college, that it was no longer automatic that children attend the same schools from which their fathers and mothers had graduated.

How strong that view was, and how deeply it had permeated that heretofore solidly ingrained commitment that the kids would follow the father, couldn't be known until at least another generation had made that decision. Some of these parents, however, had figured it all out ahead of time.

Parker himself had wished that he could have gone to one of these schools, but that was back when the standards were higher and these colleges employed a teaching staff the overwhelming majority of whom actually thought that America was a halfway decent place to be. Not today.

Duane pulled out a chair and sat down beside Parker. "Bill, I'd be glad to help out, if you need somebody. Kate and I will be here for at least three weeks; my partner is taking care of the practice; and I wouldn't mind moving about, and looking into something interesting. And another thing, too, that might be helpful. Nobody knows me."

"I didn't know you were planning to stay that long. I'm delighted that you'll be with us," Parker said with genuine enthusiasm. "Just remember, Duane, that your wife will be foaling anytime soon, and I don't want to be the only one here when she decides that 'now is the time' and that frightening phrase 'let's get moving' gets used."

"Willie, for goodness sake, show some kind of delicacy, will you?" cried Addie.

Parker, with a look of bewilderment on his face, said, "I thought I was plain and sort of classy in what I said."

Addie gave him the stare that she reserved for those occasions when she thought that her husband should be locked in the attic until all visitors had gone home.

Parker rose to his feet and announced that he would call Jan Evlin in the next few days and tell her that he would be looking into things.

"You're not going to call her immediately, Willie?" asked Addie. "Won't she be worried?"

"I don't believe so, Addie. I told her that I'd get back to her in the next few days, which allows me, and you three, too, to think about this situation. There's one other reason, too. If I call her back today, she'll know, first, that I think she may, and I stress 'may', have a problem. Next, if I call her within twelve hours of first hearing about her problem, she'll become alarmed that I seem to believe that the problem is of an urgent variety. I'm not into alarming anybody. On top of all that logical stuff, I'm going fishing on Thursday for the day. Today is Tuesday. I'll call her on Friday. That's about right for timing."

9

Parker returned home from fishing late on Thursday evening. The house seemed empty with Duane and Kate gone for a few days, seeing Duane's family up in Vergennes. Fishing had seemed a good thing to do. Addie worked during the day at one of her social projects that needed doing, and she was someone who would accomplish something. That's her, to a "T", he thought.

The trip back from his trout fishing expedition took him from the Nullhegan River, located a little way north of Bloomfield, in the Northeast Kingdom, down to Bridgeton, the Parker home place in Windham County.

Also, the Nullhegan wasn't too far from the Black Branch, where the death of Dick Obrist had occurred a year ago. Parker had wanted to go back up there to see some of the friends he'd made while looking into Obrist's death. This trip, however, also gave him a chance to fish one of Obrist's favorite streams, and he decided to take this opportunity to do just that. Also, if the truth were known, Parker wanted to see if he would have some sort of a phobia against fishing this water. A lot in Parker's life had taken place up here, much of it unpleasant.

He fished the stream, however, and found out that he had no problems on this water, although he discovered that he couldn't go all the way up the stream to where the death had occurred. He supposed that his reluctance to do so was a normal reaction. However, it was possible, he thought, that he *did* have some problem with tramping along the edge of this stream close to where Obrist met his death.

While there, he had a chance to see his old friend, Sheriff Fred Thibeault. Thibeault was of great help during Parker's murder investigation of the death of his pal, Dick Obrist, near Bloomfield. He took Parker around to the places he'd have to know about, and also introduced him to some of the local people.

That was some experience, too, Parker allowed. He would never forget these ridge runners. Real people, and brains to go with them, and people who would never be caged by a state government hell-bent on controlling them from cradle to the grave, using their own tax money to do it. He also saw again the venerable old guy John Chapman. This man had a level of silent common sense that betrayed an intellect that would rival anyone Parker had ever met.

Another person Parker wanted to see again was a young man named Bob Murray, who was the one who had found Obrist's body. A mild version of a born ridge runner, he didn't let it show too much.

And while tracking Obrist's killer, Parker had met a young female lawyer in Arizona. This woman, PG McBride, visited Vermont at Parker's invitation and met Bob Murray, who instantly turned beet red. Parker would have liked to have added, "and the rest is history", but he couldn't. The Bob Murrays of this world worked on a slower timetable than those with more confidence in themselves.

When Parker asked if he was around, Thibeault said, "The poor bastard is hung up on that McBride girl from Arizona you brought here a while ago. That's where he is now – in Arizona, probably trying to talk her into something without saying a word." Parker grinned.

"Let me know how he makes out, Sheriff," he said.

Thibeault smiled. "I don't know when that will be, Bill, but yes, I'll let you know, good or bad."

Parker enjoyed his day in the Kingdom, but the drive home sobered him.

Vermont had its first Republican Governor in years. The ProgDems, however, had taken over the Legislature, pushing the Republicans back to levels of eight years earlier. In effect, they controlled the Legislative process and the Governor couldn't stop anything they really wanted to do.

The new Governor was an intelligent man, reasonable, and determined to help Vermont become the place where people were able to work, live, and remain.

The ProgDems were beside themselves with frustration when they lost the election for Governor. They seemed to be asking "how can we give out government jobs to our friends if we no longer control the process by which they would be hired?" The state had always been, it seemed to them, the place where high paying jobs to worn-out politicians and unemployable bureaucrats of the future were to be found. That ended with the new Governor, and the ProgDems still couldn't understand, even after a full year of it, why they didn't qualify for these same jobs. After all, they were trained to leadership, so their ProgDem Generals had said, weren't they?

The real ProgDem power, however, resided in the Vermont Senate. They had captured more seats, not fewer, in the election, even with the poor performance of their party during the last two years. Vermont voters complained about high taxes, too much regulation, and an agenda followed by the ProgDems that was developed by the irrational environmental lobby. The ProgDems were now set up to resist the Governor at every turn. And the compliant news media folks were ready to defend them whenever needed.

As Parker wheeled along in his pickup, he wondered about the Vermont voters and their priorities. Windsor County had actually elected a Senator who had been, or still was, he didn't know which, a member of the Board of Directors of the Preservation Legal Association. This group was among the most virulent anti-job-creation groups in the nation. It was centered in the Boston area and attempted to stop any development in any state that its members could drive to in half a day. It now had a Vermont chapter when it became too embarrassing to defend itself against charges that they wanted to bring Vermont to its economic knees and, at the same time, didn't even have a formal connection in the state.

Parker's own Windham County, known for a Senator who only flirted with reality over the years and didn't seem to need to change anything in order to be reelected, had finally been tossed out. He tried to become Governor, or Lt. Governor, or whatever he could run for to get on the public payroll.

Parker had been encouraged to run for the Senate from Windham County many times, and always refused, knowing that Brattleboro, the largest town in the County, and certainly not his little town of Bridgeton, elected the Windham County Senators.

As Parker went through the various towns on his trek home, he could see the effects of this political and social process of the marginalizing of Vermont. Closed businesses, a few of these empty buildings taken over by socially active groups with short-term leases, and many manufacturing plants, large and small, that were dark and weed-grown. His insurance business told him about a population of aging citizens on retirement who were finding it more and more difficult to pay their ever-increasing tax bills, while the productive age groups were moving to other states where jobs needed filling. Parker couldn't avoid thinking that Vermont was heading for difficult times.

As he drove he could catch glimpses of New Hampshire across the Connecticut River. He pulled over and stopped.

It was twilight now, and the view was beautiful. The Connecticut River, shining in the rays of the late day sun, was the lower frame of a great picture. Just for a second Parker wished he could paint this scene. However, he knew that talent was needed. Parker couldn't supply it.

Another solemn thought began the process of taking him over once again, as it had on previous occasions. He couldn't explain how he felt to anyone else. They'd never understand. Addie would, of course. She understood everything.

It was simple, really. Parker had always loved the land, the earth, and the beautiful hills, valleys, and meadows of Vermont. Those different shades of green were everywhere and could be found at any time of day, even in winter. Today, though, and all the days of the past few years, that marvelous green he loved was fading away. Everything he saw in his mind turned into a dullness, almost a gritty grayness. As he grappled with this realization, fuzzy and indistinct at first, but taking shape now in his consciousness, he realized that it was the heartbeat of Vermont that was fading, but he could only see it as a variety of the colors of green. That life force he could see was losing the battle. The ProgDems had no words for it. They would only say to the citizens of Vermont, "We'll give you great programs and have the rich pay for them." What they never told us, Parker thought, was that they were squeezing the life out of everyone in this singularly beautiful state, unique in so many ways. The faded greens, ending with just the gray outlines of trees, meadows, and hills, will be all that's left. Like squeezing an orange dry. And nobody sees it, thought Parker, in frustration, except me.

Parker wondered, had the new Governor arrived on the scene too late? Were the voters too out of touch with what was happening? Was the bureaucratic system too well entrenched to be reformed?

Parker knew that he and the new Governor would not agree on some issues. He knew, however, that this Governor would discuss differences with you in a thoughtful and interested way.

This Governor would offer his arguments against your position, and then politely listen to yours. Generally, a very good man. ProgDems, on the other hand, hear, he thought, but they don't listen.

Was the new Governor committed enough to stand up to the Senators who were out to defeat him in any way possible? Would anybody be, he wondered? Does he believe, as I do, thought Parker, that the ProgDems have no ideas, and don't feel that they need any original thoughts, to win elections in Vermont? Does he think that the old ProgDem beliefs are from educators who taught them the old ideas from the old Europe, all of which failed very soon after their adoption in the real world? Does he believe, as I do, that Vermont, today, is fading away to a grayness which is the ultimate result of too much government and too little independence from it?

I don't know, Parker thought. I don't know if maybe I'm slipping off the edge of reality myself. I don't think so, but then again, it does cause one to wonder, doesn't it?

I only know, he thought, that America's system of freedom and independence is the reason why we are the most productive and useful nation in the history of the world, and that its citizens are the wealthiest, regardless of their income levels. Anybody can be anything they want to become in this country, if they simply work hard and follow their dreams. That's the only reason that makes us different from all other nations on earth – and it works, better than any other system ever dreamed up by lazy politicians who want access to power and money without doing a lick of work for it.

Parker had had all these thoughts ever since high school, and they became permanently implanted when a history teacher, in those early years, led the entire class down this road. I remember, he thought, that this woman answered questions by demanding that we answer her leading questions ourselves. At the end of that year, she had taught us something that she didn't demand of us. We had learned things that we didn't even see coming.

Parker came out of that learning atmosphere with thoughts that had guided him for the rest of his life. As a consequence, he had become anathema to many other people along the way who didn't believe that the common man had the ability and intelligence to conduct his or her own affairs. Hell, he remembered, three years ago I even got shot for it.

These creatures, he knew, would take the taxpayers' money and create unnecessary government positions for their friends to dispense unnecessary regulations that required the common man to adhere to the government line. And Vermont was fading away because of this direction.

My God, he thought, I'm going to become totally depressed if I keep this up. In fact, I'll be fading away very soon myself.

He reached for the ignition switch of his beloved pickup, started up, and rolled back onto Route 5, heading south for home.

10

When Parker pulled into his driveway it was almost completely dark. Addie walked out onto the porch as he climbed out, and said, "Welcome, stranger. Where the hell have you been?"

Parker knew he was much later than he had anticipated, and Addie was letting him know it. The worst feature of his transgression, he knew, was that he didn't even realize it. Ouch, he thought. I'll just keep that to myself.

"Sorry, sweetie, time just got away." He didn't think that that would save the situation but Addie surprised him at that point.

"I understand, Willie," she said softly. "I just get worried sometimes. That's okay. Come on in and have something to eat."

Parker draped his arm over her shoulders as they walked into the house. "Where's Kate and Duane? I thought they were coming back here after a few days."

"Willie, it hasn't been a 'few days' yet. Just because you miss them is no good reason why you should yearn like a hound for their return. I miss them, too. And I miss our other two children, who are living too far away to get here often. They're getting along fine, however – better than you are, by the looks."

"'Yearn like a hound', Addie? I don't know what you mean." Addie squeezed his hand as they sat down on the couch.

"I know you don't, Willie. That's why I love you so much."

"Be careful with loose talk like that. The Governor's Commission on Women will lock you up for demeaning today's independent woman by showing open affection for a male person."

"To hell with them," snapped Addie. "I live a natural life, and a very good one, too. Those people up there don't know the meaning of the concept."

Parker decided to change the subject. "Addie, I'm going to call Jan Evlin tomorrow, and tell her that I'll look into her perceived problem. I can't say no to her. It would bother me too much. You understand, don't you?"

"Yes, Willie, I do. And speaking of that, I have an offer to make to you. I'm sure that you were aware that I was involved in considerable volunteer work in the County over the years. Still am, for that matter, off and on." Parker nodded. He knew.

"I made many contacts around the state in the non-profit industry. Except, of course, with VNRCAUC, the Vermont New Relativism Council Against Uncontrolled Commerce, VPIRC, The Vermont People's Interest Reaction Council, CPLAG, Citizens Protection League Against Greed, TETCofVT, the Tranquility and Equal Treatment Center of Vermont, one of the most vicious of them all. There were also others like them that knew who you were, too, Willie. Therefore, they wouldn't even acknowledge my presence at joint meetings. I don't think they liked you very much, Willie."

Parker grinned, faintly. "No, they didn't. I, and many others, knew that they were a large part of the 'Vermont-needs-to-be-minimized-to-ready-it-for-social-and-political-change' bunch."

"Anyway," he continued, "what's your point that steered us in this unpleasant direction?"

"I'm going to be your 'agent-in-place', Willie. I'm going to carefully talk to many of my friends around the state. I'll go to every meeting I can for the next week. I'll expand my network to see what's going on. And I'll try to find out who 'Z' is. You're right, Willie. This whole thing, with the 'Z' business, seems to be like those awful Saturday afternoon serials at the local movie house of years ago."

Parker stared at her. He knew he couldn't dissuade her from getting nosey, but he was bothered that she would place herself in the way of bad publicity like this. It showed him another thing, too. Addie really didn't believe that Jan Evlin had received a death threat. She talked a good game of being worried about her husband, but she didn't really think that there was any danger out there. Maybe she was right, he thought. I just have to be sure, he knew.

"All right, Addie," Parker said, "you play the great detective, but you be damned careful."

Addie looked at him sharply. She wasn't used to hearing this tone from her husband. She decided that he was serious, and there was no sense in saying anything except, "You bet, Willie."

11

The next morning Parker arose bright and early, ready to do a day's work. He thought he'd be frazzled by yesterday's travels and later-than-usual contact with his bed, but he found himself feeling darn good. His first task, right after breakfast, was to call Jan Evlin. He would feel comfortable when he did as he promised her he would.

He fished around in his wallet for the slip of paper with her number on it, found it, and set it beside the phone. Then he made enough noise so that Addie would come down in her robe, say a few grouchy things, and then make his breakfast. It always worked. Addie pretended that she didn't know he was playing a game, but she got back at him in other ways, causing him a bit of discomfort when it became his turn to do something nice for her. She always came out ahead, it seemed.

"What's on your plate today, sweetie?" Parker asked.

"I'm heading to Burlington on my quest for the Holy Grail of the non-profit religion. I'll probably stay over for two or three nights with Carolyn Mercer, my old college roommate. Not that she's so old, of course," interrupting her husband's attempt at a bad joke, "but that she is in the volunteer army that works for various non-profit organizations in Chittenden County, of which there are many, many, many. She'll be talkative about them and I'll listen closely. I'll feel a little like a spy of sorts, but I'll get over it. Also, she's the most honest person I've ever met, and that counts for a lot. It's the weekends when many meetings take place, which I will attend, of course, and I'll be doing a lot of calling. I could even be gone a week. And you, Willie?" she asked.

"I'm going to call Jan Evlin and tell her that I'll look into her non-profit problem for her. I'm sure, in three days, I can get in touch with her. Then I'm going to Montpelier and see Hugh Hammond. You've met Hugh, Addie. He's one of the lone Republican Representatives from Chittenden County. A dying breed, I'm afraid. Anyway, he'll find out the things I need to know to do a thorough look-see of the non-profits up there – and maybe around the state. And I'll probably stay over, too, but not for a week."

Addie brought Parker his bacon and eggs, and asked, "Do you really think that a big problem exists for Jan, Willie? I mean is there something tangible from which she needs to be shielded? It's very hard to accept, you know. And who will believe it anyway? Especially that business of a person out there who writes strange notes and calls himself 'Z'. He sounds like a comic book character."

"We'll cross that bridge somewhere in the future, Addie. Right now, we've got to assemble facts, and not delay in doing so."

Addie went upstairs to shower and pack, and Parker went over to the phone and dialed the number that Jan had given him.

He didn't expect that she'd be there, and he was right. Her voice came over the answering machine.

"This is Janice Evlin, reporter for the Chittenden Free Progressive. I'll be away from my desk for the day, but I'll return your call as soon as I return. After you hear a series of beeps, please be sure to leave your name and number. Thanks."

The beeps ended, sounding like a hive of angry hornets for what seemed an interminable time, and Parker, for no reason he could name, hung up. Then he went to find Addie.

She was packing when he entered the bedroom. "Addie," he said, "I would feel better if you kept a very low profile while you're looking into some of this non-profit stuff. Somehow I feel itchy about all of this, but I can't tell you why."

"And I don't have a single itch, Willie. I'm really going up there to prove you and Jan are off base on this. Okay?"

Parker nodded and walked over to her and put his arms around her. "Just for me, all right? If you sense any discomfort, back away and come home."

"Of course, Willie. Just as you always did. Right? But there won't be anything like that to worry about." And she gave him a quick kiss, picked up her suitcase, and left the room, on her way to the la-la land of Chittenden County.

12

Parker went in to his office at mid-morning and was greeted by Irene Doughton, his office manager and steady supporter, and now his business partner. Ever since the end of Parker's last adventure with the lawyer/killer from Burlington, who was after Kate Obrist, Parker had looked at Irene in a different light, and with some unease. He found out that Irene had refused to leave the office after he had asked her to go on vacation when it became evident that she might be in danger. Instead, she had hauled out a .45 caliber Army handgun her late husband had taught her to use, dropped it into the top drawer of her desk, and stayed at work. Challenging most people on anything made them run away. Challenging this woman put her on her guard and *you* in the position of danger.

"What's new, Irene?" Parker asked as he stepped through the door. "Anything you can't handle?"

Irene cocked an eye his way and said, "That means you're on the road again, doesn't it, Mr. Parker?"

"No, no, Irene. I just want to be helpful in my own office. Give me a feeling of importance, you know."

Irene said nothing, and handed him the mail. "Where are you off to, Mr. Parker, and for how long, and is it the kind of business you're on where I should remain armed?"

"Montpelier," answered Parker, "on Monday, for a couple of days, then maybe Burlington, and, no, there's nothing dangerous involved, so you can leave the artillery at home."

"I don't trust your assessment of what's dangerous and what isn't, Mr. Parker. That's based on history and personal experience. Therefore, as long as I work here, and for you, I will go around armed."

"Irene," cried Parker, "that situation was an aberration, and you know it."

"Really, Mr. Parker?" she answered, cynicism evident. "And what about three years ago when you were shot? Another aberration?"

Parker sensed a possible employee revolt brewing, and he knew he would lose before it even went to arbitration. He just shrugged and picked up his mail. "At least, keep it out of sight of our customers. If they see that hardware, they'll wonder why they bought life insurance from me when they could be ventilated by asking any simple question while in the office."

With that brilliant remark, which he knew would have no effect, he trudged back to his office.

Irene smiled at his departing back, and thought that her boss was a pretty neat guy. Irene and Addie had talked about the dangers of the year before and the admiration she had for Parker. Addie advised Irene not to give him a hint of her admiration. "Otherwise, he'll be impossible to live with," she had said.

Parker was in his private office, with sloping floor and Spartan appearance, opening his mail, which turned out to be of no importance. Then he called Representative Hugh Hammond in Montpelier, an old friend who Parker knew had some knowledge of the intricacies of the non-profit industry in Vermont. Parker left a message for him to expect a visit in the late afternoon, so that he could "pick his brain" on a subject with which he knew Hammond was very familiar. Parker hoped he would have time to see him.

Then he got up from his $29.95 "executive" chair, which was the cause, he was sure, of his occasional back problems, watched the chair roll toward the outside window on the floor with the 10% grade, muttered "to hell with it", and walked out into the front room of the office.

"Well, Irene, I'm off. See you later on next week. Hold down the fort."

"Okay, Mr. Parker. Take care of yourself." Parker could tell that she didn't think he would change his ways at all, nor even recognize danger if he fell over it. Boy, was she wrong, Parker thought.

13

Parker drove his truck very carefully in Vermont's capital city of Montpelier. It seemed reasonable to him to assume that every other person on any street in this city was a lawyer; and most of them would probably sue him for violation of their rights under the equal protection clause of the Vermont Constitution, at the very least, if the breeze from his truck so much as ruffled a trouser leg in passing.

He finally found a parking place near the Thrush Tavern, that national monument in defense of saloons with too much noise, too little space and, due to the crowds, mixed-up food orders. Nobody seemed to mind in that joint, Parker thought with satisfaction.

As he hiked up to the Statehouse he noticed, once again, the security measures added since 9/11. He was in favor of these measures, recognizing at the same time that the ProgDems were a sort of terrorist group in themselves. The main difference between the two groups had to do with subtlety. ProgDems didn't indiscriminately blow up things or use people for target practice. They just started the process of spoilage of the institutions of Vermont by the legislation they passed. Polite character assassination had also become a useful election year tool. This process of destruction took longer, but it was quieter, and more permanent. Another difference, too, was that the ProgDems' upper command bunch dressed better than anybody else.

He walked into the cafeteria, which was serving no food at this hour, but had coffee available. He got his cup of coffee and walked over to a table where he could be seen by those entering.

"Bill Parker, as I live and breathe," boomed the voice of George Shaver, a Representative from the Northeast Kingdom, as he loomed up beside Parker from an unnoticed corner in the cafeteria. He was one of Parker's closest and most loyal friends. He could be depended upon, which could be the message anybody would be happy to have carved on their tombstone. He lacked that artful craftiness that dedicated politicians needed to cultivate in order to run for Governor someday. He didn't know anything about being circumspect. In short, a person always knew where they stood with George. "What trouble are you in now, Bill?"

"None, George," answered Parker, "unless you bring me some."

"Who, Bill, me?" he asked. "It's only when I get mixed up with you that I get into trouble." Then he quieted down enough to ask, "How are you and Addie, Bill? That was a rough time for both of you a year ago. Addie come back all right, did she?"

"Yes, she did, George. Most of the way, at least. I take it that you've never been questioned by anybody about that business we were involved in?"

"Just once." His face darkened as he looked at Parker. "That SOB scribbler Dieter Paine was nosing around, and seemed to know that I was doing something in the Burlington area that had to do with that bastard Benton. Told me he never thought he'd see me outside of the Kingdom and there I was, he said, hiking around Burlington, probably lost. His territory, I suppose he thought. I told him to take a hike, and who the hell is Benton, anyway? He left in a hurry, which was gratifying, and never bothered me again. He's chicken, you know, Bill. Runs his mouth and his pencil, but only writes about himself. Like Hemingway used to."

Parker was stunned by both bits of information. First, because Paine had an inkling about the Benton situation of a year ago, and secondly, because George had a familiarity with Hemingway. Of course, the possibility was strong that George meant Josiah Hemmingway, or somebody equally unknown, who ran a local hardware store.

"Nothing else, George? How did he learn about Benton and you, for God's sake?"

Shaver shrugged while Parker worried.

"And were you talking about Ernest Hemingway, the writer? Have you read some of his books?"

Surprising Parker mightily, he said, "I have a couple of them. My daughter told me he was one of the great writers of all time. So, to please her - ," and then he stopped and leaned across the table and spoke more quietly than Parker had ever heard him. "She was trying to improve my mind, you see, Bill. Well, sir, I bought a couple at the annual St. Johnsbury library book sale. The lady who ran the sale told me that she had a couple of Hemingway's best known books, and I'd really like 'em. So, I bought 'em both. Dollar each, as I recall. Well, anyway, I read 'em, front to back."

Parker was enthralled. Was this another great story from the Northeast Kingdom? "And?" asked Parker. He didn't know what to expect now.

"Wasted two dollars, by Christ. Ernie didn't write stories for others to enjoy. He wrote about what he wanted to be as a man and wasn't, and couldn't ever be. And it knocked him down, that was clear. Stories were pretty good, too, but it was plain that they could have been better if somebody else, who didn't have any hang-ups, had written 'em."

Parker smiled fondly at Shaver, and said, "George, that was a great term paper you just talked about. I don't know if you went to college, but it would have gotten you into trouble with your American literature professor if you had. However, it would have made for a lot of fun in the class."

"Never went to college, Bill," Shaver said. "Wanted to, but we were dirt poor, and I couldn't leave home. Needed there, I was. Then I got a good job, and never took the time. Some measure of regret there, I'll tell you."

Parker could identify with that story. "I think college would have spoiled you, George," he said.

Just then, Hugh Hammond walked up and put out his hand. "Bill, it's great to see you again. I suppose you and Addie are living the quiet life now, back in Bridgeton. You're all healed up from that bad day on the House floor, I hear. It's been three long years since then, you know. Three years of just sitting and working in your insurance business. Darn dull stuff. Bad for you, too, Bill. You've got to get out more, bring some excitement back into your life. Travel a little." He beamed at Parker with pleasure. Parker beamed back. George Shaver beamed at them both.

"Well, sir, Bill," said Shaver, "I'll be shoving off. Got to go up home tonight. Great to see you, Bill." He looked at Parker with a wry grin and said, "You listen to old Hugh, here, Bill. He knows what's good for you." With that, he strode off.

"There's a real character, Bill, right there," Hammond said, looking at Shaver's retreating back. "Smart, too, you know."

Parker now knew that he had badly misjudged George Shaver for years, and he didn't feel good about it either. He felt that he had been sort of a snob about George.

“I’m free now for dinner, Bill, if you can stand it. And I’ll treat. Judging by your message, you want to talk about something you think I know about. Fair enough. Let’s get going.” They headed off together toward Montpelier’s Thrush Tavern, the favorite hangout of the members of the legislature.

14

Hugh Hammond had been a member of the Vermont House for twelve terms. He was a Republican, but not so that anyone would notice. Parker thought that the definition that described Representative Hammond was somebody who "operated under the radar screen" of his constituency. His district was noticeably liberal and voted for all candidates who professed any type of socialism along with a hatred of private computer companies, and any other businesses with an "X", a "C", or an "E" at the end their corporate names.

Hammond, however, was always re-elected, and the reasons were classically political. He took care of all the questions and problems that were brought to his attention by his district. In fact, he went looking for situations that weren't considered problems at the time so he could fix them. This sort of constant campaigning was necessary when the candidate walked a political fence every minute of his day. He also had some independence of thought, an outgoing personality, a sense of humor, and endless energy. He was not brilliant, and he cast some votes that were not acceptable to a majority in his district, but the personal qualities he possessed in abundance allowed him to treat these votes with humor and his excellent preparation didn't hurt.

Parker knew that Hammond wasn't a vote that the Republicans counted on, but they always gave him center stage in their caucuses when an issue surfaced about which he knew something.

About five years earlier, Hugh's wife, Margo, died suddenly of a heart attack. She was a very successful businesswoman in Chittenden County, operating an upscale women's clothing store in Shelburne, with a branch in St. George, another in Essex Junction, a small store in, surprisingly, St. Johnsbury, and a large store in Rutland.

Most of Hammond's constituents showed up at his wife's stores at some time during the year to buy fashionable clothes that would be unsuited to their political beliefs of the "share everything you have with everybody you don't know" school of economic thought. For brief periods of time each year, apparently, "trendy" was acceptable to the political left. Parker was not surprised.

Margo's death shattered Hammond, and he had decided not to run again for the House. However, his sister, a farmer's wife from New Hampshire, was an eminently practical woman. She knew that her brother needed something to do, and reminded Hammond that his wife had always preached that when someone's wife or husband died, only *one* of them died. The other had to go on. She was convincing, and Hugh had won all of his elections since that bad time.

Parker also remembered that awful day on the House floor three years earlier. One of his most loyal and forceful supporters was Hugh Hammond, who threw caution to the winds and supported everything that Parker said, even in his own district. That could have been his political demise, and he knew it. He told Parker that he believed he won because of the energy he used to defend Parker to his voters and the absolutely nuthouse positions his opposition ProgDem candidate took when attacking Parker. They apparently admired him for his loyalty to Parker even though most of them didn't agree with his support of Parker. Some, Hugh told Parker later, even hated Parker, but still voted for Hammond. Voters are hard to understand sometimes, Parker decided.

They entered the Thrush Tavern in early evening, battling their way through the crowds of people who were entering with them or were trying and, it seemed, showing some desperation, to get out. When Parker and Hammond had successfully plowed along this hall they were confronted by a door. They opened it and could have stepped straight into the main coatrack less than three feet away. Veterans of this fight to enter the dubious pleasures of the Thrush were always able to avoid stepping into the coatrack. In fact, some of them even used it for its intended purpose.

Parker himself had never hung his coat on this rack. It would have either been mistakenly taken out of the place by somebody else, possibly to be later returned to the Thrush, or it would just be swallowed up by all the other garments crammed in there, never to be seen again. Like some low budget horror film, he thought.

Parker and Hammond moved into the bar and each ordered a beer. The beer arrived with unexpected speed and they grabbed their glasses as if they were really intended for somebody else, which was a definite possibility, based on Parker's personal experience. They were delivered by the guy who ran the place, who yelled at Parker, "Where the hell have you been, Bill? All the excitement has left our little world here in Montpelier."

"Good", said Parker emphatically, while smiling at Paul Chumley, an old friend from Parker's days in the House.

Parker and Hammond stood in the middle of the room and shouted at each other. Other old friends greeted Parker, as Chumley moved back to his post behind the crowded bar. Hammond made introductions of new members of the Vermont House Parker had not met. A couple of these new people, upon hearing Parker's name, blinked, looked closely at him, mumbled, and moved away smartly, as if he was bearing a disease. "They wouldn't like you, Bill, if you were still here," Hammond yelled, with humor, as two scruffy ProgDems moved away, clutching their wine glasses. "They would say that you had slowed down the historic process toward socialism."

"Socialism, Hugh?" shouted Parker. "That no longer has any relevance at all, does it?"

"It means something where those two birds come from, Bill, which is right from around here. They run as Progressives, but they are definitely socialists, probably worse."

"Haven't learned a thing, have they?" said Parker.

"Nope," said Hammond. "They were inoculated, when very young, against receiving any real and useful knowledge. It was good for the rest of their lives as long as they got an annual booster shot each school year. At the end of their Sophomore year in high school, they were fully protected against any logical brain waves for the rest of their lives."

Parker smiled, shook his head, and said, "Let's go into the dining room, Hugh, and let me ask you some questions."

Hammond nodded and they made their way down the hall, carrying their coats, of course, and entered a surprisingly lightly populated room.

The term "dining room" placed a gleam on this room that it definitely didn't deserve. It was clean, however, and had enough tables in it so that when it was crowded, almost no one was comfortable but not so uncomfortable as to cause people to leave in disgust. It was a game, also, ducking the platters of the famous Thrushburgers being passed around, hoping that they landed where they were supposed to. Parker knew for certain that, over the years, he had paid for a number of them that he never saw.

Parker, however, loved every minute he spent in this historic watering hole, and so did the a majority of the General Assembly members.

Only the ProgDems, in their fashionable clothes, or their "I don't have to dress up for anybody" clothes, stayed away. It was beneath them, it seemed, regardless of their station in the ranks of the compassionate people of Vermont's left.

The room had drab plastic tablecloths on the tables, and nothing else - unless you wanted to count a classic fireplace, marble trim and all, which hadn't had a fire lit in it for a period of years longer than the age of the most ancient of legislative mariners. And every time a person sat at a table directly in front of it, the marble mantelpiece got in the way of your head, no matter what a person did to avoid it. Parker had sometimes left the Thrush with a ringing in his ears due to the occasional skull beatings administered by that hunk of marble.

An interior decorator would lose his or her mind in this place, he thought. The room obviously was set up to resist and foil any of their ilk who came in carrying a signed contract that said, "do what you have to do, but clear out all old political demons, memories, and smells of stale beer, and make it acceptable to young families with their children."

The Thrush would always win, and another decorator's career would be ruined. The present owners simply did what the Thrush Tavern seemed to want. They got along together just fine.

Parker and Hammond sat down at a small corner table. Parker judged that they could hear each other and probably no one could hear them.

Hammond looked curiously at him for a few seconds. Then he said, "What do you have on your mind, Bill?"

"I'm doing a favor for a friend, Hugh, regarding the non-profits in Vermont. I won't go into any more detail than that, and it's important that you not mention our conversation. Okay with you?"

"The last time you tried to keep things quiet, Bill, you ended up on the floor of the House, ruining the carpet. However," he said resignedly, "we'll try again. Yes, I'll keep it quiet. What's up?" Parker thought he noticed a slight hesitation in Hammond when he had mentioned the purpose of his visit.

Parker drew a big breath and said, "The central thing, I guess, Hugh, is that a friend of mine was researching the non-profit industry in Vermont, and this person ran into some unexpected opposition from a direction that was also unexpected. Let's leave it at that right now." Hammond nodded.

"I need some details and background of this industry," continued Parker, "what types of non-profits there are, the names of the ones that you think are important and influential, and are they real?"

Hammond looked up at Parker at that. "What are you really driving at, Bill? What do you mean by asking if they are 'real'?"

"Look, Hugh, I'm not sure what I'm looking for. Maybe nothing. Maybe after we talk I'll just drive home and my work will be done. I owe this person some effort, though, both because they came to me and because I feel an obligation to them for past favors. They helped me out once when I was up here and in trouble. I have to do something. I'm sure you can understand that."

Hammond looked again at Parker, nodded, and started talking. "This industry in Vermont, made up of non-profit organizations, is the state's largest employer, and one of the most profitable, Bill, if you can believe that." Parker jumped at that. He was remembering Jan's comments about the profitability of non-profits.

"What the hell do you mean, Hugh? Revealing my ignorance, I want to know how they're profitable when they don't have profits!"

"Cool down, Bill. Clever accountants call *profits* in this industry by the name of *fund balances.* A nice, acceptable name for money made beyond your expenses, but not calling it profit, which is a terrible word anyway to the ProgDems. No sense reminding anybody that non-profits pay no taxes and their contributions are all tax-deductible. What a great deal for all concerned, except, of course, for the working men and women of Vermont who pay taxes on all their income and enough more to make up for the taxes *not* paid by these birds. And the regular people have no political power to match the lobbyists for the non-profits."

Hammond was speaking in a surprisingly aggressive manner. Parker couldn't remember Hammond being this worked up about anything. He had the reputation, at least when Parker served with him, of being a very balanced and thoughtful person, and never boisterous in his comments. Apparently, that condition of his life was over, at least for tonight.

"And these non-profits," continued Hammond, "collectively have very strong fund balances. Nationally, fund balances are extremely healthy. There are some, of course, that don't attract much money, but they aren't influential either. None of them pay any Federal taxes – and no Vermont taxes, either, of course, except payroll taxes by their full-time employees. That, by the way, is why they have so many volunteers. They have convinced thousands of Vermonters that their cause is just and they should volunteer as a social obligation. What they're really doing is cutting down drastically on their full-time payroll. And that leaves just that much more for the officers to split up as salary increases, bonuses, and the like. In answer to your unasked question, Bill, they're not on the level – many of them are corrupt, too, to one degree or another."

"It sounds as though the volunteers are being used, rather than being useful, Hugh. Have any of them figured this out yet?" Parker asked.

"Some people have, Bill, but others respond that they will feel like traitors to these non-profit efforts designed for the common good, and they would be betraying their responsibility to the less fortunate. That reasoning works every time, I'm told."

Hammond leaned across the table. "And non-profit organizations can take in money from almost any source, and from anywhere, and in any amount. Nationally, that's about 15% of their revenue. In Vermont it's closer to 30%. The rest of their income comes from fees for services and goods, government grants and contracts, and their own investments."

"Sounds like a sweet deal, Hugh, even if you're legitimate," said Parker. Hammond looked up at Parker. The usual smile was missing.

"To continue, Bill, there are almost 2700 non-profits in Vermont, and many of them do a terrific job. I'm sure you know that. In addition, there are the private foundations, which control a hell of a lot of money, and exert tremendous influence in Vermont, especially in the Legislature. And then we have the groups that call themselves non-profits, but don't even try to get official non-profit status. These are the ones that use the generic 'non-profit' title in order to attract donations from people who hate the word 'profit'. Of course," Hammond said with disgust, "these contributors earn their income from profitable companies all over this country. But that's beside the point, isn't it?"

"A whole other subject, Hugh," said Parker.

"I think I know what you're driving at, Bill, with your questions. Maybe I agree with you, if I'm right about what you're thinking. Just remember, though, that there are many non-profits that are religiously affiliated. I believe them to be okay, although I've never looked into them too closely. Are they on your list, too?"

"If I get led there, Hugh, I'll go there. Until this moment, I never considered churches as a non-profit."

"Well, they always have enjoyed non-profit status, Bill. I don't know if they handle the money well, of course. Churches don't get too closely looked at by the Feds at tax time, or at any time, for that matter. In Vermont many of the non-profits we're talking about get away with murder."

Parker would remember that comment many times as the days marched along.

Parker nodded. "Okay, I'll trust that, Hugh. However, have you noticed strange, and different, views of these religious groups that have formed churches by absorbing some of the failing traditional churches? They preach the gospel of the hard left of the 30's. I know about that because a church in my hometown of Bridgeton, which called itself the 'Life of the New Meaning', was passing out literature on a Sunday morning that demanded that Vermont eliminate all businesses in the state made up of more than five people unless they were involved in the 'home economy' requirements."

Hammond had a look of alarm on his face.

"I know, I know, Hugh, that that sounds ludicrous, but it's true," said Parker, holding up his hands as if to block a blow.

"I need to interrupt you, Bill, with a question. What are the 'home economy' requirements, for goodness sake?"

"These are the demands of some kind of 'life cult' that this group brought with them when they moved here. It says that people are allowed to grow what they eat, barter for the rest, and create no businesses that use more electricity than they can generate themselves on their own property." Hammond just stared at Parker.

"Let me get back to the 'Life of the New Meaning' church, Hugh." Hugh could only manage to nod.

"Some of their worshippers became upset and they came to a friend of mine, Marvin Bailey, the wisest man in Bridgeton, as far as they were concerned. He gave them the advice to get out of that church. They apparently agreed, left him and went home to stay. Then Marvin came to see me, and filled me in. The church is still there, right now, with about half of its congregation gone, but they do very well on their non-profit status income, so my wife was told. A lot of their income comes from outside Vermont."

Hammond sat there motionless for a few seconds. Then he seemed to make up his mind about something because he gave a quick look around the room, and then shifted forward in his seat, his face a study in concentration. He placed his elbows on the table and asked, in a low voice, "Do you know what you're getting into, Bill? Do you know how deep this sort of culture runs in Vermont; how many different types of organizations are active in the non-profit world in Vermont, whether they're registered with the state or not? Do you know how much money they control, and how many people are on their payrolls? And how many charitable foundations there are that are controlled by today's people who are entirely different from the original founders of these charitable institutions – and using the money, after their cut, of course, to support all kinds of non-profit enterprises and initiatives? You've heard about the ProgDem Party that receives 95% of its income from out of state at every election? That's only half the story, Bill. The hundreds of thousands that the non-profits in Vermont receive is the campaign funding money that no campaign finance law will ever suppress, or even report."

Hammond then leaned in again toward Parker and, after looking around, said in a low voice, "And here's a big one for you Bill – bigger than any of them, I think. Check out the state-funded Continuing Tradition Trust for the Victims of Capitalism. You'll have to do it, Bill. I looked at it about six months ago. I had a tip, you see, and some evidence, too. And then a good friend told me, in the nicest possible way, to stay away from this Trust. Well, I did, you know." Hammond was perspiring freely, he seemed to be shaking.

Parker was surprised by this outburst. It was almost as if Hugh Hammond was unloading some things that he'd been carrying around for years. He was not the same Hugh Hammond that Parker remembered from just two hours ago.

"You want a good example of what happens when a non-profit gets a foothold in the consciousness of the public, Bill?

Listen to this." Hammond's delivery was accented by jabbing strokes of his hands. Parker had never seen him so animated.

"What do you know about The Helpful Medics, Bill?"

"Not a thing to speak of, Hugh. My wife does some volunteer work for them around Bridgeton, and tells me they do a good job."

"And she's correct, Bill. The Helpful Medics are so well known that the majority of all town budgets in Vermont actually vote to give them money each year."

"Yeah, I've noticed that Bridgeton certainly does," said Parker.

Hammond again shifted forward in his chair. "About ten years ago, or so, two private, for profit, nursing associations tried to compete with them in Chittenden County and in Rutland County, I think it was. Anyway, these two groups attended a meeting of some health panel or board in Montpelier. I was there. The potential competitors to The Helpful Medics were denied a permit to compete against them through the process called a CON, even though their prices were lower than the Helpful Medics' prices. In some cases much lower."

"Hold it, Hugh. What the hell is a CON?" asked Parker. "I suppose I ought to know, but I don't remember."

"A Certificate of Need, Bill. It's the instrument by which the state holds a gun to the head of every would-be competitor who would like to provide those state-run health services so beloved by the ProgDems. And permission to compete against the state in health care services also means that this private company would receive their payments out of the Medicaid money – and no good ProgDem would allow that money to go anywhere except to their friends." Hammond almost seemed to run out of breath.

He gathered himself and started talking again. "It's also what they use to control hospitals who want to upgrade their level of competence and offer additional services, even if these forward-thinking hospitals propose an arrangement to share revenues with other hospitals in the region that can make use of these new programs and leading edge medical machines. If this bunch in Montpelier wants to help its friends, it simply says that there is no need for more services in this area of health care, and turn them down flat. A CON process is an excellent way to legitimize lousy operating practices and poor management. It's also a curtailment of opportunity for not only a new business but the possibility of better and less expensive care for Vermont's elderly. Hell of a note, wouldn't you say, Bill?"

Parker wasn't surprised to hear about this CON requirement. In effect, the ProgDems had their hands at the throat of every private company that could do a better job for lower costs. Parker gestured his agreement to Hammond.

Hammond plowed on inexorably. "Preservation of the state monopoly in health care is the real purpose of the CON process, not the loftier motive of doing things better and less expensively for the Vermont taxpayer and the patients. Under the state method of operating, the cost and prices just keep going up. Use Canada as your guide and you'll see exactly what I mean. And, speaking of Canada, do you know something else, Bill?" Hammond looked as if he was ready to stand up and shout.

"Go ahead, Hugh," said Parker, with a calmness he didn't feel.

"You must know that our Medicaid program is bankrupt. You do, don't you?" Hammond seemed to be testing Parker on these details. Parker nodded. "If costs are rising, Vermont simply adds more charges to the bills of the other, non-Medicaid patients. If costs continue to rise, they eliminate the service itself. If the services aren't provided, the state doesn't have to pay for them. Right?"

"That's true, Hugh, but how do you know this is true?" asked Parker. "This is serious business, Hugh. I'm sure you know that."

"Of course I do, Bill," he said loudly. "But all the ProgDems shout about giving us the Canadian Health system. And the way the Canadians have attempted to control costs is to eliminate services."

"And that's why the older Canadians are coming to the U. S. in droves?"

"Damn right it is," said Hammond, staunchly. "That's how Canada does it, and our CON process is the way we do it."

Parker nodded, having forgotten about this sort of manipulation of public and private money and services. A perfect example of state services that can't stay alive without state protection from good, less expensive, competitors. A ProgDem solution all the way, no matter what the cost. And the ProgDems don't have to pay for it.

“What are some of the other influential organizations that call themselves non-profits, Hugh?”

Hammond paused to think about this question. “I’ll give you some of the more important ones, Bill. I didn’t bring my list because I didn’t know that you wanted to talk about these types of organizations. Well, anyway, here are ------,”

“Hello, hello,” came a slightly nasal voice, “what’s this big meeting about, Hugh? And this is Bill Parker, isn’t it? Former Representative Parker, who can’t seem to stay out of Montpelier.”

The voice was accompanied by a forced and unreal chuckle. The person uttering these words squeezed through the increasingly crowded room to stand beside Hugh Hammond. Parker had never seen him before.

“Bill,” said Hammond, having difficulty maintaining his composure, “this is Reginald Naughton. Reggie, I guess you know Bill Parker, then.”

“Never met him before, Hugh, but I’ve heard *of* him and *about* him. How are you, Bill?” he asked, putting out his hand. Naughton was one of those people who talked down his nose to everybody. Parker supposed that he was expected to feel grateful for Reggie taking the time from his busy day to lower himself and speak to him.

Reginald Naughton was a head taller than Parker, and twenty-five years younger, and looked fit. He weighed about 220 pounds, Parker calculated, and looked as though he could run all day without breathing hard. When he leaned forward to hear Parker and Hammond and speak to them in the crowd noise, he smelled like new pine trees and old moss. He was dressed in that indefinable way that characterizes the fashionable woodsman. Parker also noticed that his hands were not used to hard work. In fact, they were downright perfect, finished up with what looked like a recent manicure. Parker, if he allowed himself to do it, almost felt inferior.

Parker took the proffered hand. He was right. Smooth as a baby’s lower extremity, looking from the back, and eight times cleaner. “How do you do?” Parker asked.

“Oh, I do fine, Bill. It’s I who should be asking you how *you* are,” Naughton said, effusively, and wearing a grin that was somehow smug. “I’ve heard that you’re the one who was shot in the Statehouse a few years ago?”

Parker just looked at Naughton and was about to turn back to Hugh as a sign that he was already tired of this exchange when Naughton put a heavy hand on his shoulder.

"Well, I've got to get along. I'll let you resume your meeting. Remember, you two, that up here you should be very careful what you say. Sometimes words can come back to haunt you." A broad smile covered his face. He looked directly at Hugh Hammond.

"*Nice* to see you again, Hugh, and *good* to meet *you*, Bill." Parker hated to be called by his first name by someone he had met just thirty seconds before.

Parker turned to Hammond and asked, "Who the hell was that guy, Hugh?"

Hammond's face was flush. "He's a teacher, I think, at some high school around here, I don't know which one. I've heard that he gets all over the state, talking to students about personal devotion to doing good things for people and for the state. He seems to spend a lot of time in the Statehouse during the sessions, so I guess he doesn't have a heavy schedule. Or maybe he has outside money coming in. You know, a trust funder. Or maybe he works at night. Whatever. He has an office somewhere in Montpelier. He seems to turn up all the time, but I don't know what his interests are. Quite a few people in our government seem to know him, though. There are a lot of people around here just like him – although they don't talk so strangely." Hammond showed nervousness as he spoke that wasn't apparent before.

"Let's get back to the subject, Hugh. Give me some names of these non-profits that are so profitable."

At that moment, their Thrushburgers arrived, excess fries falling off the plate and the decorative pieces of lettuce fluttering down after them. It's good to see that the important things don't change, he thought.

15

"As I started to say, a long, long time ago, Bill, here are a few names of some groups and associations that evade paying taxes legally. Let's start with the VPIRC."

Hammond looked at Parker, then smiled slightly, and continued, "That's the Vermont People's Interest Reaction Council, for you veteran legislators who have not only forgotten, after retirement, who your friends were, but also who your real enemies were when you were here. It's a far left, anti-business, coalition group that uses the children of the next generation as the excuse to ruin the present one. They are one of the many front line groups around the state that recruit candidates for the ProgDems on a year-round basis, and are paid by outside money to do so. A vicious and demanding master, if I can believe the former volunteers who worked for them." Parker showed an expression of disbelief, along with anger, that Hammond noticed.

"Am I wearing you out, Bill?" he asked.

"Just keep going, Hugh," said Parker. "I'm hard to exhaust."

"Okay. Then we have the VNRCAUC, which stands for the Vermont New Relativism Council Against Uncontrolled Commerce. These folks are also way to the left, Bill, and do the same types of things that VPIRC does, sometimes together. There is no real difference between these two. Both VPIRC and VNRCAUC actually hate both 'things' and 'people' in Vermont and America. These are two of the major non-profits, Bill, and they lead the pack in doing all they can to shut down commercialism in Vermont. And there are many of these groups. And all of them financed almost totally by outside money."

Parker was frantically writing down these names and a few notes on his napkin. He paused and looked up at Hammond. "Those are harsh words, Hugh. How accurate are they?"

"They aren't harsh enough, Bill. Let me give you a few more, just to make the trip worthwhile. How about the CPLAG? Heard of that one?" Parker shook his head. "That row of letters stands for the Citizens' Protection League Against Greed. Their mission is to protect us from ourselves by bringing in very highly paid lawyers from places around New England to stop any development that requires moving any soil at all from where it is to where it must go to start a project. Doing that will eliminate the possibility of any greed popping up, you see, and we'll all be better off, including the children. And they lead the charge in demanding that the schools train their students to resist greed, too. Of course, they will also have eliminated any job creation for the parents of these children, too. But they don't give a damn about that. The term of 'job creation' embodies a concept that's foreign to them, I'm told."

Parker was on his fifth napkin when his scribbling caught up to Hammond's dialogue.

Hammond sat back in his chair, hooked his thumbs in his belt, and said, "And we, you and I, supported, through a lack of attention, the very Act that gave us a permit process that allowed anybody, no matter what interest they may have in a project, or no interest whatsoever, to appeal to a new court, the Environmental Court, here in Montpelier. This phony court killed more jobs and families in Vermont in the last twenty years than the black plague would have."

"Our new Governor will make some changes, won't he?" Parker asked. "In fact, he's already made a change for the better, hasn't he? Something to do with party status, and being able to appeal? And he's changed the Environmental Court, too, I've heard."

"Yes, he did get something through, using the rules. He knew that he'd never get legislation through the ProgDem General Assembly to do much because the hard left has taken it over. Vermont is considered the most liberal and anti-job state in the country. The Governor is very popular, Bill, as you may know, and the media haven't received their orders yet on how to attack both him and the Lt. Governor. That will be issued, you may be sure, and soon, too." Parker was appalled.

"The Governor's powers are limited to nibbling around the edges of the environmentalists' control of the job creation process. And those people who are appointed to the various Environmental Commissions around the state have had a positive impact, too. And certainly not all of the people who are employed to run the nuts-and-bolts of the Commissions are against job-creation, either. However, the majority are. And at the end of it all, the ProgDems still retain the ultimate power in allowing any development." Hammond continued. "The Governor will do his best, Bill, but have you gone over the credentials of the ProgDems who run the legislature today – especially the Vermont Senate? A number of them came from these non-profit groups who don't like Vermont – or, in some cases, it seems, even America, very much. Some of them were actually on the Boards of Directors that ran these non-profit groups."

There was a level of disgust coming from Hammond that surprised Parker. He hadn't seen it when he was in the House and serving with him. Parker also noticed that Hammond was speaking in a different, almost compulsive, way, as if he just wanted to get as much said as he possibly could in the shortest time span. Parker sensed that something had changed for Hugh.

Hammond continued, "The Governor is intelligent and aware, Bill – he loves Vermont, which is something new for us, but these people he's up against, and thousands like them in Vermont, will do anything to stop him and they will be defended by such stalwart supporters of the 'truth' as the Mid-Vermont Bugle, the Chittenden Free Progressive, the Bennington Beacon, the Brattleboro Opposition, and the North Country Times Revisionist. All are daily papers, and all are instruments of the left's agenda."

Parker thought, this is like my time, three years ago, revisited. What I touched on then was just the tip of the iceberg. And I was shot for it, for God's sake. What Hugh Hammond is talking about is the machinery of how it all works. And how deep it goes. Nothing is changed except we have a Republican Governor, but a ProgDem House and Senate. The Senate is especially far left. What that all equals is struggle. And maybe some legislative changes that the Senate ProgDems can be embarrassed into letting go through, but not without their fingerprints on every inch of it. And they will be portrayed by the media as heroes, fighting against the extremists who will sacrifice the environment or the children, or whatever works best for them at the moment. And some of these Senators actually teach our children in our schools right now, or used to until they had been anointed as Vermont State Senators. It was at times like these that Parker felt very tired from the pressure of a constant, daily, hulking presence from some arm of government.

"Had enough, Bill?" asked Hammond, interrupting Parker's reverie. "Maybe this will give you something to take away from our quiet, subdued, and tranquil dinner tonight. My best guess is that 40% of the 2700 to 3000 non-profits in Vermont are set-ups for continuous recruiting and campaigning for ProgDems. They also employ many of these ProgDem politicians on a year-round basis, using outside money. They are in almost every town. They launder donations that are then used for ProgDem campaigns. There are probably 8,000 paid people, maybe more, and thousands of volunteers, working all over Vermont to elect ProgDems, and to lobby up here in Montpelier. A large number of the volunteers don't even see what their non-profit is doing. They have leadership from the most extreme groups, some of which I've already mentioned."

Parker was thinking furiously. All of this could be checked, of course, and the first tier of this vetting process would be the research being done by Jan Evlin.

"There is, however," Hammond said, "a central leadership council of some kind. I'm not sure of this, but there has to be, because all of these politically active associations switch direction instantly during campaigns, and all at the same time. You know what I'm saying, Bill. Like the national news media and their columnists and editorial writers, and the other 'independent thinkers' in that herd. Do you recall when the word 'gravitas' was used in the last presidential campaign? It was a 'snob' word that the ProgDems used to try to convince the American voter that one of the candidates didn't have the 'breadth' or 'depth', or some damned thing, to be President. It took almost two weeks for these strange people to figure out that the American voter didn't know what the hell the word meant. And this central authority never figured out themselves that those who were ordered to use the word didn't know what it meant either." Hammond eyed his Thrushburger, and then started talking again.

"Well, anyway," Hammond said, "it was used on a Friday evening news show for the first time, and then every one of them used it all weekend. Well, both CBS and CNN, and then VTEliteTV used it at about the same time. It was the columnists, and other members of the left, who served as guests on their news programs who used it, and all at the same time. Remember that?"

Parker nodded. He did remember that word. He was one of those who didn't know what it meant. The ProgDems who used it were working hard to make everybody feel inadequate because they didn't understand the term. Parker never told anybody except Addie that he didn't know what the word meant. Addie knew everything. When she said that she didn't, either, Parker was secretly delighted.

"Where did the orders come from, Bill? They had to have come from one source. Same thing in Vermont. Somebody is calling the shots."

Parker leaned back in his chair. My God, he thought. Is Hammond losing it?

"Hugh," Parker said, "do you know how you would be branded if you were to go public with this? A crazy man, an alarmist, and a conspiracy nut. I know. I've been through it, as you know. You were around when I spoke on the House floor, three years ago. What went on during the days before that made many of those whom I considered as friends run away from me."

Hammond blinked and looked around the now crowded room. Parker doubted that he saw anything. "Yes, Bill, I know. I'm afraid that I don't have the courage to go public. In fact, I even received a sort of warning about my innocent digging into the non-profits in Vermont. Did you know that?"

"No, I most certainly did not, Hugh. Of course, I haven't been up here for quite a while. What kind of a warning did you receive?" Parker was thinking about another warning, just received by Jan Evlin, for her excavation work on the same subject.

"Just a note, Bill, a couple of years ago, actually. It was left on my desk in the House. An envelope with my name on it, marked 'Personal'. I saved it, for some reason."

Parker had this eerie feeling that he was hearing Jan Evlin, speaking in her nervous way, the slight lisp becoming just a little more pronounced, the way it did with her. "Do you remember it, Hugh? What it said?"

"I can do better than that, Bill," as he reached for his inside jacket pocket and withdrew a leather wallet. He gazed around the room again, then dropped his hands below the table edge. He came up with the wallet and replaced it inside his coat and, at the same time, slipped a folded piece of paper across the table to Parker. It was enclosed in a clear plastic envelope.

"This really bothered me, Bill. I told nobody about it. I've been carrying this piece of paper for two years, not knowing what

I should do with it, but not wanting to throw it away. Maybe I should have, and just tried to forget it. But I couldn't. When you left your message for me the first thing I thought about was this note. I know I can trust you with this. We all know we can trust you, Bill. I don't know what it will add to your knowledge. Maybe nothing. I would, however, like your opinion of it. Read it, and when you're through, answer just one question: was I right to be worried about this?"

Parker put his hand over the folded plastic envelope on the table. "Wait here, Hugh. I've got to go to the men's room. I won't be long." Hammond inclined his head and Parker stood up and looked around the room. Nobody was looking at him. He started to walk past Hammond, stopped and squeezed his shoulder. "I'll be right back, Hugh." Hammond didn't seem to notice.

He had to wait outside the Thrush's tiny men's room for a couple of minutes, and it was all he could do to remain calm. Those days in Montpelier three years ago returned to his memory. It seemed, in those past days, that he always had had to watch his back. He found that the hours of tension of those days became intermixed in his mind with these present thoughts. He tried to dismiss them. No good. They wouldn't go away. Then the door to the men's room opened and a dimly remembered face went past him. A House member, it was, and feeling no pain. Parker silently wished him well, and hoped that his day wouldn't turn out to be as bad as Parker's seemed to be.

He stepped into a room in which you couldn't swing a cat, turned around and half sat on the sink edge and unfolded the paper. His memory told him that the paper was the same. He brought it up to his nose, just as Duane Emery had done, but the smell of disinfectant in the tiny space was too strong. He did see that the top of this note had been cut off, resembling the note that Jan had received. It was the neat handwriting that made him certain that this note came from the same source, but Duane would tell him that. The note, dated in February, two years ago, read:

Dear Representative Hammond,

It's very important that you heed the message in this note. Your work regarding all of the not-for-profit organizations in Vermont is casting a shadow over your otherwise distinguished legislative career. If you decide to have public discourse with anyone about the information you may have thought was interesting, in regard to our Vermont industry of service-above-self, it will render the rest of your career meaningless and of no account. I can make your presence in the Legislature difficult in a way that will place your reputation at risk and, therefore, anything else you may claim will only contribute to your ultimate downfall. If you refuse to take seriously my message, I have other ways available to me to silence your public utterances.

You have embarked on a course the end of which will remove you from any further public notice.

Z

Christ, thought Parker, feeling chills. This "Zorro" character is living in a dream world of misbegotten power and supposed influence. In any case, he scares the hell out of me.

Parker returned to the table, having decided that he wouldn't tell Hammond that this note was not the first one he'd seen with essentially the same message. As he slid into his chair he asked, "Have you shown this note to anyone else besides me, Hugh? Anyone at all?"

"My God, no, Bill. I told you that there's nobody else I know who would keep their mouth shut. What did you think?"

Parker had been thinking about his response to that very question, knowing that it was coming, surprised if it didn't.

"Hugh, I think this is the message from a sick person who has probably sent this same sort of thing to hundreds of people who he, or she, thinks are getting into his, or her, private business. Maybe this nut can do something drastic, but I don't think so. Just another screwball bred in Vermont. They pop up whenever something foolish needs somebody foolish to talk about it. Don't worry. Two years have gone by and nothing has happened, don't forget."

Hammond thought about Parker's words, then seemed to brighten. "You're right, Bill. There is one other thing, though. When I got this note, I did back down from further noticeable investigation, but I kept myself involved in the comings and goings of the non-profit world. I was very, very careful - until tonight. I need to trust you, Bill. Can I?"

"Of course, Hugh. But don't forget this - you're off this nut's radar screen. Problem over, solved, and forgotten. Move on. In fact, I'll keep the note, if that's okay. I have a friend who looks at handwriting with a different mindset than you or I have. Maybe we can get a line on this note writer. I'll return it in a week or so, if you think you really need it."

Hammond looked at Parker in a way that was unsettling. He knows, thought Parker, that I had just come out with a line of bull of which even a Vermont Senator would be proud.

"All right, Bill," he said, in a subdued voice. "You don't have to return it."

"Great, Hugh," Parker said in a tone that tried to express a confidence he didn't feel, and started to get to his feet.

"Just another minute, Bill."

Parker sat back down. Hammond looked around the room again, as he had a number of times during the evening, then turned back to Parker and said, "Bill, I don't want any comment or argument from you on what I'm going to say next. It's just this: if anything, anything at all, causes me to become incapacitated, or out of the game in any way, I have some information in the form of some snapshots that I have stored in a locker under the floor of my barn in Underhill. I need to know that if this general subject we've talked about tonight suddenly becomes important, you should know that this material is available. It was provided to me by a good friend." Hammond hesitated and looked around the room.

His voice was low when he said, "When he showed a little of this information to me, I just knew it might somehow be important in the future. I decided, therefore, to put it away somewhere. Under my barn floor, right under the center, horizontal, beam, where the second floor, overhead, ended, seemed logical. Nobody knew I had this information, so it's reasonable to assume that nobody would come around looking for it." Hammond had taken on the skittish look of a nervous animal, looking this way and that, fidgeting with his food.

"This friend of mine is dead now in an accident. Just keep it in mind that I have this material and where I've got it hidden." Parker nodded. Suddenly Hammond cried, leaning across the table, "You know where I live?"

"Yes, I do, Hugh. I don't think that anything like that will be needed, but if you feel better, that's fine." Hammond seemed to have come unglued somehow.

Hammond stood up suddenly, as if to say that dinner was over and he had other places to go. "Thanks, Bill. I really feel better now." Abruptly, he turned and left, skirting Paul Chumley, who was bearing down on the table with the check in his hand.

"You two have an argument, Bill? He left with a determined look on his face."

"No, no argument, Paul." Parker sat very still, only reaching up to take the bill.

“Well, it was nice of you to buy his dinner,” said Chumley.

Parker nodded, looked up at Chumley, forcing a slight smile, and said, “Yeah.”

Hammond not only forgot about buying the dinner he had promised, and he had the reputation, Parker remembered, of being a strange politician because he always kept his word. But he also left the Thrush at warp speed. Why? Important? Maybe, maybe not. Probably not. Parker’s imagination was trying to get out and play tricks on him again. But not tonight, old friend, he thought. You’re going to stay tucked away. I don’t want you adding to my questions.

Parker, as he thought about everything that went on, was convinced that as much as was discussed tonight, there was still much more that wasn’t brought up.

16

Parker awoke the next morning in frazzled condition. He was in the LaGue Inn in Barre, a place he knew well. It had served as a sort of hideout during those days three long years ago when he felt both hunted and haunted while trying to avoid both friends and enemies until he could get to the Vermont House Chamber, where he would be safe. That he was very wrong in that assumption was no fault of the Inn, and that's why he had come here to rent a room.

The owner of the LaGue Inn recognized him as soon as he stepped through the door. He bought Parker a beer, and some peace and quiet. Parker was grateful.

As he was having breakfast, Parker wondered how Addie was doing on her sojourn into Chittenden County and the city of Burlington.

No one really feels wanted and comfortable there, coming from outside, he had decided years ago. Parker stayed away as much as possible, but he did keep in touch with a few friends he had met a year ago during some very bad days for himself and Addie, and for many others, too. Addie could handle the sophistication of Burlington better than he could, primarily because he was stubborn. Addie, on the other hand, could be stubborn as well, but she knew, in that special way of hers, that being flexible because the surroundings demanded it, without breaking, was the mark of a classy lady. Parker knew that he wouldn't even see that the surroundings were demanding anything at all.

Parker had set himself a simple task for the morning. He would visit the office of the VNRCAUC, which was not far from the Statehouse, and ask for a copy of their last year's report to the IRS. Then he would travel up to Burlington and visit the offices of the CPLAG and ask for the same documents. He'd walk around their establishments for a while to see what he could see, as the old nursery rhyme had it. This should make for an interesting morning.

He was folding up his Chittenden Free Progressive so he could read it without dragging it through his eggs when he saw the headline in the Editorial section of the paper and he stopped what he was attempting to do. The CFP, as it is known by those “in the know” in Vermont, contained another editorial that was sure to make the hard left fizz. This one supported school choice for Vermont parents. It was as well written as the first one Parker could remember from them – and he remembered it because it was written very soon after a major change in the management of the paper had come to pass.

The Vermont Teachers United Associated went crazy and called on all the other papers to support them in their fight against this direct attack on the union’s power. The VTUA needed to hold parents, their children, and the members of the education union, in the position of enforced taxation. With this money the VTUA could defend the status quo, leaving Vermonters and their children with limited expectations and results. And, amazingly, this defense didn’t stop even when it was discovered that the President of the VTUA sent his own kids to private school. And apparently the union members didn’t mind, either.

Parker got to his feet, attempted to fold the newspaper into its original shape, recognized futility, dropped it on the table, and walked to the cash register. He told the young lady behind the register that he had left his newspaper on the table, having lost the battle of refolding, and that she was welcome to it. He knew that he had met her before, and her name badge told him when. She was “Nikki” and she had been instrumental in giving Parker a free dinner when he was hiding out at the Inn during those awful days of three years ago.

“Mr. Parker, isn’t it?” she asked.

“Yes, it is, Nikki. And how are you?”

“I’m fine, Mr. Parker. I read about your bad days up there in that madhouse. Anyway,” she said, “you’re here and in good shape, aren’t you? I saw you with my boss when you came in last night. I hope he gave you a beer, or something.”

“He did, he did,” answered Parker, “and I thank you again for your help, Nikki.”

As Parker paid his bill, Nikki put out her hand. “Shake, Mr. Parker. It’s not often that a real celebrity comes in here, and one I helped a little.”

“I’m certainly no celebrity, Nikki.”

"You are as far as my boss and I are concerned, Mr. Parker," she chirped, with a bright smile.

"I'll be sure to tell my wife about this," said Parker. "She may call you to set you straight." Nikki laughed, turning away to lead another couple to a table.

A terrific way to start the day, thought Parker.

He drove back into Montpelier, intent on invading the central command post of the VNRCAUC, when he thought of another friend whom he hadn't seen in a year, or more. That was Peter Morgan, a Supervisor in the Montpelier Police Department, who had very probably saved Parker's life at least once, and probably more than that, three years ago.

Parker pulled into the visitors' area outside the MPD and walked into the brick building. He was greeted by Officer Catherine Morgan, Peter Morgan's wife. "Mr. Parker, how nice to see you again."

"No, it isn't, Officer Morgan. This is the most dangerous man in Montpelier." Superintendent Peter Morgan was leaning out of the doorway of his office, wearing a wry expression. "And when he leaves Montpelier," he continued, "he'll be the most dangerous man in the next town, too." Morgan grinned at Parker, and waved him into his office.

"Good to see you, Peter. I'm just passing through and wanted to say hello." Morgan still looked like Jimmy Stewart. I, however, just look older, thought Parker.

"What are you up here for, Bill? You don't like Montpelier much anymore, I understand."

"Just passing through, Peter, as I said. Just passing through."

Morgan changed the subject. "I had a letter from Duane Emery a month ago. They seem to be doing well out there. Kate is pregnant, expecting any time in the next month, if I have the timing right. Correct?" Parker nodded.

"You know, Peter, that young man is really clever." He told Morgan about Duane's ten minute inspection of the note from the barnyard that Jan Evlin had received and what he learned from it.

Morgan seemed to become more and more interested as Parker related the tale. Morgan wasn't fooled for a second. "So, that's why you're nosing around Montpelier. I knew there was something."

"Now, Peter," Parker started to answer when Morgan interrupted him.

"Cut the crap, Bill. What's going on?"

"Honestly, Peter, nothing. A friend asked me to look into something for her, which I've done. A little more looking today and I'm headed home."

"Tell me about it, Bill. Just keep it to five minutes. I'm late now. Another few minutes won't matter."

So Parker told him the whole story. He was used to doing that with Morgan. It didn't take five minutes. He started with Jan Evlin, the threatening note she received, and ended with where he sat at the present. What he decided *not* to tell Morgan was the tale of the box under the floor in Hugh Hammond's barn in Underhill. He didn't know why he felt it was important to keep that piece of information to himself.

"What's that editor's name up there in Burlington – you know, the one with the Free Progressive?"

"His name is Hal Birdsall. I've never met him. Do you happen to know him, Peter?"

But Morgan had already turned away and started up his computer. He nodded, grunted, hit "copy", and the magic of the computer age was once again demonstrated. Then he spun around to his computer again and typed something with impressive speed, printed it out, added it to the three sheets previously copied, folded the papers once and handed them to Parker. "Don't say I never gave you anything, but forget I did. Savvy?"

"You bet, Lone Ranger. What *did* you give me?"

In a low voice, Morgan answered. "The police report from the law enforcement network organized by the Spillman System to which most police departments are tied. This report gives the basics of the death of Birdsall's brother, Gilbert. I heard some things, very recently, about what's in the report – thoughts that were put into my head by a meeting I attended and a conversation I had with a buddy in the Sheriff's office up that way. Don't read this stuff here. Put it in your pocket and read it when you can be alone. Give me a call at home sometime. We'll talk about it."

They shook hands, wished each other luck, and Parker walked out to his truck, the folded papers in his pocket and trying to burn a hole in his trousers.

17

Parker drove west along State Street for a few blocks. When he reached the Capital Plaza Hotel, he turned into the large parking area in the back. He knew he wouldn't find a parking space. This was the only single level parking lot he had ever seen where there were never any open spaces, regardless of the time of day or night. Denizens of Montpelier and of the Legislature became expert at parking illegally out there, as well as everywhere else in the city. Parker simply stopped his car in one of the travel lanes in the parking lot (called "perch and search" lanes, for those who hadn't figured how to park illegally), and dragged the papers Morgan had given him out of his back pocket and unfolded them. He did this while watching for one of Montpelier's finest trying to sneak up on him and give him a ticket for parking in a travel lane.

What Morgan had given him was the Essex County Sheriff's initial, and brief, report on the death of Gilbert Birdsall of Burlington. It was just the basics. It included, however, the narrative report of the first officer on the scene. No Medical Examiner's report, and no information from the investigating officer.

He craned his neck to look around outside his truck and then settled back in his seat to read the details.

Gil Birdsall had been the President of a small public policy think tank located in Shelburne, an upscale town south of Burlington. His body had been found on the edge of the former Champion Paper Company land in Brighton. Parker had never seen the town on any map, but it was there, all right. He had been shot through the head. It was called a hunting accident. The matter was under investigation, according to the report. Parker shook his head. If it was an accident, which this apparently was, probably nobody would come forward. Not really surprising, he thought. They'd just get the hell out of there, and feel guilty for the rest of their lives. And probably never hunt again either.

Then Parker shifted over to Morgan's brief notes, which were concisely and logically listed, with no excess words.

Former Representative,

It was great to see you today, and your subject was a huge surprise to me – at least your interest in the accidental death was a surprise. Re that, EVERYTHING is wrong with this incident. Think about the following:

1. Victim was dressed in brand new hunting clothes, apparently never worn before. Unusual, in my experience. Hunters I know like to take care of their woods clothes, and enjoy the reputation of doing so.

2. Victim was wearing no pink or fluorescent color patches.

3. Ask to see the contents of his pockets and all the debris taken from his clothes. Might be important.

4. Based on your comments to me today, somebody knows that you are getting nosey in the non-profit world, and they don't like it. Where have you been and who have you irritated that would have given them that impression (and not an impression that's in any way misguided on their part. You are naturally nosey.) You should find out how they got on to you.

5. Victim's car found about three miles away. Dress clothes found in it, indicating that victim had changed to new hunting clothes in the car. Why?

And maybe the most important question is the spot where he was found. I happen to know that there are those who think that that's the key.

Your friend,
Clouseau

P.S. Good luck.

Good old careful Peter, thought Parker. Ever the policeman. Is he telling me something? Does the Birdsall accident look strange to him? Whatever it is, I can't catch on yet, Parker mused. But the fact that Morgan used no names in the note implied that there was more to this than met the eye.

He started his truck and weaved slowly out through the illegally parked vehicles behind the Plaza. Back onto State Street he headed west for another two blocks, turned to the right and drove up the hill to the offices of the VNRCAUC.

The offices of the VNRCAUC were located in what had been a home at one time. Parker walked up onto the wide porch of this house that had to have been built around 1900, and apparently intended to outdo the grand and imposing marble capital building just down the street. It had all the usual castle-like pieces of the period, almost all of which were out of place, attached to the basic building, probably well after the completion of the home. Things like round, turret-like corners in front, fancy pillars that wanted to have the visitor believe that they were actually holding up the building, and incredibly ornate glass panels in the front door that indicated that the original owners weren't concerned that somebody would break in. They just wouldn't dare.

Added to all this were three round windows, and one immense oblong window, all located on the front wall of the house in different spots, causing it to look exactly like a huge, and extraordinarily tall, toad. All in all, thought Parker, one of the more ugly edifices he had ever seen. He was sure that no insurance company in their right mind would write a fire insurance policy for it. The firemen could find a way inside, without question, but the chance of them getting lost and never being seen again was an immense risk. And the building would still burn down.

The house was no doubt revolutionary in its layout when conceived, designed, and built. The designers of the house, however, never had an idea that 100 years later it would provide protection from the rain for another revolutionary concept – the planned stagnation of Vermont by various groups attacking our traditions, Parker thought, while cleverly making us all feel guilty for believing in freedom for the individual. And they did all this by telling us, over and over, that what they stood for was all for the children and the environment.

Entering the building, Parker was greeted by a woman in the uniform of the feminist left. She wore a long skirt of subtle dark greens, blues, and reds, held together by a faint purplish thread running through it in different directions. And the open end of the skirt was held together by an immense designer-type safety pin. Parker knew that Addie would have said something like it being a symbol of the folk-singing farmer who never waded through cow crap in her life, except by accident. Parker didn't find the skirt that awful.

However, the top destroyed anything positive that might have been in his mind. It was a tee shirt, dirty in the front, carrying the uplifting message "Kill All Republicans". To complete this sartorial ensemble was the pageboy cut (Parker thought that was the correct term) of her slightly graying hair and her Dutch-type shoes that made it almost dangerous to walk anywhere at all and remain upright.

"Good morning," said Parker as he advanced on this formidable personage.

"Good morning," she squeaked. "What can I do for you?"

Parker found her voice to be the strangest he'd ever heard. It was like fingernails being dragged across a chalkboard. He decided to get right to it and, in order to preserve his sanity, leave as soon as possible. Listening to that voice would be like undergoing the Chinese water torture.

"I would like to have copies of the IRS financial statements of your organization for the last two years. Particularly your list of contributors. I believe that all that is public information."

"I don't know anything about that sort of thing," she squeaked. "I'll have to ask my Supervisor."

Parker wasn't surprised. "Please ask your Supervisor for me. I can wait."

"She isn't here right now, Mr. Parker," she said. "Let me have your address and we'll mail the information to you." All of a sudden Squeaky seemed very nervous. He wrote down the required information, thanked her, and left the building.

What do I make of all that, he wondered? She called me by name, and I didn't give it to her. Parker could not find a satisfactory explanation except that the VNRCAUC must have had a rogues' gallery of unacceptable people behind the counter. And he was on it. Parker didn't know if he should be concerned or proud.

When he got to his truck, he found it trapped in the middle of a crowd of protesters, apparently furious about something or other, and it couldn't move before they did. There must have been better than three hundred people, as best he could figure, marching toward the capital. They were an interesting group. There was a large group of children marching along, dressed like some of the adults, which ranged from trendy casualness to intentional shabbiness. Then there were those who looked shabby and dirty and thought it was the norm.

It became apparent to Parker, after only a couple of minutes, that most, if not all, of these grownups never really did make that difficult climb to the status of contributor to the betterment of Vermont and its citizens. It seemed that they had stopped progressing at about twenty-one or so, figuring that they had all the knowledge they would ever need. Their kids were just like them, although they had stopped progressing somewhere around fourteen. Brainwashing starts early these days, he thought. Their self-esteem was, however, a wonderful thing to behold.

Parker couldn't help thinking about a letter, just last week, that appeared in the River News, a paper in New Hampshire, but located right on the Vermont border. This paper supported everything that the town of Norwich stood for. Parker had always believed that this upscale community, across the river from Dartmouth College, displayed, at all times, a group of the best educated people in the world who didn't know anything about most things that mattered.

The letter was from a thirteen-year-old girl who had written to say how she hated the current President of the United States. She used all of the talking points of the American left very well and the letter was grammatically perfect. However, what it proved to Parker was how easily a thirteen-year-old mind could be distorted and blinded, helped, no doubt, by extremely well-educated parents and teachers, most of whom were misguided and empty.

Parker realized that this young lady could never leave Norwich. She was not equipped to cross the town line and enter into the real world. She was like a rare flower, raised under the overwhelming influence of ignorance, and she would figuratively wither away if allowed to escape and hear any external news source other than Free Public Radio. The additional damage that television would do to this tender shoot wouldn't bear thinking about.

The crowd was moving sluggishly and Parker decided to tag along on the edge. Might be fun, he thought. Certainly not educational. Lemmings on parade was about right, he thought.

The first item of business for Parker, in order to enjoy his day with this bunch, was to find out what they were protesting against or for, or if they were just hiking along for the hell of it, as the case may be. So he headed for the front of the pack as they moved toward the Statehouse. As he approached the front of the mob he moved in beside a well-dressed and stylish younger woman who was carrying a sign that read, "All Goverment is Bad for Childrin". Her self esteem was probably terrific, but it didn't help her spelling.

Parker sidled up beside her and, pointing at her sign, asked, "What's better for children than having government?"

She looked at Parker, and then at her sign, as if she didn't know what it read, and then said, scathingly, "Simply no government at all. We'll just select a group of our most brilliant people and they can tell us what to do, and we'll do it. Then we can get on with our lives."

"Where did you learn that concept?" asked Parker, doing all he could to keep from laughing, or maybe crying.

She seemed to loom larger as she surveyed Parker from on high. Then she said, in a high-toned voice, straight from Radcliffe College, "I've attended three different schools in the Vermont College system, buddy," she shouted. "Now, move your ass out of my way. I'm involved in something meaningful today."

With that she swept by him, waving her sign with a sort of desperation. Parker marveled at this demonstration of modern higher education in Vermont.

Parker found that the messages contained in the signs were giving a lot of different signals. One small group, apparently from the Gay and Lesbian community, huddled by themselves and carried signs reading "Marriage Now!" and "Vermont – the Leading Edge State".

Parker went over to an attractive young woman in this group and asked her what she was protesting for or against. "We want the term 'Civil Unions' changed to 'Marriage'", she hollered. "That's all." Then she looked quizzically at Parker.

"What TV network or news organization are you from, sir?" Parker said he represented none of the news media. She turned her back on him and marched away. Oh, well, thought Parker, some people have different motives assigned to their public demonstrations.

The next person he spoke with was a young man who, even in the outdoors, smelled like he had chosen to lead a life without baths and was making that project his ongoing protest. Parker tried to determine where to stand in order to be upwind of him. When he selected the best position, he shouted at the young man, hoping to overcome the growing noise of the crowd, "What are you protesting, sir?"

The young man pointed up at his sign which read, "Don't Mess with Teachers". "My name is Bryce, sir, and I'm protesting the loss of my job."

"What did you do for work, Bryce?" asked Parker, at top decibel output.

"I was a humanities teacher in Spring River High School."

"What does that mean?" asked Parker. "What did you actually teach?" Parker was still at high volume. He was professing an innocence that he didn't feel. He just let Bryce talk, as they shambled along.

"I taught *humanities*, sir. Probably the most *important* subjects in *life* are *captured* by that title. It includes philosophy, literature, the fine arts, personal leisure, and their influence on the culture of Americans. Nothing is more important to our young people." Bryce seemed to be on his full-sized hobby horse and riding it at full speed at this point. He spoke in a sing-song kind of way, employed, no doubt, to add emphasis to his statements. To Parker he sounded like a refugee from the kitchen of a Chinese/American restaurant.

"Were you fired?" Parker asked.

"I dislike that word, sir. I was asked to leave by an ignorant school board that was stuck in the dark ages. They even wanted to test my pupils at the end of the year. I told them that no test could find the real worth of my teaching because it was about *feelings*, not measurable course content."

Parker was really astonished by this personal commitment to the ridiculous. "So, what happened? Did your subject not meet with the approval of parents or the Board?"

"That's just it, sir. I had scrapped the state and local school guidelines for my subject matter and I took the class in a new and more challenging direction."

"Really?" said Parker, trying to show an interest he didn't feel, but fascinated by ignorant people with advanced degrees. "What did you teach them, Bryce?"

Bryce was really getting into his stride now. He apparently was excited by Parker's seemingly close attention. "I taught them that free enterprise shuts off opportunity for the poor and was unfair to those who have decided on a career of art, writing, and the theatre. How are these artists supposed to live, anyway, I ask you? I taught them that school choice for their parents would ruin their local public schools and was unfair to the teachers of lesser abilities who needed their jobs. I taught them that government programs for directing more money to fund education in Vermont would be sure to raise the SAT scores. Other things, too."

"How did the students react?" asked Parker as they trudged along.

"Just fine, other than about five young people who began to disagree with me. After six weeks, I gave them an exam on what I had been teaching. These five got nothing out of my lectures, and their answers showed it. So, I showed them that I meant business and I flunked them. The other ten students in the class did fairly well, although I found that they would require special attention from me in future classes. I was committed to the thought that complete freedom for the individual is too much responsibility for Vermont citizens. They need guidance from people selected by the Vermont Department of Education, with the advice and approval of the VTUA."

Parker almost visibly reeled at that thought. "What happened then? Did somebody object to your taking this path with their children in tow?"

"I had parents in Spring River practically storm the school. I don't know why. I also had some teachers I thought were friends who stopped speaking to me. The parents in particular were so adamant that they frightened me. And they also had the nerve to tell me to clean myself up. They said I smelled bad! Can you believe that? Mr.----- what is your name, sir? You look familiar."

"My name is Parker, Bryce, and you need to know that you *do* smell as though you should start standing closer to moving water on a regular basis." Bryce looked shocked and angry.

"Do you realize, Mr. Parker, that there are cultures in the world whose citizens never take baths? That their odor is accepted by their friends and neighbors as normal? That's the symbol of true freedom in a physical way. Take people the way you find them, not as you want them. That's also the message I was bringing my pupils."

Bryce looked at Parker almost dreamingly. "Spring River's school system allows, by inattention, almost anything to be taught, and is very tolerant of students who need to act out their frustrations. I have many friends who teach there, and we teach the students that the reactionary Neanderthals of the school board and their parents, who are stuck in time, are in the way of real educational progress. Control by a benevolent government is the wave of the future. Government guidance and direction is needed. No - - - ".

Bryce stopped. He stared at Parker. Parker stepped back to stand outside the circle of odor created by Bryce. "I know you now, you son-of-a-bitch," he screamed. "You're former Representative William Parker, aren't you? You're the one who put back our timetable by five years."

Bryce was angered and moving to the outside edge of self-control very rapidly. "Get away from me, you bastard. We were just told about you. I know your face now!" Spittle was flying from his lips and he was screaming. Parker stopped walking and let the herd push Bryce along with them. No one paid him any attention at all.

As he watched Bryce move along, still screeching, Parker said to himself, Good Job, Spring River. You dumped this loony before he could infect many more children. How about the other teachers down there who are the friends of this idiot?

And what about the very good teachers who had to associate with this guy? Bryce must have totally discouraged them because he was kept on the staff for even an hour.

Parker thought about his conversation with this mixed-up and ignorant ex-teacher. None of it made any sense. The whole direction of this guy's life was totally without focus and without a goal of any kind. He simply took up some of the earth's space without giving anything for it.

It was evident to Parker that people like Bryce had chosen teaching as a profession because the requirements were so easy and the jobs were so permanent. Teachers like this clown make the dedicated and talented teachers look bad, he thought. Well, anyway, when this guy goes to that great teacher's lounge in the sky, no one would even notice he was among the missing, although they might notice a nicer smelling environment. A vacuum would be the legacy for Bryce. What a waste.

What puzzled Parker, however, was the loony's recognition of him, and the hysteria it generated. Parker had been out of the Legislature for three years. He had done nothing during that time to raise the awareness of any enemies he may have made while he was in the Vermont House. In fact, Parker knew that the ProgDems were ecstatic when he left. He had been back in Montpelier several times and nobody paid the slightest attention to him. Then why the hell would some nondescript and useless empty vessel like Bryce suddenly be warned about him? How wide-ranging had these warnings been? And, for that matter, what had they been warned about? Parker reasoned that if Bryce knew about him in some detail, then a lot of people had been told about him and to beware of him. It was upsetting to Bill Parker that such apparent enmity was out there and he had no idea why he should be the target.

And Addie was loose in Burlington, thought Parker. Addie will be more than a match for any strange person up there. I wonder if it's known in that foreign Chittenden County that she is the wife of the infamous William Parker, crimes unknown at this time, of course, but to be concocted and revealed at a later date in the ProgDem newsletter called the Mid-Vermont Bugle.

Does anyone care, Parker wondered? Most people in Vermont wouldn't believe what he had just seen in this amorphous protest march. Otherwise perfectly logical, sensible people would call me a traitor to progress if I mentioned it in public, he thought.

Parker had begun to believe that these people who consider themselves sensible are the ones primarily responsible for letting Vermont down. They are the ones who vote for ProgDems almost every time – and then complain about the Legislature and its actions. They are the ones whose union tells them to vote for ProgDems because their parents did. So they do. They are the ones who wonder why businesses can't leave Vermont fast enough, taking the jobs with them, and then vote for the ProgDems - who don't really care that the jobs are leaving.

In fact, Parker thought, these ProgDems don't even understand that jobs are critical, and not just a sidebar, to life. They are of the utmost importance to our families and their quality of life, and for our state as a whole. No, he thought, the truth of this matter would be unbelievable to these habitual ProgDem voters. In reality, it was most of the Independents, a few Democrats, all of the Republicans and Libertarians, who made up the group that was the only true friend that these ProgDem voters had.

And then a thought hit Parker. Voting for ProgDems and harboring doubts about doing so is like being on a bad drug. You know it's not good for you but you just can't break the habit.

At the end of it all, it's really very simple, he thought. Vote your *true* conscience, not how you've been instructed to vote. It's not hard to understand - but only a few people get it. What a shame.

18

Parker's next step in his course of action would be to travel up to Burlington and try to see Jan Evlin at the Free Progressive. In the best of all worlds he would catch her at her desk and she would take him by the hand to see Hal Birdsall. In the real world, however, he would find neither, and no one would know when they would be back at their desks. Well, he thought, it's only a forty minute drive. Not much time wasted. And Parker wanted to see, once again, how the city mice lived, as viewed from the perspective of a country mouse like himself.

Parker left I89 at Exit 14 in Burlington and headed west on Route 2. It didn't take long for him to reach the center of the University of Vermont campus and the green. This is where he had taken his next educational step after high school.

He remembered, after graduation from the university, his thoughts about how naïve he had been when he had first arrived at this seat of higher learning. He was seventeen years old. He had mistakenly thought that all the elements of the next phase of his learning would be laid out in front of him - like a cafeteria at lunchtime. He thought that all he would have to do was to attend his classes regularly and absorb information that was all new to him. He thought that he had only to decide if he agreed or disagreed with the instructors, state his points as he saw them, find acceptance or learn why he was in error, study his new and original material, and take his exams using what he had learned and what he thought was still correct.

It took only about a month for him to discover that he was debating half of his instructors who, he decided, couldn't defend what they were advocating.

This argumentative time in his college life bothered Parker. He then went through the phase where he, personally, took all the blame for not finding acceptable what they were saying. He thought that possibly he just wasn't suited for college. Maybe he just simply wasn't smart enough. Then he moved to doubting his own thoughts and ideas, even when he had no real reason to do so.

He was also concerned that his stupidity, along with his natural stubbornness, would be a learning barrier for him. These were bad days for young William.

Then everything changed. He met a professor of world history, English literature, and world economic systems. An odd combination, but this man had decided, and the University agreed, according to another professor who was acquainted with him, that all three of these disciplines had to be taught as a unit. They all intertwined. Each had profound influence on the other two. The work required to have a Doctorate in each of these specialties awed Parker.

This man, Dr. Mead, demanded that his students think about what he was saying to them and then debate any and all questions with him and all the other members of the class. It was at this point that Parker knew what education was really all about. He itched for every class to begin. He took all the advanced courses Dr. Mead taught. He monitored some of Dr. Mead's classes, when his schedule permitted, just to keep fresh in his mind the original thoughts of this man.

It was in these classes that Parker first learned that, in problem-solving, objective thought and reasoning had to be brought to bear on every known fact that could be considered relevant, along with the known outcomes of the application of these facts in the real world. That's when Parker begin to shape his life.

It was not an uneventful time at UVM when he mixed his personal beliefs with his stubbornness and took this resultant attitude to the rest of his classes. Some of his other instructors thought him to be too argumentative and, in some cases, unaccepting. Parker didn't wish the experiences he was having on anyone else.

In those days a student could, if he chose, hand in a self-addressed post card along with the final exam for the purpose of learning his semester grade as soon as possible. One professor wrote on the postcard a comment that stayed with Parker all these years. "Mr. Parker, you are not brilliant, but if tenacity and singleness of purpose mean anything (and they do) you will be proud of your life."

As Parker daydreamed about the "old days" he suddenly found himself in downtown Burlington. The Chittenden Free Progressive offices were located just off Church Street on College Street. He pulled his pickup into a downtown parking garage, noticing the strange look the attendant directed at his 1986 vehicle. Parker paid no attention and hoped that his truck didn't notice. He parked, locked everything he could find on his truck (not trusting the big city, apparently), and stepped out into the modern, leading edge, socialist world.

Downtown Burlington was as close to an upscale village market area as a leftist city government could make it. No cars allowed in the main street. A definite plus to the city fathers or mothers, who were apparently looking for something out of old eastern Europe. A co-op food market was in place just around the corner from the Chittenden Free Progressive offices.

This socialist/progressive effort, in order to escape the terrible label of a "capitalist" profit-making venture, turned down a legitimate bid by one of the larger food chains to put a modern market in this spot, even though the privately owned food market would pay all the costs of start-up.

The city of Burlington, however, didn't want that kind of market which, as they put it, sold "fake food". Instead, they opted for a market exclusively designed for locally grown organic foods and vegetables. In this attempt, the Sweet River Co-op, as it was called, suddenly found itself losing its customers because the prices were high, the variety of products limited, and much of the "help" somewhat unhelpful. All in all, a perfect example of why socialism, wherever and whenever it's been tried, has always failed, thought Parker.

The problem in Burlington, however, was that socialism was unlikely to be voted out anytime soon. The University students voted the socialists on the city council back in office every two years. Parker used to become upset when he thought about Burlington, the Queen City, but not any more. Instead he looked for the humor in the situation, and usually found it. The Sweet River Co-op was a brilliant case in point and could be used by the University Business School as a case study in a guaranteed business failure.

Parker entered the Free Progressive building's front entrance and was greeted by a frail appearing young man sitting behind a desk. He asked the receptionist if he could speak to Jan Evlin.

"I don't know if she's in, sir. May I have your name, please?" he inquired, with a sort of twitching of his whole body as he spoke.

“I’m Bill Parker, from Bridgeton, in Windham County. Jan is an old friend and, since I had some business in Burlington, I thought I’d stop by. If she isn’t in, perhaps I could see Mr. Birdsall, her editor. I think he’ll know me.”

The receptionist dialed a number. It was answered by a voice that could be heard all over the entire area under Mr. Twitchie’s control. It even startled Parker, four feet away from the receiver. It seemed to him to be a loud version of Jackie Gleason.

Mr. Twitchie visibly shrank back from the receiver as if he was being pounded by it. When the voice noise stopped, Mr. Twitchie thanked the voice nicely and replaced the receiver gently, in spite of increased agitation.

“You can go up, Mr. Parker,” indicating the stairs. “Second floor, go left and you’ll either see a door marked Keefe, or hear a loud voice that will *be* Mr. Keefe. He’s an assistant editor who can take you to Mr. Birdsall.”

“Thanks. I won’t be long and I’ll try to withstand the blast effect from Mr. Keefe.”

Mr. Twitchie smiled painfully. It was more like a grimace. Probably the first smile, or whatever it was, this week, thought Parker.

Parker hiked up the stairs to the second floor. When he was halfway up the staircase, he began to hear again the voice of the forceful Mr. Keefe. He seemed to be berating someone for doing something that seemed to be close to burning down the building, or mentioning the free-enterprise system at a Burlington City Council meeting.

Keefe was standing in the doorway of his office talking to a young woman about the weather or what he had for lunch. He was at least six-and-a-half feet tall, and he must have tipped the scale at a solid three hundred pounds. Well, Parker thought, maybe “solid” wasn’t the word.

He was still loud, but he wasn’t using words that were threatening. The young woman, about five feet tall in heels, just stood there as if she had heard it all before. She probably had, Parker reasoned.

Then, she did an extraordinary thing. With a big smile, she put her two index fingers into the appropriate ear while looking up at Mr. Keefe. Keefe roared with laughter, and as he did so he caught a glimpse of Parker.

"Mr. Parker, I'm Mel Keefe, the head of this newsroom. What I say goes. Right, Maureen?" He turned toward the young woman.

"Absolutely, Mr. Keefe," she said, fingers still in place. "Fine, Maureen, just fine. Now, back to your kennel."

She retreated from view. "She's in my training program," Keefe said to Parker. "I'm learning a lot about employee supervision and the management of a department from her. She's not learning anything from me except when to have lunch and where the Ladies' Room is located. She's going to be a good one for the paper if she learns that politicians are usually wrong, and that most of them really don't know what's going on, and don't care too much, either. There are some terrific politicians though, to be fair, and they're the only ones who actually do things. The others, who do nothing, run on the accomplishments of somebody else."

He suddenly turned to face Parker. "God, I'm sorry to have lapsed into reverie like that. Where are my manners? So, you're Bill Parker," Keefe said, "all healed up from your days as a Legislator, I bet."

Parker smiled faintly and nodded. "Mr. Keefe, if you feel that way about politicians, and you're one of the managers of this paper, why are the editorials mostly in favor of the ProgDems?"

"I don't know, Mr. Parker," he said, with a gleam in his eye. "I guess they don't ask the people who are right under their noses. I'm trying to educate that young lady you met a minute ago to the fact that she might not be listened to, either. But I'm trying to do it subtly, so as not to discourage her. Of course, she figured me all out from the beginning. She said to me, 'Don't worry, Mr. Keefe, they'll pay attention to me.' How the hell can I attempt to tell her to cool her jets and look at the Burlington world as it really is, rather than the Burlington world she's been told is out there?"

Parker shrugged and smiled. "Tough task, Mr. Keefe. I wouldn't make a dent in her self confidence and idealism. Impossible job. Wouldn't want to, actually. On the positive side of things, maybe she's just the right kind of person to start the revolution in Burlington that's so desperately needed. What do you think?"

Keefe thought a minute, grinned, and shook Parker's hand. "You may have the right of it, Mr. Parker. I feel a little better somehow." Suddenly he switched gears. "And you want to see

Jan. Correct?" he bellowed. Parker nodded. He wouldn't be heard above Keefe's sound level if he merely spoke.

"I haven't seen her myself for three days, Mr. Parker. Then I thought she might have had to make a quick trip to see her parents. They're getting on a bit, you know," with a knowing look at Parker. "My boss, Mr. Birdsall, wanted to talk with her yesterday, in fact. She hasn't called in yet, so I called her folks. About an hour ago. They haven't seen her and didn't know she was planning a visit. Apparently that wasn't strange, though. Jan usually just popped in with no warning. I asked them to have her call me as soon as she came through the door."

"Is this kind of absence typical for Jan? Just dropping out of sight, I mean?"

"Not since I've known her, and that's about three years now."

Parker scribbled his name and number on a piece of notepaper he fished out of his pocket, and handed it to Mr. Keefe. "Have her give me a call, if you would, please, when she has a minute."

"I will, Mr. Parker, I will. Let's go to see Hal Birdsall now," he boomed.

19

Hal Birdsall's office was about what Parker expected, judging by the basic construction of the building. The Free Progressive had spent some money to make it passably attractive not too long ago, probably to everyone's surprise. Parker could also see the back entrance that Jan had called the "escape hatch".

It was a room, because of the wall of almost all glass, with a feeling of airiness and light. That feeling deteriorated quickly when a visitor looked at the furniture and other trimmings. It was furnished with what had to be the leavings from some store that bought and sold furniture from the University students. It wasn't beaten up, exactly. It just fit the definition of "used". The couch, which had an old blanket thrown over its back for color and probably to deflect attention away from the beer stains in the fabric, was probably only twenty-five dollars on the open market. The three easy chairs were about the same. The small tables that were alongside each of these fine period pieces was also unintentionally decorated by college students. Parker knew what that sort of decorating was all about. He'd done some of it himself during his stay here 35 years ago. It's nice to know that some things never change.

Hal Birdsall was a tall man, a head above Parker. He could look Mr. Keefe right in the eye, and did. "Thanks, Keefer," he said. "Let me have a quiet few minutes with this guy. You okay with that?"

"Absolutely, boss," and walked to the door. Then he turned and said, "No word yet from Jan. I'll let you know," and left.

Hal Birdsall came over to Parker with his hand out and said, "It's a pleasure to see you again, Mr. Parker. When my secretary told me who was here to see me, I actually got a little charged up about seeing the famous Bill Parker again, and this time in more positive circumstances." He shook his head in mock disbelief. "And me a cynical and used up old newspaper man, too."

Parker was shocked. “My God, Mr. Birdsall, don’t get carried away. I was scared down to my shoes all the time I seemed to be a target. I try never to think about those days.”

“Then I won’t bring them up ever again, Mr. Parker,” he said with a smile. “Have a seat and tell me what I can do for you.”

Parker looked at the easy chairs with trepidation, selected the one that looked like it might stay together for the duration of his visit, and dropped into it. Surprisingly, it was firm and fairly comfortable. Hal Birdsall sat in one facing Parker, waiting expectantly.

“Mr. Birdsall, I don’t know how to start off with you. But I guess I want to first thank you for your help during those days of three years ago. Something I never had a chance to do when everything was over.” Birdsall waved his hand in dismissal of the compliment.

“I don’t want to be mysterious about this sit-down with you. However, I‘ve been advised about something that you know about. And it’s something that might be upsetting to you if you knew that that ‘someone’ you took into your confidence ‘let the cat out of the bag’, as they say. So I don’t know what to do next, but something told me that I had to come here today. How’s that for beating around the bush, and me a *retired* politician?”

“Brilliant, Mr. Parker, but I don’t know what the hell you’re talking about.” He looked at Parker pleasantly. “Out with it, if you please.”

“Jan Evlin, Mr. Birdsall.” Birdsall’s head came up. “She sought me out in a very private and quiet way. I also met with Representative Hugh Hammond on the same subject. Anyway, to continue, Jan was afraid of something up here and she came to me. In fact, she drove all the way down to near Woodstock - that’s in Windsor County, you know –“ Birdsall nodded curtly, - “to find me and to tell me about a situation that she believes might have gotten out of control.”

Birdsall studied Parker for a few seconds, and then asked, “Why you, Mr. Parker?” He suddenly jumped up and started walking around the room. “Of course, I should have thought of it. You were giving her the information to use to write her articles during your bad days in the House, weren’t you? Got to know each other then, did you? Some trust there, wasn’t there? That’s why she went down to see you.”

Parker nodded. "I think that was it, Mr. Birdsall. You had a meeting with Jan five days ago, didn't you? And you gave her an assignment that was a very private one. One she started working on almost immediately, I think, and once she-----," and Parker stopped speaking abruptly. Birdsall looked up with a surprised expression on his face.

Now it was Parker's turn to get to his feet. He approached Birdsall with an index finger across his mouth. It was the universally accepted sign to be quiet. He then went over to Birdsall's desk, tore a sheet of paper from a writing pad, and hurriedly wrote, "You'll think I'm crazy, but it just hit me that we should talk somewhere else. Let's take the back way out and talk where we can be completely private. Please leave the light on. Just nod if okay and we'll simply leave."

He handed it to Birdsall. He read it, then stared at Parker for a number of seconds. Then he took his coat and hat from the chair beside the door, handed Parker's coat to him, and gestured to Parker to follow as he walked to the "escape hatch". Thank the good Lord for people who will trust without calling their lawyer first, thought Parker.

Parker followed Birdsall out the "escape hatch" door. It opened onto a short hallway that led to a set of steel stairs which were attached to the outside wall of the brick building, like an old fire escape. The stairs were protected from the weather by a rough wooden shroud of plywood. Nothing fancy here, thought Parker, and probably not legal, either, but it works.

They walked along College Street without a word, then ducked into a bar and grill called "Mickey's". There was a "Closed" sign hung on the door, but it opened for Birdsall. He looked at Parker and said, "My son-in-law owns this place. Great pub-grub and beer. We won't be disturbed."

They walked down the length of the room and took a booth at the back. A fresh-faced young man came out through a swinging door next to the booth and stopped at the table. "How about some coffee, gentlemen? How are ya', Hal?"

Birdsall looked up, smiled, and said, "That'd be swell, Danny, and I'm fine. Meet Mr. Parker, Danny, from the southern end of the state, about which he believes I know nothing."

"How do you like Burlington, Mr. Parker? Different from the wilderness in the south?"

"No real difference, Danny," reaching up to shake his hand, "except the wilderness down there has trees in it. You have people instead. Trees, you may be aware, don't make noise, don't leave a mess where they live, don't use drugs, and don't demonstrate against McDonald's and Wal-Mart."

"Ouch," said Danny, smiling broadly, and left them alone.

Birdsall turned to face Parker directly. He looked irritated. "Tell me all about it, Mr. Parker, and you'd best make it good. But start off with the silent routine in my office. I can't even guess what you were thinking. What the hell was that all about?"

Parker shifted to face Birdsall. "As I was sitting in your office talking with you, I was thinking that all of the warnings I had received or heard about regarding Jan were surprising to me. I had only talked to Jan, and that was in the privacy of a car, parked at a hamburger stand near Woodstock. I learned that Jan got a warning note that morning. Three days later I was given the cold shoulder by a woman in the office of the VNRCAUC, who called me by name when we had never seen each other before. And I was shouted at not fifteen minutes later by a screwball ex-teacher from Spring River. There is only one place where that ball got rolling and that information regarding your secret assignment for Jan got started, and it triggered everything else that's happened." Birdsall was eyeing Parker steadily, without blinking.

"Well?' snapped Birdsall.

"It was in your office when you met with Jan."

"What the hell are you talking about, Parker? I certainly didn't tell anyone about that meeting, and I swore Jan to secrecy, a pledge she obviously didn't keep. She blabbed to you."

"I wouldn't call it blabbing, Mr. Birdsall. She was afraid," Parker said. He looked at Birdsall with a challenge in his eyes. "And she had no one else to talk to." Parker slid the note Jan had received across the table to Birdsall. "She considers that this note was a direct threat. What do you think?"

Birdsall read the note. His expression became one of concern. He had lost the media look of stoicism. "It definitely is a threat, Mr. Parker," he said heavily. His voice sounded tired.

"You're right, Mr. Birdsall. I know that the timetable is a little looser than I'm describing. That is, maybe the knowledge of your secret assignment for Jan became public in another way. But my explanation suits the facts better, and I can't ignore it."

Birdsall was busily thinking about Parker's words. "And?" he asked, irritably.

"Tell me, Mr. Birdsall," Parker continued, "how long have you had your secretary? And have you had any extensive rebuilding in your office in the last three years?" Parker knew that he'd just made a mental leap that was unjustified. But it was a start.

Birdsall seemed to be getting larger somehow. Growing in size. Sitting up straighter. Turning a light shade of reddish purple. And he was glaring at Parker.

"You're a brassy bastard, Parker, do you know that? I know what you're getting at," he said, with anger in his face. "I've worked with this secretary for three years. She's never given me any thought that she might be compromising the paper in any way. I don't know how she could, in fact, or why. You're being totally unfair to her with this speculation! In addition to that, Mr. Parker, my secretary was taking some vacation time on that day. I know because that's why I chose that day for Jan to come up and see me. I wanted no one to know that I had a very quiet meeting with her." Birdsall was very angry.

Parker leaned across the table and said, "Mr. Birdsall, I know this is difficult for you. But if we believe there's any danger to Jan, we have to face it. How about the rebuilding and refurbishing? Was any work done to your office and, if so, when?"

Birdsall sat back against the seat. He seemed to have changed in appearance. He was no longer furiously angry. In a way, he looked deflated. After a few seconds he nodded. "Yes, about two years ago the paper decided to spend some money for certain offices where advertisers, and special visitors, might come to talk. That sort of thing."

"And yours was one of them, I take it?" asked Parker.

Birdsall nodded. "In fact, it was the only one in the Free Progressive complex."

"How about the secretary?"

"She'd been there longer than that. She served the guy who I replaced when he retired. I'd say she's been in there for about eight years, so there's no correlation."

Parker sat silently, watching Birdsall, and adding up days before he met with Jan. Suddenly he asked, "Who do you know who's in the electronics business who might be able to check out an office for listening devices?" asked Parker. And hurriedly said, "This may be very important, Mr. Birdsall."

Birdsall had started to come out of his seat again, seemed to think better of it, and just as quickly sat back down. "Okay," he said, resignedly. He called out to Danny, who appeared almost immediately. "Who do you know who is an expert in security matters, who could check out a room for a listening device – and keep their mouth shut forever? That includes you, son-in-law," Birdsall said pointedly.

"I knew that, Pops," he said, with a grin. After a minute he said, "I know a couple of guys. You get to know them, in my business. When?"

"Now," said Birdsall. "We'll wait for them right here."

"Wow," said Danny, whistling soundlessly. "You really serious?" Birdsall nodded emphatically.

"Possible?" asked Birdsall.

"I think so. They're used to working on short notice. Let me make a call or two."

While Danny was gone, Parker decided to bring up another subject. He thought that Birdsall was now in a mood to talk about other things, but he didn't know for certain how he would react to talking about something very close to home.

"Mr. Birdsall, I want to get into another area. I don't have confirmed connections between your meeting with Jan Evlin, the Vermont non-profits, and this subject. However, the source of this question came from a very close friend. He cannot afford to be identified, but I consider him an unimpeachable source for information of this type. I've been involved with him in other situations where I wasn't comfortable. He is a cool and objective professional. He gave me some information. It didn't seem to bear on our subject. It was, however, *because* of what we're talking about that he provided it. I'm sure he wouldn't have, otherwise."

Birdsall didn't say anything. He just sat very still and gazed at Parker. Then he said, almost in an attitude of surrender, "Nothing will surprise me today, Mr. Parker. And, in listening to you now, I know how you got in trouble in the Legislature three years ago."

"What do you know about the death of your brother, Mr. Birdsall?" Parker asked, deciding that plowing ahead without stopping was the correct course.

The suddenness of the question seemed to shock Birdsall, and caused him to look at Parker in an almost demented way. He was agitated again. "Why is that subject coming into this conversation, Mr. Parker," he cried. "What does that matter to you?"

"I don't know, Mr. Birdsall. Maybe it means nothing. Or a lot. But I have to ask to make sure what it does mean."

Birdsall shook his head slowly, as if thinking hard at the same time. "You first, Mr. Parker. I need to know why you were even thinking about it, and I have to know what you may know about my brother's accident."

Parker looked steadily at Birdsall. Then he decided to go all the way with this man.

"I have to start back before that, Mr. Birdsall. I think everything started for me with your meeting with Jan. The secret one in your office. The word got out about that quiet assignment you gave her. Almost immediately, too, I think. You know what the subject was – the non-profits in Vermont. If I understood what Jan said, it was a meeting that you tried to keep secret, even from your own paper and your own secretary. Did you wonder about her back then? Is that why, just now, you immediately agreed to have Danny find an electronics guy to determine if anything is wrong in your office? My request isn't exactly a run-of-the-mill query, you know."

Birdsall nodded, face composed in a grim expression. "I thought there were some things I noticed, not long after I took over my present job, which I couldn't explain, I'll admit. Little things, you know – probably not noticeable to outsiders, but I wondered about them. You know, Mr. Parker," he said suddenly, "these things were going on before I came into this job." Birdsall looked down at the table top, rubbing out an imaginary blemish on it, and seeming to attempt to organize his thoughts.

Then he looked up at Parker and said, "Things like the previous editor's secretary, who now works for me, still at her desk, even though it was after hours, and I hadn't asked her to work late. She tried to suggest that I had requested her to be available. I knew I hadn't asked her to be in the office, but I had just enough doubt to believe that there might have been a misunderstanding. I told her that I expected her to finish her workday at the regular time. However, she came back one evening, shortly after that, and as I was leaving, claiming she had left something in her desk. I faintly wondered about it, but that's all I did. We didn't talk about it again."

Birdsall looked tired and worn out. It was as if the last hour had been like two days without sleep. "I believe that it was the occurrences that were out of the norm that caused my predecessor's retirement. He called me and asked me to drop by his house soon after he retired. He was very worried about the lack of security in the news department, he told me. However, in order to make the change from him to me a smooth one, it was decided to keep the same secretary. I had no problem with that. She could help me fit into my new job - and she did, too."

"So, do you think that there's something going on in the paper's operation that compromises its integrity?"

"I really don't think so, Mr. Parker. But I'm uncertain enough to agree to have my office checked out."

At that instant a huge, black man of about thirty, maybe a little more, appeared from the kitchen door, accompanied by Danny.

"Gentlemen," said Danny, in a stentorian voice, "meet Hugo Barkley, of Barkley, Barkley, and Barkley, snoops of the first water, and inventors of the term '24/7'".

"For goodness sake, Danny," said Hugo Barkley, "why do you do this to me? I'm trying to make a good, and lasting, first impression."

"You already have, Mr. Barkley," said Birdsall. "You make my son-in-law look like he's never had a good meal in his life."

Barkley looked at Danny and said, "He does look undernourished, doesn't he? Are these the two sneaky ones, Danny?" looking first at Parker, then at Birdsall.

"Yep," said Danny. "Did you ever see two more shady people in your life?"

Hugo dropped his bulk onto the booth seat with some difficulty, fixed his gaze on Parker, and said, "Danny, I know of your father-in-law. I don't know this gentleman – and people in my line of work need to feel easy about who they're doing business with."

Hal Birdsall said, "Hugo, you won't know this guy. He's from the southern half of the state - the wilds of Windham County, to be specific. Meet Bill Parker."

Hugo eyed Parker with a steady gaze for a few seconds. "Windham County, eh?" he murmured. "From Brattleboro?"

“Absolutely not,” said Parker, decisively, a slight grin at the corners of his mouth. “Bridgeton. What’s on your mind, Hugo? Bad vibrations about Brattleboro?”

“Yep, you bet. Want to hear why? Well, I don’t care whether you do or not. You’re going to hear anyway. Question first. What’s the first thing you noticed about me when I came through the door?”

Parker could sense that this was no idle question, but he couldn’t see around corners well enough to penetrate the reason it was asked. “The light from the kitchen was suddenly blotted out. The next thought I had was that I want to stay on the happy side of you. You’re a hell of a size, Hugo, and I’m not. Now, why the question?”

Hugo looked steadily at Parker again. “I’m from New York City, originally. I went to that great university on the hill, here in Burlington.” Hugo’s tone was derisive. “I knew nothing about Vermont. I just thought that it was far enough away from the City to satisfy me. Graduated with a degree in Electrical Engineering. I didn’t indicate a choice of a roommate, and I got this guy who turned out to be a silly, big talking lightweight from Brattleboro.”

“There’s a lot of them down there, Hugo,” said Parker.

“Yeah, I know. This particular one was dumb as hell, too. Well, anyway, this guy was delighted to have a black roommate. Considered me a social rehabilitation project without knowing a damn thing about me. I’m sure he thought I had to be the child of a single mother with no education. Decided to use me as an object in ‘show an’ tell’ to the other guys in the dorm to make him look benevolent, good, and kind. What a God damned jerk. You know something, Mr. Parker? He even invited me to spend a weekend in Brattleboro. Wanted me to meet his friends and his mother. Mother was divorced. All of a sudden I knew that I was being hauled around Brattleboro like his damned slave that he had freed. I was on a bus back to Burlington within two hours.”

“Well, Hugo,” said Parker, “you can’t leave us hanging. Did you get rid of this guy when he returned, or did you have to dump his broken body out of the dorm window?”

“Got rid of him. I told him what a hypocrite I thought he was. He got all teary and apologetic, then blamed me for misleading him. Then he said he was transferring out of the dorm to an apartment where he ‘could be himself’.”

“So, why the question, Hugo?” Parker inquired. “What the hell were you after? Maybe you’re too sensitive about that experience. Possible?”

“Maybe, but the words ‘Windham County’ seem to flip my trigger.”

“Super-sensitive blacks trip mine,” said Parker. “I was brought up on a farm, so I never had any feeling about blacks, or Chinese, or Vietnamese, or Mexicans, or anybody. They can be bright blue, for all I care. People are okay, or terrific, or total jerks. You were being a total jerk just now.” Parker couldn’t contain his frustration.

“Let me tell you something, Hugo, just for information for you to take away from here and chew on. I was in Vietnam and my best buddies were two Asian career soldiers, a black F-104 pilot, a white snob who we had to train, and two helicopter pilots whose background nobody knew. And nobody cared about, anyway. All of us hung out together. Both pilots and the white snob were killed. Nobody could have mourned them any more than we did. So don’t pull the downtrodden ‘nigger’ test on me. It won’t wash.” Parker was angry to the point of feeling a buzzing in his ears.

Hugo reached across the table and patted Parker’s arm. “Okay, Mr. Parker, okay. I’ll never try it again.” Hugo was smiling.

“Now,” Hugo asked, suddenly all business-like, “what’s going on?”

Parker and Birdsall both gave him their suspicions, with Birdsall showing more hesitancy in giving his comments than Parker did his.

“That’s it, Hugo,” said Birdsall. “Parker, here, thinks I may have a listening device in my office. I admit that I got angry at him when he suggested it, and I really feel that nothing will turn up when you check things out. Who could believe that a listening device would be at work in the Free Progressive? And in my office, too. Nobody. The CFP is an honorable institution from bottom to top.”

Hugo just sat back and watched the byplay between Parker and Birdsall. When they finished, he said, “That’s it? No more to say, you guys?” They both nodded.

“You don’t need me. You can do whatever needs doing yourselves.”

Birdsall looked disappointed. "You mean that's it? Nothing more to say? Does that mean I have a listening device in my office, or not?"

"Oh, I'm pretty sure you've got one all right, Mr. Birdsall. But you guys can find it without me."

"You mean you're not even going into my office to find it?" cried Birdsall.

"You got it, Mr. Birdsall. I don't take on work for which I'm not needed – at least today. Listen," and Hugo leaned his massive body across the table, "I'm going to tell you guys one thing about this whole business of 'bugged' rooms, especially in this state. If this bug was placed by an expert, you'd never know it. You only found out that a bug might be present because of the timing of certain pieces of information. You didn't see that anything physical had changed in your office – and I'm sure it hasn't." Birdsall nodded.

"So, let's get really practical and real. An expert not only would have placed a listening device where you never would find it or suspect its presence, but the information retrieved, *because* he was an expert, would be used so subtly that you wouldn't even notice that things were different. You'd probably say to yourselves that your opponents are very smart and ahead of you."

Parker was fascinated by all this. An experienced person treats as routine the things that the amateur sleuths wouldn't even consider.

"Apparently, however," Hugo stated, with emphasis, "and I've seen a lot of this sort of thing, boys, they are just amateurs, like yourselves, Mr. Birdsall." He looked hard at Birdsall. "Except, maybe Mr. Parker, there," cocking an eye in Parker's direction. "I'll guess that he's close to being convinced that a problem exists."

Hugo inexorably continued on. This was his home field advantage. "If I'm right, and I'm fairly certain I am, the listeners are both amateurs and clumsy. So the device is amateurish and clumsy, too. Just look along the walls, baseboards, and door casings. Look for something obvious, like a little microphone somewhere – something like that." Birdsall physically started at that.

Hugo held up a huge hand. "I know, I know, it sounds outlandish. But, mics come in a variety of shapes and sizes. Just look for something out-of-the-ordinary. Something that's different or seems changed, even if you don't know what it is. Clear? Hell, I even read about one that was battery powered and could record a conversation while stuffed into an olive that sat in the bottom of a martini beaker. That might be stretching things a bit, but it could be done, I think."

Parker said, quietly, "It's not called a beaker."

"We slaves don't know that, boss", said Hugo, smiling at Parker. They both knew they were playing a game with each other with the rules agreed upon without a word having been exchanged.

Birdsall still looked unimpressed. "How will we know that something is different if we don't know what it is?"

"If there's a wire hanging from it, you've found it," Hugo drawled.

"How do we know that there's not another device present?"

"You won't," said Hugo, "unless you look. But, just so you'll feel better, I'll slip into your office tomorrow night. How do you want me to get in?"

"On the east side of the CFP building, there's an alley. Just walk down that alley to a staircase that leads dircctly to a back door to my office." Hugo nodded.

"Meet me at that back staircase of yours, Mr. Birdsall, and let me in. I'll look at what you've found. Then I can present my healthy bill to you having actually done some work."

Birdsall nodded. "About 8:00 PM, Hugo. Okay?"

Hugo looked in a thick book he carried in his hip pocket. It was banged up and scruffy looking, but it held what Hugo seemed to need. "Fine," he said, with finality, and made a note.

Parker had a thought and spoke to Birdsall. "When you had meetings in your office, were there things that always seemed to happen, or conditions that were awkward? Things that were not noticed when you were working alone?"

Birdsall thought about Parker's question. "Not really. That office is comfortable enough. Every once in a while it gets very cold in there during the cold months. I'm always complaining, but nothing is ever found wrong with the thermostat or the furnace. Same story in the summer. My cool air always seems to have trouble when it's the hottest. So I haven't mentioned it again. Just work through it."

Hugo smiled at Parker. "Good question, Mr. Parker. You might use it as a guide when you hunt down this bug. It will be very ordinary looking, and probably in a place where you'll wonder why you never noticed it. One thing that I can't answer, though, is why anybody would take the trouble - and the risk, which is considerable - of bugging your office? Not to downplay your importance, Mr. Birdsall, or the importance of your newspaper, but what could you possibly be discussing in your office that is so critical that you'd be the target of eavesdropping? That's something that should be considered, at some point."

Birdsall was silent for a few seconds and then said, "I can't think of a damned thing, Hugo. We like to be out front on certain articles and news items, but there has never been any subjects of the level of importance that I think you're talking about. Not on my watch, anyway."

Hugo nodded toward Birdsall and got to his feet. "I'll see you tomorrow night, about 8:00, Mr. Birdsall. And don't say a word to anybody, especially in your office." He lumbered out, pausing only to direct a parting comment at Parker. "You're not unknown to me, Mr. Parker. You're the guy, two or three years ago, who took a helluva chance in the Vermont House, and got plugged for it. Right?"

"Right, Hugo," replied Parker. "Forgot to duck."

Hugo stopped and looked directly at him. In a knowing voice he said, "Yeah."

20

Parker started to get up from his seat in the big booth, but Birdsall stopped him. "Before we do any spy work, Mr. Parker, we're going to continue our talk about my brother's death. You brought it up. Tell me why."

"Your brother's death isn't connected in any way to this non-profit assignment you gave Jan, Mr. Birdsall. It's just that when I talked to my friend about Jan and her story, and when I mentioned your name, he immediately gave me some information on the death of a Gilbert Birdsall. I don't know why. Please tell me all you know about your brother's death. Then I'll see if anything you say lines up with the note I got from my friend."

Birdsall sat down in one of the conference table chairs, took a deep breath, and started talking. "I don't know a lot about it, Mr. Parker. It's all understandable. He was a hunter. He had at least twenty classic rifles in three gun cases at home and he was very proud of them. He had a special gun cabinet built big enough to hold some rifles and his hunting togs, too." He stayed silent for a few seconds, obviously thinking about what to say next.

"He kept all of his equipment in first-class condition. I gave him a camo jacket for Christmas about ten years back. It was the best I could find. Had pockets everywhere, zippers on all of them and in places where I wouldn't put them, but I'm not a hunter, either. He was really pleased. Two years later I wanted to give him some first-rate boots for his birthday. At that time, by the way, he was just getting his business started and couldn't afford the good stuff that he enjoyed so much. So I stepped in to help, using gifts on holidays to disguise what I was doing. I was going to buy him something else, about four years ago, and when I checked with his wife, she told me that he wasn't hunting any more. She thought that it was getting a little dangerous in the woods now, and had told him of her concerns. He told her that he agreed and he'd stick to shooting range competitions. Surprised me, Mr. Parker, I can tell you." The alarm bells had started faintly ringing in Parker's head, and he hated to hear them again.

"But here's what I really don't understand, Mr. Parker. Why was he up there? And his wife didn't know about it until they called her. I went up there to identify him – his wife was all to pieces – and another thing looked strange, too. I didn't recognize the rifle. It just looked like a standard run-of-the-mill .30 -.30. Sort of beaten up, and not his style. But I couldn't be sure, so I didn't say anything. Actually, I didn't know what I'd have said if I even wanted to. Everything was rushing by, and I couldn't keep up. The investigating officer talked to me and to my brother's wife by phone." Parker could see that this was hurting Birdsall, but Birdsall kept talking, so Parker let him go.

"Another officer, or I guess he was, anyway, seemed to be questioning the location of the body. It was down a bank, and in some small trees. I couldn't see anything that was worrisome about it, so I didn't concern myself with it. In any case, it was judged an accident. The police didn't seem to miss anything, and I figured if they were on the case, I'd be of no help anyway. So, I came home and helped his wife cope. She's in Florida now. Couldn't get away from the land of the whitetail fast enough. Can't say as I blame her."

"Where is this equipment now, Mr. Birdsall? I mean what was on the body when he was found? Did his wife just throw it all out? What about the guns in the cabinets? In fact, all of his hunting equipment?"

"If I had had it sent to her house she would have thrown it all out without looking at it. That's why I had it sent to my place. I figured she'd settle down and then be sensible about it. She told me to keep it, and that she didn't want to see it again, ever. I've still got it here – at my home, that is – not at the paper. I've got an appraiser coming next month so we can sell it or have an auction or whatever he suggests. I'll get the money to her through her bank. It's the last item that needs to be settled in order to close the estate."

Parker asked, "Could I see the guns and clothing? I don't want to be intrusive, but it would mean I could close this little chapter of this non-profit exploration, and tell my friend 'thanks, but no thanks'."

"Sure," Birdsall said, "and here's my card with my home address on it. Know where that is? Good. Come on out to the house for breakfast, and then you can look over all this hunting paraphernalia. But first we'll get this present search behind us, one way or the other."

"More than fair, Mr. Birdsall, let's do it." they got to their feet and headed for Birdsall's place of business.

The short walk from "Mickey's" was taken in silence. Neither man seemed willing to break the quiet interlude.

They walked into Birdsall's office and surveyed that which was about to be ransacked – or at least that's what Parker surmised were Birdsall's thoughts.

They stood in the middle of the sizeable office. The two doors that entered it were cut into the two long walls that opposed each other. One door exited to the escape hatch and the other out to the reception area where Birdsall's secretary had her desk. Entering by that same door would give the visitor a view of a long office, half of which was taken up by a long table and numerous chairs. This was obviously for conferences. The other half was Birdsall's desk, and the three easy chairs. The carpet added some color to the room but it had worn out a few years ago. Parker could see by the wear patterns that periodically, somebody cleared out the furniture in the office and turned the rug to cover new patches of wear.

"Well, Mr. Parker, where do we start?" Birdsall asked.

"Based on what Hugo had to say, I think we should look at the most obvious of hiding places. You know, Mr. Birdsall," Parker continued, "I think that Hugo would judge us complete simpletons if we don't find a bug in the next thirty seconds."

"I agree," said Birdsall. "And if we don't in thirty minutes, there isn't one. And if there isn't one, then everything you've said is knocked into a cocked hat." Parker nodded gloomily.

"Well," said Parker, "let's get on with it. Our self-imposed time limit is draining away."

"Let's each take half of the room. We'll need to look in the obvious places, maybe right in plain sight, if it's an amateurish job. And Hugo was very convincing on that score."

Parker and Birdsall went on their assigned tasks. They checked all the baseboards and door casings. They looked behind the many pictures that Birdsall had hung on the wall, including one showing Parker lying on the floor of the Vermont House Chamber "ruining the carpet", as Hugh Hammond had indecorously put it.

They moved some pieces of furniture about to expose possible hiding places. Nothing was found. Parker was glum and Birdsall looked a little more comfortable. It was hard for him to believe that anyone on the CFP staff would listen in to private conversations.

After about forty-five minutes they met in the center of the room. "What do you think, Mr. Parker?" asked Birdsall, cautiously.

"We haven't found it yet," said Parker abruptly.

Parker turned away from Birdsall, and then turned back to him. "Mr. Birdsall, you said that you had air conditioning and heating problems off and on in this office. Correct?"

"Damn right. Always seemed to happen at the wrong times, too. The experts couldn't tell me what was wrong, either. Then, all of a sudden, the system began to work properly. Strange goings on."

Parker snapped his fingers and abruptly turned and looked again along the common wall with the reception area. "I forgot something." He stopped and knelt down. "Got a screwdriver, Mr. Birdsall?"

"Yep," said Birdsall and went to his desk and started rummaging about in various drawers. "Right here," holding up the desired instrument for Parker's inspection. He carried it over to Parker. "What's on your mind, Mr. Parker?"

"Just something I forgot to check. Where's the thermostat for this office of yours, Mr. Birdsall?"

"Outside the door. In the reception area. It was moved there about five years ago. I kept forgetting to turn it down at night when I left, so I decided to move it where the cleaning service could get to it after I'd gone home. It controls both the central heat and the central air conditioning." Parker nodded.

There were four 8"x 8" ventilated panels let into the wall, flush with the surface, and painted the same color as the surrounding wall. From a standing position a person would hardly notice them at all, except for the vent openings. Must be the decorator's touch, Parker thought.

He removed all four of these vents. Birdsall moved to look into the two that were located at the end of the room that contained the conference table. He found nothing and looked relieved. One other was located in the center of the room, next to the door into the reception area, and the last one was placed in the wall behind Birdsall's desk.

It was in the third vent opening that he found the microphone. Its wire, trailing into the square duct and then moving straight up and disappearing through a split line where two pieces of the duct work were joined, was almost invisible.

It was an interesting little microphone. It was tiny and round – about the diameter of a wood pencil. It was stuck into an upper corner of the duct, right behind the removable panel. If a person wasn't looking for it, it might have been missed altogether.

Birdsall, who was looking over Parker's shoulder during Parker's inspection of the vents, took on a ghastly color, and slumped into one of the easy chairs directly behind him. He said nothing.

Parker sat on the floor, still trying to study the mic and its position.

Finally Birdsall stirred and, in a slightly broken voice that didn't sound like his own, said, "Well, pull the sonovabitch outa there."

Parker hesitated. "No, I don't think we should. I think Hugo should see this just as we found it. In fact, I think that you should leave it as it is from now on. It might be handy to allow it to record things that we *want* them to hear – whoever 'them' is."

Parker struggled to his feet. "Just like in the old spy movies in World War Two. I really shouldn't comment, though, Mr. Birdsall. I don't know a damn thing about this stuff. Hugo would have some advice for you on what to do. I'd follow it, if I were you."

Parker stood up carefully, stretching out, and waiting for a muscle to cramp or pull. Nothing happened to him. That proved that he was in top shape, he reasoned. Then, he set his heels at the middle of the heat duct opening and stepped off the distance to the edge of the entrance door to the reception area. Then he went into the reception area and stepped off the same distance back along the wall to where the duct was probably located. Except that he couldn't get there. There was a fairly small, but deep, bookcase in his way. Right next to the bookcase was Birdsall's secretary's desk. Handy, thought Parker.

He knelt down and began pulling books out of the lower shelf. He only had to remove a half dozen when he found what he knew would be there.

The small recorder was propped up against the back wall of the bookcase. It was the type that was voice-activated, and recorded on those tiny tape cassettes. Parker also saw another wire with a plug end that would fit a recorder like this just hanging in space. Parker knew what that was and where it led. He'd have Birdsall find this one.

Birdsall was standing over him, leaning in towards the book-case. Parker looked up at him and saw a man who was shattered. Birdsall still couldn't believe it.

"Mr. Birdsall," Parker said, firmly, "take this screwdriver and go over to your desk wall. Pull off that little panel over there – the one like this one. Let's see what's there, if anything." Parker spoke deliberately and slowly. Birdsall was taking this very hard, and Parker knew he had to get through to him. Make him do something. Get him involved.

While Birdsall was in his office removing the panel, Parker disconnected the recorder and rewound the tape and then hit the "Play" button. The recorder might be small but it had a high level of quality. The conversation between Parker and Birdsall was very clear, even though they were sitting at a point that was at the extreme end of the room away from the mic. He rewound the tape and removed it from the recorder and put it in his pocket.

Then he got to his feet and began a methodical search of the secretary's desk. He was looking for something that he absolutely knew would be there. It was in the back of a bottom drawer that he found it – a pack of six cassette tapes with two missing. Parker knew he had one in his pocket. She must have the other herself, thought Parker. He hoped she didn't keep a record of each tape. If she didn't she wouldn't miss one of the tapes. I have to take the chance, he said to himself.

Parker put a fresh tape from her secret hoard into the re-corder and set it back in its place. He left it unplugged for the moment.

While Parker was at work, Birdsall had walked over to his desk, and then to the wall behind it, in a kind of trance. But he did what Parker wanted. And it was very easily done. As he was removing the front panel, Parker walked over to him. When the vent cover was out of the way, Birdsall looked inside the opening. With a deep sigh he shifted his gaze up to its top and over to, and just inside, the upper corner. He reached out and touched the tiny mic gingerly, as if it was an explosive. "Here, you look, Bill," he said, in a muffled voice.

Parker wasn't surprised. The mic was placed into the corner of the opening, as was the one that Parker found. As in the first find, too, a person might not have seen this mic, either, even though it was in plain view.

The location of the speaker wire, in this case, was brazen. It simply traveled straight out to the interior wall of the office, traveled down the wall in the space made by the tongue-and-groove wood paneling, made an abrupt left turn across the top of the baseboard, through a drilled hole and into Birdsall's secretary's office. Its color matched the shade of the paneling very well. Open to the view of anyone. But only if that someone was looking for it.

Parker walked into the secretary's office and easily found the wire, hiding behind a perfectly awful looking green object called, in some circles, a potted plant. It stood at least six feet tall and looked as if it would reach out to you and take your coat and hat when you arrived. No wonder no one had seen the wire in her office.

Then the wire dove behind the bookcase. He had already seen the other end of it, with its ready plug, hanging inside the lower section of it.

He knew how both the heat and cool air could be controlled. He had only to prove it to himself. The thermostat was one of those units that had to do only two jobs – control the air conditioning in the summer, and the heat in the winter. And it was in a position where it would be easy to cause it to malfunction. Then, when the noise of the blower was stopped, the mic would pick up anything in Birdsall's office, no matter where the conversation took place. Clever, and simple, at the same time. As he looked around, he wondered if there was any other way to interrupt the blower.

And then he saw the circuit breaker box. The breaker could be manually tripped. No, that won't work. That's too dangerous and awkward. Also, for reasons of safety, the panel was locked.

Back to the thermostat. If the thermostat could be subtly sabotaged, the meeting would continue on, until someone noticed that it was becoming too warm, or too cold, as the case may be.

Parker removed the thermostat cover. All looked normal. He poked around with his finger, checking to see if the things that were supposed to move around and up and down, actually did. And then one of the screws that held down a wire felt loose.

Suddenly all became clear to Parker. All someone had to do was to move the wire slightly from under the loosened screw, maybe with a small screwdriver, or anything like that, and the circulation of conditioned air would stop. Then the recorder would go into action. It probably had a lot of noise on it from the blower whirring, but Birdsall's secretary wouldn't have to enable the recorder very often. Just during the day when Birdsall was in the office, and maybe occasionally at night. And that's why Birdsall found her working late when he hadn't authorized it, Parker suddenly realized.

It may be crude, he thought, but quite safe for her.

Parker replaced things as they were. She can't know that anybody had been snooping around. She was the only one who was allowed to snoop in this office. He walked back into Birdsall's office. He was sitting in his desk chair, holding in his hands the front vent cover from the wall.

"I'd replace that panel for now, Mr. Birdsall. Show it to Hugo tomorrow night. See what he has to say. And I think I'd ask him to bug your secretary's phone. I'd like to know who she talks to occasionally. That might be interesting."

Birdsall looked up at Parker as if he'd never seen him before. It's not easy to deal with the problem of broken trust, thought Parker, and Birdsall was having the symptoms of one betrayed.

His chair squeaked as he turned it toward the air vent opening in the wall, stood up, and started the process of refastening it.

Parker sat at the conference table, waiting for him to finish.

When Birdsall came back to him, Parker said, as quietly as he could, "You've got a very big problem here, Mr. Birdsall. It can be fixed quietly, but first you've got to be an actor. You've got to give an Academy Award performance for the next few days when you are around her. You have to act as if nothing is wrong. Can you do that? It's the most important role you'll ever have to play."

Birdsall looked at Parker in a way that made Parker believe that he was coming back to life. "Yes, I can, Bill, and I will. But only for a few days. There's a limit to my patience."

"Fine," said Parker. "Talk it all over with Hugo tomorrow night. I might even try to be here, if that's okay. All I want to know is one thing: who does she report to? Call me at home when you know. It would be good if you could hear more than one message from her. I'm headed out right now. Say hello to Hugo for me." Parker dropped a piece of scratch paper on the table with his number on it. "Keep your chin up, Hal."

Birdsall nodded. Parker walked out.

21

Hal Birdsall lived in South Burlington, on Lake Champlain. He had bought the property many years ago, thinking that he could retire on the lot and just fish away those golden years. The problem with that, he discovered, was that the taxes would become the "golden" part of his declining years. He knew that he'd have to sell when trying to live on his retirement income.

He was up and about on this morning of Bill Parker's visit. His wife was visiting her mother in Canada. She would be gone for about two weeks, so he fumbled around the kitchen opening cupboard doors and shutting them again, pulling open drawers and closing them again, too. He finally got some toast ready to go, decided against any form of eggs, and elected to serve coffee and toast. Maybe juice, too, which must be in the refrigerator, if he could find it in there without spilling other containers that surrounded it. Parker would just have to be satisfied.

Birdsall was impressed with Parker. Parker didn't talk too much, but what he said usually was right on point. He had a mind that worked, too, and yesterday was the proof of that. He worked out where these mics would be located in his office. Birdsall knew he couldn't do that and was glad he had a Bill Parker to figure things out.

The knowledge that his secretary seemed to be the one who was eavesdropping on him and his employees unsettled him and caused a sleepless night. What he couldn't understand was why *his* office was the target of a snoop. He sensed that when he learned who she was working for, he'd learn why his office was targeted, too.

And then he wondered what the connection could possibly be that was a link to the death of his brother. That one really bothered him. Well, that's why Parker was coming for breakfast today. It wouldn't take long for Parker to look this stuff over, and then Birdsall might know much more.

As Birdsall was thinking about all these things, he saw an old pickup truck, with Parker in command, wheel into his driveway. My God, where did he get that old wreck, anyway? Parker had a few strange ideas and qualities, and this was certainly one of them.

Parker knocked on the door, and Birdsall opened it almost immediately. "Hal," Parker said, "good to see you this morning."

"Come in, Bill," he said. "I'm afraid that I'm no good at fixing breakfast. I hope coffee, juice and toast will suffice. Sorry about that."

"No problem, Hal. I don't eat anything but what you're serving anyway, so that's perfect."

"What do you expect to find when you go through my brother's hunting things, Bill? Am I allowed to know or will I have to go outside?"

Parker chuckled. "Nothing like that at all, Hal. In fact, I don't know what I'll find. More than that, I might find something that a smarter and more experienced person might recognize right away as the key to the puzzle. Hell, I don't even know what the puzzle might be – or if we even have one. I just know that a very good man has asked me to check a few things. Then bring back the results of my search and call him. And, with your help, that's what I'm going to do."

"Well, I'm ready, Bill, if you are."

Parker got to his feet, walked over to the kitchen sink and poured the remainder in his cup down the drain. He said, "I'm just coffee'd out, Hal."

Birdsall eyed him and then walked over to the sink and poured out his coffee, too. "Pretty bad, isn't it?"

Parker remained silent.

"Let's go down to the basement, Bill. That's where the loot is stored."

Birdsall's basement was neat, organized, cool and moisture-free. Parker thought of his dirt floor basement that had none of those qualities.

The first items were the three gun cabinets, with all the rifles inside. Birdsall didn't know enough about rifles to know anything about scarcity and value. Parker, on the other hand, had some knowledge in this area, along with stamps and coins and other collectables. He had written insurance policies for some collections and learned to look at the items from a different perspective than the uninitiated person. The rifles looked to be in immaculate condition – except for one. Birdsall opened that cabinet and took it out for Parker to see, close up. It was an old Remington .30-.06 lever action rifle. Remington had made many of them and they had no particular value, especially this one. It was in poor condition. The bluing was almost gone from the barrel and action; the stock was dull, showing scrapes and gouges that a careful owner would not have allowed to exist; the butt plate was cracked, as if the rifle had been use as a hammer at one time in its life; and it hadn't had a rod, with its customary oiled patch, run down the barrel in too many firings to count. Overall, the condition of the rifle made it a probable safety hazard, and not a firearm used for one of the most enjoyable hobbies in the history of the country. This was the rifle that Gil Birdsall had carried into the woods on the day of his accident, as the attached yellow evidence tag told him.

Parker set aside this poor excuse for a rifle, and reached into the next cabinet for another rifle. This one was also a Remington. It was a Long Range "CreedMoore" .44 caliber model. It was a firearm that had been often used, judging by the slightly darkened areas where the hands of the user had changed the shade of the grip and cheek plate. This evidence only added to the beauty of the firearm. There was no sign of neglect. The other rifles were all in perfect condition, even the oldest ones – except that lousy Remington, Parker thought. Why?

He checked another, a beautiful Colt-Burgess lever action .44-40. He looked at a Winchester Model 86, lever action, .33 caliber, which was at least one hundred years old. Another was a Ruger Model 77, MKII .338 caliber. A beautiful gun. All had very decent value Parker knew. Except one. All were in beautiful shape. Except one.

Birdsall watched Parker handle the rifles with confidence. It reminded him that Parker was a Vietnam veteran. Parker never made anything of that, but many of those in politics did strut their stuff about their military service when they really didn't do much, and Birdsall had learned that almost all of them were phonies. Some of them had never been in the armed services at all, and they assumed that their claimed military service would never be checked. Or if it was, their friends in the news media would not report it or would discredit any person who did. Some of the ProgDems, who wanted high office, actually claimed that they had achieved academic degrees from high-sounding institutions that they never attended. Most of these ignorant people were typical of the left in Vermont. They wanted to have handed to them positions of great status, along with a damn good paycheck from the taxpayers of Vermont, but actually earning this through hard work in school, personal application in the workplace, and determination, was too much effort. They looked for a shortcut. And the news media gave it to them.

Birdsall knew that if he wrote anything that pointed out these phonies, or wrote in defense of America's soldiers in Vietnam or Iraq, he would be hauled in on the carpet. Maybe not literally, but he'd know the message when he saw it.

Birdsall was proud of the troops in Iraq. Most people didn't know that he had a son over there who was a Colonel in the infantry. Most of those who ran things in Burlington, or who attended the university, hated the President for going in there. They hated the troops, too. These ignorant people, regardless of their ages, didn't think beyond the next second. In public, however, they sounded like Socrates.

Birdsall didn't feel anger toward these unthinking people. They were never equipped by their educations to think about anything in an objective way. He became depressed when he thought of the many teachers who taught to a political agenda rather than true course content.

These are our terrorists inside America, Birdsall thought. They want America to fail. They want an elite to run things. They want the UN to be the "big momma" on our planet.

Birdsall felt strongly that he and Parker were on the same page. Birdsall knew much more about Parker than he let on. They both knew that the weakness of these ignorant people was that they spoke in sound bites. People who really thought about the comments of these shallow activist people knew that they were dangerous and ignorant. They had no understanding at all of the consequences of their words if these words ever became reality.

These America-haters, when they spoke in public, revealed their own intolerance, hatred, and ignorance. The New York Times, the Los Angeles Times, and the Boston Globe, loved them. Equally as intellectually corrupt were NBC, CBS, ABC, and CNN. Birdsall was ashamed of the news industry on which he had based his whole career.

He had always admired those people who went to Vietnam, especially those who had volunteered, and he had learned that Parker was one of those. But, that was a long time ago. Maybe he would, after all, write an Op-Ed piece on phony politicians and teachers, necessary wars on terrorism, real heroes, and what was at stake today. Of course, the CFP wouldn't touch it. No daily newspaper in Vermont would print it. Some of the weeklies might. The Caledonia Counselor came to mind. That was a newspaper that was worthy of the name, he knew. They weren't afraid of anything.

Parker was now rummaging around in one of the drawers in the bottom of one of the gun cabinets. It contained the usual items common to all well organized gun people. All sorts of cleaners, cloth, lint-free, patches, and small containers of oil. Some display patches for memberships and awards, and some parchment citations. All in all, a drawer with all the correct and expected items for taking care of firearms.

Parker moved to the second cabinet. This one had two separate and smaller drawers in the bottom of the cabinet. This cabinet contained two pairs of hiking boots, both top quality, as far as Parker could tell. The were spotless, shiny, and with only moderate wear. They looked perfectly maintained.

The third cabinet had a series of drawers up one side to about waist level, and the top section was open for its full width from that point to the top. The top section was reserved for the outdoor clothing. Parker saw the camo outfits, including the fancy one that Hal had given his brother, all lined up, on hangers, cleaned and, surprisingly, pressed. Who the hell would do that, anyway? These outfits would be wrinkled as soon as the wearer sat down for three minutes.

These garments wouldn't be worn to a formal dance, that's for certain. People, however, had different levels of comfort regarding care and feeding of the essential items for their essential hobby. Obviously, Hal Birdsall's brother was a maniac about "neat" and "organized". Parker was uncomfortable around people like that. They would remind him of his own failings in those two departments.

The four drawers up the side of this cabinet held nothing but ammunition. He checked every box, then closed the drawers, one after the other, with a manner that told Birdsall that he was looking for something and not finding it.

"What's the problem, Bill?" he asked.

"I don't know much about these beautiful rifles, but I recognize a man, Hal, your brother, Gil, who was an expert on them.

And there's something missing that he should have had here. I have an insurance business and I have insured many collections of firearms. They all had this item front and center. But, not here. I mean that it isn't absolutely essential, but I guess I'm very much surprised that it isn't here. And there's another item that isn't here, Hal, and I'm really wondering about that. too."

"What are they, Bill?" he asked.

"First, a written inventory, and a running record of the cleanings and firings of all these guns. People like your brother should have it with their guns. A diary of hunting trips. Photographs. That sort of thing. I don't see them here. I know that this type of record could be in another place – a safety deposit box, for instance. But I don't think so because it wouldn't be valuable to anyone except Gil. And real hunters like to look at those things once in a while. The absence of this logbook ties in to the other missing object."

He was right, of course, thought, Birdsall. Gil was like that. Mr. Organized.

"Do you have any papers or records of anything that your brother might have saved and filed? I don't mean personal things. Just a box of papers that we could look at." Parker looked grim.

"Sorry, Bill," he said, "I didn't notice anything like that. Maybe Polly did. That's his wife. She had all his paperwork with her. She and her lawyer went through it when closing the estate. She told me that they burned everything except for a few papers that she took to Florida. I'll send for them. Polly will be glad to get rid of them." Parker nodded. He felt disappointed and grim.

"This is important, Bill?" Birdsall asked. "Critical, maybe?"

"Oh, I don't know. I'd just like to see any records like that, but it seems too late, anyway."

"What's the other item, Bill? You mentioned two things that you expected to see, but don't. What is it?"

"I don't know how much importance I should attach to this, Hal, but there's no ammunition for the .30-.06 rifle your brother had with him on his 'hunting' trip." Birdsall noticed the emphasis.

"Maybe that's explained in a very simple way, but some of it should be here," Parker said reasonably. "If you know where it might be found, let me know, will you, Hal?"

"Why is that a problem, Bill? I can't see the reason for your interest."

Parker turned and faced Birdsall. "Your brother was a very organized person, Hal," and he gestured at the gun collection and its associated cabinets. “And he loved hunting. He was killed in a hunting accident even though he’d stopped hunting three years earlier. He had a rifle with him that was probably dangerous to fire because of its condition. He had no ammo for it in his pockets when he was found. There’s none here. His wife didn’t know he’d returned to hunting – if he did. That’s strange. I wanted to see his inventory today to see if this old Remington is listed. And were there any shells in the tube of the rifle Gil took into the woods that day?” Parker looked puzzled and mystified. “That’s why I want to see the inventory and some shells for this weapon. I came here today thinking I’d find everything I expected. I didn’t find anything I just knew should be here. Why?”

Birdsall knew that Parker was correct. “I’ll try to find them, Bill,” he said, “and I’ll let you know.”

They walked upstairs. Parker turned to Birdsall. “Thanks for all your help and patience, Hal. I’m heading back into Burlington, then to Montpelier, then home. If you run across anything out of the ordinary, would you let me know? Maybe Gil’s lawyer has something?”

Birdsall caught Parker’s arm as they headed toward the door. “There’s something else, isn’t there, that’s bothering you, Bill? What is it?” Parker shook his head. “I’m seeing Hugo tonight, Bill, as you know. You said that you might be coming to my office, too. Why don’t you show up? You know where. It should be interesting. And we could all talk about what we’ve found – or didn’t find.”

Parker shook his head again. “No, Hal, I don’t think so. Look. I might be there, but I’ve got other things to take care of. Call me, though, and tell me about your evening.”

“Well, then, let me ask you a question before you jump into that truck of yours, which by the way, will cause talk among all my neighbors, and I will be questioned for days about my new ‘old car’.”

Parker grinned, trying to shake off the blues he felt. “They simply are not aware that this country reached its peak in the production of quality trucks in the year the Red Sox lost the World Series in ‘86. And it’s been downhill ever since – except now, of course.”

“Well,” said Birdsall, resignedly, “I’ve got a question that has been bothering me from the beginning of all this. Why is *my* office bugged? We really don't talk about stuff that's really important in there. Why just my office?"

Parker turned back to Birdsall. "First, let me thank you for all your help, Hal. I appreciate it very much." Birdsall waved a hand dismissively.

"Now, before I ride away into the sunset, let me give you a possible answer to that question that might cause you some additional loss of sleep. You asked why the CFP? It's *the* question, Hal." Parker moved around the fender of his truck.

"Here's a possibility, Hal. One that feels right to me. What if the people who are behind all this have a really simple agenda? What if they only want to keep up to date with what's being said about them? What if they are hiding something very important to them? Or maybe they are ready to make a big move and need to know what they're facing – you know, who's getting too inquisitive, who knows more than they should, who's lining up against them, what are the institutions who have access to the public and which of them has significant influence? That sort of thing. Maybe all they want is to steal a march on their opposition. Stay ahead of the curve, you know. What if the CFP is only one of a number of groups and individuals that have the responsibility of protecting their clients' interests? What if there are many phones and meeting rooms all over Chittenden County, or the state, for that matter, that are bugged? Think about that, Hal, and then you'll get a possible idea of how scary this all might be." Birdsall looked aghast.

"Bill, the first thing I've had to do is to get used to my own conversations being listened to by somebody. I thought you were just a conspiracy freak when you first talked to me. I'm a believer now. But, it's too much for me to grapple with. Even if more than just the CFP is being bugged, I can't do a single thing to prevent it."

Parker looked steadily at Birdsall. "Maybe somebody thinks the CFP is important. I would, I know, if I had to be aware of what was being said about me and my organization in Chittenden County – or around the state, for that matter. But, you're right. You can't find out who the others are, if they exist at all, by yourself. But Hugo can, can't he? Why not mention it to him? See what his reaction is."

Parker walked around to the driver's door on his unusually traditional vehicle. He liked that term, rather than "old". He climbed up into the saddle, and made ready to ride off. In his mirror, Parker could see a new and different Birdsall - one who looked like a man who had lost, in a very few seconds, all of those illusions that had shielded him from reality for all these years.

22

It was 11:30 in the morning as Parker drove onto I89. He felt better right away. He wanted to leave Chittenden County as soon as he could. He felt that too much exposure to the wisps of strangeness that floated over the County could cause emotional damage that couldn't be cured by the bone-rattlers of the local mental health community.

He knew a sense of light-heartedness as he headed south. This feeling lasted only about five minutes and was replaced by thoughts of the city of Montpelier to which he was headed. Parker decided that if he could write a book about this short journey, he'd call it "Trapped in the Northeast Quandary". Or something wonderfully clever like that. Fitting.

It was early afternoon when he arrived in Montpelier. He thought he'd have a sandwich in The Thrush right after he'd checked in with Peter Morgan at the Montpelier Police Department. He hadn't found the time to try to call Peter at his home regarding the information about the death of Gil Birdsall in the hunting accident. This would be his chance.

When Parker walked into the MPD, he saw a harried Catherine Morgan talking and listening on two phones. Officers were going in and out, and there was no Supervisor Morgan. Catherine Morgan looked up, saw Parker, scribbled on a pad, and shoved it across the counter toward him. It read: "Peter at Cap. Bldg. Suicide. Go up."

Parker waved a "thank you" at Officer Morgan and ran out the door.

As he drove toward the Capital Building he thought that Catherine Morgan must have been told that if Parker showed up, he was to be sent immediately to the Statehouse. That means, thought Parker, that I probably know the suicide.

Parker swung his truck around behind The Thrush Tavern and parked. He hopped down to the ground and started walking at a fast clip up to the Statehouse.

There were police officers everywhere, it seemed, and he was surprised to see Morgan standing on the top step of the eastern entrance to the Capital Building.

"Peter, what's going on? Is it okay for me to be here? I wasn't stopped as I arrived."

"No problem, Bill. Catherine called me to let me know that you were on your way. I just passed the word for the officers to look for you and to pass you through."

"I assume that you had a reason for that. Do I know the suicide?"

"Yep, you do, Bill. It's Hugh Hammond. He slit a wrist in his committee room and bled to death quietly and quickly." Parker felt a disbelief that numbed him.

"Hugh Hammond, Peter?" he croaked.

Morgan nodded. "I let you through because you were one of the last people to see him alive, and I wanted to talk to you about that last meeting."

Morgan took hold of Parker's arm and began leading him down the hall toward the central junction point of the building. Then up the winding staircase to the House and Senate Chambers. After that, it was only one more minute, up the stairs, and down the long hall, to the committee room. It was crowded with police, both uniformed and in plain clothes, a doctor, others with the telltale equipment of the forensics unit, official photographers, and curious politicians, who were being shooed away by the police. There were even a few lobbyists trying to see into the room. Parker recognized that Naughton person among them, playing one-upmanship by wearing a fashionable raincoat, and just as interested in the scene as those other beings he looked down upon when he was doing his real-life thing, whatever the hell that was.

"Hammond was found slumped over in his chair, with blood concentrated under his left side on the floor, and on the chair, too, as you can imagine," said Morgan. "He'd apparently simply slit a wrist with a single-edged razor blade, which we found on the floor, and sat there until he died. Of course, the forensic people are still performing their magic, but that's how it appears, unconfirmed."

Morgan grimaced as he said that, Parker noticed. No matter how often you see a dead body, you never get used to it if you've got any imagination at all.

"You saw him this past Monday evening in the Thrush, as I understand it," Morgan said. Parker nodded briefly, still shaken by this inexplicable event.

It wasn't long after Morgan and Parker had arrived at the committee room that the photographers, the forensic people, and the police were showing signs of being done with their investigation of the scene. The body was still sitting at the table, as if waiting for this interruption to be over and the meeting to start again.

That idea unnerved Parker. It was so different from what he had expected. He had seen death before. Vietnam was the first exposure of William Parker, the college graduate but still the farm boy, to death in all its forms. He thought that nothing about it would ever shock him again. He was mistaken. This one did.

The gray color of the face, the vacant look of surprise in the staring eyes, and the pool of blood under Hammond's chair, caused Parker to turn away. This is dreadfully different, he thought.

In Vietnam, death was a constant companion, casting its shadow over everything. Many of those serving in that fight ended up joking about the possibility of dying. Others pointedly ignored the specter of it. Parker was one of the latter ones. He took the fatalistic approach, which, he knew, was as unrealistic as all the others. He just decided that if he was going to die, it was already preordained, and he couldn't do a thing about it, so he wouldn't concern himself with it. It provided a kind of shield, with inconsistent results, against the anguish of the loss of friends. The real difference between Vietnam and this moment was that the deaths of some of his companions was almost never seen. It happened somewhere else. The friend simply was gone.

Hugh Hammond's death, however, reached into Parker in a much different and ghastly way. This death was, to Parker, completely unexplainable. Its physical appearance, and just the presence of the body in that chair, was horrible. He found that he was unable to push it back behind his mental and emotional curtain so that he could deal with it with a certain calmness later on. The curtain either wasn't there anymore, or he had forgotten how to use it.

Parker turned away, swallowing hard, and vowing not to look at Hammond again. "Any note, Peter?" Parker gulped. He found that attempting to draw any kind of breath was difficult.

"Not that I know of," Morgan answered. "I'll have a chance to look around after the official group has cleared out. It's strange that there isn't one right on the table, but maybe only to me. Let's walk outside for a while and talk about your meeting with him at the Thrush."

23

Parker and Morgan walked down the Statehouse steps. The sun had a calming effect on Parker. He didn't know if Morgan even noticed it.

"When this conversation ends, Bill, most of it we never had. Okay?"

Parker knew what Morgan meant. "Of course, Peter. And part of this deal is that you give me any connection you may see between this suicide and the accidental death of Gil Birdsall."

Morgan stopped walking and slowly turned toward Parker. "What gives you the idea that there is a connection, Bill?"

Parker was exasperated. "I'm not the sharpest knife in the drawer, Peter," Parker said, "but even I can recognize that the Gil Birdsall information that you handed to me, without my asking, by the way, had something to do with Jan Evlin, along with the non-profits, and Representative Hugh Hammond, who is now dead by suicide. Understand this, too, Peter," Parker said, showing some heat of anger, frustration, confusion, in his voice, "I know that you have doubts about the Birdsall death, and that you also are bothered by the fact that no suicide note was left behind by Hammond. And I have something to tell you, too, after you've admitted all and have told me everything."

Morgan said nothing and resumed walking. Then suddenly he said, "Yes, Bill, I do have doubts. I had them before you came to my office the day before yesterday. I had them after I had a further conversation with my Burlington PD buddy who was at that meeting. It was only academic at that point. I didn't even know who Birdsall was. I just have a general interest in things not being what they seem – reinforced, I might add, by my experiences with you over the last three years. And then, as I was churning all this over in my mind, you dropped in, as if right on cue. I should have known that you would be somewhere in all this, even though I hadn't heard your name in over a year." Morgan grinned slightly as he said this, showing Parker that he wasn't angry at the Parker intrusions of the past.

"Is the suicide real, Peter?" Parker asked, with some hesitation. He didn't want to set Morgan off against him because of his inquisitiveness.

"As far as I know, Bill. Forensics and the Chief Medical Examiner will let us know." Morgan looked at Parker. "Why? Do you have some earth-shaking news that no one but you understands in all of this?" Parker decided that Morgan was suddenly impatient with him. He thought that he'd tread carefully.

"My only contact, in the last three years, with Hugh, was a rather strange dinner with him last Monday at the Thrush," said Parker. "It didn't start off that way, but the evening ended with Hammond abruptly walking out, leaving me with the check for a dinner he said he'd buy. That's not like him, Peter."

"What did you two talk about?" asked Morgan.

"The non-profits in Vermont, which was my subject, not his. When he agreed to have this dinner, he knew that I had something on my mind to discuss with him and about which to pick his brain. But he didn't know at all what the subject was to be. Maybe he guessed something, because he knew that I considered him an expert on the non-profit industry in Vermont. Not very likely, but it's possible."

Morgan stopped walking. Without looking at Parker, he asked, "Why is that so important to you, Bill – that is, to make sure I know that Hammond didn't know the subject before the dinner?"

Morgan hasn't lost a step, thought Parker. He's right on the beam with that question. There aren't many people like him, Parker knew.

"It was a series of things, Peter," Parker said cautiously, "that started with the dinner at the Thrush, and subsequent occurrences, too, that got me to thinking that somebody, or some group, or some other damn thing that I can't come up with, is very sensitive to anything that disturbs its web. Then it rushes out to see what's going on. If it sees something it doesn't like, it takes care of it."

Morgan stopped in his tracks and turned and looked Parker squarely in the face. "For Christ's sake, Parker, what's happened to you since I've last seen you? I admit that there was corruption when your buddy, the Representative, you remember, Kermit Mayes, I think it was," as Parker nodded, "got whacked in the Statehouse." Parker winced at Morgan's rough-cut, cop-like choice of words. "And I remember that you were on that scent like a hound, and you were right to be so. But this has *nothing* to base *anything* on, for goodness sake. Nothing at all." Morgan was being very direct with Parker. "If you go on with this, you'll make a fool of yourself, you know."

Parker had faced the situation of appearing the fool before. He had just followed his instincts in those times. That approach had put him in some interesting predicaments. He couldn't change anything now. "Well, Peter, I wanted to be sure that Hugh would be unprepared, so to speak, to defend the non-profits, or at least avoid covering up anything about them. It was important to me that we just have a conversation about them, with our hair down. That's all."

"Did he cooperate?" asked Morgan.

"Yes, beyond what I expected. I discovered that there was a deep distrust of many of the non-profits in his mind. In fact, Peter, he seemed to jump at the chance to tell me more than I asked for. Then, all of a sudden, he jumped up and left. I was completely surprised."

Morgan pondered this information. "Maybe you'd better tell me what's happened since we talked in my office – which was only, what? Two days ago? Three? Things have been piling up. It may be important."

Parker thought it *was* important. He mentioned no names, but told Morgan about his meeting with Birdsall and Hugo. He then told him about the "bugs", which shocked Morgan, and the apparent recognition of Parker by the cranks in the protest march. He also told Morgan about the non-breakfast with Birdsall and the confusing signals that were given off by his brother's hunting gear. Parker could almost see Morgan's ears pick up at hearing about this. Morgan continued to walk along, shaking his head in apparent wonder.

"Nothing has changed for you, has it?" Morgan murmured. "You just move through life doing a few good things, selling insurance, fishing for trout, being nosey when it suits you, and being bewildered when you occasionally run into people who don't like you very much. I was right when I told my wife that you were the most dangerous man in Vermont."

Parker was appalled. "Peter! You can't be serious. I never asked for those intrusions into my life. I've simply been in places where sometimes awkward things happen."

Morgan chuckled. "'Awkward things', indeed. Is that how you put it? Well, all right, Bill. I give up." He looked at Parker with affection. "Anything else?"

"Not that I know of," said Parker. "I just can't help but think that all of this ties together somehow. And don't forget, Peter, Birdsall hasn't heard from Jan Evlin in about five days. That says to me that something has scared her off her story."

"Maybe," said Morgan, skeptically. "Tell me, Bill, should we start worrying about her?"

"No, I'm not worried, Peter. Why would we worry? She's street-wise, and just got a little shaken when she got her note. I told you about her note that she thought was a threat, didn't I?" Morgan nodded. "She's probably with her family and they took a few days' holiday," offered Parker.

"I can't get it out of my head that she thought that the note was a threat to her," Morgan said, "and I'd like to remind you that you called her 'street-wise'. No, Bill, I'm not worried, either. However, to mystify you, I am going to start out by being 'concerned' rather than 'worried'."

"That's your weakness, Peter. You cops usually start out worried and then take it to new levels. We mortals blissfully walk along, being practical at a low level."

"Yes, sir, Bill. And we're happier than you mortals because we don't have so far to fall when reality finally kicks in."

"Umph," mumbled Parker, as if he didn't hear Morgan clearly, and as if he thought Morgan was the ultimate example of a heart attack waiting to happen. A fretter, if I ever saw one, he thought.

"Let me go back to the committee room with you, Peter. I won't tell." Parker and Morgan looked at each other, and then both looked slightly sheepish. "Like recess in second grade, Peter. Is this what we've come to?"

They walked further down the street, away from too many people walking by. "Including you in a police investigation is highly irregular, Bill. My career could be over if a legal sharp-shooter saw you with me."

"Would it help you at all if I told this mythical legal beagle that you and I were very good friends, and that I was brave, patriotic, steadfast, honest, and easy to like?"

"I think you would have made a strong case to get me off the hook until you got to that last alleged attribute. Then it would be all over for you as a character witness for me. But thanks for trying," Morgan said wryly.

Parker asked, "Can I go up to the room alone, Peter?"

"You can't possibly think that I would trust an out-of-shape insurance salesman from some little Vermont town nobody has ever heard of, to look around a death scene without an escort, do you? Yes, of course you can come with me. You might even be of some help."

Parker and Morgan headed back to the committee room just as the last photographer was exiting. One of the crime scene crew saw Morgan, and walked over to him. "Room's all empty except for the blood, Mr. Morgan. Samples have been taken."

"Thanks, Steve. Anything special we should look at before it turns up in the initial reports? I'd like to know so I'll look smart."

"Not that I know of, Pete. But we'll still consider you a smart guy." He grinned and walked out. Police certainly can be callous in the room heavy with death, thought Parker, knowing all the time that it's *their* protective device at work. We all have some form of shield against bad things, he thought.

Parker was walking around the committee room as this exchange was taking place. Nothing had changed since his days in the House. The rooms were still small and, with chairs set around the perimeter for lobbyists and citizens, cramped. The same messy desk surfaces, covered with notes and other scribblings, and the same cluttered floors, with piles of legislation in their awkward binders and seemingly indecipherable language. Piles of reference materials were also in evidence, used more to prop up another column of books, papers, and folders that were of more importance at the time of construction than the pile providing the support. Added to all of this were professionally-bound booklets containing statements from lobbyists and other politicians, and the occasional old food container, under the table and roughly in the area of the one who put it there. If it wasn't for the cleaning staff's work every evening, the committee rooms would be so messed up that they would be condemned by the environmentalists as unfit for human habitation.

And then Parker stopped moving. There was something very odd about this setting. He continued to look around. What was it that was out of kilter? At that moment Parker glanced down to the floor.

Under the table of the Chairperson was an object that shouldn't be there. He bent down and picked it up.

Morgan was also surveying the small room. He saw eleven small desks set up in a "T", with three forming the horizontal cross of the "T", and the remaining eight desks set up in twos, facing each other, the four two-desk sections making up the vertical main stem of the "T". From the doorway a visitor could look right down the vertical post of the "T" and right into the eyes of the committee chairman, seated in the center of the shorter "T" section, facing the door and seeing all.

Then Morgan noticed Parker, who was standing stock-still and looking at the object in his hand. "What's the matter, Bill?" he asked.

Parker waved the object he found on the floor toward Morgan. "Hammond wasn't found in his regular seat at the table. He was in another chair."

Morgan didn't understand. "What of it?" he said. "He could have just sat down at the table after he got up from his own chair to stretch, or something."

"Yes, it could be like that, except that Hammond's assigned chair is on the corner of the rectangular table, near the door into the hallway, and easy to get to. He chose, instead, to sit down in another chair that required him to *walk* around and *past* his own chair on the near corner to do it. That's strange, Peter. Believe me. During the session it's almost unheard of for members to sit in the chairs of other members. Honorable people will sit only in their own seat."

"Why?" asked Morgan. "Everything's the same for all of them, isn't it?"

"No, it isn't, Peter. Most definitely not. At each place there are various notes, phone messages, letters, materials like that, and you just don't read them. It wouldn't be ethical. I don't doubt that some people do, but I never knew anybody who did." Morgan continued to look disinterested.

"You also don't sit in another person's chair," Parker continued. "Well, that's not quite true, Peter. You could sit in another chair once in a while, if you're meeting with a few people at one end of the room. Or maybe just sit on the arm of the chair. But, unless he were a snoop, a person would always sit in his or her own chair. It also just *feels* strange to sit in a chair not your own, that's all." Morgan knew that Parker still had something else or his mind.

Morgan pondered this unexpected ethical behavior of the members of the General Assembly while they gave away taxpayers' money for uncertain results. Buying votes from the Vermont citizens, and using their tax money to do it, was big business in Montpelier.

"Therefore," Morgan said, "it *is* odd that Hammond's body was in another chair – especially when, just about an hour before his death, he was sitting in his assigned seat, as were all the committee members. Then they all left for lunch, and Hammond stayed behind, in his regular chair – or we think that's the way it was, to be confirmed when we interview the committee members."

"You've got it now, Peter."

"How did you know where Hammond's desk was, Bill? And now that I mention it, they should have a sign, or a placard, or something, hanging on the wall that will tell everybody what the committee is, and who the members are, and where they sit. It would be helpful to people who are in the room to talk to the committee."

Parker said, darkly, "The committee rooms always do have a classy sign to give visitors that information, Peter – except this one. The sign hangs right above the Chair's spot so that everybody can see the organization of the committee when they enter."

"Where's this one?"

"Right here." He held it up for Morgan to inspect. "It was under the chair of the Committee Secretary, on the floor. That's how I knew that Hammond was in the wrong chair."

"How come it wasn't on the wall?" Morgan asked.

Parker held up the sign. "It needs repairs. The wire on the back has come out and it needs to be reattached before it can be hung up again."

"Oh," said Morgan, without interest. "Well, I've seen enough. You ready?"

Morgan suddenly stopped walking, and turned toward Parker. "Speaking of signs, Bill, there was a handwritten sign hanging on the doorknob of this room when we got here. The forensics people probably have it now. I don't know who wrote it, but it said," and he consulted a small notebook, "'Keep Out, Please. I'm Resting'. Hammond left a note and then killed himself,

Bill. Is that the way it happened? And why here, for goodness sake?"

Parker looked at Morgan steadily for a few seconds. "Peter, I've never heard of that sort of thing before in a committee room. I was here for twelve years, and I never saw a committee room closed off like that during the day. They may be closed once in a while, but I never saw it." He looked around the room before turning back to Morgan.

"And that's how Hammond bought enough undisturbed time to do away with himself?" cried Parker.

Parker was walking toward the door, not really hearing or seeing anything. His mind was clipping along at a furious pace. What the hell was this all about, he thought?

"What's on your mind, Bill? I know there is something eating at you. I've seen you before."

"Nothing, really, Peter. Do you suppose you could let me look at the reports from your people when they become available? Even the CME's report? I know that's not proper, but maybe you could deputize me, or something."

Morgan chuckled. "Deputizing you would be the same thing as saying to the world, 'I've given Bill Parker something to read, which I'm not supposed to do, and now I'm covering it all up'. No, but I'll tell you what's in the reports when I see them. Couple of days."

"Fine, Peter," as they walked out of the Statehouse. "One more big, big, favor, Peter?" Parker held up an index finger, showing Morgan that he really meant it when he said "one favor".

"What is it now, Bill?" Morgan answered warily.

You usually take samples of any bodily fluids at a scene like the one we've just looked at – right?" Morgan nodded, watching Parker steadily.

"Have you finished taking samples in the committee room? This may be important, Peter."

"I think so, Bill, based on what Steve just told us. Why?"

"Here's the favor. Can you order them to check for any of the victim's blood being anywhere else in the room other than under the chair in which the victim was sitting?"

"You have that 'bee' in your bonnet about Hammond not being in the right chair, don't you?"

Parker gave a quick nod. "Please check for other places with blood, Peter. I believe this could be really important. And you'll talk to all the other committee members, won't you?" Morgan gestured that he would. "And you'll ask each of them if they find it strange that Hammond is not sitting in his regular chair, won't you? And if any of them had *ever* seen Hammond in any other seat but his own?"

Morgan was leaning against the door casing and staring at Parker. Then he absently scratched one hand with the other. Then tried to button a coat that was already buttoned. Then he removed his hat, looked it over, then gazed down at the floor, and said, "Okay." He walked over to the doorway and called out to the officer on watch. "Herb – get Steve back up here, will you? Thanks."

In two minutes, Steve Bell, Montpelier Police Detective, appeared in the doorway. "Yeah, Pete, whatdoyawant?" he asked, all the time eyeing Parker.

Morgan told him. "I think we did it, Pete, when we did the room initially. However, I'll check with the tech to be sure," and retreated down the hall.

"Thanks, Peter. I really appreciate it."

"I'm truly sorry about your friend, Bill, but I can't do favors for you just because you get an off-the-wall idea once in a while. You know that, don't you?" Parker gestured with a hand that said he had gotten the message.

"I understand that he was a good person," said Morgan.

Parker nodded grimly.

"We'll do what we can. What's next for you, Bill?"

"I'm heading back up to Burlington where the protests are more geared to single-issue topics, and not, as in Montpelier, multi-directional and scattered. In Burlington, for example, I would know immediately which protests to avoid. Impossible here in Montpelier."

Morgan smiled tolerantly at Parker. "The irrepressible William Parker at work. Well, just keep your head down, buddy."

Later, Parker would remember that comment.

24

Parker arrived in Burlington a little after five o'clock in the afternoon. As he drove across the city line he suddenly realized that he hadn't eaten since the non-breakfast at Birdsall's. An active day, capped by Hammond's tragic suicide, had driven everything else from his mind. Food, at this point, became important.

Parker had never met anyone who was more helpless in the home than Birdsall when the chief of the whole operation was away. He would be lucky if he wasn't found on the floor of his kitchen, thin and starved, when his wife arrived home from her visit.

Parker, on the other hand, credited himself with coping very well when Addie was away. He hadn't, however, figured out how she could walk into their home after being gone and immediately tell him that he had lived like a slob while she was away. And she hadn't even taken off her coat yet. There were no indications of that condition at all – and he had looked carefully around the house before she arrived.

This is an example, thought Parker, of Addie making snap decisions without enough information. There was no doubt, in Parker's view, that she had simply made up her mind that the house was messy before she arrived and that's the way it was. He knew that she'd have to get over that problem of quick decisions without real investigation. Parker was sure that he could offer suggestions that would assist her in this endeavor.

However, he knew that he had to come back into the present if for no other reason than to try to help Jan Evlin. Hammond's problems would never be known by anyone now. There were strange overtones to his death, thought Parker, but he assumed that the same could be said for any suicide.

On a whim, he pulled into the parking lot of a South Burlington fast-food emporium named Heavenly ChickenBurger and Other Stuff. It looked fine from the outside, and he decided it would pick up his day.

He sat down in the almost empty table section, wondering why, at this the peak hour, it had almost no patrons. Probably it was new, he decided, and hadn't been discovered yet.

The first indication that his choice of restaurants might be flawed was when he picked up the menu. He had to scrape its surface in various places to see what was available. He ordered. He picked up a Chittenden Free Progressive made available to the patrons. It was three days old.

The food was terrible. The coffee had to have been made yesterday. There was no napkin provided. The waitress seemed to be about twelve years old, and chewed gum. The cook, certainly not overworked, came out of the kitchen to inquire of Parker how the meal was. Parker told him. The cook swore at him. Parker left enough money to cover the bill and escaped into the twilight. He drove to a familiar quick food stop and ate a very good supper. He wondered why he had such bad luck in selecting restaurants.

25

It was just before eight o'clock when Parker arrived at the alley leading to Birdsall's office. He ascended the rickety-appearing steel stairway, which was illuminated by one low wattage bulb about halfway up. Now he knew how it must have been back in Prohibition. He kept looking around for a roaming police officer ready to snap on the cuffs and run him in.

He reached the top landing facing the door. Light showed around the door frame, and Parker was glad that he had arrived at the last minute. He wanted Birdsall and Hugo to have a chance to talk before he got there.

Parker tapped on the door. It was immediately opened by Hal Birdsall who welcomed him in with a smile. "Bill, I'm really glad you decided to come. We've just been having a chat before I discussed what we found."

Parker smiled at Hugo and crossed the room with his hand out. "You haven't gotten any smaller, Hugo," Parker said.

"It's only been twenty-four hours, Mr. Parker," he answered, with a solemn expression. "All my hard work to get smaller won't be noticeable this soon. Thanks for thinking of me, though." Parker grinned. He really liked this guy.

"So, tell me, you pair of sneaks, what did you find?" Hugo asked.

Birdsall looked at Parker and gestured for him to begin.

Parker sat down carefully on the arm of one of the better appearing stuffed chairs. "You were right, Hugo. Exactly. We found two little gizmos that appeared to be microphones in the air and heat ductwork – right behind the vent covers that are set into the wall. We traced the wire and it came out behind some books in a bookcase right at the desk of Hal's secretary. We'll show them to you."

As he said that, Birdsall was moving toward the first vent cover with screwdriver in hand. In two minutes he had both covers off. "I'm not proud of this – you know, my own secretary listening in to my office meetings, and then reporting information to somebody we don't know. I didn't have a clue, and it's apparently been going on for quite a long time."

"That's just how everybody feels when this sort thing is found. You're not any different, Hal," said Hugo, as he put on his New England Patriots cap. Parker thought he was leaving when Hugo suddenly said, "Let's take a look."

He moved quickly over to the first location and dropped to the floor with a surprising gracefulness that belied his large bulk. Parker was surprised to see this agility. He looked closer at Hugo and found that he didn't look as though he had any fat on his frame at all. Parker decided once again to be nice to him.

Hugo took out a tiny clip-on flashlight from his belt pouch, snapped it on to the bill of his cap, and crouched in front of the wall opening. He turned, grunted, lay down on his back, then his front, then on his side as he reached as deeply into the duct work as his arm would allow. All the time he was carrying on a conversation with himself, then some humming, some faint whistling sounds that sounded like the "Blue Danube", and then a chuckle or two. Parker was fascinated by the focused attention Hugo showed.

Suddenly, Hugo jumped to his feet and moved swiftly into the reception area, all the time mumbling, whistling, and making other noises that seemed to bring him comfort. He went immediately to his knees in front of the bookcase, pulled out the same books that Parker had, looked intently at the recorder, head swiveling this way and that, and then stopped, remaining completely still. His head came up and he scanned the room, while getting to his feet.

He seemed to be like a mountain man hunting for game, and hearing it close by.

Then he rushed back into Birdsall's office to the other duct-work opening, and followed the same procedure. Parker doubted that Hugo was even aware that he and Birdsall were present.

Hugo's next stop was at the thermostat on the wall of the reception area. He popped off the cover and looked critically at the innards of the device. Then he practically ran over to the desk of Birdsall's secretary, pulled open the large, centrally located, drawer, rummaged a little, and then exclaimed with a sound that, with some imagination, could be defined as uncontrolled delight.

Birdsall looked at Parker with complete mystification. Parker returned the look.

Hugo removed something from the drawer and then rushed over again to the wall thermostat, skipping around the desk, three wooden visitors' chairs, and a large and battered coffee table. He resembled, to Parker's mind, a Cape buffalo in a tutu. He put the object up to the surface of the inside of the thermostat and held it in place, viewing it from various angles. Then he seemed to deflate slightly, slow down, become more measured, and then, after a brief stop at the secretary's desk, sauntered into Birdsall's office and sat down at the conference table. He said nothing.

Parker and Birdsall walked in after him and sat down, facing him.

"What do you think, Hugo?" asked Parker.

"What do I think?" he bellowed, startling both Parker and Birdsall. "You've got a damn spy working for one of the more sensitive areas of one of the main sources of information in Vermont, that's what I think! And it's been going on for at least three years – probably more - and nobody tumbled to it. Your newspaper, Hal! And nobody was bright enough to wonder how some bits of information got out onto the street before they were supposed to."

Hugo gazed at Birdsall as if he were seeing a mental misfit with a bad disease.

"Hal, you should be ashamed of yourself. You're in charge of receiving information. You have private meetings in this office to discuss much of it. You plan what has to be done to verify it, and you reveal your sources in these meetings, and anything else that's pertinent. But you didn't question anything that got out into the public that you thought was private. You probably asked some of your people if they had inadvertently let something slip and they said 'No', with their feelings hurt. You didn't go any further – didn't try to find out anything further. If something like this had happened in the Statehouse, this paper would have hollered about checking things out, yelling that our Governor was incompetent – unless he or she was a ProgDem, of course. That's why most of the daily press is considered hypocritical by most of us." Hugo and the hot flame of anger suddenly burned out. He became quiet and subdued.

"Sorry, Mr. Birdsall. I got carried away with my own frustrations, because my profession has been used against us. I had no right to say what I did and I apologize."

Birdsall smiled and said, "You're forgiven, Hugo. You couldn't make me feel dumber than I already do."

Parker leaned forward and asked, "How did they do it, Hugo? What did you discover when you were running about?"

Hugo looked questioningly at Parker. "I was running about? Was I making noises, and singing to myself, and those sorts of things?"

"I'm afraid so, Hugo."

Hugo grinned sheepishly. "My wife says that I resemble a bloodhound when I'm looking into something. Sorry, again, you two."

"Well?" said Parker.

"Oh, yes, yes indeedy," Hugo said, like a man coming out of the fog of reverie. "Well, first, you should know that the two mics are really very good units - first class, in fact. Surprised me." He seemed to lose himself in contemplation for a few seconds. Birdsall and Parker maintained silence.

"Secondly," Hugo said, "you should know that these little mics weren't available on the market until last year. This means that what was in there before had been replaced. How do I know? Because the wire was reused from the first application but there was a *second* spot of adhesive still in the duct from the first mic, but in a slightly different spot. Same for both mic locations. Everything became obvious when I saw that. Either the original wire was still okay for the new mics or the person who installed the new mics didn't have enough time. Actually, I'd vote for the latter. What does that mean? It may mean that the secretary herself installed the new mics, but I doubt it because the connections were done by a pro."

Birdsall grumbled, "She couldn't change a light bulb without breaking it. No talent for mechanical things at all."

Hugo nodded emphatically. "It would be interesting to see the record of who worked in or around this office in the past year. Maybe when you were on vacation, Hal, or sometime when somebody knew you were going to be gone for a day. Something like that. You could check the invoices, too. You may have paid for the work to bug your own office, Hal." Birdsall started to turn red.

"Now," Hugo said quickly, deciding that he may have gone too far, "to the other part of your question. I know exactly how it was done. I don't know why, of course. But the process of stopping the blower, and therefore the noise, so the recording could take place, then recording the conversations, is very simple - and I thought it would be. Amateurs, you know." He looked like the professional who silently dismisses the work performance of the unskilled and clumsy. He no doubt had a right to do that, thought Parker.

"Are you interested in all the details, gentlemen?" asked Hugo.

"Ready when you are, Mr. Edison," said Parker. Hugo looked at Parker and smiled.

"Or, in my case, 'Doctor Livingstone', Mr. Parker?"

"Watch it, Hugo. Don't cross that line again," said Parker. "I may have to hurt you if you do." Hugo smiled again, broadly.

"Okay," Hugo said. "Here's what would happen when Hal had all the big shots in for a meeting. His girl Friday would give them about five minutes, I think, and then she'd interrupt the action of the thermostat. Then she would run back to her desk. After half an hour, or so, somebody would come to the door, probably you, Hal, and complain about the temperature, and then close the door. Your girl Friday would sit there for about five minutes, then call building maintenance and say that they were needed, but it wasn't urgent, and I'll bet she asked them when they would be up to fix things, and it was important that they be accurate because there was a meeting going on and it shouldn't be interrupted – something like that. You know, Hal, you might be able to find that out. That would be one of the things you could mention when you fire her butt out of here."

Hugo cooled himself down, again, with some effort, and continued. "Maintenance would write the number of the office that needed help on the repair list, but probably near the bottom, and wouldn't consider the problem important because that's the direct impression they'd get from your loyal employee," Hugo said, voice showing some sarcasm. "If Hal came out to complain again, your girl could say that she had called them, and they would be right up. You would nod and go back to the meeting."

Hugo stared at Birdsall. "How'm I doin', boss?"

"Uncomfortably close to what probably happened, and right on the money with the things I know about."

"Why did you open her desk, Hugo?" asked Parker.

"To find what I was pretty certain I'd find, Mr. Parker," he said. "A nail file. Want to see the tool of a criminal – and how I know that it's the real McCoy?" He got to his feet and gestured to them to follow out the door to the reception area.

"Mr. Parker, pop off that cover of the thermostat for me while I get hold of the 'tools of the trade', as they say."

As Hugo walked over to them, he said, "Mr. Parker, check those two screws there," he pointed at them, "to see if they're loose." With Birdsall looking on, Parker checked one lead and found it tight. He already knew about the other one, but he checked it anyway. It was still loose enough so that the wire easily slipped out from underneath the screw head.

Parker looked up at Hugo. "Is this what you found?"

Hugo nodded. "When I found it, it wasn't really tight. That's when I went over to the secretary's desk and opened the desk drawer. Right in front of the drawer, but right up against the inside, front, surface was this little jewel." With a slight flourish, he brought up a metal nail file. "A lot of slimy deeds have been accomplished with one of these little beauties," announced Hugo. "Another warning signal was these connections themselves. Usually, they're soldered. These weren't, so I looked at them carefully. They had been soldered in the past. But not now."

"I'm confused," said Parker. "What led you to look in the secretary's desk in the first place?"

"Mr. Parker, Mr. Birdsall, take a look at the insides of this thermostat, and tell me what you see." Parker and Birdsall followed dutifully over to the thermostat.

Birdsall looked. "I don't see what the hell you want me to see, Hugo. It can't be very obvious to the stupid."

Hugo ignored him. "Mr. Parker?" He gestured toward the thermostat, like a headwaiter showing a patron to their seat. Parker looked. He could see nothing out of the ordinary. As he was turning away, the lights in the area gave him another view of the surface of the small platform inside the thermostat.

"Oh, I see, Hugo. The scratches." Hugo beamed.

"You're not just a pretty face, are you, Mr. Parker? Yes, the scratches. And what do they tell you?" At this point, Birdsall had looked and seen what Parker had observed. A look of understanding came over his face.

"My secretary used the steel nail file to loosen the screw. And she wasn't very smooth at it, was she? The scratches are all around that one screw, and the wide end of it fits the screw perfectly. That stopped the power to the blower, no matter what time of year it was. And it was easy and quick to do, too. And because she knew almost exactly when the guys from maintenance would be here, she could hook things back up in less than a minute, likely less." Birdsall had a look of anger that would not be comforting if his secretary could see it.

"Hold it, Hugo, hold it right there. How do we know that this nail file is the instrument of doom – or that a nail file was used at all? It could be a small screwdriver that she carries in her purse. This had better be tight. Hal is going to mention it when he kicks her out. Or takes her to court."

"Let's look, gentlemen," said Hugo. They crossed the aisle to the desk. Hugo opened the drawer and showed them where he found the file. "Look at the wide end of it," he said.

Both Parker and Birdsall could see the slight distortion of it. "Put it in the screw slot and match the distorted wide end with the screw slot length. I know that the screw heads on the thermostat aren't unique, but they will be convincing enough in a face-to-face meeting with a wrong-doer, I'll bet. Also note the plating on the nail file. You'll see flecks of it on the screw head of the thermostat."

"You've got me convinced," said Birdsall.

"Same for me, Hugo," echoed Parker.

Hugo replaced the thermostat cover, and went to the desk to return the nail file, in exactly the place where he'd found it, thought Parker, based on the way he looked things over before he set it in the drawer.

They went back into the conference room and sat in the three easy chairs in Birdsall's office.

Hugo said, "I suppose that you've talked over what the next step should be for you both in this mess?"

"Bill thought that I should leave everything just as it is, do a hell of an acting job for a few days, and have you put a 'bug' in her phone to find out who she reports to. I told him that the acting job would be difficult for me, because I'm so damned mad, but I could do it for a while."

Hugo nodded. "And I can do that 'bug' part easily, and the recording hook-up, too. And she'll never hear the recorder switch 'on' when she begins to speak. That's old technology, actually, but I can talk about it with you two, and you'll be impressed. And then I look good. Clever, huh?" He looked at them both. He detected something that made him say, "What's on your mind, gentlemen?

You want something else, don't you? Out with it! I don't have all night."

Parker told Hugo his theory about a possible network of "bugs" in Chittenden County, and in other parts of the state. How could they sample that possible network to see if it exists? Could he make any suggestions?

Hugo knew exactly what they wanted. "You're asking me to destroy the sterling reputation of my small company. A company, I'll remind you, that has as customers most of the banks, lawyers, and other influential institutions in this county and around northern Vermont. But, do you care? No. You want to use my talent to illegally and unethically extract information from my customers without their knowledge or permission. I'm ashamed of you both."

"All we're asking, Hugo, is if they have 'bugs' in their systems. Surely they'd want to know that," said Parker.

"I would think so, too, but I have certain responsibilities for their computer security, and illegal entry items. But nothing else. And I'm not going to try to enlarge my sphere. Savvy?" They did.

As if to lay Parker's crazy idea to its final resting place, Hugo added, "If I start monitoring areas which are not part of my many and various contracts, and these are very smart people, mind you, they would pick up on it sooner rather than later. They would not only cease their business dealings with me, but they would see to it that nobody else used me either. My business would be kaput, finished, over, and down the tube. Comprendez, comrades?" They both nodded, awestruck by the vehemence of this very large and intelligent man.

"One last item before I go, boys," Hugo said, in a calmer tone. "If Hal takes his secretary to court, she will become the victim, and the CFP the villain. This is Burlington, located in the state of Vermont. Everything is backward in this state, with Burlington more backward than anywhere else. I want you to know it, Mr. Parker, and I want to remind Hal about it. The CFP won't admit that the state of Vermont is wrecking our workers, their kids and their jobs. His paper has this screwed-up sense of who's guilty and who isn't, and his editorial board is willing to continue this charade so that the ProgDems and their minions can continue to sue, regulate, and strangle the people who just want a chance to have their own businesses. How do they do it? By blaming these same little businesses for oppressive behavior against their employees. And then when these same employers pick up and leave because doing business in Vermont is too much of a hassle, the ProgDems yawn and say that the State will create jobs better than the private sector anyway, so leave. And if you check the results of this last election you'll find that the ProgDems have Vermont right by the throat. The final message? If you go to court, the ProgDems will see to it that you'll lose, and you'll look bad in doing so."

"Now just a minute Hugo," said Birdsall, vehemently. "Our editorials come from that editorial board which is a cross-section of Vermont sentiment."

Hugo stared at Birdsall. "No, it isn't, Hal, and you'd better figure it out. Or you won't have much of a state left to criticize, and the ProgDems won't have much of a state left to bleed. And do you know what else is happening? Our lovely Green Mountain state is starting to slip away." Hugo left with that sentiment hanging in the air.

Both Birdsall and Parker were stunned into silence.

Parker broke the silence first. He had gone through all this before, and what Hugo said brought him no new information. What startled him was where this kind of thought came from. Maybe the word is getting around, he thought. It was Birdsall who hadn't heard this sort of talk before. He just sat there, with his mouth slightly open, gazing at the door. "Bill, do you think he really believes what he said? About Vermont fading, or slipping, away – he really meant dying, didn't he?"

Parker sat there quietly for a few seconds, deciding how to answer that question. The direct approach was best, he thought.

"Yes, he did mean it, Hal. And this is a bright young man, who gets around. He sees it. I do, too, for that matter, in my own limited sphere. I lived through it, as you'll remember, and you were the only one of the major dailies, in those days, who supported me. And even your paper was very low-key about it, for fear of making your ProgDem friends angry. It was then that I had confirmed that the CFP and The Mid-Vermont Bugle, just to name two, were the front line troops for the ProgDem Party. To the credit of the CFP, you people aren't as malleable as the Mid-Vermont Bugle, but your editorial people generally support all the ProgDem propaganda that is sent to them."

Birdsall started to object, but then just sagged back into his chair and said nothing.

Parker again broke the silence, and changed the subject at the same time. "Well, nothing of our great plan worked out very well, did it?" said Parker. "He walked out angry at us. At you because he doesn't like your paper, and me because he thinks I'm too dumb to figure out what's happening to Vermont."

Birdsall looked around the room, and then said, "He's right, you know, Bill - I mean about looking around in his employers' systems to find listening devices. He can't do that. I hope he's not right about what's happening to Vermont."

"I know, Hal," Parker said. "It was just that he would be the only chance we had to find out about a possible network. And about Vermont. I know he's right. And I happen to believe that our present Governor was needed about five years ago. It may be too late for him to save us from the ProgDems now."

Birdsall countered with, "Don't give up on Vermont yet, Bill. And I can ask around a little bit to see if anyone has any experience with these kinds of devices. That's all I can do, of course, without being thought of as a nut. I'll let you know."

"Thanks, Hal. Just do your best. And now it's time for me to head home. I've been away long enough, and my circulating around has only depressed me more than I can say. All in the last four days we seem to have lost track of Jan Evlin, I don't know why my name is spread around as an evil person, and I really believe that there is some sort of a network – or at least somebody who is influencing what goes on in the non-profit world - and that person, for some reason, scares the hell out of me."

"You've had a tough week. Take care, Bill. I'll call you with anything that comes from the answers to your questions that I'll put to the committee members."

They shook hands and parted ways.

26

When Parker arrived home, Addie hadn't returned yet. The dogs greeted him casually, as if they didn't realize he'd been away.

Parker felt blue. His wife had gone away and he didn't know when she'd be home. The dogs didn't like him anymore. There was no fire in the fireplace, and no tea waiting to be poured. An old acquaintance had taken his own life – maybe with somebody's help, although he hadn't told Morgan his thoughts on that. A human slug from the educational system in Spring River had shouted a bunch of inanities at him, and others in that protest had just discouraged him with blind acceptance of the items that made up the ProgDem agenda. And what should I think about Gil, Birdsall's brother? Why did Morgan give me that information on his accidental death, Parker wondered?

He had heard so much. Did it tie together somehow? And his rear end was stiff from some unexpected exercise crawling around Birdsall's office and then sitting in his truck for nearly three hours to get to home base. All in all, a bad four days in Chittenden and Washington Counties.

Then he caught himself sliding into self-pity, grabbed the lifeline of positive thoughts, and hauled himself out of the clutch of his favorite sofa. He headed for the woodshed to make up the beginnings of a fire. The ProgDems almost got me, he thought, but, not yet, by God, not yet.

He split up some kindling, brought it back into the house and started the fire. Even though it was giving off no heat at this point, it was agreeable to just look at it as it grew. However, he thought, none of this meant anything until Addie walked in. Then things would take on a purpose.

It was beginning to become late, and Parker thought that Addie's return wouldn't be tonight. If he didn't see her by noon tomorrow, he'd call her friend in Burlington to find out what she was doing and when he'd see her again. Just as he began to consider other measures to find out when she would be home, he saw the headlights of a car swing through the yard, and he jumped to his feet and strode to the door. When he saw Addie pop out of the car, he felt that his anchor had arrived.

He stepped out onto the porch and gave her a hug that satisfied him, but caused Addie to squeal that he was hurting her and what the hell was he doing, and other subtle things like that.

But she was smiling as Parker hauled her, and her suitcase, chased by two dogs, through the door into the kitchen.

"It's about time, sweetie," he exclaimed. "I was starting to worry."

"And I felt the same, Willie. I wanted to talk to you."

"I didn't see you in Burlington, Addie. I thought I would."

Addie stared at him, amazement showing through. "It's a big town, Willie," she said, calmly, amazed at her husband's naivety. "It shouldn't surprise you that we didn't see each other, you know." Parker's face carried a disbelieving look.

"Well, maybe," he mumbled. "It was a lot smaller when I was living up there." Addie smiled tolerantly.

Parker's mood suddenly changed to one of concern. "Are you hungry? Are you tired? Is it too late to talk? I have a lot to tell you."

"No, I feel fine," said Addie. "I had dinner in Burlington with Carolyn. That's why I'm later than I planned." Then she turned solemn. "I heard about Hugh Hammond, Willie. It was on TV. Why would he take his own life? I never met him, but you knew him, didn't you? Wasn't he one of the people who publicly supported you during that awful time in the House three years ago? I seem to remember the name."

"That's him, Addie," said Parker, grimly. "I'll tell you all about it, along with other things, when we get comfortable. How did you do, up there in the wilds of Chittenden County?"

There was a seriousness in Addie's demeanor when she said, "Willie, this industry of non-profits in Chittenden County, maybe in all of Vermont, and maybe in the whole country, is not what it seems. Not all of them, of course, and not even a majority of them. Many of them, and most of the big ones are troublesome to me."

"After talking with Hugh Hammond, I, too, believe that they are definitely 'odd'," Parker answered. "What do you think is going on, Addie? Did you learn anything from your old roommate?"

"Yes, I did, Willie. However, I really think she learned more from me than I did from her. In fact, my dear, the non-profit mentality that pervades this industry has turned into a type of corruption that the leaders of these untaxed groups believe will never be uncovered. Carolyn never knew it. Now she does. And if Carolyn didn't know that funny business was going on, then nobody else does either. Or if they do, they wouldn't say anything for fear of being ridiculed."

"What is going on, Addie, for goodness sake?" cried Parker. "How bad is it?"

"It's really clever, Willie, and simple, too. Some of the big ones are definitely playing a big 'con' game. They were set up by a ProgDem-controlled Congress in Washington years ago. That Congress allowed tax-free corporations to be established, created for a purpose of helping children or seniors, or protecting the environment, or for the 'public interest', or anything else they could think of, for that matter. It didn't seem to be important back then." Addie took a ladylike sip of the beer that her husband had handed her.

"Most of them are controlled, or at least affiliated with, some big national non-profits. Many of them are just money-laundering schemes for the hard left in America. And Vermont is the test tube for most of their national efforts. These people don't like America, Willie. And they are using the freedoms America gives them to help them in their quest to take away from us those very same freedoms, believe it or not."

"How sure are you of this type of corrupt activity, Addie?" Parker asked. "These are serious charges, if true."

Addie looked at her husband "Do you know what many of them were really doing, Willie? They were raising money and recruiting ProgDem candidates for elections. Not just in Vermont. All over the country, too. They also actually ran some campaigns, and that is absolutely against the rules in the Internal Revenue Code that established them in the first place. And do you know why they worked for ProgDem candidates? So that they could protect the ProgDem majority in the state legislature, which would then pump more and more money into their operations in any way they could. And in the days that the ProgDems controlled the United States Congress, the national non-profits knew that whatever they did with their money wouldn't be checked by the Federal Government. The Feds wouldn't follow their own rules and check them out because the Congress was controlled by the left. And the very same is true in Vermont. The non-profits that exist on State Grants have *no rules at all* to govern where that money goes. No rules were ever established, Willie. Do you know what that means? It means that taxpayer money was thrown to many non-profit organizations to spend any way the non-profit wanted and they would *never be checked*."

Addie looked tired and frustrated. Parker seated himself beside her and took her hand.

Seeming to gather herself up, Addie said, "And do you know what's really tragic about all this? The thousands of volunteers in Vermont are being used to keep the non-profits afloat and looking like what they're supposed to be, while the very well paid leaders of some of the non-profits go on with their quiet political work."

Then, in a sudden switch of attitude, Addie moved into some details of specific non-profits that Parker didn't expect.

"Ever hear of the New Reality Defense Committee, Willie?" Addie asked.

"I think I've heard the name, Sweetie. Why? Do we have them in Vermont?" asked Parker.

"No," answered Addie, "but they have similar operations through other non-profits."

"What about them?" asked Parker.

"Guess what they pay their President and their Executive Director."

"I can't," said Parker, hoping the Addie would get on with it.

Addie referred to a slip of paper for the details. "Their President makes $368,000- plus expenses. Their Executive Director makes $250,000- and his expenses. And these people don't do anything, Willie. I mean, anything constructive. It's a rip-off. The biggest 'con' of all time. And here's another. Ever hear of Nature's Environmental Defenders? We have hundreds of non-profits in Vermont that pay their top people as well as anybody in any industry anywhere. And the volunteers do the work – except the quiet work of recruiting, dispensing campaign funds, and running campaigns for ProgDems."

"Addie, settle down, dear. Remember, you've started something that needed doing - questioning the honesty of non-profit operations in Vermont. But, how about better known ones, like Greenspace, for example.

"I even have something on them, believe it or not. They reported that they pay their President $71,000-. Sounds reasonable, doesn't it? What we found out, however, is that Greenspace is set up in various separate groups or divisions. Each of those divisions pays a part of the salaries of the top, full-time officers. In reality, the top people in Greenspace are making four to five times more than the public knows about." There was a terse and angry edge to Addie's voice. Parker had not seen her so upset in years.

"Addie," Parker said, in a calm voice, "these kinds of statements will cause the leaders of these non-profits to go into a frenzy. And you'll be a target - once they get through with me, that is. The defenders of this industry will come out in droves to lambaste anyone who attacks the basis of their ProgDem campaign teams and the money they receive. They'll tell everybody in Vermont that we said that *all* the non-profits are corrupt. You know that, don't you?"

"Yes, I do. However, Willie, the volunteers will not donate any more time to some of the larger and more influential non-profits, once they know that they're being used. And I intend, along with my friend Carolyn, to see that they do know. She is one angry lady, Willie. She will start the campaign to inform the volunteers, and the contributors, too, of just what's been going on, and how they have been taken. "

"How many of them do you think are in the real business of corrupting things, Addie?" Parker asked.

"Oh, Willie, how do I answer that question? I had a chance to glance through the current financial reports for about a thousand non-profits in Vermont. Almost five hundred of them in Chittenden County alone. I did that for about fifteen hours a day for two days. It helped that I knew what to look for. Carolyn looked at their applications to become a non-profit as we went along. Guess what, Willie? We found about 150 of them that didn't measure up to what Carolyn and I set as a reasonable standard. Many of these non-profits were organizations for which Carolyn had done some work. She knew something about them. With her newfound knowledge, her memory, and an old, and tattered, personal phone list she culled up from the depths of her cavernous desk, she called some friends who knew about them."

"And you know about this accounting stuff, Addie," said Parker. "That's terrific."

"Willie, I was an accountant and a financial planner long before anybody else had even thought up the title. Long before you came along, too. It really came in handy, especially in the last few days."

"Addie, I remember." Parker knew that she had graduated from Champlain College in Burlington near the top of her class. Addie was on her way to becoming a real success, sought after by larger companies, who wanted smart people for responsible positions.

Then she met me, Parker thought. Quite a comedown. Addie seemed happy, though. He decided to ask her if she *had* been happy while married to him. But not today – or tomorrow. Maybe someday. If I really want to know, he thought.

Parker asked, "So, how much information did you get from Carolyn's old friends, sweetie?" he asked.

"Many of her old friends were no longer working for the non-profits, and many more weren't volunteering. They found that the political center of almost all of them had become homes for the old and young socialists, the old and young college communists, when it was fashionable to call yourself one – you remember those goofy people I'm sure - old politicians, too, and all the other flotsam and jetsam left behind by an empty educational experience." Addie glanced out blankly at the wall.

"You know something, Willie? Ignorant instructors and professors who taught in high schools and in colleges in the sixties, seventies, and eighties have given us forty years of graduates, the majority of whom are about as dumb as their teachers. And for all we know, the educators have only gotten dumber since then." Parker knew what she was saying.

"You know, don't you, Willie, that there are different types of non-profits?" She eyed him to be sure he was listening to her. "There are religious non-profits, mutual benefit non-profits, public benefit non-profits, even golf courses, and others of less use. The ones we were looking into are public benefit non-profits."

Parker nodded. Those non-profits were the ones that had shown themselves to be out of control.

"The Tranquility and Equal Treatment Center is certainly a strong leftist organization, which is not afraid to violate the law because nobody ever checks on them. They are really a hard, bitter, and ignorant bunch. In fact, any state-employed lawyers who might check on their suitability are probably members of it, or strong sympathizers. This is the outfit that was selling bumper stickers with messages that showed that they opposed a national Presidential candidate. They know that they won't be checked, and if they are, they won't be charged with anything and their designation as a non-profit won't be jeopardized." A look of disgust showed on her face.

"There's another one, too, Willie, that will come to your notice very soon, I think. It's called the Trust of the Progressive Naturalist. This is a really dangerous group of people who will stop at nothing to buy and control more and more land in Vermont – and in other states, too."

"You two did a lot of work on this, sweetie."

"Oh, there were more than two of us, Willie. After a couple of phone calls, one of those she talked to called back, to ask what she was doing. Carolyn told her and she wanted to help. So she came over with six friends. By the time we were through with our cross-referencing, double-checking, and comparing experiences, we had a list of about 150 non-profits that I told you about. Some of us knew a lot about a few of these crooked non-profits, and all of us knew something about all of them. When we finished - after two days, I'll remind you, Willie - we had over a hundred non-profits that were without question violating the non-profit rules. They are certainly representative of the best campaign funding apparatuses in existence, including the political parties in Vermont. They have identified themselves as ProgDems, and they find the candidates to run against the hated Republicans, Independents, and traditional Democrats. And they recruit and raise money on a year round basis."

Parker wondered if that was their only purpose.

"We all agreed, Willie, that these leaders of their respective non-profits all use the English language beautifully, but they speak fluff, and don't know anything worth hearing."

Parker thought about all he had heard. "What did your buddies say about that?"

"They were incredibly angry, Willie."

Parker turned toward Addie. "I assume that you've got the list of the one hundred?"

"Of course. Here it is." Addie handed to Parker four lined sheets of paper, which were copies of an original set.

"Addie, I've heard of all of these. Except this one: SASSY. What's that group?"

“That’s a UVM-sponsored student government club. It stands for Student Activists for Sympathetic Socialist Youth. It was started by a group of UVM professors. It was for the ‘disaffected’ students who had ‘no political voice’. They lead the student get-out-the-vote drives at the University during the elections in Burlington and Chittenden County, and statewide, when needed.” Parker slowly shook his head. “They also enlist Winston College to set up very large phone bank to get out the votes for ProgDem candidates every two years.”

“Winston College? That’s here in Windham County,” cried Parker. “And nothing is being done?”

“I didn’t say that, Willie. Right now, I’m happy to report, over 2000 non-profits are being investigated by the IRS for violating their charters. Nothing ever made me happier.”

Parker was astounded. This was corruption on a grand scale. And they were using the efforts of thousands of volunteers to provide the top people with lots of money and lots of perks.

Finally, he asked, “How many copies of this list were made? Do you know?”

“I don’t know, Willie. Is it important?” asked Addie.

“When I tell you what went on in my life in Chittenden and Washington Counties over the last four days, you might think so.”

Parker told Addie everything. At the end of half an hour, Addie looked panicked, Parker thought, and I haven’t even told her of my questions about Hammond’s “suicide”.

“Willie, I have to call Carolyn right now. If this list gets out, and the wrong person sees it, it could be very embarrassing for Carolyn. She signed the damned thing.”

Parker thought that the word “embarrassing” was inadequate to cover this situation.

Addie came back from the phone and flopped down in one of the old wooden chairs that surrounded the immense kitchen table for which the Parkers had become mildly famous. “I talked to Carolyn, Willie. She made eight copies, and seven of them were given to me and our helpers. I asked Carolyn to call the others and tell them to keep their list from getting into the hands of anyone else. She agreed to do that. I told her that the daily news media would be ordered to discredit her friends, so our information shouldn’t be known by others outside our little group – for now,” said Addie, ominously. Parker felt better.

By this time, Parker was up and moving around the room. "You see, Addie," he said, "there's an awful lot that we don't know and probably never will. I'm very concerned that what we don't know will be the trigger that causes things to happen and we won't have any warning."

"Willie," she said sternly. "What 'things'? What kinds of 'things' are you talking about? What in the world have you gotten us mixed up in?"

Parker shrugged his shoulders. "I don't know, Addie, but there are unknowns out there. And they may very well resolve themselves naturally, and I will have been concerned for nothing."

"Willie," Addie said, looking at her husband sternly, "let me know if I've got this right. You went to Montpelier, on your way to Burlington. You stopped to see Morgan, just on the off chance he'd be in. He was and during your visit you happened to tell him what you were doing up there. By the way, you're a real blabbermouth sometimes, do you know that? As soon as you mentioned Gil Birdsall's name, he gave you some information about his death. And he wouldn't tell you why. Correct?"

Parker gestured that she was correct.

"So then you traipsed up to Burlington and you decided to become a troublemaker and you visited the VNRCAUC. You were surprised that they seemed to know that you were in the area and snooping."

Parker interrupted, and said, "Well, I wouldn't go so far as…." when he was in turn interrupted by Addie, who said, "I would, Willie. You have to be realistic or the truth will never come out." Parker hurriedly agreed. Best not to irritate the wife, he thought. And she did have a point.

"Then this bimbo in the office of the VNRCAUC revealed that she knew who you were, and clammed up. Right so far?" Parker again allowed that she was on the mark.

"Your next little adventure took you out into the street where you joined a damned protest march heading toward the barricades at the Statehouse. The protest was apparently for a wide variety of reasons, none of which made any sense to you."

Addie looked at Parker with a steely eye, and said, "That was the moment at which you should have left town, you know. But not you, William Parker, oh, no," she said scathingly. You had to stir things up even more. Willie, you have to stop blundering around. You have to think about what the consequences of your actions might be. You obviously irritated everyone you talked to during this fact-finding tour, to the extent that the last person you talked to actually screamed at you when you brilliantly told him your name."

Addie exhaled loudly, and then said, in a soft voice that Parker hadn't heard in years, "Willie, Willie," she said in frustration, "honesty, in that case, was not the best policy."

Parker then told Addie that she was describing his day in words that were too stark and gave no texture to the picture. Addie would not let him get away with that. She looked at him in horror.

"What the hell are you talking about, Willie? 'Texture to the picture' indeed. That's right out of a conversation with a mindless dumbbell from the '60s. Why didn't you use the word 'compassion', and be done with it? Don't go to Montpelier again, Willie. Only a few hours more of exposure and nobody down here would understand a thing you were talking about."

Parker was disappointed with her reaction to his use of that phrase. He had seen it in a little weekly newspaper called "Three and a Half Days", the same paper for which Deiter Paine wrote his unending ProgDem tributes. Parker was rather pleased that he had found a spot to try out that "texture" phrase on someone during a conversation. Addie's lack of appreciation caused him to reconsider his attempt at incorporating Chittenden-speak in his communications with his friends. He must have sounded like one of the Burlington elitists. Maybe he wasn't as forward thinking as he had hoped.

"Next, you went to the Chittenden Free Progressive and talked to some snoops," Addie firmly stated.

Parker jumped in again, at this point. "Addie, there were no snoops present. Just normal people with a problem."

"Really, Willie? Just what do you think your new buddy Hugo was? Oh, sure, he had a security business and he was as honorable as 'The Virginian'."

Addie's exasperation showed through plainly at last. "He was a snoop, Willie – maybe he likes you, and he may be honest, but he's a snoop and maybe he's just a snoop on a part-time basis, but he's for hire." She shook her head.

Parker hadn't thought about her point of view. Hugo and Addie would have to meet. He'd observe that get-together carefully.

"And then you started for home, stopping off to see Morgan again – you know," she said with biting sarcasm, "your old partner from your wild west days of just three years ago. That decision took you to the Statehouse to view the body of a suicide in one of the committee rooms. Good Lord, Willie, the Three Stooges never had more odd experiences in their whole careers than you had in three days."

"Addie, you are stretching things out and in different directions than they really should be portrayed," said Parker, in a slightly lofty way. His tone was a mistake.

"Willie, what has happened to you? You talk like a fund raiser on VTEliteTV – you know what I mean. Right down their nose at us, their humble, ignorant, and grateful subjects, thirsty for their rendition of wisdom."

"Okay, sweetie, I guess I got off the rails a little. I'm concerned about a few things. I'm concerned that we haven't heard from Jan Evlin. I'm concerned that I couldn't find any ammunition for Gil Birdsall's old rifle. I worry about what I think I noticed in the Committee room, something subtle enough that the police might not pick up on it because it's not their world. I'm thinking about the fact that some real kooks knew that I was up there and were rude to me. In fact, they became almost frantic." Addie rolled her eyes at the word "rude".

"And here's a big one, Addie, I think. Hugh Hammond told me that he had some information that he had received from a friend, now deceased, that I would be interested in seeing. I think this info regards non-profit organizations in Vermont, although I'm not certain. He thought enough of this material to seal it in a box and hide it under the floor of his barn." Addie was staring at him without blinking. "I haven't told anybody about this. I simply didn't know who I could trust. I'll be honest, Addie. I began to be a little spooked about all this."

Quietly she said, still staring at her husband, "My God, Willie, what's next? Do we just wait for Morgan to call? What direction do we take?" Parker thought she looked as though she'd had a shock.

Parker looked down at the floor, as if in deep contemplation. "I'm going to wait for a couple of days, Addie. I want to hear what Morgan finds out about Hugh Hammond's suicide, if anything. I look at that suicide as a key event in this whole thing. If what I suspect is confirmed, then a whole set of speculations goes out the window – and lots of other things come into play. Things will become simpler, too, I think. So we wait for a bit."

Addie reached out and took Parker's hand. "Whatever you say, Willie," she murmured quietly. Addie knew that this was her husband's sphere, and not anyone else's. She also knew that her husband was terribly naïve about some things, but wise and decisive about those situations that demanded action. And she loved him for that innocence that cropped up unexpectedly, and for his natural decisiveness when it was absolutely needed. Her life was good because of her Willie.

27

Irene Doughton looked up from her desk as Parker entered the office reception area of his insurance empire. Irene was a fiftyish woman, still attractive and energetic. It was her mind, though, that fit the definition of "active".

She came to Parker's small insurance office after she had retired from teaching in the public school in Bridgeton. The frustration she felt, and what ultimately drove her out of teaching, was the acceptance of diminishing academic standards, the willingness of the majority of teachers to push their own biases onto the young minds in their care, and the hypocrisy of the Vermont VTUA when they talked about the children's needs coming first. While the VTUA said all this, they, at the same time, demanded that no testing take place that would expose the teachers who didn't teach. She was brilliant, determined, and needed in the Parker Insurance Agency. Parker, himself, didn't know that until unceremoniously advised of it by Addie.

Irene came to work for the agency, proved invaluable, studied for her license, and became a partner. It was the best thing I ever did, Parker often said to himself, even though Addie was the one who decided that Irene should be working there. Parker never suspected that his wife thought that Irene would be perfect for his little company.

"Good morning, Irene," Parker said. "Sorry I've been out of touch for a few days. Are we busy? Are we profitable? Are we serving our customers well? Do they still like us? Can I still receive a paycheck?"

"Good morning, Mr. Parker, and 'yes'," she answered.

"Good," Parker shot back, trying to stay even in the exchange.

"I'll be in for the next two days, and then I'll be heading for Burlington again, I think. Depends on who calls me, if anybody does."

"What are you into now, Mr. Parker? Is it dangerous – again? Should I carry a concealed weapon - again? Are you going to send me away again for my own safety, an order which I will refuse to obey?" asked Irene, her face showing that ironic sense of humor for which she had become known in the community.

"No, no, Irene. I'm simply looking into a few things for a friend." Parker could tell that he wasn't convincing Irene at all of the benign nature of his activities.

"That will be a change, Mr. Parker, won't it?"

"Well, yes, now that you mention it. I'll be in my office if you need me," he said, with transparent joviality.

"Fine, Mr. Parker. I'll call if you are needed." Her expression said that "I can handle things". Then she smiled at Parker. "You do have some mail in there."

Parker entered the "Executive Suite" as the real estate agent termed it when Parker first bought this small building. His office would not impress anyone. The floor sloped alarmingly, the furniture was secondhand and was cheap when new. Parker didn't care. He didn't even like this back office, feeling that he was out of the mainstream when he was encamped back there. Trying to be modern, however, in case anyone cared, seemed important at the time. He remembered that at the end of the pitch by the real estate guy, he thought that his business would fail if he didn't have a private "suite". Parker had increasing doubts about that ever since, but was too lazy to move his desk back out to the front.

He sat down and faced his mound of mail. Most of it was unimportant, he decided, as he whittled it down to size. He wished he'd receive something that would truly occupy his attention for five minutes. When he had exhausted the pile, transferring it to the wastebasket, he picked up the last envelope. It was one of those standard manila shipping envelopes, letter size. The envelope was thin. It was hand-addressed and marked "Personal", with no return address on it, and had been mailed four days ago, which happened to be the same day that Parker had driven to Burlington to meet Hal Birdsall and to talk to Jan Evlin. He slit it open with his pocket knife and, peeking in, breathed a sigh of relief when he noticed that the single sheet was a handwritten note, and he could see that it was signed "Jan".

She's around somewhere, he thought. One item crossed off the master list of concerns, he said to himself.

By habit he withdrew the paper carefully, thinking that the envelope and the notepaper might be important. Sherlock Holmes would do it that way, he was certain. Parker always wanted to emulate Holmes. The postmark was from Hardwick, Vermont. What in the world was Jan doing in Hardwick, he wondered?

The note was written in pencil with the scrawl of the professional reporter. It read:

Dear Mr. Parker

I've been invited to spend a long week end next week with an old friend in a section of the state I've never visited before, so I'll be going. I need a break. I've been backed up and bogged down by bull for too long. I'll be out of touch until I get back Maybe Ill meet a knight, who also has a squire, who will be as good a friend to me as you are. Ill explain all to you and the provider whose been where I'm going when I call you on my return. Please let my husband know.

Your friend
Jan

This is really odd, thought Parker. The last thing he expected was this little trip of Jan's for a few days. And the note was not like Jan, he thought. And the punctuation was terrible. Also, what was this crap about a knight and a squire? And the strange way it seemed to be written – not with the precision of the Jan he knew - and the provider? He hadn't any idea what that meant, if it meant anything at all. And why did she send her note to him anyway? Her husband must be out of town, he thought. He was a mining engineer or something like that, working in Bolivia, or some South American country, he thought. Parker wasn't her guardian anyway. Her note tried to sound upbeat. However, Parker didn't feel happy for her. He felt uneasy. This was not a note to inspire comfort.

He'd show it to Duane, Kate, and Addie tonight. Duane and Kate would be returning for dinner and a continuation of their vacation with them. Duane will figure everything out, thought Parker.

Parker wished he knew where Jan was right now. He needed to speak to her. He needed to compare Addie's report with Jan's information.

Parker carefully pushed the note back into the manila envelope and dropped it into his briefcase. He then worked his way through a pile of new policies, set on the corner of his desk by Irene, checking them for errors (there never were any), and initialing his approval (technically not required). Irene just placed them on his desk to make him feel needed, he was sure. Addie double-checked things when he was away, anyway. Irene refused to send them out without the approval of one of them. Parker had noticed that ever since she had been made a partner, she had become difficult to deal with when office procedures were threatened by any lack of attention on Parker's part. Hell of a thing, thought Parker. Whose business is it, anyway?

After a dozen phone calls to customers - Parker didn't like the term "clients" because that sounded to him like some law firm that was trying to dress up its image - and listening to unasked-for gossip for at least ten minutes each, Parker felt that he had the pulse of the community and of his customers, too.

This is the way to survey customers, he thought. Go right to them and they'd keep him "in the know" about the area, the politics, the new businesses in town, the inside of the Select Board meetings, the school situation, and who's fooling around on the wife, or on the husband - or on both, for that matter. Parker could never quite figure out that last combination, even though it was usually explained very clearly and graphically. He always got lost on the first quick turn of the explanation.

He walked out to the reception area, dropped the pile of policies on Irene's desk, and announced that he was heading home. Irene smiled at him and said, "Duane and Kate are here, aren't they, Mr. Parker? Please tell them to drop in before they go back to Colorado, will you?"

"Of course I will, Irene. In fact, come out to the house for supper tonight. If you did, we'd all enjoy ourselves more, and I'm bringing up a subject for discussion that you might be able to help unravel for me. How can you refuse an offer like that? Good food, good conversation, good mutual friends, and a great puzzle that needs solving."

Irene had this warm feeling when she heard Parker's invitation. Including her in his personal business told her that she was valued. She had always thought that Bill Parker was unique among the men she had met. His social skills needed further upgrading, but maybe Addie had stopped just before she became in danger of spoiling the essence of the man who was Bill Parker.

She could certainly take him out in public. In fact, he was fun to be with, even though fairly quiet. He didn't rile easily, but once on the boil, he would tackle the problem and take care of it.

There aren't too many people like him around, thought Irene. Most men found a way to avoid confrontation, no matter what the provocation. “I’d love to, Mr. Parker,” she said with obvious pleasure.

“Wonderful, Irene. Call Addie for me and tell her that you’ve been invited for supper,” and walked out the door.

28

The supper was an event for Addie. She cooked, drank a little wine, and cooked some more. She moved through the kitchen and around the table at high speed, looking for glasses to fill and crackers and cheese to keep supplied. This routine was interrupted by Irene, who told her that she wanted to do something. Addie should tend to the cooking, she said, and Irene would take care of the pre-supper eatables.

Irene and Duane and Kate were delighted to see each other again, and they rattled on about what had happened to them since they had last been in each other's company. Irene commented on Kate's size, saying that she hoped that she would get through supper before she had to go to the Grace Cottage Hospital in Townshend.

"Nonsense, Irene," Kate said. "I've got another month to get through, and I'll be back in Colorado then, anyway. I just look oversized. I don't feel too big."

Parker was nervous just looking at her. Why didn't *she* look nervous?

The entire evening was fun and the supper was a treat. Parker joined in, and enjoyed the frivolity, while all the time wanting to get to the subject that this morning had started his worrying ways.

When he sensed that the evening was beginning to slow, he jumped in. "All right, everybody, let's talk about a puzzle I've been presented. I want to tell you about my last five days. In doing that, I'll be including Addie's trip into Chittenden County as my agent-in-place. Correct me where I stray, Addie, or take over if I get lost." Addie nodded.

"It all started about ten days ago, folks. Here's what happened, nothing left out," and off he went.

At the end of about twenty minutes, Parker stopped. He had just told them about the note he had received that day in the mail from Jan Evlin, and what the note had to say. The room was totally silent as he talked. The only sounds came from the two

Parker hounds, Minnie and Malcom, initiated when they changed positions while sleeping and snorting, or got up and drank some of their water, which really made a hell of a racket.

His audience was in a state of awe, and silent and restive at the same time, as they recognized that Parker had once again stumbled into a situation that was anything but ordinary.

Duane finally broke the relative quiet. "Let me see the note from Ms. Evlin, Bill, please," he said, and Parker passed it over to him.

This was the point of the whole evening as far as Parker was concerned. He had had a good time at their dinner. The conversation was fast-paced and interesting. He loved all of these people - but, he thought, let's cut to the chase and read Jan's note.

Duane looked at the piece of paper as though it were going to explode. He took it in his fingertips, using as little of the margins as he possibly could, and turned it back and forth, upside down, and then tipped it to the light, both sides. Parker couldn't tell what he was doing all this for, but then he remembered the conjuror's tricks pulled off by this young man when he first read the note written to Jan by the crackpot "Z". He kept quiet.

"Bill," Duane asked, "do you still have the note that was written by that 'Z' mystery man to Ms. Evlin?"

"Sure do, Duane," answered Parker, as he walked over to the file cabinet behind the kitchen table.

"Here it is. Perform for us, if you will, your investigatory wizardry." Parker set the note down in front of Duane with a grand flourish. Addie rolled her eyes. Her husband didn't notice.

Duane read the two-year-old note sent to Hammond once, and then again. Then he reread the note written to Ms. Carnovan-Bloom, the President of the Burlington non-profit, that led to the firing of Jan's friend. Then he sat back, stared into the distance, and then came back into the present.

"You know, folks," Duane said, "I don't have available all the evidence that the first note I saw gave me. I will be much less certain of what this note is about than the opinions I offered regarding the other note. I will give you a heavily guarded opinion of this note that you just received in that envelope from Jan, and these other older notes to Hammond and to the President of the Truth, Prosperity, and Sharing Coalition of Northern Vermont. This note," holding up the note just received from Jan, "was written by her under some stress. At the very least, she was afraid that it would be read by somebody who she didn't want to see it."

"What makes you say that, Duane?" asked Kate. "How can you be sure?"

"My point was, and is, Katie," said Duane, "that I'm *not* sure. But I'll tell you this. I noticed in this note that it's very different from the previous note from Jan. There are many punctuation errors. And the strange references she makes. You know what I mean. Jan was a very good writer, I'm told, not only in content, but in the precision with which something was written. That's her real message. Not what she wrote. She's telling us, I believe, that she feels uneasy about this trip to wherever, but she's going anyway. That's all I can say."

"What about the reference to a 'squire' and a 'knight', Duane? Is it important?" asked Parker. "And the 'provider', too. And 'bull'. I can't make anything at all of that."

Duane shrugged his shoulders. "Means nothing to me. You know her, Bill. Does she refer to things that mean something to her at the time, and maybe to her listener? Some people seem to talk in circles, you know, and all the time they're delivering a message. Sometimes a funny one, sometimes not. Was she one of those?"

"I never really knew her beyond her work and my connection with it when I was in the House, Duane. I know that she was considered a terrific writer by the rest of the news corps in the Statehouse. She was serious about her work, but I don't know anything else about her. She certainly was a student when it came to using the English language, I've been told. A real expert, apparently."

Irene Doughton shifted in her chair, then leaned over toward Addie and whispered something to her. Addie looked down at her hands, clasped in her lap, obviously pondering Irene's words, then looked up, and said, "That's worth thinking about, Irene."

"What's that, sweetie?" asked Parker.

"Irene was asking if she could borrow Jan's note for a few days. She has some ideas about how to read it."

Parker turned toward Irene and said, "You certainly can, Irene. Help is what we need here. But," he added, "will you have any time? I mean you're working yourself into exhaustion as my partner, and you need to keep that up while I charge out in my truck, rescuing damsels, and --------"

"Willie, for goodness sake, be quiet," cried Addie.

"Addie," said Kate, "remember, I'm one of the damsels myself."

Addie moved over to her and squeezed her hand. "I know, I know, Katie. It's just that my husband makes light of what's gone on in the past, and it bothers me to think about some of the close calls he's had."

Grimly, Kate said, "Addie, it's his way to deflect his concerns. You should know that."

Parker, listening to all this, felt like a side of beef just before the auction started.

Addie shrugged, and smiled at Kate.

"Willie," said Addie, trying to get them all back on track, "let's go back to Jan. What are we looking for? There are a dozen reasons for Jan Evlin's absence. Yet, you're worried about her. Why? There's been no violence, something we *have* faced in two other situations over the past three years. I'm just frustrated by the lack of a clear direction – or the real possibility that no direction is even needed. And I'm very concerned that the non-profits will be blamed for things to which they had no connection. That, in itself, is very dangerous ground."

There was a silence following this outburst from Addie. Nobody could doubt the sense of what she said. And yet Parker was still convinced that a consistent logic in all the occurrences he'd witnessed did actually exist – and that the non-profits were tied to it in some way. Then he decided what had to be done.

"I'm heading for Montpelier tomorrow, folks, and then on to Burlington. There are things that I want to check again. It's a trip to settle those things that Addie just talked about – and other things, too. I'm sorry, Kate and Duane, but this can't wait. And I will be home in a couple of days."

"That will be a good thing to do, Willie," offered Addie.

"Then you'll be home again and not antsy, as you are now. When you get fidgety, the whole atmosphere around here gets out of kilter."

"And I never see him at the office," added Irene.

"And we," said Kate, "don't have a settled vacation while you're pacing around like a rooster just before dawn. We're in this, too, remember."

"A rooster just before dawn?" asked Parker. "You weren't brought up on a farm, Kate. You're a city mouse."

"No, but my husband was, Mr. Parker. He may be a dreaded lawyer, but he can't help revealing his background, no matter how well he dresses. I just pick up on it once in a while."

There were muted grins all around, and the evening ended on a high note.

As they made preparations to clean up the kitchen and go up to bed, Parker looked at them all out of the corner of his eye, and said to himself, this is my family. They make me whole. The definition of the good life, he thought.

29

It was 5:45 the next morning when the phone rang in the "Great Hall", as Duane called it, which was otherwise known to everybody else as simply the "Parker kitchen". It surprised Addie, who was humming along in great style readying the kitchen for the rest of her family to have breakfast.

Feeding the dogs was also part of her daily routine, and Minnie and Malcom were on point at the bottom of the stairs, tongues lolling, when she descended into the kitchen. Addie always felt that this early part of the day was their peak. It certainly wasn't hers.

Both dogs raced around, intentionally brushing into knees, table legs, chairs, and each other, apparently hoping to dislodge any bits of food that happened to have been placed in a precarious position and fall to the floor with the proper amount of jostling. The ringing of the phone also upset their food preparation process. They didn't understand the delay.

Since her husband had retired from the Vermont House of Representatives three years before, all early-morning calls had stopped. It was an unexpected benefit of being out of politics, although Parker had to get used to it. It seemed to Addie that he felt unimportant, all of a sudden.

"Hello?" Addie said, in a questioning and hesitant manner. "Who's calling, please?"

The Jimmy Stewart of the Montpelier Police Department, Peter Morgan, said, "Good morning, Addie, and I'm sorry to have called so early, but I have to speak to Bill right now."

There was a seriousness about his tone that was completely different from in the past. He usually had some light-hearted comments for her before he got down to business. Not today. "Peter," exclaimed Addie, with pleasure. "I'll get him to the phone immediately."

"Thanks, Addie. I appreciate it."

"Willie", she called from the bottom of the stairs. Her husband appeared out of the customary gloom of 6:00 AM. He was wearing a bathrobe and was barefoot.

"Who the hell is that, Addie? Do they realize the time? I haven't even had my transfusion of coffee yet."

When he arrived at the bottom of the stairs, Addie handed the walk-around phone to him. "You'll be pleased," she said, "I think."

Parker looked at her for any clarification of her remark. None came. "Yep," Parker grumbled into the phone.

"Bill, it's Peter. Can you meet me at the Red Kettle before noon? It's important."

Parker was instantly fully awake. "Of course I can, Peter. I'll be on my way inside an hour. Be there no later than eleven. Can you give me a hint?"

"That situation you and I were very recently involved in – you were bothered about something, if you'll remember – well, you had a right to be bothered." The receiver clicked its farewell in Parker's ear, and he set it carefully back into its cradle. His mind was racing.

"Willie, what's the problem?" Addie asked.

He walked over to her and put his hands on her shoulders. "Things are a little deeper now than they were, my dear," he said. "Maybe everything has suddenly started moving in an entirely different direction."

"I'll get your breakfast ready. Get yourself ready to go and pack." Addie immediately started to bustle, as only she could.

A half hour later Parker was back downstairs with a cup of coffee in his hand, while Addie inspected him closely.

"Willie, try to be presentable at all times when you're away, will you?" Parker vowed to do exactly that. "You don't want people to think you're a slob, do you?"

Parker shook his head as Addie finished straightening his tie. "Now you can go out and play," she said, smiling with affection at her husband while she also worried about what he was heading into.

Parker jumped into his pickup and churned out of the dooryard, headed for the main road.

He headed north and just before he crossed the town line, he stopped at the only service station in Bridgeton. It was operated by Hollis Bagley, a refugee from the People's Socialist Republic of

Maine, as he called it. Hollie, at 71 years of age, was a rough-cut individual, not afraid to address any issue or person with straight-to-the-nub comments. Accuracy was not his strong suit, but he was fun to listen to. However, he was very bright and perceptive, an ex-logger, ex-farmer, and an ex-husband of a woman who had suddenly decided that the stars, the winds, the temperature, and the thoughts of the Grateful Dead, should guide her every act of living. Hollis decided that she was nuts, told her so, and moved to Vermont. He hadn't heard from her in fifteen years.

As Parker glided his truck up to the double set of pumps, Hollis came rushing out. "It's big Bill Parker," he bellowed. "Needs gas, intelligent conversation, and a cup of coffee, I'll bet."

"Hollie," said Parker, "I just stopped in to ask where I could find one of those things you just named."

"Right here, Bill, right here," Hollis yelled, as he unscrewed the gas cap of Parker's truck. "Got a few other things that will thrill you, too. A brand new cribbage board, a fairly clean men's room, and the old easy chair that you know about, that I've moved to another place near the stove. Got to keep modernizing, you know."

"Hollie," said Parker, as he jumped at the barrage of high-decibel words from Hollis, "I don't have time for anything except gas today. I'll take a rain check on the other delights."

"You young people are in too much of a rush. Got to slow down, Bill, and get downwind of a springtime cow once in a while. That experience will give you some real life, by God."

Parker walked around the truck, looked at the pump gauge, and handed Hollis some money for the fuel. Hollis looked at the pump, then the cash, and moved with alacrity into the office.

"Owe you $2.46, Bill. Stay right there. You just watch a demonstration of a new service of the station," he said as he practically ran into the office. "Instant change for a customer without them having to go anywhere – and without them having to use some damned machine that loses your money and screws up your bank account. Life will get better when everybody sees what this gas station gives them."

Parker enjoyed listening to another, and new, Hollis. It was another lesson in what's old is better, in many ways, from what's new. Parker wondered if the Hollis Bagley approach to all things would take hold, slowing down the rush to modern mediocrity. Time, as they say, would tell.

Hollie opened the driver's door for Parker, standing at attention, but wearing an expression that said, "You just heard wisdom, buddy. Pay attention."

Parker headed out for Route 5, then to I91, and north to the Red Kettle in Northfield. What kind of a day was it going to be, he wondered? He didn't feel good about it.

30

Parker walked into the Red Kettle a little after eleven in the morning. Peter Morgan was sitting at a corner table. The dining room was not crowded, the breakfast people having left an hour ago, and the lunch group not yet filling up the small room.

Morgan got to his feet as Parker approached, holding out his hand. "Glad to see you again, Bill. I'm about to break law enforcement rules again by talking to you about something that's none of your business."

Parker understood what Morgan was really saying. Keep your mouth shut forever.

They both ordered a sandwich, and then Morgan got right down to business. In a quiet voice, he said, "You were correct when you had uneasiness about Hammond's death, Bill. We used a Blue Maxx light. It showed the blood traces in places where we didn't expect them. There was blood in that wine-colored carpet near the corner window – right in front of the blackboard hanging on the wall. The forensic people said that someone had tried to clean it up, but it's impossible to get it all, as I'm sure you know."

"You mean that he was murdered?" gulped Parker. "That was a stupid thing to ask, Peter. Of course he was. Have you questioned everybody, Peter? Anything noteworthy?"

"Forensics says that his wrists could have been slashed right there. Then he was hauled the four or five feet into the chair in which we found him."

"And that's why he wasn't in his usual chair," murmured Parker. "And maybe that blood near the blackboard was from his nosebleed."

"Yes, Bill, and what you suggested to me about committee room chairs and their sanctity was confirmed by the committee members. Hammond was sitting in his usual chair when they all went to lunch. They all were surprised when they learned that he was in a different chair when he was found. Not enough to mention it initially. Just a little surprised. They also told us that they didn't go to lunch that day until about 12:20. Almost everyone else had gone to lunch. Hammond was totally alone."

"Not quite, Peter."

"No," Morgan said, quietly, "not quite."

Parker frowned as he tried to set up the possible sequence of events that led to Hammond's murder. "Who did you question, Peter? I mean, was it everybody who might have been upstairs where he was killed? Or did you include more people than that?"

"We threw a net around the whole building, Bill, starting at about 1:45. We questioned everybody from that moment forward. I didn't expect much. And we didn't hear anything useful. The killer had about a 45-minute head start. He or she could have been gone for a long time before Hammond was even found."

"When *was* the body found, Peter?" asked Parker.

"The body wasn't found until 1:30 in the afternoon. That means Hammond had been dead for about an hour. Possibly less than that, but not much more."

"You said 'she', Peter. It would take a strong woman to subdue Hammond."

"We are being very PC here, Bill. I'm sure that it was a man, but I can't be completely certain, of course. There are some very strong women out there these days. They are in very good shape, they are strong, and they know enough about the ways of defending themselves to be really dangerous if they want to be. These women will not be a victim of some screwball rapist. He will pay a very big penalty if he tries to mess with one of these ladies."

"Addie has told me about the training some of the women are taking. It's got to be a help to law enforcement to have young women in society who can take care of themselves."

"It's not just 'young' women who are ready to maim some over-the-top dopehead, or some other kind of crazy, Bill. There are grandmothers out there who want to guard their grandchildren from other nutty people. I saw a demo of what they all can do. Pretty amazing, really."

"In any case, a strong woman, taking Hammond by surprise, could possibly be the perpetrator. Right?" asked Parker.

"Yes, but this kind of speculation gets us nowhere, Bill."

Both men were silent for a few seconds. Parker spoke first. "Peter, have you thought of the incredible gall and luck somebody had to have had to kill Hammond in that upstairs committee room, with no exit except the same way he came up to that damned firetrap arrangement, then walk down a long hallway, then down two flights of stairs, and out of sight? I mean, if a person was planning to kill someone, he'd do it where the chance of discovery was almost non-existent, wouldn't he? To murder someone inside the Statehouse, and in a messy way, too, smacks of desperation, wouldn't you say? The killer would need some insurance that he could leave unnoticed, wouldn't he?"

Then Parker stopped talking, as if a minor revelation had hit him over the head. Then he mumbled in a low voice, "And that's the reason for the handwritten sign, wasn't it? The killer hung it on the door knob before he walked into the room where Hammond was waiting for him."

Morgan emphatically agreed. "The killer had one advantage, Bill. He chose the day when party caucuses are held. Nobody would be returning to their committees. They'd be meeting at 1:30 PM on the first floor. It just so happened that a member of the ProgDems decided not to attend the meeting of his party. He came back to the Committee Room, and found Hammond's body." Parker stared glumly at Morgan.

"To get back to the killer and the chances he took, he'd need to leave unnoticed, too, because of the possibility of being covered with blood from his victim. What does he do with himself in that situation? All of this, of course, hinges on the fact that the killer was very confident that he could at least get out of sight fairly quickly, leaving behind him an apparent suicide. We're the only ones who know it was a murder. And then. . . . .," he stopped.

Morgan said, as if to himself, "Bill, I've been a fool. There are two questions to which I needed answers, and I never got that far in my thinking. The killer may have decided that the Statehouse was the *best* place to kill Hammond if he wanted to also send a message to others who shared Hammond's knowledge. And here are the two questions, or propositions, that need answers and confirmation."

Morgan leaned against the back of his chair and looked up at the ceiling. "First, did our forensics people look for blood in the small bathroom at the head of the stairs? The killer might not have gotten enough blood on himself to leave traces on the carpet, but he almost certainly got some on himself somewhere. He could kill Hammond, walk down the hall, step into the bathroom, lock it, and clean his hands and any other area of his body where blood was found. He could leave when the coast was clear, or totally crowded, for that matter, free of bloodstains, and nobody would be any wiser. He'd have to be fairly speedy, of course, so he wouldn't waste that time when the committee rooms are always empty of people. I think that's a reasonable scenario."

"So do I, Peter. I think that's exactly what happened. Can you ask the forensics people to check that bathroom?" asked Parker.

Morgan nodded. "Will do, Bill."

"What's your second proposition?" asked Parker.

"I think that the killer also hid himself in that bathroom before noon, and just waited. When the coast was clear, he just walked down the hall, looking around to make certain that he was completely alone, hung his 'No Trespassing' sign on the door, stepped into the committee room, murdered Hammond, and then retraced his steps. And the proposition is this: did anybody, who was on the same floor where the murder was committed, try to enter that bathroom at any time between, let's say, 11:00AM and 1:15PM and find it locked? It's a bathroom for both sexes, so it locks. That's what I want to know."

Parker added, "And about what time did each of these people try? Many of them won't remember too well, but you should get enough responses to find out if there was a single period of time when *nobody* could get in. This wouldn't be noticed, of course, by anyone because those who tried would say to themselves that it's occupied, so I'll go to lunch, using the bathroom outside the cafeteria. You know, Peter, this line of questioning might yield the exact time that the killer hid in there, waiting to walk down the hall to commit a murder. That could happen if someone says that they *were* able to use the bathroom at a certain time *before* 11:00AM. And maybe there will be someone who says that they were able to use it sometime *after* the murder."

Parker suddenly got up from the table and walked around it, and then sat back down. "There is a problem, though. How would the killer know that Hammond was in the committee room, and alone, too. And why didn't Hammond go to lunch with the rest of his committee?"

"Maybe he had made a previous arrangement to wait there to meet with the killer. Of course he wouldn't know that his visitor was a killer, would he?" offered Morgan.

Parker agreed. "Did Hammond have a pocket calendar?" asked Parker. "Were any notes found on his body, or on his desk? And even if there was a message of some kind, wouldn't the killer take it and destroy it? I'm sure he would. In order to be completely clear, the killer would have made an arrangement by phone. If anything went wrong, he could say that he had no meeting with Hammond even if Hammond's date calendar said he did. You should check Hammond's e-mails, even though I'll bet that you won't find anything from the killer. But Hammond might have a list of his engagements in there that might tell us something."

"I'll check on those things, Bill."

"Please let me know the results of your prodding, Peter. This murder has really changed everything for me. Who knows that it's not a suicide, Peter?"

"Just you, me, and the forensics guys. I think the ME has a strong suspicion, because he found an unexplained bruise on the side of Hammond's neck. That bruise makes sense, by the way. It tells us that Hammond was probably standing in that corner, looking out the window, or something like that, and when the killer walked in, Hammond somehow knew what the killer was there for. He struggled, the killer hit him, stunning him. That's probably where the nosebleed occurred, too. Then the killer hauled him to the first handy chair, and cut his wrist. Then he left. We'll probably never know with any certainty."

Morgan had a look of distaste on his face. He hated loose ends. "I asked the ME to delay his report for another three days, if he can do it, and when he does release it, give me a heads-up. And that's what he'll do, I'm sure, but he won't go any more than that. And I wouldn't either, if I was him."

"So," Parker asked, "how much time do we have to nose around before the truth is out there? It's going to explode in this state. You know what I'm saying, Peter. A second murder in the Statehouse in three years? I can hear them now: 'What the hell are you running up there, Mr. Governor, a murder-for-hire ring?' And the Mid-Vermont Bugle will blame it all on the Governor because he's not a ProgDem."

"How much time do we have to look around before it all blows up?" Morgan mused as he repeated Parker's question. "At best, four days," he answered. "Maybe a little more, because the media in this state are lazy, and also don't understand anything new. They need it to come from some ProgDem source who has already suggested to them what to write. We'd best get cracking, Bill. Time's a'wastin'."

31

Parker left the Red Kettle at 1:00PM. He had placed a call to Birdsall on his private line and he picked up immediately.

"Yes?" Birdsall answered. "What's your business?" This curt reply was not like the Birdsall that Parker knew.

"It's me, Hal. I'll be up there in the next hour, or so, and need to see you. Will you be at your office?"

"Ted, I'll meet you where we met before. Come straight there. Then I'll decide if your story is worthy enough for us to print it. And I have news, too."

"Right," said Parker, and hung up. Double-talk is one way around an eavesdropping Secretary, thought Parker. Hell of a way to have to live, though, he thought. The "Ted" has to be the first name of Ted Williams, the Red Sox all-time great. Birdsall had an autographed picture of him on the wall of his office. That's as close as I'll ever get to the Hall of Fame, Parker thought, as he headed toward Mickey's.

The "Closed" sign was on the door as before, but opened to Parker when he pushed on it. In the semi-darkness of the closed restaurant, seated in the same booth as before, was Hal Birdsall. He got to his feet when he saw Parker and advanced through the gloom to shake his hand.

"Good to see you, Bill. I've brought along another friend of ours. He has some interesting things to tell us."

The impressive bulk of Hugo Barkley rose up and advanced on Parker. "Mr. Parker, the obstinate one, as I've called you since we first met, it's a pleasure to see you again."

"Hugo, you haven't changed at all, have you? Apparently weight loss is not a top priority for you, is it?" Hugo gave a wide smile.

"I may be large, but in great shape, Mr. Parker. You, however, need some help."

"I've never doubted it, Hugo," said Parker.

As they sat down, Birdsall asked, "What did you want to see me about, Bill?"

"I have to swear you to secrecy, Hal, and you, too, Hugo. You can have your story ready, Hal, and I'll give it to you. You only have to wait about four days to run it or talk about it. Agreed?" They nodded.

"Do you know a Member of the Vermont House of Representatives named Hugh Hammond? He's from Underhill Center." Birdsall nodded. Barkley shook his head.

Parker related the sad story of Hammond, his death, and the current knowledge that he was murdered. Hugo sat quietly, watching Parker. Birdsall, however, was visibly shocked, and jumped to his feet.

"Why are you telling us about this, Bill? What does it have to do with Jan, or my Secretary, or Hugo, or God only knows who else?"

"I believe that Jan's assignment to look into the Vermont non-profit industry eventually led to Hammond's death - and to her disappearance when we need her the most."

Birdsall abruptly sat down. "You'll have to tell me why you think so, Bill, because you seem to be blaming the non-profits for his death. And that's not ever going into the CFP, I can tell you that right now." Parker nodded in agreement. He knew what Birdsall was really saying.

Parker looked around the dark interior of the restaurant, then questioningly at Birdsall. "My son-in-law is in the back," said Birdsall. "I told him that if he had to come in here, to make a lot of noise before he arrived. We'd shut up until he left. Satisfied?"

Parker nodded. "You bet, Hal. Well, let me start with the facts and occurrences as I've experienced them. Then you two can give me your opinion." With that, Parker told them both everything from the night Jan Evlin tracked him down on the Chateaugay trout stream to the present moment. He even included the information that Hammond had a box of information hidden under the floor of his barn. It was the first time he'd mentioned it to anybody, and he didn't know why he'd shared with these two that piece of information, except that somebody had to know it and he decided that they could be trusted. "And I'm going after that box tonight."

When he finished, both Birdsall and Hugo seemed speechless.

"Why are you telling us this, Bill? I'm a news reporter, for God's sake, and this guy," pointing a thumb at Hugo, "is an information guru, and professional sneak." Hugo winced at that description.

"Because I want this story told to a wide audience, and accurately, Hal. And that will be your job. Tiny, here," looking at the large physique of Hugo, "will be providing a lot of information, none of which can be attributed to him. Right, Hugo?"

Hugo shifted his huge frame toward Birdsall, and said, without looking at Parker, "Right you are, Bill. Right, Hal?" he said, with a tinge of menace that would be unmistakable to anybody paying attention.

Birdsall, resigned to it all, gave a gesture of agreement.

"When are you heading out tonight to do the dirty deed, Bill?" asked Hugo.

"I'll be leaving my motel, the Winterhaven, here in Burlington, pretty late, Hugo. Never stayed there before. Picked it out based on its address, which isn't in the best part of town. It's probably not a five star dwelling, but that's what I want. Anonymity. I'll get underway probably no earlier than midnight. I'd rather stay out of the way of any citizens when I go out to steal something." Birdsall visibly reacted to that statement.

"And why did you tell me *that*, Bill? Just the thought of that adventure gives me the sweats. And if you're caught? I'll bet you'll want me to come to the jailhouse and bail you out, or something. Me, an upstanding citizen, CFP editor, and objective observer of the truth."

"Hal, you don't even have to admit that you know me. I'll just tell them the truth. I'm sure I won't have to spend more than a day in the jug. When my wife arrives on the scene they'll wish they never heard of me. She's my secret weapon." If he was caught, Parker shuddered to think about what Addie would say to him in the aftermath of his midnight requisition of the box under the barn floor. Parker thought that the whole damn thing sounds like a Hardy Boys mystery from long ago.

Parker yanked himself back into the present, and said, "Besides, I'm known around the state a little bit, and I have a few friends in law enforcement who will at least vouch for me – I think. But, that box was given to me, in effect, by Hammond, and its importance may be crucial to what I'm doing for Jan."

"Do you think the box is heavy, Bill?" asked Hugo. "Hard to lug around, maybe?"

"Oh, I don't think so, Hugo. I certainly didn't get that impression when Hammond told me about it."

"Have you ever done anything like this foray before, Bill?" asked Hugo. Parker noticed that Hugo was being very persistent with his questions. Parker thought about the scheme of events of the last two years in which he was scared out of his wits at least five different times, and merely petrified for the rest of the time. He could be direct, open, and honest in answering Hugo's query. Or he could be slippery and evasive. Parker selected the latter.

"Nothing like this, Hugo," Parker said, not looking directly at Hugo. Hugo gazed at him for a long moment, then looked at Birdsall. Birdsall shrugged as if to say, "I don't know how his mind works either."

"Now, Hal," Parker said, "why is Hugo here? I didn't expect him. You must have issued the invitation. No offense, Hugo. Why, Hal?"

"Hugo called me a couple of days ago, Bill. He wanted to talk to me, privately. By coincidence, we set it up to meet today. And then you called. So, here we are." Birdsall seemed almost glad that he could jam all the bad news into one secret meeting in the shadowy confines of a shuttered restaurant, rather than two.

"Does your information have to do with what we've just been discussing, Hugo?" asked Parker.

Hugo nodded. "I think so, Bill. In fact, I think all of this ties together, especially since I heard your dissertation a minute ago."

"Let's hear it, by all means, Hugo," said Parker, with enthusiasm.

"It's about phones, recorders, stupid minor-league spies, and information-gathering networks in Vermont. Altogether, very interesting stuff."

Hugo suddenly lurched to his feet. "I think better on my feet," he said, sheepishly.

"In the days since we first met here at Mickey's, I've taken it upon myself to give extra time to many of my most public customers. By that I mean those who have constant contact with clients and customers all around Chittenden County and, at the same time, probably have contacts in other parts of the state. I did a lot of guessing, but I was able to check them out for the things we discussed, along with the normal surveillance activities for which I am being employed. That way I feel that I'm doing something honorable and for which I charge an honest fee, and to provide cover for the nefarious work I'm doing for you two." He smiled at them.

"Actually, what I do for you guys is a service for my clients, too, and they don't have to pay me for it – yet. I even checked out four non-profits for incoming private lines that were hooked up to recorders, and not phones. I also did my dirty work on three banks. Two of them had a common non-profit for which they did work. It's the Guardians of the Earth. Now there's an interesting group. They handle a hell of a lot of money, and they buy up the development rights of a hell of a lot of land in this state. And they've been doing it for years."

"Hugo," said Parker, "I'm very happy that you checked things for funny business where you could. But I remember being chewed out by you because we asked you to do the very thing you have apparently done anyway. How come?"

"I didn't want you to depend on me for anything, Bill. You might get lazy, and do nothing, while waiting for me to find something. It worked, too, didn't it? You guys plugged away and now you have what you didn't expect, and it may pull your theory along faster than you thought. That's an example of how smart I am. And it's a perfect example of your political philosophy, too, Bill." He smiled at Parker.

"Besides," he added, "you both looked so down when I was giving you my 'honor and loyalty' speech when I refused to get involved that I couldn't stand it, which demonstrates my compassion for the downtrodden."

Parker grinned at Hugo. "Okay, okay, enough. Let's see how smart you are by talking about the details of what you found. You're bragging too much, Hugo. It makes me nervous." Another new game with Hugo, thought Parker. He is bright, though, he admitted to himself. Never underestimate him.

"What I found bothers me a lot, Bill. Much of it has to yield to supposition, I'm afraid, but the physical evidence is too much to ignore. I found the exact same problem that I found in your office, Hal, in two banks I do work for. A secretary who records certain meetings, and a Department Manager of the bank who is advising somebody outside the bank of what's going on in the bank. And how do I know that? Most of my work is done for the majority of my clients after hours. I usually come in through a side or back door which has a code. The bank authorizes me to use the numbers of that code as part of its agreement with me. In fact, I create them for the client. I can come in any time, but I usually have a fixed schedule."

Parker said, "You must have had to pass a pretty rugged examination and background check to warrant that sort of freedom, Hugo. If you were a real crook, which you are now, temporarily, at least, because of your work for us, you could really foul them up."

"Correct, Bill," said Hugo, "but I'm an honest and trustworthy person, as you know." Parker smiled at Hugo, and gestured for him to continue.

Hugo walked around to the other side of the table. "So, I changed my schedule, at least for the first trip. I slipped into the bank at a different time and different day. And what do you suppose I found?" He left a gap of time, waiting for somebody to say something.

"Hugo," blurted Parker, "stop, in the name of heaven, playing games. Just give us the information. What did you find?"

"Mr. Workaholic himself, a guy with ponytail, who probably doesn't do crap during the day, sitting at his Manager's desk at 11:30PM, listening to a tape recording, and jotting down notes on a pad."

"Ponytail?" said Birdsall. "You mean the guy is a beatnik?"

Hugo looked fondly at Birdsall for a moment. "You just dated yourself big time, Hal. Today's hiring practices dictate that you must give everyone a real chance at improving themselves. The bank receives credit from the politicians and social activists, in various unofficial ways, if they demonstrate 'diversity' and a 'global' attitude in their personnel policies. Where the hell have you been, anyway?"

"Certainly not in that world," mumbled Birdsall.

"To continue," said Hugo, "after being interrupted by a Neanderthal," looking at Birdsall, "I couldn't hear the tape because he was listening to it through an earphone. So I stepped back into the hallway and started to make innocent noises from the corridor – you know, as if I was starting regular work. He came out, saw me, and said that this wasn't my usual night and that I had disturbed him during a very important task for the bank. He was pissed, I can tell you. I apologized and told him that I also had an important task for the bank, and I was going to by God do it. It had nothing to do with him. He blinked, and for a moment. I actually thought he was going to cry, and then he retreated to his desk. I stayed where I was, but was able to observe him through a small window in the corridor door. He hurriedly jammed the earpiece into the side of his head, snapped on the recorder, jotted notes furiously, stopped, ejected the tape and slipped it into his pocket, put the recorder into his desk, tore off the paper from the pad and put it into his pocket, locked everything up, and left. Not even a goodbye for me, his new friend."

"So, he didn't leave you with any way to find out what he was doing?" asked Parker. "Why did you explain all this to us, but can't produce any hard evidence that he was doing anything other than his job for the bank."

"Because he left the best record in the world for me," answered Hugo. "And I took all that time because I wanted you to know that it's the real McCoy." With that he produced a sheet of blank note paper and handed it to Parker.

"Thanks for the paper, Hugo," Parker said with exasperation. "I'm sure I'll need it sometime."

Hugo smiled. "Take it over to the light coming in from the kitchen, Bill. Hold it sideways and look across it at an angle, and tell me what you see."

Parker walked over toward the light source and did as Hugo suggested. Then he squinted across the surface of it. "Christ," he said to himself. He was looking at the written notes that Mr. Ponytail had written on the sheet above this one. The impression of the pencil point had made an additional copy and Mr. Ponytail never knew it. He had been in a hurry, too, and that might help to explain it.

"Reading it is tough, but I did get the gist of it. You're mentioned in it, Bill. Notice that?' asked Hugo.

"What?" cried Parker. "No, I didn't get that far. What the hell kind of a meeting did he record, for goodness sake?"

Parker was alarmed that his name would be in a bank meeting, the subject of which was stolen by a damned disloyal pony-tailed spook – a spy, and this really angered Parker, who worked for the bank.

Parker suddenly realized that he was generalizing, or whatever the sensitive ones would call it when dealing with pony-tailed people. Well, what the hell, he grumbled to himself, these same socially cognizant nitwits would protect the right of a damned pony-tailed terrorist to come into the country and blow somebody up. They'd be unhappy about that particular event, but they had done their job by protecting his rights to do just that.

"Hal, can you ask your son-in-law for a couple of wooden pencils, nicely sharpened?" asked Hugo.

Birdsall called to his son-in-law, and presently he appeared with the requested pencils. Parker knew what Hugo would do now. All kids did it at some time in their lives, and older folks did it when they were collecting ancient gravestones. Rubbing with a flat carbon stick, or a pencil, usually brought up the images very quickly and easily.

Inside a minute, Hugo handed Parker the sheet of blackened paper. Parker took it by its edges and started to read. The notes were very clear because of the force of the pencil being used, although some imagination had to be used because most of the writing was in short phrases and single words, and therefore artificially shortened.

Mtg 5-7

Pres/stf tlkd re 4 cntbtns frm frnds. Pres tnks suspcios. 2 bg, dnrs nt reptbl, chk out be4 acptg. Smg wrng?

Rmr re B. Park lkg at us. Hmnd dfntly ded. No other cntcts.

cll Z@ north point.

Birdsall was looking intently at the words revealed by the rubbing.. "This is like a code, isn't it? A speed writing code, but none like I've ever seen before. Sort of homemade speed writing."

"I think you're right, Hal," said Hugo. "It's probably very simple. Let's not even call it a code. I think that the guy who used it didn't have the sense of a lemming. We can figure it all out."

Parker said nothing. He seemed to Birdsall to be in another world. Parker just continued staring at the strange message.

After a minute or two Parker suddenly said, "Boys, we have a very big problem. Much of that problem will become more clear when we hear the rest of Hugo's report. What else do you have, Hugo?" he asked, turning toward him.

"I went to the other bank. Changed my routine there, too. There was no one there at midnight when I went in. I had a new security program to install for the bank computers, so I wasn't just sneaking around. Because no one was there, I really checked the place out, including the office of the President. It was clean. However, being a normal human being, I had to use his can at that moment and I went in to his private privy. Makes me feel like a real insider, I can tell you. A person like me doesn't just stand there, no matter what he's doing, so I looked around, as I usually do." The mental image of what Hugo described brought grins from both Parker and Birdsall.

Not noticing this reaction from his audience, Hugo continued. "The first thing I saw was another door, on the opposite wall, leading out and into an adjoining conference room. I've seen this arrangement before. If the President of the bank uses the conference room for clients or bank meetings, he'll unlock the bathroom so that those in the conference room can use it if needed. Otherwise it stays locked on the conference room side. The door is locked from the inside, as you can imagine. I expected that this one was, too, and I wasn't wrong." Hugo was pacing again, and on a roll.

"In the corner, behind the door, was an 8"x8" square wood box, about eight feet long, running from the floor up to, and through, the ceiling. You know what I mean. Some people, who have a party room in their basements, will case in, or build a wooden box around, a pipe, or whatever it is that can't be moved. Makes things look nicer, you know. Got one myself, for that matter." Hugo plopped himself down in the booth beside Birdsall. The room seemed to tilt slightly.

"I thought that the casing job was well done, so I looked at the place where it entered the false ceiling, because mine looks sort of sloppy where it disappears through the ceiling, and I'd like to do something about it – or, to be honest, my wife would like me to do something about it. I thought "here's my chance to get a bright idea". So, I stepped up onto the toilet cover, stood tall, pushed up the ceiling panel, and shined my flashlight in the space above the ceiling."

Hugo had a pleased look on his face. "Guess what? No support column. Just a bunch of wires that came to this central place in the bank from lights, phones, and computers. I looked them over and found no strange type of a wire that shouldn't be there. As I was getting ready to lightly drop to the floor, I happened to glance down at the backside of the case, which was about a foot from the wall and behind the door. There was a little panel there. I almost missed it. As I said before, I dropped to the floor and ran my hand over the surface, found the panel, and put my light on it."

Parker found himself fascinated by this blow-by-blow description of Hugo's evening in the bank. He surprised himself. Usually he would be bored to tears by any long-winded talker.

"I got down on my knees, reached in, grabbed the edge of the panel, and pulled. It popped out easily. I had just enough room to shine my light in the opening and look around. And what do you think I found, gentlemen?"

Oh, God, here we go again, thought Parker.

"Tell us, Hugo, please," he said, sarcasm dripping from his voice. Hugo looked at him with innocence.

"I found one of those large suction-type pick-up mics on the back wall of the casing, which happened to be the common wall with the conference room. These types of mics can be damn sensitive, boys, and I was able to look it over enough to determine that it wasn't the latest type, but probably adequate for the task. I also found another little voice-activated mini-cassette recorder hanging on a nail next to the suction-mic. That little recorder was exactly like the one in your office, Hal. Probably bought 'em by the gross. That spare recorder allows them to keep the conference room under surveillance all the time."

"I didn't touch anything. I put things back together, and then went into the conference room. There was a hole drilled in the paneling that apparently allowed enough sound through to record. Must have been close, but just enough."

"Will you tell the bank President, Hugo?" asked Birdsall. "He should know right away."

"Yeah, I'll tell him that I stumbled on to the recorder by complete accident. I'll profess ignorance, and will try to convince him that we should let it run. This will allow us to find out who is responsible for this sneaking around. I'm sure I can get him to help us, just as you're doing, Hal."

Hugo walked over to Birdsall and threw a larger-than-life arm over his shoulders. "How are you doing, by the way, dealing with your secretary? Any ideas who she contacts? Nothing has turned up so far on the bug I put in the phone, I know."

"No news, Hugo. Of course, I'm not giving her much to chew on. My acting job extends only so far. I can't wait to fire her."

"Okay," said Parker, bringing the meeting to a close. "We each have jobs to do. I'm checking out the connection between your brother's death and Jan's absence. Hugo, please keep checking your clients for us. Hal, let me know when you hear from your brother's wife about the rifles, and for God's sake, start feeding your secretary information that will cause her to call somebody."

"I already have, Bill. I mentioned, in a fake meeting I held in my office just two days ago, that I had hired you to take up where Jan had left off. I figured that your name would get somebody excited. I thought that was pretty clever."

"What?" yelped Parker. "You didn't even check with me?"

"Well, I didn't think I needed to. I thought the plan was to get them riled up, whoever 'them' is. So I did. It's not dangerous, you know. You said so yourself." Parker would have chosen another message, but too late now.

"Hugo, please check your wiretap on Hal's secretary's phone again before you go," asked Parker, still thinking about Birdsall's act of dangling him in front of somebody who might not like him very much. He was also thinking about the murder of Hugh Hammond. "I may get run over before I get to my truck, and I'd like to know about it beforehand if possible."

The check on the tap yielded nothing but the usual newspaper business. "It's clean, Bill. Nothing about anything we're interested in. I would guess that that's probably the proof that she contacts somebody when she's out of the office." It was the "somebody" that worried Parker.

"One last item of business, gentlemen," said Parker. "Hugo, you mentioned that you checked out four non-profits for being snoops. Find anything?"

"No funny looking wires and cheap mini-recorders, Bill. I checked these offices of four of my non-profits. All I usually do for them is to go through their computers to update their virus and threat protections, install new programs, and make certain that their door lock installations are working the way they are supposed to. Every month I change the lock codes on all internal doors, leaving the new code numbers for the Executive Director in a locked box with a slotted cover. Very routine. I didn't know what they would have that's valuable enough for them to hire an expensive guy like me to make certain that low-budget guys like you don't steal from them. The offices in the non-public part of the operations are usually messy and dirty. Out front the conditions are a little better. Gotta keep up appearances, you know."

"So you didn't find anything that would aid us in our little investigation, Hugo. That's disappointing," said Parker.

"Did I say that, Bill? Did I even imply it?" Then Hugo's face took on a look of triumph. "I found something in all four of them that may have nothing to do with what you're looking at. Or a lot. But, as a citizen and a taxpayer, I'd be furious."

"Something apparently set you off, Hugo. What did you find?" asked Birdsall.

"The first non-profit to which I paid a very, very late evening visit is called "People's Revolution Against Profits, Production, and Private Property. Better known as PRAPPPP. Catchy, huh?" Hugo spelled it out, and handed Parker a brochure and a bumper sticker as he did so.

"PRAPPPP?" asked Parker, sounding out the letters as he said them.. "It sounds almost like something unmentionable in polite company. I have heard of it, though, probably because of its acronym. That's pretty distinctive."

He went over the brochure. "For goodness sake, Hugo, these people want to overthrow the state government. They don't like anybody. Where do people like this get educated? Cuba? California? Libya? No, no, I've got it. Some Ivy League school."

"Bill, I only know that it's just a few Vermonters getting together to protest against certain people who they don't like at all – like you, for instance." He wore a pained grin as he looked at Parker.

"Hugo, what have I done to them? I know nothing about them."

"Who knows, Bill? When I opened a file of candidates recruited by this non-profit, I knew they'd never contact you to run. And you're a good man, as far as I know. I think I'd trust you to represent me. Maybe." Parker was surprised. He'd never expected any kind of even a partial compliment from Hugo.

Hugo, as if embarrassed that he had said anything like that to Parker, hurried to fill the brief and empty space with more words. "You'd be surprised at some of the names who are on the 'take' and the amount of money that non-profit contributed to their chosen candidates. In addition, you'll find a campaign plan for one of the most left-wing candidates in the state's history. That means that the non-profit was providing financial help to all candidates of their own leanings – and managed campaigns for them. In addition, the overwhelming majority of their income came in from outside the state. Fantastic," he said, as if to himself.

"No one challenges them when they break the law that gives them their non-profit status?" asked Parker.

"I understand that some of them are being challenged," said Hugo. "And they're all upset about it. Calling those who want to take away their tax-exempt status 'Nazis', and the daily press goes right along with it."

Parker was reading the bumper sticker. "What is this crap?" he yelped. The bumper sticker read, "The UN and Our Children - The Education of Diversity".

"Oh, you mean turning our children over to the UN?" said Hugo. "Standard stuff for these people, Bill. The problem we have is that Vermont has thousands of people who love that idea. The Vermont Teachers United Association leadership supports that line. Most of the teachers don't, however. My wife is a teacher, Bill. She absolutely detests the VTUA. It took her a while to cotton on to their drift. When she did, she went wild. Publicly accused her union of having another agenda that has nothing to do with children. Boy, did she get it in the neck from that bunch."

"I remember that, Hugo," said Birdsall. "I think we did an editorial on her. Is she still working?"

"She is working, Hal, and yes, I have a copy of that ignorant and toadying editorial. Put it in a picture frame, my wife and I did. Hung it on the wall in her office at home. Put a small sign on it, too. 'Beware of the Non-educators Who Want to Educate our Children'. That was the start of her determination to change things for herself and our own children."

"Based on what you've said, that must have started a firestorm in Vermont education circles," said Parker.

Hugo grinned. "My wife had a teacher-friend who used to visit often. When she saw that sign, she never came back. We got the word a month or so later that my wife scares her."

There was a silence in the darkened room that amounted to an attitude of gloom. "I used to hear that the VTUA put thousands and thousands of dollars into campaigns of members of the ProgDem Party, just like these non-profits do. True, Hugo?" Parker asked.

"Absolutely, Bill. And the majority of teachers in the union don't like it, but they don't say anything. They just blindly, and in a half-hearted way, follow the orders of the head of the union, who, by the way, sends his kids to a private school."

"I heard about that, too," said Parker. "What's the matter with the members of the union, anyway? They're supposed to be aware of things. They teach our kids, for God's sake." Parker had to work hard at calming himself down. He never could abide ignorance, socialism, and cowardice, and he saw a lot of that combination in the VTUA.

"Hugo," Parker said in as quiet a voice as he could muster, "if your wife is still working, what school board dares to hire her?"

"She's teaching in a private school, Bill. Its name is the Lech Walesa School. It's a school for families who distrust the public schools. It has a fund into which families from all over the state contribute money. Those contributions include many from families who will never be able to send their kids to the school because of geographic reasons. In mostly modest amounts, of course, but it allows people to borrow the tuition money and then repay it at terms they can afford. And there are a couple of big financial supporters, too, who choose to remain anonymous. Terrific people, my wife tells me."

This sort of individual initiative fascinated Parker. "What kind of a fund is it, Hugo? How does it work? I assume it's legal." Parker had to hear more.

"Of course it's legal, Bill," Hugo said, with a hint of exasperation. With a slight grin, he calmed down enough to speak carefully, no doubt saving Parker from a punch in the nose.

"It's a type of revolving loan fund," he continued. "It all got started when my wife began to visit business people for contributions. The results were amazing. They have over two million dollars in this fund, and she's only been at it for about a year."

"How does she like it, Hugo?" asked Parker. "Is it a school for low-income families? Is it made up of minority families? Is it accredited?"

"Mostly white people, Bill. Income level is not a barrier. The loans are granted on a sliding scale, so wealth, or the lack of it, plays a big role. Of course we don't have many minority families in Vermont, but more are coming here because they want this school for their children. My wife is the only black teacher, but they have Hispanic teachers, Vietnamese teachers, and teachers from Germany and England. My wife is sort of their unofficial leader. She's an impressive lady, you guys. I've decided not to debate anything with her. I come away feeling inadequate."

"I know the feeling, Hugo. I have a wife like that," said Parker. "How's the school doing?"

"Space has become limited, and expansion is in their future. And she loves teaching in this school. She tells me that it filled out her personal career because the school demands that the basics be taught and mastered before the students are allowed to move to the next grade. My wife tells me that every student really works very hard – and they all succeed, some with additional help where needed, of course, but they do succeed. All the teachers have made themselves available during vacations and summers for extra coaching."

Good for her, thought Parker. Addie and I are going to meet this lady before we're done.

"You asked about accreditation, Bill," said Hugo. "Of course it's accredited. It was a hell of a fight, though. The ProgDems and the VTUA went to court to stop them. The school was afraid of that move, I can tell you. They had no money to hire lawyers. And one night the people who started the school were meeting at our house. They were wondering how much money they could raise to pay for attorneys. I wasn't in the meeting. I was sitting in the living room and I heard a knock at the front door. I answered it and it was two well-dressed guys I didn't know. I thought they were a couple of troublemakers from the VTUA." He looked at them in obvious embarrassment. "That tells you my state of mind, doesn't it?"

Parker knew that feeling well, based on the last three years. He was beginning to sense it again and it wasn't pleasant for him.

"They asked if they could speak to my wife. I asked them what their business was because I told them that my wife had enough troubles without inviting more. They said that their business was the law and they wanted to ease the troubles of the school rather than add to them. It turned out that they were prepared to put their law firm behind the accreditation effort, and at no charge. As you can imagine, I took them right into the meeting. The school became accredited."

"What was the reaction from the State Association of School Directors, Hugo?" Birdsall asked.

A look of disgust came over Hugo's face. "They fought the school all the way, writing irrational letters against it that not even they could understand. My wife was told by a former member of that august body that the VTUA wrote the letters and various dopes in the Association signed them and sent them out."

Birdsall looked extremely uncomfortable when Parker glanced at him. He should, he thought. It's only recently, after a change in management, that the CFP supported school choice. That caused a shock that the VTUA hasn't gotten over yet. They apparently don't know how to directly attack a former supporter.

"That's one of the most biased and ignorant groups in the state, Hal. The VTUA runs them, telling them that if school choice is allowed, they will lose students. And possibly they are correct, of course. However, that's their only issue. A student's education doesn't come into it for them."

Parker said, "Hugo, I had no idea of the depth of this education problem in Vermont. This whole education lash-up in Vermont is really corrupt, you know. I pity the good and decent teachers. They must be terribly frustrated." Parker hesitated, and then said, "However, we've got other things to cover now. What are these non-profit clients you 'visited'?"

Hugo seemed to snap back into the present. "Oh, yeah, Bill. The first one is called 'The Global Association for Geopolitical Solutions', or GAGS for short. I don't know what 'Geopolitical Solutions' means, unless it's some kind of code that's understood by their believers. Actually, I'm afraid to ask what it means. You can read their pamphlet. It won't tell you what they really do."

He held the pamphlet up for Parker to see. "They were established primarily to recruit teachers to run for the Legislature, to raise money for them, and to operate their campaigns for them."

"How can you be so sure of that, Hugo? It's really critical that we have proof of this kind of thing."

Hugo slid another booklet across the table. "This little devil is what you're talking about, Bill. This tells the staff how to recruit, what types of people to recruit, how you can get them elected, and to be quiet while you're doing it."

Parker picked up the thin booklet. Its title was "How to Build a New State". It was a numbered copy, this one he held carrying the number "48 of 50". Just two left in the warehouse, Parker thought, and not issued, by the look of the newness of this copy he held.

"Hugo, won't this be missed?" asked Parker. "It's brand new."

"As I was doing the honorable work for which I'm being paid, Bill, I saw a copy of this booklet, opened up, right in the middle of a desk. It wasn't hidden at all. And I knew it could be important. It was very well used – ratty, almost. I looked it over, noticed that it was numbered – number "37" of "50", in this case - and realized that there had to be thirteen more of them somewhere. They weren't hard to find. They were in a bookcase located in the back of a closet. So I did the dishonorable thing and borrowed number 48." He smiled. "We'll run off a copy of it for our use. They'll never miss it for a day or two."

"Who published it?" asked Birdsall. "Does it say in the front somewhere?"

Parker opened the booklet at the front and in the back.

"Ah, said the doctor during his examination," said Parker, hoping for a chuckle from somebody, which he didn't get. Not in the front, my man, he said to himself, but on the inside of the back cover – and the publisher's name wasn't printed when the booklet was. It's just hand stamped. And a sloppy job it is, too.

"It's Freebird Publishing, Basement Productions, South Burlington, Vermont, Hal. It even has a little statement under the address. Get this," Parker said. "'Publishing/Printing for all New World Material. Don't Wait in Line'." Birdsall shook his head.

"J. Walter Thompson Advertising it ain't," said Hugo. "Is it significant that the publisher's name wasn't printed in the booklet when the booklet was produced?"

Birdsall spoke up at this point. "Probably not. What I thought of, however, was that there are many copies of this book around – many more than 50 - and some of the purchasers didn't want the name of the publisher to appear on their booklets. I don't know why."

"Maybe this publisher has an unsavory reputation to some people," said Parker. Birdsall shrugged.

"What other non-profits did you visit, Hugo?" asked Birdsall.

"The third one I visited was the People's Order of the Religious Keeper, otherwise known as PORK."

Birdsall sat straight up in his seat at the mention of that name. "PORK? Is there a problem with them? My wife does volunteer work for them once in a while. We've even attended their church occasionally. A little strange, but interesting."

"This one is really a leading edge hard left church with a religious non-profit program," said Hugo. "I looked up their activities information that qualified them for non-profit status as a religious institution. They met the test at that time. Today, however, nobody checks them for adherence to the non-profit line." He shook his head in frustration.

"Some friends of ours were members of one of the well-known, traditional, churches," Hugo continued. "Not any more. They told me that their church and most of the traditional religious systems in the northeast have been taken over by strident, far-left, religious cults, made up of people and new-wave ministers who preach against other churches, against certain politicians, in favor of non-traditional beliefs, and against America on many occasions. This support of these strange beliefs has been designed to split these churches. This automatically purges the traditionalists."

Hugo was grimly set on his course of telling Birdsall and Parker just how much they'd missed in the last ten years.

"Then the new wave people take over complete control, often set up religious non-profits, where needed, and extend the far-left message in wider circles." Hugo was distressed. He gazed down at the floor, saying nothing. The sudden silence seemed deafening. "And a large piece of their money comes in from outside."

"I'm not a very religious person," said Parker. "The ministers I've come in contact with over the last fifteen years *are* somehow different. They don't speak to me anymore. They just speak at me, and in a tone that suggests that they are in contact with their God, but I can't go there. I will get my contact with God only because they grant me permission. That sort of thing, you know? My wife and I stay away from church because of that high-and-mighty attitude. You've just given me a more powerful reason to distrust churches of the past. Their future lies in indoctrination of their flock, not leading it on a path from which people can make choices as to how much of it they want."

Parker hesitated, and then said, bemusedly, "I sound like what I dislike about the single-issue people on the right, don't I? Except that they are essentially harmless. It's the socialist-type that concern me. They are vicious with a religious twist."

"Have you looked for different churches, Bill?" asked Hugo. "They're out there, you know. Churches that help you believe, rather than the new ministers who demand that you give up a lot of your religious philosophy to join the 'new approach'."

"No, I admit that we haven't. It seems almost beyond our energy to go through the process. I guess it's partly discouragement - and the rest is laziness, Hugo. Not proud of it."

"What you guys are really talking about, you know," Birdsall said, "is the same thing going on in all levels of education." Parker and Hugo turned toward Birdsall, surprised to hear from him. They both assumed that he was from the same general outlook as the newspaper for which he worked, and he wouldn't have much to say when the subjects swerved toward the more general.

"What's being taught," Birdsall continued, "is designed to change America from a place where people can grow, live, and find wealth if they work hard, into an 'Old Europe' type of country. You both know what I mean. The Old Europe is represented by Germany and France, for example. Those are two nations that are dying right before our eyes while, at the same time, trying to convince themselves and the rest of the world that they are the model nations for the rest of us to emulate. In America, the process of dumbing us down is being accomplished through our school systems. What these educators are doing in this country is designed to change our people and their children from citizens who expect their right to live and grow to exist forever, to those who expect government to tell them what they can do and who is qualified to do it.

Parker pondered what those words meant to him. "Hal, what's their motive? What do they gain by diminishing this country? These people call themselves intellectuals, don't they? Don't intellectuals look objectively at something and then support it or reject it based on clear-eyed investigation? I know *what* you're saying – I don't know *why* it should be true."

Hugo shifted in the booth, leaning against the backrest. "I agree with Hal. Here's what my wife says, Bill," he said, "in a nutshell, as she puts it. I think she's talking in simple terms so I'll understand. She says that the 230 year history of America is the result of 2300 years of European history, where all the countries and non-countries had kings, queens, and all the other fancy people running things. So a lot of people in England got fed up, got in some leaky boats with their families and everything they owned, which wasn't much, and came to America. That was a hell of a trip, by the way, boys, from what I've read," said Hugo. Parker gestured to him to keep going.

"Then, after a fracas with this same England, and which these tough colonists won, they had to decide what kind of a government they wanted. I'm sure you can imagine what a huge decision *that* was. Then somebody made a rough list of the things that made them leave England, and they simply went in the opposite direction. You know what I mean," as he looked at them.

"Instead of a Church of England, these tough colonists said a person could worship God in any way they wanted. Instead of some jerk with fancy silk drawers on telling everybody that if their fathers were shoemakers, then everybody in that family forever would be shoemakers – or farmers, or well diggers, or stonemasons, or whatever. So they changed that, too, and anybody could be anything they wanted to as long as they were willing to work hard and then work even harder after that. Everybody would take care of themselves and their families. Nobody had to give a large chunk of what they earned to Mr. Silk Drawers, you see. We didn't allow any Mr. Silk Drawers in this country – or if somebody showed up who wanted to be *something* without doing *anything*, they'd starve. They got the message real quick."

"Although some did starve, so I've read," Hugo said quietly. "They got what they asked for, though," he said firmly.

"Of course, they did allow slavery," he said, "and it took 175 years to get rid of it. However, my father used to say that the basic beauty of America was that, after huge struggles, death, and hatred, slavery *was overcome*. In Africa, where most of our ancestors came from, they still have it after 2000 years, or more, and there's no end in sight. The killing still goes on. "

Parker was enjoying this small speech from Hugo as much as anything he'd ever heard. This guy knew what America was all about, he thought. Birdsall was sitting in his place, totally transfixed, and still.

"And that's the problem, boys. ProgDems are the Old Europe people. They consider themselves the next generation of kings, queens, and dukes, although they won't ever use terms like those. They consider themselves the elite, the brightest of the bright. They say they represent 'the people' instead of 'special interests'. They think that they are entitled to take our money, pay themselves well, and run Vermont. They're hypocrites, too. They are probably socialists, but want to be royalty. That would enable them to do very little in the way of productive work and sit in offices in Montpelier, handing out business cards."

Birdsall was now making a note or two as Hugo walked around in the dim light.

"And your paper, Hal, actually had kind words to say about an ex-Vermont State Senator who resigned from the Senate because this Senator needed more money, and got a government job dreamed up by a fellow Senator." Hugo glared at Birdsall.

"This job paid this ex-Senator more money than they ever made in their lives for two years - before the Legislature caught up with the sham. So this ex-Senator is now running for a statewide office, liking taxpayer money more than working at something worthwhile. A perfect example of what I've been running off at the mouth about. What the hell is the matter with your paper, Hal? This person is a charter member of this ProgDem elite corps. And your paper can't see a thing like this for what it is. Good Lordy, Hal, you've got to wake up the CFP."

Birdsall was speechless. Parker loved every second of it.

Suddenly Hugo seemed to run down. He looked embarrassed as he said, "I'm awfully sorry Bill, Hal. I just got off on one of my favorite subjects, and didn't even know you were still here for part of it."

"Wouldn't have missed it for the world, Hugo," said Parker.

Birdsall was seemingly in a slight state of shock. Then he suddenly got up from his seat and walked over to Hugo and threw an arm over his shoulders. "Thanks for telling us so much about yourself, Hugo. And for giving me an approach for an editorial on what's happening in Vermont."

"Think you can get it into the paper, Hal?" asked Parker.

Birdsall shrugged. "A better chance now than in the past, Bill. But, objectively speaking? Probably not. Our editorial supporting school choice drove the Burlington City government wild. An editorial describing what Hugo has just told us would bring down our house around our ears. I'll submit one on the day I officially retire."

Parker decided to change the subject, although he could have discussed the subject for hours. "Hal, you said you had some information for me. Now's the time."

Birdsall snapped his fingers. "Yes, Bill, I do," he said. "I don't know how important it is. I heard back from my brother's widow, now a resident of Florida. She called yesterday morning and told me that two days before she had mailed an envelope to me that she said 'might be of interest to you.' And then she said, 'That's all I have, Hal, and all I want to have'. And then she hung up. Very strange, but then she probably is completely worn out. I know I would be."

"Let's see this information, Hal. This could be of interest," said Parker.

"It's at the office, and my secretary is already gone for the day, so we'll interrupt her recorder and then be comfortable."

"You're welcome to come with us, Hugo," said Parker. "You're into this whole confusing mess as deeply as we are."

"Don't mind if I do," agreed Hugo, amiably.

It was after 5:00 in the afternoon when they arrived at the Chittenden Free Progressive offices. As Birdsall had indicated, only the night staff was there in the production areas, and a few reporters working to finish their stories to meet their deadlines. No one saw them enter Birdsall's office.

The first thing that Birdsall did, after giving them a silent signal to be quiet, was to place two homemade, insulated, panels firmly against each heat duct opening. He seemed pleased with his anti-spy efforts. Foiling the sound recording microphones in those ducts seemed to be Birdsall's calling in life.

"What have you got, Hal?" asked Parker.

"Two things, Bill. First, here is the envelope I received from my sister-in-law." He set a 9x12 manila envelope in front of Parker. "I didn't see anything of major significance in there, but maybe you can tell me how you view it from your vantage point."

Parker pulled out the contents of the envelope and spilled them on the table. The inventory list of firearms, contained in a small notebook and written in a neat style of printing, was the first item of importance. Then there were two sales slips that Parker set aside for further examination. The last item was a piece of crumpled notepaper that showed signs of an unsuccessful attempt to flatten it into its original condition. And that was it.

Parker had a feeling of disappointment. He had expected that a widow, asked to go back through her late husband's papers would make very certain that she had found them all. Maybe this is truly all he had left. Parker, however, didn't believe it. And he didn't know of a way to squeeze the last drop from her. She'd been upset enough.

Then Parker had a thought. "Hal," he asked quietly, "who has been through your brother's house since his death? Many people? Only a few? We've been in there, of course, but who else?"

Birdsall thought for a moment, then went to his desk and removed a thin file folder from under his desk blotter. "I almost forgot I had this, Bill. The police gave it to me when they began their investigation. It lists those people who are authorized by the police to go through the house as part of their official duties. If someone else wanted to go in, I was not to allow them access."

"Anybody not on the list try to enter, Hal?" asked Parker.

"Yeah, I remember one guy, who was already in the house when the police and all the other agencies that had a role in this sort of thing first came here. At the end of that exhausting day, they handed me this list, and introduced me to each of the people in the room so I'd have at least a chance to recognize them. Standard stuff, I think."

Maybe standard, maybe not, thought Parker. But why did so many people show up? Is that usual for these situations? He'd have to ask Morgan.

"Do you mean that this guy was in the house with you before the local police arrived?" asked Parker.

"That's right," Birdsall said. "He said he was from the state police. Showed me his badge, in fact. I remember thinking that this guy was right on the ball with his timely arrival."

"Did that guy appear on the list?" asked Parker.

"No, Bill. I know that because I met everybody within the first hour of the police arrival and he wasn't among them on the list. In fact, I asked the police about him, telling them he was here from the state police when I got to the house. They didn't know him, but didn't show any more interest in him. But he did try to get in a couple of times during the rest of that week. I had to escort him out of the house."

"Do you remember what he looked like, Hal? Any details at all? I'd be interested."

Parker could just feel Hugo looking at him.

"You know, Bill," said Birdsall, "I do remember this guy left an impression on me after he was gone. He was younger than you or I. Older than Hugo, here. I didn't note his name, although the way you're questioning me, I wish I had." He grinned uncomfortably. "I also remember that this guy could be the poster boy for state police officers everywhere. You know, in great shape, looking great, and smelling like new-mown hay - or something like that, anyway."

"You mean he had an odor that was like that, Hal?" asked Hugo, incredulously. "A real smell about him?"

"You bet, Hugo. Interesting, huh?"

Parker listened carefully to this exchange, knowing that there was something that it should be telling him, and unable to grab that "something" as it flitted by in his memory.

"Hal, I think you said that this guy was in the house when you got there. You mean standing inside the house, or waiting on the porch?" Parker's sense of the scary was working overtime.

"Oh, he was inside the house, Bill. Definitely. I asked him how he got in, and he showed me some sort of small tool and said something like, 'we in the state police can get in anywhere. Part of our training'. It made me mad as hell, but I didn't take it any further. I didn't think anymore about it."

Parker looked at Birdsall with despair, and then at Hugo, who just stared glassily at Birdsall, with his mouth open.

Attempting to move the subject along without letting Birdsall know that he was a damn fool, Parker asked, "Hal, was there anything strange that you remember about that visit from the state police guy? Just anything at all."

"Well," said Birdsall, "it was all quite a while ago, Bill, but there was one thing that I wondered about. This state police guy seemed very familiar with the house. I mean, not just generally, but specifically - like anybody who builds houses, or is an experienced real estate broker. They can look at a strange house and tell you where everything inside is located while sitting in their car on the street."

"I know people like that," said Hugo. Parker did, too, and agreed.

"The incident as I remember it is this: while we were standing in the living room, this guy wanted to see my brother's firearms. Now, as far as I knew he'd never met my brother and had never been inside the house. And the door to the basement is located behind a closet off a hallway into the garage. Almost in the opposite direction from where it would be traditionally located – and where it was located until they enlarged their basement a year ago and then moved the firearms to their new basement. Not readily apparent, you see, is what I'm trying to say. But, you know what? He walked right to it."

Parker couldn't shake the feeling that he should know this phony state cop. No reason why, he thought, but it was nibbling on the edge of his consciousness. "What did you do, Hal, when he started for the cellar door?" asked Hugo.

"I told him to stop. He didn't seem like the type to obey anybody, but he stopped, which surprised me. I walked up to him, angry because it looked to me like he was taking advantage of his position as a state cop. I told him to wait until the Shelburne Police got here, and I asked him for his name. But he was headed for the door and probably didn't hear me. I stayed in the house to wait for the local cops. When they arrived and came in, he wasn't with them. I didn't bring the matter up because I never thought of it until you asked me about him, Bill. Is this important, do you think?"

Parker felt like strangling Birdsall. The lack of detail in his information did not speak well of experienced and hard-bitten newshounds.

Gritting his teeth, Parker said, "Probably not, Hal." Hugo was looking at Parker and seeing his frustration.

"By the way, Bill, I've heard from Jan Evlin. Only by a phone message on my answering machine, but she's returning to work soon."

"That's great news, Hal. Is she okay? Has she been ill? Are her parents okay? Where's she been? Can I be of any help to her? I was beginning to worry, to be honest."

"I don't remember the details, Bill. She has a hell of a cold, and she was sneezing and blowing while leaving her message. I suspect that she's been under the weather. In fact, if you hit that red button on that infernal machine right next to your elbow, you can listen to it yourself. In the meantime, I'm heading for the latrine." And with that, Birdsall strode from the room.

Parker looked at Hugo, finger poised over the red button of the answering machine, and Hugo said, "What are you waiting for, Bill?" Parker, uncertain of what he might learn, jabbed at the button as if he were sending a rocket into space.

Jan's voice came out of the small speaker in a nasally, and rough-surfaced way. "Mr. Birdsall, this is Jan Evlin. Sorry I haven't contacted you before but I've been away, and sick at the same time. I'll be back in a few days, and then we can talk. Bye, bye."

When the message had ended, Parker just sat there, staring out a window.

Birdsall walked into the room at that moment. "Well, Bill, did you hear her message? I think things are okay now. And she's going to finish her article. Then I can get her back on her regular beat of Montpelier and Burlington, and other legislative efforts. I was a little concerned, to be honest, but things seem to be back in line now. She sure sounded sick, though, didn't she? She really sounded in bad shape. I'll be glad to see her when she walks through that door, I can tell you." Birdsall was rattling away non-stop, seeming to be afraid to stop. "Bill, what else can I do for you right now?"

With a lifeless voice Parker said, "I'd like to take this tape from your message machine with me, Hal, if that's all right with you. Just for a few days. Also, I'd like to borrow this envelope of material from your sister-in-law. I'll have that back to you in a week, or so, too." Parker felt as if the energy in his body had suddenly drained away. Like Vermont, in its own way, he thought.

"Fine, fine, Bill," proclaimed Birdsall. "Keep 'em as long as you like." He was really joyful now, Parker noticed.

Hugo took the ball this time. "Why are you so pleased, Hal? I don't even know this woman, but it was, at the least, a strange and awkward message."

"She's sick, Hugo, and it showed. Don't worry. I'll find out all when she returns."

Parker slowly rose to his feet. "I'm heading back to my motel, and then out on my midnight ride, like men of old. Good night, and thanks to both of you. I'll be in touch."

Parker walked down the back stairway from Birdsall's office and out to the street where his truck was parked. He was glad that Birdsall was so pleased.

32

Parker arrived at his motel, The Winterhaven, at a little after 10:00PM. It was in the north end of Burlington, on one of the more down-at-the-heel streets. The population of this area consisted of a few college students, low income housing residents, drug dealers, and undercover cops. He hung around the front of the motel in his truck for enough time to see if anyone he knew was coming and going and to check out the person behind the front desk. Based on the location and appearance of The Winterhaven, he was sure that this short-term living establishment wouldn't attract anyone who knew him, or anybody else of his acquaintance, for that matter. In other words, it was perfect for his purposes.

Parker got out of his truck and walked across the road to the motel. As he pushed open the entrance door, he could see that some temporary tenant had apparently not been happy with his accommodations and had put his fist, or something like it, through the large glass section of the door, which comprised about two thirds of the door's surface. Finding this sign of displeasure in the quality of the motel surprised Parker a little because that implied a clientele that was more demanding than he supposed. The only thing Parker had seen of a positive nature in this first thirty seconds of his arrival was that the broken glass in the door had been very neatly and precisely taped back into place.

No one was present behind the service counter when Parker looked in that direction. He spotted a buzzer on the wall by the entrance door and pushed on it. The door behind the counter slammed open and a man, small in stature, but making up for it by being as unkempt and messy as a man six and a half feet tall would be, slapped both palms on the counter and said, "Welcome to the Winterhaven, sir. What can I do for you?" This battler against clean sheets and towels had a stained name tag on his shirt that announced that he was known as "Chugger" to his friends.

Parker was about to ask for room rates, when the little man suddenly leaned forward and asked earnestly "You'd not be the law, would you, sir? Or the Governor's Commission on Women? I mean, you don't look it, you know, but today we in the motel business can't tell any more."

"What if I was a cop?" asked Parker.

As smooth as glass, the old guy said, "Different room rates, sir, for our friends in the law enforcement community."

"No, I'm not law enforcement," answered Parker, "but I know a lot of people in that line of work." That ploy was unsuccessful, Parker could see from the expression on Chugger's face. That look said that he had seen and heard it all.

"$29.99 each night, sir. Includes fresh towels and clean sheets at least once a week."

"That will be fine, Chugger, but I'd like a room away from the street. I've been on the road a long time and I need some sleep."

"Can do, sir, can do," cried Chugger. He turned the registration book around for Parker to sign, looked at Parker's name, then up to his face, squinting as if to sharpen his vision, and then said, "Cash before use, sir. That's $29.99, plus tax. Then you'll get the key, sir. Sorry to seem rude, sir, but there's a lot of bad people out there preying on honest businessmen like me. Hope you'll understand, sir."

The look Chugger gave Parker was one of recognition, Parker believed. On an impulse Parker asked, "Do you know me, Chugger? Have we ever met?"

Chugger looked intently at Parker for several seconds. "I have a hobby of keeping up with politics in this state, sir," he said carefully. "In this business it's important. Yes, I know who you are. You got shot in the Statehouse a few years ago. Right? A year ago I was also working part-time for a caterer. We had a contract to do the food at a stamp show a year ago, right downtown here in Burlington. You were there in the balcony, weren't you? You chased a guy out of the auditorium. He died that night, from what I read in the paper. You seem to attract bad company. That's why I want my money up front." He looked nervously at Parker.

Parker fished two twenties out of his wallet and handed them to this old sleazeball. My God, he thought, nobody else has put two and two together on all that mess of a year ago – until now.

"Chugger, I don't know what the hell you're talking about. I wasn't up here to see a stamp show. I've never collected stamps, or anything else, in my life."

Chugger looked at Parker keenly. “Okay, mister, okay. Let’s leave it at that.” He tossed the key to Parker and walked back to his inner sanctum.

Parker waited alone in the lobby of the motel for a few seconds, and then walked to the door behind the counter and shoved it open. Chugger looked up suddenly from his porno magazine. For an instant Parker thought he could see fear in his eyes. He hoped so.

Chugger popped to his feet. “Need anything else, sir?” he asked. He seemed nervous and hesitant.

“A few seconds ago, you said to me that we’d ‘leave it at that’. Correct?” Parker put on his most menacing face. Chugger mouthed a “yes”. “I suggest that we agree to that without question. Understood?” Chugger tried to speak, couldn’t, and nodded vigorously. Parker left.

He drove his pickup around to the back of the motel and parked at his room location. It was 11:00 at night. He had a couple of hours to kill before he departed for Underhill, never to return to this dismal place.

The room was everything he knew it would be. Musty, barely clean, and equipped with questionable linen, and inadequate lighting.

Parker took off his jacket and sat down on the bed. At the instant he hit it with his full weight, the phone rang. He jumped to his feet, thinking he’d triggered some kind of alarm. Then he picked up the receiver carefully, heard a muffled “click” on the line, and said, “Yes?”

“Bill, is that you?” asked Hugo.

Parker’s mind was racing. “Yes, and come on over. Room 19.” He hung up.

That muffled click he heard was a great big warning sign. Parker ran out the door and to the front of the motel. He stopped at the front door, pushed carefully on the door and stepped up to the front desk. Then quietly went to the door to the back, which was slightly ajar. He listened at the one inch space between the door edge and the jamb. He could hear the phone receiver being lifted off the cradle. Changing his position, he could see the phone and Chugger’s hand, hovering over the buttons. He was starting to punch in numbers.

Parker stepped quickly into the room and gently removed the receiver from Chugger's nerveless fingers and disconnected the phone.

"Who were you calling, you son-of-a-bitch?" rasped Parker. "Especially at this hour, and right after you just listened to my caller and me talk briefly. Better tell me now, Chugger. I'm not going to wait around for your answer."

Chugger looked panicked. He's not half as panicked as I am, thought Parker. "A friend," he answered sullenly.

"Chugger, you'll call no more 'friends'. You've made your last call to 'friends'. That all stops now. I have another question for you, too."

Menacing look once again.

"What if I had stayed in another motel? Just picked another one at random. There's a lot of them in this county. An upscale motel. Not one like this. I wouldn't have faced a blackmailer like you, would I?"

Chugger looked up at Parker and managed a faint smile. "I don't know this for a fact, Mr. Parker, but I think the odds are that you would have been spotted at many motels in this county. I don't know how many."

Parker was aghast. "What makes you say that, Chugger?"

Chugger seemed to become more confident. "My three kids work in three other motels in the Burlington area. That's why I'm living here, in fact. This kind of work is all any of us have ever known. Not in the nicer motels, though. We couldn't get work in those places. Ones like this, or better, up to fairly decent places. Those are the places where the people go who want to hide away for a night. Just like you, Mr. Parker."

He smiled again at Parker. It looked like an attack of indigestion had hit Chugger when he tried to perform this feat.

"My kids tell me that many of them have an arrangement to report arrivals to somebody, they don't know who. No, I'd say that you would probably have been seen, Mr. Parker."

Parker moved toward Chugger, with a look of fury on his face. He didn't have to act for the effect. "I want all the details, Chugger. Right now."

"Look, Mister Parker," he blurted, backing away from Parker and darting glances around the room as if he expected someone to be listening. "I have a deal, you see. With a guy who pays me a retainer, as he calls it, to report if some interesting people stay here that he should know about. He gives me a list of names every once in a while. When I got the new list just five days ago, I checked my guests against that list. I'm supposed to call him if someone on the list comes here."

"What if people use false names?"

"I told him that a lot of the people who stay here *do* use fake names. He said that that was okay. Couldn't be helped. He'd provide pictures when possible. Just do your best, and it had better be accurate, he said." Chugger looked sweaty.

"Who is this louse, Chugger? How often have you called him? What's the number? You see, I have to have this information. You'll give it to me, I'm sure." Parker tried his menacing look again. He felt stupid.

"I've called him about fifty times in the three years I've had this arrangement with him. The first dozen or so were false names, but I thought they were somebody I could identify, and I called. You, I knew right off."

"Who were you trying to call?" asked Parker, softly. "I need to know, Chugger." Menacing look trotted out again.

"I don't know his name, Mr. Parker. Honest. I got a note from him once in the mail – just before we started our arrangement. Signed with an 'N', Mr. Parker. He sends me $200.00 a month to keep me on his string."

Yes, I was right. Blackmail, thought Parker. Simple blackmail. Parker waited a few seconds, and then asked, "What's he got on you, Chugger? What does he know about you that causes you to provide this kind of service for a crumby $200.00 a month?"

Chugger looked as edgy as Parker felt. "He knew that I had a record. What I did was not pretty. I'm not an idiot. If it got out that I was here and where I'm located, it wouldn't be pleasant for me. Look, I've served my time, Mr. Parker. I'm not a crazy guy who can't leave crime alone. But this guy knew somehow that I was getting out of prison and where I was heading. So, after I took over this bankrupt motel for the loan payments, he called me. If I didn't help him, he'd tell the people in this area who I was and where I was working. People get really angry at people like I'm supposed to be. I'd never be able to work in Vermont again. So, I said okay. What else was I supposed to do?"

"Why would he call you and this crumby motel, Chugger? I mean who the hell would ever come here that was important enough to have secrets that this guy would want to know about? It doesn't make sense."

Chugger grinned tightly in a nasty sort of way. "You'd be surprised about who comes here, Mr. Parker. This is the last place anybody who is anybody would come to. Right?" Parker just watched and listened.

"Wrong," announced Chugger, in answer to his own question. "Some of the people who everybody thinks are the most high-minded come here to make deals, meet a woman or a man, or generally do things that they can't be connected to. I've never seen you here, though, since I've been here. Why is your name on my list?"

Parker just stared at Chugger. It was getting more and more difficult to keep the look of menace intact. "Don't ever ask that question again, Chugger – not of me or anyone else." Chugger nodded vigorously.

"I'm not, and I've never been here," Parker said. "But I want to have that phone number. And another thing, Chugger. You're going out of the dirty information trade. Right now. I mean immediate. Because if I hear anything negative that is attached to you after this day, and you can believe me when I say that I *will* hear, I'll come after you in any way I can. The only difference between this 'N' character and me is that once I've finished with what I'm doing, I'll drop out of your life. Your worries will be over – unless somebody else knows who and where you are and wants to make your life miserable. Personally, I want to wash my hands of you. You make me feel unclean. Phone number, please."

Chugger wrote it on a card and handed it over. "That's the number, Mr. Parker. You will get another number to call when you call this number. That other number changes pretty often, and so does this one. That second number puts you onto a voice mail account, and you simply speak your message. What do I do if he calls me and demands that I give him information?"

"Chugger, that is your problem. Now," Parker said sternly, "is there any kind of a phone code you have to give? You know what I mean. Some kind of a rite of passage? Another number when the phone is answered? I need to know that, too."

"Not from my end, Mr. Parker." Chugger was stiff with fear.

Parker turned and walked out, with a parting shot across the bow. "Just say that nobody has showed up. Remember, another phone call from you to this creep, and stuff is going to happen to you that you've never even dreamed of. Understand, you creep?" Chugger bobbed his head frantically.

Parker left, feeling that his acting was terrible and unconvincing.

When he got back to his room, Hugo was waiting for him. "Where the hell have you been, Bill?"

"Dealing with a real creep, Hugo. You don't want to know about it." Parker opened the door to his room and entered, followed by Hugo. Parker then cocked an eye at Hugo. "And why are you here?"

"Well, I felt a little guilty when I watched you decide, up in Birdsall's office, to take on the risk of this midnight escapade of yours. So I thought I'd help."

"I wouldn't call this an 'escapade', Hugo. I'm just going out to retrieve something that's probably mine, anyway."

"Bill, anybody who does something as simple as you just described it doesn't need to do it at midnight. I'm here to help."

"Does your wife know about this 'help' you're offering?" asked Parker.

Hugo grinned at Parker. "Does yours know about this brilliant plan of yours?" Parker was silent.

After a few seconds, Hugo said, "I didn't think so."

"You don't need to get involved, Hugo," said Parker, secretly pleased that Hugo was there. "If there is any trouble, which you know I don't expect, it's better that you stay clear."

"Bill, to be perfectly honest, I didn't even think about getting involved," said Hugo. "However, when we parted company in Hal's office, you'll remember that you left first. Right?"

"I guess so. What's the point?"

"I wasn't very far behind you – maybe a couple of minutes, at the most – but I left from the front door while you left from the servants' exit in the back. I could do that because all anybody has to do to leave that building is push on the door. Getting *in* is the problem for any nefarious people."

"Hugo, what the hell are you getting at?" crabbed Parker. He was tired and irritable, and his day wasn't anywhere near over yet.

"When I got to my car, I saw you and that truck leaving from the back entrance. When you turned into the street, another car, parked about four or five cars ahead of me, immediately started up and jumped on your tail. You were being followed, my good man, by a guy in a rented car from New York state. I hung around for a while, from a distance. Then I decided that you were in over your head and didn't have a clue about it."

Parker was stunned. "Followed? You mean followed, as in 'trailed'? How do you know? Are you experienced in this sort of thing?"

"My grandmother would agree with my assessment, and she's the kindest and most forgiving person I ever met. She never saw anything bad in anybody or in anything. Even she would have said that you were being tailed. Believe me."

Parker got to his feet. "Hugo, I have a story to tell you. I think you should know it because you're here. It's going to test you, because it's so outlandish, but it's real." Parker told Hugo what had happened to him at the motel. When he finished, Hugo simply stared at him, then lurched to his feet.

"What else does that tell you when you connect what I told you with this crazy tale of yours?"

Parker looked puzzled. Then he said, almost to himself, "Oh, my God almighty," he breathed. "Hugo, we have to leave. That SOB who followed me could be sitting out there, waiting for me to appear."

"You can depend on it, Billy boy. Why do you think I came here? You're very capable of taking care of yourself when the action is starting, if I can believe your buddy, Morgan, of the Montpelier PD - but totally incapable of realizing when you're up to your hips in alligators and about to become the main course."

"You know Peter Morgan?" asked Parker, incredulously.

"In my kind of work I get to know a lot of people, Bill. Especially in law enforcement. I've made it a point to find out who can help me or hurt me. I've read over the news reports of your exploits when that guy got knocked off in the Statehouse about three years ago. I concluded that you had to have had police help to do what you did, and Morgan seemed like the right person to talk to. I know him well enough to call him, so I did. He trusts me, and he told me about you."

Parker said, "You can't believe what he tells you, Hugo. He's a sensationalist. He should be writing novels. Now, let's get out of here."

"Not before we call on your friend, Chigger, Bill,"

"Chugger", offered Parker.

"Chigger, Chugger, whatever. He's got to be a first class bum, Bill. And because he *is* a bum, we're going to take your name off that motel register. Did you get a receipt?"

"No, he just pocketed the cash."

"That isn't a surprise, is it?" Hugo muttered. "Let's go," and shoved Parker through the door. "We'll walk to the front office, but up the opposite side from the one you used. There's got to be a door at that end of the motel. We'll go in through there. Surprise him again, in a manner of speaking."

Parker and Hugo moved silently through the dark, occasionally tripping on some piece of trash, apparently held for safekeeping in this unlit back lot. Hugo then gently stopped Parker and pointed at a back passage door, so loose and ill-fitting that the light from inside shone out around its edges. They might not have seen it, without this help offered by poor maintenance by the motel owner.

They slipped in to the storage room behind the office and slowly opened the door. Chugger was seated in a dilapidated stuffed chair, looking at his poor excuse for a magazine, totally absorbed. He became suddenly unabsorbed when Hugo snatched him out of his chair and clapped a hand over Chugger's mouth.

"My boss, here, Mr. Chigger, isn't sure of your loyalty. He's funny about things like that. We want to see your register of guests. His name is coming off your rolls. If you decide to play games with my boss, he won't come around. But I will. Where's the book, shitheels?"

Chugger couldn't gesture fast enough toward the desk. Hugo whipped Chugger over to the desk as he walked to the counter. He held on to him as he leafed through the register with his other hand to find the last page. He found it, checked that Parker's name was there, and simply tore the page out of the register, jamming it in his pocket. As Chugger began to make noises as if he was choking, Hugo shifted his grip so that Chugger absolutely *knew* that he was choking.

"Let's get out of here, Hugo," whispered Parker. "Our luck can't last much longer."

Hugo wasn't listening. He was looking at the previous days and weeks of registrations. Then he dragged Chugger, along with the book, over to the light, and shook him a little. Then he looked straight into motel manager's eyes and asked, not pleasantly, "where are the other copies of registers?"

Chugger was by now turning a ghastly shade of puce, but he wasn't too far gone to point toward a floor-level cabinet. Hugo dropped him on the floor, where he remained, quiet, motionless, and barely breathing, held in place by one of Hugo's feet across his throat. Hugo gestured to Parker to open the cabinet.

Parker went over to the cabinet and opened the door. There must have been fifty registers covering a number of years, standing on edge, apparently supported by a layer of dust so thick that a fiber mask would have been useful for health reasons. As Parker leaned forward to investigate one of the books, Hugo shoved him aside and quickly cleaned out the entire cabinet of registers. Hugo took half, and gestured to Parker to take the rest. Parker was going to protest, but one look at Hugo's face indicated that picking up the registers was a terrific idea.

Hugo moved over to Chugger and snatched him to his feet again. "One word, Chunker, to anyone, about tonight, and living to a ripe old age won't become one of your options. Get me?"

Chugger nodded rapidly and with enthusiasm. "Fine," said Hugo. "I'm sure we understand each other." He dropped Chugger again and moved through the door to the storeroom and then to the outside. The smell of the trash and garbage out there was bad, but the air seemed clear and fresh to Parker. They retraced their steps and arrived at their vehicles, winded and sweaty.

"What if he had hidden cameras?" asked Parker, as they stopped by their two vehicles.

Hugo looked with amazement at Parker. "Are you kidding, Bill? Cameras in that place? Come on. Even if he did have them, the dust would make everything into non-evidence. However, he didn't have cameras. I know something about security cameras. Trust me." Parker did.

"Hugo, I don't want you to get into any trouble, so don't go with me when I visit Hugh Hammond's home in Underhill tonight and pick up my property."

"You're still going to go? You're an idiot."

"Maybe, but this has to get done, and delaying it won't make it any easier."

Hugo looked at Parker for what seemed to Parker as a long time. Then he nodded, as if to himself, and said, "I'm going with you, Bill."

"Why do you want to, Hugo? I can deal with this without you."

Hugo, in exasperation, said, "I think you can, too, Bill, as long as nothing surprises you. But I'm not sure that this midnight requisition plan of yours is as simple as you may think. A lot can go wrong, you know. And I know this, too," he said. "I'm going with you because I won't sleep at all anyway while I know that you are stumbling around in the dark. And there's another reason, too," he said, his expression and voice altered by what seemed embarrassment. "I kind of like you, Parker, difficult as it may be for you to understand."

Parker took a few seconds to take in that sentiment. Then he said, "Let's get going, Hugo. And what about that guy who is probably out front, somewhere, waiting for me?"

Hugo looked around the trash-littered expanse of the back lot of the Winterhaven. Parker followed his gaze, and then began to look more closely at the board fence that shielded the Winterhaven from the prying eyes of its neighbors, if anyone back there cared. He walked over to the fence and saw a car-width double door let into the fence. It was difficult to see in the dark, and the only sign that something was different about that section of fence was its sagging outline, shown up in relief by a streetlamp behind it. He checked the middle of the two doors and found a padlock hanging on a clasp. He grabbed the padlock and pulled. The metal closure came away in his hand, wood having rotted away by years of inattention. He pushed on the two doors and, screeching a protest, they swung open to reveal an alley that was open to the next street, about half a block away.

"This is the way out for us, Hugo. Let's go. We can head straight to Underhill, retrieve my property, and get out of there, no one being the wiser."

"Forget that crap, Bill. We're going to my house first, drop off your truck, and then the both of us will go to Underhill in my business van."

"I don't understand why you should expose your presence in that way, Hugo. My pickup wouldn't be noticed in the rural charms of Underhill. There are a lot of them there. I'd just fit right in."

"Bill," said Hugo, showing real frustration with Parker, "how long has it been since you were in Underhill?"

Parker sensed that he was about to receive another lesson. "About ten years, during daylight hours. I went to Hammond's house one night about three years ago. Didn't see much, but I could tell it was rural, where he lived."

"Underhill," stated Hugo, "is now an upscale rural town. All the natives have been squeezed out by the well-to-do computer generation. There are SUVs everywhere, even though the owners of many of them tell us that they are dangerous and use too much fuel. Another large part of the Underhill population drives pick-ups as a second vehicle, but not like yours. Your pickup would not only be noticed because it isn't leading edge and modernized with all the flimflam of the computer age, but because almost everybody in Vermont knows that truck of yours." Parker blinked at the meaning of what Hugo was saying.

"Don't you remember the newspaper article about you after you leaked blood on the carpet of the House Chamber?" asked Hugo.

"'Man of the People' was one headline I read during my recent trek through the history of William Parker. 'Drives an old pickup everywhere' another said. What crap. Pictures of that old wreck of yours were in anything that printed words for public consumption, for God's sake. And those pictures, cut out of the local papers three years ago, are still hanging on walls of diners, service stations, and rod and gun clubs around Vermont. You are remembered by people all over this state, Bill – primarily because of the unique way you debated on the Vermont House floor that day." Hugo was making his point, and it completely surprised Parker. He had no idea that he was remembered by anybody. Except Addie, of course.

"And you want to take that truck into Underhill, thinking you would fit right in. Hell, a Constable in Underhill would pick you out when it was pitch dark before you got a mile across the line."

Parker was figuratively reeling from this attack on his pre-conceived notions. He decided to change the subject.

"Won't your wife be upset by your connection to me and what I want to do?"

Hugo looked once again at Parker with that baleful look of the loyal old hound dog who can't believe that his master is so damned dumb. "Didn't you listen when I described my wife to you, Bill? She's bright, determined, and brave. She scares the living hell out of me because of her commitment to things in which she believes. The only reason she wouldn't go with us tonight is because she couldn't find a babysitter in time."

"Okay, okay, Hugo," Parker cried, lifting his hands in submission. "I'm glad to have your help. Honest. By the way, how much does your wife know about all this?"

"She only knows that I've met you, and she knows who you are. For some inexplicable reason, she's looking forward to meeting you."

"Well," said Parker, "we'd better get going. We've stayed here longer than smart people would have. You lead the way, Hugo, and let's be as quiet as we can – you know, no speeding away with screeching tires, and that sort of thing. If there are any neighbors who would notice it, let's let them sleep in ignorance tonight."

Parker walked over to the room, unlocked the door, and tossed the key inside. Pulling the door closed, he turned and walked to his truck. "You first, Hugo."

They drove slowly out of the back area of the motel. As soon as Parker was through the opening in the fence, he stopped his truck, got out, and walked back to the rotting doors and pushed them shut. With that simple act he felt that he had closed out something old, useless, spoiled, and rotten – a place, like this motel, used by people who had chosen never to contribute anything to the world of which they were a part - no matter how attractive they looked, how well they spoke, how accomplished they seemed, and how compassionate they appeared. They were running on intellectual and ethical "empty" and, as long as they could control the citizens of Vermont, they would continue to control the legislature and its institutions.

33

Hugo Barkley and his wife lived in South Burlington. Their home, completed about fifteen years before, was in one of the former farm areas. During that time, a person could strike a deal with the farm family for more than a quarter acre on which to build. The Barkleys had about two acres, located on the height of land. They could actually see Lake Champlain on a clear day. The Everance family, farmers for generations, had been good people to deal with.

Time had been kind to the ground where about twenty-five homes had been built. The trees and shrubs had grown rapidly and undisturbed in that rich soil, giving their neighborhood the appearance that it had been in place twice as long as it actually had.

Even though it was dark when they pulled in to Hugo's place, the headlights of their vehicles showed off the homes very well. Hugo had done well for himself, thought Parker. God bless him.

Hugo had parked just off the street in front of his house and stepped out of his car as Parker pulled up beside him. In a low voice, he said, "Pull that truck of yours out behind that three-car garage standing off to the left of the main house. Be as quiet as you can, if that truck of yours is capable of it, so my wife won't wake up."

Parker nodded and crawled into the driveway and out behind the garage. With the bushes and trees surrounding the house, his car would be almost invisible.

While Parker was doing this required task, Hugo had driven his car into an open bay in the garage. Then, as Parker was walking out to the front of the garage, Hugo backed out of another stall a black, windowless, van. The magnetic signs on its two sides read, "Barkley, Barkley, and Barkley, Inc., Security Systems and Full Time Support", followed by his address, phone number, and web site information.

“Wow, Hugo, pretty impressive stuff. Who are all the other Barkleys. Members of the Board?”

“Not yet, Bill. they’re not old enough. But they will, in time and with some luck, be running the company someday.”

“Does that mean that all the Barkleys, needed to fill these slots, are not with us yet?” asked Parker.

“Yessir, but they’ll be along.” He smiled at Parker. “Now, let us be on our way.”

At the careful speed Hugo was driving, the trip to Underhill Center took about 45 minutes. Parker, impatient in the extreme, knew that it couldn’t be more than a dozen miles to the village, and another mile to Hammond’s deserted house. It took a lifetime to cover that ground.

Hammond’s wife had died three years ago, Parker remembered. That was the only time he had visited Hammond’s home, but he could still recall the location.

While they trundled along, as Parker would have described it, his itchiness grew. “Hugo, for goodness sakes, can’t we get a move on? My truck would have been there by now.”

“And so would the local police, Bill. No, we’re doing just fine.” He drove steadily, ploddingly, Parker thought, onward.

They crossed the line into Underhill at nearly 2:00AM. “Do you know where the hell we’re going?” asked Hugo.

“Of course I do, Hugo,” said Parker. “We’re looking for a road off to the right, and not too far from here. Don’t you have any confidence in me?”

“Frankly, no, Bill, I don’t,” said Hugo. “Anyone, all alone, who would take on a job like this, doesn’t rate any confidence being bestowed on them.”

They continued on the local road, heading toward Underhill Center. Suddenly, Parker yelled, “Here it is, Hugo! Turn right.”

Hugo jammed on the brakes, causing the van to shudder to a halt.

Hugo put his forehead down on the top of the steering wheel, and gripping the wheel in a death grip, said, “If anybody is paying any attention at all in this burg, they’ll know we’ve arrived. How about some kind of warning next time?”

Parker wasn’t paying any attention. “Yes, this definitely is it, Hugo. Head right up there. Let’s get this over with.”

"I don't think we'll do that, Bill. Let's do a little scouting around first. Are there any turns into the woods off this road? Somewhere we can stash this van, out of sight?"

Parker shrugged. "I've only been here once, Hugo. Be happy that I found the driveway."

"Oh, good," Hugo muttered sarcastically.

They drove, at moderate speed for another quarter of a mile. A 'hmmmm' from Hugo got Parker's attention, and then suddenly Hugo turned off to the left and down a slight pitch to what seemed to be an old log landing. But it couldn't be a log landing, could it, thought Parker? None of the people in this town would allow anything made of steel, with an engine attached, and with sharp teeth, anywhere near a tree. However, the secondary growth did a fine job of hiding a black van.

They clambered out of the van, shutting the doors quietly, and stood still for a moment while their eyes adjusted to the dark.

They were wearing dark clothing and Parker felt like one of the Brit commandos on D-day – forgetting for the moment that he was a slightly out-of-shape insurance salesman from a little town nobody had ever heard of.

"Let's go," he whispered, and started toward the road.

After looking both ways, they quickly crossed it, then trotted along the road edge to a point where they knew that the driveway entrance was only a short distance ahead.

Before they reached the drive up to the Hammond house, they found another drive. This one led to Hammond's neighbor's house. It was set back from the road about 200 feet, and the lights were blazing, even at this hour in the morning.

It seemed to be one of those new places, with glass, sun rooms, multi-vehicle garages, and 8 bedrooms. All in all, a house that a town Lister loves. And the admirers of the statewide property tax were not far behind them. More loot for Montpelier. The main point of interest, however, was a sedan parked at the edge of the climbing driveway to the house.

"What do you think, Bill?" asked Hugo. "Is this an indicator that a bad guy has preceded us to Hammond's?"

"I don't think so, Hugo. It's parked close enough to this house to make me think it's simply an innocent person who arrived home and parked before he got to the house. And it's not hidden at all. Just parked where anybody can see it. No, I don't think we have to be concerned about it. Besides, if a criminal type was checking the house for midnight visits from me, he'd have put it away. Also, how would he know that I'd visit Hammond's at all? In fact, nobody would know."

Hugo appeared to be thinking long and hard.

"How do we know what Hammond told his killer before he was murdered?" he asked. "He may very well have told the killer the same thing he told you. That there was information in the barn and here's where it is. People do strange things when they're threatened, you know."

Parker knew that Hugo was right, but in this case, the killer would not have delayed.

"If the killer got the same information from Hugh that he gave me," said Parker, "he'd have moved the night of Hammond's death. He would have already been here, grabbed the stuff, and disappeared."

"I agree, Bill. However," and he pointed toward the barn, seeming to lurk in the back-lit gloom up ahead of them, "if Hammond decided that he'd tell the killer that the information was in the barn, but gave him the wrong place to find it, then the killer would have to follow you around until you led him to it. A cow barn is a big place. And he's been following you, I think. Just like tonight. If this crank decides to commit mayhem, this is the perfect place to do it."

"Then we'll just be damn careful, Hugo – and quiet."

They went into the woods, heading toward the Hammond place. The moonlight gave them enough illumination when they were on the road edge. In the woods, however, it was a different story. They used a mini-beam light to allow them to move.

"Bill, let's understand what we may be walking into. I'm assuming that that 'somebody' is watching for an intruder to arrive."

"How do you know that somebody has been watching, Hugo? I could have been coming here for any reason and at any time of day since Hammond was murdered."

"How do I know? The simple answer is that I don't. But I'd bet a hefty sum that I'm close to being right." Hugo looked at Parker, and said, "And another thing I've discovered, Bill. And that's that the rural charms of Underhill have slipped downhill, in my estimation."

Parker thought about the word "rural". That neighbor's house was only 200 yards away. Parker decided that this qualified as rural to former city dwellers.

"Maybe this car does belong to that house in that direction," Parker said, pointing back to where they had come from. "But I'll humor you, Hugo. We have to keep going. As you said, we'll just be damn careful and quiet. I don't want any surprises." Hugo agreed.

"Let's disable the car," Hugo said.

"No, leave it. We're not in any position to deal with the outcome of that action." Parker was thinking of a similar act a year ago. It resulted in a memory that wouldn't completely go away. And he'd found another weakness in the Bill Parker he used to know.

Hugo looked quizzically at Parker for a moment, then nodded, and turned toward the Hammond place.

As they approached the house, which seemed to suddenly appear before them like Dracula's castle, Parker whispered, "Let's keep away from the house. We'll stay in the woods and head straight for the barn, pick up my stuff, and depart."

"One question, Bill, before we get to the barn. Do you have the keys?"

Parker looked at Hugo for a few seconds. "A locked cow barn? They don't exist, Hugo."

"Yeah, but this one hasn't had a cow in it for a good many years, I'd bet. City dwellers put locks on everything they own, no matter where they are."

Parker said, "Yes, that's right, Hugo. But cow barns are things I know something about. There is always a way into a cow barn. And I know them all."

34

Parker moved as silently as he could through the dark. The barn seemed to loom up in front of them like an ancient fortress accented by the moonlit sky. Hugo followed right behind him, exhibiting that same sort of speed and smoothness that he exhibited in Birdsall's office when they found the listening device. Parker found this unusual for a man of his size.

He headed to a small attached building on the eastern side of the barn which Parker believed was the milk house. This would probably have windows in it if the door was barred.

But the door wasn't barred. In fact, it was ajar, which, under normal circumstances, probably wouldn't be unusual. Tonight, however, with senses humming and nerves pulled tight, the position of the door was of great interest to Parker. He gestured to Hugo to take notice of this door. Hugo got down on his hands and knees and, after looking over the entire circumference of the door frame, using his mini-light, looked carefully at the top corner of the door and its frame.

"I think there's somebody who has very recently been in this barn," Hugo whispered, "but I can't determine exactly when. Just very recently. Not knowing the habits of spiders very well, I can't be sure."

Parker looked at Hugo in the faint light. "The habits of spiders? What the hell does that mean?" he rasped.

"This barn spider, up here in the corner of the door frame, is busy rebuilding his web. See him?" He gestured toward the upper corner of the frame on the opening side. A large brown-black spider was rushing around and working hard.

"Oh," said Parker, worriedly, "I see what you mean. You feel that there could have been somebody here before us. Right?"

Barn spiders and his days on the Windham County family farm came back to him. He remembered them, all right. And spiders were pretty handy to have around in a barn, too.

Hugo nodded, and said, "The key question is how long ago that someone was here. I'll bet not very long ago."

"Hugo, I think that right now somebody could be in this barn, waiting for us, or somebody, anyway, to come calling. I'm changing my mind about that car. Now I'm guessing that the vehicle we found in the woods on our way in here tonight is the wheels for the early visitor."

Parker sometimes wondered if he had lost his wits, finding himself squatting in the dark in an old retired cow barn in rural Vermont, with a youngish man whom he didn't know very well or for very long. This was one of those times. He knew he was too old, too set in his ways, and too easygoing to be here. He should be home with Addie, and the greatest crisis in his life should be the decision of where he should go fishing in the morning.

"Hugo, do you know of the children's book called 'Charlotte's Web'?" Parker wheezed.

"You mean the book about the spider and the pig?" he asked. Parker nodded.

"Sure I do. My mother used to read that book to me when I was a little kid. My wife and I have read it to our kids. Why?"

"When did the spider do all her work making webs that could be read in the morning?"

"At night, Bill, of course. What's on your mind, anyway?"

"I think we can rely on the accuracy of 'Charlotte's Web', don't you? That being the case, here's what I think. Someone has been here just tonight, and came this way to get into the barn. On the way in, this person disturbed this barn spider, and this little guy, or big guy in the world of spiders, just told us that we are the second visitor today, and we are breaking up his web, and he's not happy about it."

Hugo looked at Parker in the dim illumination of the tiny flashlight. "Do you charge money for reading the minds of spiders, Bill? Don't get carried away, for God's sake."

"Here's what I think, and I'm not an alarmist," Parker said quietly, without seeming to hear Hugo's comment. "It's as I said a minute ago. This intruder is still in there," Parker said, gesturing toward the door. "Maybe he's waiting for us, or maybe we'll surprise him in the act of something. I don't care. I want to know who it is."

Hugo stared at Parker. This was a man he hadn't met before - the Bill Parker that Peter Morgan had described was now very clear. He was a warrior, and warriors took on challenges the ending of which they couldn't know. Hugo knew they were a rare breed. In some ways he was glad he wasn't one of them.

"I wouldn't be so curious if I was alone, I can tell you that, Hugo," said Parker, in a low voice, "but your presence makes a big difference to me." Hugo now wasn't so sure that Parker would have hesitated even if he had been alone.

"Well, Bill," he whispered, "let's go inside and see what surprises are waiting for us. I hope this damn door is a non-squeaker."

35

It was. When pushed open it slithered silently.

"That's one quiet old door, Bill," Hugo muttered. Using his tiny light for guidance, he murmured quietly as he gave a close examination to the old door and its hinges.

"I don't know about all the other doors in this barn, but somebody has very recently chosen these hinges for heavy lubrication. Look at the floor under the inner edge of this door."

Parker could see that the floor actually glistened with some form of lubricant, and that the amount used was far and away in excess of the amount needed. "He was going to make sure that the hinges were quiet, and would make no sound, wasn't he? That means that he decided that he must be able to come and go through this door without warning anybody that he was here." Hugo nodded, grimly.

They stepped into the barn and froze just inside the door. Parker listened as if it was the only thing he was born to do. Complete silence. Nothing could be heard.

The interior of an old barn is unique in its feel and atmosphere. Having no source of natural light, the sounds, or lack of them in this old building, became the focal point of the mind. The imagination runs wild, helped by the odor accumulated over 100 years, never to be eradicated. Parker was almost afraid to snap on his tiny flashlight for fear that the ghosts of many years would suddenly appear, changing quiet into chaos. He then cursed himself for too much imagination. It will weaken a man.

After about two minutes of standing still, making no sound, Parker knew they had to move. He remembered his military training at the strangest times. Although it was well over thirty years ago, one thing that invaded his mind was that a person could freeze through uncertainty. The instruction he had received before traveling to Vietnam insisted that a man be aware of this dangerous lack of action and that the solution was to force himself to move – to do something - anything.

He could feel Hugo standing close to him, his breath coming rapidly. Parker forced his arm up and snapped on his flashlight.

He gasped and recoiled from the objects that confronted him. The barn was full of silent people, staring at him, but not moving.

Hugo said "Christ," in a yelp, and ducked down. Parker snapped off the light, grabbed Hugo by the arm, and moved quickly toward the center of the barn.

Once again standing stiffly and quietly, Parker whispered to Hugo, "Be quiet and be ready. I'm turning on my light again."

Hugo said nothing, and Parker, without waiting, snapped on the light, and shone it at the side of the barn through which they entered. Same ghostly figures. Same lack of movement. Then Parker saw what they were and laughed quietly and felt Hugo do the same. The entire side of the barn contained mannequins. Clothing dummies, for God sake, he thought. So many he couldn't even estimate the number. They were everywhere in the huge main floor space of this old barn. They were the remains of the estate and business of Hammond's wife. Parker felt ridiculous.

Hugo expelled his breath in a raspy swoosh and whispered, "This setup scared the living hell out of me. What's this exhibit all about, anyway?"

"Hammond's wife was in the women's clothing business," Parker whispered. "The last thing I expected was that her business equipment would still be around to haunt friends of her husband."

Hugo stood up to his full height, looking around the interior of the barn, his eyes following the small beam of his light.

"Okay," he said, with a breathy voice, "where is this carton or box that was left for you? Let's get it and disappear from here. Let's also hope that there's no one here looking at us. I haven't heard a sound. Have you?"

Parker shook his head as he began to move his light toward the horizontal ceiling beams while he walked back toward the main entrance doors of the barn. "Hammond told me to look for a horizontal support beam 'where the upper floor ends', as he described it. Directly below the center of that beam we'll find the box. I'm pretty sure I got his instructions correct."

"If that's the case," said Hugo, "then you're walking in the wrong direction. The floor ends just a couple of beams this way," and he pointed his light in the opposite direction and up at beams and the floor they supported. This upper floor ended at one of these supports.

Parker retraced his steps and stopped under the edge of the partial floor. “The floor up there probably rotted out over the years from the storage of hay. Tells you why hay has to be really dry, and not what somebody hopes is dry enough. Of course there are other problems, too, that wet hay can give a farmer.”

“Well, here’s the end of that upper floor,” said Hugo, gazing after his weak shaft of light. “And here’s about the center of it. And I don’t need a lecture on spontaneous combustion, either. Let’s get going. I’ve never been in a spookier place in my life.”

Parker swept away the little bits of debris, old hay and dirt that was on the floor, revealing a sort of trapdoor. It was about two feet square. It showed no sign of hinges, and the edges were faint and tight-fitting. It was evident to Parker that someone had taken the time to make certain that this section of floor would not be noticed by just a casual glance. He stood up, stretched, and shone his beam up to the floor above, checking his location. As he did, he saw a flash of a movement and a creak that gave him an instant chill.

He yelled, “move!” and slammed into Hugo, pushing him away from the trapdoor in the floor. As they both hit the barn decking, Parker yelled, “Roll, for God’s sake, roll away!”

A large object hit the floor with a huge, slamming, BOOM, bounced once, grazing Parker’s shoulder and back as it went by him, then fell back on its side with another solid whamming sound.

Parker lay on his back, stunned by the sudden calamitous change from silence into chaos. He heard Hugo move.

“You okay?” wheezed Parker.

No sound for a few seconds, and then Hugo said, “Parker, you son-of-a-bitch. A quick trip in, pick up your stuff, and a quick exit. Remind me never to listen to you again.” Parker could hear him rolling over. Then he asked, “You all right, Bill?”

“I think so,” whispered Parker.

“What the hell was that thing, Bill? It sounded like it could have squished us both like bugs.”

At that moment, they both heard the rapid scraping of muffled footsteps on the floor above, and then, in a corner of the barn, coming down to the main floor.

“Get to your feet, quick,” urged Parker as he struggled to do the same. “Let’s get that bastard!”

The stairs were located in a corner of the barn on the same wall as the milk house entry door, and someone was rapidly moving along the wall, obviously heading for the way out.

"After him," shouted Hugo, and he started toward the exit door, driven by fear and, at the same time, a towering fury. Parker was behind him when a rumbling sound started rolling along the barn floor like a drum concert – first the snares, then the marching band drums, graduating into the full-voiced and deep crescendo of the bass section.

What the hell was happening, Parker asked himself? And then he saw the answer. The damn clothing dummies were falling over, he thought, and they were creating a domino effect like nothing else could. And the sound they made became deafening as they fell.

There must have been a dozen rows of dummies paralleling the long wall of the barn, and there were probably fifty dummies in each row – and they were all falling over, and right in their way. Hugo blasted into this maelstrom like a defensive tackle.

The dummies started to hinder him when he was about halfway through the defensive shield created by the women's clothing industry, and finally he fell sprawling, plowing naked mannequins, and their various body parts, in all directions. Parker, behind him, couldn't stop his forward motion, and he fell on top of Hugo, knocking the wind out of them both. They were struggling to their feet, tossing dummies aside, when they heard the closing thump of the door. And then silence.

They stood up, shakily, and looked at the sea of naked ladies waiting for them to try running through them again. Hugo was limping noticeably as he tried to navigate out of the chaos.

"We're going no further, Bill. It wouldn't do any good anyway. He's got too much of a jump on us, and I can't run." He was rubbing his lower left leg. He looked around with his small light. "Let's see what the hell it was that fell from the heavens. And then we're out of here."

"I can't find my damn flashlight," groused Parker. "It's got to be in this mess somewhere." His back felt as if he had broken it. "Have you still got yours?"

"Better than that," Hugo said. "I almost forgot I had it." With that, he reached into one of the deep pockets of his stylized urban barn coat and withdrew a small flashlight, and snapped it on. The illumination put out by this industrial strength light was incredible, and even more so by its comparison with the puny beams they had started with.

"Good Lord, Hugo, that's some lamp."

"Never leave home without it, Bill," he said, still whispering. "Useful in my work, you see."

They limped back through the grasping arms of the naked women, finally reaching open space, and Hugo swung the light around to the object that had scared the bejeezus out of them.

"Wow," breathed Hugo, when he saw the object. It was a 275-gallon oil drum of the type used in homes for heating oil.

"That could have done us in, old buddy," he said.

Parker was looking at the tank, studying it, and then bent over and tried to lift it. He couldn't, although he was able to shift it slightly. He turned and looked at Hugo. "Hugo, my friend, let's get my stuff that Hammond left me from under the floor and, with a slight delay for something else, get out of here."

Hugo was already prying up one edge of the trapdoor with another appropriate tool, this time a folding pinch bar, dug from his magic coat of tricks. Suddenly the section of floor popped up and was in his hands. He set it down and went down to his knees and looked into the hole it left. He shone his lamp around. "I don't see anything, Bill," he said, his voice showing some anxiety. "Not a damned thing."

Parker had a sinking feeling as he moved over to the hole and followed the light beam around. All he could see was the underpinnings of an ancient old barn. "Oh, man," he said quietly, "what's going on here?" Suddenly he walked to the edge of the hole in the floor. "Give me a hand, Hugo. I want to look around down there for a minute."

Parker was down under the floor of the barn with Hugo's powerful light, streaks of illumination showing up through the cracks in the floor. His back was killing him. After a few seconds he came up to the hole and stood up, just his head showing.

"Hugo, I don't get it. I was so certain of this cache of Hammond's. Do you think that that bird who tried to end our days got here first?"

Hugo thought for a few seconds, and then said, "No, Bill. He was waiting for us, or somebody, to come along. Remember that his car was cold, which means it had been there quite a while. If he had already gotten his hands on whatever this stuff turns out to be, he'd be long gone, as you said. And he'd never have tried to do us in. He'd just wait until we were gone."

Parker nodded grimly. "Well, help me out of this hole and we'll get out of here. We've already been around too long."

As Parker turned toward Hugo for a hand up, he stopped and reached for the trap door, lying close by the edge of the floor opening. He flipped it over onto its back. "Well, well, what do you know, Hugo, me lad? Give me some light, Watson, and I'll reveal all."

Hugo looked at Parker as if Parker had lost his damn mind. "What in the world are you – ?" and he stopped, seeing what Parker had seen. It was a thin, flat plastic container about two feet square and about an inch thick. It had been painstakingly handmade, no doubt by Hammond, for a very special purpose. It was attached to the underside of the trap door by metal clips on the corners, also handmade.

"Sorry, Bill," he said. "I had the loot right in my hands and never looked it over."

"We both almost missed this, Hugo," said Parker. "And now, do you have one of those magical things you use in your work called a screwdriver? And if you do, would you kindly take this cover off the underside of this trapdoor?"

Hugo couldn't believe Parker could suddenly be almost jaunty. His evening had included a nerve-wracking expedition at two in the morning to an old barn, then almost being killed by some weirdo, and being scared out of his wits while all of this was going on. Or at least Hugo knew he was damned well scared. He wasn't so sure about Parker anymore. Parker could keep his head. Hugo had learned that much about him.

"Hugo, while you're doing that, let me borrow your light. I want to go upstairs for a brief visit to see what I can see, said the great seer."

With that, Parker bounded away, if you could describe it that way in Parker's case, and disappeared from view, kicking the naked ladies out of the way. Hugo marveled at the new Parker. His bad back was obviously forgotten.

When Parker arrived at the upper floor of the barn, he went immediately to the edge of the floor that was over the trapdoor. What he saw was not really what he expected. Parker thought he might find something that would help identify the man who had tried to kill them. He found nothing like that.

He did, however, find that there were a few other objects up there that could have done the job on them, too. There were all kinds of store furniture that would have been adequate to the task. The display cases could have been really good at killing people from a height, Parker thought, and they were all lined up close to the edge of the floor, too. And then it hit him that the killer couldn't know where Parker and Hugo would be. But somehow he must have known that they were going to be under this floor edge at some point, and therefore within range of these lethal weapons from the ladies' clothing business.

It was a clumsy idea on how to kill somebody, but if he hadn't expected two people he would have had another way to kill somebody alone. I guess he was desperate to kill me but I showed up with a friend. Damn glad of it, too, he said to himself with a feeling of reverence.

But why would these heavy objects be on an upper floor of the barn? Nobody in their right mind would go to the trouble of hoisting these big objects up and setting them in place where some sort of crazy accident or occurrence might cause them to fall off the edge of this partial floor. As he was letting his mind chew on that line of reasoning he was shining that powerful light of Hugo's around the floor. There were only small things stored in the rest of the space. All the heavy stuff was here where it had no business being.

He looked up where the light shone and suddenly he had his answer. Coming from two old hay hooks in the dead center of the barn roof was a steel beam and on this beam was an electric hoist, complete with chain and various kinds of belts and wires that would allow a person easily to lift anything from down below and place it up on this level. And all with just pressing a button on the remote controller that hung down to floor level. If I hadn't looked up, Parker thought, I'd have missed all this.

Parker gave the space a quick once-over before heading down to Hugo. "Hugo, we're out of here right now."

Hugo knew that Parker was now concerned about something, and Hugo had no desire to know what it was until they were well away from this Vermont example of Transylvania. He also knew that the Secretary of Tourism, and whatever else they called it, would be very upset with his comparison.

36

Hugo and Parker got back to Hugo's house in South Burlington at 5:00 in the morning. As they turned into the driveway Hugo muttered, "Oh, crap."

"What's the problem, Hugo?" asked Parker.

"The light's on in the kitchen. That means that Connie is up and will demand an explanation of where I've been tonight."

Parker was puzzled. "Aren't these your normal work hours? Why would she question tonight in particular?"

"I told her I'd be home early because I was all caught up on work. Also, she might guess that I was with you, and that would worry her."

Parker was surprised at that remark. "What kind of a person do you think I am, Hugo?" Parker asked. "All I want to do is live my life and stay out of the way of troubles that are not of my making." Parker was irritated that anybody would believe any other description of him. Hugo made no answer.

As the van stopped in the driveway, Parker could see the figure of Hugo's wife silhouetted in the doorway, back-lighted to show her in the position of arms crossed and probably angry. Parker was an expert at identifying this type of wife behavior. He could almost see her toe tapping on the floor.

She opened the door for them, standing aside for Parker, who gave her a slight smile and entered. She didn't smile back.

Hugo gave her a hug, and said, "Honey, this is Bill Parker, a new friend and already a good one. Bill, this is Connie." He was gesturing between the two of them almost wildly, as if to hurry along their friendship. Parker guessed that Hugo could sense that his wife's acceptance of him was tepid, at best, especially at 4:00 in the morning.

"Did you have a nice reunion with your new friend, Hugo?" Without waiting for his reply, she said, witheringly, "How nice for you, dear. And how about you, Mr. Parker? Did you have a nice evening, too? No troubles? No close calls? Nobody shooting at you, eh?"

Connie Barkley was in her mid-to-late thirties and looked ten years younger than that. She was a strikingly beautiful woman with a bearing of confidence that would be intimidating to anyone who had any guilt in their heart at all. Parker knew this because he had plenty of guilt in his heart on this night.

"Connie, that's unfair, and you know it," said Hugo, firmly. "I helped Bill out after I'd finished my work for the night. That's all."

Hugo's wife looked at Parker. Then she walked over to him and placed a hand on his arm. "I apologize, Mr. Parker. My only excuse is that I took the time to visit the archives at our local library today. I carefully read the newspapers of the last three years. What that means is this: I've been reading about you. You've had an eventful life, haven't you?" There was no sarcasm in her demeanor, Parker could see. She just wanted him to know that she was somewhat acquainted with his public past, so don't try to fool her.

"Apology accepted, Connie, although I don't know that you owe me one. I know that if it hadn't been for me, he'd have been home much earlier. But," Parker said, with enthusiasm, "here he is." Parker's attempt at some ice-breaking humor drew not a wrinkle of a smile from Connie Barkley. She simply plowed right on into Parker's background.

"The papers very thoroughly covered your escapades in Montpelier of three years ago and your adventures in Burlington a year ago, Mr. Parker." It was as if she hadn't heard a word Parker had said. She smiled sweetly, and continued. "No, I didn't concentrate on that particular Montpelier adventure. I'm talking about the death of a Burlington lawyer in an auto accident up in the Islands."

Parker felt a sudden numbing. That bit of knowledge was the last thing he expected to come up. That episode still bothered him, and even more so since he had just learned that a bright person with an inquiring mind could put two and two together and not be too far from the truth. In fact, he had found out just seven hours earlier that even a weirdo motel operator could do it. Quietly Parker asked, "What makes you think that I was in any way involved with an auto accident in the northwest of Vermont?"

"Well," Connie said brightly, "when I looked up anything to do with your name in the archives, I found all that information about the death of a Vermont Representative and, of course, your name was everywhere."

Parker nodded. "That's to be expected, Connie. There were a few things my wife and I did for his widow. Except for one small incident, nothing too exciting."

Connie Barkley smiled broadly at Parker. "You bet, Mr. Parker. I'm sure you'll agree that enough of those 'small incidents' can hurt you. But that's not what I was talking about. When your name was being searched on Floogle – do you use the internet, Mr. Parker? – if you don't, you should - it also popped up in connection with a postage stamp show in Burlington. You were only mentioned twice. First, as an attendee to the stamp show. A reporter recognized you and thought it odd that you'd be ambling around at a stamp show. Secondly, as a person who was seen on the floor of the show when this lawyer I spoke about ran out the door. You were on his heels, I think. The next thing I read in the archives was that the lawyer was dead. No mention of you again."

"Connie, for God's sake," yelped Hugo, "that's enough!"

"That's all right, Hugo," said Parker. "You make it sound like I murdered this lawyer, Connie. We've all known some of that breed we'd like to have murdered, haven't we?" Parker looked knowingly at Connie. "I knew him from a previous association, but that's it."

"Let's talk about that whole thing, Mr. Parker, but later. Now, what do you both need right now?"

"At least a sandwich, honey, and some hot chocolate. Okay with you, Bill?"

"Perfect," said Parker.

"And then we'll talk about your evening together. I'm very interested."

Suddenly, Parker became wary. He pitied Hugo. He will be chewed out by his wife, which won't be pleasant to witness, and I will be made to look like a demented beast, he thought.

Hugo tried a tack that Parker had attempted in the past with Addie. On all occasions it was loudly unsuccessful. "Connie, we're totally whipped. We'll get a nap and then some breakfast and then well discuss our evening with you."

"Sleeping because you're tired, Hugo, is not going to happen for a while. And do you think that you're the only ones who didn't sleep? Personally, I'm exhausted, but I won't sleep until I know what you two were doing at midnight. Spill everything while I'm putting together a couple of sandwiches." With that she turned and headed into the kitchen. Dutifully, Hugo and Parker followed. Hugo looked at Parker and shrugged.

Parker dropped down into a padded chair in the corner of the kitchen and found that it was the most comfortable chair he'd ever known. He was completely frazzled, to the extent that he felt fuzzy. He hadn't gone this long without sleep in many years and his aging body was telling him all about it.

"Bill," Hugo said, "I've got to tell Connie most of this messy situation, from the beginning. It can't be avoided. I'll feel better, anyway, if I do." Parker nodded and gestured to Hugo to go ahead.

Connie looked up from her sandwich production line. "I want to hear *everything*, Hugo," she said firmly.

Hugo started his tale from his personal beginning in "Mickey's" restaurant and bar in Burlington, where he met with Birdsall and Parker. When he talked about the tapped phones, recorders, and the bank spy, Connie came over to the table and stood behind him to rub his shoulders and back. She looked distressed. Parker felt badly for her because he knew that what was coming next would be a real shock.

When Hugo told her about Hammond, and that he had been murdered, tears welled up in her eyes. "Oh, Hugo, my dear, this is all too big for my experience. You're talking about corruption, spying, and murder. And it's all true, isn't it? I mean really true. Going on right now. And you two are in the middle of it."

Parker sat up in his chair at that remark. "No, Connie, Hugo isn't in it, as far as I can tell. No one can identify him as being with me in tonight's goings-on. And when I slip out of here after breakfast, that will be the last contact between us, I promise."

Connie Barkley looked at Parker in astonishment. "You don't know us yet, do you, Mr. Parker?" she asked quietly. "You don't know what I went through in setting up our private school, do you? The VTUA and its pet legislators fought me at every turn when I was trying to start my educational facility. They brought in their high-priced lawyers. They told their legislators to halt me with action by the legislature. They brought in their bought-and-paid-for politicians to testify against any move like mine to remove students from the public school system. And all they did was lie, and quote the results from studies that had no integrity, written by people who had only an agenda but no knowledge. And I won, didn't I? And what all that means is that we're going to help you in any way we can." Hugo's expression was one of astonishment.

Parker smiled at this determined, bright, and committed lady. "And I'll bet that you still aren't very well liked by anybody in the brain-washed education industry in Vermont. Correct?"

Connie smiled. Parker decided right there and then that he never wanted a Connie-type smile like that directed at him. "They lost, Mr. Parker. I won. And there's another fifty schools being started in Vermont – all going through what I went through. The difference is that hundreds of public school teachers are lining up to help us."

"Really?" asked Parker. "Hundreds? Connie, I hope you're correct, but those teachers who are helping you are in for some rough treatment by the VTUA, you know. And by the subtle actions of the School Boards Group, not to mention the bureaucracy of the State Department of Education."

Connie Barkley straightened up and walked over to the window, looked out at the faint beginnings of the dawn streaking the dark sky. Then she turned back toward Parker. "Mr. Parker, now is the time to educate you about education."

It was at this point that Hugo spoke up. "Connie, for goodness sake, Mr. Parker is out on his feet. So am I, for that matter. Leave him alone."

"What do you think, Mr. Parker? Are you too far gone to listen. Or are you just being polite because I just made you a sandwich?"

Parker had come alive listening to this terrific young woman, and loving her commitment. "I'll never forgive you if you stop educating me, Connie. Keep rolling."

Hugo settled back in his chair and said to Parker, under his breath, "You asked for it, Parker." Connie didn't notice.

"Okay, here we go, Mr. Parker. I'll begin with one item. Most teachers who are the true educators – not the inadequate ones who are strewn through our systems – would love to go to a school where they could teach kids without the state bureaucrats and the politicians telling them what to teach and how to teach it. They want to respond to the parents' wishes. They *want* their students to be tested. Unbelievable, right? They all want to work with parents, showing these kids that they can have a wonderful life if they learn the basics. And parents who become involved in the education process become supporters of the school. And do you know why,

Mr. Parker?" Connie Barkley didn't stop for his answer. "Because they are being listened to, and points of view are shared, and from just that simple approach, the kids win." Parker decided that Connie Barkley would be a formidable opponent, regardless of the subject. She was wound up on this subject and was totally convincing.

"What about 'hundreds' of teachers, Connie? Do they exist?"

She nodded energetically. "Let me give you an example, Mr. Parker, but a big one. The St. Johnsbury Academy is a private school in the Northeast Kingdom. It's really the high school up there, too. I'm sure you know something about it." Parker nodded.

"Here's something I'll bet you don't know, though," Connie said. "The school has a waiting list of *six hundred* teachers for any teaching job that opens up."

Parker was astounded. "Six hundred, Connie? I've never seen anything in the news media about that. That would be a big story." Connie smiled faintly at Parker. "You're joking, aren't you, Mr. Parker? Our daily media are in the pocket of the VTUA."

"How about your school, Connie?" Parker asked. "Do you have a waiting list of teachers who want to teach there?"

Connie looked at Parker in triumph. "We presently have twelve full-time teachers, Mr. Parker and, at last count, 117 applications on file. Most of them read like a cry for help. They all want to teach where they are wanted. They want the school to care that they are there, because they care about the students. All of them seem to feel that their reward will not be a piece of paper issued by the VTUA or the Vermont Education Department. They all seem to be committed to developing students and knowing the parents."

"Connie, what you've told me bowls me over," said Parker. "The Legislature has a lot to answer for, doesn't it, for all of the unneeded mandates placed on schools that discourage the good teachers and give the poor teachers an excuse for the failure of their students. But we haven't seen the loss of pupils, have we? Even I, who haven't been in the General Assembly for over three years, would have heard about that. Of course, I haven't been paying a lot of attention, either, I admit."

"No, until three years ago, we hadn't. The combination of home schooling and people with kids moving away is now starting to be felt. And the legislature has been the cause. Whether or not these legislators know it, they started the destruction of the public school system themselves when they passed the statewide property tax in Act 60. You do remember that awful legislation, don't you? It authorized the state to raise taxes in about 50 towns in Vermont in order to pay the education costs of the other 200 towns. I guess it's called Act 68 now, and they had to raise taxes again to pass *that* version of a school funding measure." It all came back to Parker.

"Ah, you *do* remember, Mr. Parker," she said with enthusiasm. "The Legislature assumed that the public would just sit there and take it. All Socialists think that way, you know." Parker did know that piece of Legislative arrogance.

"However, they didn't, Mr. Parker. They didn't and they won't. The Legislature just shifted the taxes around. It was the only thing the present Governor could do. He could never win what he thought was needed with that terrible Senate we have. And this type of school funding is destroying the vitality of our towns, Mr. Parker, not just our schools."

Connie looked at her husband, who had drifted off to a fitful sleep. "First and last lesson for the day, Mr. Parker. My husband is in la-la land right now, and I'll bet you could use some shut-eye yourself. Just stretch out on that couch. I think a couple of hours will recharge your batteries enough so that you can get out there on the trail after the bad people." She smiled at him.

Parker smiled back.

"You know, Mr. Parker, I'm really glad Hugo brought you to the house this morning. He had told me that he'd met you, and since I remembered your name from three years ago, I wanted to meet you – you know, to see if you were real. I read that your wife – Addie, is it? – calls you Don Quixote. Is that true?" She was still smiling.

"Not really, Connie. She came up with that during my last term in the Vermont House. It referred to a couple of dumb things I did that didn't please her. Nothing more than that." Connie's smile broadened.

"Get some sleep, Mr. Parker. I won't let you stay out too long."

37

Hugo gently shook Parker's shoulder. It didn't work. Parker grumbled a little, then "harrumphed", and continued snoring.

Connie walked into the room at that moment. "I have the magic formula, dear. No one can resist my bacon, frying and sizzling, in the pan. And some fried eggs and hash-brown potatoes. I guarantee results." She walked into the kitchen area of the large room and began to bustle.

Hugo strode along after her. "How come you're so helpful with this guy, and I have to fight to get the same kind of breakfast from you?"

"The children will be down in a few minutes and I want them to meet Mr. Parker when he's in a good mood. My breakfast will provide that assurance. Besides, dear, I think Mr. Parker may be somewhat unique. He's always in the middle of trouble, I think, based on my reading about his public life. It seems to me that he sort of bumbles along, trying to do the right thing, and not straying off course. He's very determined when he gets the bit in his teeth."

Hugo stared at his wife. "The 'bit in his teeth'? Where did you pick up that saying, Connie? That's right out of the Farmer's Almanac, for God's sake. The first edition, too."

"I got that yesterday from a man who is a retired psychiatrist who volunteers at my school, and others, too, each month. He actually knows Mr. Parker. He told me so. His name is Dr. Malcom. He lives in the next town to Bridgeton, where Mr. Parker lives."

Bill Parker seems to be known all over this state, thought Hugo. "What did he have to say about him?"

"I simply happened to mention to Dr. Malcom that Mr. Parker, from Bridgeton, was a friend of my husband's. He seemed surprised. He said he was acquainted with Mr. Parker."

"So I proceeded to tell him about my thoughts and the death of this attorney in Burlington last year. Dr. Malcom looked at me very strangely, Hugo, and then said that he would not discuss any alleged happenings in Mr. Parker's life. He also said that I should never talk to anyone about my guesses regarding Mr. Parker and his past. He hinted strongly that if the wrong person, or people, should hear about this connection I made, it could be troublesome for Mr. Parker. But he told me about Mr. Parker's life, or as much of it as he knew. He's quite a person, Hugo – and so is his wife. The two of them are quite a pair, he said."

"Then let's keep it all to ourselves, shall we?" Hugo said, with a firmness that surprised Connie. He was uneasy about this supposed knowledge his wife had deduced. However, he thought, it sounds as though that "knowledge" could very well be an exaggeration. Hugo really liked Parker and didn't want to see things coming out of his past that could be "troublesome" for him, regardless of whether they were true or not.

Connie knew she had stepped over the line and her husband was angry with her. At that moment Parker shuffled into the kitchen. He looked terrible.

Parker felt as if he had been run over by something large and heavy. He knew at this moment how his eyes would feel if washed out with gravel. "What month is it?" he mumbled, and tried a grin. He couldn't make it happen. "Where's the bacon I smell?"

"I think you're on the road to recovery, Mr. Parker," Connie chirped. Parker, with a superhuman effort, smiled. A death mask, he was sure.

Connie filled up two plates with a heaping breakfast, set coffee down in front of each of them, and said, "I'll go down for the paper. Got to keep up with the bad guys, You know."

As the door banged behind her, Hugo looked up at Parker. He had a slightly sheepish expression as he said, "I didn't give you sufficient warning, Bill. She got right after you, didn't she?"

"Hugo, it was wonderful. I love people who are committed to things, and are knowledgeable, too. So many people complain, but they don't get involved. There's absolutely no reason to apologize."

Hugo grinned at Parker. "She's a handful, you know. She's been the best thing that ever happened to me, I can tell you."

"I've got one like that, too," Parker answered. "Way ahead of me, I'm afraid."

Connie bounced into the kitchen, looking at the front page of the Free Progressive. "The Vermont left is showing its true colors, boys. They've picked their idea of a middle-of-the-road candidate for Governor. He's a socialist, a member of the ProgDems.

Beautiful," she chuckled. "And his Lt. Governor is a woman from Windsor County with exactly the same pedigree."

Connie sat down to skim the news of the day, as altered by the personal leanings of the reporters and their editors.

She looked up at them. She seemed to be reading an article at the bottom of the front page. Looking up and pointing at a small headline, she said, "These are the happenings that make me want to get out of Vermont, you know."

"I know the feeling, Connie," said Parker. "But then I bury those thoughts and decide to fight back, in my small way."

"Here's an example, Mr. Parker," said Connie. "There's been another murder in Burlington. A motel owner was found at one o'clock this morning. He was killed by a blow to the head. Apparently he was found by one of the people staying there and they called the police. When the cops got the call a CFP reporter happened to be in the station and followed the cops to the motel. He probably called in his story in time to make the deadline."

Hugo and Parker looked at each other. "Is there anymore detail, honey?" asked Hugo quietly.

"What do we care about detail, Hugo?" Connie asked. Then she looked at Hugo. "Are you acquainted with the victim, Hugo?"

"Sort of," answered Hugo.

"Through your business?" she asked.

"Sort of," he answered.

Connie saw right through her husband's evasive behavior. "Spill it, my dear. What's going on? And you'd better tell me everything."

And Hugo did. At the end of his tale, his wife looked bewildered. And then she surprised Hugo and Parker. No anger was displayed. She got up and walked over to her husband and hugged him. "I don't want to lose you, Hugo. And my feminine intuition tells me that you were very close to a killer. In fact, I think you had left the motel only about a half hour before the killer shot the motel owner. And you, too, Mr. Parker, were in danger."

There were tears in her eyes. "And I think that he would have killed you both if he could have. He certainly tried in the barn." Parker silently agreed.

"We don't know anything about the guy in the barn, Connie," said Parker. He turned toward Hugo. "Hugo, did we have any cars passing us while we were motoring along leisurely toward

Underhill last night? It seemed to me that the road was empty at that hour."

"Yes, we were passed by three or four vehicles on our way, Bill. A couple of them were really moving, too. I think he got by us when we stopped here to change vehicles."

Parker shrugged. "Could have happened that way, and we could have been passed, too, while on the way. Doesn't make much difference anyway. He got there ahead of us."

"Yes, and if he passed us on the way, he didn't recognize my van, did he? But he'd know that damned pickup of yours, wouldn't he?" Parker remained quiet. Hugo was right, though, he knew.

"It doesn't sound as if you two left anything incriminating behind," Connie said. She was really asking them a question, rather than simply stating a fact.

"No, we're all right on that," said Hugo. "I made certain."

"And I never mentioned Hugo's name," said Parker.

"Good," Connie said firmly. "It sounds as if he might know yours though, Mr. Parker." Parker was sure of that, too. "I'd keep my head down for a few days," said Connie. "Out of the limelight, you know?" Then, with obvious and businesslike finality, she said, "Now, what's on for today, boys?"

"I'm going to get some sleep during the day, and then go to work at my usual time," said Hugo. Then he looked up at Parker suddenly. "Bill, for goodness sake, we had an adventure tonight, or last night I guess it would be, to find a box of something that was left for you. Let's look at it."

"No, Hugo, let's not. It will keep. If that box contains flammable stuff, I don't want you to know anything about it. You're out of the game, and right now."

Parker was determined, and it showed in his voice. And then, almost as an afterthought, Parker said, "Hugo, you know that that attempt to kill us tonight could not have been planned. If he knew where the package was, he'd have simply taken it and be gone before we got there – if he wanted it, or even if he knew about it. If, on the other hand, he planned to kill us, it was a damn poor plan. I mean that he didn't know that we'd even be there tonight, he didn't know that we'd be standing right where we were, which was the only place we could stand to be in line for something heavy to drop on us. No, Hugo, I think that what he did tonight was an act of a desperate man. Something has happened that has panicked him. That something is probably not known to us." Hugo nodded in understanding.

"What am I going to do next, Connie?" said Parker, suddenly, in answer to her initial question. "I'm going to see Peter Morgan, Montpelier Police, as soon as I get up from some sleep."

He walked over to where Connie was standing. "I want to thank you for providing a terrific husband. He was very together tonight. And I hope it's all right that I get a little sleep here, Connie."

"Of course, Mr. Parker. Sleep as long as you like. I'll be at work, so you won't be disturbed. Hugo sleeps like a log. I'll wake you both at 4:00PM."

"Oh, I'll be up and gone long before that hour. I'm a light sleeper," said Parker, with certainty. "Then I'll see Peter, and then head for home."

"Try to stay out of cheap motels in the future, Mr. Parker, will you?" said Connie. Nobody smiled.

38

Connie Barkley shook Parker awake at 4:15 in the afternoon. He had slept for almost six hours. Even then it was touch-and-go as to whether Parker would come to the surface and be human again. Then, in a sudden burst of sleep-plagued urgency, Parker ran through a shower, shave, and a fried egg sandwich provided by Connie. Hugo arrived on the scene just as Parker was aimed toward the door. They passed each other in the kitchen with "good mornings, good byes", and "we'll talks", all led off with a couple of "howdaya feel"s.

It was 6:30 in the early evening when Parker finally arrived at the Montpelier Police Department. He had called ahead and talked to Catherine Morgan, Peter Morgan's wife, and also a police officer. He told her that he'd be arriving and hoped that her husband had some time for him.

He thought about the relationship he had with Peter and Catherine Morgan, and with the Montpelier Police Department as a whole. He'd gotten to know most of them over the past three years and he learned that it wasn't only Peter Morgan who had guided him along when he was tracking a killer. It was the many people in the Department who had done off-duty things that seemed small by those who did them but together were a powerful force – and probably saved his life. Trust from both parties to the other gave Parker comfort when he walked into the MPD, and they didn't have a problem with Parker entering their world at any time. This has to be a rare thing, thought Parker. He hoped it wasn't illegal.

He pushed open the door of the MPD and the first thing he saw was Catherine sitting at a table behind the front counter looking at a man who had to have been at least sixty, dressed like he was a sixteen-year-old high school student who was having a bad day. Catherine Morgan was making notes as another officer addressed questions to this young/old scraggly person.

"Officer," this apparent prisoner stated, in a flighty tone, "I object to answering your questions. You are invading my privacy.

I was merely conducting a survey of youngsters for a class I teach in the Vermont college system. You fascist thugs arrested me, and you'll hear about this from my attorney," announced the scraggly one.

"Ricky, cut out the crap, will you?" said the young officer, completely out of patience. "You haven't taught anybody anything in over a year. Even the state college system got rid of you, and they seem to keep anybody who comes along. You're collecting money from about three different charities, along with some damned state program that rewards losers like you just because you're still breathing. And that income allows you the time to attempt to do inappropriate things when children are around." The officer was obviously tired and looked frustrated, too. Probably pulled an all-nighter, thought Parker.

"I resent that, Officer," Mr. Scraggly shrilled. "I'm on sabbatical for the purpose of research. Just check the record." Mr. Scraggly sniffed as he talked, giving the impression that he either had a problem with his nose or he didn't think much of the law enforcement community. Probably both, thought Parker.

"I *have* checked the record, Ricky. We all have. You're a bum with a hang-up, and I'm sick of seeing you roaming around at all hours doing God-only-knows what. We all know you, Ricky. You talk as if you were going to be placed on the Vermont Supreme Court at any time."

Mr. Scraggly whipped around. He shouted, "I *was* being considered for the Court, you know, and then the Governor betrayed me and decided to retire from office and try for something bigger. And don't call me 'Ricky'. My name is 'Ricardo'. Ricardo Rudolfo Murch, Professor of the Discipline for the New Future. That's an advanced course in geopolitical social organizations, you know, that will govern the world for our children. And it's a non-profit, too, for you doubters." He seemed very proud of something, but Parker couldn't make out just what it was.

Catherine looked up, sensing Parker's presence. "Hallo, Mr. Parker," she said pleasantly. "Chief Inspector Morgan is at the Statehouse, and he'd like to have you join him, if you could." She talked quietly and with steadiness. Parker was impressed. He had no doubt that dealing with "Ricky" for five minutes would throw him into deep despair.

Ricky whirled around toward Parker when Catherine said his name. He looked frenzied. "You should have died three years ago, Parker," he screamed. "You are one of the reasons that I developed the Discipline for the New Future. Your type won't be allowed to live in any community in Vermont when the Discipline is established."

Parker was incredulous. "Ricky, how do you know me? I've never seen you before in my life."

"*My* people know who you are. *We* even know your truck. *We* have all been warned to avoid you. You're dangerous." Ricky was starting to babble again in a high volume, sing-song way, like some failed modern third rail music group that always sounded like they were still warming up when, in fact, they were halfway though their concert.

"Ricky, all I want to know is who talked to you about me?" At this point Ricky was beginning to keen in an unintelligible and mournful way.

And then Parker heard something that astounded him. Ricky seemed to howl words into the air. "My friend told me about you," he said, pointing at Parker with a grubby index finger.

Then he drifted off into disjointed and unclear mumblings. Phrases were used that had no meaning for anybody except, presumably, the followers of the Discipline for the New Future.

And then Ricky said, clearly, "Spelling test knows about you. He is last. Last, I tell you." His voice was quiet and Ricky was perfectly lucid, which gave the whole setting in the Montpelier Police Department an eerie cast. A sort of tableau effect that seemed to Parker as almost evil.

"What in the world is he talking about, Catherine?" asked Parker, startled by this change in the atmosphere.

Catherine turned to the officer. "Denny, what's all this drivel? You've had the most experience with Ricky. Ever heard this stuff before?"

"Nope," said the officer. "All new to me. Usually he just talks about his eminent appointment to the Supreme Court. By the way, my sources have told me that the ProgDems are actually considering this jerk for the short list for an appointment to the Vermont Judiciary when they win back the Governorship." He shook his head. "If this scumball is ever in a position to dispense justice in Vermont, then you can bet that the Discipline of the New

Future will be calling the shots. Then it will be time to move out, friends."

Denny couldn't hide a look of sadness. "Sometimes I think that the beautiful green of Vermont is changing. Ever had that feeling, Mr. Parker?" Parker just looked at Denny. He couldn't think of any words that would be suitable. However, Parker decided that Denny was a kindred spirit. Parker felt sorry for him.

Denny walked around Ricky's chair and over to the window. Parker thought that Denny was changing the scenery and his blue mood. Looking out onto State Street, Denny said, "One thing he ranted about, though, that truly *was* new. He talked about the 'spelling test'. I haven't heard that one before."

"Yes, yes," Ricky shouted, blasting away the quiet in the room. "The spelling test. The last. The real last." He yelled. Then he slumped over the table and seemed to instantly fall asleep.

"Does he sleep here sometimes?" asked Parker, unsettled by the wild and unproductive statements of Mr. Scraggly, in contrast with the calm and quiet responses of these officers. Parker never knew which was coming next.

"Many times, Mr. Parker, many times," said the officer. "We can't hold him for anything. He's just a nuisance. Or at least that's what we think. If he's not causing trouble, we let him alone. However, this is the second attempt to be near children, and we're afraid that his mental health profile we have on record will be accurate. That is, the kid stuff will come out."

"Interesting, or at least I think it is. How did he know me?" asked Parker. "Any ideas on that?"

"None, Mr. Parker," he answered.

"Well," said Parker, "I can't let this jerk slow me down. I've got to get going. Have fun with Ricky when he wakes up. Sorry for the interruption, too, folks."

Parker turned to go. Catherine walked over to Parker. "How do you like those shoes Ricky's wearing? Stylish, wouldn't you say?"

"I noticed them, Catherine. What are they?

"Bowling shoes, Mr. Parker. Ricky thinks they're the latest. Wears them all the time. Like the varied colors?"

"Lovely," said Parker.

"Catherine, could you call Peter and tell him I'm on the way?" She nodded. "Thank you very much," as he headed for the door.

"You're welcome, Mr. Parker. Come back and talk with some of our other guests sometime. Maybe you have other acquaintances who live in Ricky's world. They certainly are seen in this city, and increasing at a high rate. And you seem to have taken to him." Her broad smile belied the ridiculous nature of those inhabitants of "Mr. Scraggly's world".

As Parker drove to the Statehouse his mind and his memory were hard at work on the problem of the word on the street about former Representative William Parker. Apparently everybody who was anybody in the hard left of Vermont politics had been warned of the impending doom that would be visited upon them because of being seen with me, thought Parker. He simply didn't understand any of it. What connection did he have with any of these people and organizations?

He tumbled this puzzle around in his mind. It had all started, as far as he could tell, in the offices of the VNRCAUC and the little lady with the unbearable voice, then moved on to the ex-school teacher from Spring River who had the aversion to soap and water, and ended up with Ricky, the mental invalid from Montpelier.

All were stellar citizens who were the products of the modern instructional wing of a know-nothing educational establishment in Vermont. To this group, any solid knowledge containing incontrovertible truths was to be avoided because it might damage the self-esteem of both the students and their instructors. But what Parker couldn't figure out, was why? He had had no direct contact with the subject of politics for three years. He had busied himself with his Addie, his insurance agency, and his trout fishing. He had written no letters to the press, and even if he had, who would print them anyway?

He smiled to himself as he automatically thought of the Mid-Vermont Bugle. He had heard from some friends who were still in politics that this paper would print none of their letters, which was not news to Parker, of course, but would print letters in opposition to theirs, in spite of the fact that their letters hadn't appeared in the Bugle, but had appeared elsewhere. That was a new twist, Parker thought. But then he knew the answer: The paper realized that printing their letters would get in the way of the Bugle's role of being the daily trumpet section for the ProgDems.

No, he thought, there's something else going on, and he hadn't any idea what it could be. Somehow, however, he felt in his bones that the murder of Hugh Hammond, the disappearance of Jan Evlin, the hunting accident of Gil Birdsall, the murder of the motel owner, and the notes from "Z" and "N", were all tied in together.

Probably far-fetched, he thought, but he couldn't stop the idea from popping into his thoughts when he least expected it. It was just a feeling, after all, almost an expectation – but not quite. He hadn't talked about his thoughts in this area with anyone else.

Maybe Morgan, he mused, at some point, would get the benefit of this bizarre concept.

Parker arrived at the Statehouse area in less than five minutes, and he pulled around to the back of the Thrush Tavern and illegally pulled into the empty parking space belonging to the Chief Justice of the Supreme Court. He felt good about that. If the Supreme Court decided that they were going to interpret *my* Constitution in *their* strange ways, thought Parker, then I could take one of *their* parking spaces for *my* purposes. It all made sense to Parker somehow.

He walked up the slight hill to the Statehouse and walked down the marble hall to the office of the Sergeant at Arms. The present holder of that title was an old friend of Parker's. As Parker turned the corner toward his office, he came out. "Bill," he said pleasantly, "I got the word from Mr. Morgan. They're upstairs in the Committee room where the suicide took place."

"Thanks, Herm," said Parker, and headed up toward the wing where these rooms were located.

Peter Morgan was standing in the hall outside the secured Committee Room where Hugh Hammond's body had been found, talking with a uniformed policeman. As Parker approached, the patrolman walked past him and down the hall. Morgan was alone.

"Hello, Peter," said Parker. "I see that this room is still off-limits. How come? You must have all you need from it for your case file."

Morgan took Parker by the arm and pulled him into the room, closing the door. "Because, Bill, when it hits the papers that this is a murder, the press will be all over it. And all over me, too."

"Well, Peter, what can I do for you? I can't imagine that it's too much," said Parker.

"I wanted to talk with you about the answers we got from our Statehouse interviews. I also wanted to try to re-create the crime scene. And in doing that, I use all sources of information. You're a part of my information buildup."

Parker grinned at Morgan. "It's a thin resource, Peter."

Morgan returned the smile.

"Let's sit a while, Bill." They moved over to the long, central Committee Room table and both flopped down in the chairs, facing each other. "You've probably been nosing around Burlington for a couple of days, just as I've been doing around Montpelier. Anything to report?"

Parker glanced up at Morgan. "Idle question, Peter, or is there something behind it?"

Morgan seemed uneasy. "You, or rather that damned pickup of yours, was seen last night outside a crumby motel in a seedy section of Burlington by a Burlington Police patrol car. He knew it was yours. Nobody else would drive anything like it. He talked to my buddy in the Department about it and he called me. I've sworn them to secrecy, but I don't know how long that will last. He also reported that there might have been someone with you. True?"

Parker had a sinking feeling when he heard what Morgan had to say. He hadn't made up his mind about telling Morgan about his escapade last night. He hadn't thought about Morgan's pipeline into the Burlington PD. He also noticed that Morgan hadn't mentioned that the motel clerk had been murdered shortly after he and Hugo had left. Is it possible that Morgan didn't know about that? Dream on, Parker, my boy, he thought. He knows.

"Peter, this is a very troubling time for me. It doesn't bother me that my truck was seen outside that motel. In fact, it might be the best thing that could have happened. However, in order to explain that statement I'll have to go back to the start of it. It's a lot of facts that didn't seem connected when I was exposed to them. They came together in one period of about five hours last night. And all of it was totally unexpected. But you need to know all of it, from the beginning."

Morgan's expression didn't change. He just stared at Parker. "Let's have it then," he said quietly, "every little bit."

"Some of it you already know," said Parker. "In fact, you were on the edge of it at the very beginning. You'll remember when I walked into your office recently and told you what I knew, which didn't take very long. Just that I was going to follow up on the information given to me by Jan Evlin, the reporter for the Chittenden Free Progressive." Morgan watched Parker closely.

"So I went to the only person I knew who could shed light on the core issue – the non-profit industry in Vermont. I met with Hugh Hammond for dinner at the Thrush. That was a strange couple of hours, Peter. Hammond was ready to talk about this business of the non-profits, and he did. I still have the notes from that meeting. And suddenly he decided to leave with no explanation."

"I don't see anything yet that I need to know, Bill. Keep going and make it quick. I don't want to be interrupted," he said, glancing at the Committee Room door. Morgan was itchy.

"Let me start off this way then, Peter," said Parker. He reached into his brief case, removed a folder and took out the note from "Z" that Hammond had given him. "What's your opinion of the intent of the writer?"

Morgan held the note up to the light that was streaming in from the west windows of the Committee Room. As he read, Parker looked around the room. It was not a Committee Room where he had met when he was in the Legislature. But, then again, all of the Committee Rooms were essentially the same.

Morgan was reading the note a second time when Parker allowed his eyes to drift over to the corner of the room where Hammond had been killed. It was almost impossible to avoid that spot, knowing what he knew.

And then he stopped. He looked again, changing his position, and looked again. He got to his feet and what he had seen wasn't visible from that angle. He sat down again and it reappeared. At this point, Morgan was looking at him.

"Bill, he said, "this is a ---," and then he stopped. "What's the problem, Bill? What are you looking at?"

"Peter, swap chairs with me, would you please? Don't question me yet. Just come on around here and sit down." Parker got to his feet, allowing Morgan to slide into his chair.

"Just look into that corner of the room where we believe Hammond was killed. Below the blackboard, close to the corner. On the wall there. Where the angle of the sunlight puts everything into sharp relief. Move your eyes around a little, if nothing jumps out at you right away. There's something on the wall. Do you see it?"

Morgan still had the note in his hand. He stopped moving in his chair and stared at the wall. Then he looked at the note.

"You see it, don't you?" cried Parker.

Morgan said nothing. He got to his feet, leaning this way, that way, then walking over to the corner for closer inspection.

"My God Almighty," he breathed. "That's very plainly a big "N" on that wall."

He took his automatic pencil out of his pocket and uncapped the eraser. He tried to draw a smudged line on the wall, near to the "N".

"You've done it, Peter," said Parker, excitedly. "Same mark exactly."

Morgan went over to the desk and picked up a thick file marked "Hammond" and withdrew a paper, which he scanned closely.

"This is a list of what was found in this room at the same time Hammond's body was found. There was a wooden pencil on the floor, right under the body." He shook his head, obviously upset with himself. "I missed the significance of it at the time."

"Good Lord, Peter, don't berate yourself for that. Who would ever consider that the corpse scribbled something on the wall with the eraser of a damned pencil just before they died? And also it's probable that the marked wall is only visible for fifteen minutes a day, and only during this time of year. And you'd have to be standing in exactly the right place to see it. I was simply unbelievably lucky."

Morgan wasn't listening. He had picked up his cell phone and dialed a number. "Curt," he said into the phone, "is the photographer still here? Good. Send him right back up here." Morgan listened impatiently. "Yes, immediately, and have him bring all his camera equipment – fast! No coffee breaks!"

Morgan looked at Parker with an agitated expression. "I know we were lucky, Bill, I know that," he said in exasperation. "This room was getting a coat of paint tomorrow. I authorized it myself. Not now, after this," and he swung his hand toward the corner. "This find would have disappeared forever if you hadn't seen it."

The photographer entered the room at that moment. He looked irritated. "I've shot this room from every angle you can name, Mr. Morgan. What the hell else is left to shoot, for God's sake?"

Morgan patiently pointed out what he wanted. The photographer seemed bored, looked at the wall, then looked again, bounced around the room looking at the wall from every angle conceivable, and then enthusiastically began the process of setting up his equipment. "Never done this type of shot on purpose, Mr. Morgan," he said, "so I don't know how it will turn out." Parker and Morgan stood aside and watched the cameraman at work. He knows what he's doing, thought Parker. Thank goodness he was still around.

After 20 minutes, the cameraman announced, "I hope I got what we want, Mr. Morgan. I can't tell you until these are developed, but I did take a few shots with my digital shooter, and I think I could see what you wanted. I'll let you know in the morning. I'll develop them tonight, try to highlight this area," he said, as he pointed at the wall, "and have the photos on your desk first thing." When he left he was very polite.

"We haven't discussed what we think happened," said Morgan. "I mean, how did this happen, or how do we think it happened? That's why you're here, Bill. An expert witness." Morgan was still upset at how close he came to missing this vital piece of evidence.

"How much blood did they find in that corner, if any, and where was it?" asked Parker.

Morgan opened the file again and removed another piece of paper. "There was blood there, but not much. The body had evidence of the nosebleed, by the way."

"I'd forgotten the nosebleed," Parker said. "Had he been hit in the face, or something like that?"

"No visual evidence of it that I could see. We'll check with his doctor. If he had high blood pressure, the excitement of the moment may have triggered one. Certainly not unknown."

But Parker wasn't listening. He was staring off into space. Morgan noticed this odd behavior and asked, "What now, Bill? Something else come to the top of your strange mind?"

"I was starting to wonder if I had been too close to all these details. I was starting to get confused, Peter. I want to continue my story to you."

Parker went through all the happenings from the beginning. When he got to the business of the motel and what he and Hugo found, he mentioned the man who called himself 'N' who had pressured Chugger. It got Morgan's attention.

"Is this the same 'N' that we see on the wall?"

"I can't prove it, but I'm sure it is," Parker said grimly. "I kept running into the letter 'Z' from the beginning of all this. And then the letter 'N' pops up – and not just today, marked on the wall with a pencil eraser. I was wondering if I should disregard these letters. But it's all clear now to me."

"Enlighten me, Bill. What are you thinking about?" asked Morgan.

"Think about Hammond's position when he scraped that letter 'N' on the wall. He was no doubt lying on the floor – maybe dying, I don't know. Maybe just on the edge of consciousness. He knew who was in the room with him. He must have known what was about to happen. Somehow he was able to smudge that 'N' on the wall before he was dragged over to the chair."

"And he was lying down on the floor when he did it!" cried Morgan excitedly. "It's really a 'Z', isn't it? Of course, that makes all kind of sense. It's the simple things we miss because we try to make them too complicated."

"I'm sure of it, Peter. I also believe that the 'N' that Chugger told me about was really a 'Z', too. Chugger was just nuts enough to read a handwritten 'Z' as an 'N'."

Morgan opened his mouth to speak when Parker said, "I know, I know. Nothing could be more shaky than that leap. But I just know it's right."

Morgan stood up and looked at Parker with intensity. "If you're right, and I happen to think you are, then this bastard 'Z' is tied in to everything that has happened, isn't he? Including that note to Hammond." Morgan still had Hammond's note in his hand. "By the way, this is a threat if I ever saw one," Morgan said, holding up the note.

"You bet, Peter, and there's nothing that we can offer as proof – at least not yet. And, even then, it will probably take a confession from the killer to have anyone believe it."

"Too bad that Chugger was murdered last night, isn't it?" asked Morgan, in the mildest sort of way. He was studying Parker intently.

Parker looked at Morgan. "Yes, it is, Peter. I read about it in the morning paper."

"You realize, don't you, that the killer was waiting for you to appear and then you would have become the next victim?" he asked. "What stopped him, I wonder?"

"I had a friend with me, Peter. A big guy, too. Maybe he saw him and backed off."

"If that killer could find a way to tie you to the murder of that motel clerk, he'd do it, you know."

Parker said, "I know, Peter. But he'd have to come closer to the radar screen to do it, and he's been very careful for a very long time. I don't think he'd risk it. And, Peter, I didn't murder anybody."

Morgan grinned. "I *know* that, Bill," in exasperation.

Then Parker asked a very important question of Morgan, in as casual a tone as he could muster. "By the way, Peter, what's your buddy in the Burlington PD going to do with the knowledge that I was around the motel where the murder of our close friend Chugger took place?"

"Nothing. He simply saw your truck across the street from the motel. It was gone when he came back through. But he knew it was your truck. That's why he called me. And of course you didn't murder anybody. But sometimes evidence can be made to be anything for somebody who wants something accomplished." Morgan sat thinking for a moment. "You're in the clear on that one, Bill. Let's move on."

Parker agreed, and took the conversation in another direction. "What about your interviews with the people who were in this building when Hammond was killed?" asked Parker. "His Committee members. Anybody at all? Anything important come up?"

Morgan looked toward the door and then turned toward Parker. "That's why I'm glad you're here. You were very accurate with your concerns. Before I go further, I should say that between the apparent time of the murder and the time we got here was about 45 minutes, as best as we can figure. Therefore, the killer could have disappeared during that time and nobody would have noticed. That's a gap in time that we thought we could never fill."

"A lot of loose ends and various people wandering around that makes for confusion and unpredictability," murmured Parker.

"You're so right," said Morgan. "But we were able to tighten up a few things. First, we interviewed over 350 people, all of whom were in the building between 11:00 in the morning and 2:00PM. We had completed securing the building at about 1:30 in the afternoon, so we were able to overlap the times by about a half hour to make us feel some comfort that nobody would slip through the cracks. Not very scientific, I know, but the best we could do."

Morgan began to walk around the room, gesturing with his hands, and generally becoming more animated than Parker had ever seen him. "Then we checked with security here in the Statehouse. We asked if anybody had left the building during the hour just before 11:00 in the morning and the hour after 2:00 in the afternoon. These would be those people who we had not questioned. Actually, there were three, and we talked to them. Without question, they were cleared. They had just left the building not knowing what had happened."

Parker thought about what he had heard. "Are you convinced then that the killer was still in the building?"

"Yes, the odds are that he was still here," said Morgan. "Of course, he may have just walked out earlier, missed by Statehouse security and us, too. I don't want to automatically assume that we didn't mess up."

"What about the Committee members? Were they surprised that he was found in somebody else's chair?"

"Absolutely, Bill. They agreed that it isn't unknown for a member to sit in another member's seat for informal chit-chats, but never in any official capacity. Also, Hammond was never known to sit in another chair, no matter what the circumstances were. He apparently was quite square about that."

Parker thought about that for a few seconds. "Okay, Peter. Now comes the big one, at least as far as I'm concerned. Did any of the 350 people try to use the upstairs bathroom on this floor during the times you established?" asked Parker.

Morgan's face changed from one of extreme seriousness to almost gaiety. He grinned at Parker. "Bill, the reaction to that question was hilarious. Picture this: the Montpelier Police were conducting interviews about a suicide in the Statehouse. We were, of course, very official-like, as you can imagine. We would ask the kinds of questions that you would expect, but still making everybody nervous along the way. And the answers were predictable, too, to those questions that pertained to where they were, what they were doing, and did you see anybody where they shouldn't be – things like that. And then we'd ask if they had tried to use the bathroom on the floor where the body was found? In most cases, they just gawked, wondering what the hell that was all about. All but nine said they hadn't tried, with most saying that they weren't in that area of the building and why would they trek up there when the best thing government does is to provide restrooms everywhere you look."

"But the other nine people? What about them?" asked Parker.

Morgan's face became serious again and he said, "All of them tried to use that bathroom during the period from 11:00 AM to 2:00PM. All tried, as best they could remember, to give us the exact time they rattled the door. None of them were as certain as I needed them to be. None of them stayed around waiting for the bathroom to become available. They just moved downstairs to the other facilities."

"Well, Peter, all this tells us one thing, at least. The bathroom was tied up during that period of time that seems to be important. Any way to determine if it was the same person during that long period of time? I mean, could it have been, say, five people who used it, and they left when nobody was around?"

Morgan frowned and said, "I thought of that, too, Bill. It's possible, but the odds are strongly against it. There were....let's see," and he opened a small notebook and riffled through some pages, "yes, here it is. There were a total of 159 people, including Legislators, who were in this committee room area from about 10:00 AM. Sixty-six were committee members. Seventeen of them left the area and came back during the period in which we're interested. The nine I mentioned before came out of this group, of course."

"What times did you get from these 159 people, Peter? I'm thinking that their memories probably are faulty, but that's because they didn't have any reason to look at their watches when they felt the urge. They simply wanted to use the bathroom. They tried. They left and went elsewhere. Standard stuff. Suddenly the police are asking them if they remembered the exact time they wanted to use the facilities on that day. Let's assume they all have memories that are equally faulty in cases like these. Even if wrong they might provide a pattern."

"I decided that same thing, Bill. In fact, it's not unknown in these types of occurrences. Here's the pattern, as you called it." He handed Parker a piece of paper with a kind of hand drawn spreadsheet displayed on it. Very neat, thought Parker. As expected, the nine times were clustered in a half hour period – from 11:45AM to 12:15PM.

“Any luck with the bathroom itself, Peter?” asked Parker, now discouraged by the lack of information that would point them in a direction. “The forensic people have anything to report?”

“Ah,” said Morgan, his spirits suddenly on the upswing once more, “now we do have something to talk about.”

He hauled out of an inner pocket the intrepid notebook once again and flipped through the first pages in it. “We got here within an hour of the estimated time of the killing, Bill. The cleaning crew hadn’t been in there, so we got a good look at it. It’s not a large bathroom. Therefore, if someone normal had waited in there for upwards of two hours, they’d be stir-crazy when they got out. But not this guy, Bill. He had the strength and ability to wait for two hours, not being able to move around, ignoring the knocking on the door from nine people who wanted to get in and, all the while, maintaining total silence.”

Morgan hesitated, seeming to think about that feat for a few seconds, and then righted his personal ship and continued speaking. “Then he had to check the hall to see if anyone was around. If it was clear outside in the hallway, he’d slip out, walk down the hall and into the committee room where Hammond was waiting. He’d kill him, and then go back to the bathroom.” He shook his head. “This is one cold customer, Bill.”

Parker nodded. “How do you know that the killer went back into the bathroom again after killing Hammond, Peter?”

“Because we found traces of Hammond’s blood in the bathroom, Bill, and he would have only had blood on him if he had first killed Hammond.”

Parker felt like a dunce. He shook his head, grimacing at his stupidity. I hope it’s because I’m tired, he thought, and not because I’ve started that long, steady, decline into senility at an early age. “Where did you find the blood, Peter?”

“Two places, Bill. Under the lip edge of the wash basin counter top, and in the trap in the drain.”

“And you’re sure it’s Hammond’s?”

Morgan looked at Parker in his infuriatingly tolerant way – as if he were dealing with the village idiot – and said, “Bill, would I say that if I didn’t know absolutely that it was Hammond’s blood?”

“No, Peter, you wouldn’t,” answered a contrite Parker.

Then, changing the subject, Parker said, “Peter, I’m beat, I’m sure I don’t have anything more for you, and it’s time for me to head home. I'm getting out of your way. I do have one more question."

Morgan assumed an overly-tolerant attitude and said, "Please, Bill, I can't wait." Parker knew that that look from Morgan, along with his expression, was saying, "I've got a limit on my patience, Parker, and you're reaching it right now".

Parker decided to get right to it. "Since Hammond's death, has any of the family, or the family lawyer, gone into the house – or anyone else, for that matter?"

Morgan looked totally surprised. "Why do you ask, Bill?" he asked cautiously.

Parker didn't want to talk about the attempt made on his life in the barn last night. He didn't know why he didn't want to bring it up, but maybe it was that too much death had already occurred in the last very few days. But now he felt he had to. So he did.

Morgan was very angry. "What else have you held back from me, Bill? Can I believe you when you say that I now know everything?"

Parker said, "Peter, there's nothing else. You can believe that."

"Why did you ask that question, Bill?"

"It occurred to me that this bastard was waiting for me, or somebody, to come into the barn. Hammond had told me at dinner that he had some information hidden in the barn and he told me where it was. I didn't know what it was, but if he thought it was important, who am I to argue?"

"I wondered if anybody had broken into the house since Hammond's murder," continued Parker, "because somebody was waiting for me in that barn. It made me wonder if Hammond had been forced to tell his killer where and what information he had and the killer was in the barn, looking for it, when I walked in."

"That means that Hammond was broken by his murderer, and the killer went straight for the barn. However, if the house had been broken into, it means that the killer was on a wild goose chase, sent on it by Hammond. I'd like to know."

"Yes, they did," Morgan said. "Two days after Hammond's murder my friend in the BPD called to say that Hammond's kids, both married, so there was four of them, went into the house to see what was there. The next morning they reported to the BPD that the house had been broken into during that night. Nothing taken that they could see."

"And that also means that Hammond was brave under the most severe kind of strain. I just wanted to know, that's all."

With that knowledge, Parker walked out of the committee room. He now knew a lot more about his enemy. The knowledge wasn't pleasant.

He was trailed down the hall by Morgan's voice echoing, "Keep your head down, Bill."

39

Parker arrived home at about 9:30 at night. He was tired, his back was sore, and he was worried. He backed his truck into the shed and slid out of the cab clutching the flat container that he'd removed from the barn. He liked the word "removed" rather than "stolen". The word removed lent a certain dignity to what otherwise would have been called, by a more objective soul, a criminal act.

He hadn't looked at its contents yet, but would in the company of Addie, Kate, and Duane.

He thumped up the steps to the porch while Minnie and Malcom tore around his legs at top speed, checking him over to see if he was suitable to enter the house. Parker didn't believe that any dog loved him. They simply tolerated him in a distant sort of way. He couldn't understand why.

Addie greeted him at the door with a cup of tea, a smile, and a kiss. "It's been a while, Willie," she said fondly. "Have an interesting few days in the wilds of Chittenden County, did you?"

Parker greeted them all, ignoring Addie's usual comment about the oil-and-water mixture of Parker and the Chittenden County culture. He was surprised to see Irene sitting there, dropped the container that held probably nothing interesting on the big kitchen table, and flopped down in an armchair nearby.

"Addie, my dear," Parker said, "I *did* have an interesting time up there. And Irene," he said, "I'm glad you're here to hear this." He described the events in detail, except for the time in the barn when he was frightened stiff, and indicated the container he'd picked up while in the barn.

"You haven't looked at the contents yet, Bill?" asked Duane. "It might be very important. Mr. Hammond thought so, and I'm sure he thought that the material was important to the subject of Vermont non-profits, too. Let's take a look."

"Okay by me, Duane," Parker said. "Give it here, Addie, and I'll open it up."

What spilled out onto the table was a package of photographs and a note written by Hammond and dated the previous November. It was signed "H. H." Parker gave the photos a quick look. Most of them looked very clear and were almost surely taken with a more than decent camera.

The note, scribbled on the last photo copy page, was very brief. It said:

> "In the forbidden land. Whose farm is this? Does anybody care?
> From G."

Parker had never heard of any forbidden land in Vermont raised to any kind of notoriety. A "farm" wasn't surprising, of course. It could be anywhere, but logic says it was located in Vermont. To Parker there was no doubt of that.

Some people, from the large cities and towns from almost any state you could name, who wanted to be thought of as intrepid rustics or farmers, called their homes a "farm". Without doing the actual work required to be farmers, they just felt good about themselves when they purchased their first box of personalized stationery with "Windswept Farm" or "Colonial Days Farm", or something similar, in old English script across the top. And they were particularly impressed with themselves when they sent their first letter to friends in, or around, New York City, Boston, or some other large metropolitan area. For these folks, e-mail was out. Handwritten letters were in. Quill pens were on the horizon.

Parker spread the photographs out on the table, under the strong light which hung down from the ceiling. They each looked at them in turn. There was silence in the room, as if they all could sense that they were at a crucial moment in this whole episode.

Parker was the last to look at them. What he saw, and what the others had seen before him, was a series of 24 shots with a 35mm camera, from a variety of angles, of an irregularly cleared area hacked out of the pine forest. Some of the other pictures were from a distance away. The close-up pictures looked to be three log dwellings of some size, tucked back into the immense pines on the edge of the cleared area. In the background was the hint of a body of water, with a forest of small black spruces growing along the shore. In fact, Parker thought, if it wasn't for the clearing, and the light it allowed to penetrate to the forest floor, the pictures would not be clear enough to really see anything that was meaningful.

Parker stood upright and asked if everyone had seen all the photos. “Not yet, Willie,” said Addie. “Your son-in-law has held back the last few and he’s hoarding them.” Parker could see that Duane was not hearing a thing being said. He was focused on the three photos, moving from one to the other and back again.

“Do you have a magnifying glass, Bill, the larger the better?” He didn’t look up as he said this.

Parker allowed as how he did, and went to dig it out of his fly-tying kit. When he brought it to Duane he asked, “What are you looking at, Duane?”

There was no answer from Duane. He just started gazing intently through the glass at the three prints again.

Then he sat back in his chair, setting the magnifying glass down on the table as he did so and said, in a tired voice, “It’s important that all of us look at all of these photos, and especially these three prints. Then we’ll talk about them.”

He got up from the table and walked away from the group, and then stepped out onto the porch. It seemed that he had seen something that distressed him to the core. Parker hadn’t seen him act this way since he first knew him when he was a police officer for the Montpelier PD, working for Peter Morgan.

When Parker’s turn came, he sat down and pulled the three prints toward him and scanned them initially with the glass to determine the best distance to see what could be seen. Then he moved the glass over the first one and looked.

He couldn’t see anything strange in the first group of photos except that the photographer took too many shots of essentially the same subject. When Parker started to look at the last three photos, he wasn’t sure what he was seeing at first. Then he saw that it was of another person who was walking toward the camera. What was strange was the slightly blurred image of this person and the off-center location of the subject within the borders of the frame. All the other pictures were taken with a steady camera, well centered, and very clear. This last image was of a person about fifty feet away. The other two shots were of the same uncertain quality, except that the blurred image seemed farther away from the camera. Parker could make nothing of them. One picture was of just the ground. “Duane, do you think that the hand numbered pictures were in the order they were actually taken?”

Duane, who had re-entered the room, said, “Yes, I think so, Bill. There were 24 photos, and there would have been no reason to number them at all if it wasn't for the fact that the photographer wanted us to know what the order was. We just don't know why that was important."

Parker leaned back in his chair and looked at the faces of the group. "Who wants to tell us what they saw in the photos, especially the last three?" he asked.

Irene Doughton cautiously raised her hand. "I'm not sure I'm correct, Bill. In some ways, I hope I'm not. This is all new ground I'm on. But, here we go. I noticed that they were numbered, too, Duane. So I organized them so I could get a sense if there was any kind of a pattern."

As an aside she said, with a slight smile, "I learned that from you, Duane. I remember that you were a great one for 'patterns'." Duane nodded acknowledgment. He remained grim.

"The first two shots were not as clear as the balance of the pictures. To me, it looked as though the photographer wasn't quite sure of what he had for a subject, and he wasn't used to the camera, either. He figured it out after those first shots. Then, staying back away from the area and the log homes, he moved around a little to take some other shots. Then the photographer left the scene. I have no idea why the last three were a little out-of-focus, unless he had camera troubles." She looked around the room. "That's the best I can do, folks. Who's next?"

Parker said, "That's about as far as I got, too, Irene. I'd like to hear from Duane. I can tell you've got something on your mind, and it's not a happy thought, is it? Tell us what you think about these pictures."

Duane stood up and began to walk slowly around the table and then up and down the room. The size of the room almost put him out of earshot once in a while. "I won't take long, folks. I think I have a plausible scenario to offer for your consideration, but I need to try it out on all of you for your comments."

Parker thought it might come down to this – Duane Emery giving us a lecture on a subject that is considered unclear to us mere mortals. It made Parker happy to sit back in his chair and watch and listen. And that was a rare thing for Parker, because he didn't know anybody else, other than his friend Marvin Bailey, the wisest man in Bridgeton, who could glue him to his chair by just talking.

"Irene," Duane began, "I think you're correct, as far as you went. However, I don't think that the photographer wanted to be seen near those log buildings by anybody. In other words, he was in there, with a camera, but didn't walk boldly up to the door and introduce himself." Duane was off in another world, talking to them and to himself, too.

"He went in quietly, stayed back in the trees, took a lot of pictures, tried to get closer, did, took more pictures, and then was seen by somebody. The photo guy then ran out of the area, while being chased by somebody, and tried to take a picture of this guy while running. And got what? Three, is it? They are not too well focused and are not of any practical value, right? Except for one thing. Look closely at the top of the photos. Can't see his face too well – certainly not so well that we could identify the stalker - but look at his head."

They all crowded up to the table, each picking up one of the pictures, closely examining it, and handing it on.

Suddenly, Addie yelped, "I know what you're getting at, Duane. It looks like one of those Tyrolean hats that men wear in the Alps. They're worn in the US to bring a touch of class to the person who has the courage to wear one all the time." Addie was looking at the third photo. "And do you know what, ladies and gentlemen? That dark line in this picture is probably the fancy feather that is jammed into the hat somehow. Taller than usual, but it's there. See it?" She was brandishing the photo in front of the others. "And I don't know what that white streak is, either. See it? It's a fringe of white of some kind, on the hat, I think."

"You're right, Addie, there is something there. But what it might be is too straight to be a feather, I think – and a feather for one of these hats is not that long. I'm convinced that that projection is not a feather in the hat, standing up straight. It's the barrel of a rifle, held upright as he ran after the guy who took the pictures."

There was a buzz at this statement and, in order to bring things back under control, Duane said, "However, I don't know what that means. I mean, it was probably hunting season when these pictures were taken, based on the color of the leaves of the few hardwoods that are there. What it says to me is that these log cabins are a casual retreat for somebody or some group. And they don't want anyone to know about them. All of a sudden, somebody was found taking pictures of this place in the wilderness, and the cabin owners didn't like it, and chased our Steven Spielberg off the place. And I'll close by saying that I'm convinced that you, Bill, and maybe Addie, too, are known to be snooping around on some project that irritates them, and it's very possible that some rough people know of the existence of these photos – remember Chugger - and they may very well know that you have them."

There was a silence in the room that greeted Duane's comments.

Parker broke it. "That's fine reasoning, Duane. I think I agree with it. Addie and I can take care of ourselves."

Parker stood up and stretched, and then said, "But it doesn't do us any good, does it, because we don't know where the hell these pictures were taken." Parker was completely exasperated. "It could be anywhere in this country, Canada, or even Europe, for goodness sake. Why were these pictures so sacred to Hammond? Why didn't he leave a hint of the location? If we assume they were taken in Vermont, that's all it is – an assumption. What's their importance? And as far as rough people being involved, I disagree with you. If there are any bad guys out there, they couldn't know that I have the pictures because they don't even know there are any pictures." There was silence in the room.

Then Parker decided that he had to force the conversation forward to change the atmosphere. "And what about the last picture? The one which just shows the ground."

Duane said, simply, "The photographer dropped the camera. I think it's as simple as that. That film was bad, too. As for the white streak you saw, Mrs. Parker, I haven't a clue."

Irene piped up. "As long as we've become frustrated over some pictures, let's get hot-under-the-collar about a note, written by Jan Evlin to our esteemed Mr. Parker." Grins all around.

Parker snapped his fingers and exclaimed, "Irene, I'd completely forgotten about that note. You borrowed it to experiment with – trying to figure it out, and all that. Any luck?"

"I have a couple of observations, first off, before we get into the meaning of the note. And here they are: I thought I got the impression from you, Mr. Parker, that she was a journalist. I mean, doesn't that imply that she could write? Addie told me that she was excellent in her craft. You know what I mean. She could put her thoughts down on paper, using language we all could understand, perfect punctuation, and all that sort of good stuff?"

Parker smiled faintly. "Irene, you need training in the newspaper business and newspaper writing in general. Almost none of the reporters and correspondents can write properly. Somebody else proofs their material, if any proofing is done at all which, in many cases, I doubt. They are a product of public education systems around the nation. I'll say this, however. I spent fourteen years in Montpelier and Jan was the best at the writing craft of anybody I met up there. And I'd know, too. Jan was the reporter I gave my information to when I had those busy times about three years ago. She'd - "

"Willie," said Addie, interrupting, "those 'busy' times were almost fatal for you, you'll remember." Parker paid no attention.

"She'd write it, as I was about to say, and I'd proof it, to the limited extent I could. What she wrote was always perfect, as far as I could tell. She seemed to be a careful writer, never resorting to fanciful ideas to try to convince us that she was something special. She was very good at her work. Why the question?"

"Did you really read this note when you first got it?" asked Irene. "We were all in this room, you'll remember."

"I don't think I did – anyway, not really, Irene. I listened to Duane try to make sense of it. I remember I was tired, and I didn't have my heart in it at the time because I wasn't convinced that there was a problem. I tried to read it in the office, got the gist of it, and never thought of it again, because so much else was happening. My memory tells me that there was an almost total lack of punctuation. Why?"

"This note is oddly written, phrased in an uncommon way and, as you said, the punctuation is spotty. Do you remember that?"

Parker was out of his chair like a shot. "Let's see it again, Irene." He took the note and read it again. He knew he had been stupid not to notice that the note Jan had written was unlike any other writing he had seen from her. He had noticed it, he remembered, but had placed no importance on it. I'm a damn fool, he thought.

"Yes, Irene, I can confirm that Jan is an expert. This note is not written with her customary precision. In fact, it's terrible. Lead us through your conclusions, please." Politeness became his watchword. The last person he wanted angry at him, personally, was Irene Doughton.

"At first I could make nothing of it," Irene said. "Of course, I was going on the assumption that she was not herself when she wrote this note. I wondered at one point if she had even written it, but I discarded that notion when I felt strongly that the note is written as a warning flag to the reader about something, and not just a poorly written letter. It was her way of sending that signal."

Parker stirred uncomfortably and looked at Addie, who was listening to Irene with total concentration. Duane was sitting back in his chair with his eyes closed, but obviously listening intently. Kate had fallen asleep. Being eleven months pregnant will do that to you, Parker thought.

Irene was looking down at the tabletop and seeming to not see anything.

"Since I needed a starting point in this puzzle," Irene continued, "I simply decided that, from this moment forward, I had to consider the note to be an intentional warning to Mr. Parker and not just a rambling discourse without any meaning. So I started looking for the obvious messages from a writer, Jan in this case, who was not given to trickiness with words. Right, Mr. Parker?" she asked.

Parker nodded emphatically. "Right," he said.

"Since subtlety was not her style," continued Irene, "I shouldn't look for anything too smooth. If she thought that her note might be read by somebody before going in the mail, she would send her warning in such a form that this person would accept it and, more than that, send it on its way."

Irene rose to her feet and started to walk around as she spoke. "This note is odd from our point of view, but not so odd for someone who hadn't seen her previous writing ability on display from her past career. The note obviously passed review, if that was her motive, which tells me that whomever she's with doesn't know her very well." That caused Duane to open his eyes and look at Irene. He smiled.

"So I thought that a thesaurus would be the way to start out."

"Addie, you'll have to tell me again what a thesaurus is," interrupted Parker. "You told me once, but I don't remember much. A sort of dictionary, I think?"

"Well done, Willie," Addie answered, "you were very close, but it's not a dictionary, really. It's a book that allows you to look up a word and find other words that mean about the same thing. Writers use a thesaurus a lot, even if they won't admit it."

She turned toward Irene. "Irene, what you've done so far is really terrific. Keep going."

Irene beamed with pleasure. "I just listed the words that seemed odd; you know what I mean. The words not in Jan's way of writing, as I understand it. Here's my list of these words," she said, and spread a piece of paper out on the table. "There are probably others, folks. Don't hesitate to bring them up. By the way," she added, "we can add the misspellings and poor punctuation to the list, too, although I don't know what she had in mind."

Parker looked at the list and saw written the following words and phrases: "backed up", "bogged down", "bull", "knight", "squire", "provider". Parker was glad that he wasn't selected to solve this puzzle. Maybe Irene wasn't on the right trail, although Parker thought that she was. And if so, Irene might have found that dangling string which, when pulled, causes all the pieces of the puzzle to come together.

"Next, I tried out the thesaurus idea by looking up the words 'backed up'. I actually found 'back up', so I went through the words given as possible substitutes. There were eight of them and I chose two of them: 'be behind' and 'back'. Then I moved to 'bogged down'. I found 'bog' and chose 'marsh' and 'mire', for no other reason than that would be two out of the three possible choices. Next I ----------,"

Parker listened with admiration as Irene took them through her reasoned approach to solve the conundrum.

"So," she said, "what I ended up with were these words, in no particular order; that I gleaned from the thesaurus: 'behind', 'back', 'bull', for which I have no word to give you, 'kingdom', and that's from 'knight', and I'm doing some guessing on that one, my friends," Irene said, "and 'squire' which is an 'armament specialist' in days gone by, and 'provider', which has other words that indicate that taking caution would be a good thing. You know, provide for yourself, etcetera. Add to that list the obvious errors in punctuation, and you have a list of words that make me feel bewildered and a little uncomfortable."

There was silence in the room. Parker knew he didn't feel like saying anything because he didn't think that he had anything to say that would add to the understanding of what Irene had done.

Then Duane sat forward and said, "Irene, did you use any of the other choices of similar words that you chose to leave out and try them in the list? You know, to see if they were compatible with any of the other combinations? You'd have to do it by sampling, of course. It would be impossible to dream up all the combinations of all the words and then look for similarities in each list. You'd have a nervous breakdown. Almost like the code breakers in England during World War Two. There were a lot of them at an estate called Bletchley Park, and they probably averaged two breakdowns a week. But you could have worked there, Irene, if you'd been around during those days, I'm sure. You've done really well." Irene studied Duane for a few seconds before accepting his words as complimentary.

"I tried a couple of combinations, Duane, and the overall impression of the note didn't change for me. I also used a thesaurus from thirty years ago, along with a new one, just for objectivity's sake in a very subjective process. And I still don't have a clue about 'bull'."

"Maybe 'bull' isn't in the thesaurus as we think of it, Irene," Addie said.

"Oh, it's in there, Addie," Irene said, "in all its various glories. You'd be surprised."

Parker stood up, stretched, and walked about the floor for a few steps. "This is all very tenuous, you know. We are making some jumps in logic that could be considered really stupid by almost anybody else. That being said, I believe Jan *was* warning me to be careful if I traveled to some place in Vermont, and I think that the poor punctuation was the signal flag for me to see. And she believed that I'd see it, but she had too much confidence in me, didn't she? Somebody else had to tell me to look at it. I won't tell her when I see her that I almost missed her very obvious clue."

"But where is this place in Vermont, Bill?" asked Duane. "How can we proceed without that vital piece of information?"

"Let's take it in steps," Parker said, in answer to Duane's question. "First, did Hugh Hammond take these pictures? If not, then we know that someone else took them and was in league with Hammond on his project, or whatever the hell he was working on. We need those answers and I think I know right where to begin."

The National Life building housed one of the larger insurance companies in New England, although only half of it was used by National Life. The rest was leased to the State of Vermont, with a few offices leased to smaller organizations. It was located right on the city line of Montpelier. Along with its primary use of providing a space to park a car, it also doubled as a meeting place, both planned and unintentional. Parker had heard that many clandestine meetings had been held in the dark of night in this parking lot – and in the bright sunshine, too, apparently. This was where Don Flanders held meetings that never happened.

"Why not your office, Don?" asked Parker, when he called Flanders after learning that Flanders was Hammond's lawyer. He listened intently. Then he said, "here's the sort of information I need, Don," and he spoke about the pictures and cameras and any other information that dealt with non-profits.

Then Parker said, in a dry voice, "Thanks so much." He hung up and turned to the group.

"That was Hugh Hammond's lawyer, Don Flanders, by name. He was a help to me when I was in the House three years ago. That's how I know him. I'm going to see him at 1:00PM tomorrow. Not in his office, though. Apparently he doesn't want to be seen with me. I don't understand that." Parker trudged back to his chair, looking a little down.

"That's all right, Bill, nobody who is anybody wants to be seen with a lawyer. Now, what's on your mind?" asked Duane.

"I just want to track down the person who took these pictures. I know it's probably impossible. That person, though, and maybe it's Hammond himself, which won't help us any, has a lot of answers for us and probably doesn't even know it. And then, after I see Don tomorrow, I'm dropping off at the home of a friend of mine who is a forester. I'm going to show him these pictures and see if we've missed anything that would tell him where these pictures might have been taken. Anyway, I want to see him and his family again. Good time to do it."

Addie said, "I know who you mean, Willie. It's Bob and Ruth O'Sullivan, isn't it? Please give them my best. Their kids must be growing up fast. We haven't seen them in quite a while."

"Why don't you come with me, Addie? It might be a good day for you."

"You've forgotten that I have volunteered to work on the planning for the eighth grade science and environmental fair for next weekend. I'll bet you've also forgotten that you are to be a judge at that same fair."

"I haven't forgotten, my dear. I'll be there at the school at the appointed day and hour," with an assurance he didn't feel. "When is it?" he asked, with some trepidation.

"If you go to the school, Willie, you'll miss the whole damn thing. It's a week away – next Saturday, and it starts at 4:00 PM - and it's at the Community Center, not the school." Parker could sense some slight irritation coming through along with the words. He didn't know why.

"Of course sweetie, and I'll be there." Parker wanted to change the subject but was having a difficult time finding a way through all the barriers Addie was throwing in his way.

"Now I have one more phone call to make, folks. Won't take a minute." It did, of course, take fifteen of them, but at the end of the call, Parker was pleased.

He had called Hal Birdsall at home. Surprisingly, he was there. After checking to see if his secretary was still on the job, which she was, and not for much longer, apparently, Parker asked him to contact his brother's widow again and ask her to check, once more, for any papers, letters, business meeting minutes, and any other sort of correspondence at all that she might have found since she sent the first small package of information regarding her husband's gun collection. And please make it fast. It was that particular request that gave Parker the distinct impression that Birdsall would have strangled him if he'd been in the kitchen with him.

But when Birdsall had finished speaking, he agreed to do what he could, and then jammed down the receiver so hard, and so inaccurately, that it could be heard all around the kitchen as it banged around before finally breaking the connection.

"He was a little put out I think," said Parker. "I don't believe he relishes the task of calling his sister-in-law again."

It was very late, and Irene stood up, and walked over towards to the door. "Late night, everybody. Time for me to get on home. I have a tough boss." She turned and thanked Addie for the company and the information. She kissed Duane and Kate on the cheek. "That's in case I don't see you again before you head back to Colorado."

40

Parker drove into the huge parking lot of the National Life building, and began the search for the dump area, called by the ProgDems a "refuse collection and categorizing center". Everything was a "center" for some purpose or other, to the ProgDems. Centralizing everything meant to them that the problem was bound to be solved.

No problem was ever solved by any government program, Parker knew. The first obstacle to any governmental success was that the people who were hired to run the effort had no incentive whatsoever to fix anything. If they actually did what the legislation required, they'd be out of a job.

The next obstacle was created by the politicians, who didn't want to get rid of any program, even though it was an obvious failure, because it might be used against him or her in the next election.

Don Flanders told Parker he would meet him in the parking area devoted to the state offices, and would be parked behind the "refuse collection and categorizing center" dumpsters at 1:00 PM. Parker thought the location of the meeting was odd but maybe appropriate. Leave it to a lawyer, he thought.

Parker pulled his pickup around the dumpsters and stopped behind a fence that provided cover for the trash. It occurred to him that Flanders must have used this spot before for quiet meetings. Parker didn't consider his request so special that he had to meet a lawyer in this secret place. Maybe Flanders wanted to talk about something that deserved to be hidden by trash, thought Parker. Well, we'll find out, he thought – maybe.

Parker leaned against the driver's door, enjoyed the warmth of the sun, and wondered what was going on behind all those glass windows. Was it productive? Did it mean anything to anybody? What if all those windows were only for one use – allowing nosey people, who should be working their fingers to the bone, a perfect perch for viewing the outside world, which, in this case, was a damned parking lot.

Parker looked down the open aisle of the parking lot and saw a sedan rolling into the far end of it and then heading straight down the main row for the trash receptacles. The driver pulled in behind the dumpsters and nosed up against Parker's truck. He carefully got out of his car, looked around, and then walked over to Parker.

Maybe Parker should have wondered more about meeting in an out-of-the-way place. Maybe Flanders didn't want to be seen meeting with a pickup like Parker's in the area. Or maybe he had other things on his mind. It couldn't be Parker himself, he decided.

Flanders seemed different today than Parker remembered from three years before. He looked just slightly on the scruffy side – as if he didn't really care how he looked, but knew he needed to try to match his profession. Parker also noticed that Flanders seemed slightly on edge.

"Afternoon, Don," said Parker, perhaps just a little too enthusiastically. "Long time."

"Hello, Bill, and yes, it has been a while." Flanders forced a miniature smile which disappeared quickly. "What are you working on now? Can you tell me?" as he and Parker shook hands. "The information you wanted to see tells me that you have some task in front of you, and it involves Hugh Hammond. Anything about the Hammond estate is confidential, you know."

"Of course I know that, Don. I'm simply looking into another problem that someone else thinks they have and Hammond's name came up."

"Really, Bill?" Flanders exclaimed and, because of his tone, he may as well have said "I don't believe a word of it".

"What's the general subject of your interest in seeing some material of one of my clients? After you answer that, maybe I'll talk with you," said Flanders curtly.

Parker looked down at the toe of his shoe, then the trees, and then the sun – anywhere but at Flanders.

He may look a little shabby, thought Parker, but he's still a lawyer. Parker cast a fly over the Flanders pool. "I think it has to do with some unethical people in Vermont. I'm not sure, mind you, Don, but it's the only subject that my friend and I talked about. I felt I owed this person a favor for past services and I'm helping him now."

"Come on, Parker," said Flanders, showing impatience. "Out with it. You see, I've been doing some very careful research in some matters that Hammond knew a great deal about. I didn't like what I've found so far."

Parker thought about that comment from Flanders. It had become suddenly apparent that he needed to trust Flanders in this. After all, Flanders worked for Hammond and without doubt he would know something about Hammond's interests - possibly in the same subject that had interested Parker. So Parker eased ahead a little more forcefully.

"I'm just looking for some general information on the non-profit happenings in Vermont, Don. Trying to help somebody out. You know how that is, as a lawyer. Unlike you, I'm not billing my hours to anybody." He smiled as he said this.

Flanders looked steadily at Parker for a few seconds. There was no answering smile. "I hope you can understand that this meeting never took place, Bill. If you don't understand that, then I'm leaving."

Parker was surprised by this remark. "Don't worry, Don. Not a word."

"But I *do* worry, Bill. I worry about this subject much of my time. I worry even more because I learned just today that my ex-client and good friend, Hugh Hammond, was murdered, which you didn't think to mention, and I also learned that you were involved in some part of the police investigation. So, what's the story? Why are you here, asking questions? Why did you call me? Why do you need this information? I need to know this, Bill. Then maybe we'll have a frank discussion."

Parker was not ready to hear that the word was already out on the street that Hammond's death was murder. His face must have shown his alarm.

"Oh, you've still got a couple of days before this is generally known," remarked Flanders. "I just had the information from an interesting guy who I do work for on occasion." Flanders changed position so that he was looking directly into Parker's eyes. "Tell me all about it, Bill."

What could I lose, Parker asked himself? In fact, I might gain something.

Parker started at the beginning and brought Flanders into it fully. He did it because it seemed that Flanders had information that was more than just about cameras. And he told Flanders everything because Parker might need a lawyer and an ally at some point in this whole mess.

Flanders walked over and stood beside Parker and looked up at the sun, too. Parker thought that Flanders probably never noticed the comfortable warmth it gave because he was too busy digesting everything Parker had told him. He'd be a terrible trial lawyer and poker player, Parker thought. I can read him like a book, and I'm not very good at that kind of thing.

Finally, Flanders turned toward the parking lot, and looked it all over carefully. And then back toward Parker.

"I'm being watched, Bill," he said, quietly. "Somebody is watching me and following me. I just know it. Some people can tell that sort of thing. I'm one of them. My office was bugged – in fact, it still is. Can you believe that?" Flanders was very agitated about that and it showed. It seemed that he felt violated. In fact, he had been, in the most comprehensive way.

"My security company found it. They were brilliant."

He pointed over his shoulder at his vehicle. "And this is not my car. I borrowed it from a friend. These clothes are not mine. They represent something I would never wear. I came here today from a motel I stayed in last night. I haven't gone into my office yet. I'm here only because your call intrigued me, and because I was advised by my security guy to meet with you and to follow this routine before I did. It seemed at the time a way to find out what was going on in this Hammond business. Because something truly is. I'm also here because I'm very worried and I took the chance that you might be providing the only life raft I can see out there."

Flanders hesitated for a few seconds, and then it seemed that he decided to go all the way. "Or maybe you are involved in this shadow work and this is your way to deliver a message to me – a message I won't enjoy hearing. Which is it?" he asked abruptly.

Parker looked carefully at Flanders. This man was really on edge, thought Parker. Maybe he really is being followed. Maybe it's his imagination. But I won't lose a thing by siding with him and it might provide some solace for him.

"I'm not following you, Don. I know nothing about anything that's troubling you. You're correct, though. Something is wrong in the non-profit world. I have no idea what's going on. I'm just pulling at threads until something unravels. You were one of the threads. I need you to trust me, and I need the information you may have in Hammond's estate file. It may be useless, but I need it."

Flanders opened the door to Parker's pickup. "Let's talk inside. It will be quiet and easier to talk."

After they had gotten settled, Parker asked, in an off-hand manner, "Who's your security service, Don. Maybe I know them."

"Oh," Flanders said, "a small company out of South Burlington. Barkley, Barkley, and Barkley. I helped him set up the business when he first got started. Know them?"

"No," said Parker, deciding that Barkley, Barkley, and Barkley, Inc. should be left out of things. "They must be good to find out you were being bugged."

Flanders nodded. "It all happened so quickly, too. Hugo Barkley, a terrific person, by the way, Bill, and President of the company, always came in to my office late in the afternoon to do what I wanted. All of us in my firm looked forward to it because he was so pleasant and also very smart. He and I would occasionally go out for a beer after he got done." Flanders stopped talking, seeming to wonder what to say next or, maybe, if he had said enough.

"All of a sudden," he blurted out, "one day, the week before last, he called and asked if he could come in after midnight that night because he had a scheduling problem. Of course, I told him. When I came in the next morning, there was a sealed envelope on my desk. It was a handwritten note from Hugo. It said that he was parked across the street in a black van and would pick me up on the street one block over from the back of my building five minutes after he had seen me enter my law office. As you can imagine, Bill, this behavior was beyond anything in my experience with him. But, as he obviously wanted to keep our meeting quiet, I did as he asked. We talked for about ten minutes while he drove around the downtown of Montpelier. Then he dropped me off some distance from my office."

Flanders turned toward Parker. "Is this too much minutiae, Bill? I don't want to bore you."

Parker, unbeknownst to Flanders, was riveted by this story. "Please keep going, Don. I'll tell you if it's too much."

Flanders gave a quick nod and said, "He told me that he'd found a tiny microphone in my personal office coupled to a wire that ran down through a hole in the floor and into a voice-activated recorder in the basement. He told me that he had an expert working on this sort of problem and he needed me to keep quiet about it for about a month. But to try to find out who, inside my little office, was the damn traitor. So I have kept quiet and I have found the traitor. Except for you, I've told no one else. And I think you needed to know this."

Parker hoped that Hugo's "expert" didn't turn out to be one William Parker, master of no-trades-at-all.

"In addition to this office bugging, Don, what makes you think that you are being followed?"

"The office invasion only made me look at things around me with more care, Bill. And I saw things and people that wouldn't have been worrisome a year ago. Today they are. That's all I can tell you. Maybe I'm overdoing it, but I'd rather do that than the reverse."

Parker was tempted to tell Flanders about Hugo's finds in Burlington and elsewhere, but he didn't think it would advance Flanders' emotional stability so he remained silent about Hugo.

"So, Bill," Flanders said, "now we both know everything about what we both are thinking about. What's next?"

"Can you tell me about how long you've been followed? Any idea at all, Don?"

"I've been thinking about that, Bill, and I think it's been for a long time – maybe as much as a year. That's much more of a guess than a certainty, but probably ever since the Governor named me to our District Environmental Commission. But I'd guess about that time frame. Not too long after the big fire at the new manufacturing plant being built over near the Interstate. That was so terrible that I unconsciously time everything of importance from that date."

Parker thought about all this information. In a way, Flanders had had the same experiences that he had. Different order of events, maybe, but everything seemed to fit.

"Don, what have you got for me to look at? I won't need to keep it – just look it over and try to learn enough to guide me from this time forward."

Flanders reached into his inner jacket pocket and pulled out an envelope. "This is a list of the items that are in his estate and that are more general in nature. Not cash, stock, and items like that. These could almost be in the category of special bequests."

Parker scanned the list. He found the camera, which was a 35mm Nikon. "Do you know if the camera was used, or loaned out, at any time during the months prior to his death?" asked Parker.

"The camera was never used by anybody, Bill, at least during the seven months before his death. It was damaged, and there was a tag on it when I got to listing the contents of the house. The tag read," and he pointed to the last page of the inventory where, in pencil, were the words, "Damaged, November deer season, 2003. Send repair costs to G." Parker looked out the window, figuring dates and times. "When I saw the camera, Bill, the lens was either scratched or cracked, and the camera was dirty, as if it had been dropped in the dirt and rubbed around a bit. I brushed it off and listed it."

Parker handed the list back to Flanders. "I'm glad to know about the camera. It doesn't say if it was loaned out, but I'd guess it was at least used by somebody who didn't treat it very well. But, anyway, it was in November of last year."

"Anything else, Don?" Parker asked. "You've been carrying that folder since you got here. I hope there's something else for me."

"There is, Bill. This is a file of letters, announcements, replies, and information regarding his memberships and associations and other non-business information that I worked on for him. Hammond was never one for saving anything except the most essential papers. I discussed this with him because I always thought that a person needed to keep information about dealings with other people. Memories are no good after ten minutes have elapsed. He wouldn't hear of it. He used to say to me, 'Don, nobody ever looks again at 99% of the papers they save. All they are is a few markers along the road we're traveling and they don't mean anything after a month goes by.'" Flanders shook his head.

"So," he continued, "I saved a few of the important ones which I had something to do with, and shoved them in his file at my office. He didn't know I was doing it, of course, but lawyers save these types of things. It's a trademark of being thorough."

The file was thin. "This shouldn't take long, Don, and I'll let you go on your way."

Parker looked through the file. There was nothing in the file that could point Parker in any direction. It was just the normal collection of random pieces of paper, as Hammond would have put it, that were of no help to anyone. Murder certainly wasn't involved.

One of the notes was a quick handwritten communication to Flanders from Hammond, thanking the lawyer for recommending him as a member of the Board of Directors for a small non-profit organization called The Northeast Government Watch Institute.

"Don, what's the Northeast Government Watch Institute?"

"It's just a small non-profit set up to watch Vermont government and to write monthly reports to its members, op-ed pieces, and to give interviews on radio and TV," answered Flanders.

Parker nodded. There seemed to be dozens of them like that in Vermont. At least all the facets of the political spectrum were represented. He put the papers back into the file and handed it back to Flanders.

"Anything of help, Bill?" asked Flanders.

"I guess not, Don, but thanks very much for agreeing to meet with me and breaking your lawyer's oath of silence to do it." Parker was very disappointed. This elaborate set-up for a quiet meeting yielded nothing.

"Well, I'm glad we had this meeting," said Flanders. I guess I've been helped even if you haven't."

Parker smiled without humor and said, "Let me give you my phone number, Don. If anything does come to mind, please call me, and I'll do the same for you." He jotted his name and number on a piece of notepaper and handed it to Flanders. True to his lawyerly nature, Flanders folded it carefully and slipped it into his wallet.

They shook hands and went their separate ways, Flanders to the life of an active and worried attorney, and Parker back to the life of a semi-retired insurance man. But one who still had many questions, and who was determined to find the answers to them.

41

Parker left Montpelier and headed south on Interstate 89 and then onto Interstate 91. At Exit 6 he cut across on Route 103 to Chester, heading for the home of his friends the O'Sullivans.

Parker could not travel on a road in Vermont that went through the towns with ski areas without thinking about the days of Act 60, Vermont's destructive school funding law.

This road connected with the fabled Route 100 that went through the majority of the towns that were forced to pay a property tax rate that was established by the state, and not their local Select Boards. About 50 towns were initially required to pay school taxes that were higher by up to 500% into the state coffers. With those taxes the state forced them to pay, it became impossible for these towns to maintain the quality of their schools. These target towns were forced to strip their schools of all the programs that made them some of the best in the state.

The ProgDems told every town that these fifty towns would support the school spending of the remaining 200 towns and life would be wonderful again. These target towns with ski areas in them would be required to be "understanding" and "sharing".

Within three years the number of towns forced to pay into the state had tripled, and school spending was completely out of control. And Vermont had wrecked three tax commissioners and dozens of the best schools in the process, thought Parker. Needless to say, the ProgDems avoided these towns whenever they were on the road. However, the angry residents of these towns continued to elect ProgDems. Amazing, thought Parker.

The only good thing that possibly came out of all this chaos caused by the ProgDems was that one of the Senators who was an architect of this terrible legislation ran for Lt. Governor. This ex-Senator had been clobbered. This Senator probably hoped that her Senate reputation had preceded her. The Senator's hopes came true, thought Parker.

These tax increases were no surprise to normal people who had lives grounded in realism and experience. However, it always surprised the ProgDems who had had the idea driven into their heads by high school and college teachers that socialism was splendid as long as the populace gave them enough money to pay for it. And the self-esteem of these leaders would be elevated wonderfully, thought Parker, with disgust. As his father used to say, just "follow the money". He could have added "and watch whatever it touches rot away before your very eyes".

Parker was now on the Green Mountain Turnpike, just on the eastern edge of Chester, and headed to the O'Sullivan spread.

For down-country people, who had not seen this Vermont local road, it probably sounded like a high speed road that would bypass Route 103, the main clogged artery in the heart of Vermont each Sunday afternoon during ski season.

Actually, it did allow a driver to avoid a small piece of Route 103. That was a good thing, unless you had an aversion to a dirt road that changed with the weather and knocked hell out of your car and its passengers while heading home to Massachusetts, New York, or New Jersey.

Parker had unexpectedly met the O'Sullivans five years before during one of his many House campaigns in Bridgeton. The O'Sullivans happened to be visiting friends in Bridgeton when Parker knocked on the door to hand out a brochure, hoping the householder would vote for him, and ask if they had any questions. Usually no questions were asked by Parker's constituents, and he would move on. The folks in this particular house when Parker came calling had no questions, as usual – but the O'Sullivans did.

Parker gently reminded them that they weren't in his district and that their questions would be better asked of their own Representative. The O'Sullivans accepted that as being quite true, and then began to pepper him with questions anyway. Even some of their children did, which surprised and pleased him. Parker did the best he could in answering these queries, and hoped that they didn't think he was yet another political dunce.

Parker found his way into the front yard/parking lot of the O'Sullivans. He climbed down from his truck and stopped to look at the O'Sullivan castle.

It was one of these rustic houses, built by the owner, added on to as needed, and very comfortable to be in. In fact, it was great fun to just stand inside the house and see all the different items of interest that the O'Sullivans had accumulated. That happens, decided Parker, when you have taken on the responsibility of the education of a number of children, all of whom ask a lot of questions – about everything.

As he trudged up to the front door, it opened, revealing Rose O'Sullivan, who launched into her greeting by asking, "Have you eaten, Mr. Parker?"

Rose O'Sullivan was the ultimate housewife, worker, planner, and stage manager for a very busy playhouse. Parker thought that an Oscar should be given out to Rose every year, to be stopped only when all the children were on their own. She did all this while her husband worked as a forester.

Other than marking trees to be cut down, Parker was never sure what that term really meant until Bob explained it to him. Then Parker had an entirely different view, and part of that view reinforced Parker's total lack of trust in the ProgDems because of the sale of the Champion Paper Company land in the Northeast Kingdom to environmentalist interests.

At the time, the methods and untruths used to accomplish this purchase were never understood by opponents of the deal, and understood only too well by the small number of lobbyists and "experts" who told the ProgDems to vote as they would be instructed to vote.

While these thoughts were rolling around in Parker's mind, suddenly the O'Sullivans' well-used front door opened and the O'Sullivan kids rolled in from outside. Bob and Rose had six children. They were handsome kids, and very well-mannered, energetic, active, and interested in everything into the bargain. This attribute was clearly shown when one of the boys of about five years old suddenly popped up in front of Parker and recited the preamble to the Vermont Constitution. Never missed a beat either. It was at that moment that Parker suspected that these children were not educated in the Vermont public school system.

He was correct. They were home-schooled and doing very well, by the looks. Of course, their parents were still paying education taxes in their town to support a school in which they had no confidence. That was okay with the ProgDems. They just wanted to control the money and use some of it to hire their friends who were otherwise unemployable. Parker and Addie, who had also met the O'Sullivans, always considered that that sacrifice was the ultimate test of commitment to children.

He was greeted noisily and cheerfully. A lot of words were flying around that everybody heard and understood - except Parker.

Rose was doing her four jobs and talking to Parker, Bob, and each child, too. Amazing, thought Parker. All the kids looked as though they had grown at least six inches since he had last seen them. Impossible, he thought. Nothing but mushrooms grow that fast.

"What are you doing at our door, Bill?" asked Bob. "Glad you're here, of course. What can we do for you – or are you just sick of driving and pulled off the road and here you are?"

Parker grinned. "Sorry to just drop in like this, Bob. I won't stay long but I need your expertise. I feel lucky, too. You're not usually home. Usually running around in the woods identifying things."

Bob looked at Parker quizzically, smiling all the while. "What's going on in your life, Bill? What are you doing now? Still nosey and playing strange games? Oh," he said, "Addie called. So we knew you were coming. Even washed our faces and hands for the big event. She wants you to call her before you leave here."

Parker laughed and then lied through his teeth. "Thanks for the information, Bob. And, in answer to your nosey question, I'm just helping out a good friend, that's all."

Bob nodded and said, "As I recall, that's what you were doing the last time you helped someone – and were shot."

"I have some photos, Bob," Parker said, paying no attention whatsoever to O'Sullivan, "and I wanted to pin down where you thought they might have been taken. I'm convinced that they were taken in Vermont," Parker added with enthusiasm.

"Wonderful, Bill" he said, in mock cynicism. "And that's all the information and guidance I get? Parker, you're an idiot, do you know that? Nobody can answer something that you can't describe any better than that."

Again, Parker seemed to have lost his hearing. He spread the pictures out on the dining table. "Any ideas, Bob?" Parker winked at Ken, the older son.

The two O'Sullivan parents, along with their oldest son, began to look the photos over. All three of the onlookers were careful with them, as if they were the only copies available and could never be duplicated. As it happens, Parker thought, that's true. All he had were those prints. He decided that copies had to be made as soon as he could get to a camera shop.

O'Sullivan seemed to be arranging them in an order that meant something to him. It was entirely different from the arrangement that Duane had settled on. Abruptly, O'Sullivan stood up, waved toward a door that Parker hadn't seen before, and said, "To the dungeon, Bill. We have some work to do," and walked away.

Parker followed dutifully, along with Ken bringing up the rear. He hoped that this meant that Bob had something to add to the scant knowledge he already possessed. He not only was right, but he was overwhelmed by the perspective that O'Sullivan brought to the problem Parker had presented to him.

In the cellar Parker was confronted with what O'Sullivan called the "nerve center". It contained a computer, a printer, or maybe two, Parker was never sure of that, what looked like a drawing table, but used for whatever purpose was called for, and other mystical symbols of his trade. To say it was neat and orderly was to place an undeserved grace on this work area. It wasn't. But O'Sullivan knew where everything was and could lay his hand on the implements of his expertise in an unerring way. The purpose of the orderliness of any work area, Parker knew, was its usefulness to the owner and not the reaction of House Beautiful magazine.

Parker himself could lay claim to some of the greatest areas of work space wreckage in the universe. His problem was that, after he had completely organized things, he couldn't find anything he needed. He never talked about his case of the cluttered mind syndrome with anybody, including Addie. Of course, he suspected that he didn't need to mention it to her. Addie knew everything.

O'Sullivan sat down at the desk, turning toward Parker as he did so. "Are you certain that these shots were from the same roll of film, Bill? I know they're numbered, but that was done by hand."

"I'm assuming so, Bob. But only because of those numbers."

While Parker was answering the question, O'Sullivan was setting aside four of the pictures. Two from early in the roll and three at the end, just before those that were out-of-focus. There was a long-distance shot showing a couple of mountains, then one showing a steel gate across a path or road with some water in the background. The later shots told Parker nothing at all. Just trees on the edge of a clearing, and water in the distance.

"Bill, this is really odd. I actually think I know where these pictures were taken. It so happens that I'm certain I've been in this area for survey purposes a few years ago." Leaning forward, O'Sullivan handed the long distance picture to Parker. "See anything that jumps out at you?" he asked.

Parker looked carefully at the snapshot. He knew there must be something that caught O'Sullivan's eye and he was being challenged to see it, too. But he couldn't see what O'Sullivan saw. "It just looks like uninterrupted forest to me, Bob."

"This little exercise is probably unfair, Bill." With a pencil point he directed Parker's gaze to the middle of the photo. "Can you see that very faint line running across the face of the picture? Left to right, just below the middle?"

Parker thought he could, and said so. "But I don't know what it means."

"That's a major power line swath cut right through this forested area," said O'Sullivan. His tone of voice left no doubt.

Parker looked steadily at O'Sullivan. "Then you *do* know where this area is located, don't you?"

"I think so, Bill. And I think I can show you some pictures that I took awhile ago and, if my memory serves, you'll see the resemblance right off."

Parker was shaking his head. "It seems incredible to me, Bob, that I could walk into your house with some mystery photographs, knowing nothing about them and, within 15 minutes, you can show me where they were taken in Vermont. I guess I'm having a hard time with that. And the reason I bring it up is that it's so critically important to me and what I'm working on."

O'Sullivan settled back in his chair, pulled at his beard, and smiled at Parker. "Remember, Bill, if I hadn't had the chance to walk around in this area some time ago, we'd be doing too much guessing about where your pictures were taken to be useful. It's not really odd, though, that I know where these photos were taken. Most of us who are full-time foresters, and work to be better at our business, have been in this area where your pictures were taken at least once. And I made a few trips into this area. I know where they were taken. I have many friends who could tell you where your happy snaps were taken, too, as I said, but they would have to be contacted and you'd lose a month to learn what I've just told you. And you've been incredibly lucky that I have my own pictures of this area. All this is my professional opinion, Bill. If I didn't know this stuff, I wouldn't be a trusted forester for very long." Parker smiled at Bob.

"And I don't have a clue," Bob continued, "about an insurance policy covering anything of value. Insurance policies confuse me and that makes me nervous. But you can look one over, I'll bet, and tell me the makeup of the family that would buy this sort of policy, what company is selling it, and about what it costs. Correct?"

Parker answered in the affirmative. He saw the point Bob was making.

"Are you ready to be impressed with modern technology and my special brilliance in the manipulation of these gadgets?" asked O'Sullivan, grinning at Parker. Parker allowed as how he was.

O'Sullivan poked at his computer keyboard and a screen came up that had small images of many photos of woods, trees, trails and paths, and water. "I have, in this magic box," patting the top of the monitor, "a software package called DeLorme Topo Quads. Pretty jazzy name, wouldn't you say, Bill? Even the uninitiated, Mr. Parker, will note the significance of the quasi-word 'Topo'. Correct?" Another big smile followed this proclamation. Parker nodded and grinned, noting O'Sullivan's obvious enjoyment of this moment.

"This little beauty will tell us everything we need to know, and will set you on the path to success – which, I'm sure, based on your history, goes through some anxious moments." O'Sullivan wasn't smiling as he said this last bit. Neither was Parker.

O'Sullivan tapped keys, shoved the mouse around, and suddenly Parker saw his long-distance photo appear on the screen. "How in the world did you put my picture on your screen?" he yelped. "I never saw you open your scanner."

Another smile from O'Sullivan. "I didn't scan anything. That's not your photo. That's mine. Yours must have been taken from somewhere around where mine was – and that's at a spot that has sort of a pullout for viewing. There are thousands of photos taken from this spot, by thousands of tourists, over many years."

Then O'Sullivan started moving the picture around. Parker moved closer to the screen. He was transfixed.

"Bob, this is wonderful," he said. "I suspected that all kinds of technology was out there, resisted by people like me, of course, but I'd never seen it."

The image on the screen was a view of the forest from high, low, and sideways. It wasn't Parker's photo, of course, because that photo was only one plane. Also the computer image was not as well defined. However, the first view, as purposely established by O'Sullivan, was very close to Parker's photo.

"Let me show you something else, Bill," said O'Sullivan. He began playing with things on the keyboard and with the computer mouse. Images were moving rapidly on the screen, as if in a hurry to get out of the way of the next group in line. Parker thought that all that was needed was a background of some weird and haunting music and deep drums and some incantations from O'Sullivan while all this activity was whipping by.

And suddenly things stopped. The screen revealed the satellite imagery which fixed the location of the area exactly. The aerial photos, put at the mercy of this brilliant computer program, allowed O'Sullivan to tip, turn and elevate the whole area that O'Sullivan thought would be helpful. The silhouette of West Mountain, matched against one of Parker's photos, was the final proof for Parker that O'Sullivan had identified the area where Parker's photos were taken. And by doing so, a loop was closed around this strange treasure of photos, obtained by Hugh Hammond through somebody else's efforts, hidden in an old cow barn in Chittenden County, and rescued by Parker. They were of the highest importance to Hammond. Therefore, they must be important to Parker, too. The problem for Parker was that he still didn't know how to begin to find out their secret.

"Where is this location in the Northeast Kingdom, Bob?" asked Parker.

"I'm betting that the area where your photos were taken is in Ferdinand. A nasty hike east of Ferdinand, will take you to the Ferdinand Bog, right into the core area of the former Champion Paper Company land. Ferdinand itself is pretty close to being a gore, I'm told. In any case, very few people live in the town."

O'Sullivan fiddled with his computer again. "Here's the clincher, Bill. See the power line on my computer-created image of the land?" He tipped the image down, giving Parker a type of aerial view. It instantly reminded Parker of his days in Vietnam, flying his vulnerable little 120 MPH puddle jumper over terrain like this, and being shot at by people who didn't like him very much.

"And if you need anything else, notice the trees in this shot." He pushed one of Parker's pictures toward him. "These trees are all tamarack and black spruce. Just what I saw when I was up there. To me, they positively confirm the identify the area as the Northeast Kingdom. The pictures tell us pretty close to *where* in the Kingdom."

Parker could see it all clearly.

"Now, look at this picture of yours." He handed Parker another one of his photos, taken near the beginning of the roll. "Upper left corner, Bill." as he pointed again with his pencil. "Right there," as he hit the photo with an index finger. "See that straight line through the branches of the tree? And see how straight the tree trunk is?"

Parker had seen the straight trunk in his kitchen the first time he had opened the container of pictures. "What of it?" he said.

"That's not a tree, Bill," O'Sullivan screeched. "That's a power pole! And that straight line is the wire! And this location is just west of Ferdinand Bog. More proof, you see."

Parker was just as excited as O'Sullivan was, but he tried to show a calm demeanor. "I won't disagree, Bob. Now my question to myself is this: why did my friend hide these pictures so carefully and completely – and then suddenly blurt out where they were and that I should pick them up if anything should happen to him? Which it did."

O'Sullivan stared at Parker for a few seconds. "So that's what this is all about, is it? That's why it's so important for you to have the location of your pictures nailed down tight. And that's why you came to me – on the off chance that I could get things started for you without drawing a lot of attention to yourself. Or me, for that matter. What you're into isn't very pleasant, is it, Bill? Unless I miss my guess, there's some very bad business going on here. Am I right? Typical Bill Parker business that's not very healthy for anyone involved."

Parker was gazing at the wall, and not seeing it. He nodded slowly at O'Sullivan's questions and comments. "I'm getting away from you and your family right now, Bob. Just to be safe. I still don't have an idea of what's going on. However, it's possible that I now know where something is located that will tell me what I need to know." He got to his feet, picking up his coat as he did so.

“You’re not leaving quite yet, Bill,” said O’Sullivan. “I have one of my own pictures to show you. Not a computer-generated one. I didn’t realize that there was a small sign in the foreground when I took it. Even when I saw that I had included it in the picture unintentionally, it was okay. I didn’t give it any more attention other than to blame my amateurish talent with a camera. In fact, it gave the picture a nice contrast, you know? A sign just stuck in the ground. If we assume that my pictures were taken in the same area in which your pictures were taken, then it might be interesting to look at it.” Parker leaned forward, looking interested.

“I can blow it up to a certain magnification,” said O’Sullivan. “Then we’ll use a magnifying glass to see what it says – or give us a good idea what it might say. Sometimes this works, and sometimes it doesn’t.” With that, more screen action, some muttering from O’Sullivan, and the sign appeared.

“Hard to read the words, even with the glass,” murmured O’Sullivan.

“It’s not words, Bob, it’s just capital letters, I think,” said Parker. “The words come later, right under these letters. The words are easier to read because I’ve certainly seen these two words in my line of work. ‘KEEP OUT’ is what I think I see. I’m sure you’ve seen them, too.”

“Yes, you’re right, Bill. And the letters above ‘keep out’ are NPF II.”

“Bob, do you woodsy types use letters and numbers like these to indicate an association or group, or something like that?”

“Yes, we’re as guilty of that as many others, but I’ve never seen that one, and I’ve seen a lot of acronyms in my time. But that’s not even an acronym. That’s just letters that probably stand for something, but I haven’t any idea what. There’s the Roman numeral ‘II’, also. I draw a blank there, too. All I can think of is that there’s a Roman numeral ‘I’ out there somewhere.”

Parker frowned. “So now I know where these pictures were taken, and about when – certain enough, anyway, to assume it until something gets in the way that changes my mind.” Parker turned toward the wall again. “My problem is that I don’t even know why I want to know where they were taken. I just feel that something is very wrong.”

O’Sullivan studied Parker for a few seconds. “You’re going in there, aren’t you, Bill?”

Parker nodded. "Yes, at some point I am. I have to see what the photographer saw who took these pictures."

"Well," O'Sullivan said, his voice soft, "take along black fly dope and keep your head down. A hunter was killed there last hunting season."

"Really, Bob? Well, this isn't hunting season, so that concern is not a worry," said Parker. "Another hunting accident in Vermont," Parker remarked. "Pretty soon we'll get a bad reputation, Bob."

"Friend of mine, John Chapman by name, would argue with you, Bill."

Parker sat straight up in his chair as if he had received an electric shock. "John Chapman, you said?" he yelped. "From Bloomfield?"

"Yes, that would be him. Do you know him? He told me that he had law enforcement experience that allowed him to make a judgment different from the Sheriff's regarding that body. I only thought that John was a part-time farmer, part-time guide for hunting and fishing, and full-time story teller."

Parker laughed out loud. "You've got it right, Bob." Parker knew what Chapman's "law enforcement experience" consisted of. A job as an unpaid and nosey informal amateur law enforcement officer is what he was. At Parker's instigation, too, a year or so ago, during a dangerous time looking for a killer in Burlington.

"And also Chapman has attracted an older lady who comes over to see him every once in a while. Can't believe it," Bob said, to himself. "She's from Burlington. Has to be at least 75, maybe more. So is he, for that matter. And he goes to see her, too, once in a while. Add the two together and they see each other a lot."

"She a classy lady, is she, Bob?" It was all Parker could do from visibly showing how amusing all this was to him.

"Oh, yeah, she is, Bill. Opposites, etcetera, you know."

"So John is still in good health?" Parker said.

"He certainly seems to be. Even stopped smoking that terrible pipe of his. Bought a suit, too. He told me he'd never owned one. I'm sure the lady had something to do with that. And she's a wonderful fly fisherlady, I'm told. Every bit as good as John. Cleans her own fish, too. That's probably what attracted him to her. He never met one like her before, I'll bet."

"I'm going up to see John. Haven't seen him in a year, probably."

"He have something to do with this business, Bill?" No flies on this man, Parker thought.

"No, I can't imagine that he does," Parker said, while being completely unsure that he knew what he was talking about.

Parker wasn't skilled at lying, and O'Sullivan saw right through it. "Right," he said, quietly.

"One more thing, Bill?" holding up an index finger.

"Of course, Bob." Parker settled back into his chair. "Shoot."

"The other pictures you brought in here? The ones showing the three large log cabins?" Parker nodded.

"If I'm right about the location of these cabins, and I think I am, then these buildings, which were not in the area when I was up there three years ago, are built in the core area. No buildings were allowed to be there. They're illegal. They were built without any permission, which they wouldn't have gotten if they'd asked."

"What would they be used for now?" Parker asked.

"Probably a playground for the Vermont left. You know what I mean, Bill. Take over some prime land for their followers, denying anyone else the right to do the same, and tell the strange people who use it that they have a right to do this because they are merely taking back what's rightfully theirs from the extremist businesses who stole it long ago. The national Planet Protection League has apparently been found to be giving some of its 'untouchable' land to its officers and board members for very private homes. This may be the same thing, right here in Vermont."

"I know you're not serious, Bob," said Parker. "You couldn't be, you know."

"No, probably not, Bill. I'm just tired." He stood up and stretched, and clapped Parker on the shoulder. "I'm really not serious."

"One last thing, Bob?" Parker asked, hesitantly.

"Sure," said O'Sullivan. "What is it?"

"This is tricky, Bob." Parker lobbed three pictures over to O'Sullivan. "Last three in the roll, Bob. A few people before you have looked at these. As long as I'm here, I'll give you a try. What can you tell me?"

O'Sullivan looked the pictures over closely, compared them to all the other pictures in the group, and handed them back to Parker. Parker felt almost sorry for O'Sullivan. Parker had, in a way, tricked him and it wasn't fair. "Well?" asked Parker.

"The photo guy was working very hard to get away from somebody who was chasing him and shooting at him. But he didn't get the picture he wanted, which was because he was running fast and then stopping for a split-second to try to get a picture of the shooter. That's all I can see with any certainty." Parker was flabbergasted.

"How in the world did you determine all that, Bob?" Parker exclaimed.

O'Sullivan seemed surprised that Parker sounded so amazed by what he said. "Easy," he said. "All the other pictures are very clear and focused. These three are blurred because he was running away, and the guy is chasing him. That's in the picture, but too blurred to make out, as you already know."

"What about the photographer being shot at?" asked Parker.

O'Sullivan reached across the table and picked up the three pictures, selected one, and dropped it down in front of Parker. "Take a look along the left side on the picture, Bill. Notice how the camera seemed to tip sharply to the right side when the picture was taken?"

"Those people who have looked at these pictures before had decided that the photographer tripped while running."

"That's sort of correct, Bill, but not anywhere near the truth."

"Well, what *is* the truth, Bob?" he asked, his exasperation starting to show through.

O'Sullivan decided that he'd better tell Parker now or else he'd have a stroke victim on his hands.

"Let's get practical, Bill. A person can't be running if they're facing in the direction from which they were trying to escape. You agree?" Parker indicated that he did.

"Have you looked along the left-center of the picture yet?" O'Sullivan asked.

"Yes, I have. I can see spots and slivers of light, as if the film was bad, or moving too fast, or something like that. That's what the other people said who looked these pictures over. I agree with them."

O'Sullivan took the picture again and pointed at the spots and slivers. "What this picture shows is not a section of a picture that was taken with bad film. For the most part, bad film is a thing of the past. No, these spots and slivers are slivers, all right. They're slivers of wood, caused by a heavy slug into the tree right beside the photographer, who had stopped to take another picture. No wonder the camera tipped off to the right. He stopped to take a shot with his camera and so did the guy with the rifle. Came damn close, too, but no brass ring."

It all made perfect sense to Parker. And all very discouraging, too.

"Can I use your phone, Bob?" asked Parker, troubled by this open display of attempts to kill somebody. "I need to call my wife." O'Sullivan handed him the phone.

Addie answered immediately. "I expected you to call earlier than this, Willie. Busy day?"

"Yes, it was, and I found out a lot about the pictures, sweetie, but I don't know, when I put everything together, what it all means. You probably know almost as much as I do right now and we haven't even seen each other. Any news from your end?"

"Yes, some. Hal Birdsall called this afternoon. He has received some more information from his brother's widow in Florida. And he said something strange, too. He said to tell you that 'the well has run dry'. What did he mean by that?"

"He means that Gil Birdsall's widow has told him not to bother her again. He must have caught hell from her for making continual requests for anything she may still have of her husband's that may be useful to us."

"That's odd," Addie said. "Why would she be unwilling to help her brother-in-law when it wouldn't make any difference to her?"

"She probably wants to forget her life in Vermont," Parker said, "because of the way her husband died. A hunting accident must seem such a useless pursuit to cause such a devastating loss."

"Anyway," Addie continued, "Hal wants you to stop in his office on this Sunday afternoon. He said he can't make heads or tails of the material she sent. He wants you to come to this meeting, if you can get there. He's called a meeting 'of people who have the same interests that you do', whatever that means. I told him you probably could."

Parker groaned. "Another trip to Burlington isn't what makes me excited, Addie. But, I'll go. I'll make a few calls tonight that should be made. I'll call Peter after this meeting of Hal's. I want to see Peter Morgan anyway. Are you okay, sweetie? Anything I'm not doing that I should be accomplishing? Anything urgent?"

"No, Willie. I just want to see this business you're involved in brought to an end. This is not my idea of semi-retirement for you."

"I agree," said Parker. "We'll get there, sweetie."

"I know we will," said Addie. "Will you be home today, Willie?"

"Yes, ma'am," Parker said. "I should be on my way from Bob's in a matter of minutes."

"No word from Jan Evlin?" asked Addie.

"Nothing at all, as far as I know. When she happens back on the scene I think she'll call our house first, so you'll know before me."

"You know, Willie, I'm getting worried about her."

"I know. So am I. I just can't figure out what scared her off."

"Get home as soon as you can, Willie. The dogs miss you."

Parker stretched out as well as he could in the unfamiliar chair, feet crossed and receiver held up to his ear by a shoulder. "You know, sweetie, I'm tired. And frustrated. There are so many loose ends to bring together. Hell, I don't even know if they *are* loose ends. I'm swimming in fast water and everything is rushing past me."

"You'll catch up, Willie. But come home now."

"Okay, take care, sweetie, and I'll try to be there in an hour, or so. I have the judging in the school coming up tomorrow and I won't miss that. How are the little monsters coming along on their science projects?"

Parker was secretly pleased that he remembered the judging of the middle school science projects that Addie had volunteered him to do. Mentioning it to Addie would no doubt win him some points for his civic duties remembered.

"And how is the big judge-detective coming along trying to become the Sherlock Holmes of the new century?" she said, chuckling. "I know what you're doing, Willie, and it won't work."

Parker sighed. Life goes on, he thought. Unfortunately, it sometimes doesn't include dragging the likes of me with it. However, he realized, too, that life doesn't go on for Hugh Hammond at all, does it? And others? We'll have to see, won't we, he thought.

42

For once in his life Parker arrived home about when he said he would. Addie must have decided that this rare occurrence would actually happen and she handed him a fresh cup of tea as he walked through the door.

"Are you ready to be the big-time judge tomorrow, Willie? I know the kids, as well as their parents, are looking forward to having you there. It seems that your reputation precedes you."

"What's that supposed to mean, Addie?" Parker asked. "I don't sell insurance to all of those people. How would they know me, or at least look forward to seeing me?"

"You apparently have some sort of reputation as being a giant-killer. These last three years have gotten you some notoriety, I believe."

"Oh, man," he breathed. "I'll keep a low profile, sweetie. Then neither of us will be embarrassed. What kinds of exhibits will I be seeing? And will the young exhibitors be there? It can be a lot more fun if they are."

"Oh, yes, they'll be there with bells on, as I'm advised by the parents. And the other two judges are known to you, too. Marvin Bailey will be there, and Dr. Malcom. They invited him because the science and art teachers in the Bridgeton Elementary School thought that he would lend some objectivity to the process. The heavy hitters are in town, as they say." She smiled broadly as she said it.

"So," Parker said, "we'll being viewing science projects of varying subjects and art work, too. Is that it?"

"Exactly," said Addie, "and you three are going to be in the center of a very competitive exhibit."

Parker sighed. "You mean that the parents all expect to win an award of some kind, is that it? And woe be the judge who doesn't bestow great honor on their child. I thought this was merely to show the students' progress in these two subjects. Not a damn competitive anthill."

"Willie, that's what it is. It's just that some parents want their offspring to do well. You know how that is."

"I definitely do, Addie. Yes, ma'am." Could be a rough day, Parker decided.

"How are you doing on the disappearance of Jan Evlin?" Addie asked.

"Well, she hasn't surfaced yet, if that's what you mean. And we don't know where she went. She was even more frightened than we thought, sweetie."

"Carolyn gave me the word that a couple of things have come to light since we last spoke, Willie. Many of these totally corrupt non-profits are being looked at by the Federal government for non-compliance with their stated purpose. And are these outfits angry? You bet. They're calling these investigations smear tactics, run by extremists, and the doubts being cast on their operations are going to harm the down-trodden population who they serve so loyally. Your name even came up when an ex-teacher from Spring River mentioned that you were to blame. He also said that you made a suggestion to him that was harmful to his self-esteem, and he's been tortured by your comment ever since. He's going to sue you for diminishing his status as a complete human being, and for intruding on his methods of living. Who in the world is this person, anyway? And what did you say to him?"

Parker thought for a spell and then snapped his fingers. "A couple of weeks ago, when I was just getting into this non-profit mess, I met this jerk in Montpelier. He was in a protest of some kind – I never did find out what he, and the group he was marching with, were mad about – so I joined it and talked to a few of them. His name, as I recall, was 'Bryce'. He was really out in left field. My remarks to him were respectful, Addie, really. At the end of our brief conversation I told him that he needed a bath and that he should take one regularly. He told me that I wasn't in tune with his sensitivities, which was true, of course, whatever they were, and we parted company. By the way, he knew who I was and he certainly didn't like me. That's it, Addie. That's all."

Addie smiled at her husband. "You've gotten into trouble before, you know, by offering suggestions that don't go down well. Also, how did he know you?"

"My impression was that he had been warned that I was looking into something or other. That's all I could find out. I really didn't look too hard, Addie. My first impulse was to get away from this idiot."

Addie had an expression on her face that told Parker she was concerned about something. "What is it, sweetie?" he asked.

"Why would a person like this know about you, Willie? And who would send out a warning that you were in the area to some silly little man like this teacher? At the least, any warning about you should go to somebody who knows that taking regular showers is important. Not some uneducated noise-maker."

"Who knows, Addie? Let's not be concerned about anything that came from this guy. He lived on another planet, anyway."

This didn't cause a change in Addie's concern. "Please watch out, Willie, from here on in. Please?"

"Of course, sweetie. You know that you don't have to worry about me." Parker decided that he wouldn't mention Ricky, the drugged out nit-wit with the bad social habits that he'd had the questionable pleasure of meeting in the Montpelier Police Department. He'd been told about me, too, Parker thought. This sender of the warnings should clean up his employee list, and soon.

Parker went to bed that night with visions of people with squeaky voices, aversions to baths, and a loose grip on reality, dancing in his head.

43

Parker and Addie arrived at the Community Center an hour ahead of the time that he was asked to be there to act as a judge. Parker wanted to get a feel for the order of the exhibits, and the overall quality of them, too.

The Bridgeton Community Center had started out life as a large one-room school in the village. When the town built its new school to replace it, the teachers were happy because it was a proven fact that better surroundings for them and the students would result in better educations for the children. Parker was part of the committee that studied the issue. It was ultimately approved by the committee. The voters agreed and a new and modern school was built. Parker was always of two minds on this whole thing, but he voted for it.

The teachers' union, the Vermont Teachers United Association, was pleased because Bridgeton was entering the modern world of education and they could now make the case for higher wages for its members and, therefore, although unsaid, higher dues income for the union treasury. The results, five years later, showed that one of the goals had been reached, and one hadn't. The teachers had been awarded noticeably higher paychecks, but the students had flat or lower achievement scores.

By then it was too late. Bridgeton demanded school choice so that their children could attend schools with proven higher results. The ProgDems in the Legislature refused. The citizens then demanded that they be allowed to establish a Charter school. The ProgDems refused. The school population decreased by a third. No teaching jobs had been eliminated.

However, as the school population dropped each year, the inevitable pressure to reduce the number of teachers in Vermont rose. In order to protect the union's jobs, and therefore its dues income, the union's pet legislators pushed through an amendment to include pre-school pupils as part of the school population figures. There was no legislative debate in either the House or the Senate on this issue. The ProgDems simply pushed it through.

This enabled them to demand an increase in the number of teachers employed. Tax revenues to the state that came from the statewide property tax could be used for pre-school education, thus diluting the amount of this tax money that went to the traditional grades of Kindergarten through 12.

The Vermont left had triumphed again. Parker decided that Vermont had reached the tipping point, and the taxpayers would begin to see even higher education tax bills in the future. The Bridgeton School, among many others, had become a kind of high income welfare colony for unneeded teachers. Parker wondered why a revolt wasn't brewing in Vermont.

Parker knew that within the Bridgeton School system there were some extraordinarily gifted and committed teachers. They talked to Parker very privately about the school system in Bridgeton, the intellectual corruption at the state level, and how discouraging it all was. They made it very clear, however, that they would say nothing publicly.

Their union, the VTUA, could see what the declining enrollment meant to their union. Did they tell their teachers to be prepared to lose some jobs because the number of kids to teach was falling dramatically? Not on your tintype, thought Parker. They just told the ProgDems in the Legislature to authorize state-run and state-funded pre-schools, and to hell with the privately-run pre-schools in the state. Putting them out of business was perfectly acceptable to the union and its legislators.

The ProgDems didn't want a legislative debate on this volatile subject either. One of their Committee Chairmen just slipped the money into the state budget on the orders of the VTUA. Tricky stuff, and with other people's money, too.

Parker was glad that his children were out of school and on their own, having missed this "wonderfully modern educational experience", as the teachers' union leadership called it.

As Parker and Addie were standing in the middle of the room, waiting for the exhibit to open, Marvin Bailey and Doc Malcom came walking over. They shook hands and exclaimed that none of them looked a day older. Then Doc Malcom, ever the objective observer, said, "Except you, Bill. You've been under some stress, I think. What's going on in your life?"

Doc Malcom was a well-known psychiatrist, as was his wife. They both had retired about ten years earlier but, about a year ago, had done some unofficial psychiatric work for Parker during a particularly bad and dangerous time. They'd probably checked me out along the way, too, he thought at the time.

"No, I'm fine Doc," Parker had answered. "My life is uneventful and stress-free."

"Let's have a talk very soon, Bill," Dr. Malcom replied glumly, as if he hadn't heard a word Parker had uttered.

Marvin was not as insightful as the Doc. "Bill, you look great. Just a tad tired, I think, but healthy."

Marvin was a very close friend of the Parkers, and he generally was thought of as the wisest man in Bridgeton. He had played a small, but pivotal, role in Parker's first adventure, setting in motion a sea change, at that time, in the ProgDem control of the Legislature.

"Done any fishing, Marvin?" asked Parker.

"No more fishing for me, Bill," he said. "Doctor said that my ticker wasn't to be trusted. Just be careful, she said."

"'She', Marvin?" Parker exclaimed.

"No matter what your age, Bill, a person has to change with the times. I'm not an old fogy, you know."

Parker smiled, showing great affection for this wonderful man. "You're the youngest man of eighty-one I've ever known."

"Eighty," Marvin said equably. "I'm only eighty."

"Sorry, Marvin," said Parker. "Your life doesn't seem to advance as fast as mine does."

At that moment a young woman came up to the four of them. "Addie, I'm glad you're here a little early," she said breathlessly. "Can you give me a hand helping Jesse set up his exhibit. It's a map of our country showing all of the locations of every Indian tribe that ever existed. Painted on it, in different colors, for goodness sake. And a tiny doll dressed in the ceremonial garb of each particular tribe. The whole thing fell apart as he was bringing it through the door. And it's set up on a plywood platform that's 8' x 8'."

"Of course I'll help, Liz. First, though, let me introduce you to our three judges." Addie turned to the three "judges" and said, "Boys, meet Liz Boyer. Liz, meet your three judges: Marvin Bailey, Doctor Malcom – I don't think I ever knew your proper first name, Doc – and my husband, Bill."

"Gentlemen, I'm so glad you agreed to be our judging panel. It's really nice to meet you all, finally." Liz was beaming at her three trophy panelists, her enthusiasm palpable in the room.

"I don't usually display nervousness, but I was pressed into service at the last minute to oversee the exhibit. I'm the math teacher in our school."

Parker looked around the large room. "This is a science and art exhibit, Liz. Where are the teachers for these two subjects? I don't see them. It seems to me that they are needed here."

"Oh, the union members in our school called a meeting for this morning. That's where they are. I'm glad to help out here, anyway, of course."

"Why aren't you at that meeting? They didn't give you a dirty job because you're a rookie, did they?" Parker said this with a smile, but inside he was beginning a slow boil.

Liz continued smiling, but it had a "fixed" look to it, as if it was a cutout smile pasted on her face. Parker picked up on it. He was sure that his fellow judges, and Addie, too, of course, were on his wavelength. "I'm not a union member, Mr. Parker. I was approached last year, my first year in teaching, to join the union – it's the VTUA, you know."

Parker knew, all right. "Yes, Liz, I know them quite well," he said, grimly.

"I just couldn't join, Mr. Parker. My mother was a teacher, now retired. She tried to talk me out of teaching, if you can believe that. She intensely dislikes the union. She told me that it only wants money and control of the schools in Vermont." They all murmured their agreement.

"But I love teaching, Mr. Parker," as she looked around at them all. Almost in desperation, thought Parker. "I wanted to do something to help children really be ready for the rest of their lives. And I decided that knowing how to read was the key to everything that follows."

"Children need that ability, it's very true. Are you succeeding, do you think, Liz?" asked Addie.

"Oh, yes, Mrs. Parker. I'm even having brief classes for fifteen minutes every day for anyone in the school who wants extra instruction. That fifteen minutes is the time available from the end of the last class of the day and when the buses leave. In addition, I've sent a note home with the children to their parents. I offered to spend time in their homes, if they'd let me, teaching all the reading and writing skills. It's very satisfying for me and, I think, for them." For Parker, her enthusiasm was great to see.

"You see, Mr. Parker, I believe there's a huge difference between knowing *how* to read and *enjoying* reading. My goal is to have my students have a book on some subject present in their homes and occupying every free minute of their lives."

The three judges were astounded. "That's a remarkable goal, Liz. How are you doing so far?" asked Doc Malcom.

"Wonderfully, Doctor," Liz said energetically.

Addie looked steadily at her. "And you got into trouble with the other teachers, too, didn't you?"

Liz admitted that she had had some complaints. "They were concerned that I would use teaching methods that wouldn't work and, as a result, the students would be further behind than if they had had no instruction from me at all. They also reminded me that my subject area was math."

"Who's 'they', Liz?" asked Parker, in a cloud of anger growing by the second.

"A half dozen of my teaching associates took me aside, Mr. Parker, 'to explain the way of things'."

"Did they give you any specifics about what you might do improperly?" asked Marvin.

"No, not specifics, Mr. Bailey. They let me know that I might be violating the union contract with my methods and the extra instruction I was offering. They had contacted the union about what I was doing. I was led to understand that the union is sending a representative down here to let me how I was endangering their negotiating processes with school boards all over Vermont. I find that hard to believe, don't you?"

"Are the half dozen teachers members of the union?" Marvin asked, gently probing a sore spot.

"Yes, they are all members. We have fourteen teachers in our school. Eleven of them are in the union. Three of us are not. I'm told I'm the last independent soul to continue to 'stand up to the union', as they put it. The other two non-union teachers gave up fighting them long ago. Sometimes my husband says he's concerned about me. He says maybe I'm taking this all too seriously. He's afraid it will take its toll on me. To tell you the truth," Liz said, her voice lower, "I enjoy the battle. Keeps me sharp." She smiled.

Addie looked at her husband. "Don't get involved, Willie," she said, noticing the thunder cloud building up on his face. She knew what that meant. “You’ll only make things more difficult for Liz.”

Parker looked at his wife, but Addie wasn’t sure that he actually saw her. But he heard what she said.

“I won’t make things any more difficult for Liz than they are presently. If I do something right now, it won’t be for Liz. It will be for me. And you. And probably a lot of others in this town.”

“I don’t know what you have in mind, Mr. Parker, but I don’t want to have this exhibit spoiled,” she said. “And I don’t want anyone to think that I told you about this situation only so you would go to bat for me.”

“No blood will be spilled in here, Liz. Trust me on that. Elsewhere, maybe.” Parker then turned toward Doc Malcom. “I’m going to look into this, Doc, and maybe you should take notes. I may need to lie down on your couch and admit all to my personal medicine man and bone rattler.”

“I have all the notes on you I’ll ever need, Bill. Now climb aboard your white steed and charge out to do good. We’ll see you back here in---,” he checked his watch, “twenty minutes.”

“Good Lord, Doc, I’m not going to hit anybody. I’m going to quietly discuss a subject with a few people having to do with loyalty to their students and to their school. I’ll be back well inside twenty minutes.”

Addie looked concerned as she watched her husband stride out the door and head down the road toward the school and the union meeting.

“Should we be concerned, Mrs. Parker?” asked Doc Malcom.

Addie forced a pained smile and said, “No, I don’t think so, Doctor. What do you think, Marvin?” she asked.

“I think somebody else needs to feel concern, Addie. He’s definitely on the warpath.”

“Let’s get Jesse’s exhibit repaired, Liz,” Addie interjected, deciding that bringing the conversation back to the present was a needed ingredient to improve the atmosphere. “My husband won’t embarrass you, I’m sure.”

She wasn’t sure at all.

44

Addie saw her husband arrive back at the Community Center well inside the twenty minute time frame established by Doctor Malcom. He strode through the door and walked straight over to Addie.

While he spoke to her, a young man and woman came through the door, one hurrying, and one with an "I-don't-give-a-damn" laziness to her walk. Children used to do this, Parker remembered, and probably still do, when they were damned well going to do as they were told by their parents, but were going to show a sense of independence by going about their terrible tasks in slow motion.

Parker walked over to the slovenly one and said something to her. Things speeded up for this teacher. Parker returned to the judging panel and his wife.

"Okay, Willie, what happened?" Addie asked. "Give us the bad news."

"No bad news at all, Addie," he answered. "I simply pointed out to them that their loyalty lay with the source of their paycheck and with the children of the parents who pay the bills. They did as I asked very well, I thought."

"Except for the woman who came through the door looking like she'd chewed on a persimmon," said Marvin.

"Well, I must admit that she got a second dose of my logic. I told her that I heard about this union meeting through one of the teachers who let the cat out of the bag quite innocently. I told these two teachers that I don't expect to hear anymore about it. Probably will, though. She's a hard-edged revolutionary-type of person." He grimaced.

"The woman," he continued, "was one of these people who thinks she already has learned all of life's lessons. The young man seemed to understand and was eager to take on his newly-learned responsibility. If I were on the school board, I'd call the young man a keeper, and I'd throw the young woman back till she grew some."

Addie wasn't pleased with her husband for getting into what was none of his business. But she tried without success to hide a small smile at his description of his "logic".

When Parker had finished his low volume talking he discovered that the room had suddenly gone from almost empty to almost full.

"I think we're ready now, gentlemen," Liz said, as she bustled over. "Just circulate, look at all the exhibits, speak with the young artists and scientists, and make a note of their exhibit numbers and their names. When you're ready, give them a score from one to ten in each of the three categories shown on your score sheets. All clear?"

They all nodded, and set off on their appointed rounds. Parker started at the end of the line, so to speak, thinking that these youngsters with the last numbers would think that it would take hours for them to be judged.

He enjoyed his judging experience very much. Parker was heartened by the thought and work that went into most of the exhibits. Of course there were always the amateur slackers who didn't work at their exhibits and it showed. They were trying to get a passing grade without doing any work. Parker didn't like that and his scores showed it. But the large majority of the exhibits were really enjoyable, and it was obvious that the creators of the work had entered into the spirit of the thing.

Parker had gotten through a little over half of the exhibits when he visited the table and display of a young artist. There were a number of people standing around and looking at the picture this young man had painted, so Parker had to wait for a bit until he could get a decent view of the work.

Even though Parker's sight line was from off to the side, he could see it was a landscape - but not an ordinary landscape. It showed an open meadow in the foreground, with a small stream running through it, surrounded by the green of the soft wood forest. It was really well done and Parker was impressed.

When the crowd had dispersed somewhat, Parker walked around the painting to stand directly in front of it. The idyllic view of meadow, stream, and forest that he had seen from off to the side came into sharp focus. It had as a backdrop a huge castle that seemed to just appear out of the clouds, not quite real, and not quite seen as part of the painting if you had too shallow a perspective. It might, in fact, be just a mist in the mind of the person viewing the painting.

Parker was not a person overly sophisticated in viewing art, but he appreciated this painting, done by this thirteen-year-old. The red and yellow flowers in the meadow and alongside the stream seemed to be very real to him. It was a wonderful job of work and Parker said so. The young artist was embarrassed but appreciative.

"Sometimes I get kidded because I'd rather paint than do anything else, Mr. Parker," he admitted. "But I play golf and do okay."

A man stepped up to stand beside Parker. He said, "Don't let him get away with modesty, Bill," said Marvin Bailey. "He's a terrific golfer. Meet my grandson. He's Chase Clarke. We call him 'Chatty' because he likes to talk some – don't you, Chatty?" Marvin put a hand on his grandson's shoulder, real affection and pleasure showing in his voice and expression.

"I guess so, Gramps," the young man said. "Not too much, though."

"Yes, that's true, Chatty," Marvin said. "And you make sense all the time. Do you know Mr. Parker, Chatty?"

"No, I've never met him, Grandpa, but I've heard you talk about him a few times. I remember that you told me that he was one of the unknown heroes in Vermont." Marvin's expression took on one of embarrassment. Parker's, too.

"Don't believe all you hear, son," said Parker, easily. "Your grandfather has been known to exaggerate." He turned toward Marvin with thunder clouds in his expression.

"Tell me about your painting, Chatty", Parker said. "It's really very good, I think. I'm sure there's a story about it you can tell me."

Parker looked at Marvin as Chatty turned toward his work. Parker gave Marvin a motion of his head that said "Go away, Marvin, I want him to talk without you hemming him in." Marvin grinned and slid away and out of sight.

Chatty looked at his painting in what seemed to Parker to be a critical manner. He hesitated for a few seconds and then said, "I wanted to paint something realistic and, at the same time, something out of a fairy tale. I know I have a lot to learn before I can ever paint what I really want to see, Mr. Parker, but I enjoy painting and I'm going to keep going with it. I guess I just wanted to try to paint something for this exhibit that was too much for me at this stage, but fun to try."

"So that's the backdrop with the castle, is it, that seems to bleed into the real world? What's it telling us, Chatty?"

"Exactly what you just said, Mr. Parker. What we have today came from what we were given thousands of years ago. That's what I tried to paint. I really don't know how to do it yet, but it will come, I'm sure."

But Parker wasn't really listening to Chatty, the next Andrew Wyeth, he was sure. He was leaning forward and looking closely at the painting. "What's this supposed to be?" he asked, pleasantly.

"Oh, that's some of the realism part of the painting. It's a 'KEEP OUT' sign. Probably not too well done, but I'll get better at it, Mr. Parker."

"No, no, that's not what I mean, son. You have even put letters on the sign. I can read the 'KEEP OUT'. I can't read the rest of it. What does it say?"

"It won't make any sense to you, Mr. Parker. A visitor at our art class, suggested that I should put on the sign the letters for NPF, and Roman numerals for 'II'. Present day realism, he called it. So I did. I'm searching for that sort of thing so I'll try most anything." Chatty stood beside Parker and looked at his painting.

"He said it stood for North Point Farm, where he has 'spent some time', as he put it. I don't know what the Roman numerals 'II' mean. He laughed out loud when he saw the sign on the painting. He laughed a lot, I thought. More than a person would laugh normally at something so small. I asked him where this farm was located, but he had already gone off somewhere. He was still laughing. I didn't care anyway. As far as I could see, he had left. I never caught his name. Maybe he never told me."

"Ever see him before?" asked Parker.

"No, this is the first time I've seen him. Some of the kids had seen him before, but they didn't mention any kind of a name. I only remember him because of the sign."

"And the sign had 'NPF' on it," asked Parker? "That's an odd sign, isn't it? I mean I've seen all these acronyms before when I was in the Legislature – but not that one," Parker said, almost to himself.

"I painted what he requested, Mr. Parker," Chatty said, continuing, "because it was 'different', if you know what I mean. And I wanted something 'different'."

And NPF might mean something important, thought Parker. "I understand, Chatty."

"Why the interest, Mr. Parker?"

"Just curious, Chatty, that's all." Parker was thinking about "North Point Farm". What did it mean?

He brought the conversation back to Chatty's painting. "Why the backdrop of a castle, son? That's the unrealistic part of the painting, isn't it?"

The young artist nodded. "Mr. Parker, haven't you ever been up in the Northeast Kingdom? Kingdom? As in 'castle'?"

All of a sudden the lights came on for Parker. And a strong connection with Jan's note really came into focus. Castles, kingdoms, princes, knights, squires, and the bull. Could that be Ferdinand, the name of one of the unoccupied towns in the Kingdom? Was Jan's note a poorly written warning note, or did she write it in a reporter's shorthand? Hell, I don't know, but I'm going to talk about it with Addie. She'll know. And I'll bet that my partner, Irene Doughton, will know, too.

Tomorrow I'll turn these guys in Birdsall's office loose on it. Parker knew that when he described his thoughts regarding the kingdom, bull and all the other connected bits of information, he risked total embarrassment, along with shaking heads and a damaged reputation for logical thought. Because, Parker admitted to himself, this train of thought is pretty wild. He decided to try to calm down. Thoughts should flow rather than jump out at a person.

Something, however, kept Parker's excitement growing. He looked around the large room: what an unexpected place to give him a whole new way of thinking about Jan Evlin's note, the Northeast Kingdom and the North Point Farm, and all of the other bits and pieces of this crazy, and perhaps murderous, conundrum he was facing. He hoped against hope that he wasn't just allowing his imagination to carry him away – which, he was well aware, had happened before.

Parker thanked Chatty, told him to keep on with his painting, and keep playing golf, even though Parker himself hated the game. It had made him depressed, angry, and irritable, the few times he'd tried it.

He moved on to the rest of the exhibits. He was becoming restless now to get his task for the school completed so he could talk about this possibly nutty idea with Addie.

45

Parker and Addie were happy to be sitting at their kitchen table with a cup of tea an hour after the exhibit closed, the prizes given out, and thanks received from Liz.

Chatty had received an art prize for originality. The two teachers who should have been there from before the beginning didn't say a word to anybody. They just left as soon as the last prize was given out. Parker decided that they didn't care too much for him. I hope they weren't policy holders in my insurance business, he thought.

"Okay, Willie," Addie said, "what's on your mind? I know you're sitting there just waiting to invade my tranquility with something."

Parker jumped to his feet, wincing as he sloshed hot tea on his hand. "Addie," he said excitedly, "I ran into Marvin's grandson today. He had a wonderful painting on display. Did you see it?"

"Yes, I did, Willie. You mean Chase Clarke. A lot of talent there, I think."

"Let me tell you what happened when I stopped at his exhibit."

Parker starting out by explaining the photographs with which O'Sullivan had performed his magic. And then he told her about his conversation with Chase, and the sign in the foreground of his painting. "That sign, Addie," his enthusiasm mounting, "I'm convinced, is the same sign that O'Sullivan picked out in the blown-up picture that I took from Hammond's barn. You'll remember that the letters 'NPF' were on that sign. If I'm right, that sign up there in Ferdinand stood for 'North Point Farm'." Parker placed his hands palm down, on the surface of the table. "How about that?"

Addie eyed her husband speculatively. "Willie, my dear, aren't you making a very big leap? I mean, it all seems so thin – so darned ethereal, almost."

Parker didn't know what "ethereal" meant, but wouldn't admit that to Addie. "I was afraid you'd say that, sweetie. That's exactly why I wanted to have your thoughts about my 'leap', as you call it. So let me show you another 'leap'. Chatty gave me a new direction from which to view Jan's note. You remember Jan's note? Generally, I mean?"

"Yes, of course, Willie. Sort of strange, I remember."

"Then how about some of the crazy words in her note? Like 'bull', and 'backed up', and 'bogged down', and 'knight', and 'squire' and 'provider'? These words are the key, Addie, I'm sure. They directly link up 'knight' with the Northeast Kingdom, 'backed' and 'bogged', and all the rest. It was a message to me. I'm convinced that she was telling me that she was in the Northeast Kingdom, and probably behind the Ferdinand Bog. Writing this note also said that maybe someone would be reading it before it was sent."

Addie was silent. Then she said, "Do you think that that note would fool someone who was holding her captive? That's what you implied just now."

Parker became uneasy. Her comment was accurate. "Addie, I don't know. There may be a dozen reasons why she wrote this note, and in the fashion she composed it. I just don't know. Maybe she wrote it before she arrived wherever she was going, knew the destination and was worried. So she wrote this note, and hoped that, if her companion read it, he wouldn't understand what she was saying. But he didn't read it and she dropped it into a mailbox in Hardwick. Hell, I don't know. All I do know for certain is that I received this note and I think she was telling me some important things."

"I'm not saying you're wrong, Willie," Addie said. "It's just something you'll have to be careful with in the way you use it. But, my dear, as you were talking, I thought of my own 'leap', even bigger than yours. Did you ever think that 'Z' might be connected to her note to you? After all, he wrote a note to her, and to others, and the notes were the same style. It seems to me that we can't separate 'Z' from NPF. Now there's a championship 'leap'," she said.

Parker gawped at his wife. He sat down again at the table and then hopped up again. To Addie, he seemed speechless. His own feeling was one of astonishment, along with some shame that he couldn't see this obvious signal.

Of course, Parker thought. That's the next "leap". Then he rushed around the table and planted a kiss on the top of Addie's head. "You brilliant, beautiful, clever, Holmes-like creature, you," he yelped. "That's it, Addie, that's it!"

Parker was still on his feet, walking around in aimless circles, hands clasped behind his back. Holmes would have done it that way, he knew.

"And 'Z' was in Bridgeton, for goodness sake – about two weeks ago, probably. I just know it."

"Are you sure, Willie? It seems odd that he might be here. Let's start calling him 'Z', whoever he is."

Parker didn't seem to hear his wife. "I think 'Z' helped Chatty with his painting. But, nobody, including Chatty, could remember him. None of the teachers at the exhibit today knew who I was talking about when I asked them. They often had art instructors come in to help the kids, but that wasn't allowed within 30 days of the exhibit – got to be fair, you know, Addie, level playing field, and all that. Or if they did know anything, they wouldn't tell me after I had treated those two teachers so badly." Addie smiled.

Then Parker quieted down. "I wonder what he was doing here, Addie? And why would he insist on putting that sign in the foreground? Who is he? And, most importantly, am I off base? Am I letting my imagination run wild, I ask again?"

Addie got to her feet and walked over to the counter where the teapot was waiting for her.

While she was pouring, she said, "Willie, I've been very bothered by everything you've told me about this situation of Jan's. What's not easy for me to believe is that we have a murder that seemed to come out of her attempt to write a story about non-profits. In fact, probably more than one murder. I simply cannot believe that anybody in the non-profit culture in Vermont would have the sick courage to kill to protect their organization. It doesn't make any sense to me."

"Why not, Addie? Aren't they capable of being just as loyal as anybody else to something that's crooked?"

"Oh, sure, they are, Willie. I could see them lying, and hiding contributions so they could be used to support campaigns of ProgDems, and managing political campaigns of ProgDems in direct violation of their charter, and lying some more to get the legislature to give them taxpayer money, and generally violating their legal parameters. In fact, they're doing that now. You have to remember, though, that most of the full-time employees of the large non-profits are not employable by the private sector." Parker looked up at her, mystified expression showing through to his wife.

"That's true. They are not decisive, and they are not people who function very well while working to the normal standards of private businesses. Hard decisions don't come easy for them. They have to 'feel' good about their work – not perform and make progress." Now Addie was on her feet.

"I know, Willie, I know," Addie said, gesturing at Parker. "There are some people who can exist anywhere they work and do very well. They are there only to work, however. They are capable of separating agenda from missions. They don't have a political agenda as their first order of business, as a large proportion of the prominent non-profits do." Addie poured herself another cup of tea. Rocket fuel, thought Parker, for this smart lady.

"I know a lot of leadership people in the non-profit world, Willie. I have not met many who had that kind of a decisive nature. I have met some who do, but they are scarce, and are part of a declining number. The bulk of the full-time people are sort of 'empty' people who write 'mission statements' for their group, and vicious letters against people they see as a danger to their agenda – whatever that might be. And they see those kinds of efforts as 'work'. But they are very reluctant to venture out into the world of direct debate. Facts always make them look bad, and they know it. They will let others provide their public face – like the politicians they help elect. And don't forget, Willie, they don't have to develop an income stream through innovative work. Their non-profit enterprise was set up by other, outside, interests – interests that send them the money to carry out an agenda that's very different from what the public knows about."

Parker was quiet for a moment. Then he said, "What's the alternative, Addie? You're on to something. Let's hear it." Parker knew he sounded discouraged by her words.

Addie took a deep breath and said, "We are either terribly wrong, Willie, and no murders have been committed, and there's no 'NPF' signs – just a crank designation – and there's nothing in Ferdinand, Vermont, that warrants our attention."

Parker started to splutter, as he did when the words were coming out faster than he could articulate them. Addie held up her hand to quiet him down. “Or,” she said, “the problem is a lot bigger, more dangerous and, for that reason, more carefully hidden, than we had any right to expect. It may have started with hundreds of non-profits, the majority of which are corrupt to a greater or lesser extent, but I think Jan Evlin got too close to something else. And that’s why I’m worried about her.”

Parker listened intently. After a few moments of silence, he said “You’re right, you know, Addie,” in a low voice. “And that’s why whoever is involved has set up the spying network to keep track of some of the information sources that could harm their efforts – whatever the hell they are. Maybe just the actual attempt to set up these listening devices tells us that we really *are* into something that is very big, very secret, and very dangerous to whoever finds it out.”

“I’ve wondered about that,” said Addie. “Willie – what’s the lineup of victims of this wholesale info theft? Who, or what businesses are being listened to by spies?”

“Well – a few banks, a number of lawyers’ offices, the Chittenden Free Progressive – probably only a sampling of these types of mainline trafficking in rumors and facts.” Parker thought for a few seconds. “You know, I wouldn’t be surprised if every large county in Vermont has this sort of encroachment into what was always considered truly private and confidential.”

“Willie, we have no proof of that. And it would be a huge risk for them, too,” said Addie. “It wouldn’t be surprising if somebody else was as nosey as you are, and stumbled across just what you did, in all the other counties in the state. But there aren’t too many people out there like you.” Parker hoped that that comment was a compliment.

Parker waved away what he considered as nonsense. “Don’t forget, my dear,” he said, “I just had a wild hunch, based on nothing whatsoever, and tried it on for size. In this instance it worked. But the stars have to be perfectly aligned.” Addie nodded.

“And there aren’t very many Hugos around either, Addie,” Parker continued. “He’s the one who really saw what was going on because he knew how to check things out. I had no idea what I was doing. He did.”

Addie nodded and asked, “What’s next, Willie? What do you have nagging at you? Things can’t be allowed to go on like this forever.”

"I haven't thought beyond tomorrow's meeting in Birdsall's office, Addie. When that's over, then maybe we'll know. I'll take along clothing for a couple or three days, just in case." Parker decided not to tell his wife what else he had in mind. There was something that was pulling at him in ever stronger waves that he could no longer ignore.

"I'll help you pack, Willie. Then, 'early to bed and early to rise, makes good sense when you're dealing with spies'." She chuckled to herself, kissed her husband on the cheek, and went to the door to let the dogs out.

Letting the dogs out was the last ritual act of the day and the dogs knew all about it. Parker realized, after all these years, that he didn't know it, until that very moment, that an "end-of-the-day" routine was always in play, and lent a certain finality to activities. Always watch your dog, he mused. They know what's important and what's not.

46

Parker left his house earlier than he would under normal circumstances for a drive to Burlington. He wanted to see the Malcoms first. They had helped him in the past when the strange happenings he encountered were too much for him. Both Doc and his wife, Agnes, were psychiatrists, retired and living the life of unobtrusive down-country transplants in Vermont.

The Parkers and the Malcoms knew each other only casually in the beginning. It was when Parker, involved in his past adventures and confused about what he was really facing, sought them out.

And they scared the hell out of him. Their advice had been right on-the-mark and had probably saved his life. Ever since that time, a year ago, Parker and Addie had reserved for the Malcoms a special place in the Parker pecking order.

Because of that history Parker decided that he should bring them into the present situation. He had called them, probably too early in the morning, because they had invited him up to their place for breakfast. When he arrived, Mrs. Doctor Malcom, Agnes to the insiders, was waiting for him on the back porch with a cup of morning tea in her hands.

"Good morning, Mr. Parker," she called out, as he slid down from the cab of his truck. "Have a cup of tea to start the day." She seemed very jovial, Parker thought. He'd change that very soon, he thought.

In reality, Dr. Agnes Malcom and her husband were looking forward to yet another problem brought to them by this most interesting, but odd, man, as she thought of him.

"Good morning, Dr. Malcom," Parker said. "This *is* a great way to start the day, and I thank you for the personal service." He gratefully took the cup of tea.

"It is, it is, the only way to start the day, and you're welcome," she exclaimed. She was looking Parker over as if he was to be slaughtered and made into sausage and the weight of the beast had to be determined by the local slaughter man. She seemed to make up her mind about something and then waved Parker up the steps onto the porch and into the kitchen through the back door.

Doc Malcom was frying up bacon, and a bowl of scrambled egg potion stood at the ready. "Come in, Bill, come in," he warbled. "Breakfast coming up." He turned toward his wife and said, "Was I right or was I right?" he asked.

"You were terrifyingly accurate, my dear. We have to do something about it."

"We are. I'm cooking the best breakfast he's probably had in a month, and then we'll dazzle him with our charm. Sit down, Bill, right over there," as he waved a pancake spatula in the general direction of the side of the table, spattering himself in the process.

"Mr. Parker," Agnes Malcom announced, not to Parker, but to her husband, still slinging hash and "stoving over a hot slave", as she occasionally and irreverently put it, "only comes up here to the hill country to see us when he's in trouble – and I perceive that he's in trouble again. Did you notice that, Gerald?"

This was the first time that Parker had ever heard Doc Malcom's first name. He felt "included" somehow.

"I did indeed, my dear. Well, we're good for something in our declining years, I suppose."

"Including coming very close to talking too much to a Mrs. Barkley, up in South Burlington," said Parker.

"Ah," Doc Malcom chirped, "you heard about that, I surmise?"

"You surmise correctly," said Parker, firmly. "You succeeded in causing a strong and determined young woman to tell me about her encounter with you and to promise me that she would never utter a word of her knowledge about me. I think you actually scared her – and I didn't think there was anyone alive today who could do that."

"She's very imposing, isn't she? You made an impression on her for bravery and intelligence, you know," said Doc Malcom. "Apparently for something that went on just that night. True?"

"Doc, I was scared out of my wits most of the time – and her husband was with me. We did fine. I'll try very hard not to tell you anything about it."

Doc laughed as he served up the eggs and bacon.

"What can we do for you, Mr. Parker? Do you have another person who is 'different' and who is upsetting your life? Is that the reason for your visit?" queried Agnes Malcom.

Parker said, carefully, “I think so, Mrs. Malcom. We may very well have another coo-coo on our hands, and I need you two to ‘read’ him for me.”

“Coo-coo? Mr. Parker? As I recall, that word, or words, is as close as you’ve ever gotten to the technical terms that define our previous employment.”

“And I won’t get any closer than that, Ma’am,” he said.

“Tell us about this person, Mr. Parker,” Agnes said. “In truth, we can’t wait.”

“I really don’t know much about him, folks, but here I go, just as we’ve done before.”

He plunged into the description of the murder of Hammond, the murder of Chugger, the probable murder of Gil Birdsall, along with the spy system of keeping track of the important information that may have an effect on an agenda of some sort, which is coveted by somebody unknown, and the general shape of the mystery surrounding the non-profits in Vermont. Also, Jan’s note was not only described, but delivered to the Malcoms for scrutiny.

He finished with the odd notes that kept showing up, all signed by “Z”. He even told them about the guy who talked Chatty into putting in the sign in the foreground of his painting, and then laughing about it more than its importance required.

The Malcoms were silent, each digesting what he had said in their own way. Both were note takers and they were staring at their scribbles. “Since you are heading for the Northeast Kingdom, Bill,” offered Doc, “I wouldn’t go alone.”

Parker was rocked back on his proverbial heels. He wondered how Doc could make that mental journey and end up where Parker had decided to go, and not having told a soul about it.

“How did you know that, Doc? I wasn’t going to tell you about that until I’d actually gone up there and seen what was in the pictures.”

“It was a calculated guess, Bill. Not difficult, however, for anybody who *sees* things, rather than just *looks* at them. It was just that you were heading north, I guessed, because I’d seen your truck leaving town at least half a dozen times in the last two weeks, heading north. Also, your shoes. Those are not Chittenden County shoes. Those are rugged hiking boots. You’re going hiking and climbing. And since I’m quite sure you don’t do any real exercise activities like rock climbing, it just seemed logical to me that the Kingdom was your ultimate destination, but it would be difficult for you to head north without seeing your friend Peter Morgan. How did I do, Bill?"

Parker was always impressed with the way the Malcoms' minds worked. Never more so than now, however.

"All of the above is true, Doc," Parker said glumly. "Nobody knows it, though – including Addie. Except, of course, you. You really bother me with your hobby of reading things around you and coming up with these startling conclusions. I don't feel safe, somehow."

Doc Malcom quickly rose to his feet and scuttled around the end of the table and sat down beside Parker. "Please, Bill, it's only for you that I try that kind of exercise. It's good for me, you see. And I never tell anybody else. Never. If you are uncomfortable with my using you as a target, I won't do it again." Doc was upset, Parker could see.

"No, no, Doc. It's just that I can't let anybody know what I'm doing and where I'm going – at least until I get back. And I've been careful not to spill the beans myself. I've said nothing to anyone. And then you rattle off all the items of my little agenda and about when I'm going to be doing them – well, you can imagine my surprise. But, please, Doc, don't stop using me for an experiment. It's terrific. It just amazes me that you can do it at all."

"He's just showing off, Mr. Parker," said Doctor Agnes Malcom. "Don't worry. He won't say anything. We never do."

Doc Malcom looked relieved. "One question, Bill. Have you read the Jan Evlin note? I mean really read it?"

"Well, I think so. I mean that I think I saw a meaning in that note – a strong message within a message. Actually, my son-in-law saw it first for what it was: a veiled warning that would be noticed by someone who knew her. He's pretty quick, and he hasn't ever met Jan. It didn't come to me until yesterday, when I talked with that young man at the Bridgeton School Art and Science exhibit, that things fell into place for me. I just couldn't figure it out at all until yesterday. And I'm very concerned with her whereabouts – and, to be frank, her well-being, too."

"You should be, Bill," Malcom said solemnly. "And you know that somebody could have been looking over her shoulder when she wrote it, don't you? Although I think she wrote her note to you beforehand, and got a chance to drop it into a mailbox when she suddenly knew that she was heading into the unknown. It obviously made her nervous, you see. And now we know definitely that you're going into the wilderness of the Northeast Kingdom. We also know why, too, don't we?"

Doc Malcom was looking intently at Parker. "I'll just say one more thing, Bill, about the note she wrote. We are doing a hell of a lot of stretched guessing. You know that, don't you?" Parker nodded. "In this case, and these situations are rare, it's better to guess at what should be done to keep things and people safe, rather than doing nothing and allowing something to happen that's infinitely worse."

Parker did know. "Yes, I've got to try and find her."

Doc Malcom gazed at Parker for what seemed a very long time. "Don't go alone, Bill. Don't go alone," he said again, his voice trailing off.

"Now, Mr. Parker," Agnes said, brightly, "I hope you remember our routine when working on the puzzles you bring us?"

"You mean that I'm banished to the backyard until you take my story apart and both agree to the educated guesses that you feel comfortable with, I believe," said Parker. "Is that it?"

"Your memory is excellent, Mr. Parker. We'll beckon in a while," said Mrs. Malcom. Parker walked out into the springtime air.

Parker always enjoyed walking around the property of this old hill farm. It came from a time when hard work was survival. It was never questioned by anyone, as it would be today. Everyone in the family worked. They were brought up on it. Parker was doing his chores on the family farm at four years old. It never stopped after that until his father died. His mother sold the farm and moved, with a widowed friend, to better weather. She had died ten years earlier, having a beautiful stretch of retirement years as payback for the relentless work schedule of a farm wife. Parker was happy for her.

It was only about 30 minutes later that Parker heard Mrs. Malcom's call to come on back in from "banishment", as she called it.

"Have a seat, Bill," said Doc Malcom. "What you talked about today is very interesting – although your information is less developed this time than on previous occasions. Mrs. Malcom and I agree on many things," Doc continued, "and, not surprisingly, we disagree on some. But we agree wholeheartedly that you, a small town resident and business person, have run up against some really strange people in the last few years. Your information at that time tested us, you see. Made us stop and consider possible ramifications of what you told us with more attention before we gave you our opinions. A couple of your subjects have actually had real lethal tendencies, which of course, is a couple too many. This one, who we will call 'Z', as you and Addie have done, has other interesting impulses not as prevalent in the lawyer from Burlington of a year ago."

"Is he dangerous to me and my friends, Doc?"

"Absolutely, Bill," said Doc. "In fact, he may be more dangerous than the lawyer because the lawyer was slipping out of control as you applied pressure. And he then became more predictable. 'Z' has seen the pressure mount, and he probably is aware that you are causing this pressure, but he hasn't done anything in desperation. He just answers back in his own, controlled, way."

"My friend and I thought he was acting in desperation when he tried to kill us in the cow barn at Hammond's house in Underhill," said Parker.

Mrs. Malcom shook her head. "No, Mr. Parker," she said, "we don't agree, and we had quite a discussion on that point. We believe that he tried to kill you, but it was such an unfocused attempt, we also believe that it wasn't important enough to the killer. He didn't need to try, did he? You suspected he was there in the barn. But you didn't know. He just applied some pressure in opposition to yours. Different from our kind of pressure, but the result would be the same. It simply was his kind of pressure, applied so you would notice it. He also knew that he could leave the barn without you two stopping him."

"He was right about that," said Parker. "Scared the bejeezus out of us both."

"You see," Mrs. Malcom continued, "this person is someone who needs complete control over his world. He feeds on this control. If he ever lost control – if he ever felt that he couldn't direct the events around him – he would lash out at whomever he believed was responsible. You, for instance, Mr. Parker. It would, however, be very well planned, and not just a wild reaction."

This wasn't pleasant for Parker to hear. "You mean when you say 'lash out' that he wouldn't necessarily wait for me to show up. He might very well go for whomever he saw handy that he knew was working with me? One of my friends helping me in this situation, for instance?"

"You've got it, Mr. Parker," said Mrs. Malcom. "You would be better for him, but anybody will do, if it comes to that. Killing you or, if that wasn't possible at the moment, sending you another warning that you would notice. That's enough for this guy."

There was a quiet moment in the cozy kitchen. Nobody even moved. Then Parker said, "What about this story from the young man who painted the picture? Remember? I mentioned it to you. The business with the addition of the sign, suggested by some guy who definitely needs to be checked out."

"Yes, we were coming to that interesting occurrence," said Mrs. Malcom, consulting her notes. "It was the laughter at what the sign looked like in the painting from this strange person that interested us, Mr. Parker."

"You mean because he laughed? You find that interesting?" asked Parker, mystified.

"Oh, yes, Mr. Parker. You described his laughter in a way that made both of us want to know more about that."

"Chatty gave me the impression that the laughter was over-the-top. More than was called for. I think this guy is a real whack job, Mrs. Malcom. I tried to accurately describe to you what Chatty said to me. I thought that to do that was important to you."

Doc Malcom nodded. "There you go again, Bill," said Doc. "Using technical terms. 'Whack job', indeed. However, we both want to believe your description because that sort of reaction shows a certain sadism that we've run into before. You should ask Chatty again – that's his name? Chatty? – if he thought that the laughter was sort of beyond expectation. Do that to confirm our first thought. Will you?"

"Of course, folks. Now, I've got to be----". He was interrupted by Doc Malcom.

"There is something else, Mr. Parker," said Doc, quietly. "It's difficult to show you definite proof because we don't have enough indicative evidence. It's better, however, to tell you about something that may not come to pass, but if it does, you had better be aware of it. It makes him a little less predictable, you see, to us – not to him. If what you have told us about this killer is accurate, and we believe without question it is – you've never let us down in this regard before, Mr. Parker – then this is a person involved in something very nasty. Something that's bigger than anything you've tackled before. In fact, bigger than we've ever been involved with, ourselves. We won't go any further because that goes beyond even speculation." Doc Malcom sat back in his chair for a few seconds, as if to get rested for the rest of the tale.

"The point is this," he continued. "This person is driven by beliefs that make him immune to being afraid of death. That makes him even more dangerous. He won't back away. He will take chances, or what we may call chances, and will enjoy it. That's the 'laughter' Chatty heard from his visitor. He will kill, and we think he has killed, in places and situations that would be considered too dangerous to any other person capable of murder. The reasons are that he doesn't think we're capable of catching him, he also has a plan for these things, and he's driven by the urge that tells him that we are standing in his way of some goal that is irresistible to him."

Parker was listening intently. He didn't think it was possible that someone could be more dangerous than the killer in Burlington the previous year, but he was changing his mind.

"You said that you two had been on the edge of something like this? What did it turn out to be?"

"It was a group, a cell, really, of people who hated all forms of authority. They hated America. They hated people. They were Americans, but they had become radicals, and were part of an international movement. The name of the group was 'The Saviors of the Earth Movement'. We were called in by Federal officials to help profile these people." He glanced at his wife. She nodded emphatically. "Keep going" she seemed to be saying.

Doc sat up and started talking again. "We found that they were the old leftists who had joined the new international terrorists, well funded by different Foundations in this country as well as wealthy people in Europe. They were not necessarily Muslim, which might be what you'd think initially. In fact, the groups were not driven by any religion at all. They used a false religious devotion to join other religious institutions. In some countries that's where solid information can be found, telling them if anybody has gotten wind of their activities which, it was discovered, was assassination, destroying businesses, burning homes, distorting voting processes, and other forms of mayhem to destabilize a town, a state, or a nation."

Doc Malcom looked at his wife once again. She gestured for him to keep going. "It was popular, at the time, to mask their intentions by hiding behind what's 'good for children', or against 'global warming', or against world trade. Heard of those excuses for wrecking things, Mr. Parker?" Parker said that he certainly had.

"They still do, of course, because the word 'children' is the key to reaching people with their message. In reality, of course, they couldn't care any less than they do about children."

"Then they moved to 'global warming'. They destroyed many businesses and their products by blaming America for over-producing and being rich." Doc grimaced as he sat quietly in his chair.

"'Global warming' was much more difficult to explain for them because that required the use of long words. They kept mixing up the global warming arguments, and the words that went with them, especially when our winters didn't cooperate and continued to stay cold. On top of that, their argument supporting the presence of the phenomenon called global warming is not only bogus, but is, in fact, a calculated lie." Parker thought the Malcoms might be kidding him but they were deadly serious.

"Now they are backing away from that tripe because more and more people are learning that 'global warming' is not real, and the reports to support this false idea are produced by people who have no technical background – only a political agenda. It served a purpose that for years enabled these radicals to stop a lot of development in America and start the process of bringing America to its knees. One great example for you, Bill: America hasn't built a new refinery for over 20 years. Just to keep up with demand we should have been building two a year. Part of the 'destroy America' movement."

"You both were looking at these kinds of people?" asked Parker. "It must have been creepy for you."

"Oh, yes. What we learned has never been very far away from the fronts of our memories. It was one of the reasons that we chose Vermont as our retirement destination. It would be a state providing us with some protection from these groups that other parts of America and the world had to confront. But not Vermont." At that comment, Doc Malcom reached out and squeezed his wife's hand.

"Then you told us that you had come across an eavesdropping system here in Vermont," he continued. "It was this information network right here around us that made us wonder.

Why would it be in Vermont? And then we asked ourselves, why not?"

Agnes Malcom was gripping the table edge with both hands and staring down into her lap. She said quietly, "We had a friend working with us on tracking these insane people. She was shot through the head at point blank range by a young man in Albany, NY, after church. Perhaps you remember reading about it. The young man was caught. He didn't mind. He told the authorities that he did it in order to save the planet for the wild animals."

Doc walked around the table to the back of his wife's chair. He placed his hands on her shoulders and massaged them, much in the way a dog owner would massage their animal to quiet them down during a thunderstorm.

"This bunch has provided people for every international demonstration that fought anything that had to do with the United States,' Doc Malcom continued. "They were, in our professional judgment, unhinged. We have no way of positively knowing that your killer is connected with anything like this, but your description and our experience tells us that you should be very aware of this possibility."

Parker rose to his feet, saying nothing. He walked over to the kitchen window. No one spoke. Parker gazed out across the Malcoms' acreage. It was a little after nine in the morning. It was Sunday. People were going to church. They were out for a drive. They were spending a good day at home. And all the time things were moving along inexorably under the surface. Evil things and people, who hated these trappings of stability, family, and the future. And they hated America with a fervency that defied any reasonable logic. Parker knew, without any additional thought, that this was what he was involved in. This was what Addie had suggested to him, just last night. He had no proof at all. It just somehow made sense to him. Maybe not to anybody else. But to him, it did.

Parker turned back to the center of the room. "I want to thank you very much, folks, for your expertise and your willingness to use it to help me. This is a very upsetting time, but we will get through it." Parker walked out onto the porch, deep in thought. There was so much to do. It was very possible that there was not enough time.

He turned around to face the Malcoms. Then, on an impulse, he stepped forward and hugged Agnes Malcom. She was surprised. She hugged back. And then he shook Doc's hand. "I'll see you soon. I bet I'll have a lot to tell you. Thank you for all your help."

As he walked to his pickup he was tempted to turn around, go back, and tell them how sorry he was that they had to find out this distressing information from him. But, on reflection, he thought that maybe it was better this way.

47

Parker arrived in Burlington on Sunday afternoon, early enough to be at the Birdsall meeting at its start. He wanted to be able to tell everybody at the meeting that they were nearing the end of a trek, a difficult and hard-to-believe, migration. And everything would soon become a police matter. As time went along, however, things had become very cluttered.

The police would enter, if they hadn't already, into the investigation of the murder of Hammond, but would they, or even *could* they, connect all of the other occurrences that Parker had witnessed that seemed to emanate from that death? That's what he wanted to talk to Morgan about.

Parker drove to the area of the Chittenden Free Progressive building, watching in the mirror to see if he was being followed. It seemed to him that everybody connected with the Hammond mess was being followed, or at least thought they were. He knew how they felt.

He parked his truck in an alley behind the Onion River Co-op and hoped that the police wouldn't become curious.

Parker remembered that the Co-op was put through the Burlington City government primarily because of an argument put forth by its supporters - that low income people could walk to it and do all their shopping, just like "days of olde", saving money and buying the best quality at the same time.

In reality, the Co-op was a publicly-funded outlet for the organic farmer bunch, so that they could sell their produce at high prices, while telling everyone that not buying organic products was close to being unpatriotic. They felt this organic approach was extraordinarily desirable for every living soul because it was untouched by terrible mass-produced chemicals. They believed it and, therefore, they were certain that all the rest of the public would agree with them.

They also believed that the Onion River Co-op, and only the Onion River Co-op, mind you, was the answer to the biggest problem the supporters of socialism had; and that problem popped up when shoppers could make direct side-by-side comparisons with the much less expensive items offered in the traditional supermarket – especially when many of the products offered by the organic farmers didn't look as good and cost noticeably more than the usual supermarket offerings. The progressives found that shoppers simply resisted the prices that were charged by the organic farmers. It turned out that only the members of the ProgDem Party ended up buying the stuff. Then the ProgDems were shocked when they found that many of their own people would sneak out to other grocery stores. Unbelievable.

The answer to this problem was the usual answer supplied by progressives – eliminate the competition. And that's what they did. The Burlington powers-that-be and the Burlington voters wouldn't allow the private supermarket to come into the downtown area and build a store.

This progressive approach had been honed to perfection when the ProgDems eliminated private health insurers in Vermont, leaving the way open for a health care system run by ProgDems from Montpelier and paid for by all the residents in Vermont. They'd done it with schools by denying school choice to parents, and now they did it with food sources.

Then another problem cropped up. The word that was going around Burlington was that the Co-op was the most expensive grocery store in Burlington and it might last for another year, at the most. The ProgDems had no public relations people who could counter this report.

What ProgDems couldn't figure out, but what was happening all along, was the dreaded free enterprise system. In its inexorable way, it had been exerting its influence through the choices made by customers who still had the power to decide where, and for what, they spent their money. They refused to pay the prices for the marginal quality of the products. The operators of the store couldn't figure it out. If they couldn't change the way things were going, their Co-op would go the way of all the progressive, and non-competitive, dinosaurs.

This power of individual choice was wonderful. However, it's only a matter of time before the Burlington city government will outlaw the power of citizen choices, he thought. Then the beauty and uplifting atmosphere of "directed choice", as some ProgDems have called it, would be apparent to all. What ignorant souls they were, thought Parker.

ProgDems knew one other tidbit regarding their publicly-funded organic farming movement. They didn't talk about it because it was a believable and devastating comment on their entire culture of being able to trash the chemical industry that was part of a recent government study.

The accusation was that gene-spliced food is considerably healthier than so called "health food." This bombshell was that produce grown without the protection of the biotech additives produced its own poisons. These are called "mycotoxins". One of these toxins was labeled "fumonisin", which Parker struggled to pronounce, but what was not lost on him was that this toxin is extraordinarily dangerous to mammals, birds, and fish. The last bit of this study showed that the evidence indicated that this toxin was also found as a cause of fatal birth defects.

When Parker was reading this study, sitting in his big kitchen, he had just finished a dinner mainly consisting of vegetables proudly grown organically by a friend who gave them to the Parkers.

Parker remembered a feeling of unease and he found himself experiencing an upset stomach. It soon evaporated, of course, but the new-found knowledge, if true, didn't. Just do your homework, Parker thought, and all of these warmed-over and failed initiatives by the ProgDems would be tossed on the scrap heap. Maybe sometime it will happen, he hoped.

Parker knew he had let his mind wander for a couple of minutes. I'd better get back on the beam, he thought.

He glanced around occasionally as he walked to the back of the Chittenden Free Progressive building. He was looking for anything out-of-the-ordinary as he made his quiet way to see Hal Birdsall.

Parker couldn't imagine that he was on anybody's radar, but his memory of the strange people he'd met in Montpelier who inexplicably knew who he was, was still fresh in his mind. And, according to Hugo, he had been followed when he left Birdsall's office a few days ago. Could be that Hugo was mistaken, of course, he thought, but no sense in tempting fate now, is there?

Parker could see Birdsall's office, up on the third floor. A window was open. He's there, he thought, and wants to talk. I hope he's had word of Jan.

Parker was beginning to truly be worried about her physical well-being. What he couldn't understand is why she would be in any danger. We're only talking about the non-profit industry in Vermont and, anyway, everybody knows that it's been corrupted by people who are from outside Vermont, and always will be from outside Vermont, no matter how long they might live here, he said to himself.

Parker, however, now believed that the problem of corrupt non-profits had been supplanted by a larger and more sinister corruption.

Corruption is always distasteful and unsettling but the knowledge of this non-profit corruption won't keep anybody from going to work the next day, enjoying their bowling night and, generally, living their life that the state of Vermont might choose to allow. And it's not as if we're being attacked, is it? So, he asked himself, why was Hammond murdered? It has to be for some other reason not immediately visible from the limited range provided by the non-profit industry. It *is* something else, and very much bigger. Addie was one smart lady, he thought.

Parker stopped in the depth of a doorway and looked across the alley at the stairs that led to Birdsall's office. It was afternoon, but this back alley seemed very dark to Parker. He looked up to the top of the back stairs, seeing the door to Birdsall's office. So much had happened in that office in the last few days. Just a few days, he asked himself? Seems like years, for God's sake.

Parker strongly believed that Birdsall was one of the keys to unwinding this business. After all, it had started with his innocence in giving Jan Evlin the quiet assignment to look into the non-profit industry. And his eavesdropping secretary, of course, knew it at the same time and told – who?

As Parker started to take his first step to cross the alley toward the stairway, a faint scraping sound came from above. He slid back into whatever darker patch of the doorway was provided by the alley walls and remained motionless, hardly daring to breathe. From twenty feet above his head he heard light steps coming down the stairs.

He expected it to be Hal Birdsall. It wasn't. It was a tall woman, wearing dark glasses and a dark raincoat that had a sort of shine to it. She stepped from the stairs into the alley, cursing as she fought her way through a collection of trash cans, and then retreated to the front opening of the alley and disappeared. Parker hadn't heard profanity like that since he had left Vietnam.

Then there was silence. Parker didn't move for a full five minutes. Then he moved over to the bottom of the stairs, glancing around once more as he entered the open spaces of the alley. Was Parker the one being followed, he wondered, thinking wildly and rapidly? Or was Hal Birdsall the target? Maybe he'd have an answer to that, too, before too many more days had passed.

Move, he said to himself. Don't hesitate. Parker stepped quietly onto the bottom stair, and then quickly ascended to the back door. He knocked and the door opened almost immediately.

"Bill, it's good to see you. Come on in," Birdsall said, as if he really meant it, obviously having forgotten the phone-slamming incident after he had agreed to do something for Parker that he didn't want to touch. If phone smashing had been an Olympic event, Birdsall would have medalled.

Parker walked into the room and found that it was not empty. Sitting there was Hugo Barkley, President of Barkley, Barkley, and Barkley, Incorporated, local electronics expert and snoop. Also present was someone who Parker would never have guessed would be there. It was Peter Morgan, Supervisor of the Montpelier Police Department, and totally off his legal range of professional responsibility. And some people thought *I* was nosey, Parker thought.

And he saw Don Flanders, more than slightly disheveled, and seeming to look more worried than the last time Parker had seen him. Parker turned to the group.

"Well," he said, "a proper meeting of the clans, I'd say. Why are we all here, gentlemen? I had a private meeting planned with Hal, here," waving his hand in Birdsall's direction, "and I see all the professions represented except the VTUA, the Vermont Trial Lawyers, and the Conservation Law Foundation – and I am really surprised that they aren't here." His smile brought several chuckles from those in attendance. "What's going on? And who brought all you guys together? I didn't know you even knew each other."

Birdsall got to his feet, stretched, and said, "There's a common denominator in our midst, Bill. We've all been affected by the non-profit industry in one way or another." He gestured toward one of the group. "You know Don Flanders, here, I think."

Flanders also got to his feet. He looked, close up, like a man who hadn't changed his clothes, hadn't slept, and hadn't shaved. Parker had just seen him fifteen hours earlier, and he didn't look anywhere near as shabby then as he did right now. "When you told me your story, Bill, at our meeting at the dumpsters, it was very interesting in an academic way, but certainly nothing I'd have a contact with, even if I wanted it. That all changed when I got to my office. I'll bring you all up-to-date later."

"What's the purpose of this meeting? To find out what each of us knows and to see what's next?" Parker asked.

"That's it exactly," said Hal Birdsall. "We're convinced that Flanders will be the next target. We're not afraid to be on somebody's list, Bill," Birdsall said earnestly. "If, at the same time, we can set up a trap that would expose the killer, that's what we want to do."

Parker walked over to one of the slightly dog-eared easy chairs and flopped down. He turned toward Birdsall. "Be careful what you wish for, Hal." He looked at Birdsall steadily. "Understood?" Birdsall nodded.

"And what about your secretary, Hal?" asked Parker. "Is she still on the payroll?"

Birdsall frowned. "Yes, Bill, she is. But I hope I have your permission to can her - which I'm planning to do next week anyway."

"Under the right circumstances, Hal, only then, please," Parker answered. "I think we may have a use for her, starting tonight. Have you told the others here tonight about what we found in the heating ducts in this office of yours?"

"Yes, Bill, Hugo just got through telling everybody about that. I wanted to wait until you got here, but I didn't know when that would be. What he found is the reason why I invited him. He's filled us in on what he's found in other parts of the city – and Vermont, too, for that matter. Right, Hugo? You're finished?" Hugo nodded.

"Hal," Parker interrupted, "is the recorder still working as she expects? Nothing has changed in that routine to warn her off?"

"It's still as she expects it to be, Bill, except that I've unplugged it for tonight's meeting. I'll plug it back in when we're through."

"That's exactly right, Hal."

Birdsall continued the introductions. "And Peter Morgan, of the Montpelier Police Department, is here, too."

Parker grinned at him. "I saw you here, Peter. Will you be run out of town if the wrong person sees you?"

"Probably, Bill. To guard against that, I've let my buddy in the local PD know I'm here for a brief meeting. In fact, I'm including him in this get-together." He craned his neck over the back of his chair to one of the darker corners of the room. "Bud, come on out now. I want you to meet Bill Parker and his hole-in-the-wall gang."

Pulling himself up from one of Birdsall's stuffed chairs in a far corner and stepping out of the semi-gloom was a figure who must have stood six and a half feet tall, and eight feet wide. He was even larger than Hugo, Parker could see, and that's going some. "Bud" lumbered over to Parker and stood in front of him. Parker felt instantly miniaturized and powerless.

"This is Bud Small, Bill, a detective in the Burlington Police Department."

Parker reached out to shake his hand. As Parker's hand disappeared, he had a thought about the size of "Bud" that prompted him to say something that he just knew would be hilarious. As he opened his mouth to speak, he was interrupted by Detective Small.

"I've heard all the jokes and witticisms before, Mr. Parker. Please don't waste your time."

Parker decided, as he looked up at "Bud", that he would follow the Detective's advice.

He turned toward Morgan and asked, "How much does Bud know about what we're doing? Come to that, Peter, how much do you know?"

Morgan grinned slightly, sensing Parker's discomfort, and said, "Hugh Hammond's murder brought me into it, Bill."

At that announcement a restlessness became evident in the room. Morgan plowed on, not seeming to notice it. "Because of my work on that case, I've run into people, some of whom are in this room, who seemed to be busily engaged on a parallel course – your buddy Hugo being one of them. And Hal Birdsall, sitting over there beside you, who couldn't stop himself from calling me to inquire about you. He wanted to know if you were brave, honest, trustworthy, true, and a real scout in all ways. I, of course, told him the truth." He smiled at Parker.

"I don't want to know what you said, Peter," said Parker. "You're the first untrustworthy cop I've met." Morgan's expression of muted happiness was obvious.

Flanders stood up and walked over to Morgan. "You've done a hell of a job keeping this quiet, Mr. Morgan," he said. "How did you accomplish that?"

Morgan replied. "As you can imagine, it wasn't easy. But I had some help from my Department. The logic for attempting to keep things quiet for a few days is simple. If the killer knew that we had determined that Hammond had been murdered, he or she would disappear - or that's what we thought at the time. I happen to believe that what we did turned out very well. It certainly helped this group accumulate information without endangering itself. How we did it isn't important. Nothing was illegal." He let that thought hang in the air.

After a few seconds had passed, Flanders spoke up. "This bothers me a great deal, Supervisor Morgan. Not that you held back the information. I understand that. It's that I met with Bill Parker just yesterday and we discussed this murder. I wasn't aware of it until then. What causes me trouble is that when Mr. Parker and I met, Hugo suggested to me that I try to meet where no attention would be drawn to me. And to dress in a way that strangers wouldn't get curious about a person who was surely down on his luck. He also suggested that I drive another car, which I did. Quite melodramatic. But I followed his advice. I left my car in the service area of my car dealer. You all know the rest of the story. My car burned up. It took two new cars with it."

Flanders looked truly nervous as he related his story. "I call that an attempted murder."

There was a silence in the room. This was an important event, leaving aside its possible problem for Flanders and a long life. It could be a turning point in this problem.

Parker said, "I don't think it was an attempt on your life, Don. I'm sure it was just a warning. I'll tell you why I believe that later."

Then Morgan leaned forward in his chair. "I agree. I don't think you are in any immediate danger, Mr. Flanders. Staying alert is important, but I think that this destruction of your car was a warning to you of the clearest possible kind. Pardon my bluntness, but I think that if he or they wanted you dead, you'd be dead now. Now, an important question. What have you done or said, out-of-the-ordinary, that makes you a danger to anyone? Any change in your routine is important, too. Think about it."

After a minute or so, during which time the room again was silent, Flanders said, “The only thing I’ve done out of the ordinary in many months is to meet with Bill Parker this morning in the National Life parking lot – way off to the side, behind the dumpsters and the small trees. I don’t think anyone saw us. Even if they did, I was dressed differently and drove a different car.”

He was most probably right, thought Parker. However, Parker didn’t want to keep traveling on this path.

“Peter,” he piped up, “let’s get something straight. There *has* been a murder, really two. We all know that. However, I don’t want us to become paranoid, looking under every bed in the house before we crawl into it. We really only know for sure that Hammond was killed in the Statehouse. And Chugger was murdered in his motel. They could be completely unconnected. And that’s all we know. A lot of fact-checking has to be done before we bring in the cavalry. This is the problem we had, past tense, you’ll note, as I saw it: nothing fits a pattern, and nothing seemed to be related to any other event. I believe that’s changed.”

Morgan looked long and hard at Parker. “Obviously, you have new information, Bill. All the same, let’s just not forget to keep our wits about us from now on.”

At that moment, Birdsall spoke up. “Let’s get back on track, gentlemen. Time’s short. Bill, I have two things to bring up before we part company. First, I had a call from Jan Evlin’s husband, Herbert Evlin. He asked if Jan was here. He got no answers to his many attempts to talk to her. He called her parents and they’ve got the two kids. So he called me. I told him she was on a special assignment of a quiet type for another week. I asked him where he was and he is in Iraq. He’s some kind of an engineer, working there under contract. I told him that she would call him as soon as she got back. He said okay but to call him immediately when she got ‘off the road’, as he put it.” That guy was probably out of touch somewhere for the last week, thought Parker.

“I also received some more information from my brother’s widow, and the flat statement that I was not to call her any more. She’s through with Vermont. And apparently through with me, too, although I can’t for the life of me tell you why. We always got along, I thought. She didn’t even take the time to put these pieces of paper in an envelope. She just faxed them to me.”

“Did your secretary see it?” Parker asked abruptly.

"No. The FAX came into my personal FAX machine in this office. Here it is." He handed the pieces of paper to Parker.

Morgan and Small had left their chairs and surrounded Parker as he laid the three sheets on the table. The FAX showed a type of paper that seemed to be lined, like the writing paper from a tablet.

The top sheet, with "Page 1" written on it, was full of unexplainable entries. Same for the second sheet with its "Page 2" at the top. Parker skimmed the two sheets. He read a typical entry:

"349WQ4D10Sa"

All of the entries were different, and yet they all had this same sort of mixture of letters and numbers. They were all done by hand. No computer records for this info, thought Parker. There were at least 75 entries on each sheet. And I don't have a clue what they are telling me. Hell, thought Parker, they could be the layout for a bowling team schedule organized by a math teacher.

He looked up at Morgan. "Any ideas?"

"Nope," he said. "Not at the moment."

Small agreed.

The third piece of paper was a formal communication, in the form of a proclamation, announcing the addition of Hugh Hammond to the Board of Directors of the Northeast Government Watch Institute. This is interesting, thought Parker. I just heard about this bunch from Flanders at our noon meeting behind the trash bins at the back edge of a huge parking lot in Montpelier. It was what was printed at the bottom of this announcement that really got Parker's attention. The president of this non-profit institute was Gil Birdsall. And he had asked Hammond to be on his Board. And that meant they were friends – or at least Gil Birdsall knew Hammond well enough to know he would make a good member of the Board of his fledgling organization.

Parker rolled this information around in his mind. That's the connection, isn't it, he suddenly realized. It must have been Gil Birdsall who took the pictures of the compound in the Northeast Kingdom. And, therefore, it was Gil who was shot at and ran away. And that's why the pictures were so carefully protected and hidden. Gil knew they were critically important. He knew that he was a target now because of the attempt on his life among the trees behind Ferdinand Bog.

It must have scared the hell out of him, thought Parker. It sure would have scared me, he knew. And if Gil was afraid, and there is every reason to believe he was, it would explain why he gave his pictures to a friend and Board member of his organization and told him to hide them very well. I'll bet that's exactly what happened, Parker mused. He decided that this was important enough to tell the others.

When he finished, he asked for comments.

Don Flanders said, "That's as good an interpretation as we'll get, Bill. It ties a lot together, and it's perfectly reasonable." There was agreement from all the parties.

Morgan had one comment. "Bill, we are assuming that Gil took these pictures, was shot at, and escaped. Right?"

"Yes, Peter, that's right."

"My question is this: why would Gil go back up there? I mean, if he was frightened, and I'm sure he was, and he already had the photos, why would he need to tempt a killer to have another try at killing him?" Parker watched Morgan at work. The cop at his best.

Morgan continued. "I don't think Gil took the pictures, Bill. He was killed in late November of last year. You got into this mess in late April of this year – five months later? Something like that. If this was hardwood growth, we would have a decent idea of about when these pictures were taken. But the trees are softwoods, and it's much more difficult to tell when the photos were taken – especially as the photos don't show much expanse of the land."

"What's your conclusion, Peter? Where are you heading with this?"

Morgan took a deep breath, shook his head, and said," I don't think Gil took these pictures. I think that Hugh Hammond took them, got shot at, escaped, and got back home, scared out of his wits. He then told Gil what he'd seen and photographed, maybe at one of the Board meetings of Birdsall's organization, and said he wanted to take a breather for a few days or weeks. Having been shot at is a real traumatic experience and not something that an amateur handles very well. Hell, cops don't like it either."

Parker was gazing out to the far wall of Hal's office, seeing nothing. "So," he mused, out loud, "you're saying that the pictures were taken a few months before we thought. Then Gil went up there disguised as a hunter, not too long after he'd seen the photos, whenever that was, to see this compound. He was murdered. Hugh, of course, was shocked by this - his nerves were in bad shape anyway. They certainly were when we had dinner together, I know."

Hal looked up. "He was behaving strangely, Bill, during that time. I noticed it, too."

"Then I came along," said Parker, "and met with Hugh. I asked him questions that made him nervous. So nervous that he walked out of the Thrush. He was dead a day after that."

"That's it, buddy," Morgan said.

When he was done talking, Parker felt tired, but in a strange way. It was more an empty feeling. Maybe he was hoping to feel better – take on a lighter mood because he'd told others about the details he had carried in his memory, almost totally alone, for two weeks. Talking about them with these people didn't work. He was simply too disgusted by the corruption that seemed to be all around them, and it pulled the energy out of his body and mind.

"I wonder what these big non-profits want, at the end of everything?" asked Flanders, absently.

"Money," said Morgan promptly. "Money and control. Just follow the money, my old man used to say." Parker's father had said the same.

Parker asked Birdsall if he'd make copies of these sheets of paper for the police in attendance and for him. Birdsall took the papers and retreated to his desk where soon leading edge whirring could be heard. Soon he reappeared with the copies.

"Hal, the reason I asked about your secretary and if she saw these papers is because I saw a woman coming down the back stairs from your office just before I arrived. Was she invited to the meeting and then had to leave?"

"What?" cried Birdsall. "What did she look like?"

"Tall, and dressed in a dark raincoat, I think. Hard to tell much detail in the limited light in that alley. Wearing shades, and swore like a trooper, too."

"There was no woman here that had to leave, Bill. And that's the last straw, by God. She's out of here tomorrow!"

"Don't be too hasty," said Morgan. "This could be a big break. Tell me, Mr. Birdsall," he said, "how much information has she been allowed to hear through her little recording device?"

"None, by Christ!" Birdsall said, firmly. "Any important meetings I call now I hold outside this building."

"She's probably starved for information. Nothing to report to Mr. Big, you see?" said Morgan, reasonably. "He's probably pushing her to give him something. Sign of panic? Maybe. Probably too much to hope for. He believes he has other sources, although most of them not as good as this one, I think."

Morgan shifted in his chair in order to look directly at Parker. "Bill, if we all agree - and we may not, of course - that the murder of Hammond, the murder of that little motel owner here in Burlington, and the fiery end to Mr. Flanders' car, the abduction, if not worse, of Jan Evlin, and the murder of Gil Birdsall----," Hal Birdsall lurched to his feet at that matter-of-fact comment.

"Wh-what do you mean the *murder* of my brother?" he quavered. Birdsall was pale, shaking, as he stood in front of Morgan. "That's never been mentioned anywhere, Mr. Morgan. Not even hinted at!"

"Mr. Birdsall," Morgan said, voice quiet and calm, "it became a real possibility to me after I learned about the secret parcel of pictures that Hugh Hammond told our friend, here, Bill Parker, about. There was no way to be sure, of course, so I didn't mention it to anybody. But it seemed to me at that time that the death of your brother was probably the first killing of all of them. We now have at least two others to list and the definite warning given to Mr. Flanders. I decided to bring all this out into the open right now. I couldn't wait any longer. I'm truly sorry for upsetting you like this."

Birdsall slumped down into one of the easy chairs, made vacant for him by Bud Small, who guided him to the chair. He stared at the floor with glazed eyes.

Morgan looked up at Bud Small. "Bud, I think that Gil Birdsall's body was found in the town of Ferdinand. Right under the power line, in fact. Close to the eastern border of Brighton just over the line from Ferdinand."

Small consulted a small notebook, which all policemen seemed to have. "Yep, Brighton, right on the Ferdinand line, if that's important to you, Mr. Morgan."

Parker felt a fizzing in his mind. Too much information. Not smart enough to bring it all together and make sense of it.

"Who has spent time up there near Ferdinand? Anybody here?" asked Parker.

"Well," said Bud Small, "I have. I used to hike all over that part of the Northeast Kingdom with my family. Loved it up there. We used to camp at Maidstone Lake. It's been about five years since I've been up there, but I don't imagine too much of it has changed – except access to it, of course, which was eliminated by the Legislature, and the sudden appearance of this compound, the purpose of which has remained a mystery."

Parker got up from his chair. He was stiff and needed to move. It had been a long day. He was not surprised to hear Morgan state that Gil Birdsall's death had been murder.

He walked over to the conference table, poured a cup of coffee, sat on the edge of the table, and turned to the group and said, "I was in the Vermont House when the Champion Paper Company put the land up for sale. One of the saddest days I spent while in the Legislature was the day when the first parts of the plan were set in motion to make the Champion land available to the Protection League types. In fact, the state of Vermont took six million dollars from Vermont taxpayers and kicked that in to the pot, too. I don't know how many of you, if any, know the sequence of orchestrated events in the Legislature that led up to this huge land grab, using money from outside our state. It was very simple at the outset. Is that knowledge useful to us?"

There was a subtle rumbling of agreement in the room as people got comfortable. "We need to hear it, Bill," said Hugo. "We'll decide on its importance."

"Thanks, Hugo. This won't take long at all. We should also remember that this same sort of effort is working in almost every state in the country right now. Vermont is the test tube for many of these radical initiatives in the country. Even our Governor at that time played a key role in the Earth First Amendment Coalition organization's plan to take a large part of our state for themselves and to remove from the hunting camp owners an entire way of life. I'm going to tell you because you need to place this takeover of one of the most beautiful parts of Vermont into the context of the overall plan for the country – determined by people we don't even know."

Hal Birdsall looked up from his position of despair. He hadn't said a word since Peter Morgan had told them all that Hal's brother, Gil, had not died from the results of a hunting accident, but rather from an act of murder.

"And my newspaper supported this effort," he said, in a low voice. "Left the impression that a group of hard working people had scraped up the money and they should be rewarded with the opportunity to buy up the 140,000 acres." He shook his head in disgust. "That was pure garbage. These big environmental groups like the Trust of the Progressive Naturalist, the Bitterroot Group, and this Earth First Club, will never run out of money. They are wealthy beyond belief. And they are buying up our country."

"That's right, Hal, they are," said Parker. "And your paper has had so many opportunities to do a terrific job for Vermont by telling what's really going on, but instead your editorial people chose to follow the ProgDem agenda."

"I'm being very blunt, Hal," said Parker, "but it galled me then, and it still does. And I think we're running out of time. The CFP surprised me when their new managers wrote a couple of editorials supporting school choice. The extreme left in Vermont was really furious at that. That was a few years ago. Haven't seen another, though. But don't feel alone, Hal. Every left-wing news source in Vermont wanted this land to disappear from private ownership. They didn't care about the destruction of a way of life, along with it." Birdsall didn't seem appeased at that sharing of the blame.

"Let me continue," said Parker, "so we can get on with our meeting. I remember sitting in the House in 1997, I think it was, and the first piece of legislation that came up called for the restriction of clear-cut logging to no more than 40 acres. That would mean that the Champion Paper Company immediately lost the right to control the harvesting of trees cut from its own land."

"And that one little bill," continued Parker, "caused half of the workers in the forest industry to lose their jobs. And this was a *renewable* resource. It's the type of resource that the ProgDems are always supporting. The hypocrisy of that was what has lingered with me ever since. Most people in the southern two-thirds of the state didn't even know what the fuss was about."

"They do now," said Flanders. "Vermont is now, believe it or not, a net *importer* of timber products. My God almighty, we are 80% forested, and we have to import timber. I've got a couple of clients who were in the wood products industry. They've closed their businesses and moved out."

"That was just the sledgehammer of the ProgDems, my friends," said Parker. "The obvious and public move. What came next was cute and clever. It came about an hour after the limitation on how much they could cut without state permission. They passed another piece of legislation – it was either a bill or an amendment to some other bill – I don't remember, that prevented the owners of timber land from aerial spraying a clear-cut area a few months after a clear-cut was complete. Does anyone here know what the argument was that the ProgDems used to sell this destructive idea?"

"Something to do with the chemical glyphosate, as I recall," said Flanders. "They said it was poison. Was there something wrong with that, Bill?" he asked.

"Other than that their statement was a lie, no," answered Parker, bitterly. "Glyphosate, when sprayed over the clear-cuts, would fall on the broad leaves of the hardwoods that were trying to take over where you want softwoods to grow. When glyphosate descends as a spray, it will land on the broad leaves of the small hardwoods and stops them from growing. But it won't affect the softwoods because the glyphosate won't stay on the needles. The softwoods are allowed to grow up to be a renewable resource. Simple, wouldn't you say?"

"I remember that, Bill. Weren't the ProgDems saying that glyphosate would poison the ground?"

"Yes, they were, Don. Another lie. When glyphosate hits the ground it becomes benign. Do you want to know something else really aggravating? The ProgDems called glyphosate a poison, but I'll bet that they all had some in their garage or barn. Almost all of the members of the House that day admitted that they had some, and used it often. It's called 'Round Up'."

Hugo blurted, "You mean that the chemical they sprayed was Round Up? I use it a lot around my place. Hasn't bothered anyone in my house in any way."

"And it won't," said Flanders, stirring in his chair. "So, Bill, we were sold a bill of goods and we all bought it, is that it?"

"Yes, that's it, Don. Only five months later, Champion put all their Vermont land up for sale. One hundred and forty thousand acres. The whole thing was orchestrated right from the beginning. And the ProgDems worked it like a dream."

"These supporters wanted to test this approach," continued Parker, "test the public relations approach used to sell it in Vermont, and then take the result out for national environmental campaigns designed to buy up more and more of this nation.

Vermont had drifted so far to the left that they really didn't have a big fight, of course. They had the votes in the House and Senate, so they passed whatever they wanted. And they had a Governor who was also from the left and supported these radical initiatives."

Parker started to walk slowly around the room. He didn't do it to be more dramatic. It was simply that his rear end hurt from leaning on the table edge. "And they had enough voters in their districts or counties who would complain about their legislative agenda - even write letters against their Senators or their particular Representative - but then vote for them again anyway. And today the ProgDems have regained their strength in the Legislature, allowing them to pass the same sorts of things. So, hang onto your hats, folks, and your wallets. You've already lost the power to control your own land."

There was silence in the room. Parker broke the quiet and moved the subject along. "Sorry to take so long, everybody. But I thought that you should know what happened to the Champion Lands, and how it happened. And I think that behind the Ferdinand Bog, and in the core area, is where this compound is located. Now, let's talk about whatever we need to discuss regarding this mysterious track we're on."

Hugo got to his feet and stood beside Parker. "Now," he said firmly, "here's what I see. Hal gave an assignment to Jan Evlin. She apparently became upset because she thought she'd been threatened. Now she's disappeared. She skedaddled, no doubt. Where to? We don't know. Then Parker, here, gets into things. He talked to Hugh Hammond. Hammond is killed. Oh," he snapped his fingers, "and Mr. Nosey, here," waving a hand at Parker, "also finds out that some goofy people he meets were warned that he is on the prowl. Also, just after Parker leaves the motel up here in beautiful Chittenden County, a disreputable little man named Chugger gets his head caved in." He looked at Parker. "You really do attract the strange-o's, don't you, Bill?"

Bud Small looked at Parker, just as Parker was turning toward him. Small couldn't hide completely his faint smile.

Hugo turned back to the group. "And while all this is going on, other people get warned with these strange notes, written by 'Z', who might very well be anybody. Then Flanders is warned, in a most direct way, to stay out of whatever is going on. At least, I think that's probably safe to say. Then Parker and I invade Hammond's old barn to retrieve some papers that Hammond told

Parker to pick up if he is ever out of the game. I go with the intrepid Mr. Parker one night and we come close to being flattened permanently inside this barn."

Morgan is startled. "You never gave me any details about this, Bill. What's Hugo talking about?"

"I'll tell you later, Peter. It just scared the hell out of us, I'll tell you."

"I want to know now, please," announced Morgan.

Parker turned toward Morgan. "Hugo and I were on the main floor of an old cow barn behind Hammond's house, and somebody from the second floor pushed a large and heavy oil tank over the edge, aiming at us. It missed but, like the old song, the memory lingers on." Parker's attempt at levity to defuse the electric atmosphere had no effect on the group.

Morgan thought about this abbreviated rendition of that night in a cow barn. "Well, you two must have been close to the killer's activities, or at least the killer certainly thought so. Maybe the potential killer thought that this might be the best, and maybe the only, opportunity to take care of the problem you presented. Desperation? It sure seems like it. I'd like to think so, anyway. Bud, what do you think?"

Bud Small hesitated, obviously churning the question around in his mind the way people in the law enforcement community tend to do, and then said, "I agree. Your reputation, Mr. Parker, is one of over-inquisitiveness, you know. Many of us in law enforcement know that. The one way a person wearing a black hat can take care of the problem you represent is the elimination of your presence. 'Striking while the iron is hot' was probably the idea in the mind of this coo-coo in the barn." Parker wasn't happy about this scenario. "What information did you and Hugo come away with that night, Mr. Parker?" asked Detective Small.

Parker thought that the brief description rendered by Hugo was enough for the group. Now was the time to describe this unclear batch of pictures. "Just some photos. No identifying descriptions. But now I know where they were taken." Parker went on to describe what he had learned from Bob O'Sullivan.

When he was near the end, he brought up the sign that was posted at the rough entrance road to the edge of the core area of the Champion land. "Anybody recognize the letters 'NPF'?" he asked. "And also the Roman numerals 'II'? Any great guessers here?"

After many attempts by the assembled participants to make these letters arrange themselves in a useful way, the buzz stopped. "The only thing that's apparent to me is that there probably is an 'NPF I' somewhere," said Flanders.

Parker stood up again and said, "I think I know what the letters mean, but I wanted all of you to think about them. In fact, I thought that one of you might absolutely know what they stand for, and what you know as fact might eliminate my information, which is secondhand, or confirm it. I was looking for confirmation from you folks. And I got it, I think. Here's what I think they mean," said Parker. "'NPF' stands for North Point Farm."

Morgan straightened up in his chair. "That rings a bell for me, I think. I heard that name, or one like it, three or four years ago, in the Montpelier and Barre area. I can't tell you in what context, but maybe I can find out." He made a note in his cop-like notebook.

Parker related his experience at the middle school exhibit, detailing as well as he could his conversation with Chatty. "It's possible that our bad guy was actually in Bridgeton a few weeks ago."

"Bill," said Morgan, "I think you're tying things together quite well. Anything else?"

Parker then passed along the information from the Malcoms, without mentioning their names. "That's why I think you got a straight-out warning, Don, and not an attempt on your life."

Flanders nodded, and then added, "Glad to have the opinion of your two pet shrinks, Bill. All the same, I'm keeping my head not only down, but out of the way completely."

"Well, what do we have to do next, Bill?" asked Birdsall. He looked as if he was still very "down", but his voice was stronger and he seemed to be recovering somewhat from the shock of learning that his brother had probably been murdered.

"Well, Hal, I think you'd be the one, along with Peter Morgan, who may have friends and acquaintances who might be able to shine some light on what this damn sign is telling us – which might be precisely nothing. But this is an example of where we are right now. Lots of information and only now is it starting to connect. If you two could do what you can to unravel the mysterious sign, compare notes, and then let us all know, we'd know if that sign is useful to us." They agreed, although Morgan wasn't happy about talking to a non-law enforcement person, especially a newspaper man, about information essentially in the sphere of the police. Parker knew that Morgan would be very, very careful about how much he said to Birdsall. Parker didn't think that was the worse thing.

Peter Morgan spoke up next. "Bill, I'll work on Hammond's murder. I'll have to do that, anyway, of course, but now I have extra incentive and another Parker-assigned job, too, to do. I have you to share my information with." He grinned.

Bud Small rose up out of his over weight-limit easy chair and announced that he "would follow up and dig around regarding the murder of Hal's brother".

At this point, Parker told him about John Chapman and his apparent theory that Gil Birdsall was murdered rather than having met with an accident. "No matter what you learn from John," Parker said, "you'll enjoy hearing him tell you all about it. But don't sell him short. He's smart and he has one of those practical minds that seems so rare in Vermont these days."

"I'll check him out," said Small.

"How about you, Bill?" Flanders asked. "What do you have as an action plan?"

Morgan spoke to Flanders before Parker could draw a breath. "He's going into the Champion land and nose around."

"How do you know that, Mr. Morgan?" asked Flanders.

"Because I know Bill Parker."

Parker said, in response to this conversation to which he'd added nothing, "I *am* considering a trip in there in the future. But not until I get the time."

"That means, for those of you who haven't had the PE treatment, that he's going in there tomorrow," said Morgan.

"What's the PE treatment, Mr. Morgan?" asked Flanders.

"That's the 'Parker Experience', Mr. Flanders. You may be on the edge of involvement in this life-changing sensation, so pay attention."

Parker finally slipped in a word. "Don, don't pay any attention to him. Law enforcement people don't choose to talk too much during their normal workday. They use as few words as possible in an attempt to give the impression that they are serious, and are devoted to objectivity. When they leave that cloistered atmosphere, however, they sort of expand, losing control of their brains and their tongues every once in a while and sacrificing common sense – like just now."

Parker continued. "In answer to Superintendent Morgan's comments, I have another assignment for Hal. Yes, Don, I'm going into the core of the Champion Land, but only after we have a conversation in this room that will be picked up on your secretary's sneaky recording machine. If she's at all anxious to hear something she can pass on, then we'll give it to her. Our little talk will take place right now, Hal." There was a babble of sound in the room. Morgan was silent, looking at Parker, with a pleasant expression. A sort of "I told you all about Parker and what he'll do when you least expect it" expression.

The room settled down when Parker started to talk again. "It will be one in which I will announce that I'm going in to the Ferdinand Bog area because I have some pictures that tell me that something is going on up there that has to be looked into. I'll also say that law enforcement wants nothing to do with it, so to hell with them, I'll go alone. Also, and this is very important, Hal, we have to be sure she gets the word on her little tape that I'll be going in on this Wednesday morning. In reality, I'm leaving early tomorrow morning in order to get up there well ahead of time, and will be back tomorrow night. Also, I'll say that I have enough information so that I know what I'll be looking for and what I have will blow the roof off this scheme. It could be dynamite, etcetera – that sort of thing - on her tape that ought to cause a real stir. So let's get on with it."

It took only about twenty minutes to plug in the recorder and record the misleading message. Everybody was completely quiet while this was going on, but all were fascinated by the plan that the devious mind of Bill Parker had concocted. Parker noticed this unordered silence and thought that it was because nobody wanted to be connected with him at this point. Can't say as I blame them, he thought.

Hugo watched the tape machine to make certain it was doing its job. He would unplug after the fake message was recorded and then reconnect it after everyone had left.

Everything worked like a jeweled watch. "Anything else? Is that it?" asked Hugo.

It was. Everybody got to their feet and slowly filed to the door, speaking in low tones with some of the others. Bud Small drifted up beside Parker and said, softly, "What time do you take off in the morning for Ferdinand? I want to know because I'm going with you. I need a day or two of vacation anyway. Also, assuming that there's been one murder up there already, going up there alone will not be the smartest thing you ever did."

"I can take care of myself, Bud," said Parker, firmly.

Small looked at him intently. "I know the signs, Mr. Parker. It's my business to know how people like you react to situations. I'll be with you. Believe me, you will not be going without me."

Parker decided not to argue. In truth, he was glad that he had someone like Bud with him. "Give me your address," he said. "I'll pick you up about 3:00 AM tomorrow. That will give us each a chance for a little sleep. Wear rough country clothes and footgear – and be sure it has dull colors so it doesn't announce our arrival to anyone who doesn't like us."

Bud smiled at Parker, made a gesture as if he were tipping a hat, and left.

48

Parker arrived at Small's house in Jericho shortly after 2:00 in the morning on Monday. He felt groggy. He had gotten about two hours of sleep, and that was accomplished while lying on one of the UVM student-rejected couches in Birdsall's office. After he had tried to sleep on this bed of nails, he came close to checking himself into a homeless shelter somewhere nearby. That would have been much better than that damn couch.

As he pulled into the driveway of the neat ranch home, the porch light came on and Detective Small, larger than life, stepped out onto the porch and down the stairs to Parker's truck. "Pull over there, Mr. Parker. We're taking my vehicle. Take whatever you brought for this trip and throw it into the back of that rig over there."

He gestured toward the side of the garage. Parker could see the dark color of the sizeable "rig", and decided that there were only a few automobiles available that could accommodate someone of Bud's size for any length of time. An SUV like this one was one of them.

"We can take my truck, Bud. It will move along very nicely," Parker announced.

"Great, Mr. Parker," said Small. "However, let me tell you something of which you're apparently not aware." Parker noticed that Small used the English language in the same way that Addie had been forcing on him. So far he'd been able to fight her off, but every once in a while he caught himself actually doing the tricky stuff the way she wanted it. I'll have to watch that, he thought.

"We don't know what's ahead of us today, but one thing I do know might be very important. I want something that will move along a hell of lot better than 'nicely'. Also, I would be cramped up for a week if I had to spend three hours in your truck, especially on some of the tracks we'll be on today, if my guess is correct. And last, my rig fits right in with that territory in the Kingdom. There's nothing up there but pickups and SUVs. Your 'pickup' is different from any other 'pickup' that exists up there –

or anywhere else, I think. I want to fit in, you see – not be followed by people who will be asking us where the antique car meet is going to be held. I hope I didn't hurt your feelings, Mr. Parker, but this is something on which I insist."

There he goes again, thought Parker. Saying things correctly. "I understand, Bud. No problem at all."

Parker decided, when this murder stuff was all over, that he would look at this pickup of his with an objective eye. Maybe he needed to change his transportation method from classically inconvenient to modernly useful and appealing. Maybe. Change, however, his father used to say, may not be good for some people.

They slipped out of Small's yard and headed east.

It took Parker and Small almost four hours to reach the area near the Ferdinand Bog. They came across using the Interstate 89 highway, then onto Route 302, and east to Interstate 91, and then north to Route 114, which took them to the area just below where the track heading into the area where the Ferdinand Bog should be.

There were no general stores in Ferdinand. There were no health clinics, police stations, non-profit offices, or citizen protests against a housing development. It would, however, be a "gold town" under the Vermont ProgDem legislation that sucked the money out of all the prosperous towns in the state in order to give it away to "poor towns". It also ruined towns that had a low ability to pay any tax bill at all. It appeared that there were no decent roads, with the exception of 114, other than grown-over logging roads.

To Parker and Bud it was beautiful. To Parker, however, it was also tragic, because the national leftists had found a way to buy up this productive land and put hundreds of people out of work – and to cause Vermont to become a net importer of wood products, saw logs, and lumber. When Flanders told him that, Parker had almost cried. God, what a terrible waste of our resources, both human and natural. The collective and long term effects of this takeover of private land would be felt most strongly by the families who had worked in the Kingdom for generations. The heart of this area of Vermont was ripped right out.

Parker couldn't help himself. His mind was never very far away from the various blights the ProgDems had visited on Vermont and its citizens. The evidence of the work of the left was everywhere. No lasting jobs, marginally educated children, Vermonters unable to afford health care insurance, and a spoiled voting process that allowed out-of-state visitors to vote for the state's leaders and then leave town. Parker also thought that when the ProgDems began to regulate the uses of all the land, regardless of the acreage, there wouldn't be enough alarmed people remaining in Vermont to mount a serious challenge to them.

These kinds of emotions caused Parker to become blue. He knew he shouldn't let this train of thought invade his otherwise practical and easygoing approach to life. With effort he put these thoughts to the back of his mind while he considered what lay ahead of them.

It could be a very quiet and peaceful trip, and they'd be on their way back toward home in four or five hours. Or they could meet a man with a rifle. It all depended on whether or not the phony message was reported to the Boss Man from Hal's secretary.

Small began to slow down and pulled over to the edge of the road. He stopped, and then asked, "Do you have a firearm, Mr. Parker?"

Parker was startled. "A firearm, Bud? Why would I need a firearm? We're just going for a walk in the woods." He could feel Small's eyes on him.

"*We* know that, Mr. Parker. However, what if somebody we meet in here hasn't had that explained to them? I have one for you, in any case."

He pushed a holstered .38 Police Special across the seat divider. "It's loaded, the safety is engaged, and I want you to strap it on your belt in the small of your back. I'm not heading into a murder zone without both of us being armed. I'd like to come out of here today and see my family again. I know that you have had experience with handguns. Morgan told me about your past – some of it, anyway." He continued to look at Parker.

"Okay, Bud. I'm sure we won't have any need of them, but I'll go along." He picked up the holster and set it on his lap.

Then he said, "Let's get something settled right now. You told me just now that I had to be armed while up here. That's settled. Now, stop calling me 'Mr. Parker'. You're making me nervous. The name is 'Bill'. Okay?"

Small smiled slightly, seeing Parker's method of defusing the slight tension that existed, and said, "You got it, Bill. Let's charge into the woods, listening for the sound of trumpets, just like the old days." With that, he pulled out into the highway and, as Parker thought of it, they were off on their great adventure.

Parker had enjoyed his trip from Burlington in Bud's SUV. It rode much better than Parker would have guessed. It was roomy and, as they say in advertising lingo, user-friendly.

Parker remembered meeting an Addison County ProgDem Representative during his first term in the Vermont House. It was about the same time that the Vermont left had unleashed a series of attacks against SUVs. These attacks disgusted Parker's new friend.

Parker's friend told him that he had many owners of SUVs in his voting district. He told Parker that he had not surveyed the owners to see what the reasons were for their purchase of an SUV. But his impression was that these owners were in large part an older population, many retired, who needed the type of vehicle represented by an SUV. Hospitals, and other essential destinations, could be reached in almost any kind of weather. They could haul their grandchildren around and feel perfectly safe. These folks, as they became older, needed the assurance offered by the SUV. Rather than Sport Utility Vehicles, a title ridiculed by the leftists, these older people called their SUVs 'Special Use Vehicles'. Parker loved that term.

The "compassionate" ProgDems in Vermont, however, had received their marching orders. They were to follow the national agenda of the radical left. The SUV was to be the symbol of all they hated about America. And this agenda was to be followed to the letter. After all, the national left had poured into Vermont 90% of all the ProgDem campaign money over the last fifteen elections. They had "bought" Vermont. They expected a return on their investment.

So, the ProgDems contacted all their letter writers around the state, giving them the talking points to be used in their letters to their newspapers. When Parker read these letters the first thing he looked for was the name of the writer. They were the same cast of characters, without exception. They'd better find some new recruits, he decided, to put out this fiction. It was all too obvious.

The same talking points were then used when members of the ProgDem Party visited the editorial boards of the various daily newspapers around Vermont, urging them, in a much more subtle way, to use the talking points, which they called "basic facts", in order to write editorials on various subjects. For the most part, they always met with friendly receptions.

The ProgDems of Vermont had no problem with following the lead of the left. Many of them were already following the radical agenda. A few of them were just blindly wallowing along, too lazy, or too stupid, to look into what they were supporting. But the rest of their party was made up of hardcore members of the left.

This national agenda called for the installation of the Prog-Dem "elite" leadership in the Legislature and, as soon as possible, the Governor's office. The SUV controversy they created was just one more item to cast doubt on the system and institutions of their country. They already controlled the important courts, so they were almost there. And the Vermont ProgDems assumed that *they* would be this Vermont "elite". Maybe, thought Parker, but if the national leftists do control Vermont completely some day in the future, Parker and the new Independents both expected that the new rulers of Vermont would be from out-of-state.

Parker's friend switched parties during his second term and joined Parker's party of one. They doubled their membership in one day. He and Parker became an unofficial caucus. Their meetings, held in the Statehouse cafeteria, were always well attended, and they enjoyed it immensely. They swapped the Chairmanship title before every meeting. The official press never attended one of their meetings, of course. They missed some great debates, thought Parker. And the coffee was okay, too. Kind of expensive, though.

According to the map that Parker had received from O'Sullivan, they arrived about where they should start to look for a place to hide the car and start hiking.

"Anywhere along here, Bud, we should look for a trail. That was East Haven we just went through." Bud nodded, then suddenly swerved off the road and onto a faint track heading into the tree line. When he stopped, he backed around so that the vehicle was headed out again. He pointed across the road into the wilderness and said, "Somewhere in that direction there's a gravel road that the map says is 'drivable'. Hell, that wasn't drivable when my family and I used to hike in these parts, and I'll bet that the lefties have torn apart what road existed to prevent anybody from going in there."

"Bud," said Parker, "there has to be a way to get where we want to go. If those three log buildings actually exist and are used by people, then all kinds of supplies will be needed. That will take a road."

"Then we'll look for one," Small said simply.

"It's now 6:00 in the morning, Bill, Small said, checking his watch. "Starting to get light around the edges out there. How do you feel? Beat, I expect. Here, have a sandwich and a cup of hot coffee. My wife made them up for us." He reached into a small insulated metal box that had the name "Piel's Beer" on it, followed by "Bert and Harry say Hello", and produced the items.

Parker was really pleased with the food. He'd never given it a thought. "Bud, where the hell did you get that beer cooler? That's older than the hills."

Small smiled and said, "My father gave it to me. Told me to take care of it because it had some kind of historical significance for him, although I never found out what it was. Darn good cooler, though, even if it is a little old." Parker was amused by that. A *little* old, indeed. Bert and Harry were my generation, not yours, my friend.

Parker took his bearings to coincide with where he thought Unknown Pond was located, hoping that the topographical map was accurate – or that he was reading it properly. They had crossed under the big power line and hidden the vehicle. Then hiking was called for and they struck east, on foot, hoping to hit the undrivable "drivable" road, and follow that around to the back of Ferdinand Bog. When the road ended, the forest would really begin. That's when decisions would be made as to how they would proceed.

If they found some sort of a supply road they would be pleased, but only because they would know that, according to the map, they were in the proper place. Parker was certain that they would also stay the hell off it. If there were any unfriendly people in this area, things would rapidly come undone if they were seen.

And, Parker was certain, this was the place where Gil Birdsall was murdered, and his body then dragged out to be found by John Chapman. Parker would urge Bud to talk to John when he got home later today.

The light was just bright enough to see by, but not enough of it to be easily seen. They slipped into the trees, being as quiet and unobtrusive as they could, in the remote possibility that someone was around to see them.

They were standing at the edge of some young softwoods, tall enough to hide them, but easy for them to see from. All of a sudden Parker jumped as he heard a "beeping" sound. He saw Small reach in to his military-style backpack and drew out a cell phone. "This will be Morgan," he announced. And it was. Parker was impressed.

"Yeah, Pete, we're here, just ready to hike into the Bog area." He listened. "You've found 'NPF I'?" Bud exclaimed. "Great going, Pete. And it's not far from you? When are you going to go there?" More listening. "Parker? Here's right here. Want to talk to him?" Small passed the cell phone to Parker.

"Peter," said Parker. "Tell me about NPF I, please."

Parker heard an amazing tale from Morgan. Morgan had simply asked one of his veteran Sergeants if he had ever seen a sign with "NPF I" on it. "Sure," he had said. "Before my father retired from Barnes Lumber Company in Danville, he drove truck after truck down to East Calais to deliver all kinds of building materials to a place on the east side of the town. Some guy had apparently bought an old farm and 200 acres and was fixing the place up." His father said that a couple of lumber supply businesses right within shouting distance of the place were really upset because they didn't get the work.

When they questioned Todd Barnes about it at a meeting somewhere, Barnes told them that he didn't cut any prices at all to get the job. In fact, he said, he loaded up some prices just because he knew he wouldn't get the job because he was too far away. He thought that the new owner wanted to get a quote from away to use as a bargaining tool against the Barre lumber yards when the final price was negotiated. That way the Barre businesses would benefit if he gave this guy higher than usual prices. Todd thought he could shaft the new owner, who he didn't like the look of, rather than this new SOB shafting the lumber yards in Barre. Thought it was the least he could do. He said that nobody was more surprised than he was when he got the order.

"You follow all that, Bill?" Morgan asked. Parker said he did, but where the hell was all this taking them, he wondered?

"So when his father was making his runs down to East Calais, he noticed that the barn was the first item of reconstruction – not the house. The old couple was still living in it. I guess that was part of the deal when they sold it. Well, near the end of the work on the barn his father saw a bright green sign hanging on the front wall. Big one, too. 'NPF I', it read. Interestingly, when the work was all done, the 'NPF' was gone when he drove in with the last load later on. But a big 'I' was painted on the barn wall. Weird, huh?" Morgan said.

"What's the name of the owner, Peter?" asked Parker.

"It's still in the name of the old couple. Davidson is their name. The new owner has an apartment in the upstairs barn. We'll be checking him out some more tomorrow. I have a friend who works for the Expert Nurses Association who is willing to drop in to see how the old folks are doing. No box number for this new owner at any post office in Barre or in any surrounding town. If he has a phone in his apartment, it's unlisted. The Davidsons still have their phone in the house."

"Don't you think that this guy is being unnecessarily secretive, Peter?"

"Not unusually so, Bill. There are many people in Vermont who simply want to be left alone by the rest of the world. This is one way it's done."

Morgan hesitated, and then said, "The rebuilding materials for the house and barn from a business in Danville is different, though. And along with that we found out that the people who did the rebuilding work were actually from Canada. How about that? No locals. They apparently came down here, lived in trailers until they got the barn done, and moved into the barn while they worked on the house. They finished, got paid, and went back to Canada. We're trying to track them down through friends on both sides of the border. It's only been about six years since they did this work. It will be interesting to talk to them, I think. I'll call you later in the day with whatever new information we come up with."

As Parker was about to close the cell phone, he heard Morgan say, "By the way, I think that having carpenters from Canada and materials for the rebuilding job brought all the way down from Danville exceeds normal precautions taken by out-of-staters who want to be left alone."

Parker thought about what he had heard. "Peter, it may be very important that you talk to those people. I agree with you that what they say could be interesting. And one last thing before we disconnect – can you have someone watch that barn. I'm concerned that whoever lives there will learn that we're up here and will try to do something about it. In fact, he may be the one who Birdsall's secretary reported to. What he could do, I don't know. He's at least three hours away, but if he leaves the barn, looking like he's headed out on a trip, you should call us so we'll know. It will be a help to us."

"Will do, Bill. I'll set that up. Take care of yourself. See you soon." With that he hung up.

Small and Parker crossed under the power line and hiked through some rugged country for an hour, and suddenly reached a road that was running approximately north-south.

Bud remembered this road from his family-camping days. "I'm pretty sure this is the Paul Stream Road. I think we'll head north from here. We should run right into that 'undrivable' road. We'll head east then and that road will take us around to the backside of the Ferdinand Bog. And then we shall see what we shall see, won't we?" Small sounded excited about the prospect of going where they shouldn't be, and then leaving unseen.

Parker wasn't.

49

Parker and Small made much slower time than they planned for. They stayed inside the tree line all the way to the road that would take them to the NPF II. Without saying so, they both knew that it was very important to go into the core area of the Champion lands and back out again and leave no trace of their visit.

When they finally left the Paul Stream Road it was the middle of the morning. Parker thought that they were about an hour behind the time which he had planned.

They moved carefully along the edge of what seemed to be an old log road. But Bud remembered it as the road he had hiked on ten years before with his family.

"I remember when we first came up here to camp. We camped in the state park on the eastern side of Maidstone Lake. Always had a terrific time, too.

One day I decided that we would take a ride in the car to explore the western side of the lake. There were camps there and some of them were really nice. So we hopped in the car and went over to the lake road on that western side. It was a beautiful gravel road. I hadn't ever been on a better one. And it was wide, too. Had to have been at least a 60-foot-wide road, just like main roads in the rest of the state – except this was private property. Champion Paper Company land."

"Sounds impressive," said Parker. "Do you think this road we're on was as good, in its day?"

"Looks as if it was as wide, anyway," answered Bud. "Well, to continue my story, I, in my innocence, headed up the road on the western side to see what was there. We hadn't been on that road ten minutes beyond the lake camps when I saw, bearing down on us, a fully-loaded log truck, heading down the mountain at sixty miles an hour – maybe more. Bill, sixty on a good paved road is one thing. A log truck with all it can carry, traveling on a gravel road and coming off a mountain, in the wilderness, at sixty, is another thing entirely – especially meeting it with your whole family in the car. I'll tell you right now, it was all I could do to hide from my family how completely petrified I was. When we got back to the campsite I realized that what we had seen over there was exciting, big time, logging at its best. As you can tell, I've never forgotten that experience. It was great. And now gone, thanks to the leftists in the Legislature."

By this time they had reached the upper end of Paul Stream. Paul Stream was the main drainage for Ferdinand Bog, as far as Parker could tell from the map. And the road from the past, if it was a road that they had been following while still in the trees, ended abruptly at that drainage. It had been cleaned out with heavy equipment, probably at the time the theft of the land took place in the Legislature. No wheeled vehicles could go further.

This was interesting to Parker, but what really caught his attention was a yellow sign, about three feet square, that read, in block letters, "KEEP OUT" and under that command were the letters "NPF II". Parker snapped a picture of this most revealing indication that this area was important to somebody. And he thought of Chatty's painting, too.

Crossing the Paul Stream here was impossible.

"Well, we have no choice, Bill. Let's walk downstream until we find some shallower water, and we'll try to cross there. We'll probably get soaked, but we'll get over to the other side and complete our mission."

"Lead on, Watson, lead on," said Parker.

Small looked at Parker for a moment, but decided to say nothing. He'd ask Supervisor Morgan about Parker when they got back. Morgan knew him quite well, Small learned. Parker seems to be a real weird dude in some ways, he thought.

They walked south on Paul Stream's edge for what must have been a half mile. It was not easy walking. The curious would get discouraged by this terrain and head home. Only those with a mission would try to cross and wear wet clothing for the next few hours. Even some of them would probably turn back. Only determined snoops would continue.

All of a sudden Small stopped. He looked down at the water and said, "Well, lookie there, Bill," and pointed down to the water's edge. Lying at the edge of the stream, but also snugged up against the bank on which they were hiking, was a log bridge, in excellent condition, with length enough to cross the stream when placed in position. It would take at least one of the big pickups of today, a ton and a half would be Parker's guess, equipped with a sizeable winch, to be able to do it. All it would take would be enough of a roadway to allow a truck to get here. And Parker could see that where they had been walking, still inside the tree line for most of the half mile, dropping down to the stream edge occasionally to check the depth of the water, didn't allow them to recognize the relatively flat ground along the stream. They only saw it by luck when Small chose this section to slip out of the woods to look at the water.

"Well, well, well," said Parker. "Whoever uses this place doesn't want anyone else to use it, do they?"

"We'll be among the first, Bill. We're going to get wet, but I think we'll get across just fine. Let's go," he said, and strode into the stream and powered his way across the thirty feet of moving water.

Parker, not to be outdone, followed, barely making it without being knocked over by the surprisingly strong current.

They both were soaked to the hips, something neither of them had planned on, but they knew they could overcome the discomfort and keep moving with a purpose.

Now they were definitely close to the old road. The map showed it to head almost north-north-east for half a mile and then plunge sharply south for another half mile before it turned north again and headed up to the back side of the Bog. The jog in this road allowed the traveler to avoid what Parker considered as the real definition of a "bog". And a bog is not the place to hike and move fast at the same time.

About a three and a half mile hike had to be negotiated to where this old road ended. Beyond that will very possibly be some rough territory until we reach the compound, he thought.

It was turning out to be a clear day. Good for hiking, thought Parker, although when you're not used to it, a long hike can grow old very quickly. But he kept at it.

Bud Small just kept walking. He had a walking gait that didn't allow anything to change his pace. He just seemed to float over obstacles, even with that large pack on his back. A very formidable person, thought Parker. Good to have him along. Really glad I invited him.

50

As they labored through the fringe trees, Parker knew that they had dropped another hour behind his schedule. He hoped that this lag of two hours wouldn't leave them exposed for too long. They still had plenty of daylight, so it might not make a difference to them, but the uncertainty of what lay ahead made Parker uneasy.

Small and Parker took a short breather after an hour of steady travel. Small looked as if he could have marched all day, and was bored with waiting for just a few minutes. Parker worked hard to appear the same. A quick ham sandwich, a little water, and Small turned and, without a word, started off. Parker decided that it was a good idea that he do the same.

Another hour and Small abruptly stopped, motioning to Parker to stay down. "I think the compound is just through there." He pointed in the general direction of their track. "I caught a glimpse of it. Good idea to stop and look things over, I think."

Parker had moved up with Small and looked ahead, through the small trees and bushes. At first he could see nothing, but as he moved his gaze in an arc, he suddenly saw what Small had.

It was unmistakable. Many of the pictures, taken by Hugh Hammond, rather than Gil Birdsall, an idea advanced by Morgan, and which Parker now believed, showed the compound from the same angle that Parker and Small were now seeing it. Some of the pictures, however, showed things from other angles. He commented on this to Small.

Small was staring at the ground, obviously thinking about what they were seeing. "And what that means to me, Bill, is that Gil Birdsall, when he came up here to check this compound out, was seeing just what we are – nothing. So he went into the trees and moved all around the place, probably just like Hammond did when he was taking his happy snaps - all from different angles. Gil's mistake was to be seen by somebody. And that led to his murder, and then moving the body, so when it was found, the probability of finding the compound was really remote."

Parker nodded. "And that's why the attempt was made on Hugo and me in Hammond's barn that night. I'll bet that Mr. Bad Guy was at that barn all the time, or one of his cohorts was. I could imagine that some kind of surveillance of Hammond's barn on a very regular schedule was set up from the time that somebody had seen Hugh and me in the Thrush, having dinner. Mr. Bad Guy couldn't afford to let me learn something that he didn't know about." Parker stopped talking and thought about his next comment.

"Was I followed to the barn? Maybe, but I don't think so. This bad guy, whoever he was, was just waiting for somebody to come to the house or the barn. You know, to pick up something or to see something. It would take a number of people to watch that barn for a number of days, wouldn't it? Seems like an impossible task, but somebody was willing to try. Whatever is being protected must be very big, indeed."

"It's starting to come together, isn't it?" Small seemed excited. "That is, if what we're speculating about is the way everything really happened. One thing I'll mention now. The killer may have had somebody watching the barn, but I'll bet that you were being watched from the moment of Hammond's murder. And all the time, too."

"I didn't see anybody, Bud," Parker said.

Small grinned slightly. "But you weren't looking for a tail, were you, Bill? And even if you were, you wouldn't know *how* to look, would you?" Parker agreed with him.

And then Parker straightened up. "We're forgetting something, Bud. Yes, we are. Birdsall's non-profit think tank. His business was established to report what's going on around the state, as I understand it. Keeping watch over state government and state programs. That sort of the thing. I'll bet anything that Gil came up here, alone, to 'check things out', as Morgan said. He'd seen Hammond's photos. He probably thought that he needed firsthand information before he went public with it in his newsletter. Then he would blow the lid off this operation, whatever that is. He even had photos."

Parker hesitated, and then went on. "And the killer, or killers, knew that, or definitely suspected that somebody knew too much about the compound. Birdsall couldn't be allowed to leave here. He couldn't just disappear either. There would be people all over this place if that happened. So they killed him, and moved the body away from the compound."

"And it worked, Bill," said Small. "That is, it worked until you came along. That's when the warnings went out to the non-profits who were on the 'take'. Remember? The message? *Watch out for Parker. Let me know when you see him.* The big non-profits would become the spy network for Mr. Bad Guy. And why? Because they could be receiving the bulk of their funding from him, or he could direct money to come to them – probably from a variety of sources. And they needed that money. Then they could go on working to keep the ProgDems in power in Vermont so that their programs could be funded by the Vermont taxpayers, filtered through the Legislature."

"And Mr. Bad Guy could do. . ." Parker hesitated. "What the hell does he do, anyway, Bud?" Parker asked.

"That's why we're here, Bill. To 'check things out'."

For the first time in hours, Parker felt like smiling.

51

They kept inside the cover of the trees as they cautiously moved toward the buildings. There was an edge of the water of Ferdinand Bog that was near the compound. That was shown in one of Hammond's pictures, Parker remembered. When they approached that small amount of water they found that it was closer to the compound than Parker had realized.

They stopped and waited, lying down, for any motion that would show that somebody was there. Maybe a watchman, or perhaps guests, in attendance for something going on at this wilderness retreat. Nothing moved. The birds continued to talk to them and to each other. A family of raccoons moved out of their cover and approached the center building of the three. To Parker, these were signs that they were alone in this remote silence of the Northeast Kingdom. Everything normal.

They stayed flat on the ground in the brush. Bud whispered in Parker's ear. "We've got to stay where we are for a half hour, or so," he rasped. "This isn't easy, but we must have absolute silence and a minimum of motion, and that motion, if required, must be slowly made – no quick movements. I think that Birdsall must have come in here walking along on the old road, never dreaming that someone was here who wouldn't hesitate to kill him. Could be wrong, of course," he mused quietly, "but Birdsall was a very naive sort of person, according to my information about him. If true, it's interesting. I thought these guys who kept watch on government doings turned out to be very cynical."

Parker just nodded his head slowly and settled down to wait and watch.

Time marched. Then suddenly, Small was on his feet. "I think the way is clear. Let's get going, find out what this place is all about, and disappear. My feeling is that we don't have much time left and we have a lot to do."

They trotted through the woods and came out behind one of the end buildings. They stopped again. They waited – and watched. Nothing moved. No unexpected sound was heard. Small got to his feet and moved quickly to the back of the cabin.

The three cabins were of log construction. Each was about 60 feet long and 25 feet wide. They all seemed to have basements. Parker thought that that was strange. Depending on the use for which the buildings were constructed, a basement seemed to Parker to be an unnecessary amount of time and work. He doubted that he would have dug the holes for them but accepted the idea of basements without question as a quirk of the builder/owner.

Each building had only six windows – two in each long wall and one cut into each end. There was one door in each long wall. There was a metal chimney coming out of one end. House Beautiful Magazine had not supplied plans for these rustic-to-rough buildings. The best that could be said for them was that they were utilitarian, and only just.

The two large outhouses, set downwind, one would hope, and back in the woods, looked more fashionable to Parker than the main buildings. There's a message there, thought Parker, that I'm sure comes to us from millions of years ago, and it has to do with the survival of the first human beings and what was important to that ongoing process.

They were single story buildings with steeply pitched roofs, probably providing what appeared to be a good sized attic along with the additional benefit of keeping the snow load on the roofs down to a manageable level. All the logs were hand-hewn and that meant that people worked very hard to build these dwellings. Log buildings with no power available meant that all the sawing and drilling had to be done by hand. Unless somebody was very, very good with a chain saw.

Parker had visited a store up toward Killington, on the famous Route 100, where there were guys who created bears, moose, and deer out of stumps and large logs, using nothing but a chain saw. People from all over New England bought them and probably wowed their neighbors when these folks woke up on a Monday morning and saw a rough looking grizzly staring at them from next door.

"I've brought along the proper instruments to open up that back door," said Small, in his normal voice. It startled Parker because they had been speaking in muted tones for about two hours. "Do you care that evidence of our invasion be seen?"

“As long as nobody knows who did the entering,” answered Parker. “If you can hide it, I’d feel better, but do the best you can but don’t waste time.”

Small turned to the door with what looked like a tire iron. “Nothing fancy is needed, Bill.” He slipped the knife end into the edge of the door, right at the lock set, and pushed. The door creaked and then suddenly Parker heard a sharp “crack”. Small grabbed the door edge and forced it back and open. “Here’s where we begin to see what we shall see,” he said.

There was plenty of light, even though the number of windows was limited. “Let’s move, Bud,” said Parker. “You know what to look for.”

The room was a barracks, divided into two halves, with a passage door between. It stood open. There were wooden double bunks along each long wall, and at the end of each stood two foot lockers. There was a series of wash basins and hanging mirrors down the middle of the room. Beside each basin was a bucket, presumably to haul water for the morning cold water wake up call.

At the end of the room was a kerosene stove and tables and chairs for eating. That appeared to be it. Other than these few essentials, the room looked bare. The only item that gave them a message was a box of candles. If they had a generator for power they wouldn’t need these so prominently displayed. Especially when Small opened the box and found half of the candles were used to varying degrees. So – no generator or wires. Just kerosene heaters, lamps, and candles.

“We give it a quick, but thorough, look-see, Bud, and then we move on. I figure we have about five hours before we have to get out of here. I want to use up as little of it as possible in this place.”

Small nodded. “I’ll check out the basement, first thing.”

Nothing was found in the building that interested Parker or Small. Parker was discouraged.

“Other than about 100 gallon cans of kerosene in the basement, Bill, there’s nothing down there. Can you smell the kerosene? There have been some leakers down there at some time in the near past. By the way, there is a whole set of wood-working tools down there, along with some big two-man saws. I’m not surprised to see tools like those in this part of the world.”

A thought hit Parker, and not a pleasant one. “Show me those tools, Bud,” he asked quietly.

They descended the stairs and Bud pointed out the tools, dumped carelessly on the dirt floor of the basement. They were covered by a piece of dark-colored canvas which had been pulled back by Small. There were many tools that Parker remembered his father having: adzes, all kinds of augers, chisels, hammers, bucksaws, long planes, draw knives, hatchets of all sizes, and even an old broadaxe. These were the tools of the people who built these buildings, Parker knew.

As he shined his light on them he caught sight of four large wooden toolboxes in the back side of the pile of tools. These transportable toolboxes, if that was what they were, were the type that a rugged man was required to carry when they were packed with tools. There were some tools left in them, but all four were on their sides, unceremoniously dropped on the floor. All four boxes were marked with a name: Armand LaPierre and Sons, Drummondville, Quebec, Canada. Parker's look became grim.

They moved into the center building in the same manner as before. This was apparently the administration building for the activities, which were still a mystery. This one had a number of office cubicles, including filing cabinets, desks, and shelves.

"I'll head for the basement now, Bill," said Small. "I'll be right back up here to help you finish."

Parker gestured that he understood. He went into the first cubicle and checked out the filing cabinet. It looked as if it was locked, based on the position of the lock button next to the top drawer. He tried to open it anyway. Surprisingly, the drawer opened. In the drawer were a series of expandable folders, each carrying a label of an individual state. There were about twenty folders in each of the file drawers. All the files were empty. As Parker was about to close the cabinet, he noticed a small piece of paper taped to the side of the drawer, facing the desk. He opened the drawer to its fullest extent and sat down at the desk chair to see it.

It was a "key" of some sort, he thought. I haven't seen anything. . . . . . and he stopped. Yes, I think I have seen this before. Parker reached into the inner pocket of his jacket and removed the copies of the papers that Birdsall had received from his formerly friendly sister-in-law. He looked at the randomly selected group of numbers and letters. Let's just see if this key translates this string of letters and numbers.

Parker jotted down the number on a blank side of paper. '349WQ4D10Sa'. He then turned to the "key".

"#1," he read. "Operative's numbers (no fewer than two, no more than three)". Parker wondered if there was a list of operatives' names to go along with the numbers somewhere. Also, operatives for what purpose, he asked himself.

Next was the "W". Stands for west. "West what?", asked Parker, of no one in particular.

After that was a "Q". This was for "quadrant – national", according to the key.

Then a "4". The key tells me that this means the 4th quadrant, he thought.

The "D" stands for the month. December, in this case, he guessed.

And the "10" means the 10th of the month. It was becoming more clear to Parker now.

The "S" is for successful. Parker looked for an entry that had another letter in place of the S. He found one almost immediately. An "F". For Failed, perhaps?

The last figure in the line was a small "a", which would tell the "method".

What method, thought Parker? What am I being told by this key? God, I wish I wasn't so dense.

He tore open the other two drawers of the file cabinet. Just empty files, or nothing at all.

Parker went through the other cubicles quickly. He even looked at the blotting paper that was on two of the desks. It's not that blotting paper was needed with today's pens, but it made an excellent surface on which to write. He found nothing on the surface of the blotting paper except smudges that were not from ink. He even removed the blotting paper from its frame, which held the paper securely and flat while in use on the desk. Nothing.

As a last resort, he returned to the first cubicle he'd checked, the one that gave up the "key". He had not checked the blotting paper in its frame.

He hit the jackpot. Three pieces of paper slid out from under the blotting paper and onto the floor. He picked them up, glanced at them, and knew immediately that they were what he hoped to find. He could feel an excitement building.

What Parker read told him the following details about how to read the key. The first piece of paper was a list of people, men and women, who had spent time here during a period of time that included last deer season. They were from half the states in the union and about a dozen foreign countries. Each name had a number assigned to it. Forty-two people were here for some reason, Parker read. Good Lord, he thought, there are even two members of the Vermont Legislature on this list.

It also told him that the "mission" was in the West, and in the 4th quadrant, and it happened in December of last year, on the 10th, and it was successful. What was successful, Parker again asked himself?

He found out when he looked at the last sheet of paper. The small "a" stood for "fire", the "b" stood for "explosives", the "c" was "permanent", the "d" was for "violent protest", and the "e" stood for "other (give details, please)".

The last brief paragraph told the real story. Parker read the following:

"No person, group, or government will prevent the undersigned from achieving its goal of the minimizing of all countries that use the natural earth and water in any way that runs counter to our aims. It is without shame or guilt that we save the natural wonders of our planet by neutralizing or eliminating, by whatever means available to us, those who would compromise our beliefs and goals.

Sponsors:

1. Continuing Tradition Trust for the Victims of Capitalism
2. New Relativism Council Against Uncontrolled Commerce
3. Tranquility and Equal Treatment Center of Vermont
4. People's Revolution Against Profits, Production, and Private Property
5. The Trust of the Progressive Naturalist"

Parker sat back in his chair, knowing the outline of what this compound represented. It was a school. Or a training camp, designed to train people who would then be selected to destroy economic improvements somewhere in the world – but certainly in America first. These people hid behind whatever cause was handy and sure to illicit sympathy for them and their cause. Popular subjects for these leftists were children, the spotted owl, the snail darter, and two dozen others. And they didn't give a damn about any of them – he was now certain that they just wanted to shut down America. Who would believe this, he wondered? Who could I tell about this find?

He felt an anxiety that prompted him to his feet, anxious to finish their investigation and to be on the way out of this danger zone. He called down to Small. “Bud, how are you doing down there?”

A muffled reply came back from the basement. “Bill, I think you should come down here. I have found things that are unexpected.”

“On my way, Bud,” Parker called out, and he swung out of his chair and descended into the basement.

The smell of kerosene was as strong as in the first building. “Can’t this place blow up or burn if you light a match?” he asked.

“Well, it’s not safe, any way you look at it,” answered Small. “I can’t imagine the owners allowing kerosene leaks to continue. It makes me think that this place hasn’t been used for a while. The only thing that’s probably saved these buildings from going up in flames is the fact that kerosene doesn’t ignite very easily.”

He pointed to another part of the basement with his flashlight. There were bags and boxes, and other containers of some kind of chemicals. Also they found what were called “fire sticks” at one time, Parker remembered. Just light the fuse and you have a few seconds to toss it where it will do damage. It provided an instantaneous, and white-hot, fire that would burn or distort any material it touches. It lasts for some minutes and is a favorite weapon of people who are into mayhem. In another part of the cellar hole were some steel containers packed with a dark gray material that had just been pushed into the container and then packed solidly. A kind of putty. Is this that stuff they call *plastique*, he wondered? Real explosives? Small looked it over. He shrugged. “I don’t know what it is, Bill.”

Then Small remarked, “I’ve had some training in this sort of stuff, Bill, but I don’t know anywhere near enough for this.” He gestured toward the gray putty. “But I know a little about these chemicals we’re looking at. By themselves, they aren’t noteworthy, but together they pack a wallop.”

He looked at the pile of materials, and then moved around the edge of the pile. He spent some time taking the covers off some unlabeled barrels, dropping them on the floor, and then looking intently at the material inside. He turned back to Parker.

“Bill, what have we gotten into?” he asked worriedly. “What kind of people are these?”

“We’ll talk about it when we leave, Bud,” Parker said. “In the meantime, I’m going to take some labels from all these containers. We’ll have an expert look at them.” Parker noticed

Small lean down and pull at something. Whatever it was came loose suddenly, and Small shined his light on it.

"What in the world is this?" he murmured. He walked over to Parker with an object that was stuffed behind the pile of chemicals. "Take a look at this, Bill. Probably not earth-shaking, but I didn't expect to see this intentionally hidden behind all this junk."

As Parker reached out for the object, he asked, "How do you know it was intentionally hidden, Bud?"

"The imprint of the box on the dirt floor was under this thing, Bill. Therefore, it was shoved under the box to hide it. It looks like a woman's handbag, but a big one, bigger than I've seen in a while."

"Let's see it, Bud," said Parker. As soon as he had pointed his light at the object, Parker was gripped with an awful premonition. This was Jan Evlin's bag. No doubt about it. Parker had seen it just three weeks ago. The imprinted rose on its side was the final proof.

Parker looked inside. It was completely empty. "We're taking this with us, Bud," Parker choked out. "I've got my labels. Let's go."

Upstairs, Parker dumped all the papers he had collected into Jan's purse.

The third building was apparently a lecture hall. Parker found one odd item. It was a log, about six feet long and about thirty inches across. It was standing on its end in front of the classroom chairs. It had numerous steel spikes driven into it, and sunk below the surface. A box of these steel nails was on a table nearby. The directions for use announced that these nails would retain their physical properties when driven into concrete, which was their intended purpose for the construction industry. What in hell was this all about?

Small, again, went into the basement, leaving the upstairs to Parker. He came up quite soon, hauling after him a large flip chart. "More chemicals down there, Bill, and lots of kerosene. But I found this lecture aid leaning against the wall. This is the biggest mistake these people have made so far, Bill. This is the basic outline of the introduction speech that the new people receive."

"Bud," murmured Parker, "this is too much for me to think about right now. Later, after we've headed back, I'll look at all these papers and we'll talk."

"Bill," Small said, "let's face it. I think this is a camp for the training of international eco-terrorists. It can't be anything else. When you see these flip charts, you'll know that the recruits came through NPF I, and then were assigned here for final training."

This is incredible, thought Parker. I started out to just look into Jan Evlin's perceived ideas of a threat. Now I've stumbled into a real threat. Not to just Jan, he thought. Against all of us.

"We have to leave now, Bud. We have too much information. We must get it back to people who can act on it." Parker was busily engaged in stuffing the outline into Jan's purse, when Small's cell phone announced itself.

"Peter?" Small asked. "What's up? Yes, we're moving out now." Small listened for a moment, checked his watch, and breathed, "Damn, damn, damn. Okay, Peter, we're on our way. Thanks."

Small disconnected. "We've got to move now, Bill," as he headed for the door. "Peter just told me that a helicopter with three men in it left NPF 1, heading about northeast – our direction. Our problem is that Peter doesn't know exactly what time it left. At least an hour ago, maybe more. His amateur watcher at the farm let him down."

At that very moment they both could hear the whop, whop, whop of a helicopter.

Small exploded into activity. "Move it, Bill. Get out of here and wait for me in the woods by the old road. I've got something to do here." Parker started to speak and Small said, firmly, "Get going, Bill. Right now."

Parker jumped out the back door and ran, dragging his loot, into the woods, and then started to circle around toward the bog. He kept moving until he found the spot where he and Small had lain down and looked things over before feeling comfortable enough to finish the hike into the compound. He dropped down into this crease in the land and watched for Bud to appear. What in hell did he have to do that was so important? Parker muttered.

A half hour went by. No Small. What the hell is he doing in there? Where was the helicopter crew?

And then he saw them, moving slowly and cautiously from the east. They all held rifles and were looking about the area.

Well, Parker mused, Hal Birdsall's secretary was certainly listened to by Mr. Big, wasn't she? The timing of the arrival of the three shooters up here in the Kingdom and their mode of transportation certainly shows me that she was an agent for somebody. We'll find out. Hurry up, Bud, these guys mean business, thought Parker.

Suddenly, all three men hit the prone position. One of them fired a shot, and then another. Then Parker could see Bud Small running in and out of the trees, following the same track as had Parker. Then the rifles began to crack more frequently as the shooters could see Small more clearly.

Small had reached the side of the road and was headed straight for Parker. And then a shot and Small was down, bouncing loosely off the old road and into the edge of the bog. He was motionless.

Parker reached into the small of his back and pulled out the revolver. He wasn't even thinking how unfamiliar it felt in his hand. He was thinking that he'd drag Small all the way to the car if he had to. But first he'd get to him, regardless of what happened, and cover him. Parker jumped to his feet and started running toward Small.

The shooters now caught a glimpse of Parker, running out of his place of concealment and trying to run in a zigzag fashion. All three began to fire aimed shots at Parker. And then Parker was down. He lay in the road, just behind the crown of the open ground, and his leg was numb.

He moved his hand slowly down to his knee, wondering what he would find. He found blood. He could see blood through many small tears in his pants leg – but not as much as his fears had forced him to believe.

How bad is it, he wondered? He looked down and saw the fresh bullet scar on a rock that was in front of him, embedded in the old road surface. It had probably ricocheted off the stony surface of the old roadway right in front of him and had driven some rock fragments into his leg. It seemed also that the slug creased his leg somewhere, but he couldn't see where.

It could be a lot worse, he thought. The only problem he could see ahead was really a question: could he move? He tried to flex his knee and his ankle. They worked as nature had intended. The back of his calf seemed to be bleeding more than anywhere else, but not to the extent of rendering him helpless.

Parker knew then that he could function, and if he moved now, not waiting for the leg to scream at him that it was hurt, he would be better off. The one thing that was definite was that he could still shoot.

He had gotten away with one, he realized. Even with a small bullet hole in my leg, I'll be able to move. Don't stick your head out again, you damn fool. The next thing he thought of was, inexplicably, how angry Addie would be with him about all this.

Parker rolled back as quickly as his tired old body could manage it. He was fairly certain that he couldn't be seen by the three shooters because of the rise of land right in front of him.

For some reason it became critically important to him to give the shooters the impression that they had wounded him badly. He knew he stood no chance of hitting them at that distance with his little popgun, so he replaced the revolver in its holster at his back and crawled as fast as he could to the edge of the road. If these three killers had no knowledge of functioning in the woods, they might be hesitant and uncomfortable, especially right after shooting at people running through the trees.

Maybe they would even delay long enough for Parker and Small to get out of range and heading for their car. If, however, the three were flat-out professionals, then he and Bud wouldn't have a chance anyway.

Parker dropped off the edge of the road and slid down beside Small. He was afraid of what he'd find, but he knew he'd have to deal with it, whatever it was. What he didn't expect was that Small would be moving around and swearing as he did so.

"Bud," gasped Parker, "where did you get it?"

Small didn't answer him directly. He only asked, in a tight voice, "Check my back, will you? Tell me what you see."

Parker pulled the large pack off Small's back, and lifted his shirt. Small grimaced as he moved his shoulder to aid Parker to get to the area where he had been shot.

"Bud, I don't see anything at all except a big black-and-blue mark, but spreading as I look at it."

"You must be able to see something more than that. Look again," he growled. "The son-of-a-bitch got me right under the shoulder blade."

"Well, there's nothing here. Just the black-and-blue. That's all."

And then Parker noticed something else. There was a bullet hole in Small's pack, right over where Small thought he'd been hit. Parker reached into the pack and pulled out two steel fry pans one inside the other. Both were distorted by the lead bullet, now a shapeless lump, which ended up against a towel under the fry pans, and next to Small's back. The towel was placed in that position so the metal pans wouldn't be uncomfortable while hiking. He explained this to Small, who smiled and let out a sigh of relief.

"I'll never be able to explain this to my wife," Small wheezed. Parker didn't mention that he had already had the same kind of thought.

"So both of us went down as though shot," Small mused. "That might be of help to us, if they react the way they should."

Parker was glad that Small had had the same idea that he did. He didn't feel quite as dumb as he had just three minutes ago. "Now, let's get going, Bud. Do you think you can move well enough to make it back to the car?"

"Yes, I can, Bill. But I want to stay here for a few more minutes." He gritted his teeth as he moved his position in order to see the compound from another position. "Where are those bozos right now?"

"They've stopped coming for us, Bud. They seem to have slowed down. They won't wait much longer, though. They're going to want to get back while the light is good enough for flying. Somehow I don't think that helicopter is new enough to have the latest electronics stuff on it. That means that they have to make certain that we are very dead, and very soon, the way I see it, before they can go anywhere. So we have to get going."

"Just wait for a little bit more, Bill. It's important." Small was in pain, Parker could see, but he could still move.

As they watched their assailants, they could detect an urgency in their movements. Suddenly, with one of them staying behind to cover them, two of them jumped up and ran up to the buildings, and then disappeared around to the back. After a brief delay, during which time the silence of the woods was deafening, the third shooter got up from his firing position and dashed for the buildings, too. It seemed to Parker that two of them entered the administrative building while the remaining one went into the lecture building.

"I just thought of something, Bill," Small wheezed. "Your fake message said you'd be up here on Wednesday. Today is Monday and as soon as they got the message from Birdsall's secretary, these three show up. The reason? I'm sure it's to get rid of something they didn't want found. I'll bet that those three birds that are going into the administration building were told to check it out by somebody – buildings that are important to them, probably."

Parker could see that Small was hurting with every movement and every word. "The other bad guy went into the lecture building where we found other goodies. Just where we found something having to do with the use of the buildings. The explosives' components are a good bet, I'd say. We hit the jackpot in there, Bill, although we didn't know it at the time."

Parker whispered, "We've got to think about leaving, Bud. You may not be nervous - because I understand that professionals aren't nervous under these conditions. But I'm a nervous as a cat in a room full of rocking chairs."

"If you were really told that, Bill," Small grunted, "then you were lied to. Cops are trained, that's true, in the hope that the training works while we're nervous. That's the only difference between you and me, my friend."

Small moved his body so he could peer at the compound from under the log. "You know, Bill, I think we may have been right. They really believe that they have already killed us – or at least wounded us badly enough to put us out of action. They'll think they can finish us at their leisure."

Small seemed surprised at his realization. "That's why those three decided that we're out of the game and they didn't need to watch us. They all saw both of us shot. Now I think that they really believe we are no longer any threat to them. That's why they are in the buildings now. What do you think?"

"You might be right, Bud. Let's hope. If that's true, then that will definitely give us an edge, I think. But, make no mistake. They will be here very soon to make certain of us and then hide the results." Small made no reply which, in his case, meant that he agreed. "All I ask is that we get out of here."

Small looked at his watch. "Any minute now," he murmured.

Suddenly Parker could see smoke from the Administration building. What the hell is going on, Parker wondered? And unexpectedly, a roaring flame shot through the roof. Then the bunkhouse went up in a large thump of an explosion, followed closely by the lecture hall. The flames were so pervasive that all three buildings were going up together and very quickly, too. The bunkhouse was completely enveloped in flames. There was no sign of any of the three riflemen.

"Did you see any of those three killers?" asked Small.

"Not a sign, Bud," said Parker. "Those buildings went up so fast that probably nobody could have gotten out. The explosions must have taken care of them – if any of them were alive at that point. They're definitely all done if they were in the basements of those buildings."

"Call Morgan," urged Parker. "Tell him all that's happened and don't take long doing it. He'll tell us what we should do. Also, ask about Jan Evlin. Has anyone seen her around NPF I? And get directions to NPF I. We'll need them. And then we're out of here."

Small gazed at Parker when he asked for the map to NPF I. Then he gave a tight grin through the pain and a grimace at the same time.

While Small was connecting with Morgan, Parker had gotten to his feet. He swayed with fatigue. After a few tentative steps, Parker walked up to the burning carcasses of the terrorists' training camp. His bleeding seemed to have stopped, but his foot felt squishy inside his boot as he put his weight on it. Not good, he thought.

Parker stood in front of the three burning buildings and watched them fall in on themselves. He looked around, wondering if the fire had spread anywhere else, but enough rain had fallen in the past week to make that possibility seem remote. So he pushed off for the clearing to the east. He hadn't known that there was a clearing until the helicopter arrived on the scene.

It wasn't more than three minutes of his limping walk when he could see the machine through the thinning trees. It was a large machine. It looked as if it was an ex-military copter. It still had the camouflage colors on it which, based on what Parker now knew about this operation, were appropriate.

He moved around to the pilot's door, opened it, and painfully swung up into the seat.

The layout was the military design, but there were many empty cutouts in the instrument panel. Before the military sold this one, they had cleaned anything out of it that was current technology. It had not been replaced.

Inside the copter it was messy and disorganized. Papers were scattered on the co-pilot's seat, and on the floor behind the pilot and co-pilot were thick packages of documents inside thin folders, and two slim briefcases that looked interesting, so Parker threw them out on the ground. The last items taken by Parker were found clipped to the instrument panel by strong, magnetic-based, spring-loaded clips. This constituted the copter's bits of flight information that would be used to construct its flight log for at least the last two months, based on Parker's quick perusal. Knowing where the copter had been would be interesting, thought Parker, and possibly revealing.

When he thought of that, he checked the last note of flight time. It read, "Woman taken south in a hurry. Very early. RT." It carried today's date. Today's date, thought Parker? That means that the copter must have been here at least two hours ahead of us. We would have heard it after that.

Birdsall's fake message sure started the jungle drums pounding, Parker thought. The "boss man" was no fool. He didn't believe Parker's message. He sent his boys up early in the morning to have Jan brought down to NPF I. Then he sent them back up to intercept us, kill us, get rid of the bodies, and return home. Very neat. I wonder how many bodies are buried up here, Parker silently mused. Not healthy to think about that sort of thing.

He lowered himself to the ground, and it was not a pleasant experience. His leg had stiffened with inactivity. He gave the helicopter's interior another quick look, this time at near eye level, and saw what looked like a silver dollar under the co-pilot's seat across the cabin. He scuttled under the fuselage and walked to the opposite side of the copter and opened the door. He reached under the seat and withdrew the "silver dollar". It wasn't a silver dollar. It was a display pin and on it was inscribed 'Syria, Go Home'. Parker didn't know if he should feel happy or sad. The pointed wire that allowed the pin to be attached to something was missing.

When he found a way to carry all this material, Parker hiked back to Small, who had finished talking with Morgan.

He checked Jan's handbag and pulled the strap out of the interior – and there it was. The wire from the 'Syria, Go Home' pin. Jan was in trouble, Parker thought, but she was bravely sending messages whenever she could, hoping that someone would find them and help her.

The sun was getting low when they set off in their quest to escape from this very bad day. As they limped along, Small told Parker about his conversation with Morgan. Small said he had convinced Morgan that they hadn't been seen at any point in the day. Of course, said Small, he couldn't guarantee that no one saw them but if nobody showed up during the fires and explosions, that was a pretty good indication of that.

Morgan was especially concerned about the apparent deaths of the three riflemen, Small told Parker. Morgan had asked how he could be sure that they died in the fires. Small had said they couldn't, but the three of them didn't make a showing after the fires started. Any idea what happened, Morgan had asked? Small only said that when he was in the buildings, there was a lot of kerosene leaking in the basements of the buildings. Also, containers of what looked like explosives. Maybe the three shooters did something stupid, he offered to Morgan. Lit a cigarette, or something dumb like that. Ask Parker about that, he had said.

Finally, Small had told Morgan that they both were in rough shape and really ought to find a doctor they could trust while they were on their way home. We wouldn't want to be stopped by Vermont troopers, he had said. Hard to explain to them why we looked so beat up. Morgan had said he'd call them while they were on their way to St. Johnsbury.

It took two hours of pain-filled steps to get to the Paul Stream road. It had been a very long day, and it was beginning to get dark. They saw no one while on their trek. The smoke they left behind was dissipated by the strong west-to-east breeze that prevailed that day. That was the real definition of luck, to Parker's way of thinking.

Parker's leg was still bleeding slightly, but not alarmingly. Small was in real pain, though, and Parker guessed that he had a broken rib or two, but he wasn't coughing up any blood, so that was a good sign.

They stayed in the trees as they struggled south to the car. Both of them were silent for most of the hike.

But they were alive, thought Parker, and even if it was only by blind luck that they were, it didn't make them feel any less grateful for being able to hear and appreciate the sounds of the nocturnal birds and animals.

As Parker and Small moved along, these forest inhabitants went about their usual business as if nothing that day had been remarkable. Those sounds were saying to Parker and Small "nothing has changed in two million years around here. And nothing you went through and nothing you did this day will change that order of things. Deal with it, and get out of our way".

And that's just what they were doing.

52

Small was driving the SUV as they headed south from the compound. They were back on Route 114 and heading for Lyndonville, where they would pick up Interstate 91. Then, continue south to St. Johnsbury and the doctor they needed. As Parker began to worry about where the doctor was, Small's cell phone made a funny noise and Small grunted, "Flip it open. You'll be connected with whoever the hell is trying to find us."

"What if it's somebody we don't want to talk to?" Parker asked.

"Bill, who knows my cell phone number that we don't want to talk to?"

His tone was one of exasperation with somebody who wasn't up with today's technical progress. Parker thought he'd better get with it in the very near future. The younger generation wouldn't want to buy insurance from him if they thought that the only way they could get in touch with their insurance representative was with two tin cans and a stretched string.

It was Morgan. He gave the address of a doctor for them to see when they reached St. Johnsbury. "He's a good man, Bill," he said. "He won't run his mouth like some others would."

"Peter, what's been going on at NPF 1 in the last six or eight hours? Anything at all?" asked Parker.

"Oh, that's been a busy place. Started about 9:00 this morning. Mr. Big must have been contacted by the agent/ secretary, and that caused him to call out the troops. You guys assured me that nobody saw you, or if they did, they aren't in a position to identify you anymore. Are you two still sticking with that story?"

"Yep," said Parker.

"Okay, but remember this: he knows who you are, Bill. You can be sure of that."

"Nobody saw us, Dick Tracy," Parker snapped back.

"Okay, okay, Bill," Morgan said. "I just had to bring it up. It's very important that nobody can talk about your little visit up there. Ever."

"Understood, Peter. Sorry for my lack of manners. You didn't deserve that. One more thing, Peter. I think that Jan Evlin is still alive and has been flown back yesterday to what was called by these clowns as 'south'. Any activity there that would include a passenger on the helicopter yesterday?"

"I know that the copter was traveling around yesterday, but no detail suggesting passengers in it. I'll check on it, though. Can't guarantee anything, though. I'll let you know as soon as I can."

"One last thing, Peter? Call Addie and let her know that I'll be home day after tomorrow? I'd appreciate it very much."

"Fine, I will, Bill. But why the delay in your arrival home? You'll be back in Burlington tonight. You could be home tomorrow."

"I want to make sure that there isn't anything else that I have to do, Peter. Then I can go home knowing I've done all I needed to."

"It's Jan Evlin, isn't it, Bill? You think she's around here somewhere, don't you?"

"Maybe," said Parker, in a tone that told Morgan not to question him further.

"One last thing, Peter. Call Hugo Barkley, would you? I'd like to stay there tonight, if it's not too much trouble for them. I'll plan on it unless I hear from you. Why? It's out of the way." They disconnected.

Parker turned toward Small. He looked drawn and he had to sit in an awkward position in order to drive. Parker could see that he was in pain. "Pull off up there, Bud," Parker said. "I'll drive."

Without a word of protest, Small cranked the wheel and soon the exchange of drivers was made. They hadn't been on the road longer than five minutes when Parker could hear gentle snoring from the passenger side of the vehicle.

The doctor was waiting for them as they pulled into the parking lot of his clinic. He gestured to Parker to pull the vehicle around to the back door. Parker did so and doused the headlights as soon as he stopped moving.

He had gotten the doctor's message that he didn't want anybody to see this emergency pit stop for running repairs. He must have done this sort of thing before, thought Parker, as they were assisting Small out of the front seat. Together they moved him inside and into a small examining room.

The doctor was a young guy, and probably this was his first real job in his profession, Parker guessed. Parker was very good at reading this sort of thing. His business required that good guessing be as important as his state insurance license.

Small looked terrible. He was pale and sweating. When they moved him at all he gritted his teeth. It looked to Parker as though something was badly wrong inside.

The doctor didn't try to lay Small down. After stripping Small's shirt and jacket off he began a minute inspection of his back. Parker expected that instant surgery would be required and then the cat would be out of the bag for both of them. "What am I looking at here? I mean what happened to cause this?"

"A rifle bullet hit him in the back. Fortunately, it hit two fry pans first and stopped right there, as far as I could see."

The doc prodded and pinched in and all around the discolored area where the bullet had made such an impact. Small groaned as the busy hands performed their investigation.

While he was performing this inspection with his hands and fingers, he looked at Parker. "And how are you?" he asked.

Parker had forgotten all about the damage to his leg. He didn't even recognize that it was bothering him.

"I'm okay, Doc," he answered. "I got some rock fragments in my lower leg. And maybe a graze from a rifle bullet, too. I haven't thought to look. I can walk, and I think the bleeding has stopped. I'd appreciate it if you could clean out the scrapes and bruises, and then we'll be on our way. By the way, my name is. . . . ." He never got any further.

"No names, please," said the doctor. "I don't want to know anything more about you. No records will be kept. I insist that you not mention my name or that you stopped here for treatment for some mysterious wounds, which I don't know about, either. Clear? My contact told me that you could be trusted. Is that true?"

"Yes, it's true. I certainly understand, Doc," said Parker. "How's he?" pointing at Small.

"He has a massive contusion and I'm surprised that he didn't have something broken or sheared off. He's a big, strong, young man, and in good shape. But without those two fry pans it would be a much different story. He looks like a cop, but I don't know. His physical condition is all that saved him from really serious harm, even *with* the fry pans. I'll give him something for the pain right now, and we'll wait a few minutes to see if it helps. If it does, and it should, then you two can get under way."

He walked over to a wall cupboard and removed a syringe and a small bottle of a liquid. He filled the syringe and walked over to Small. "This won't hurt," he said to Small, "but if it does, it will be worth it." He put an exclamation mark on the subject by jabbing the needle home in Small's upper shoulder. Small didn't react.

Looking at Parker, he said, "Here, give him these tablets. If he starts to feel pain, give him a couple. At a maximum, two every two hours. Got that?" Parker said he got it.

"Now, how about you, sir? Lets see that leg. Anything above the knee? No? Good," he said with satisfaction.

The doc took a knife and slit the pant leg up above Parker's knee, squeezed, prodded, and pinched, while murmuring, whistling, and uttering a few "umm"s, "mmmm"s, and "yes, sir"s.

"Off with your boot, please." Parker did as he was told. The "mmm"s and "ummm"s started again. Then Parker could feel the coldness of the cleaning solution being applied in large quantities, accompanied with gentle cleansing pressure. More "mmm"s and "ummmm"s and now some picking around with some tweezers. Then wrapping bandages of some kind around his leg.

"That should do it, sir," the Doc said. "How does the area feel?"

"Much better, Doc. Thanks very much. And don't worry about us saying anything. We won't."

The doctor nodded. "I know you won't, Mr. Parker. I know about you and I recognize you. I won't say anything either." He grinned slightly. "By the way, you might be interested to know that, along with rock fragments in your leg, the bullet hit you, too – a deep graze, but very close. You'll feel it in the morning."

Parker was surprised. "How do you know me, Doc?" he asked.

"I was here in Vermont, just starting up my practice, when you were on the House floor at the OK Corral in Montpelier. I wish you were still there. You made sense occasionally."

"Thanks, Doc, that's nice to hear. But I retired because my idea of sense had no effect on any legislation. Three quarters of the General Assembly is made up of people who are from someplace else, and most of them don't like Vermont, and many of those don't like America, either, very much, I'm afraid."

Parker watched the Doc closely. May as well find out if this guy is like so many medical people infesting the state. Many of them, and almost all of the new ones, are great at advocating socialized medicine and not so good at the doctoring part.

This doctor was sharp. He was watching Parker watch him. Then they smiled at each other. "Don't worry, Mr. Parker. The thought police from Montpelier haven't got to me yet. And they never will. I've got this practice up for sale. When some idiot buys it, I'm gone. And you know why?"

"I might have an idea, Doc," he answered.

"I'll bet you do, Mr. Parker," he said, with a knowing smile. "This state is going to have a takeover of all medical care in the near future. When that happens, the reimbursements for everybody in the health care field will go from not high enough now to steady decline. When providers drop out and work for cash only, the state will tell us that we aren't 'caring' enough and revoke our licenses to practice unless we agree to work for the state at their rates. None of this is complicated, Mr. Parker. Anybody who is licensed by the state to work in their trade in Vermont will be fair game. It just depends on the 'hot' topic for a new Legislature. That's the way these folks are in Montpelier."

"Doctor, you can't be serious. The state wouldn't dare to go that far. That's like a protection racket," Parker protested.

"Do you know anything about the health care industry, as controlled by the state, in Vermont, Mr. Parker?" he asked bitingly.

Without waiting for an answer, he bolted into his subject. "The providers can't get reimbursed for their true costs from the state, so they take the state amount and then go after the difference from the cash-paying patients they have. That's called the 'cost shift', Mr. Parker. Ever heard of it?" Parker certainly had. His business was insurance. And much of today's insurance was affected by the "cost shift".

"It's the same for our hospitals, our dentists, all of us. I can make my loan payments for my education debts now. When the state gets into it, the marginal doctors will stay and be happy. They aren't very aggressive doctors anyway but can make a reasonable living here without a hassle. However, Vermont will lose the innovative and forward-thinking medical providers. Those doctors will leave. Whether anybody except me thinks so, I'm one of them. And when that situation occurs, you will have Canada South, right in the good old US of A. Have fun," he said cynically.

"Do you think that socialized medicine will be coming, Doc?" Parker asked.

"You bet. It's on the way. Vermont is a socialist state, Mr. Parker. These people want all the money. Then they can distribute it to their friends, most of whom cannot exist in a competitive medical services market anyway. And do you know who pays for this debacle? Our senior citizens, who are the victims of rationing of medical services. They use the expensive services, Mr. Parker. They are older. They can't help it. We'll all be in their place when our turn comes. But these are the services that get cut because they are the most expensive. You only have to look at Canada."

"You know, Doc, I agree with you – and there's no stopping them now. It's the 'Robin Hood' approach to health care, isn't it? Right on the heels of the 'Robin Hood' approach to the education of our kids. You know what I mean: strip the rich people or towns of their money, along with their quality services in education or health care, take a large brokerage fee when the money arrives in Montpelier, and give the difference to their friends in education or health care who 'cooperate'."

The doctor looked away. "That's a very good way of putting it, Mr. Parker. You mean the education funding act, of course. I shall remember that."

At that moment, Bud Small stood up, stretched a little, and said, "I'm ready to get moving, Bill, so let's go. And here is the information that Morgan gave me regarding the location of North Point Farm I. I'll forget to give this to you, I'm sure, when we get to my house, and he wanted you to have it." Parker took the piece of notepaper and shoved it into his pocket.

Parker shook the doctor's hand, as did Small, thanked him, and they went out the back door into the blackness. As soon as they were in their vehicle, the lights in the clinic went off.

"He's glad we're leaving, isn't he?" asked Small.

"Wouldn't you be, in his position?" said Parker.

"You bet. Let's roll."

53

Small did all the driving after seeing the doctor in St. Johnsbury. The pain pills worked, and they allowed Small to forget the worst of the pain and still remain alert. They saw very few cars on the trip. This was a rural world at eleven o'clock at night in the Northeast Kingdom. No one followed them.

Parker had slept fitfully for about the two hours of the trip from St. Johnsbury to Small's house in Jericho.

They had talked with Morgan on the way back. He told them that the problem that they all were working on had attracted some interest from people from outside Vermont. He took the chance of setting up a meeting at his house at 9:00 AM the following day. Could they both make it? Parker said he'd be there. Smart said he didn't know, but would try.

"I talked with Addie, Bill," Morgan said. "She wasn't too happy with you – or me, either."

"What did you say to her, Peter? You didn't say that Small and I were a little beaten up, did you?"

There was silence. Then Morgan said, "Not in those words, Bill, but I had to say something. After all, you had asked me to call her for you. She wanted to know why you didn't call her yourself. So I said that you were indisposed. That was the wrong thing to say, I found out."

"What did she say to that, Peter?" Parker asked, dreading to hear the answer.

"She accused you, and then me, of hiding something from her. And then she said that she was coming up here and taking you home. And she used some words that were somewhat unlady-like."

Oh, boy, thought Parker. She must be frothing at the mouth. "When will she be coming up this way to drag me home, Peter?"

Hesitation again. "Well, tomorrow, actually, Bill. She'll be at my house at 9:00 AM."

"Peter, you've set me up to be chewed out in front of people I don't even know. Think of my ego, for goodness sake."

Then he chuckled and said, “Don’t worry, Peter. I’ll be glad to see her, of course. She’ll add something to the meeting, I’m sure. By the way, Peter, I may be a little late for your meeting, but I’ll be there.”

“You’re going to leave me having to fend off your wife again, aren’t you? What did I do to deserve that?”

“I think you’re getting good at it,” answered Parker. “Tell her this, too, Peter, if you can work up enough courage: I’ll be at Hugo’s house early in the morning. I’ll get some sleep and then I’ll be at your house by 9:00 AM, I hope.”

Morgan audibly sighed. “I’ll do it, Bill. I seem to be a receptacle for your commands lately. Take care, old timer.” He hung up with what Parker thought sounded like relief.

At Small’s house Parker helped him out of his SUV. “How’re you doing, partner?” he asked.

“I’m a little rocky, Bill, but two more of these pills, and eight hours of sleep and I’m sure I’ll be okay – on the road back, anyway. Where are you going to stay tonight? You can stay here, you know.”

“Thanks, Bud, but I have a place to stay, and I’m on my way there right now.”

It was only a small fib. Parker had an errand to run first.

54

The only sleep Parker had been able to get was a two hour nap stretched out on the back seat of Small's SUV. He was surprised that he felt as good as he did when he hauled himself up into his truck.

He was happy to be back in the confines of the cab of this good friend. It was a loyal old beast that somehow sensed its keeper's pleasure and was able to return it. His truck would never hear about an SUV that his owner took out on a long-distance date this evening. As he was running these inane thoughts through his head, Parker knew that if anybody could look into his mind right now they would strap him up and put him away in the family's proverbial attic.

Like an old buddy, Parker's truck had served him well, and Parker was going to ask of it another task, possibly the last one, before retirement. And because of that, he would inquire of his old friend, in a most respectful way, if it was willing and able to help out, just once more, his owner and companion.

The instant start of the engine was the signal that said, 'Okay, Parker, old son, I'm in.'

Parker had told no one of what he was going to do tonight. He only knew that it had to get done without any delay.

He was certain that Small had no idea. Parker knew that he would have demanded to go along. And Small was in no shape to help anybody do anything right now. Hell, thought Parker, right this moment I'm in better shape than he is and I'm thirty years older.

NPF I was in East Calais, so the hand drawn map told Parker. It was an old farming community and located east of Montpelier. It was seething with old socialists and old members of college communist clubs, when it was fashionable to call yourself a communist, and members of the left who had an independent income. How nice for them, he thought.

Parker knew some of the normal residents of this lovely part of Vermont and they had decided that none of these odd people had ever recovered from their indoctrination in high school and college. These were the people, Parker thought, who had converted Vermont from a healthy and vigorous state, full of industrious and cranky citizens, to a state that had developed a bad political chest cold.

Then, as these old leftists grew politically stronger, this bad cold had turned into a form of political illness that needed radical surgery. And the only surgeons left in town were the voters, but they were unwilling to wield the scalpel at the polls.

All of this transformation had gone unnoticed by the residents of the town. Initially, the only thing that came to the surface from this heavy chest cold was a lack of attendance by people in their annual Town and School meetings, a difficulty finding candidates to run for local offices, and a falling school population. All of these symptoms suggested that more and more Vermonters were getting out while the getting was good.

Parker supposed that the other problem was that the election process had been corrupted by the Legislature with help from the ProgDems and the Vermont Court system. Registration became easier and easier. Rarely were investigations done by the local communities to update the voting checklist. Students and other transients, because of Legislative fiddling by the ProgDems, were allowed to appear on at least two checklists – the one back home and the one in Vermont – and, it was rumored, another one in another town in Vermont.

When that happened, the candidates from the left got elected, and the students and transients went home, leaving behind Vermonters to pay the higher taxes and try to survive until the Legislature met again - at which time, Vermonters were beginning to learn, the ProgDems could renew their efforts to chip away some more of their independence.

Parker reached East Calais after midnight. He drove along the Old Stage Road, just east of the village, looking for Town Highway #9, a local road. It was probably a gravel thoroughfare, Parker thought, and probably in pretty good shape, if their road foreman was a long-time resident. The old-timers knew how to shape a gravel road.

The village was dark, as it should have been at this hour. Suddenly, just as Parker had left the populated areas of the village, his headlights illuminated a sign indicating “TH 9”, off to the east.

He swung onto this town road. He had gone more than a mile, which had him wondering if the map was wrong. As he negotiated a sweeping turn, his headlights brushed across an old farmhouse crouching back about a quarter of a mile from the road. Behind it was a large barn. That had to be it, he decided. The map had suddenly become his friend. It was right on.

This part of East Calais was really lonely. There was nothing but open lands and some forested patches. No other buildings.

Parker continued to drive by until the farmhouse had passed from view. To Parker, there would be nothing more noticeable than a vehicle that slowed to a stop in this part of the town, and at this hour.

Parker drove along and looked intently for a place where he could hide his truck. It had to be easily reached in case of an emergency and yet not easily seen by the casual observer. This was not accomplished without some earnest appraisal of the landscape. When he found a small and dilapidated shed, half of it fallen in, Parker pulled into the rough driveway, and then around to the rear, hoping this shed could hide his ancient truck. It could, in a cramped space under the remains of a roof and two leaning walls.

Parker felt that he'd done what was possible. He had driven a mile past NPF I and that didn't make him happy, because his leg was bothering him and he didn't look forward to the hike.

As Parker trudged back to the farm, he knew that he didn't have any idea what he'd find. He only knew that it had to be checked out, especially since his search for Jan Evlin had taken on an atmosphere of danger for her, and murder of others.

Is that what the written log notes he had stolen from the helicopter meant? Taken the woman "south"? He had no idea. They could have taken her to Memphis for all he knew. His immediate reaction was, however, that NPF I was the "south" referred to. He also knew that he had to see what was at the "farm" for himself.

There was a porch light showing as Parker reached the end of the driveway up to the house. He stopped and looked around, then limped as quickly and as quietly as he could across the drive, and stood motionless against an old maple tree. He thought he was bleeding again from his leg wound, because he could notice that slight squishiness in his shoe again. But it was sure better than it had been before he saw the doctor in St. Johnsbury.

Everything was silent. And then it wasn't. A scrape sounded from the porch. And then the squeal of a door opening. Parker looked toward the porch and could see a figure standing on the porch, looking around, then retreating into the house. Parker thought that the figure had looked straight at him. Parker froze against the tree. That was probably the old guy, Parker thought. Checking things out, just as he had for 70 years, when he still owned the place. And when he had 50 head of Jerseys in the barn. A man could make a decent living in those days with that number of cows.

Parker waited for five minutes. No sound came from the house. Parker moved out into the gray darkness and headed for the barn.

When he reached it, he moved toward a dim light that showed through the side window. As Parker moved closer for a look into this lighted space, he noticed that the window was equipped with sturdy bars, anchored into a steel frame that was bolted around the window. You might need this husky steel protection if you were raising a full grown grizzly, he thought, but not for any other reason he could think of.

He moved up to the window, keeping to the side, and peered in. He gasped and stepped back from the window. Then he moved back to the window.

Jan Evlin was seated at a small table, her hands clasped together as if praying, and her head bowed down. Her position made Parker think that she had completely given up hope about everything. Parker then saw that her hands were wire-tied at the wrists. Good Lord almighty, he thought, what's going on in this place? He turned away from the window and started to look for a passage door that he could pry open.

He headed for the back of the barn because he saw only large double doors on the short end of the structure, and they were solidly bolted shut. He knew he couldn't waste time trying to open them in the dark. He felt that he had to be cautious but he was frantic to get inside and take Jan away from here. Control your fear, Parker, he said.

On the long wall in the back were two steel doors. He tried the first one he came to and, surprisingly, it opened when he turned the knob and pushed. The ease with which he opened that door made him very wary indeed. He carefully pushed the door wide open. It made not a sound. Parker had never known any door in a barn that opened silently. All the doors he remembered when he was a kid on his family's farm squeaked or rasped. Some were downright screamers. Maybe the owner had a high cost of maintenance, which also covered the task of keeping all hinges oiled. Or maybe the door was left unlocked for a purpose – and Parker was that purpose, with or without noisy hinges.

With the door fully open, Parker just stood there in the doorway, and tried to see in. All detail was lost to the semi-darkness, but he could still see enough to step gingerly over the sill and into the barn.

The only illumination was faint moonlight through the numerous windows cut into the long wall of the structure. If Parker could judge by the two other windows he had checked in that long wall, all the windows were strongly barred.

Parker could smell the familiar odors of farm life. No amount of rebuilding would eliminate it. Especially, as in this case, when much of the wood from the old barn had been reused in the renovation project. Parker loved that smell. It provided a clean, almost uncomplicated, vision of Vermont's past. And people need that past to build the future, he thought.

In addition, now he was certain that the note from "Z" to Jan was written on paper that was kept in a barn – this barn, Parker was convinced, with no proof at all. That deduction was Duane's of long ago, or was it only two and a half weeks ago? Parker was tired to the point where he didn't care.

He again stood still, waiting for the slightest noise to bring all his senses to battle stations. No sound at all.

Parker moved toward the inside room where he calculated Jan had been sitting. He would free her and they would then run as fast as they could for the truck. And then race for safety. He had it all worked out in his mind. And then reality set in.

The cold steel of a handgun, pressed against the side of his neck, woke him up.

"Good evening, whoever you are," said a soft, deliberate voice. "You shouldn't be here, you know. There are things going on here that you can't know about. I'm sure you understand."

Parker tried to turn slowly, but the barrel of the handgun stopped him. "Now, open that door and step into the room. Slowly, please – and stay on the hinged side of the doorway. That's right," he said as Parker moved through the doorway as ordered.

That last direction, the one that ordered him to stay on the hinged side of the doorway, told Parker that this guy was probably a professional mayhem-maker. By instructing Parker to pass through the door on the hinged side, he made certain that, if Parker was so foolish as to try to slam the door on his adversary, it would be very awkward for him to launch the door from that angle. The delay due to that awkward movement would be plenty long enough for the man with the gun to do bad things to him. Parker had calculated the odds and knew that he had to wait for another chance. Learning what he had so far about this guy did not please him.

When Parker walked into the room Jan Evlin looked up. She simply stared, and then looked surprised, incredulous, and then shocked, in that order. "Mr. Parker," she blurted out, "you must have read my note."

Parker limped over to her, wishing that she hadn't used his name. "Are you all right, Jan?" he asked. "Why are you here? Have you been here for the last two weeks? Can you leave with me?"

"Mr. Parker?" the man with a gun asked. "Mr. William Parker, insurance king of Bridgeton, Vermont? And the nosiest bastard in New England?"

Parker didn't answer. Instead, he continued to talk to Jan. "How long have you been here, Jan?"

"I've been here a day – maybe two, Mr. Parker," she answered dully. "I can't think," she said, head hanging down again. Then she looked up at Parker with a sort of pleading look. "Can I leave here, Mr. Parker? Can I go with you – right now?"

Billy the Kid cut Parker off before he could utter a sound. "I'm afraid that won't be possible, Missy," he said, using a mocking tone. "Neither of you will be leaving here." Mr. X, as Parker now thought of him, reached over Jan's shoulder to quickly snip the wire that held her wrists tethered to the table top.

"Just like the old couple in the house?" asked Parker. "Are they aware that you won't allow them to leave when they want to?"

"That old man and his batty wife? I straightened her out a couple of weeks ago when she started blathering about wanting to leave. Enjoyed it, too. She hasn't spoken since."

"Who are you?" asked Parker. Not that he cared. Parker was trying to buy time, desperately looking for a way out of this mess.

And he couldn't. This was a very careful man – confirming to Parker, if he needed it, that his opponent was a professional killer.

Mr. X was only about 5 foot 7 inches. He was thin and seemed wiry, and probably strong for his weight, judging by the large and powerful-looking hands. These were the subtle points to be considered about this man. The most noticeable thing, however, wouldn't be missed by anybody. His full head of hair was completely and shockingly white.

"My name won't mean a thing to you, Parker. I'm just a person who is being very well paid to do what I'm very good at," Mr. X answered.

"What you're good at, as far as I can see," snapped Parker, "is environmental terrorism."

Mr. X chuckled. "You mean eco-terrorists, to coin a popular phrase, don't you? Aren't they a weird bunch? None of them have had an objective thought about anything in years. If they weren't so pitiful, they'd be funny."

Parker shifted his weight slightly. His leg was bothering him and he thought it was beginning to bleed again. "Surely they know a great deal about the natural events of our planet. They're just extremists, carrying things too far, aren't they?" Parker was trying to goad Mr. X.

The silenced barrel followed him as he moved, not changing its aim on the location on his body.

"You go right along and believe that, buster," Mr. X said derisively. "But are you aware that they not only don't care about the 'environmental condition of the planet', but they don't know anything technically correct about the planet either? They are after a whole country – the good old U. S. of A, Mr. Parker. Hell, I know more about nature than they do, and I never made it a main course of interest."

Parker tried to show that he was extremely interested in what Mr. X was saying. And he decided that the man liked to talk.

"That's ridiculous. You can't mean that. What evidence do you have to support what you've just said?" Parker asked.

Mr. X studied Parker. Then he grinned. "You don't think I'm smart enough to see what you're doing, do you? 'Delay him and maybe I'll find a way out', you're thinking. Right, Parker?" Parker said nothing.

"I've sat in meetings with these oddballs. Not a contributor, you know, just a listener and an enforcer for my boss, so to speak.

A suggestion will be made by one of these fools as to how something can be started that will edge along their plans for Vermont. Then someone will be assigned to write a scientific paper on the subject, or they can use the letters written by somebody else in the country. That's funny, all by itself. None of them know anything about any of the subjects. In fact, they're not even interested." He smiled, as if remembering this was soothing to him.

"The daily papers in Vermont will rush to print it as an op-ed piece. Then the letter writers around the state will be assigned the task of writing to their papers announcing that it's about time somebody in the scientific community has written about this important subject." Mr. X laughed again.

"The son-of-a-bitch who will write this 'scientific paper', and the press, too, will love it and will print it, along with his bio, which will not be verified by anybody. He'll suddenly be a 'doctor' of something, or have his Master's degree in 'Sun Healing', or some damned thing. But, as I said, the money's good and that's all that matters to me."

He went on as if he couldn't wait. "Hell, this dumb state even had a state officer of some sort, and this person's bio listed some accomplishments, some of which were lies. All of these jerks lie about themselves. Just like that fake Indian college professor out in Colorado. Remember him? The professor of something that wasn't real? That's how these people do things. They don't know how to work, so they make it all up. All of these people are lightweights. But it works, at least in Vermont."

He chuckled again, shaking his head. "You know, I've been all over this country, getting good money from people who have it, to do various things for them. And of all the states, Vermont is the only one that will buy anything as long as its wrapped up in pretty paper."

Parker decided to change the subject. "Where's your boss? I assumed he'd be here. Then I could talk with him, too." It was an inane way to change directions, he knew, but he didn't trust this screwball to remain stable for too long.

"He left about 7:00 AM this morning. He'd been trying to reach somebody all night. He got no answers, I guess. So, he left, and in a hell of a rush, too. As I think about it, I guess he must have wanted to reach his helicopter – yes, we have one of those, too, Parker. We're very well equipped, you know. He'll be back any time now, I think. However, you won't be able to talk to him, I'm afraid."

He motioned with his silenced pistol. "Now, out the door. And no sudden movements, please." He looked at Parker, who was standing askew, keeping as much of his weight off one leg as he could. "Parker, you look a little like that leaning tower thing, or whatever. Bad leg, I think? You'd better not be trying to make me think you're not dangerous. I have my Master's degree in sniffing out that sort of crap, and I'm not lying about it. Now, move out, both of you," and he motioned to Jan.

As they stepped through the door and into the darkness outside, Parker thought that he might have an advantage. The night would make a lot of things easier for him and Jan and he'd be looking for it.

That thought dissipated when Mr. X switched on the outside lights as he stepped through the door.

The two lights, one on each side of the door, were not bright. The bulbs were obviously undersized for the job of illuminating the outside area behind the barn. Parker continued to look around the cones of light produced by the inadequate lamps. Beyond the splotches of light was blackness.

Jan Evlin had not said a word. Parker thought that she was numb and wasn't understanding what this crazy man was about to do to them.

"Jan," Parker said quietly, "are you okay?"

She nodded vacantly, first looking at Parker and then the pistol. Parker knew that his question was totally dumb. If she doesn't understand, that's probably better, he thought.

"When do you expect your boss to be back? He may not be very happy when he learns that you've harmed us," Parker said, as equably as he could.

"I think he'll give me a bonus for getting rid of you, Parker. And I don't think he cares about the woman at all."

"What does he mean, Mr. Parker? Is he going to kill us?" asked Jan. Her voice was showing her panic as she seemed to understand what all this preparation work meant.

"I'm afraid so, missy," Mr. X said, "but it will be. . . "

Parker could see the eyes of Mr. X suddenly open wide, and a look of what Parker later thought was one of great surprise overtake his face. As Mr. X stood in place, the gun tipped toward the ground and then slipped from nerveless fingers and fell to the soft lawn with a muffled "thump".

The low level of lighting still was enough to produce a gleam on a shiny protrusion from Mr. X's shirt front. In fact, there was a second gleaming object on his shirt front, too. What the hell are those things, wondered Parker?

Mr. X continued to stand upright as this small tableau unfolded. Parker had not moved. He couldn't. He had become, during a very small amount of time, too used to paying attention to this man. Then Mr. X began to move. Parker took hold of Jan's arm and pulled her off to the side and stood back himself.

Mr. X fell straight forward and flat on his face. As he plunged forward, seeming to pick up speed as he went, the ghastly appearance of what changed everything appeared. It was the handle of a two-prong pitch fork standing straight up from the middle of Mr. X's upper back. The body seemed to vibrate for a few seconds, and then stopped. A breath of air wheezed from the lungs of Mr. X. Parker started at the sound. Jan just stood there, looking down at the body of a man who probably brought death to many people in the past but who never thought that his death would take place in the wilds of Vermont.

It was totally silent. Parker was about to move toward the body when a shuffling sound caused Parker to step in front of Jan instead and turn and face the noise. It was a very old man, hunched and work-worn from countless years on a farm. And no complaints about it.

Parker knew the type very well. This old man had to be the original owner of this property.

"Mr. Davidson,?" asked Parker, tentatively. "Is that you?"

"Yep, it is, son. Did I kill that son-of-a-bitch?"

"Yes, I think you did, sir, and our thanks to you for what you've done. But – how did you know to come up here at this odd hour? The good Lord knows we're grateful, but how did you know?"

"I saw you when you thought you were sneaking by the house and up to the barn. Hour, or so, ago, son. If you have any more sneakin' around to do, young fella, you'd damn well better improve on the way you do it." Mr. Davidson looked at Parker with real seriousness.

"I figured," Mr. Davidson said, maintaining his serious look, "that anybody that decided they needed to sneak in here was somebody I'd like to meet. So, I let you go in, then I followed you after a little bit. Heard the whole thing. Heard this bastard tell you that he enjoyed hitting my wife. Decided right then that he was not going to live much longer. So you see, killing him was what I was going to do anyway. Better to say I 'put him down', like a poor animal. The word 'murder' is reserved for human beings, wouldn't you say? He doesn't qualify. The only difference in my plan was that killing that bastard just wasn't planned for tonight."

He hesitated, and then he muttered, as if to himself, "Never did anything like that before, either."

Coming back to the present, he said, "You and the little lady, here," gesturing toward Jan, "just happened to be there."

Parker decided right then that this old man was one dangerous little ball of energy, coupled with commitment.

"Well, old-timer, we owe you a lot, anyway, even if you didn't mean it to help us. Right, Jan?" Jan just turned to Parker with a stony face and tears in her eyes. Maybe this is what shock is all about, thought Parker.

"What are you going to do with this piece of crap, young feller?" asked Mr. Davidson, looking at the body of Mr. X .

"Well," said Parker, "I was just going to leave him, Mr. Davidson. Nobody knows that we two have been up here. Except, now, of course, you. I'd like to keep this lady out of things, if at all possible. You have any objections to that?"

"Nope," he answered clearly. "I think you'd better stay out of things, too. I'd suggest that I put him away for today. He won't smell bad for a while. Then call the cops. When the big boy comes back this morning he's going to have a half-hitch in his tail, and when he's excited he's like a bull in fly time - uncontrolled hell."

"Let me give you a hand, Mr. Davidson," said Parker.

"Nope, you get outta here. I can take care of this," and he pointed down at the body with disdain.

Parker nodded. "If you can handle this mess, I've got some quick looking around to do upstairs. Then the lady and I are getting out. You could be in a lot of trouble over this."

"Son, I'm 93 years old. What would they do? Execute me? Christ, I'm doing that all by myself. Now, I warned ya, son. Don't delay. I may have the desire to kill this boss man, too, but I don't know if I have the energy for it." He flipped Parker a key ring. "That'll let you in to his apartment."

"I'll return it."

"Don't bother, son. He don't know I have it. Along with that key, take this, too," and he handed Parker a small card. "It's the combination to a small wall safe behind his bed. Might be interestin' for ya. Took me a while to get that. Had to be slippery. Didn't know I could get around that well at my age. But I managed." He reached out for Jan's arm. "I'll take her down to the house. We'll wait for you to come by. Then get going."

Parker went into the barn and up the stairs. The key did its job and he was suddenly inside the boss man's quarters. It was rustically furnished and very comfortable looking. There were at least three bedrooms up here, he thought, and only one of them interests me.

Parker quickly rifled through the large desk. The most interesting thing he found was a stack of writing paper that was identical to all of the notes, threatening and not, that had been received since Parker got into this rat-race. This is the lair of "Z". Good, he thought. A little bit of the mystery solved.

Then he went on to the master bedroom. He pulled the bed out from the wall, and there, set into the wall, was the safe.

Parker was pretty shaky, from a lack of sleep, a bleeding leg, and just plain nerves. The combination seemed to want to get the better of him, but finally he worked it. The safe door opened easily and Parker simply scooped whatever was kept in there into a pillowcase that was conveniently left on the bed, apparently for his use.

Then he looked around, saw a photograph on the wall that showed two proud parents and two children – a boy and a girl. He took that, too, and then limped down the stairs and out the back of the barn. The squishing feeling in his boot had reared its head again.

When he stepped out of the barn the body had already disappeared. Where it went Parker didn't want to know.

He limped down the driveway to the house. As he stepped up on the porch, Mr. Davidson came out, leading Jan by the hand, as if she were a prize heifer at the state fair. "In a little time, lad, she'll be right as rain. Got a cup of coffee into her with a little somethin' in it."

At that moment an elderly lady shuffled out. She was wearing a bathrobe and slippers. She obviously was the mate to Mr. Davidson. She had a large bandage on the side of her forehead.

"Mrs. Davidson?" Parker asked.

"Good guess, Mr. Parker, and we know who you are, too. Your friend here told us. We won't say a word. Now, get out of here. Come back when this is all over. Tell us all about it then. But not now."

Parker looked at this tough old couple. Memories of his own parents flooded back to him. They were tough, too, but maybe not like these two.

Parker took Jan by the arm. "Goodbye, sir, ma'am, and thanks for everything."

He and Jan started walking down the road. "Are you all right, Mr. Parker?" Jan asked.

"Yes, but that's not the question, is it? It's you that has to be all right. So? How are you?"

"I'm coming back," she said, with a little more firmness than in the recent past. "I guess it was just too much, these past three weeks. Especially this last hour." Parker certainly agreed.

55

They reached the truck in about an hour of awkward walking, leaving Jan exhausted and Parker bleeding. A hell of a couple, he thought.

As they were climbing into Parker's faithful old companion, the sound of the helicopter was suddenly directly overhead. It flashed on its landing lights and disappeared behind a row of trees that sprouted beside the driveway.

"Time to go, Jan," he said, "and carefully and quietly, too."

He hit the starter and prayed. God was kind and his old friend rumbled into life. Parker pulled out to the edge of the road, and stopped, headlights off. Then he went to the left, rather than right. He could just barely see the road.

"I don't know where we'll end up Jan, but I don't want to retrace my steps of last night. Makes me uncomfortable to think about going back by the Davidson place. At some point we'll get to a spot that one of us will recognize, and then we'll head for Hugo's house. A little late, but we'll get there."

"Can't you take me home, Mr. Parker? I'd like to get back into my life." Jan was pleading for something that nobody could allow at this time – maybe never again.

"Your life will start up again, Jan, when 'Z' is out of commission – permanently. Until that time, you, Addie, and I are going to become kindred spirits."

After a few minutes of slow driving, Parker asked, "How did you mail your note to me, Jan?"

Jan was quiet and they drove slowly along, headlights off as much as possible. "I was becoming increasingly worried about the whole trip from the beginning, Mr. Parker. So I wrote that note to you in the motel I stayed in after I left home in the evening. I wrote it in a sort of code – you know, in case somebody else read it. Probably not a very deceptive code," she said, her voice lowered, "but the best I could do at the time. Then I stopped in Hardwick, dropped it in a mail box, and here you are, popping up, and right on time, too." She smiled slightly, Parker noticed. She's on the road back, he thought.

Parker said, "There is one thing that I want to know about all this, though. In asking it, I might upset you. But, I have to know something. You may not be able to answer it, but you may have some information that would help."

"I'm all right, Mr. Parker. Nothing will be as upsetting as what we've experienced tonight. What is it?"

Parker drew a breath, hesitated, and then said, "In my experience in this matter, Jan, a killer has been loose. There have been at least three murders that we know about. The first killing took place six months ago. My guess is that you might have every reason to present a greater threat to 'Z' than any single one of these victims. And yet, you are still alive. Why, I wonder, when they had you under their control and nobody knew where you were? Can you help me?"

Jan was quiet for a moment, and then she seemed to steel herself. "I don't know this for sure, of course, Mr. Parker. I just had the feeling that he wouldn't harm me. In fact, I thought he might know who I was. I don't know why I felt that way."

Parker was thinking about Jan's naiveté. If a person could blindly believe that she wouldn't be harmed when others had been, maybe her going off without telling anybody wasn't so strange after all. "Why did you think he might know you, Jan?" Parker asked.

"I don't know, I don't know," she said, almost in despair, "but in the two weeks I've been living like a prisoner, I've never seen the leader, who you call 'Z'. Whoever he is, he possibly is the head of a group of very odd people. Do you remember how you found me just two hours ago? Wired to a table? When I was at the farm, I was always in that room except for daily exercise, accompanied by somebody with a rifle. It felt like I could go where I wanted during the first days of my 'visit' at NPF II, but I'm sure I was closely watched. We were up in the Kingdom then – in those three log cabins? Have you ever seen them?" Not waiting for Parker to answer, she said, firmly, "Well, they're up there all right."

"You know, Mr. Parker, I really never saw him. I was in a large tent set up off to the side of the school buildings. The man I thought might be this 'Z' person you talk about would talk to me through the tent wall once in a while."

Parker was astonished. "Talk to you through the tent wall? Why did you go up there in the first place? There must have been a hint of something troubling going on," cried Parker.

Jan shook her head. "No, no warning like that. Why did I go? I was invited by my *friend*, Mr. Parker, who had resigned from that non-profit." Jan was showing some anger now.

"You remember, Mr. Parker. The Truth, Prosperity, and Sharing Coalition of Northern Vermont? Her name was Margaret Phillips. She e-mailed me to join her up in Bloomfield, at the General Store. We set a date and time and up I went."

"You hadn't seen her since she resigned from the non-profit?"

Jan shook her head. "I wasn't surprised to hear from her after a long dry spell, Mr. Parker. This has happened before. In fact, it happened the same way when she called me out of the blue to have lunch on the day when this whole thing started. That wasn't that long ago."

"When she e-mailed me to meet her in Bloomfield and we'd have a brief vacation, I was just getting over my visit with you near the trout stream. I still felt threatened and worried. I wasn't sure you would get into this situation of mine, and I just felt that her e-mail gave a wonderful place to go for a week or so. I accepted her invitation. I didn't even tell Mr. Birdsall. I did send a short letter to my husband. He's in Iraq, you know. Then I simply went away. Disappeared for a while."

To Parker the real reason then came out. "And, I was scared. The note I saw from 'Z' really bothered me. I'm not a brave person, Mr. Parker, like you are." Parker winced at that compliment. If she only knew.

"I took the easy way out and went on vacation for a few days. I even left late at night from home, thinking that I wouldn't be noticed. I knew I was spooked, but I just couldn't help it. After an hour or so on the road, I stopped overnight, and then finished my trip the next afternoon. I was met in Bloomfield by a smiling little man who told me that my friend had to go to a funeral, but she would be there tomorrow at noon. It was the man who was going to kill us both just an hour ago, Mr. Parker."

Parker was thinking that everything he had experienced over the last month was a story of slight differences and tiny incidents: in meetings held and not held; in reasons for doing something and doing nothing; in nanoseconds rolling on the ground and avoiding a bullet; of fry pans being four inches away from where they were; an old man who thought he saw someone sneaking around on his property, let him go on, and then followed him in exactly the right period of time so that he arrived on the deadly scene at exactly the right second. Tonight I used up any luck I had left, he thought.

"He told me to leave my car behind an old barn and follow him to the 'rustic resort' that my friend had picked out." Jan grimaced at that recollection. "I knew I wouldn't have any trouble following him. His hair was totally white. I had never seen anybody with hair like that."

This whole description of why she went to an unknown destination without a certainty of what it was all about was completely foreign to Parker. Maybe he was too careful, or hidebound, or stubborn, or simply unimaginative. But he knew he would have done some checking. Parker thought, to be fair, that her fear would no doubt have been a powerful motivator. Just get away, she would have said to herself. Don't hold back; leave town for a few days; things will be better when you return.

So Jan went away to leave trouble behind. What she couldn't have foreseen was that the trouble had run around her and ahead of her and was waiting for her in Bloomfield, Vermont.

Parker then asked a question that might be a key for him and this mess. "What's your maiden name, Jan?"

Jan looked at Parker in surprise. "Zederbian, Mr. Parker. A combination of Polish, German, and Armenian, all with a backdrop of Irish. Different, eh?" Parker wrote down the name, asking for the correct spelling. No idea where it would lead him.

"Can you see a connection? You understand where I'm going with this, I'm sure. What about 'Z'? And the 'Z' in your maiden name? You said you didn't see him. Isn't that odd? This guy may have written a note to you that frightened you, for goodness sake." Parker was frustrated.

"Let me start out by saying that I don't think he knew that Jan Evlin might be someone he knew. He only knew me as a meddling female reporter." Parker nodded his understanding.

"I went for a walk with this white-haired guy the next day. We walked around the front of the compound. It was pretty country up there but it was also rough living, if you know what I mean. As we walked, a man came out of one of the buildings and started to walk toward us. He had a beard and was about my age, I thought. Suddenly he turned away and disappeared into one of the buildings."

"My white-haired guard seemed to be surprised. He told me that the 'boss man' had said that Jan should be taken out for a walk and the 'boss man' would come out and accompany them. The 'boss man' wanted to see me and talk to me. Then the white-haired guy took me back to my tent."

"What about your friend. Did she arrive around noon?" asked Parker

"No, Mr. Parker. I never saw her or heard from her, either. It was at that point that I knew something was terribly wrong, but I couldn't for the life of me say what it might be. I remember thinking that maybe she didn't write the e-mail at all. Maybe somebody else did. But the implications of that were too much for me to face, I guess. I just knew that I had to get away. It never occurred to me that I might be in danger. I didn't have enough imagination, I suppose, to feel real, solid, stomach-turning fear or terror. I didn't feel real panic until about an hour ago, when I suddenly realized, standing there with you behind that barn, that this was real and that I was going to die." Jan didn't show any fear while telling Parker about her experiences. He expression was just blank as she spoke.

Parker thought about this whole scenario as he drove. It fits together with other pieces of the puzzle to form a partial picture. The problem with it was that it took leaps of faith to believe it. Parker made a mental note to check the whereabouts of Jan's friend, Margaret Phillips. If she has lived in New York state without any warnings or discomfort, then a lot of his plot calculations would fall apart.

"You said you had conversations with somebody who might be 'Z' through the tent wall. So you never saw his face. Right?" Jan gestured that he was correct. "What did you talk about?"

"Nothing very deep, Mr. Parker. During the very first conversation we had, I asked him when I could leave. He never answered. He just left."

"The thought that he might be someone I knew actually came to me in a flash," she continued, "when he kept asking me questions about my parents, where they were, how they were doing, that sort of thing. And then the conversation would be brought to a close and he'd walk away. He never talked about non-profits, or anything else, for that matter. It was like he would run out of things to talk about and then leave me."

"Nothing to do with what he was doing there?"

Jan shook her head.

"What do you think, Jan? What was going on at this compound?"

Jan squinted down at the floor of the truck, thinking about what Parker had asked her. "It was a school, Mr. Parker, located where it wouldn't be seen or found. It was training people from all over the world in something that they didn't want known. Sinister, really. The people were strange-acting individuals. There was a lot of forced laughter, loud laughter. Different languages, too, but I couldn't decide what they were. But when they all were in the buildings, there was total silence, except for the buzz of the voices of the instructors. I never heard what they were teaching."

"Did you ever go into the buildings,?" asked Parker.

"I was never allowed in them. I always had someone with me. After a while it usually was a man carrying a rifle. He was the helicopter pilot, the white-haired man told me."

"Last question, Jan. How did you know he might be 'Z'? You didn't see him at all up close. Right?" She didn't speak for a few seconds.

"Just one thing, Mr. Parker. It was a small thing. Not even recognizable to me at first. When he asked about my family, my mother and father, I sensed, as he went on, that he knew them. Little details, you understand? His questions seemed to be asked with some kind of prior knowledge of how they should be phrased." She shrugged. "Anyway, that's how I saw it." A little weak, Parker thought, but he'd file it away for the future.

Jan stared off into the distance as the truck rocketed along, putting distance between them and an old farm where danger seemed to breed.

"You know something, Mr. Parker?" Jan said. "The white-haired guy was going to kill us tonight, wasn't he?" Parker nodded his assent

"So, he would never have done that without the permission of his boss," Jan continued. "If he knew me from before somehow, that knowledge still would never have saved my life if he couldn't afford to have me around anymore, would it? He'll wish he had killed me, however, when he finds me gone from NPF I. You know, Mr. Parker, he may decide that the game is up and leave." She sounded hopeful.

Parker thought about that for a few seconds. "I don't read him that way, Jan. I think he's already started to clean up his mess on his back trail and come out of this in good shape. In fact, I think he started a while ago when he murdered a motel manager in Burlington, and then tried for me."

Jan raised a hand to her mouth and gasped, "He tried to kill you, Mr. Parker?"

"Oh, yes, Jan, and someone else who was with me. No, I don't think he'll run away. He has another problem, though, I think. Vermont is very important to him, if I read things correctly. NPF II is one of the main training camps for their international eco-terrorists. If that goes wrong, then he's in trouble. I think that that's a very rough group. They're playing for the biggest stakes that anyone before them ever went after. A whole state. Eventually, probably a whole country, although that sounds crazy. I think he'll be around. And that's why you can't go home now. You'll be with Addie and me for as long as it takes."

Jan had begun to cry quietly, with quiet sobs. Parker thought that maybe she needed to do that. Maybe she hadn't cried enough in the past few weeks. He wished he knew something about the psychology of "letting things come out". He'd read about it. He'd been with buddies in Vietnam when their tears seemed to help. At least sometimes.

Parker traveled none of the same roads to South Burlington and to Hugo's house that he had traveled before. While driving at moderate speeds to avoid having state troopers look him over, he also had to check the sky to look, incredibly, for helicopters.

He tried to visualize a conversation with a Vermont trooper right after he had been stopped for speeding or erratic driving or something else equally dastardly.

The trooper might say:

"You're looking for what, sir? Helicopters?"

"What was that again, sir? Blood running over your boot top is not a problem?"

"Your girl friend looks very upset, sir. You'd better step out of your vehicle."

"What year did you say this truck was, sir? Let me see the proof of inspection, please."

No, that couldn't be allowed to happen. Parker had no answers to any reasonable questions that anybody might pose. He slowed down even more as he entered Barre on Route 302.

Only once, to this point, was there the sighting of a searching helicopter. Parker was lucky. He had stopped, once again, on the edge of the road, and then pulled in, as close to the trees lining it as he could. He switched off his headlights and climbed down from his truck. He waited there for his customary five minutes and then reached for the door handle of his truck - and stopped.

He could hear the whap, whap, whap of the helicopter and then saw its searchlights come on. The pilot had been following the various roads from East Calais that would take him west. He was looking for headlights and at this hour of the early morning there wouldn't be many. Depending on the fire power in that helicopter, they would be dead pigeons.

Parker waited for the searchlights to disappear over the rise ahead. Then he jumped into his truck and headed back the way he had come. He took the next left and just followed the track for fifteen minutes, hoping that the helicopter had already checked this road out. Then Parker turned left again and headed generally west. This was a real chess match. And his hide-and-seek chess skills were doubtful, at best.

When he stopped again for a helicopter check, Jan got out of the truck with him. They waited in silence. Nothing in the sky, waiting for them to appear. Parker and Jan headed out again, headlights off but his attention mechanism operating on high-beam.

Another hour and a half, during which time Jan slept, saw them rolling into Hugo's driveway.

It was 5:00 in the morning. Parker was totally exhausted. The lights were all on and Addie's car was parked in the yard. Parker thought of the Charge of the Light Brigade as they walked up to the door. It flew open and Addie grabbed him around the middle and hugged him. "Willie, you idiot, and I don't even know what you've been up to. Are you all right?"

"I certainly am, my dear," Parker said with forced joviality. "When did you get here? How did you find your way? You've met Hugo and Connie, I assume?"

"Yes, she has, Mr. Parker," said Connie Barkley, walking toward them with Hugo in tow.

Addie saw, at that moment, Jan Evlin, walking behind her husband.

"Jan, my dear," she said, We've never met, but I know who you are. Where have you been?" The question of the moment, thought Parker. It was asked in innocence, but was at the heart of everything.

Addie walked over to her and put an arm over Jan's shoulders.

"Come in, Bill," said Hugo. "We've been telling stories about you and some of the stuff we've done over the past two weeks. Your wife is now part of the whole scheme."

"You've got a good woman, Mr. Parker," said Connie Barkley. "And from what I've heard tonight, you definitely need one."

"Only occasionally, Connie. Like now," and he squeezed Addie to him.

They walked into the house and when inside, Connie said, "What's that medicinal smell? Notice it, Addie?"

"Yes, Connie. Is that you, Willie?"

"Yeah, it is. I scraped up a leg and got gravel ground into it. A doctor cleaned it out, and the antiseptic is what you smell."

"Did you fall, Willie? Where were you when this injury happened? Do you have to go back to the doctor for a checkup?"

"A friend of mine and I took a trip into the Northeast Kingdom for about ten hours, total, looked around, and then we came home. I fell during that four hours of tramping around."

Addie looked up at him. "I know where you've been, Willie. You've been up to the NPF II, haven't you? The area where the pictures were taken. Did you find things that the pictures showed?"

"Yes, we did, my dear. We also hit pay dirt as far as the use of the compound is concerned. And, Hugo," Parker crowed, "you are a genius. You'll remember that we put a fake message out in Hal's office that his secretary was supposed to relay to somebody." Hugo nodded. "Well, it worked to perfection."

"I think Hal is going to land her in a lot of trouble, Bill," said Hugo, "and now we can prove what she did."

"As long as we don't go further than the passage of the fake message to somebody. We don't talk about what we did as a result of it. The rest of it is a closed book. I don't think we'll ever be able to mention to anyone that we've been up there, Hugo. I'd rather not tell you what went on, in fact. It became messy."

"Willie, we need to know," said Addie.

"No, you don't," Parker said firmly. The subject was closed. Parker was pleased he'd said that it wouldn't be discussed and that Addie had clammed up. Hugo and Connie would be impressed with his leader-of-the-pack stature. Parker knew, however, that he'd tell Addie everything on the way home because if he didn't she'd keep at him, using all her considerable woman's skills, until he did. Addie was nothing if not determined.

"Hugo, I very much need to use your phone. I need to call Peter Morgan immediately."

Hugo handed Parker his cell phone. "You can keep it for the time being, Bill. I have to go to work now."

"Are you heading in the direction of Montpelier, Hugo?" Parker asked.

"As a matter of fact, I am," Hugo answered. 'Barre first, then Montpelier on the way back home. Why? Do you need anything?"

Parker handed him the pillowcase that contained all the goodies from "Z"'s wall safe. "Could you drop this off to Morgan at the Montpelier PD?" he asked. "He's there now and I think he'll be there when you go through, and on your way to Barre."

"You bet, Bill," Hugo said. Then he kissed Connie and headed for his business vehicle, the familiar black van.

Parker walked over to the other side of the room and punched in the number for the Montpelier PD. "Peter, this is Bill Parker. Yes, we're at Hugo's house. Just got in. I need a favor. Can you send somebody up to NPF I? Right away, if you can. There's an old couple who live in the house a little away from the road. Their name is Davidson. They saved our lives. Who? Oh, Jan Evlin and me. Yes, she was there. But I'm very concerned for the Davidsons. I'll tell you all about it later today at your house in Northfield. Another thing, Peter. Hugo Barkley, of Barkley, Bark. . . . . Oh, you know him, do you? Anyway, I gave him a pillowcase full of goodies I found at NPF I. I hope they'll be useful to us. Also, thanks a lot for everything, Peter."

He closed the cell phone. He hoped he wasn't too late in calling Morgan about the Davidsons. It was at this time that he wished he had a cell phone full-time.

Parker walked back to the small group. "We'll be going down to Northfield later this morning for a meeting with Peter

Morgan, Connie, and you'll be the only one of us who is going through her day with a normal schedule. Ours is apt to be chaotic. And thank you for having us tonight. We'll be up and at 'em first thing and gone by eight."

Parker and Addie settled down on a pull-out sofa to grab a few hours sleep. Addie was holding Parker's hand and wouldn't let go. "It was rough up there, Willie?" she asked.

"Yes, it was, sweetie. I had Bud Small with me – he insisted that he go along. He saved the day a couple of times. I was serious when I said we couldn't discuss anything about it, but with you, I'll tell you everything on the way to Northfield. That okay?"

Addie murmured sleepily that it was. She was asleep almost instantly. She still held Parker's hand.

I didn't fool her at all, he thought.

56

When Addie and Parker, walking on either side of Jan Evlin, stepped through the door and into Morgan's house for his morning meeting it looked like somebody's family reunion – except that there were no smiles and laughs.

People were there who were old friends of Parker's and others were in the room who he had never seen before. Surprising to Parker was that Addie knew some of those people who were strangers to him. As she socialized with them, he knew that he had become a little thoughtless in this regard. Addie had a life, too, outside of her family. She had acquaintances, friends, and formal connections to whom Parker, through inattention and a degree of damned selfishness, had allowed to fade away in his mind. Parker, right today, vowed not to let it happen again.

Morgan walked up to them with a look of subdued pleasure. "Addie, Bill, I'm delighted to see you here. There will be a lot going on here and it wouldn't have had any importance without you." He turned toward Jan. "And are you Jan Evlin?" She nodded.

"I can't tell you how delighted I am to meet you, Ms. Evlin. We were worried about you, you know."

"I was worried about me, too, Mr. Morgan," she said.

Just then Hal Birdsall rushed over to her. "Jan, my dear, seeing you is wonderful. I certainly didn't mean for all this to happen when I gave you that assignment. However, if you really were on vacation I hope you got some rest."

He was pleasant all through his reintroduction to Jan, but it came through to Parker that Birdsall had been a worried man, and now some of his concerns visibly dissipated. "We'll talk as soon as this meeting is over," placing a hand on her shoulder.

Morgan moved closer and said, "My patrol went out to the Davidsons' place early this morning. They just got back. All quiet, Bill. Nobody around."

"Nobody?" said Parker. "Any lights?" Morgan shook his head and turned back to Addie and Jan.

Parker thought that the absence of lights was odd. He felt a frantic concern for this old couple with more courage than concern for themselves.

"Who are all these people, Peter?" asked Parker, gesturing around the room. "I didn't know that there was going to be a law enforcement convention here today, but there are many others who actually have suntans. Where in the world did they come from?" Parker was genuinely puzzled.

Morgan gave Parker a tight grin. "Many of them are friends of mine. You'll meet them all at some point. You'll find them to be useful, I think."

"Good," said Parker, "we'll need them."

"Bill," said Morgan, "I want you, Addie, and Jan, to pin one of these on and find a seat." He handed each of them a name tag, and a very brief note under the name, to help, in a limited way, to identify them to the viewer. Parker's tag read "Willing to Take Risks".

Parker gestured to Morgan to step aside for a quick talk. "Peter," Parker said, in a low voice, "can you check a name quickly, like right now, to find out if she is still in Vermont? Or if she's still alive? The name is Margaret Phillips, of somewhere in Chittenden County. Used to work for the Truth, Prosperity, and Sharing Coalition of Northern Vermont. I think she went to New York state. And what did you find out about the Canadian carpenters? Peter, I'm sorry to have to drop all this on you. I keep running into names and I have no way to check them out except through you."

Morgan made a few notes, and then said, "Okay, we'll check her out for you. Finding anything on the Canadian guys has been a lot of trouble, but we got a faint tug on the line yesterday. We might know about them today, too."

He looked around before speaking again. "About the Davidsons. My people made a quick search of the area. They probably left before the bad guy came back."

Parker wasn't at all sure of that.

"Also, you'll be interested to know, Bill, that a helicopter was sitting behind the barn." Parker didn't say anything to Morgan about this sequence of events but this "Z" character was probably watching them all the time they were poking around. Morgan's officers were probably alive right now because they *were* cops and their uniforms were a deterrent.

Parker looked around the room and saw Bud Small, sitting in an easy chair, and looking uncomfortable, but not in the way a man might look who had just barely escaped being shot to death just hours before. Seated on the arm of his chair was a young woman who had her hand on his shoulder. Every once in a while, which seemed to Parker to occur about every fifteen seconds, she would squeeze his shoulder or give it an affectionate pat.

She had to be Mrs. Small, Parker thought. Her married name fit her as perfectly as it had evaded her husband.

"Addie, Jan, I want you to meet somebody who was very important to me yesterday," he said. They weaved through the crowd and approached the Smalls. When Bud saw him he struggled to rise to his feet, saw Parker's "don't bother" signal, and sat back in his chair.

"Addie, Jan, meet Police Detective Bud Small of the Burlington Police Department. Bud, my wife, Addie, and the elusive Jan Evlin."

As they all shook hands, Parker turned to the young woman. "Are you Mrs. Small?" he inquired.

She nodded and asked, "Mr. Parker? I'm Robin. And is this your wife? Addie, I believe?" She also nodded to Jan.

Addie stepped forward and shook Mrs. Small's hand. "How much of a story did you get from your husband, Robin?" she asked.

"Only that the most interesting thing that happened was that my husband fell while walking back to the car and landed on a rock. His shoulder is all black and blue." Robin cocked an eye at Addie. "How about you, Mrs. Parker?"

"Well, Robin," she said, "*my* husband also fell, only his fall was on a hard gravel road and had to have a doctor clean it out. And he's never been to a doctor voluntarily in his life."

"Mrs. Parker, when you get a straight story, please call me – and I'll do the same. I think their memories have begun to fail them."

Parker and Bud winced as this exchange took place. Bud finally broke the silence. "It was a rough place to hike," he said, unconvincingly.

Jan moved forward and said, "You two women have very brave husbands. I think, if I read this room correctly, that we all will learn every detail of the adventures that these two had yesterday – and last night, too. Right, Mr. Parker?" Parker shrugged.

Then he said, "I still don't know who all the people are. There must be twenty people here and I've seen less than half of them before." Parker knew that he was lousy at changing a subject smoothly.

"The four of us will talk later," said Addie, ignoring Parker.

"I don't know any more than you do, Bill," Bud answered.

Parker recognized Hal Birdsall, Hugo, and Don Flanders. Good Lord, he thought, even the O'Sullivans are here. And their three older children. I'd certainly have welcomed the chance to be a fly on the wall during *that* vetting interview with Peter Morgan.

Morgan had walked to one end of the large room and said, loudly enough to quiet the room, "We all have a specific purpose for being here. However, I'll be surprised if we don't have about the same reason for all the traveling that is represented here today. Now, everybody, get your coffee and anything else we need and then let's get started."

Morgan formally called the meeting to order. His wife, Catherine, was taking notes. Parker thought that he would be surprised if Morgan wasn't taping everything said, too. An interrogation room, when all is said and done, but the most comfortable one in existence. Always the professional law enforcement man, Parker mused.

57

Introductions were made. Each person stood and gave their name, where they were from, who invited them to this meeting, and what their special interest was.

An interesting twist to the introductions was that a few people would only give their first name. They didn't trust anybody. And at that moment Parker realized how dangerous his "thrashing around" had been from the very beginning. Perhaps, he thought, I would have never started on this trek if I had been aware of what was waiting out there for bumblers like me to encounter.

When Morgan stood to briefly describe his interest in this case, he also set a small framed picture in front of the person to his left. "I'm starting this old photo around the room. I want everybody here to look at it while we're discussing our situation. I need to know if anybody can positively identify anyone in it. Please take the time to be sure." Then he sat down.

Parker could sense danger, fear, and anger in the room. Everybody he looked at seemed to be figuratively looking over his or her shoulder, not knowing or having confidence in anybody else seated here this day.

As if right on cue, this lack of trust of some members of the group began to show through. The nervousness and wary nature of at least some, if not all, of the members of this almost unique meeting in Vermont, became obvious with the comments of the first person to stand.

From California, and obviously chosen to deliver this message, he said he felt comfortable in the room except for one person. "He's a newspaper editor and in Vermont that means he's against us. He will write about this meeting, he will mention names, subjects, and actions to be taken by us. At least where I come from, that makes everything very dangerous. Personally, I didn't know anyone from the press would be here, Peter," turning to face Morgan. "You didn't mention it when you invited me to attend. If I'd known, I would have never left California."

Everyone turned toward Morgan. He stood and speaking so softly that it was all Parker could do to hear him, said, "No, you're right, Chet, I didn't mention it to you. In fact, I didn't mention anyone's job, did I? To anybody. It wasn't important. And do you know why, Chet?"

"I need to know, Peter," Chet said. "Then I'll decide if I stay."

"Do you remember the first death I mentioned? Probably not the first death that's occurred because of this business, but the first death that drew our attention to what might be going on?" Chet from California nodded.

"That victim was the brother of this newspaper editor." Morgan swept his hand around and toward Birdsall. "Best to keep that quiet, I thought. Especially because I didn't know if you'd be coming here, and it would be better not to spread that information around to people who might not want to be included in the ones who are here today. Dangerous, I thought."

Chet was about to say something when he saw Hal Birdsall rise from his chair. "I can understand your reaction, Chet. The newspapers, at least the dailies, are just the voice of the extreme left in Vermont. I include the paper for which I work and I am one of their editors. That first murder victim *was* my brother."

Chet looked down at the table top. "I'm sorry if I offended you, Mr. Birdsall. I just have to be careful. I have a family to think about."

"Let's be clear on this," said Birdsall. "When this is all over I *am* going to write it up in a series of articles for my paper. Whether they print it or not is a question. If they won't, I'll find one that will. However, I will mention no names. I will, however, identify sections of the country, actions taken, and proof found. Everybody clear on that?" He looked around the room. "It will be written so that no one can backtrack to find out who is here today. That I can guarantee. Everybody understand? Now's the time to leave if you're nervous about what we're going into. It's going to be very rough, I think." Nobody stirred.

"Fine," he said. Turning to look at Morgan, he said, "Let's roll, Mr. Morgan."

The story that unfolded that day would never leave Parker's memory. It was a tale of complete corruption; of terrorism inside the country's borders, of outside money distorting the institutions of many states, including Vermont, and of murder. But there was even more. There was undeserved ruin of reputations, with the help of a compliant and ignorant news media, and of the destruction of citizens' futures by ruining what they had built that gave shape to their dreams.

Some stories actually brought tears to some, furious anger to others. Finally, Parker told them of his involvement in this whole matter and what had happened along the way.

"You mean," the man from a western state asked, "that Vermont has almost 2800 non-profits and you only have about 650,000 people?"

"Yep," Parker answered.

"Hell, we're small fry where I live then. We've got only a third of the Vermont non-profits and we've got about twenty times the number of people."

"Remember, sir," said Parker, "that what ends up working in Vermont will soon be knocking on your state's door. And all perfected, too."

A man rose from across the room. He looked at Parker and then said, "So you're Bill Parker. I read about you when you got involved in something or other having to do with a legislator who was killed in the Statehouse."

"That was three years ago, sir. All past and forgotten."

"Mr. Parker, I'm from the state of Washington. Call me Marv. That's good enough. What I just said about you hasn't been forgotten in my state. And do you know why? It's because the State of Washington seems to be as hard left as Vermont. But it isn't. We have spasms of practical politics out there that fight off the left for another year or two. Vermont doesn't have any days of respite left. Everything here revolves around central planning – a steady, daily diet of it. You don't have a chance. Your politicians haven't learned anything in twenty-five years, have they?"

"Afraid not," said Parker.

"One of the best things that happened in Washington was the disappearance of our main ring leader for the hard left. You know the kind of person I mean. These people burned logging equipment, drove steel spikes into trees so they couldn't be cut – killed a couple of loggers when their chains hit the spikes and the chains broke up and lashed the operators. A hell of a thing to do to a man, too," he said in a thin, reedy, voice. "And they started fires in new home developments and manufacturing buildings and generally tried to destroy things they didn't like." The memories were having an effect on him.

"Well, anyway, we took it upon ourselves to find out who this creep was. We are not certain of his name. We heard that he was also known as 'Knots' in some quarters."

Parker turned quickly toward Jan, but she showed no reaction.

"We found that out through very good friends who were placed where they could research things like that," said Marv, the man from Washington. "Whoever this Knots is, the name no longer shows up in any current records. It's like he dropped off the face of the globe. Maybe he's dead – I don't know. If he's alive we don't know what name he uses. But it no longer matters. He hasn't been seen by any law enforcement people in years. Our snitches haven't seen or heard anything about him. He doesn't show up anywhere in Washington state now. Hasn't been around for at least six or seven years – maybe even longer than that. He is one mean bastard, I'll tell you. We believe he's responsible for a good many deaths. My personal opinion? He kills if it suits him. Be thankful he isn't here."

Parker looked at Jan. She knew what he wanted, and she gestured to go ahead. "Based on the little bit we knew coming here for this meeting, with strong confirmation from you just now, we think he *is* here in Vermont, running a training school for international terrorists up in northern Vermont. He's on the loose right now. A police detective and I ran into him just yesterday. I think he knows who I am, but I'm certain he doesn't know the detective." There was shocked silence. And then a ripple of the sound of curses and concern went through the room.

Parker didn't say anything about the destruction of the training school facility. It's better, he decided, to erase all ties with that incident.

"So he came here when he left us," Marv said softly, as if to himself. "Then if it's the guy I was talking about, Mr. Parker, and it sounds as if it is, watch your back more than your front. If he has any idea that you could identify him, you're on his list." With that unsettling comment, Marv sat down.

Another man from away stood up. Parker immediately knew, as others no doubt did, that this guy was from some other place and some other latitude because he had a tan. And not just a slight tinge on his skin, but a tan that must have gone all the way to the bone and had been there for all the years this man had been on earth. When he spoke, all doubt was removed. With a restful southern accent he announced, "Ladies and gentlemen, my name is Lucas Montague. I'm from Louisiana and I don't give a damn who knows it. I'm a Federal Homeland Security officer. I'm on vacation, if you get my meaning. I assume, Mr. Birdsall, that you can keep that out of your story?"

Birdsall gave this impressive man an enthusiastic nod.

Montague continued. "We in Louisiana know of this man, I believe. His nick-name in our fair state was 'Zeddy'".

Jan started at the name Montague mentioned. She gazed balefully at him across the room. He didn't notice, but Parker and Addie did. Addie took Jan's hand in hers and whispered to her.

"He spent about a year and a half there," continued Montague, "as far as we can determine. He was a point man for the Trust of the Progressive Naturalist. It's not a trust. It's a non-profit, but how they qualified to be a non-profit is beyond me. This trust and its supporters are all 'forest watchers' types. You know who they are. They are watching our forests for 'the benefit of our children'. They represent the greatest rip-off of this century. This is a vicious group of people, folks," he said.

"They were famous for a lot of damage to drilling platforms, an attempt at blowing up a dock where drilling equipment was kept, injuries to oil workers by attacking them in restaurants and bars, and threats to their families. This is a trust that is in almost every state, to varying degrees. Our snitches tell us that Vermont is the home of a very strong chapter of this outfit, and its role is to buy up as much land in Vermont as possible and ultimately combine it with huge chunks of Maine that they control. That's why I'm here. This damned trust, or whatever it is, has cost this nation more jobs and lives than any effort against us ever has." He took a sip of coffee and looked down at a brief outline of his presentation.

Parker knew he was making a very big point. It was the danger that these eco-terrorists posed to everyone – not just the equipment, buildings, and vehicles, but to anyone who got in their way. Yes, they were real terrorists, he now knew. He looked over at Jan. She sat very still, hands clasped in her lap, and stared down.

Montague straightened up and continued. "Their goal is to own and control the top tier of the United States, from the

Canadian border down about 150 miles. That came from a snitch who got out of the organization when it became clear to this person what was really going on. Their efforts are being pushed in every state across the top of the United States. We knew what they were doing, but it wasn't believed by those who counted." Montague looked angry.

"But those of us who were following their activities – as well as we could – knew that they were being trained somewhere. We just could never get a handle on where the training was taking place. We suspected that it was in California. But we couldn't find anything to prove it." Montague paused. Sipped on a cup of ice cold coffee.

"And then Peter Morgan called," he said. "When he described the situation he was facing in Vermont, it made us all realize that this man 'Zeddy' could be up here. In any case, we had to check it out because the pattern they used on us was being repeated in Vermont. And they quietly use some very rough people to help them accomplish their short-term goals. The long term plan they will take care of with their political people, already in place."

Parker finally remembered the name of this non-profit. Addie had come back from her investigative trip to Burlington with this name on her mind. The Trust of the Progressive Naturalist. What a lovely-sounding and uplifting title. They'd watch your kids for you and while they did, they'd teach them stuff that will make them unable to function in society. All for the family. Except your family would turn into something you wouldn't recognize in a couple of years. And the rest of the damage would be to the reputations of the good and committed teachers.

Catherine Morgan suddenly stood up from the table where her job as note-taker was being conducted. She had her cell phone to her ear and her face was grim. She waved it at her husband.

"Excuse me for a moment, ladies and gentlemen." He took the phone from his wife and listened intently for a few seconds, scribbling rapidly in his note pad. Then he snapped it shut and looked up at the people who were sitting silently and watching Morgan. They knew that something had hit him solidly.

"Folks," he said, his voice seeming to shake noticeably, "I had a request made of me this morning before we got started. It was to check on the whereabouts of three people – people who are mixed up, in different ways, with this 'destroy America' business which has caused this meeting to be convened. I doubt very much if any of them even knew they were involved in things that would place them in danger. In addition to those people, I want to report that Jan Evlin, the reporter from our local daily newspaper, was missing for almost three weeks. This became of real concern to us. However," he said, smiling, "she's okay and sitting in this room. Jan, please stand and say something."

Jan still looked down at her hands, and shook her head.

Addie said, "Peter, she's not well. Let's leave her be for a while." Jan was breathing shallowly, her face flushed.

Morgan nodded and began to speak again. "that's okay, Jan. We certainly understand."

Then Morgan's face seemed to darken as he turned to look around the room. "Let me give you all a report on these three people. The first person we checked on was a Margaret Phillips, who really started the ball rolling for us regarding the corrupt non-profits she knew about. She's dead. A hit-and-run accident in Schenectady, New York. Pardon me but I doubt that this is an unplanned event." He stopped and looked at Jan. "Sorry, Ms. Evlin, but there's more hard-to-handle information coming at all of us before this ends, unless I miss my guess."

Morgan again looked around the room. "And do you know something else, folks?" he said. "All of these crises are coming to a head just about now."

Jan Evlin began to cry, covering her face with her hands. She was comforted by Addie, who looked as though whatever Jan needed she couldn't provide.

Morgan went on relentlessly. "Next is a couple in their 90s – retired dairy farmers from right around here – who are missing. We're still checking that situation out. But I won't hide from you the fact that I am concerned." Morgan had an intensity of attention from the group that was palpable.

"Lastly, early this morning I was asked to check for five Canadian carpenters, a father and four sons. About seven or eight years ago they were hired to come down here to do a large amount of work rebuilding the Davidson house and barn – where the old couple are now. We think this person who bought this house and barn from the Davidsons is our suspect – 'Zeddy' or 'Z' or whatever the hell he's using now for a nickname." Morgan's frustration was breaking through his usual calm exterior. "We are waiting for that report now from our own sources and from our

Canadian police friends. These are dangerous times for us, my friends."

Parker signaled Morgan and received a nod. Parker got to his feet and said, "The reason we're showing concern about these carpenters is that the police detective and I found all their tools up at this 'school' in the Northeast Kingdom. In the basement of one of the buildings. Just junked in there. No attempt to take care of all these personal tools. The four of them probably built the three-building complex up there right after they had finished the farm in this area – the one where we hope the Davidsons are, right now. We're looking for them." He sat down.

Chet from California piped up. "Why would somebody hire builders from Canada to come down here to do this work? There's probably plenty of people within a mile of us right now who could do the work."

Without waiting for a response, he said, almost to himself, "Or did this bird want to keep everything out of the line of sight of gossipers in town?"

"That's what we think, Chet," answered Morgan. "Didn't work as well as they hoped, did it?"

Just then Parker felt a touch on his arm. He turned to find Jan who said in a whispered plea, "Mr. Parker, I have something to tell you. It's something that I now realize – and I've been trying to avoid this for too long. It's very important. It might affect everything." She was holding the small framed picture that Morgan had started around the room.

Parker gestured to Morgan who walked around the table to them. "Peter, can we take a quick break – ten minutes? It may be important."

"Of course," Morgan said. "It's probably a good time to stop for a bit," and he announced the break to the rest of the group. There were sounds of relief as the group got to their feet, stretched, and started to walk around the room, carrying on conversations in low voices.

Parker sat down, facing Jan and Addie. Morgan sauntered over, apparently not wanting anyone to know that he had overheard Jan, and wanted to see what she had to say. Also, thought Parker, cops don't "saunter". They walk directly to their target of the moment and stare at them for a few seconds, then start asking questions. Therefore, to Parker's way of thinking,

Morgan barged into the middle of the group, plopped down, and began listening and taking notes.

"Mr. Parker," Jan said, her face showing a panic that she was unable to control, "'Z' *is* my brother. I know it now." Her voice was quiet, but strung with tension. "I told you I'd continue to think about it, Mr. Parker. Now I know it."

All three listeners leaned forward toward her. Addie and Morgan were mystified.

"What's she talking about, Bill?" asked Morgan.

Parker held up his hand and said, "Wait just a little bit, Peter. What she's going through right now is very tough for her."

Parker then leaned forward and said, "Jan, are you sure? This is extremely important. What caused you to become certain?"

"Mr. Montague triggered it," she said, her voice weak and low. "He called this person 'Zeddy'." Parker acknowledged that he had heard that. His only thought was that the name had a 'Z' in it, but he still couldn't make a solid connection.

"So, Jan, what about it?" Parker asked. "What did it mean to you?"

"A lot of things, Mr. Parker. You see, that nickname of 'Zeddy' reminded me of a day many years ago. I was maybe nine. Really dumb about so many things. One morning I heard a knock at the door. I opened it and saw this scrawny guy standing there. He asked me if 'Zeddy' was there. I told him that there was no such person named 'Zeddy' in the house. Just then my brother came on the scene and said to the visitor, 'She's just my sister, Ernest. She doesn't know anything about anything.' That made me mad Mr. Parker. I said to him, 'And who is Zeddy? I don't know anybody by that name.' For some reason, Mr. Parker, he became very angry, and he hit me – hard. I fell down and hit my head. My brother just laughed and said, 'Let's go, Ernest. We've got some serious learning to do.' I didn't think I'd ever forget that, Mr. Parker, but obviously I did; or at least I did until this moment."

"But it must have been obvious to you that 'Zeddy' was a nickname, Jan. Isn't that a connection that's easily made?"

"Not by a nine-year-old dummy, Mr. Parker. and don't forget that I've been married for over twenty years and I've apparently been able to bury it because I didn't want my hatred for my brother to affect my family. I don't know." Jan looked perplexed and confused. "Whatever, Mr. Parker," she said, some anger showing through, "I didn't 'make the connection', as you put it, until now. I guess it was something I was fighting, too. And now the next step is really tricky, just like my brother used to be." Parker thought about what the Docs Malcom said about "tricky".

"What was 'tricky' about him, Jan?" he asked expectantly.

"I know that he's using another name, Mr. Parker. Maybe this name is just one of dozens over the years, I don't know. But my memory tells me that he won't get very far away from his roots. And the story of his roots start with Zederbian – or 'Z' – or 'Zed'. He's still using that connection to his real name and *daring* us to notice it." She was opening up and the words were flowing out to those who were standing around her. Mr. Montague was there, and Chet from California, and others who Parker hadn't yet met.

"And what does 'Zed' mean, Mr. Parker?" she asked.

"The British use it to refer to the last letter of the alphabet."

"And what's a word, an English word, Mr. Parker, for a number that starts with Z?"

"Zero, or naught" said Chet from California, before Parker could answer.

Suddenly the dawn broke through for Parker. "Reggie Naughton?" he said, softly, looking at Morgan. The gadabout, unobtrusively intrusive, well-dressed shadow of the legislature. And nobody knew why he hung around so much. And the killer of Hugh Hammond? And of "Chugger" of motel fame? And of Gil Birdsall? And how many other deaths was he responsible for?

Parker remembered when he was talking to Morgan in the Statehouse Committee room about Hammond's death, who had been looking through the door, along with a few others? Reggie himself. Had Reggie secreted himself in the bathroom for hours after he'd killed Hammond? And then just casually walked out of the bathroom and down the hall to look at his handiwork and to hear what was being said?

Parker remembered meeting Reggie at the Thrush when he was having dinner with Hugh Hammond. He came over, gushing all hail-fellow-well-met platitudes. And within five minutes, Hugh Hammond had walked out, and in a hurry, too. And he was dead the next day, in a very messy way. Parker didn't blame himself for failing to recognize the signs of panic when Naughton appeared at their table in the Thrush Tavern. Not even when Hammond left the Thrush in such a hurry. He didn't tie the two events together. Until now.

Parker stood up and walked around the group, hands in his pockets, and in deep thought. "Jan, let's go back a bit. I need to know as much as you can remember about your brother. What was your brother like when you both were at home?"

Jan leaned back in her chair, arms folded across her middle. "He was always different, Mr. Parker. I was two years younger and even I could see it. He argued with everybody, no matter what the subject. And people were uncomfortable with him. I stayed away from him as much as I could, which is hard to do when you live in the same house."

Parker knew what that meant. The difference in his case was that his sister wasn't really mean to him – although he thought so at the time.

"How was he different, Jan? I don't mean to pry, but if we're going to end up confronting him, we need to know what we're up against. Anything you can tell us, please."

Jan sunk her chin down toward her chest, eyes closed. After a time she spoke quietly. "We had just moved here from Canada, where I had spent my first eight years. My brother was very smart. Very intelligent. Way beyond us at home and his friends at school. During his junior high school years he received the top grades in his classes. He was still mean and argumentative but he worked to achieve those grades. In spite of everything, my parents were very proud of him. And I remember that I was, too, although I still didn't like him very much. At his eighth grade graduation ceremony he was named valedictorian of his class. He actually gave a speech and it was very well received, too."

Jan got to her feet and started pacing. Her footsteps were the only sounds in the room.

"After that eighth grade graduation exercise he took a summer course from a high school history teacher who was looking for the smartest kids from junior high in some of the schools in the area. Naturally, this teacher extended an invitation to my brother. At the end of the summer we noticed a change in him."

"Was more settled, Jan?" asked Morgan.

"No, Mr. Morgan, he wasn't. He was still contentious, but now he was quarrelsome in the extreme. It was almost as if, over the summer, he had learned how to hate. Unfocused, I think, as I look back on it, and I know that I was more than a little afraid of him. And I was only about eight years old, but I remember the feeling. I think our parents were afraid of him, too. And he was a great deal bigger and stronger then, too.

"Do you think that his summer course affected him?" asked Parker.

She shrugged. "All I know for certain, Mr. Parker, was that he had changed. He had this same teacher for classes for the rest of his years in high school. And his grades went down, too, along with his number of friends, and his arguments with our father were almost daily."

Parker thought that this situation was fairly common. The reasons came from a variety of directions: teenagers believing that their parents were intruding into their private lives; drinking by the parents to excess; parents showing perceived favoritism for another brother or sister; or parents demanding better grades in school – and a lot of other reasons, too.

"What was his reason, Jan? You don't seem to have been afflicted by anything that upset you," Parker said.

Jan hesitated, and then said, "No, Mr. Parker. My parents were great – to both of us. My brother just seemed to reach a tipping point when he entered senior high school. It was then that we really noticed a change in his behavior. I even noticed the difference in him, and I was pretty stupid about such things at that age. It seemed to me that he began to show hatred for people, our country, and our family." Parker was surprised at hearing this. Is this turn of events more common than I thought, he wondered?

"That's a surprise to me, Jan," he said. "Most of the time a freshman in high school isn't that sophisticated."

"Oh, Mr. Parker," she cried, "my brother was way beyond his classmates. They didn't even like having him around any more."

Jan's pacing became more animated. "You see," she said quietly, "he read about topics that were unknown to his acquaintances. Nobody understood him at all, according to his friends. I was only about twelve and I didn't know what he was talking about most of the time. But, as I look back on it, I do believe that it was that summer history course that set him in this direction. I can't be sure, of course, but I think so."

"What do you think he learned in that summer of study that could have changed him that way?" asked Parker, gently probing.

"It started when I was vacuuming – my weekly house chore, you know. I discovered some books hidden under his bed that seemed to be part of his summer course. They were all about Socialism, Communism, and blaming America for all kinds of things – like too much freedom for the individual. Or anyway, that's what I heard my father say after I brought them downstairs."

"In fact," she continued, "my brother even told me, his dumb sister, that a group of trained leaders were the only people who could control and direct America. He actually believed, with the exception of this group of trained leaders, that all Americans were too stupid to have any say in the operation of America. He really liked the European style of Socialism, too." She shook her head in disgust.

"I didn't really understand a lot of this stuff, Mr. Parker, but he seemed very certain about hating America. Even I could see that. And my father could, too, of course. That's what they would fight about." Jan stopped pacing, and looked at the group, as if catching her breath. Parker thought that she was unaware of how much she was revealing about herself, her family, and her brother. Then she turned to Parker with her remarks.

"My father thinks that America is the greatest county in the world. I guess you can see the reason for my father's point of view, Mr. Parker. His family came from nothing. When they came from wherever they did, America gave them a genuine chance to be what they wanted to be. None of his family ever wanted anything else. That's why they loved America. That opportunity. Nothing else. And no other country gave them that chance without government permission slips."

Jan just let all of these thoughts come out, as though they had been repressed for all these years. The room was still eerily silent.

Then Jan suddenly turned to the group. "And they made the most of it, too. They had business successes, one of them became a state Senator, one a doctor, and two of them became lawyers. All the others did what they wanted. None of them achieved the measure of success that some did, but they were happy here. Delighted, I think, would be a better word." She smiled at the group.

Parker said, "It doesn't seem as if neither your father or your brother would back down from their positions, Jan."

"No, they wouldn't, Mr. Parker," she said emphatically. "After a particularly loud argument, when my brother was in his junior year in high school, he shouted at my father that he was leaving home in the morning. He was dropping out of school, he said, and would be starting on his mission of changing America. And he left. I was listening to all of this from the hall. And he left. I never heard from him again. That was twenty-five years ago."

"So you're convinced that this guy 'Z' is your brother?"

"I am now, Mr. Parker. I wrestled with this for a long time. I knew that I couldn't afford to be wrong. I'm not wrong."

There was continued silence in the room. Parker couldn't remember a more moving series of comments in his life. And the reaction from the group in Morgan's living room was the same.

And then some subdued clapping of hands started. And the group moved around Jan thanking her for her words.

Morgan spoke up, to bring the momentum back into their meeting. "Bill, you know what I'm thinking? Remember that nut case in the Montpelier PD that Catherine and Denny were interviewing? Ricardo Rudolfo Murch, I think it was."

"How can I forget Ricky-boy, my buddy?" said Parker. "What about him, Peter?"

"He was picked up again last night and taken into the station."

"Lucky you," said Parker. "Again, Peter, why did you bring him up?"

"He talked about you again. He said that you were going to 'blow up'."

"Blow up?" asked Parker. "You mean like 'explode'?"

"Who in the world knows?" said Morgan. "But people like him bother me. He was told by somebody that he was to look out for you – and probably report back to that somebody if he saw you."

"Pay no attention is my advice to you, Peter. You have enough to be concerned about. The Rickys of this world occupy a tiny sliver of the population."

"Take care of yourself, Bill. I think that somebody out there doesn't like you at all."

Parker nodded and then turned back to Jan. "Jan, you heard what I said. This guy, your brother, is not a very nice man. And we think he's now using the name of Reginald Naughton, who hangs around the Legislature a lot during the sessions. Ever run into him?" Parker described him to her.

Parker saw the wheels turning, but she said, "I guess I've heard of him, Mr. Parker. However, I've spent most of my time in the last few years near the Governor's Office. Almost no time with Legislators. In any case, I've never met him." She then held up her hand.

"Here's the last bit of proof that 'Zeddy' is my brother, Mr. Parker." She held up the small framed photo. "Where in the world did you get this picture?"

Parker looked steadily at Jan. "It just turned up, Jan. I got it along with other things in the course of this situation. Does it mean something to you?"

"That's my parents, and me and my brother. I was maybe twelve. I've never seen this picture before. This was taken a little while before my brother left home. I knew what he looked like twenty-five years ago, and that's him," she said, waving the picture, "but I can't tell you what he looks like now."

Parker felt an excitement that was real and unclouded by other uncertainties. "He's your brother. No question now, Jan. It's funny, isn't it? I mean he must have known that when he was sent here he'd find you here, too."

"No, Mr. Parker, he wouldn't. He would have no reason to suppose that he'd ever see me here in Vermont. We came here from much different directions."

Morgan stepped in at that comment. "Regardless, Jan, we now have definite proof that Naughton is your brother. Then we have to show he's 'Z'. And to do that we have to figure a way to bring him out into the open. If he doesn't come out, then our work here will grind to a halt. Does anybody disagree with that?"

Morgan looked around the room. All of those in attendance had found their way into the circle surrounding Jan Evlin. They turned toward Morgan. No one found fault with his assessment of their situation.

"Ms. Evlin," said Lucas Montague from Louisiana, "we must act on all the information we now have. Whatever role you play in the next scene, I will have to consider you as a weakness in the plans we formulate because you are this man's sister. You understand that, don't you?"

Jan stood up and, hands flat on the table, she leaned toward Montague. Her face was deadly white except for the red of her cheeks. "Mr. Montague, I haven't seen my brother in twenty-five years. I don't know him at all, and my experiences over this last three weeks have told me that I never did. He means less than nothing to me. If this man, who calls himself 'Z', or Zed, or

'Zero', or 'Zeddy', or whatever, has any familial hold on me, that was destroyed when he argued with our father on that last day of his at home. And then he left. It made me happy when he left."

Montague said nothing. He just continued to look directly at Jan.

"But you can't have any workable plan to draw my brother out without me being involved, Mr. Montague," said Jan. "I'm the only bait to which he will respond. And he'll be very, very, careful when he does come out into the open – if he does. At the end of your planning, Mr. Montague, you must have me as the incentive."

Montague just stood there, studying Jan. He nodded. "You see, Ms. Evlin," he said, "there has been so much suffering, destruction, and sadness in my state because of this man and his followers that I can't afford to take chances on this possibility of finding him. Nobody will publicly oppose him because they hide behind a commitment of 'saving our planet for our children'. They care nothing for our children. That's why I can't afford to be casual about who is involved in his apprehension. And I won't be the only one who will feel betrayed if any single one of us is that 'weak link' I mentioned before. However, I think you're right. We need you, and you should know that whatever you do to get close to this man will be dangerous. There will be limits to what we can do to protect you. Just bear that in mind."

Montague didn't look around the group as he spoke. He continued to look at Jan. She returned his gaze for many seconds. Montague turned suddenly to Morgan and said, "Let's get planning, ladies and gentlemen," and sat down.

Parker breathed a sigh of relief. Montague had accepted Jan as the critical part of their ultimate plan.

58

When the meeting ended, four hours later, Parker felt positive, but worried at the same time. Positive because the plan was probably the best they could do. Worried because the plan might not be enough and because Jan was directly involved in the scheme to bring this dangerous man to some sort of justice. And Addie would be stationed inside the double doors of the ground floor entrance to Flanders' second floor office. She'd also be behind the fire door, next to the stairs to the second floor. Her job was to step out and meet Jan if "Z" should not arrive, guiding her to Flanders' office.

Addie's job in this plan was suggested by Morgan. He thought that Jan would need the knowledge that somebody was close to her all through this operation. He reasoned that this person could be a woman, rather than a police officer, or another man. He had too few men at stations where the action might be fast and furious. By that time, Naughton would be too busy trying to get away. In any case, she wouldn't be in the area for very long, and would be hidden from view until the last minute. Parker had listened very politely to Morgan's explanation of Addie's role in this enterprise. He thought the rest of them could manage very well without exposing Addie to the possibility of something going wrong.

"For goodness sake, Willie, don't fret," Addie said. "You guys are stretched on having enough people to do this job. This little piece of work is perfect for me. I won't be anywhere near this guy. What an old woman you are," she said disgustedly.

Then, with a big smile, she added, "I'll just be your average streetwalker, resting in an old building before my second shift starts." To Parker, humor had no place in this situation. He was still not happy, but couldn't raise any arguments to which Addie would listen.

One very satisfying piece of information came out of the meeting, aside from deciding on their approach to "Z". That was the meaning of the code letters and numbers that Hammond's widow had faxed to Hal Birdsall. Lucas Montague and Chet from California had unraveled it in two hours. It was a list of national sabotage projects that the graduates from the Vermont eco-terrorist training camp had taken on. It identified the targets hit, the agents who attacked them, what method was used, and their success or failure. In just the last five years they had attacked 127 developments, large and small, around the country, and were very successful. Only on four occasions had the letter "u" appeared, signifying failure. Montague and Chet knew that a list of this kind had to exist somewhere and they had been looking for it for five years. They came to Vermont and the prize fell into their hands.

They had decided to give all their data to the FBI as soon as they returned home. It was decided that Vermont law enforcement could have it, too, but it was a certainty that the Vermont politicians and lawyers of the left would savagely attack the Vermont law enforcement community for its role in attempting to besmirch the Vermont environmental movement and harm the children, too, of course, in the process. It was also concluded that the pet news media outlets of the ProgDems would concoct a drumbeat of criticism of anybody who publicly stated that Naughton was a menace. Morgan and Small were visibly upset by this implied criticism of their life's work, but they stated that they agreed that the ProgDem Party could at least make recruiting of new officers around the state very difficult.

Another piece of news came out of this meeting that probably wouldn't have meant anything to anybody else in the room except Parker. And to him it solved a puzzle.

Don Flanders had sidled up beside Parker while the identity of "Z" was being uncovered, and said, "Your guess was right, Bill. Our friend Reggie Naughton has an office in the National Life Annex. It faces the parking lot. If a person had a decent pair of binoculars, which, by the way, we found in a drawer of a side table, he could watch everything that happens all across the sea of cars there. For instance, lovers sneaking out to a spot where nobody could possibly see them, or seeing our meeting take place where we also felt some privacy. And anyone who would set up a spy operation in some of the state's largest businesses and organizations wouldn't hesitate to use a simple pair of field glasses. I think that's when he decided to burn up my car. He saw us meeting."

Parker moved Flanders off to one side.

Parker asked, "What was the name of his little business office?"

"The name of his organization, as painted on the entry door - a non-profit, by the way - is The New Path, and they specialize in" – he consulted a small note book – " 'active studies for new approaches to environmental compassion'. Hope this helps a little." He moved off.

Thank you, Don, thought Parker. Reggie is not as careful as he needs to be, is he? Arrogance is bad medicine for bad people.

At this point the meeting ended, and people moved toward their cars. Each had a job to do, some during the plan to bring "Z" into the open, and others to bring information back to their home states in order to prevent more attacks from occurring.

Parker's job in the plan was to get the word to the target through a believable source – or sources. He decided that he would do this job in two ways. The information to get "Z" to move the way Parker wanted him to would need to be confirmed by a second contact by "Z".

He didn't know any sensible members of the House anymore – except one. George Shaver, the House member from the Northeast Kingdom, and Representative for seven towns up there. George was already tested, involving himself in the effort to find a killer in Chittenden County just one year earlier. George was a very sensible and determined man, Parker knew, but he also was generally known to be a little short on subtlety. And that might just be the key.

As they pulled into Hugo's driveway, Parker was practically out of the vehicle before it stopped moving, and headed for the house.

The phone call Parker made to Shaver was, of necessity, evasive, even to the extent of Parker giving a false name to the Statehouse operator.

An hour later the phone rang at Hugo's and Connie picked it up. "Mr. Hingleton? I don't. . . . . oh, yes, sir, Mr. Hingleton," she announced, with a sort of forced gaiety. "He's right here, sir," and handed Parker the phone.

"Representative Shaver?" Parker asked. "This is an old friend of yours. I need to talk to you where we can have some real privacy."

"All right, who the hell is this?" Shaver bellowed. "I'm a busy man and I don't need silly games."

"George, please trust me, and if you want to guess at who this is, do it under your breath. If the word gets out that I'm in the area the autograph seekers will swarm."

Shaver caught on immediately. "I'm sorry I can't meet you. I'll be heading south from Montpelier to a favorite supper spot where I'll be working on a speech for tomorrow. Goodbye." With that he hung up.

Parker grinned to himself. George was darn sharp.

"Hingleton?" asked Connie, with a smile. "Where in the world did you get that name?"

"From the back of a feverishly working brain, my dear. Don't question my brilliance."

"Willie, I'm not sure that sounded like a satisfactory phone call," said Addie.

"It couldn't have been better," said Parker. "George told me where he would be eating dinner, and at about what time."

"Really?" said Addie, her doubt showing. "That was a very brief call. First, I think I heard him swear at you, all the way across the room. Then you spoke for about four seconds. Then he said something that took another four seconds, and then you hung up."

"George told me that he would be at a small restaurant, during the supper hour, in Northfield, and working on a speech. George has never been to the restaurant in Northfield, even when I asked him to join me several times, and he certainly has never worked on a speech for anything. His dinner hour is five o'clock sharp, no matter what. And I'll be there."

Parker looked at Addie and then Jan. "George is the one who can get our ball rolling, if anybody can. After that it's up to you two – and I'm not happy with a plan that puts you both within reach of anybody who would call himself 'Z'. I'm worried enough about Jan."

"We can handle ourselves, Mr. Parker," said Jan. "Remember, it's two against one."

When Parker looked at her he could see that she was actually serious. Parker could think of nothing to say.

59

Parker was waiting for George Shaver when he walked in the door of the Red Kettle at exactly 5:00 PM. Parker got to his feet and greeted his old friend. Only a few people were in the restaurant and none of them were familiar. That's why Parker had many meals there when he was in the Vermont House. Privacy.

"George, you always seem to come through for me when I need you," said Parker as he clapped Shaver on the upper arm.

"I haven't come through yet, Bill. Is this favor a really nutty one – like some others you've asked from me?" They walked over to a small table in the back corner of the small dining room.

"This isn't putting you into a dangerous place, George. But I need a trusted friend who can be depended upon to do something for me without asking any questions."

"Then you've come to the wrong place, Bill. I ask questions. And I want some answers before I do anything for you."

Parker looked at his old friend to see if he was kidding. He wasn't. "The reason I don't want to tell you any of this is that it may get messy at the end. I don't want you to be dragged into anything like that – or touched by it in any way."

Shaver actually looks happy, for goodness sake, thought Parker.

"By God, Bill, this sounds just like last year. I never felt better than I did when I was involved with you and that screwy guy from Burlington. Now I see that I have another chance for that good feeling. Tell me all about it, Bill. I'll be quiet."

When Parker finished the story of the non-profits, then moved on to tell him about the terrorist training camp not too far from where he lived, and the killings that had gone on over the last six months, Shaver looked uncharacteristically shocked.

"Reggie Naughton?" he asked, apparently thunderstruck. "You mean that guy who looks great all the time? The guy who sort of hangs around the Legislature, having quiet conversations with all the ProgDems? And a few others, too, like me, for instance. I bet you're surprised at that." His look was one of pleasure at Parker's expression.

"Bill, you've really made me mad. I knew that these old socialists hate America – or most of 'em, anyway. You know who I mean. Women and men with the long gray hair and no standards, trying to relive their pasts of drugs, sex, and rock-and-roll. And about that school, I heard there was some kind of rough-cut buildings in the core area of the Champion Lands. But none of us ever believed it enough to go in there and look. That's a tough hike. Against the law, too, you know." He grinned.

Then a look of determination came over his face. "I've had a few conversations with that bastard," he said. Shaver seemed to be in another world. "Bill, what do you need me to do?"

Parker described the task. Shaver listened with total attention. "So, what you want is to plant this story so he will come out into the open to get his hands on this evidence that might very well put him away forever. And when he does, you'll know that he's the bad guy. That it?"

Parker nodded.

"And who will be the sacrificial lamb for this tiger? Anybody I know?"

"Lambs, George, lambs," Parker said. He didn't want to tell Shaver, but he knew he had no choice. "Addie and Jan Evlin," he said quietly. "Addie only on the edge of things; but Jan insisted on being the bait."

"Addie's in this? You are a damn fool, Bill. I've always suspected it and now I know for sure. And Jan Evlin? She's that little reporterette from Chittenden County, isn't she?"

Parker nodded again.

"I'll do my best for them, Parker, but I don't give a damn about you. Placing those two women in harm's way," he said derisively, "should make you ashamed of yourself, nice women like those two."

Shaver, still upset at Parker, said, "So, if I remember correctly, Jan has the documentation rounded up of the proof against the person and his organizations and you're going to deliver all of it to your lawyer on Monday night. Your lawyer will certify it as genuine, and unsullied by human hands, copied, filed, and sent to the newspapers, and all that crap. That's three days from now." He thought about the timing.

“I’m not going to be delivering the information, George. Your story will be that Jan Evlin will be bringing it to my lawyer as soon as she receives it from her source. And it will be the last piece of evidence that she’s been working on before she went missing for a few days. And it’s the most important, too. Can you manage it?” asked Parker.

“Sure, that’ll work. I’ll see him tomorrow. He’s always there on Friday during the session. And he’ll certainly be there this Friday because the session could end within a week. Or sooner. He won’t miss that. That will give him the weekend to plan something – if he shows up at all. I’ll say that when this evidence is published and when the trial starts, it will blow the lid off all these crumby organizations that don’t have to pay taxes, but are screwing us in any way they can. And you can’t deliver this proof yourself because you’re in the hospital, getting a bad leg tended to that you got while hiking in the old Champion Land a few days ago. How’m I doing?”

“Just great, George,” said Parker. “Tell it as if it were gossip. That should make it a bit more believable.”

“What if Reggie won’t buy it? The whole damned thing sounds a little contrived, to me. And why are you using Jan Evlin to make the delivery? You could use anybody. You, for instance.”

Parker shrugged. “Yes, it’s sketchy, I’ll admit. I think he’ll come, though, when he learns that this proof against him was accumulated by Jan who will be delivering it to my lawyer at a certain time Monday night. Don’t you think Naughton will come out of hiding if he knows it’s Jan Evlin making the delivery, and who just happens to be his sister!”

That one got through to Shaver. “His sister?” he rasped “That nice person who I like to kid?”

“She’s still a nice person, George,” Parker muttered. “And you don’t have to mention to Naughton that you know she’s his sister. He already knows who she is.”

“Of course she’s a nice person, Bill. If she’s willing to trap that son-of-a-bitch, she must be.”

“Will you see him, George? Can you talk to him? In a group, I think, would be the most believable setting. Just be sure he’s in the group. It would probably be better if you didn’t address any of your remarks to him personally. Just make sure that he hears them.”

"I see him most every day, Bill. Whenever I can, I've always avoided him. But, in the last few months, he seems to sit down with me fairly often and plops down at my table. Very friendly sort of fella. I saw him today, in fact. He didn't look very good, now that I think about it. Eyes all bloodshot. Lack of sleep was what I thought. Tried to talk to me. I wish now that I'd let him. Getting to talk to him won't be hard to do. I only hope I can restrain myself from decking him."

Shaver thought a bit, and then grinned. "I guess my sparkling personality isn't what drew him to my table in the recent past, is it? He just wanted to keep track of any gossip drifting down from the Kingdom about that damn school of his."

"George, decking him wouldn't be the way to convince him of anything. And yes, I don't think he was planning to invite you to a quiet dinner to discuss your political philosophy."

"I know, I know, Bill," he said, still very angry. "I'll get it done for you. I'll put on a performance that will earn an Academy Award. You don't believe it, I know, but I can do it."

After a few instructions about the location, Parker ended with one more piece of information. "My truck will be parked in an alley right across the street on Sunday morning. It's important for it to be there, I think."

"You'll be lucky if it's still there after an hour, Bill. Creeps steal things in Montpelier." Then he shook his head. "No, I'm wrong. Who would steal that wreck, anyway? They haven't yet. Car thieves have the luxury of being choosy."

Parker smiled at Shaver. A good man, he thought. And I've given him a tough job to do. But if anybody can pull it off, he can. Everybody considers him a loud bumpkin. I've just learned that this is a very subtle man. Is his "bumpkinness" not what it seems? Could be.

They shook hands and parted company. As Parker walked to his truck he thought about what George had said about the plan being somewhat contrived. And Parker had to consider that Naughton might be guilty as sin, but still might not come out of hiding. I need that other confirmation. And I've got one, too, he thought suddenly, as he slid behind the wheel.

Parker drove quickly back up to South Burlington and to Hugo's house. He strode through the door and directly to the telephone and dialed Hal Birdsall's number.

"Hal, Bill Parker at this end. Can I come to see you right now? It's important. In your office? At 'Mickey's'? Okay."

"Yes? Great. No, I'm in South Burlington. At Hugo's. Is your secretary still working for you? Excellent. I'll see you in twenty minutes."

Parker put his arm around Addie's shoulders, planted a kiss on her forehead and said, "Addie, come on. You may as well see the kinds of places I've been frequenting while I've been away from your side."

Two minutes later they were speeding north on Route 7. "This is the last piece in the entrapment scheme, sweetie. And you are going to see its distribution system at work. It's in Birdsall's office."

"Where are we going, Willie? It didn't sound as if Mr. Birdsall wanted you in his office."

"That means that what we're going to talk about is important, sweetie, and that's a good thing."

While Parker was talking and driving, Addie was trying to get comfortable in her husband's pickup. She had tried this stunt before and had met with no success whatsoever. The only salvation for her physical well-being was to tilt her whole body to one side for as long as she could and then switch to the other side. This method seemed to work better than sitting the way a normal person would and getting pounded.

Over the years, the best thing she had devised was a useful string of reasons why she couldn't ride with him at that particular moment. When she reached the end of the list, she would start over, hoping that her husband wouldn't recognize a "used" reason.

Addie had attended Champlain College, so Burlington was no mystery to her. But where Parker was going was through an area that she hadn't been in during those years of sopping up her education to beat the band. She noticed that there had been attempts at gentrification in some parts of the city, and the condition of these areas looked good to her and brought back memories. However, gentrification hadn't reached the part of town where they apparently were stopping. "Mickey's" was the only bright spot in a block of blight.

Parker's truck lurched to a stop and he hopped out and ran around to open Addie's door for her. She was surprised. He hadn't done that in ten years.

"You'll like this place, Addie. Hal's son-in-law owns it. The food is Irish and good and the privacy is great. Wait till you see it."

When they entered they saw Hal Birdsall stand up and walk toward them. "Addie, I'm glad to see you again. How was your short trip?" asked Birdsall, with a mischievous grin. Addie somehow knew that Hal was talking about Parker's truck.

"It was unique, Mr. Birdsall. That's the word. Unique."

Parker didn't react.

They sat down in the same corner booth where the first meeting between Parker, Birdsall, and Hugo had taken place.

"What do you need, Bill? You look all in a frenzy," said Birdsall.

"Hal, do you know anybody who works in the Medical Center of Vermont? Somebody who would let me use a phone so that I can call you from there? And who will ask no questions and forget that I was there? And you'd need to record your end of the conversation on your secretary's spy setup."

Both Birdsall and Addie stared at him. They looked incredulous.

"Pardon me, Addie," he said. "This may get rough." Birdsall's anger seemed to swell him up again, as had happened the first time he met Parker.

"Be my guest, Mr. Birdsall," she answered levelly.

In as quiet a tone as he could find on short notice, Birdsall growled, "What the hell are you talking about, Bill? I report news. I don't create it. I'm an editor for the Chittenden Free Progressive, the most important daily paper in the state. You're asking me to do something unethical. Correct?"

"I didn't think what I asked was unethical, Hal. And it's very important. There were a lot of killings in the last six months that happened because of this man, and everything is coming to a head. This has to happen right now. Tonight." Parker knew that he was pushing very hard against Hal Birdsall.

Birdsall gazed at Parker for a long few seconds. Parker had unknowingly forced him to bring the murder of his brother to mind anew.

"As it happens, Bill," he said quietly, as if he had already bowed to Parker's will, "I do know somebody who works in the Medical Center and who is a very honorable and ethical person. This is also someone who has assisted me in the past in certain ventures which will remain closed to nosey busy-bodies – like you, for instance. How long will you need to use her phone?"

"A couple of minutes, maybe three. Long enough to tell you that Jan Evlin is delivering the evidence to my lawyer that we have accumulated against the spy network, the terrorist training camp, the location of the local area indoctrination center, and the identity of the leader of the whole shebang in Vermont. It also will clear up a few murders that have been committed during the last six months in Vermont. Delivery to be made about 8:00 PM on Monday, right after Jan has received the last bit of the evidence. The delivery will be made to Don Flanders' office, and I can't be there because I'm in the hospital having gravel dug out of my leg from my visit to the Northeast Kingdom. Got all that?"

"And I'm to see to it that it's all recorded, right?" asked Birdsall. Parker nodded emphatically.

"Do you believe that 'Z' will surface?" asked Birdsall.

"I don't think he can afford to ignore this message, Hal. If he's guilty of anything, he has to try to stop this evidence from getting into the hands of my lawyer. If he doesn't show, then nothing will bring him out. And we have no case. Simple as that."

"Nothing is simple in this business, Bill. Wouldn't he know that this evidence would have duplicates of everything somewhere? Why would he risk everything on a real chance of gaining nothing?"

"Because I'll also be telling you that these documents are the originals, gathered piece by piece, and delivered at night when things are more quiet and hard to see. Duplicating them will happen in Flanders' office before going public with them. I know it's weak, but it's all we've got. Don't forget – he'll think that if he can destroy these originals, he's home free."

Birdsall stared down at the table top. Then he looked up and said, "Okay, I'll do it. Let me make a call." He got up and stepped quickly to the phone, which was hanging on the wall beside their booth. Incredibly, Parker saw that the phone was shaped like the Emerald Isle itself. It was even green.

The Irish will do anything for publicity, Parker thought.

60

Parker and Addie were sitting in a little restaurant in downtown Burlington, having some of the most delicious soup, breads and small cakes he'd ever tasted. It was called the Flour Shop and the owners were a young man and his wife, who were bustling around the room serving an overload crowd.

One interesting feature of the business signage in the front windows of the little restaurant announced that all their ingredients were the best they could purchase and were mostly non-organic. They didn't think that organically grown produce looked as nice as chemically assisted ones, and the genetically-enhanced produce tasted every bit as good, if not better, than that which was organically grown. On top of that, the proprietor said, the organically grown ingredients provided no additional health benefits to the consumer.

"In fact," the young man said, when Addie asked him about his sign, "in some cases, organically grown foods were not as good for the consumer as those that were helped along with additives."

"My goodness," said Addie, "them's fightin' words around this part of Vermont, I would think."

"Yes, ma'am," the young man said. "But, look around, ma'am," he waved his arm around the packed dining room, "our business has grown every day since we opened. We're starting a mail order business now, sending ready-to-use ingredients for our breads, muffins, and other pastries, along with our recipes, all over New England. That part of the business is showing signs of being a bigger revenue producer than our restaurant."

"Any trouble with the organic farmers?" asked Parker.

"A little. City inspectors, although I had my doubts about that, were sent in to check out our equipment and our space for the disabled customers. For the first month, they dropped in every week. City fire inspectors came in every week for the first two months. When I asked for their identities, they did a lot of hemming and hawing. They couldn't find anything wrong. The bureaucracy is very active in this city, if they are behind these multiple checks. Progressives order things like this to be done and the bureaucracy jumps. One of them told us that there are businesses right in this area that have never been checked in the last five years. We haven't seen inspectors for a while. Makes me think they weren't real, somehow, but we did what they wanted. They know we're okay. And we keep it that way."

"Well, your food and soup is wonderful. If you keep up the quality, you'll have a total success," said Parker.

"Don't worry about that, sir," the young man said, smiling. "Our competition can't keep up with us on that score." Then he disappeared into the melee to bring out more non-organic taste treats for other consumers – none of whom seemed to worry about being poisoned by the food.

"How do you feel, Addie?" Parker asked. "Just two days more and you're on Broadway at Flanders' office. I can't help being mightily concerned for both you and Jan."

"It's the only way to protect Jan, Willie. Two people in the immediate area will be adequate. I'm just the helper, anyway. But the real point is for Jan to know she's not alone. I know we can't physically defeat 'Z', if it comes to that, but I'm betting that he won't do anything to the two of us. I probably won't even be in the scene. He'll just grab the evidence and be gone, and into your clutches. And Jan is his sister, after all. He didn't kill her when he could have, so I don't think he will do anything bad now."

It all sounded so logical to Parker. That's probably why I don't trust it, he decided. "Don't you think that he'll view it as a situation that may not be believable?" asked Parker. "I mean, it's going to be a very dangerous situation that he's walking into. And he'll know it. That's why I don't think he'll come." Parker was trying to stay calm. He didn't want to make Addie nervous.

"Willie," Addie said, with firmness, "he has to come. He can't afford to stay away. And he's a chance-taker, isn't he? I think that's what you said. He'll be there, Willie. If he believes that the evidence is real - and he'll have to believe it, what with you giving him so much trouble at both NPF I and II - he will believe that he's got only one chance to survive. He must have that evidence. He can't afford to guess about the importance of it. If he gets his hands on it, he can destroy it and then play innocent. And the press will defend him and you'll be the bad guy. He'll try to destroy you – and they'll help him."

Parker surrendered and raised his flag of capitulation. "I think he'll make his try for the papers as soon as Jan approaches the double doors to Flanders' office building," said Parker. "You agree?"

Addie nodded, her mouth full of buttered wheat biscuits. "That's the only chance he'll have," she said, after chewing a bit more. "He has no idea where she is. He'll only know where she is when he sees her stepping out of a cab in front of Flanders' office. And when he takes the papers, you'll move in. Right?"

At that moment, Addie's cell phone buzzed. Catherine Morgan had loaned Addie her personal phone for the next few hours. Maybe she was just testing it out.

Addie listened and then passed it over to Parker. "It's Peter, Willie."

Parker took this new-fangled contraption and held it up to his ear. Addie was frantically waving at him. He switched the ends around so that he could hear what Morgan had to say instead of listening to empty air. He wasn't embarrassed for his ignorance.

"Peter, what's going on?" asked Parker. He was never sure if the person he was talking at could hear him. The earpiece and the speaking end seemed to be too close together.

"Some news, Bill. Some very bad, and some very good."

Parker had a sinking feeling. "Go ahead, Peter."

"The Canadian carpenters, the father and three sons? Our friends in Canada have told us that those folks never came back from across the border. There was a big search up there, because the families had been called by the old man to tell them they were all done in Vermont and would be home the next day. They never appeared. The Mounties up there did most of their looking on the Canadian side of the border. I guess there was some checking down here, but there was no real record of them ever being here."

Parker had never felt worse in his life.

"So the search ended about five years ago. Well, the state police have been going over the site of the fire which took out three buildings up there. In one of the cellar holes, which had been cleaned out with a back hoe, the operator scraped a little too clean. He had opened up a grave. There were four bodies in there. We got the word that they were all shot in the back of the head. Assassination style. They are checking things out up there, but we know that those are no doubt the Canadian carpenters. We're letting them know what we think in the most subtle way possible. We can't go further until this is all over."

Parker couldn't speak. He and Bud Small had probably stood on that grave. This whole sickening confrontation had only grown more terrible.

"Bill, you okay?"

"Yes, Peter. What else have you got?" Parker felt down and out.

"I went up to the Davidsons' with two other officers. The house was empty, the barn was empty, and the place was silent. We walked around, knowing that we had no warrants to search, to see if there was a sign of activity at all. We saw the helicopter under some tarps, and we looked it over. Nothing to note there. And then one of my officers heard a voice from the direction of the old silo, across the drive from the barn. We went over to it and, from the low door, out climbed the Davidsons. They'd been in there for two days. They were in very shaky shape, but still feisty for 90 plus years old. Amazing, really."

"So they're okay then?" asked Parker.

"Right as rain," said Morgan. "And they told us a very interesting story."

"I'll bet," said Parker, dreading the "story" to come.

Morgan told Parker the "story", which was, of course, exactly what had happened. However, the Davidsons gave no names.

"Then this old guy told us," Morgan said, "that he had murdered somebody. Perfectly straight face, and matter-of-fact, he was. He'd dragged the body into the woods behind the barn."

"I think we all blinked at that. He took us over to the spot and, sure enough, there was certainly a body. The damn pitch fork was still in his back, for God's sake."

"Then he told us that story, too. We have no idea who was there, who the woman was who left with the mystery man, and where they went. Probably never will know. I called the department and they got the proper people up to the farm and all the procedural things were taken care of. Except who was there and then left Any ideas?"

"No," said Parker.

"Let's talk about it sometime, Bill, shall we?"

Parker didn't answer.

"The body was of a Mr. Milo Shumsky, of Chicago," said Morgan. "He had all of his identification information in his pockets, including a paycheck stub from an operation called The New Path, whatever that is. He also had a Vermont driver's license in the form of a picture ID. We took all that documentation and ran a check on him. This SOB is wanted for a whole list of things around the country, including larceny, assault with a deadly weapon, attempted murder, murder, and incitement to riot. He dropped out of sight about ten years ago. He's a really bad boy, Bill. The world is now better off."

"Peter, I don't have any information for you regarding the Canadian carpenters, or the body at the Davidsons. But the New Path has an office in the Vermont Life building. Because of this check you've made, isn't that enough to go into that office and look around? It's possible that someone may have been there ahead of you, of course. I'm not sure, but you should know about that possibility." Parker was thinking of Flanders. "If I'm right, then this person is a friend." That statement didn't, in any way, cool down Morgan. He was thinking of Parker and how to throttle him.

"We'll talk about this whole thing after we catch Naughton. Okay?"

"I'm sure it is, Bill," grumbled Morgan.. "Thanks for the info."

Parker knew that Morgan was furious.

It was just after midnight and extremely early, Parker's creaking body announced, on Saturday morning, when he stopped his venerable old pickup on the street where Flanders' office overlooked a piece of Montpelier that had seen better days. Or maybe, Parker considered, gentrification had simply passed this section of Montpelier by.

He pulled his truck into an alley formed by two old, brick, warehouses that were no longer in official use. Peter Morgan had told him that there were no real businesses in this section of Montpelier. Just an office in a slum house promoting the League for the Protection of Vermont Sex Offenders and a small theatre that produced plays of an "avant garde" nature, so proclaimed by a poster. The hand-lettered sign on the building announced that the plays were locally written, locally acted, and locally accepted as "the best New England has to offer". If that's true, Parker mused, then he would shudder to think of the production quality of the other playhouses in the five state region.

As Morgan had put it, "it's just a section of Montpelier that's waiting anxiously for the wrecking ball, but it never comes."

Perfect, thought Parker, and he shut down the engine and decided to sit there in the quiet dark for a few minutes before he took to the shadows, and disappeared. He wasn't trying to hide his truck. It would be impossible in this part of Montpelier, anyway. He just wanted it to be out of the limelight, but still handy.

He had had two interesting conversations in the last twelve hours. The first was with Bud Small, who was recovering nicely from the momentum of two steel fry pans that had tried to enter his body unannounced.

Bud talked about his phone conversation with John Chapman, of Bloomfield, Vermont, and surrounding environs. The subject was John's thought that Gil Birdsall had been murdered, rather than the official, and easier position that he met with a hunting accident.

"Well, Bud, how did that go?" asked Parker, wishing that he had been able to listen in.

"Bill, do you know this guy?" Bud asked. His voice and tone seemed to find that possibility an impossibility. Small seemed mystified that Parker, by his comments regarding Chapman, apparently not only knew him but respected him, too.

"A little," Parker answered, without any emotion.

"Well, first of all, he thinks you're the best thing since flush toilets, as he put it."

"Really?" said Parker. This was pure Chapman.

"He knew you were responsible for his appointment to the exalted position of special assistant to the County Sheriff up that way. Chapman believes you have an incredible gift for recognizing talent. That's why you have his regard."

"Oh," said Parker. "And what did you find out about Gil Birdsall's shooting death? As I recall, John didn't think much of the official version."

"Bill, you were right. Mr. Chapman is a wonderful story teller. I've never heard a better one. And that includes my father-in-law, who's great at it. However, unlike my father-in-law, Mr. Chapman never gets to any point at all if he doesn't choose to. And you have to be extremely alert if he does."

Parker grinned to himself. John would have loved to have heard Small referring to him as "Mr." Chapman.

"You have to understand, Bud," said Parker, "that John tells his *real* story to you by telling you another story. You have to be very sensitive to the little tendrils that are running through John's stories."

Parker could almost see Bud's smile. "Mr. Chapman should be in the Vermont Senate. He's so subtle I couldn't pick up any 'tendrils' at all."

"What's his conclusion, Bud?" asked Parker. "What's John's assessment of Gil Birdsall's death?"

"The body was found in a place where no hunter, or even a hiker, would be found, which was on a hillside facing east, directly into the sun at a time of day when the deer would be moving. The sun in his eyes would allow the hunter to only see 180°, and that direction was nothing but thick slash. So this combination would prevent him from seeing anything at all, including the view. If he was a real hunter, he simply wouldn't be there. Of course, Mr. Chapman is talking about the morning. I asked him if the afternoon would put a different meaning on the subject of murder or no murder. He said to me, 'No, it wouldn't, young man. Who in their right mind would be up and about only in the afternoon?' Mr. Parker, I still haven't figured that one out yet." Parker listened with total enjoyment. It was the high point of his day, no matter what else happened.

"It was obvious to Mr. Chapman," said Small, earnestly, continuing on, "that Gil had been shot in another place and dragged to the spot where he was found. Mr. Chapman also mentioned that Gil's body may have been dumped there with the idea that it not be found at all. Using his description of the place and photos that the Sheriff e-mailed to me, I tend to agree with him. He told me that he had argued with the county Sheriff for a long time about it."

"No other physical evidence?" asked Parker.

"Nope," answered Small. "I want you to understand, too, Bill, that this revealing information from Mr. Chapman was told to me by the use of his story about three groundhogs that had had a family squabble in the Spring."

"Thanks for telling me that, Bud. It puts a certain texture on it, doesn't it? Also, would you call the County Sheriff?" asked Parker. "I'd be interested in what he says."

"After I cleared my head from the talk with Mr. Chapman, I did just that. At first, he wouldn't talk to me about Gil Birdsall's death. Then I mentioned your name. That opened the floodgates. He asked me if I 'was hanging around with that disgraced politician?'"

Parker laughed out loud. Thibeault knew that the word would get back to him.

"He said that he actually agreed with Mr. Chapman's thoughts on the location of the body. In fact, he told me that he's still looking into it. Unofficially, of course. He's assigned Mr. Chapman and a guy named Bob Murray, who are his 'special assistants', to keep the heat under that pot. But he has absolutely nothing to base any other sort of opinion on except that it was a hunting accident. You know, Mr. Parker, I almost told him the whole story, but held back until I talked to you. By the way, the Sheriff wanted me to tell you that . . here's the exact quote, Bill, from my notes. Sheriff Thibeault wanted it delivered accurately. 'Tell that nosey SOB that the long-legged blonde lawyer from Arizona is in Bloomfield, visiting Bob Murray'. That's it, Bill. What's that mean?"

"Bud, my boy, it means that nature is at work, and there's no help we can provide to move it along any faster."

Parker was made happy by that message. That's why the human race will never die out, he thought. Men and women make an infinite number of choices regarding their selected mates. Even the outlandish possibilities are on the table, along with all the others.

Just think, he considered. A bright, confident, pretty, and long-legged lawyer from Snowflake, Arizona, might just select steady Bob Murray, a quiet, bashful, rough-hewn ridge runner from the Northeast Kingdom in Vermont. Some lawyers might be smart, after all.

Parker came back to the present. "That's a good thought, Bud. Go ahead and tell Sheriff Thibeault. He will be our agent-in-place in the Kingdom. Let me know his reaction, please. However, I wouldn't tell him about our little sojourn into NPF II. But maybe, just maybe, your 'sources' could have mentioned to you in passing that they heard that there was a big fire somewhere up there and could the Sheriff comment on it?"

"I'll do it, Bill," he said. "We need to know what's found after the fire is discovered – which it no doubt is, by now."

“One other thing, Bud. Can I talk freely to you?” asked Parker.

Small, knowing what Parker was really asking, said, “Yes, we’re fine.”

“When we were up at NPF II and were just getting out as fast as we could, you stayed behind. I didn’t know why, but after a few minutes, I saw you running through the woods toward me. The next thing I knew was that all three buildings were on fire. Did that surprise you?” asked Parker.

“No, it didn’t, Bill,” Small replied, his voice quiet.

“Can I ask what you did in there?”

There was a period of time when Small said nothing – and neither did Parker.

“Do you remember the box of candles we found in one of the buildings? Upstairs in the bunkhouse, as I recall. Remember those?”

Parker did. “Yes,” he answered.

“I grabbed one of those candles and headed into the cellar of that building, broke open some cans of kerosene and let them dribble out onto the dirt floor. Then I took a hell of a chance. I cut off about a quarter inch of candle, leaving a stub of wick, put a small piece of paper on the floor and set that stubby candle on it, and very carefully lit it. Kerosene actually has a flash point that makes it hard to get burning. Not like gasoline, which will blow up easily. I hoped it would burn down, touch off the small piece of paper, and get something going. I did the same thing in the other buildings, and then I ran for your hiding place. There’s a chance that that combination won’t work, but with the kerosene all over the place, it had a good chance. The candles burned down a little faster than I planned on, but they worked. The kerosene started to warm up and then a vapor of it was in the air. The vapor is all that’s needed to start kerosene going, ending in a big swoosh. It worked to perfection. I thought it was the proper thing to do.”

“You took three really bad people with it.”

Small didn’t comment. He just kept moving forward. “There were many reasons, Bill, including professional ones, why we should have left those buildings standing. However, I knew that after the daily newspapers had whitewashed the whole terrorist school thing, the ProgDems would have converted them into a vacation playpen for politicians and the leaders of their support organizations. You know, as a reward for their hard work in

Montpelier. And the terrorist training would have continued. All this goes no further. Right?"

"All what?" asked Parker.

The second phone call was from Catherine Morgan. "Mr. Parker," she said, "I am concerned about Ricky Murch – you remember him? He was one of the people who knew you were involved in the non-profit investigation. We interviewed him in the station and you happened to drop in."

"Yes, I do remember Ricky. A strange guy, who had no sense whatsoever about anything. What about him, Catherine?"

"I was part of a search team that had a warrant to look at his apartment. On another matter entirely. Among the items I found were instruction pamphlets for the building of explosive devices."

"Explosive devices?" Parker cried. "Ricky will blow himself up first. Why are you telling me? Your husband and I talked about Ricky just hours ago."

"I've called you because of those same remarks of Ricky's just hours ago, Mr. Parker, about blowing you up. We have some more information."

"Let's hear it Catherine, but I don't think he'll be a danger to me."

"I hope you're right about that, Mr. Parker. I'm referring, however, to his words about the 'alphabet', and 'the end', 'spelling test', and 'he is last'. Remember those inexplicable words?"

"Yes, I do, Catherine. Weird stuff from a really weird guy. Do drugs do that to you, after a while, or is he simply off the edge by choice?"

Catherine didn't comment, but went right on with her subject. "I think he was referring to 'Z', Mr. Parker."

"Why, Catherine?" Parker was intrigued but not hopeful. He'd been disappointed too many times in trying to nail 'Z'.

"Simply stated, because the 'spelling test' is at the 'end' of the 'alphabet', Mr. Parker, and the 'last' is 'Z'."

The light bulb flashed for Parker. He instantly knew she was correct. Convoluted as it was, Catherine Morgan had connected words and thoughts into something coherent. That is, if anything connected to Ricky could be called coherent.

"Catherine," Parker said with enthusiasm, "I think you're right. And if you are, then we should be heartened by this development rather than downcast by it. If 'Z' is Ricky's mentor, then ‘Z’ has had to reach pretty far down into the talent barrel for helpers. Let’s consider it in that light.”

“We meet some really strange people in our line of work, Mr. Parker. And those experiences make us think that Ricky is a danger to anybody he comes across when in the mood.”

“Catherine, I don’t think that Ricky will ever harm anyone with a bomb. He’ll do much more damage to people with his nutty form of government that he actually teaches to kids. And school boards allow him, and others like him, to teach junk like that. I think they’re the real culprits. Remember that subject of his? The Discipline for the New Future? I may have forgotten his other inane ideas but I haven’t forgotten his new form of government. And if he has his way, we’ll all be living in his world of the Discipline for the New Future. I don’t know exactly what it means but it doesn’t sound good for anybody who dislikes intrusive government.”

Catherine Morgan remembered the Discipline, too, but all she wanted to say before hanging up was, “Just so you know, Mr. Parker. I felt strongly enough about it to talk with Peter. He agreed with me, and asked me to call you.”

“Catherine, you’re brilliant. Does that bum of a husband of yours ever tell you that?”

“Every day, Mr. Parker, every day. I’m sick of hearing it.”

Parker slipped out of his truck after an hour of sitting and watching and walked down the alley to more open ground. He stayed out of the bloom of a streetlight and watched for any movement. He was alone.

He stepped out into the open and trotted through the back alleys and empty lots to the Montpelier PD. It took about a half hour of steady trotting for the trip. He even took care to stay out of any light there. He went to the back door and knocked. The door opened within seconds and Parker slipped through into the dark interior. Morgan asked quietly, “Okay?”

“Fine,” said Parker. Then Morgan snapped on the light. “Thanks for the special help this evening,” said Parker. “You’ve been operating over the line, haven’t you?”

Morgan just shrugged. Changing the subject, he said, "I've got an off-duty officer who's willing to drive you back up to South Burlington, if you want, Bill. Any interest?"

"That would be swell, Peter. Can we go now?"

Morgan went to the doorway and said, "Denny, are you ready to drive Parker north?"

A tough looking officer came to the doorway. It was the Denny who had interviewed Ricky Murch. "Ready, Mr. Parker? We can talk about Ricky while we go."

Parker smiled and walked out to the car.

61

The strong light of May daytime was gone at 7:30 in the evening on the Sunday of the confrontation, if there was to be one. And it was still chilly. Parker was wearing a black sweatshirt and slacks. Dark blue sneakers completed his outfit. Blending in was all that Parker ever wanted in his whole life and after 45 years of wanting it, it took until this very moment to bring it about. And he felt stupid in this costume. But Morgan had insisted.

The lights were on in the lawyer's office and Parker thought he could see movements through the front windows. Only about another half hour and the show would be on. He felt calm and yet under pressure at the same time. If "Z" came forward tonight, and if Parker and his friends were able to put him away, they could clear up at least six murders – maybe more.

Parker had no doubt, after listening to Addie, that "Z" would show up. However, he still couldn't shake the thought that the plan *was* a gamble. So many things could go off center just a little and everything would turn to dust. The other bit players involved in this plan were showing some doubt, too, but their obvious false confidence only made Parker more determined to think positively. Parker and his people tried to make provisions in their plan for all the possible ways in which "Z" could act.

Parker was standing in the shadows of a used car lot which had a few old car wrecks scattered through its expanse. Possibly it was the graveyard for cars that had been carried in inventory by the dealer, sold, and then returned as unsatisfactory transportation by the disappointed and very angry owners. By that time, of course, the dealer was out of business and probably out of the state. Maybe the car purchasers of yesteryear had decided to pay back the dealer by turning his lot into a real junkyard by dumping off the junk he'd sold them, thought Parker.

The lot was beside one of the old warehouses that also sheltered his truck, and it afforded him a decent, but not perfect, view up to the lighted windows of Flanders' office and of the whole street that passed in front of his building.

Addie was already in position, and Parker would get to her just as soon as this action was on the wane.

A block away a black van waited in the murky darkness. It was the van in which Addie had ridden to the scene, and from there had walked behind the block of old buildings to her station. She carried a surprisingly heavy walking stick.

Parker had four other watchers in the area. Mr. California and Mr. Louisiana were there somewhere, along with Hugo and Hal Birdsall.

Birdsall had insisted on being involved. "After all," Birdsall had said to Parker, with irrefutable logic, but not much common sense, "I started this whole damn thing by giving Jan this dangerous assignment, and I insist that I be in at the end of it."

How much help Birdsall would be is questionable, thought Parker. And then again, to be fair, Parker decided that Birdsall might just be able to do as well as he, himself, could.

Parker looked at his watch. It was showing that they had about twenty minutes left until the witching hour. In order to stay alert, Parker decided to call on the training he'd received while in Vietnam. For a few minutes, put your mind in another place. Doing that was restful for the main switchboard of a person's being. So he did.

Parker's view of the street in semi-darkness, relieved only by cones of illumination from streetlights of very low power, reminded him of the great Bogart movie "Casablanca".

And specifically, he thought of that great scene when Bogie and Claude Raines, at the end of the movie, were walking away over the tarmac of the airport in Casablanca, pools of lamplight charting their path, rain puddles around their feet, and Bogie saying, as far as Parker's memory would permit, "Louis, I think this is going to be the beginning of a beautiful friendship" as they both went off to 1939 Spain to fight Nazis. Parker admitted to himself that he'd like to be Bogie, for just that one sequence.

Then he shook himself figuratively, back into real life. Good Lord, he said to himself, I've never told anybody, including Addie, about that nutty fantasy.

At that moment he heard some urgent words from just up the street from his perch. "Get the hell out of here, you nitwit – right now."

Staying in shadows as well as he could, Parker moved in the direction of the sounds. It was Hugo, and he had a bedraggled looking figure by the collar. It was Ricardo Rudolpho Murch, the one and only. Murch was wearing a raincoat about eight sizes too big, a floppy hat reminiscent of Fagin's, and his fashionable bowling shoes on his feet.

"Ricky, what the hell are you doing here?" rasped Parker. "Get out right now."

Ricky looked at Parker as if he'd never seen him before. And then his face brightened. "It's Mr. Target," he said, with real pleasure. Before Parker could inquire again, Ricky said, in his sing-song way, "I'm leaving now, Mr. Parker, for good. I'm following my leader. You'll never see me again. My life is changing and I have promises. Real promises. I've done my requested work. Goodbye, Mr. Parker, and goodbye to you, you cruel and unfeeling black person."

Parker interrupted Hugo from the act of breaking Ricky's neck, saying, "Hugo, let him go. He's ignorant, stupid, has delusions of grandeur, has been strung out on drugs for years, and likes little kids."

"Drugs? No, not hard drugs," screamed Ricky. "My medicinal treatments require certain medications of an experimental nature. Not recognized by today's medical dullards. I have a prescription from my 'Mind Medicine' futurist. He knows what's best." Ricky began to sob.

"Let him go, Hugo. He won't remember any of this in an hour."

Parker felt no sympathy for Ricky. He'd met many Rickys in his life. They welcomed their own destruction by maybe graduating from high school or college in total ignorance, then complaining about their victimization by others, and moving to drugs to ease their emotional pain. They were losers by their own actions – nobody else had a hand in their demise.

Ricky wobbled off down the street, whistling, singing, and crying. Parker looked over at the lighted windows in the front of Flanders' office. When he looked back down the lighted street, he was prepared to see the retreating back of one Ricardo Rudolpho Murch. Instead he was surprised to see that Ricky had suddenly disappeared in the gloom.

It was just eight o'clock and Parker saw no movement in the street. An occasional car went by, but didn't stop or even slow.

Parker's group had arrived at about 7:00 PM and quietly and unobtrusively took up their stations. Parker had asked them to check all around Flanders' building, expanding their circle of search to three or four blocks, and look for a car, any car, that was parked anywhere in their area. They were to jot down the license number and relay it to Catherine Morgan, and she would call her husband to determine who owned the vehicle. If any vehicle seemed suspicious, they were to tell Catherine, and her husband would send around a patrol car to check things out. They had reported eleven cars but all had a reason for being where they were found.

Parker moved his gaze up the street to find out if Jan had kept to her specified time. Suddenly, a cab pulled up on the corner of the block in which Flanders' building was located. This was not part of the plan. The cab was supposed to stop directly in front of the double doors of Flanders' building, thus shortening the amount of open ground she had to walk. Jan had obviously just changed that, deciding to put herself at extra risk by requiring a 100 yard walk.

Stepping out of the cab and into a weak pool of light was Jan, striding purposefully along, with a briefcase tucked under her arm. The low capacity lights still gave enough help to his vision so that he was able to watch Jan all the way to the front doors of Flanders' building. Parker was ready for anything. His nerves were just singing with a high pitched whine.

Nothing happened. No sound at all.

Jan arrived at the doors and, after a few seconds, turned toward the double doors, pushed them open and disappeared inside.

Parker and his troop made no move or sound. Parker looked up and down the street. No movement. Damn, he thought, what's going on?

As he swept his gaze back up the street he looked up at the lighted windows of Flanders' office. They were on as before.

Well, he thought, we planned to stay out here for at least fifteen minutes after Jan and Addie had gone up to the office, so we will. And then go over to Flanders' office for an after-action meeting.

He looked up again at the windows in Flanders' office. He stopped his casual viewing. The drapes had been pulled. He could see the that the lights were on, even then, but somebody had pulled them across the windows. The plan called for the windows to be unobstructed at all times. And then he knew.

Parker started running. He reached the doors and slammed through them and pounded up the stairs, reaching the closed door. He twisted the handle and, surprisingly, it opened. He burst into the room. Addie and Jan were sitting together on a couch, hands clasped in their laps, and their heads bowed. Flanders was sitting in his desk chair, but the upper half of his body was lying forward on his desk. He was face down in a pool of blood, and in that attitude of looseness that was unmistakable.

As Parker looked around the room, suddenly Reggie Naughton stepped out from behind the open door, looking cool and comfortable. A silenced handgun was aimed directly at Parker.

"Good evening, Mr. Parker. You've arrived just in time. I expected you, you know. You tried to be clever. You aren't. But you are a damned nuisance." He had a slight smirk on his face.

"I take it that this is your wife?" He gestured toward the end of the couch on which Addie sat.

Parker said nothing.

"Are you going to kill us all, you bastard?" Parker's voice didn't sound real to him.

"Oh, I'm thinking about that, Mr. Parker. This poor excuse for a man," and motioned with his head back toward Flanders, "tried to attack me when I entered his office two hours ago. I didn't have time to negotiate with him." Cold as a scorpion thought Parker.

"You can't kill your own sister. That's just beyond belief." No matter what, keep this madman talking, he thought. And hope that a distraction of some sort would occur for just long enough for me to try to stop him from killing anybody, Parker thought.

"She's not my sister, Mr. Parker. Not really, anyway. You know that we haven't seen each other in over twenty-five years. We hated each other when we were living in the same house. No, killing Janice would not be a problem for me. Nor the two of you either."

"You've killed so many people," said Parker. "It all started with Gil Birdsall, didn't it? And then Chugger, at the motel? And the Canadian carpenters? What about them? And Hugh Hammond?"

Naughton smiled broadly. With no reaction to Parker's words, he said, "They had to die. They got too close to certain things."

"When you killed Hammond in his Committee Room, Naughton, did you stay in that bathroom for all those hours? I'm just curious."

Naughton looked at Parker with irritation. "You gave me some trouble, Parker. You guessed fairly well. I spent an hour in the bathroom before I met with the talkative Hugh Hammond, and another hour after his body had been found. It was fascinating to be in the crowd standing around and saying things like, 'how could he have done it?'" Naughton's smile was without emotion and he looked untroubled.

"I learned two items of interest when I was with him in the Committee Room, Mr. Parker," Naughton said. "The first was that Hammond was ready to talk to people I didn't consider worthy of hearing his information. That realization was unfortunate for him. And the information I needed was in that damned barn of his, so he said. I couldn't find it. He obviously gave me the wrong location, even under some persuasion."

Naughton was showing an edge to his anger. "I realized then that he had some courage. I didn't expect that. Then I lost patience, you see, and I took care of him permanently, as I had planned." Naughton kept his eyes steadily on Parker.

"So, I began to follow you, with some help, of course. I had to assume that you knew where Hammond's little treasures were to be found in his barn. I made that decision while in the Thrush that night that you and Hammond had dinner. He spoke much too loudly. I didn't think it would be too many days before you headed for Hammond's barn. All I had to do was wait and you'd lead me to the hidden information. I wasn't really concerned even if someone else had found it before I did. They would look at the pictures – that was what the information consisted of – and then stop right there, confused and deciding that the pictures weren't worth any more investigation. You, however, were a different matter. I was convinced that you'd follow them up, based on the history of your inquisitiveness. And you performed true to form. You even went to NPF II. I didn't expect that. You fooled me, you see."

Parker was overwhelmed by Naughton's willingness to open up like this. He knew, however, that it could mean only one thing. Naughton knew that he could brag, if that's what he was doing, without worrying about what Parker would say. Because Parker wasn't going to be saying anything to anybody again. And that included Addie and Jan.

"I also learned," said Naughton, "that, although you presented no threat, you were checking into things. I had my network providing me with information, and they first hinted at your presence on the scene. So you were next, but it had to look like an accident, so I took time to find the best way."

"It sure as hell wasn't the best way to kill us in the Hammond barn," said Parker. "That was pretty dumb."

Naughton's face reddened, but he quickly returned to his lethal composure.

"I knew that Hammond was going to die in the Committee Room, of course. It was my plan. What a wonderful way to send a message to those who knew things about me. And it was so easy. Kill him, back to the bathroom, clean up, wait for commotion, step out carefully, and walk back to the Committee Room. Who would ever think that the killer would go back to that room ever again? Nobody, that's who. And that's why I did it. It was great fun for me."

"But not for Hammond, was it?"

"Your hands aren't clean, either, are they, Bill?" Naughton said. "How about the three men at NPF II? Oh, I know all about your presence up there. I should kill you for burning the compound down."

"I don't think the world will miss those three, Naughton," said Parker. "And killing us won't change a thing for you, either. The word is out about your non-profit friends and your phony environmental workshop."

Naughton smiled again. "Please, Mr. Parker, don't try to mislead me. According to my information sources, and they're very good ones, you know, it's all quiet on the western front, as they say. Not a twitch on the line. I would have heard something, if it was out there. And do you know something, Mr. Parker? Some of my sources don't even know they're helping me."

A happy look spread across Naughton's face. "And I have willing support in the Legislature. There are even a few of them who hate America, too, you know. The difference is that, beyond maybe a dozen legislators, the rest of the ProgDems don't even know that they're being used. They don't really care. Completely ignorant and they work to remain that way. Most of them even have somebody in their party write their letters to their constituents. They are there to take up space and to vote the way they're told. And they do it every time. The members of the Progressive/Democrat coalition simply like to be called 'Representative' or 'Senator'. They all speak well, too. They just don't know anything worth repeating. To actually do anything significant is well beyond them. But Vermonters elect them, and then complain about what's 'going on in Montpelier'." He laughed delightedly.

Parker said nothing.

"Now," said Naughton, suddenly all business and efficiency, "we have things to do. First, Mr. Parker, empty all the contents of your pockets on that chair beside you. Hurry up. If something doesn't happen right now, I'll put a bullet in your wife's knee. If nothing happens then, it's the other knee. Get the picture? Good." Parker nodded and started doing as he was told. He had never felt so helpless in his life. And there was a hatred welling up in him that exceeded anything he'd ever felt before.

Jan was still looking down at the floor. Addie had found the energy to speak to Naughton. "You have no chance, Naughton. The area outside is covered. You can't get out. Even if you kill us all, you will lose. You're in an impossible situation."

Naughton smiled again. "Mrs. Parker - Addie, is it? You're a brave one; I'll give you that. But you're a wrong one, too. Do you think I'd come into this neighborhood without prior knowledge of its advantages to someone who wanted to get out quickly if they had to? Of course not. I'm about to pull off a disappearing act. And you're going to help me by remaining in this office. And no noise. No phone calls. Understand, Mrs. Parker?"

Addie said nothing.

Looking at Parker, Naughton said, "Hand me your truck keys, Mr. Parker. My own vehicle is well out of range of this place. In order to disappear, I will need wheels. Yours will be perfect for a short time. Oh, yes, I know where it is. I also had word from one of my helpers when you put it there. It helps because now when I leave I'll be in your truck. Who will question the driver of that truck? Everyone who sees it will assume it's you who's driving."

Parker handed Naughton the keys.

"Thank you very much," as he took them from Parker, his silenced handgun steady in his hand. "Now step back." Parker did so.

"Mr. Parker," Naughton hissed, suddenly looking grim and deadly, "every time I turned around in the last three weeks, I found you struggling along, bumping into things and not understanding any of it. You didn't even know you were close, did you? For all your stupidity, though, you are the most stubborn person I've ever met. But after tonight, all that will be changed."

"What did you do, Naughton? Follow your own instructions at NPF II and place a bomb at one of our biggest employers? To harm present workers and families by destroying their livelihoods? Or a bomb under an Interstate bridge? Do you believe that you can destroy our economy, and bring us to our knees? If you are stupid enough to believe that, then you're stupid enough to be caught."

Naughton's face drained of all color for about two seconds, and then back came his expression of grim confidence. He suddenly wheeled on Parker and hit him with the butt of the handgun.

Parker saw it coming, but too late. The next thing he knew he was on the floor with a thousand stars moving at fantastic speeds all around his head. He tried to get up but couldn't.

Jan raised her head but didn't react.

Naughton suddenly reached out and, seizing Parker by the collar of his coat, seemed to snatch him up onto his feet. "You're coming with me, Mr. Parker. Maybe I'll let you go and maybe killing you would give me pleasure. You see, it's up to me, not to you."

Naughton reached over and jerked the desk lamp off Flanders' desk and ripped the wire out of its base. He quickly tied Parker's hands behind him with it. He turned toward Addie.

"And it's up to you, too, Mrs. Parker. I suggest you do some praying. The first sign of an attempt to rescue your husband, whether you instigated it or not, and he's dead."

He looked down at his sister in disgust. "As for you, Janice, I wish you dead, but I won't need to do it. You're already dead. Look at you. You're already practically unconscious. You won't last long and every minute you have left will be hell. And you deserve it. You're worthless."

Parker heard every word uttered by Naughton, and that told him that he was coming out of the effects of the blow to the head. But his limbs felt sluggish and slow.

Naughton pulled Parker over to him and looked at him. "Mr. Parker, you're going with me. One attempt to warn anyone or to escape and you and your wife and Kate and Duane will regret it."

Parker blinked as the enormity of what Naughton was saying registered. Naughton noticed Parker's reaction. "Yes, I know who they are and how they are connected to you. And I know where they are. Do you understand me?" he asked in a sharp voice.

Parker nodded, and said he understood. His mouth felt like it was full of marshmallows. Suddenly, Naughton grabbed him by the front of his sweatshirt and shoved him ahead and out of the office. Parker stumbled along obediently.

He was beginning to revive. His head throbbed with the intensity of a strobe light, but his extremities were working a little better, and in a few more minutes he might be able to walk like a real person.

Addie, Addie, Addie, he pleaded to himself. Don't try anything brave. Just stay in the office and leave my safety up to me. I'll be back for you.

Parker prayed, for the first time in years. Maybe you only pray when nothing else is left for you to do, he thought. A situation looks so desperate that there's nothing else to do to try to find some kind of comfort. Something is really needed at a certain moment and people move toward prayer. Vietnam was the first time he'd seen that emotion displayed.

62

Naughton dragged Parker down to the first floor. He stopped, just off to the side of the double doors, and carefully surveyed what he could see of the street. Then he moved carefully over to the other side and surveyed in the other direction.

He grunted in satisfaction, turned, and dragged Parker, not through the doors and out into the street, but away from the doors and down a hallway toward the back of the building. There was a door at the end of the hall with an unlighted sign that, if operable, would proclaim "EMERGENCY EXIT". Just before that escape door to the outside was another door, set into the wall on the left. Naughton pushed on it with effort and it screeched open.

"Still needs oil, Bill," he whispered, "just as it did when I surveyed Flanders' office and this building about three months ago."

Naughton pushed Parker ahead of him onto the stair landing, and then he stepped onto it with him and pulled the door shut behind them. It was then that he flipped on the light. "Your plan was a good one, Bill. Its problem was that it had to work on me. I'm different, you know. I'm special. Nobody fools me, nobody scares me, and nobody tells me what to do. And when Vermont, and America, too, tumbles down, I'll be the one calling the shots. I'll be the big boy in class."

Parker looked at Naughton, and felt helplessness.

"You're right to be afraid, Bill, and when I've squared away the new training compound, I'm coming back. I'll deal with your wife then and your whole family, too. Also, a few ProgDems who are beginning to waver in their support of the historical process I've taken on. None of you will know when. And it will be fun for me." He grinned as he shoved Parker forward and headed him down the steps.

When they reached the floor of the basement, Parker could see that the basement had about a dozen feet of headroom. He knew that that much height was very strange, but he couldn't think beyond that. He felt "trussed up" and helpless. For the first time in his life he believed that tonight was his end.

Naughton brought him up to the basement wall, facing in the direction of the street above in front of the building, although twelve feet below its surface. In that basement wall was another door, a large one, and it had a set of what resembled miniature railroad tracks set into the floor.

"Curious, Bill?" he asked. "I've been here in Montpelier for over six years and I've made it my business to get to know the city in which I do most of my work. It's fascinating. And it's not complicated. Just get the earliest map of the city – the older the better – and look for the old buildings, or their sites, anyway. Especially courthouses and jails, churches, and other places of assembly."

Naughton was talking to Parker as if he didn't notice that Parker was his prisoner and unable to speak.

Naughton pushed open the door and pushed Parker into the dark tunnel. They were now walking under the street, as far as Parker could tell. Naughton kept up his running chatter. Maybe he was showing off, thought Parker, letting me know that his escape plan was foolproof and that he controls all events from now until he disappears.

"Many of them had secret passages, connecting one building with another. Some of them were dug as part of the underground railroad during the civil war. Courthouses, jails, and tunnels for the underground railway were common in the more settled communities. This tunnel we're in has these narrow tracks to haul court records, documents and other heavy items in small carts on these rails. Clever for the age, wouldn't you say?"

My God, thought Parker, why can't he shut his mouth? Like a damned tour guide.

"Just follow the map," Naughton remarked, blissfully, "and when you find that you can check one of the interesting buildings in a town, without being seen, of course, you do it, and you observe useful things. This tunnel, for instance. It was a real find, especially for my purposes. You see, Flanders' building was once a courthouse, or at least the site was. The County Courthouse stood on this spot 130 years ago. And the jail was across the street. So they had a tunnel built. Remarkably, they connected it up again when the buildings changed in later years. Probably because of pressure from the local Historical Society." He chuckled softly.

They had reached the end of the tunnel, at what had to be the foundation for the building across the street from the old courthouse. Naughton pushed the door open into the basement of the old jail. The door moved easily, with no sound. Then they walked across the cellar and up the stairs to the first level of the old warehouse located directly across the street from Flanders' office.

"Quiet is everything, Bill. Do you understand me?"

Parker said nothing.

"Good," Naughton said, with satisfaction, and stepped to a door near the front of the building, but still at its side, and opened it. It entered into the alley that held Parker's truck, which was parked fifty feet down the alley.

"I just knew it would be there," trumpeted Naughton, in a low voice. "I just knew it. When I saw you, Bill, earlier this evening, I knew that transportation was guaranteed. I would have escaped anyway, you know. Just at a slower pace. And why do I feel safe in driving that old wreck? Because nobody who's anybody would drive that truck except you. So, whoever drives it will be taken for Bill Parker no matter what the driver looks like. Are you listening, Bill?" Naughton jerked Parker around so that he was looking straight into his eyes.

"And that truck," said Naughton, "is my quick ticket out of here. When I leave it, Bill, wherever that is, I'll never be seen until I choose to, and you can have your truck back – or your heirs can." He wheezed a strange and quiet laugh.

They started walking down the alley toward the truck. There was complete silence in this enclosed space.

Then everything changed.

A strange figure, thin, strangely dressed, as much as Parker could tell in the darkness, came up out of a pile of old boxes and leaped in front of Naughton.

"Mr. Zed, Mr. Zed, take me with you, please take me with you," the figure cried.

"Ricky, is that you?" Naughton whispered hoarsely. "What the hell are you doing here?"

"I've done as you asked, sir. I've completed my mission. And did it well, sir. I'm reporting for another order, sir. And remember, we're going to talk about the Discipline for the New Future. You were interested, sir, remember? You said that we'd talk about it after I carried out my order. Well, I did it, sir, I did it." Ricky was almost screaming with an urgent joy.

He looked at Parker. "Is this Bill Parker? You've got him? Wonderful. He's the one you wanted me to be careful of. I've met him before, you know."

"Get the hell out of my way, you idiot," rasped Naughton, ignoring Ricky's non-stop babbling. "I'm not going to talk with you about the 'Discipline for the New Future' or whatever your stupid idea is called, or anything else."

Ricky continued to bounce in front of Naughton, who was trying to get to the truck, with Parker in tow.

"Don't go any further on this path, sir," Ricky keened. "It's not safe. You don't know it the way I do."

Naughton slammed Ricky out of their way and as he did so, Parker saw his chance. He suddenly twisted his arm and pulled out of Naughton's grip. Naughton tried to re-establish control, but it was too late. Parker broke away and ran, as fast as his numbed body and brain allowed, away from Naughton and towards the only safe place he knew – the street at the end of the alley.

He ran, hands tied behind him, and waited for the shot from Naughton that would end everything for him. It didn't happen. He could hear Ricky still screaming and shouting. Naughton was screaming back at him.

As he neared the entrance to the street he suddenly saw, in the alley and off to his left, a running figure who was heading down the alley where Naughton and Ricky were pushing and shoving and shouting.

Parker didn't stop and turn to look at this person. In fact, Parker took this shape as another enemy and avoided the shadowed image. He didn't care who it was. He only knew that he had to get away from a madman. He just kept running, lungs gasping, legs cramping, and feet pounding. He turned the corner in order to stay out of the direct line of fire from the alley and from a killer, who was probably following him.

But Parker wasn't being followed. He stumbled to a stop, gasping for breath, and looked back down the alley in the fading evening light.

Naughton had other things on his mind than Bill Parker. He was running straight for the truck, fumbling in his pocket for Parker's keys, while Ricky grabbed at him and babbled incoherently.

“Not that way, Mr. Zed,” Ricky wailed. “You’re wrong to go that way. It’s bad, very bad. That’s Parker’s truck. I did just what you told me to do.”

Naughton paid no attention to Ricky’s screeching. When he reached the truck door he turned and pushed Ricky back and then smashed him in the face with a heavy fist. Ricky dropped to his knees, dazed and crying, with blood rushing from his nose. It was at that moment that Naughton noticed a figure in the alley rushing at him.

It was Janice, his sister. She reached her brother and was pounding on the truck door with clenched fists.

“Don’t leave, brother. Come back with me. This is the right thing for you. I have all kinds of people who can help you. Don’t. . . . .”

No more time, Naughton thought. No more time. Got to go. He was humming as he shoved the ignition key into the key slot and cranked it over.

63

The immense blast blew down large sections of the two brick walls of the abandoned warehouses that had surrounded Parker's truck. And those same brick walls, located on either side of the pickup, acted to direct the blast effect of the explosion out both ends of the alley as well as straight up. There was nothing in the way of this effect in the rear of the alley, so nothing was changed from the wasteland it had been.

But, in the three buildings across the street, the blast blew out every front window, caused a frame building to slide a foot off its foundation, and actually collapsed the two double doors in Flanders' brick building. The two windows of his office, on the second floor, simply disappeared.

When her husband and Naughton had left the office, Addie stood up and walked over to look at Flanders. It sickened her, but she could see that nothing could be done for him. Flanders' computer was perched on a work table behind his desk, the screen-saver scrolling along, uninterrupted, inexorable. Addie thought that there was a certain horror about the inevitable functioning of the computer in the midst of all this chaos, never stopping, never hesitating, while death surrounded it.

Jan still sat on the couch, seemingly stunned into permanent silence.

Addie seemed to be frozen. She knew she couldn't just stand in one place. Addie forced herself to do what her husband had always told her. When under stress, do something, anything, to change the chemistry of the moment. She forced herself to move back toward the computer monitor, located against the wall on a table behind Flanders' desk.

She tapped a key and what came up was some kind of a report. She peered at it and said, over her shoulder, "Jan, take a look at this." Addie thought that Jan would be very interested. Addie also wanted to give Jan something else to think about.

It was a detailed statement, or letter, to "The Chittenden Free Progressive, attention: Hal Birdsall." It was the whole terrible period of time of the last three weeks –or maybe four - Addie couldn't focus well enough to remember – and it was being readied to go to Birdsall for publication, or at least to form the basis for a big story.

Addie turned toward the couch to bring Jan into the scene. Jan was gone; the door was open. How long had she been gone, Addie wondered? She was about to cross the room and look out at the street through the large windows when the windows suddenly seemed to pour into the room in a shower of glass shards. For the most part, it all missed Addie except for the ricocheting splinters of glass, which hit the top of her bowed head and the tops of her shoulders. Not being in the line of the windows at that instant had saved her life.

But she was stunned. Moving in a purposeful way was impossible. She stumbled away from the side of the room where Flanders' body was grotesquely leaning forward across his desk, and leaned against the far wall, away from the door, away from Flanders' body, away from the blood, the wreckage, and the terrible harshness of a monstrous explosion.

What have we unleashed, she asked herself? Is Willie still alive? Would he come to her soon? He always had in the past. Willie, she muttered, please come. I need you now more than I ever have.

It was at that moment that Morgan and Hugo burst into the room. They saw Addie across the room, standing rock still, and dazed. "Are you all right, Addie?" Morgan cried.

Addie couldn't understand him. The shocking boom had made that impossible. She gestured helplessly.

Then Morgan saw Flanders.

"Oh, Christ," he muttered, and walked through the mess to the desk.

Hugo ran over to Addie. "Mrs. Parker, are you hurt?" he breathed.

Addie didn't respond, so Hugo shouted in her ear. Addie looked at him, then asked, "Where's Willie?" She could feel the blood in her hair, running in a listless trickle down into her collar. All she was aware of was a stickiness under her shirt.

Hugo shrugged. “He’s tough, Mrs. Parker. I’m sure he’s okay.” He wasn’t sure at all, of course.

Addie looked at Hugo, and then started weaving to the door. She didn’t have to go far. She was met in the doorway by Catherine Morgan and Parker. To those in the room, Bill Parker’s embrace of his wife, Addie, seemed like a renewal of something great. Addie and Bill knew it was just that.

It was at this point that Morgan took charge. He emptied the room of all but himself and Catherine, and told the others to scatter. “I’ll be in touch with you as soon as I can bring some order to this chaos. There’s an unmarked cruiser outside, folks. It’s waiting for you. Hop into it and the driver will take you to Hugo’s in South Burlington. Now get going. Very soon now there will be a lot of people milling around and you shouldn’t be seen. By the way, Bill, your truck is no more. That was a bomb in it that went off when Naughton started it, unless I miss my guess.” Parker looked blank.

Parker, Addie still clinging to him, and Hugo, walked downstairs quickly and out to the cruiser. When they were underway for Hugo’s, Addie thought that the air seemed a little more breathable, the noise of the speeding cruiser seemed like a quiet evening at the Parker place and, thank God, they were all together. Just thirty minutes ago, that seemed impossible.

Hal Birdsall, Chet from California, Lucas Montague from Louisiana, and all the other attendees at the meeting of just three days earlier had already received the word. Those folks were hightailing it out of Montpelier, out of the state, and heading for home. They carried with them the evidence gathered by Parker, Small, and Hal Birdsall that would tear apart the groups that were hiding behind totally corrupt organizations in their states.

The only question to which Parker needed an answer was whether or not the Vermont news services would even consider this story as important for the unwashed and ignorant citizens in their Vermont sphere of influence. Probably not, he reasoned. If they did report it, it would be on page eleven of the annual flower show insert. Keeping citizens ignorant was what was keeping Vermont’s news organizations solvent.

64

Their arrival at Hugo's was very emotional. Hugo and Connie were very glad to see each other, to the point where Parker and Addie had to announce their presence.

Connie saw them walking into the living room. "Stay right here, you two," she said. "All I wanted to do was prove that this big Galumpke was my husband – and that he wasn't missing a leg or an arm. Or his head, for that matter, although I think he was in danger of losing that as soon as he went out on the trail with you, Mr. Parker." Connie was smiling as she said this. Parker studied her closely and then felt a sense of relief.

Then she looked more closely at Parker and Addie. "You two are bleeding," she said, maintaining a cool exterior while ramming around the kitchen, then the bathroom, and back to the kitchen, and opening drawers as she went. A cry of triumph was heard. A plastic see-through container was plopped on the kitchen table. Connie went to the sink and retrieved clean cloths and some water, while Hugo was snapping open the container of medical supplies. "Sit down, Addie. Let's have a look." She began to clean Addie's face and to check the places of oozing.

She looked up at Parker. "Don't go anywhere, please, Mr. Parker. You're next." The authority that accompanied that command caused Parker to stand rooted to the kitchen floor. He was too tired to do anything but follow orders. Connie looked again at him. "You can sit down, Mr. Parker. This isn't the army." Parker sat.

It was a strange atmosphere in that kitchen. While Connie Barkley worked on Addie, no one said a word.

The spell was broken when Connie arose from her Nurse Jane work. "Okay, everybody, I want to know what happened, from start to finish. And I can tell it wasn't a walk in the park."

She gestured to Parker to sit down in her makeshift operating pavilion.

More silence. Hugo spoke up first. "I don't have a big story, honey. The Parker Platoon arrived in the area at about 6:00 PM. I parked six blocks away."

Hugo was interrupted by his wife. "The 'Parker Platoon'?" she said, acidly. "Is that what it's called? The Parker Platoon? It sounds like those silly names used by the professional football people. You know, "The 'violet people-eaters', and the 'nineteen blocks of granite'. Names like that. Is that sort of thing creeping into situations where people, just like you, might actually lose their lives rather than scoring touch goals? Spare me that crap, Hugo."

Hugo had not picked up on the full anger of his wife. He said, in what turned out to sound like a patronizing comment, "That's the *Purple* People Eaters, Connie, and the Seven Blocks of Granite. And it's touch*downs*, not touch *goals.*"

Timing was everything, as Hugo soon learned. Connie leveled a gaze at her husband that would have frightened an alligator. Hugo was no fool. He decided to get back to his original subject, as smoothly as possible, and immediately.

"We each went our separate ways and headed to our stations. The first thing I did was to walk around the six blocks looking for vehicles, or anything else that seemed out of place. I called Catherine Morgan a couple of times to check some plates that I saw. They amounted to nothing. Then I went to my assigned station. It was just north of Flanders' building, in an upstairs window of a small branch bank. Actually, one of my clients. And I just sat there, twiddling my thumbs, for over two hours. Bored as hell," he said.

"I did keep my eye on the street and the front of the office, but saw nothing unusual. Flanders' car was parked in its usual space, but that was planned for. And everything was normal and quiet." Hugo took a sip of coffee.

"What I didn't know was all that had already happened during those two hours, right while I was sitting there in comfort." He shook his head in disbelief at his ignorance of what might be happening elsewhere.

"About 8:30, I saw a person, maybe a woman, run out of the front of Flanders' building, across the street, and disappear down that alley where Bill had his truck parked. I couldn't imagine what had happened."

"Then I saw you, Bill," Hugo said, "running out of that alley. I knew that the game had already started and I didn't have a clue about what was going on. I was just pretty sure that our plan was shot to hell. By the time I got to the street I couldn't see you anywhere, but I saw Morgan, running toward the office from the other direction, and I just ran as hard as I could from the opposite direction to meet him. I figured he'd know what was happening. As it turned out, he didn't know any more than I did."

Parker was wincing as Connie was cleaning and bandaging his lower leg. It had been leaking blood for the last four hours because he couldn't take the time to give it a rest.

Connie was mumbling to herself and shaking her head. "Keep talking, dear," she said to Hugo. "I can listen while I save lives on the battlefield." But despite her attempts at some levity, they all knew she was shocked at what she was hearing.

Hugo was speaking in a soft voice. "Just before we met at Flanders' building, there was a huge explosion. Morgan and I were damned lucky to be out of the way. Ten more seconds and we both would have felt the effects of that blast and we would have become mincemeat. The doors and windows of Flanders' building just seemed to disintegrate. Other buildings next door were also heavily damaged. It was as if someone built a bomb but didn't know how much of this and that they needed, so they erred on the side of large." Hugo had gotten to his feet by this time and was leaning against one of the kitchen counters, drinking a glass of milk.

"That's about it," he said. "Well, maybe one more item. I have to assume that someone was down that alley when the bomb went off. The woman was running into the alley. A few seconds after that, the bomb went off. I don't know if there was anybody else down there with the woman. If there was, I don't think they survived." He stopped then, looked at Parker, and waited.

Parker looked back at Hugo, and then nodded. He described his ordeal as Naughton's captive. "So I know that there were at least three people in that alley, undoubtedly very close to my truck, when it blew up. Made a hell of a racket," he said grimly. "My ears are still on half power."

Parker paused for a few seconds and Hugo wondered if he was deciding whether or not to go on. But Parker continued. It seemed to Hugo that his friend simply wanted to get it said to somebody rather than hold it all inside.

"The three individuals in the alley were a creepy guy named Ricardo Rudolpho Murch. He was one of the flower people of thirty years ago, if that's what you call them today, and he was so whacked out by a poor education and drugs that he couldn't carry on any kind of a conversation with anybody without suddenly beginning to sing, cry, and shout. He may have made the bomb, Hugo, but I can't envision him having the attention span to do it. I vote for Naughton, myself. I think Naughton must have made it and he told Ricky to place it in my truck. I have no confirmation of that, but Naughton was in the alley with Murch and they were fighting and yelling when I was running out. Murch was practically attacking Naughton and howling that he shouldn't go toward my truck. 'It isn't safe', he yelled and 'I've done what you wanted'. Silliness like that."

His face took on a look of sadness as he said, "I am positive that the third person was Jan Evlin. She probably wanted to see her brother before he left town. Or maybe she wanted to kill him herself for all the terrible things he had caused. In any case, she's disappeared and I have to assume that her trip down that alley resulted in her death. We'll never know the details now, of course."

Connie looked at the three of them in awe. "You mean that this all took place in little Vermont," she said. "What will the press say, I wonder?"

No sooner had she said that than the phone rang. Hugo went to it and picked it up. It was Morgan.

"Hugo, is Bill Parker with you?" he asked.

"You bet, Mr. Morgan," and handed the phone to Parker.

"Yes, Peter," Parker said.

"The four of you should be prepared for inquiries from the newshounds in Vermont. I'm having a press conference tomorrow at the department, and I'm going to tell them the whole story. I will try to keep your names out of it, but I'm not going to go out of my way to do so. I will also tell them that we have been unable to positively identify the vehicle at this time. That's as far as I'll go to shield you, Bill, and that's only a temporary delay. If I tell the truth I won't have to remember what I said, as my old man used to say."

"Fine, Peter," Parker said. "Anything else we should know, even if we shouldn't know it?"

Morgan took his time in answering Parker's question. "Here are some things you've heard from unnamed sources. Okay? After tomorrow it will be public knowledge, but not until then."

"You bet," answered Parker.

"First, Forensics found enough to know that there were three people who died in the blast. One was a woman, and it was probably Jan Evlin. They found some pieces of the coat that was undoubtedly hers. The consensus is that the other two were men. Murch was definitely one of them."

"How do you know one of the men was Murch, Peter? I'm asking because, if it was, then this crazy man is out of my life for good."

"We found his shoes, Bill. Do you know anybody else who wears multi-colored bowling shoes for everyday footwear? They were positively ID'd by my wife and another officer who had lots of contact with him." Parker remembered that Denny was the officer when Parker first met Ricky.

"The third person was another man. We're pretty sure it's Zederbian, Bill, or Naughton, if that's the correct name of the month. We found a belt buckle with 'NPF II' on it. I'll bet he wore that belt in plain view for years, and laughed to himself that he was parading the knowledge of the compound right in front of the people of Vermont. And I'll bet that nobody else ever wore that belt, or one like it." Parker thought about Jan's remarks describing her brother as "tricky".

"Maybe a court of law wouldn't express certainty," continued Morgan, "but we know he's dead. There wasn't much else left to look at anyway for more positive identification. That was a big bomb, you know." As if I wasn't aware of that fact, thought Parker. "Bill, that blast was so big that we can't even tell it was a pickup, much less *your* pickup."

"Keeping it simple was important to the planner of this operation," said Morgan. "If this Murch, or Munch person, or whatever his name was, had the job of planting it, it would have to be simple. He was an idiot, you know. Lived on an entirely different planet. Probably there would have been no loss if he'd made a mistake and it went off before he ever arrived in that alley. My forensic people told me that it was something very powerful. Something fairly modern, too. I was surprised at that, but they seemed certain."

“You mean *plastique* stuff, Peter? That’s very dangerous material. I learned the basics of that kind of explosive when I was in the army.”

“That *plastique* material is known as C-2, Bill. It wasn’t that, apparently. My folks tell me that they found the residue of what they think is SEMTEX in the blast area. This stuff is really nasty. It’s the Russian version of C-4, the next generation after C-2 or *plastique*. It’s the explosive material of choice of terrorists and those who want to destroy things and be sure of it.”

“Where can that stuff be bought, Peter? There must be records of it somewhere.”

“It can be bought anywhere within 200 miles of the east coast, Bill. It’s available, if you know where to ask.” Parker felt a surge of anger.

“Got any idea what the trigger might have been?” asked Parker, sharply. His fury was obvious over the phone line to Morgan.

“Again, something simple, I’m told. The charge was inside a steel container with an open top. We found enough of that to be sure of what it was. Just set it on the ground, under the driver’s seat, with a cord running from inside the box from whatever the trigger was in there. Probably had a lead weight tied to it. Balance the lead weight on the exhaust pipe. And walk away. When somebody started up the truck, the vibration would shake the lead weight loose, and pull a strip of plastic from between the jaws of a pressure switch. When the switch closed, a small battery would activate the detonator inside the box, and ‘boom’. That’s probably not too far from the truth, Bill.”

Parker was quiet for a few seconds. And everything to do with this murderous climax, he thought, started out as something so damned innocent. And that simple beginning cost Jan Evlin her life.

“Thanks, Peter,” Parker said grimly, “for calling. Also for letting us know about the onslaught of the Vermont paparazzi. We’ll be ready.”

“One more thing, Bill. We found a 9 MM Glock handgun in the wreckage. It was undamaged. It’s probably Zederbian’s. We had never picked Ricky up and found him carrying any kind of weapon. We clamped it in our bullet trap and fired it. The sample compared perfectly with the slugs found when the carpenters’ bodies were autopsied. We also sent the handgun up to the

Vermont Crime Lab. They've got one of these special bullet traps – some people call them 'boom tubes' – that's a tube filled with water. No damage to the slug from that device. I know it's not proof that's strong enough to say that Zederbian pulled the trigger, but the reasonable person wouldn't have any doubts – and I'm a very reasonable person."

Parker was quiet for a few seconds. "What about the shooting death of Don Flanders, Peter?"

"Oh, we'll check that, Bill, have no fear. There's no doubt that Naughton pulled that trigger. We'll see if it's the same handgun. After all this time, it seems that Naughton would have dumped it – but, maybe not."

"I wonder how many deaths he's responsible for, Peter? It just never seems to end, does it? I mean, killing those four carpenters who had worked for him is not explainable."

"We'll never know, Bill," Morgan said. "We'll never know. Many, probably. But the stakes were very high, I think. Their plan was to bring this country to its knees, as far as I can tell. I still have a hard time believing that this group could have believed they could do that."

"Anything else, Peter? We have many more holes in this web. I'd sure like to fill them in."

"Here's one that you will understand, Bill, because you got involved in this kind of thing about three years ago. We were able to search Naughton's office in the National Life building. There wasn't anything there that referred to NPF I and II, but there was a small, but damned solid, filing cabinet that was locked. And bolted to the floor, too. Because of all these precautions taken by Naughton, I got very curious. We got into it, legally, you should know, and what we found was fascinating."

"First, NPF I and II were financed by the Bitterroot Group, the Foundation for Nature Preservation, and PRAPPPP. All three are international organizations, but started here in America."

"PRAPPPP?" Parker asked. "Where have I heard that before?"

"It's a non-profit, Bill, and the acronym stands for the 'People's Revolution Against Profits, Production, and Private Property'. I'm surprised that you are unaware of it." Parker could feel the tightness in Morgan's face right through the phone line.

Then Morgan's voice became somber and quiet. "We also were able to make good use of that code, or that sort of shorthand, that you found up at NPF II. You remember the long string of letters and numbers that were finally untangled by Lucas Montague of Louisiana. The next target by the graduates of NPF II was actually two sites located in Galveston, Texas. Both are oil refineries, and both are critical to this country. Nice people, huh?"

"My God, Peter, none of us had any real idea of what was happening right on our doorstep."

"Then, in a file," continued Morgan inexorably, "was a list of 167 individuals around Vermont who were being paid by various non-profits and Foundations as full-time employees, but without any duties. That's not unknown in Vermont, of course, but the organizations laundering the money were not favorites with many Vermonters."

"In conversations with our friends around Vermont," continued Morgan, "we discovered that, of the political people in this group of 167, none of them on the 'take' had mentioned to anybody during their campaigns that they were supported by outside money."

Morgan was quiet for a few seconds, and Parker could hear papers being shuffled. Morgan was ready for the press conference and this was his rehearsal.

"I will not mention the names to the press," Morgan continued. "Probably a non-political person wouldn't even give this information a thought. Totally confusing to the uninitiated, ya' know. But people like you and me would know immediately that it was dynamite."

"Naughton was working like a deep cover agent for somebody, Peter," said Parker. "And we have no idea who."

"My guess is that it's one of the big non-profits, Bill, not necessarily an environmental organization. A non-profit with a public face of helping children, or the natural wonders of Vermont, or against sprawl, would be a perfect cover for him."

Morgan hesitated for a few seconds, as if reciting all these bits of information had exhausted him. "As far as Naughton, himself, went, Bill, he was a very careful man. He did some things along the way that we might consider 'chancy', but he didn't think of them that way. That picture you stole from him," Morgan said, with some relish, "hanging innocently on the wall of his apartment, while gathering other items, was one of the very few big mistakes he made, and it hurt him. Poor Jan Evlin recognized it and it told her that Naughton really was her brother and that he was also known as 'Z'. I think it also told her to stop ignoring the messages contained in our evidence and face the fact that her brother was a very bad person."

Morgan seemed to have a complete grasp of everything that had transpired since that evening when Jan found Parker fishing in central Vermont.

"So I asked Catherine to try to make sense of it all," Morgan said. "She's good at those sorts of puzzles. You know what I mean. What positions were represented by these 167 names. She was able to unscramble all of them. All were part of Vermont's political left who had held these positions over the past ten years. Were they actually being paid? Yes, but I can't prove it. Should we turn the knowledge of the existence of this additional income over to the tax department to compare with their income tax statements for prior years? We could, but nothing will come of that. This isn't really proof that the IRS could act on. Were all 167 of these individuals on the edge of the left? I don't know for a fact, but it seems apparent. Based on Naughton's notes, this money was primarily from outside Vermont, laundered here, and I think it enabled many members of the Vermont left to earn a good living while serving in many important positions, both appointed and elected."

Parker was stunned by the possibilities offered by this "list". However, the daily press in Vermont wouldn't touch the implications that that list provided.

"Peter, I guess I'm not surprised. Many of us in the House were aware of people who were being paid additional money from somewhere to be there. I don't remember that we thought of it as illegal, although it may have been. It just seemed strange when the average person in Vermont had no such option available to them which would allow them to run for office. As far as lousy legislation imposed on Vermonters by these people, we got Act 60 which gave them control of all the money spent on education – over 700 million bucks, at the time. Then they went to work on health care. They're after the money, almost two billion dollars a year. And they'll get it, too, based on the philosophical direction of our present legislature."

This unofficial information from Morgan made Parker feel blue. "What are you going to do with this 'list', Peter?"

"Not much, Bill. Someone did go one step further with it, though. I have just heard that it was leaked, apparently very, very carefully. A ProgDem called me, asking who leaked it, but really accusing me of doing it. I gave him a new set of brains right then. I don't think he'll call back. And I'll find the SOB who did that, too."

Parker was glad that he had never gotten Morgan angry at him. Irritated at times, but not really angry.

"But it seemed to turn about a third of the members of the Vermont General Assembly into a dither," continued Morgan. "Our legislative sources said it was almost comical. Most of the 'takers' of this money were not pleased that their constituents might find out that they were being paid by various unpopular pressure groups. You'd be surprised who they were, Bill."

"However, the list is hand-written and unsigned, so we can't prove anything. And I won't release it for political speculating during an election year anyway."

"Why not?" Parker asked, irritably. "The ProgDems release phony crap all the time against their opponents."

"But their sources, Bill, are from other politicians, inside and outside the state, and their campaign managers. Most of it certainly unreliable and, for the most part, probably made up. However, sketchy and unproved information like this will not be coming from my law enforcement people. I won't have it. It doesn't mean that I don't believe it, Bill. I do. But political spinning is for others. Not cops."

His answer caused Parker a flush of irritation for a brief moment, but he understood it. He also realized that Morgan's sense of ethical behavior was why he admired him.

"Best of luck tomorrow, Peter. All of the hard left press will be there and their words on the written page the next morning will make you wonder if they were at the same press conference you were."

"I've given press conferences before, Bill. Their reporting was okay the next day. I'm not concerned about that."

That's fine, Peter, as far as it goes. But you will be attacking one of the left's icons. Reginald Naughton: interested citizen, defender of children, and dispenser of funds for pliable politicians. He represented the environment, our children, and tomorrow's world. They will not let you get away with casting a shadow on his memory."

"That's your experience, Bill. Mine will be different."

“Peter, I hope you’re right. I didn’t mean to come off sounding like some old negative curmudgeon sitting in a nursery home rocking chair and trying to be relevant.”

Morgan laughed. “You’ll never be anything like that, Bill, even when you *are* sitting in a rocking chair somewhere. I suspect that you will be a bit of a curmudgeon, though.”

“Thanks, Peter,” said Parker, dryly. “See you soon,” and hung up the receiver.

65

Parker and Addie left South Burlington at 4:00 the next morning. They just wanted to get back to their home and the surroundings which they knew well and appreciated, now more than ever. They both felt a renewed sense of well-being. The cloud of danger that had hovered over them both for a month had dissipated. Parker himself felt free and he had put aside that caution that had been governing him for such a long time.

The only shadow on his memory was the death of Jan Evlin. Her brother had caused so much havoc and incomprehensible destruction to so many people, and in doing so, had pushed her into danger's path. She had paid the penalty for the hatred and extremism of others.

They made the trip in Addie's vehicle. Parker noted that it was a three-year-old minivan in excellent condition. He hadn't actually been in Addie's van more than a half dozen times since she bought it. He didn't really feel as if he was traveling anywhere unless he was in his pickup. Just because his truck was not the sort of vehicle that would please everybody, did not, in any way, diminish his affection for his former mode of transportation. He was convinced that everybody would appreciate it if they had just spent some time riding in it. If they didn't want to avail themselves of the experience, then to hell with them.

One of the general attributes of his old pickup that was not present in Addie's van were the handy places to put things. He could think of numerous examples of the useful modifications he had wrought in his truck that should be incorporated into his wife's van. He promised himself to discuss it with her when things had settled down a bit. He was sure that she'd immediately latch on to his ideas. Addie was really smart that way.

One of Parker's inspirations was a homemade clip that held a large flashlight. It was located at the top of the front window. Just reach up and you had it in your hand, he thought. Its problem was that the clip was not strong enough to hold something that large and heavy on a rough road. It kept falling out and landing on his thigh and knee, and it hurt just to think of it.

Even when he added an additional clip, the flashlight fell – just not as often. Addie, however, kept her small flashlight in the glove compartment. You knew where it was, but you couldn't grab it quickly enough to suit Parker. When he pointed out to Addie the handiness of his arrangement, she asked, somewhat sharply, he thought, "Willie, when have you ever had to grab hold of the flashlight in your truck on an emergency basis?"

He told her that he had never had to do that, but he wanted to be ready if the situation ever came up.

Parker thought about another practical piece of work he had done in the name of creativity. It was the addition of a series of straps behind the driver's seat that held in place a gravel shovel, the handle of which had been shortened so it would fit in a vertical position.

After this job had been done, Parker noted that he'd lost the ability to adjust the driver's seat fore and aft. Well, he thought, mildly irritated, all of the great inventors had their disappointments, too. If his work in designing this eminently practical modification wasn't appreciated, he reasoned, he was the only one who ever drove this truck - so the hell with them. He was especially proud, however, of exhibiting deference to the modern world by using wide Velcro for the straps. The only problem was that they held together in an almost inhuman way, causing him to beat up his knuckles every time he removed the shovel. Addie just shook her head when she saw what he had done.

The one change Parker made, however, that pleased him the most was his personal recognition of the value of steel tire chains. Although scoffed at by his friends for resurrecting these valued and necessary safety implements, Parker went ahead and purchased a brand new set of welded tire chains. He knew that when these were needed, the situation was probably critical. He stowed them under the passenger seat of his truck.

This had been almost fifteen years ago when his truck was a very new second-hand vehicle. He'd never had an occasion to use them. And Addie stopped riding in his truck about a dozen years earlier, telling Parker that "I can stand the truck all right, Willie, but those damned tire chains under my side of the cab rattle, even with a blanket over them, so much that they make my teeth ache. You decide, my dear. You can ride with me by your side as your faithful life's companion or you can ride with your new and, I'll remind you, never used, chains, rattling at you every inch of the way."

Parker was never one to enjoy ultimatums, regardless of their source. He patiently explained to Addie, once again, that chains were a necessity for emotional stability while on the road in the winter. She patiently explained that that was perfectly acceptable to her and that her Willie was to have fun when on the trail - alone.

On their way home from South Burlington, they stopped for breakfast at his favorite diner, the Crossroad Cafe in White River Junction. It wasn't really a diner, as the term "diner" implies. It was a single-level frame building, but it had all the other amenities of the good diner. Terrific food and service, an open area that allowed people to walk around if they wanted to, and very reasonable prices.

Parker had gone in there often during the year because he had a lot of customers in the White River Junction area, and just servicing their needs allowed him to know many people in town – including the owners of this great diner. He saw the same people enough times during the year to get to know some of them.

Parker was known as *Mr.* Parker by the regulars in this diner. That term of respect (and Parker hoped that it was just that, and not an attempt to fool him for their own enjoyment) started right after he had "messed the carpet" on the Vermont House floor three years before.

He thought that these people used the Café as a part of their routine every day. Most of them knew almost everybody else. They knew that they would always find friends there.

Everybody in the world should have a place like that, Parker decided. It would do more than anything the United Nations had ever done. In fact, he thought that a couple of the regular patrons, whom he saw practically every time he stopped, actually lived in the diner, and the owners didn't know it.

They made one other stop when they were within shouting distance of home. That was at Hollis Bagley's Garage to fill up Addie's van with gas. This was a reality check that Addie had to experience, thought Parker, knowing that she had never been there before.

"Bill Parker," cried Hollis, as they rolled in. "I recognize you but not the vehicle. Don't tell me you've finally thrown your pickup out with the trash."

"Nope," said Parker. "It just died in Montpelier, Hollis."

Addie gave him a sharp glance.

"Pretty much everything does, Bill," said Hollis. That's a bad place for anybody with sense. They don't know us. They just pass whatever the old socialists want."

Then Hollis spied Addie. "Bill, is this the Mrs.?" he cried. Without waiting for an answer, Hollis ran around to the driver's side. "Mrs. Parker, I believe," he said, two grease-bearing hands clutching the bottom of the open window.

He's damn near bowing, thought Parker. Hollis was exhibiting a respectful manner that Parker had never seen before.

"What can I do for you, ma'am? Fuel, perhaps, a cup of coffee, maybe? I just cleaned up the rest rooms. Is that timing or is it?"

"Just gas, Mr. Bagley, and thank you for asking." Addie spoke to Hollis in her way of conveying appreciation of having the opportunity to meet him. If Hollis had had a tail it would have been swatting flies and cleaning road dust off the van.

"Immediately, ma'am, immediately," cried Hollis. As he clattered around to the gas pumps, he called out to Addie. "Do you admit in public that you're married to this insurance swindler, ma'am?"

"Only when absolutely necessary, Mr. Bagley," she answered calmly.

Hollis apparently hadn't been called "Mr." in many years. His tail started wagging again. Parker was witnessing the making of history as it concerned *Mr*. Bagley. The transformation from irreverent to reverent was breath-taking.

Hollis collected his money from Addie, practically groveling. Then he turned to Parker.

"Say, Bill," he said, "did you ever see that fella who stopped in here looking for you? Couple days ago. Maybe three. Strange name. Knots, or somethin' like that." He paused. "Never was good at remembering names," he mumbled. "I think he said he had some business with you, but didn't quite know where you lived. He saw the sign for your insurance business, he said, but the lady in your office was not very bright and didn't know much about your whereabouts."

Parker stared at Hollis. "What did you tell him, Hollis?" he asked quietly.

"Well, sir, when he said that about Irene, I decided that that bastard was up to no good – sorry about the cussin', ma'am," he said, turning toward Addie. "Irene's about the smartest person I ever met. And one of the most helpful, too. Outsmarted me, for sure, and I ended up buying insurance from your agency, by God."

"Hollis," said Parker, levelly. "What did you tell him?"

"I told that son-of-a-bitch, pardon, ma'am," practically knuckling his forelock in respect, "that I didn't know you or anything about you. I told him I keep to myself, and he'd better start doing the same. I think I sort of startled him, Bill. He asked me where he could eat and I told him. That's when he left."

"Did you tell him to go to Lizzie's Luncheonette, Hollie?" asked Parker, levelly. Hollis nodded his answer.

Parker was glad that Hollis had shown that sort of horse sense, even though he had no idea that he was dealing with a madman. He also noticed that he, himself, was still jumpy from the experiences of the recent past, as shown when Hollis told him that someone who was now dead had been looking for him.

"I'll do my best to get in touch with him, Hollis. Don't know how successful I'll be, though. Thanks for the message." He turned toward Addie, who was watching him steadily. "Let's get going, sweetie. I'm real anxious to get home."

66

When they arrived home Addie backed the van up to the porch, rather than put it away in the shed. Too far to carry the luggage when both of them were among the walking wounded. She could see that her husband was brooding about something.

When they finished unloading the minivan, Addie moved to put it away, but Parker stopped her. "Let me look around first, Addie," he said. "I want to check things out. Don't call the Lutzes yet for the dogs, either. The dogs will keep for another hour. Why don't you sit on the porch for a few minutes while I look around."

Addie gave an emphatic nod and did as requested.

The first item of inspection was around the front door, and then under the porch. Nothing.

Next, he placed a phone call to "Lizzie's". Lizzie, the owner, answered the phone and told him that somebody fitting "Knot's" description had been there and had asked for directions to his house. Something about business, confided Lizzie, speaking softly, as if imparting an old family secret. "I told him where you lived, Mr. Parker. Was I wrong to do that? Maybe you don't want to have to do business at home. I'm real sorry if I did something wrong."

"No, that's all right, Lizzie. Thank you," said Parker.

Addie eyed her husband. He has a bee in his bonnet, she thought. It's best not to argue with him when he's like that.

Parker roamed around the house, checking this and checking that He found everything as he had left it. He went outside and walked around the porch, and looking under it for anything out of place, or simply different. He found nothing. He even checked the van over, still parked at the back steps, although he had just been riding in it. He was beginning to think that he was going to need the Doctors Malcom for a little out-patient head shrinking to calm him down.

Simply because he had found nothing suspicious caused Parker's personal warning system to automatically go to full alert. But after looking around the house for a while he decided that he was probably just nervous from the last few days. But he still knew that being careful was being prudent. At least for a little bit longer.

He walked to the shed, located about twenty feet from the house. He was about to haul the doors open when he thought that "being careful" demanded that he check the shed closely before he even thought about entering. You don't open anything, twist anything, or push anything, Billy, me boy, he said to himself. You just look. And then you look again.

He checked all around the outside of the three-stall shed. Then he went to the back of the shed and slipped in through the small passage door opening. He looked that door opening over, too, very carefully, before walking through it.

He wouldn't admit to anyone that he was "checking things out". He had never gone to these lengths before on his own property. But Naughton, or Zederbian, or "Knots" or whoever the hell he was, had been alive just three days ago. And the knowledge that a crazy dead man had visited Bridgeton in the last three days, looking for him, was enough.

He stood rooted to the spot, just inside the shed. There was enough light through gaps between the boards of the walls and the open spaces between the roof and the top of the side walls to see fairly clearly most everything not in deep shadow. His first careful trip around the inside perimeter of the shed showed nothing.

He was about to shove the outer door open on its overhead track when he stopped. He saw something right in front of him. What was that? Whatever it was it shouldn't be there.

And then he knew. He was practically standing close enough to it to brush it with his arm. He felt fear of the gut-wrenching type. Vietnam all over again.

It was just a spot of gleam in the shadowy light, unnoticeable if you weren't looking for it. But Parker was looking for it, or something like it.

It was a steel box, leaning vertically against the inside of the door, balanced precariously on one of the horizontal 2' x 6' door supports, about waist high, its open side facing to the outside of the shed. Trailing from its side was a heavy cord that followed along the top surface of the 2 x 6. The cord was tied to the outside sliding door. When that door was pushed open, it stretched the cord until the trigger inside the box was activated.

Parker backed away carefully, horrified by how close he was to being vaporized. He didn't know very much at all about explosives beyond the basics. But this device, following on the heels of the powerful bomb of last night, was what that bomb must have been.

After what seemed to be a lifetime of tiny steps, Parker slid through the passage door and walked steadily back to the house. Addie met him at the door. "It feels good to be home, Willie. I needed to be back here."

"Addie," he said, in a manner that made her look at him searchingly. "Get your bag and your coat. We're leaving for a while."

"Why, Willie? What's wrong?" She was putting on her coat as she questioned Parker.

They got into her van and slowly drove out of the yard. After they had traveled almost to the main road, Parker stopped the van and got out. He dragged some log chunks and brush across the driveway and piled it up, hoping that it would dissuade any visitors for long enough to have his road blocked and manned by professionals. When they were all the way out on the main road, Parker pulled over to the side of the road and stopped. Addie could see that he had a sheen of perspiration on his face.

"Please tell me, Willie. What did you find?" Addie pleaded.

"Another bomb, sweetie, probably like the one that went off in the alley across from Flanders' office. I've got to call Morgan. I'm heading for Marvin Bailey's house. I think he's still a Constable. He'll help us."

"Willie," said Addie, "more bombs? It doesn't seem real to me. It wouldn't seem real to anybody."

"I know, sweetie, but it does fit a pattern started at NPF II. Bombs, I mean. That's what they taught at that damn compound. Other things, too, of course. But that seemed to be the specialty of the house. How to make bombs. And some other types out of materials that, by themselves, are easily available. But Bud and I thought that we had found the plastic stuff, too. Big bombs are made from that." He stopped and wiped his face with his handkerchief. "Addie, all bombs are murderous, whatever they're made of."

Parker started talking again, as if it made him feel better. "As these strange groups gained support in the country, they became more aggressive. These environmental extremists are the terrorists inside the country, Addie. And they diminish the interests of groups and non-profits that have honest concerns over these same environmental issues. Honest opinions are held by the people who are willing to discuss things to reach reasonable conclusions. The extremists are another kettle of fish. They don't discuss. They indoctrinate and, from our own experiences, throw around things like bombs if they don't get their way."

"But, Willie, bombs are so final and impartial and are so easily seen and tracked, aren't they?"

Parker looked fondly over at Addie. She was the smart one in the family, but there were some things that she hadn't experienced. "Don't forget, my dear, that it took those folks at Morgan's meeting, from Louisiana, California, and the state of Washington, at least six years to find tangible evidence of this corrupting force. And they had to travel to Vermont to confirm it." Addie went quiet.

Parker started the van and they headed out.

It was only a ten-minute drive to Marvin Bailey's home. Marvin was an older man now, but still active in the Bridgeton community. He was the chief of the local volunteer fire department, and also a Constable in the town. He had been a Democrat all his adult life. Or he had until the ProgDem Party had been formed. But he still was the principle reason for Parker running, and winning, a seat in the legislature.

Marvin had no use for phonies and had decided that his party was not being honest with the voters. Bill Parker, an Independent, was Marvin's gift to what he perceived as the dishonest politicians in Montpelier. And it was from that modest beginning that the influence of people like Parker started to be felt in those hallowed halls of government control, high taxes, and ruined school systems.

The ProgDems saw this, too. So, in the election of 2004, with the help of the Vermont news media, they simply destroyed the elections of independents, Republicans, and any turncoat ProgDems they could find. They swept into office, decisively controlling the entire General Assembly.

Vermonters had chosen their path. As long as somebody else was paying for it, give me socialized medicine, they seemed to be saying. What they hoped for was that the facts from Canada regarding that socialized medicine system wouldn't be publicized in Vermont. Canada's high court had said that private insurance should be made available to their citizens when the government-controlled system didn't provide them with needed services. And the services provided by the Canadian government were shrinking every year.

Marvin was sitting on his front porch, with his morning coffee, when they drove in. He got up and walked down the steps.

"Bill and Addie Parker, I do declare," he cried. "You haven't been here for a few days, have you? Or is it months? What can I do for you? It must be important, sure enough."

Parker shook his hand and Addie gave him a hug and a peck on his grizzled cheek.

"Marvin, I don't have time to tell you what has been happening in our lives. But I will, as soon as things settle down."

"Well," said Marvin, wearing a grin, "as long as you haven't been trying to blow up Montpelier. Did you hear about that? Last night? People died, too, I hear."

Parker ignored this, and said, "You're still a Constable in town, aren't you?"

Marvin glanced sharply at his friend. "Yes," he said guardedly.

"Marvin, I'm going to ask you to do some things for me and I need you to stay away from questioning me about them. Okay?"

Marvin looked down at the floor. "Okay, Bill. What do you need?"

"Call the State Police and tell them that you have a trustworthy friend who says he has a bomb in his vehicle shed." Marvin's head snapped up. He studied Parker.

Parker knew this moment was all built on trust, and the years they had known each other. "And that you need the bomb squad immediately deployed."

Marvin didn't say anything. He walked up on his porch and into the house. He gestured for Parker and Addie to follow.

Marvin sat down at a small phone table and dialed.

"Hello," Marvin said, "this is Constable Marvin Bailey, calling from Bridgeton. I need some officers here right away. And I need the bomb squad here, too, just as soon as you can do it."

Marvin listened for a moment, while a voice squawked at him. Suddenly, the screeching voice had gone away.

"Bea, this is Marvin. Thanks for coming on the line. I don't have enough time to talk to you now. Please get some officers out here. Where? At Bill Parker's house, of course. He's with me now. What? Yes, it's the same Bill Parker. Hold it, Bea, hold it. Right now. Tell the officers to arrange for blocking off a road, too, going to the Parker place. I need it done official-like."

"When?" Marvin cried. "Now, Bea, right now, for God's sake." Marvin was showing irritation. "Great, Bea, and yes, it's very important. I'll meet your troopers there where the Parker's road meets the main highway."

He hung up. "Anything else you need, Bill?" he asked.

"Let me use the phone, Marvin, for one call." Marvin handed Parker the phone.

Parker dialed and Marvin heard Parker say, "Peter, is that you? I'm glad I caught you. We're at home, that's where we are. And I found a bomb in our vehicle shed. And it seems that it might be something like the one that went off in the alley – or like the one about which you speculated. Troopers are on their way here now."

Addie and Marvin could hear the phone buzz, and then Parker said, "That's a good plan, Peter. If you can postpone the press conference until tomorrow, you might have some firsthand evidence." Parker listened for a few seconds. "I know you can't keep my name out of things. The only thing I'm concerned about is the identity of my truck. If they identify it as belonging to me, I'm afraid that I don't have very good reasons for parking it there."

Parker listened some more. "Well, Peter, I'll be ready. And you know something else? I don't care if my truck is identified. It will open the door to a whole new way of relating what happened to us. You will simply use facts. Just facts, dust dry, with no meat on them. I will give them a narrative. I'll be irresistible and brilliant."

Peter made a comment that only Parker could hear. "Peter, that's unkind," said Parker. "Just keep everybody out of it if you can. As far as I'm concerned, let 'er rip."

Parker ended with, "Let's get up there and wait for those troopers."

The three of them piled into Addie's van and headed for home.

“What’s the timing on the bomb squad, Marvin?” asked Parker.

“With luck, we’ll see them in about four hours,” he answered, “and half of that will be driving time. That’s very good for them when they have a sudden emergency. And do you know why, Bill?”

“No, why? Asked Parker.

“The law enforcement people depend on each other. I’m sure you know that,” Marvin said. Parker nodded.

“Well, some of them know who you are. I’ve heard your name used often. And those who know you want to help you. Those who have never heard of you soon get the word.”

Parker looked blank. “Hard to understand,” he said. “I’ll have to talk to Morgan about that.” Marvin just smiled as they rode.

The troopers arrived not long after Marvin, Addie, and Parker did. They could hear the wailing of sirens for three minutes before two of the familiar green and yellow cars came to a dust-covered halt. Five troopers piled out.

“Bill Parker, I presume,” said one of the troopers. “In trouble again, I see. Sergeant Dan Tofel, Mr. Parker. Brattleboro barracks. I’m sure you know that we don’t have bombs in Vermont. But you’ve found one, is that it?”

Parker grimaced as he thought he detected some doubt in Tofel’s tone. Well, I don’t blame him, Parker thought.

“Where is it, Mr. Parker?” he asked quietly.” Tofel was showing some patience, but there was an edge to it. Parker understood. Bombs don’t go off in Vermont.

“In the detached vehicle shed, at my place,” Parker said, pointing down the long road toward the house. “Can you block off this road until the bomb squad gets here?”

“We’re good at that. Bomb squad? When did you call them?”

“A half hour ago. They should be here sometime after noon.”

Sergeant Tofel nodded, and then walked back to his troopers. They immediately went their separate, and well-trained, ways. In a matter of minutes the road was blocked by their distinctive tape and a State Police vehicle.

"We'll wait here until those guys get here. Marvin," he cried, as he spied Marvin Bailey standing apart from the group. "How are you? It's been a while."

"Tof," Marvin said. "I'm glad to see you, but not on this kind of business."

"Mr. Parker, what did you see in there?"

Parker described the bomb and where it was located. Sergeant Tofel jotted down these facts in his ever-present law enforcement-type note book. "We wait," he said, with finality, "for the bomb boys."

Then he looked at Parker with intensity. "Lots of bombs around these days, wouldn't you say, Mr. Parker?"

Parker shrugged. "If you say so, Sergeant."

It was just over two hours later that another car could be seen hustling along toward them.

"That's a cop," said Tofel, gazing at the pedestrian-looking vehicle speeding toward them. Parker couldn't see anything distinctive about this vehicle and wondered how Tofel could be so certain.

The car skidded to a stop and out jumped Peter Morgan. "My God almighty, Bill," he yelped, "you just can't stay tranquil, can you?"

"Peter, I just wanted to get home, and that's all. I was nervous about something that had occurred on our way, and took a careful look around the house. That's when I found it."

Parker decided that this was a good time to change the subject. "Peter, this is Sergeant Tofel, Vermont State Police. Sergeant, this is . . . .

"I know who he is, Mr. Parker. We've had our run-ins before. How are you, Peter?" asked Tofel.

"Good to see you, Dan," said Morgan. "The bomb squad is on its way. I got ahead of them when I tore out of Montpelier."

"I'm surprised to see you, Peter. How come you're here?" asked Parker.

"When I heard that it was Mr. Bailey who made the call, that was very persuasive, Bill. Plus I've learned to listen to him over the past three years. And if this bomb you've found, if you really found one, is a match to the remnants of the one we scraped up in Montpelier, then we have a chance to tie the two together. That will be powerful information. You see, we were able to take some very good fingerprints off a piece of steel that was imbedded in a brick. Remarkable, really, but our print guy is very good, and he knew where to look."

Sergeant Tofel looked at Parker and Morgan. "So there *was* a bomb in Montpelier – and you two were involved. Very interesting."

Before Morgan could respond, Addie moved in to the attack. "Please, Sergeant Tofel, let's have a quiet talk. Okay?"

Tofel was surprised, but walked off with Addie, head bent down, and listening intently. When they returned to Morgan and Parker, Sergeant Tofel was more respectful.

Less than an hour had passed when the Bomb Squad arrived. They were all business. Very serious business. They talked to Morgan first, then to Marvin Bailey.

When they approached Parker, it seemed to Parker that they didn't believe that he had found a bomb. Nobody uses bombs, especially in Vermont – except the one that went off in Montpelier last night, of course.

The leader of the squad, Corporal Helm, asked Parker to describe what he had found. Then to draw a sketch of it. And then to describe exactly where it was. When all the information had been drained out of Parker, Corporal Helm told Parker, off to the side, that one of his best friends was Bud Small.

"He told me everything that's been going on, Mr. Parker, including your trip into the Kingdom to find NPF II." Noticing a change in Parker's expression, he seemed to hurry to add, "Don't worry, Mr. Parker. Bud uses me to bounce things off of, and I use him for the same purpose. We never talk about what we know."

Parker said nothing. He was concerned that the word of his involvement would taint others who could not afford to be known.

"That's why we got here so quickly," Helm said. "When the bomb squad got the word of what you had found, I called Bud immediately. He said that if 'Bill Parker said he found a bomb, then you'd best believe that he really has found a bomb'. That's exactly what he said, Mr. Parker."

Parker stayed silent. Helm turned and called out to his people. "Okay, we're going in. I have the location details. Touch nothing until we confirm visually. We will follow the initiating procedures and check for bombs and other unusual devices in and around the dwelling and out-buildings. Questions?"

There were none and they set off, moving rapidly up the long drive, leaving Parker, Addie, Marvin, Morgan, and the troopers, to sit and wait.

It was late afternoon when the squad came trudging back down the drive to the main road. They all looked exhausted. They were dirty and sweat-stained, their specialized coveralls filthy. Helm had, under his arm, and wrapped in plastic, the steel box that Parker had seen mounted on the inside of the sliding door. Another squad member had a cylindrical object about the size of a broom handle and about four inches long. It had two wires hanging out of it. That, too, was wrapped in plastic.

"Is that a bomb you have there, Corporal?" asked Parker.

"It sure is, Mr. Parker. Enough explosive here to level the whole area. It's plastic of some sort. I think I know what it is, but it's best not to guess at this stage. It's a very crude explosive device with a trigger of basic and elementary design - but it's big and certainly would make a big bang. You have a very upset adversary out there somewhere, Mr. Parker. Are you sure you paid your local taxes?" Helm tried to bring a lighter mood to the assembly, but not even he could smile.

"And we found this, too. Right on the ground under the lower edge of the door. Was it left there, or was it dropped in haste? Or does it have any connection with bombs? Hell, I don't know."

He had a piece of paper, also wrapped in plastic, that was unfolded. Helm held it out to him. Parker could easily see through the clear material. Written on the paper was a single statement, "Sweet dreams", and signed with a jagged "Z". Parker walked away. Nothing could be any more chilling than that simple message from a man now dead.

"Any idea what this means, Bill?" called out Helm. "Or does it mean nothing at all? And what about the strange little number somebody used for a signature? Looks like a '2', maybe? I don't know," he said with frustration.

Parker stopped and looked back. He shrugged.

67

It wasn't until 7:00 that night that Addie and Parker were able to enter their house. It had been a day of bomb squad work. Patience, training, and incredible focus was what made up an excellent specialized unit like that. These guys had it all, thought Parker.

When they said that the house was all clear, Parker knew that it was completely ready for them. And yet that feeling of hesitancy, doubt, and anger mixed together would be with Addie and Bill Parker for a long time. What should have been an occasion for happiness was an atmosphere of a kind of gloom and mistrust. I guess we should expect to have those kinds of feelings, Parker thought, but somehow this situation was different. Visits from the dead were eerie. What Parker knew, and only a few others also knew, was that this intruder was no more. Of that, at least, Parker was confident.

He backtracked in his mind the sequence of events that allowed that bomb to be placed in his shed. It had to have been set during the night before the Montpelier bomb. Naughton had been a busy man during that last 48 hours. And somehow he knew that both Addie and Parker would not be at home. He made a big error, however, during those hours. He asked Hollis Bagley for directions to the Parker house. A stupid error, Parker thought. Out of desperation, he wondered?

Addie showed, more than her husband did, a heightened nervousness upon entering the house. Parker, himself, was affected by the past danger just as much. He just wanted to appear cool and collected in order to set an example. He hoped he looked the part.

Somehow they both began to settle down when Minnie and Malcom, their two dogs of indeterminate breeding, were dropped off by their neighbors.

The dogs went crazy. They spent two hours sniffing out the intruders. By watching them, it was obvious to Parker where the bomb squad people had been. And they had been everywhere.

Parker was certain that any enemy, faced by those two big mutts, would have been backed into a corner and would have starved to death while looking for a blood-free way out.

Addie and Parker went to bed at midnight, exhausted and sleeping in an off-and-on way. He was not feeling any better after two hours. At that point Parker slipped out of bed and went down to the kitchen. He boiled some water, made a pot of tea, and sat down in an easy chair to look at the television news remnants.

He always turned to public television, VTEliteTV, first. He wanted to see what the spin had been on the news of the previous day. By this time VTEliteTV would have disseminated to the viewers what their talking points had instructed them to say.

Morton Draft, an old hand at telling Vermonters what they needed to know, would have filmed his "take", and that was what Parker wanted to see.

Morton didn't let him down. He started out reporting the huge blast in Montpelier. Someone had said that it was caused by a gas leak. Without any more information than an apparently self-generated rumor, he jumped on it as if that was the proven cause. He added that all energy companies should be considered as suspect because of the poor quality of their delivery mechanisms. He also mentioned the death of Don Flanders, but not that he was shot in the head, assassination-style. That was the end of his report.

Then he got into the big fire in Ferdinand and the "intentional" destruction of the "vacation camp", used by "protectors of our environment" in the former Champion lands. He was particularly upset by the apparent death of three "volunteers for nature" in the fire, which was "possibly set by the angry people who lost their hunting camps when the sale of the Champion land was completed". He went on to say that a detailed investigation would be launched to "uncover the perpetrators of this heinous crime".

Parker was not surprised by any of this. He was sure that VTEliteRadio would get into the act, too. This radio arm of the ProgDems would call on Daniel Beach, from high on his perch in Washington, to give his rendition of what happened. Parker always enjoyed Beach. He had never heard anyone who could show such immense snobbishness by only the use of his voice. Parker always enjoyed this part of VTEliteRadio programming. It kept him aware of this lost generation of the aimless and clueless.

Parker had kept the volume of the television down to its lowest point so as not to disturb Addie, but he could hear her padding around upstairs. She appeared a minute later.

"Couldn't sleep, Willie?" she asked.

"Nope," he answered. "Tea?" he asked. Addie nodded.

Parker got to his feet. "Let me get it for you, sweetie."

As he was pouring it, she asked, "Are you going up to Morgan's press conference in the morning?"

"I'd like to. I'll just sit in the back and watch while the ProgDems go nuts."

"You might be recognized, you know, and if Morgan has to mention your name, you might be mobbed. You're still, after all these years, not liked by the denizens of the left in Montpelier."

Parker grinned, for the first time, it seemed, in days. "That's okay. Morgan might need backup, and I'm the one to do it. He's backed me up too many times to count."

Addie was standing beside him now. She put her hand on his arm. "I thought you'd say something like that. I'll stay home, Willie, if it's all right with you, and listen on the radio."

The press conference was held in the Capital Plaza Hotel, across the street from the old Pavilion Building. It was also across the street from the entrance drive to the Thrush Tavern, a much more interesting place than the Plaza. Parker wished he was there now – or that the press conference was being held there.

He was standing in a back corner of the large room. It was noisy from all the talking and clanking of chairs. All the Vermont news media were there, it seemed, and cameras were part of the uniform of the day.

Morton Draft and Dieter Paine were there in the full plumage of the professional news gatherers. Paine was just slightly disheveled, like some loveable old bumbling and forgetful college professor out of the thirties, wearing the obligatory tweed jacket, and the fashionably long and graying hair. And he had just enough beard to remind them all that it was okay for the brilliant ones to forget to shave once in a while. Image was everything. Under this exterior, Parker knew, was a writer as vicious and ignorant as they come.

Draft, the VTEliteTV icon, was just the opposite. He wasn't a casual clotheshorse like Paine. Nothing looked good on him. And he didn't seem to care, mused Parker, even when he was on the silver screen (or whatever they were making them from these days).

The Vermont Information Bureau was there in force, too, and a more dependable carrier of the water for the Vermont left couldn't be found.

The daily newspaper in Barre, the sister paper to the Mid-Vermont Bugle, was also represented. Two dinosaurs in the last dance of their existence, thought Parker. That idea made him feel good. It couldn't happen soon enough.

The newspapers from the Kingdom were there, too, as Parker had expected. They would get it straight, or as straight as Morgan could make it. Unlike the other sources of news in Vermont, Parker believed, the Kingdom press actually tried to report what happened. That was embarrassing for the everyday media when comparisons were made showing the diametrically opposed reports from the Kingdom. Questions about this difference in the news stories between the Kingdom and the rest of the media in the bottom two-thirds of the state were asked, and when no answers from the left-leaning media were forthcoming that made any sense, the statewide media sources looked a little shabby. Hard to believe that the left hadn't taken over the Kingdom news sources years ago. Parker was certain that they were trying.

Half of the General Assembly, it seemed, was also there. Many of them walked in with that subdued swagger, expecting that deference was due them because they represented power. Some of the press ran around taking down the statements from them. None of them knew what actually had happened, but they suspected that it wasn't good for their agenda. They still had statements to make, however, based on spin, intentional ignorance of the facts, and arrogance.

Then Parker saw Hal Birdsall. He was talking to Hugo Barkley, of all people. Parker would have guessed, had he been asked, that this was the last place Hugo would be found. Hugo seemed to appreciate anonymity more than most. Then Birdsall, in his turn, saw Parker. They both walked over to him.

"Good morning, gentlemen," Parker said. "Hugo. What the hell are you doing here?"

“Playing in the dirt, like my kids do,” he said. Parker didn’t think he was trying to make a joke.

“Bill, before I forget, Mr. Morgan asked me to give you this.” He handed Parker a folded piece of paper.

Parker wanted to rush away and read this note, but he needed to know something else. “Hal, what happened about your secretary-spy?”

Birdsall’s expression immediately turned from pleasure at seeing Parker to one of grim reality. “I sat down with her the morning after the bomb went off in Montpelier, Bill. When I lost Jan Evlin in that terrible thing, I vowed that those who had caused that to happen, directly or indirectly, would be exposed. I told her that I knew about her spying on me and my meetings. I told her that she could leave my employ immediately. I told her that I’d be suing her and others for violation of my civil rights to privacy. I told her of the deaths that she had directly caused by her acts of treason. I told her . . . . . . Well, anyway, I really unloaded on her. I was furious then and I still am.”

“Can you sue somebody for violating your civil rights to privacy?” asked Parker.

“Hell, I don’t know, Bill. That’s what I told her, anyway. And I really am bringing a suit. Thanks to Hugo’s customers, who were advised to check certain things in their places of business, we have nineteen people we are suing.”

“What was her reaction?”

“You know, Bill, she almost looked pleased at what I was telling her. Then she said, and I’ve remembered this because it struck me that this may be the real central theme that guides all the ProgDems, ‘Mr. Birdsall,’ she said, ‘I’ve done my part in bringing down Vermont - and America, too. It’s what I was trained to do from the time I was in high school. Our school system in Vermont is the great breeding ground for those of us who hate a person’s freedom of choice. What right does anybody have to make personal choices? All decisions have to be made by a Central Committee, appointed by the majority party. Then decisions that affect us all will be made by people who have our best global interests at heart.’”

Parker watched Birdsall while he was speaking. This was the real awakening of a responsible news chief in Vermont. This is an upset man, he thought.

Birdsall resumed his troubling thoughts. "I told her that I thought that was what we had – a General Assembly, not a committee, made up of two different bodies, and representing all the people in the state of Vermont based on their free vote. Bill, she looked at me with a face that made me feel that she had to lower herself to talk to an uneducated clot like me."

"Wow," said Parker. "And she admitted this philosophy to you, Hal?"

He nodded, vehemently, and continued. "She said, 'Voters are too slow and ignorant to do a proper job of it'. She actually told me that we'd still have the General Assembly, in order to make the old-timers feel comfortable, but their duties would be sharply curtailed. All decisions involving taxes, regulation, and business development, would be given to their Central Committee, for goodness sake," cried Birdsall. "I told her, and I was really shocked at this point, Bill, that the Vermont Economic Progress Commission, making a hash of everything as it has, sounds just like the Central Committee she described."

Birdsall hesitated for a few seconds. His expression was one of a combination of anger, disbelief, and disappointment.

"Then she told me that that Economic Progress Commission, enacted in 1997 as part of the Education Act that gave the Legislature the power to set local education tax rates, was the first step in the plan to enact this Central Committee, and to limit the powers of the Legislature, as we know it."

"Hal, even our Vermont Supreme Court, as agenda-driven and far-left as it is, wouldn't let that happen," said Parker, really alarmed now. "They may be a strange bunch, but they couldn't accept anything like what you're describing. It's crazy to even talk about it."

Birdsall looked at Parker. Then he said quietly, "She said that the legislation to restrict the powers of the Legislature and set up this Central Committee is being written right now."

"What?" cried Parker. "You can't be serious, Hal. Our Constitution wouldn't permit it. And the federal court could stop it, couldn't it?"

"I don't know about the federal courts, Bill. But she said that our Vermont Supreme Court would find another way to discredit our Constitution. They'd done it before and they could do it again. That's exactly what she said. And she hates the Vermont Constitution, Bill. 'It gets in our way,' she said." Parker blinked.

“Can’t you write a series of op-ed pieces to expose this plan?” asked Parker. “You’re in a position to do this. Have you written any editorials or op-ed pieces for your paper about what we experienced, Hal?” Parker carefully asked.

Birdsall seemed to change color and expand like a prairie chicken. “Yes, three of each, Bill,” he sputtered. “My publisher not only wouldn’t print them, he told me that the ProgDems in Chittenden County would make things difficult for the paper and its advertisers.”

Parker was shocked. “You mean that the old protection racket still exists up there?”

“I don’t think it’s that, Bill,” said Birdsall. “I think he was truly concerned about possible letters to the editor - both those sent to us, which could be ignored, of course, but to other publications against our paper and its people. Our advertising revenue isn’t what it was, you see, and we can’t afford any glitches in our income stream.”

“Hrummf,” grunted Parker, irascibly. “Protection is protection, however it’s run.”

68

The note from Morgan, unsigned as Parker knew it would be, was brief.

> "Glock 9 mm slug found in F's head matches the slugs found in carpenters' bodies. Same weapon used. Can't prove that "Z" was the shooter in either killing.
>
> Fingerprints on big banger you found at home do match prints taken from the piece of steel we found in Capital blast. Looking everywhere for prints from Z. Not hopeful.
>
> Clouseau"

Parker had a diluted sense of satisfaction in knowing that Naughton was the mainspring in all the havoc that had been uncovered in Vermont. However, the death of Jan Evlin cast a pall over his positive reaction to this note. And it always would be with him, he knew.

The press conference was handled very smoothly by Morgan. His remarks were to the point and very clear. He told everybody in attendance the sequence of events, finally bringing Naughton's name into it. He gave them Naughton's real name. He told them about NPF I and II. He told them about Naughton's past work in different parts of the country. He told them the proof he had to support his comments. There was an angry ripple from the news media gallery and the political people.

Morgan knew that this was not standard police protocol, but his Chief had decided that this was a big enough case and the use of a bomb too noticeable to be professionally coy about it.

"I hope you can prove that Reginald Naughton was the terrible person you make him out to be, Mr. Morgan," said one of the newest members of the Vermont press. Parker recognized her.

It was little Maureen whatshername, showing that her boss, Mel Keefe, of the Chittenden Free Progressive, hadn't yet been able to protect her from the effects of the ProgDem-style of thinking.

"We know him as a committed environmentalist, a supporter of children's activities, a man who lectured in our schools all over Vermont, and an interested observer of the Vermont Legislature," she said, with some force.

"Did you ever meet him, Miss? Did you ever interview him? Did you ever check into his background?" asked Morgan. Maureen shook her head to each question.

Morgan was not a man who appreciated his honor being questioned by the ignorant. Because of that, he had never felt the need to develop the social skills necessary to ignore ignorance and move on.

"I think you should stop believing your own articles, little lady," Morgan said, with some heat, "and those of your editorial writers. There are some very bad people out there and Mr. Naughton was one of the worst I've ever dealt with. You'd better get yourself into the real world. It's very interesting out there. It's less comfortable than your world of make-believe, but if you do start to observe what's going on, instead of what you're told is happening, it would help your writing, and your articles could be something that people just might enjoy."

Parker suddenly noticed that Mel Keefe, her boss, was standing on the edge of the crowd, and grinning broadly. The education of a young reporter had begun.

There was a stunned silence at the words that described Naughton as something other than a wonderful human being.

But it was the "little lady" that really got to them. Dieter Paine lurched to his feet, caught his balance, dropped his writing pad, and then bellowed, "You are the sort of law enforcement person that I thought we had purged from the system years ago, *Mr.* Morgan. I will *personally* contact the Governor's Commission on Women. That will effectively end your career. And it will end your persecution of Reggie Naughton, who was one of the truly great people in Vermont."

Morgan walked around the podium and stood in front of Paine and looked him in the eye. "*Mr.* Paine," he said scathingly, "there's a time in everybody's life on earth when they need to see things for what they are. You've got to stop writing your articles and columns using the old talking points of the Vermont radicals. I read some of the junk you put out. You ought to be ashamed of yourself. But the least you can do, before they screw you into the ground, is to decide that you will finally grow up and use the sense you were born with. If I were you, I'd research the real Naughton, and I'd look at the evidence we have and maybe, just maybe, you'll understand what kind of a monster we were dealing with. If you won't do that, then there's no hope for you."

Then Morgan walked around the podium to continue the press conference. The applause for his remarks surprised him, and it showed on his face. Dieter Paine's face showed that he was surprised, too. And it also was a deep red color, like a setting sun at day's end. Parker was delighted.

Morgan spoke for a few more minutes about bombs and environmentalist extremists, and was about to bring the press conference to a close, when another reporter interrupted him.

Parker learned later that it was a youngish man named Brent O'Toole, apparently newly arrived, he said, from California. He looked like a beach person, wearing no socks and a pair of tastefully scuffed loafers. All tannish, slightly longish blond hair, a faintish smell of a redwood forest, and clothes that would foreverish mark him as someone of the Species California. Can't wait to see how he winters, thought Parker.

O'Toole was a free lance reporter. What the hell he was doing in Vermont was anybody's guess, thought Parker. Probably transferred in to help the ProgDems win elections.

"Supervisor Morgan, you must have had another person involved in this before you got into things. Usually the police don't get involved in something this messy without the public knowing about it. Who was it?"

Morgan glanced quickly at Parker, still in the back of the room. "The initial contact was made by a reporter from the Chittenden Free Progressive. Her name was Janice Evlin. Along with Mr. Naughton, Ms. Evlin died in the explosion."

There was a collective moan in the audience. Everyone knew Jan.

"And there was a third person there, too, who also died." Morgan was speaking to the whole assembly now. "His name was Ricardo Rudolpho Murch. Technically, he was unemployed, but there's evidence to support the belief that he was working for Mr. Naughton."

"How about the vehicle that got blown up, Mr. Morgan," asked Dieter Paine, in his testy way. "Whose was it?"

"The vehicle was a pickup truck, owned by William Parker of Bridgeton. Mr. Parker was not present when the bomb went off."

This information caused an uproar. "Is that former Representative Parker that you are referring to?" asked the editor of the daily paper in Barre. His voice was right through his nose and sounded like breaking glass. In answer to Morgan's nod, he said, in a confidential manner, "He's trouble, you know, Mr. Morgan. Caused all kinds of problems during the past three years around here, I can tell you. And elsewhere in Vermont, too. Actually murdered somebody in the Statehouse. You probably know all about him. If you don't, call me. I can fill you in."

Suddenly Bud Small, plain clothes and all, moved in behind the editor and whispered into his ear for several seconds. Mr. Big Time Editor looked stricken, and then silently melted away to the outside of the group.

Captain California, however, took up the gauntlet. "And where is this mysterious William Parker, Mr. Morgan?"

O'Toole spoke as if Morgan were a Vermont dunderhead who had to be re-educated in the California style. O'Toole had selected a "listen carefully, Mr. Morgan, and you may learn something" tone. "He *does* exist, I trust."

Captain California stood there with an expectant look on his face, knowing that his way of demeaning people always worked to scramble his opponents' minds. That was when their mistakes showed up.

"Oh, he exists, Mr., Mr. . . . what is your name, sir?" Morgan asked. He was in his extremely respectful mode, his voice quiet and, to those who knew him well, on the edge of blowing a gasket. Parker watched all this, remembering that when Morgan was like this, he was already at battle stations and ready to counterattack.

"I'm Brent O'Toole, Peter. I'm a. . . . . ."

"Hold it, O'Toole, right there," snapped Morgan.

Parker, from his vantage point, could see that Peter Morgan was beyond angry. This is a great spectator sport, he thought.

"My name is *Supervisor* Morgan, or *Mr.* Morgan. I prefer '*Supervisor*'."

Then Morgan turned away, and looked at the reporter from the Caledonia Counselor, who was standing on the outside of the group, and who Morgan had noticed a minute before. He beckoned him to step through the ring of reporters and come over to him. He whispered in the reporter's ear, "Don't look over there now, but Parker is standing in the back of the room, in the far corner. While I keep these nitwits busy, why don't you scoot over there and tell him that I sent you over to interview him?"

The reporter backed out of the group. Nobody noticed him. They were too busy with their own images and their jobs of discrediting Morgan. He slipped through the crowd to Parker, gestured for Parker to please follow him, using the old Chinese sign of clasped hands and a slight bow, and an old American sign of "follow me" by an exaggerated head nod, and they both left the room.

Parker and the reporter, Carl Johnson, walked down the hall together. There was not a soul around. Everybody was in the room where the press conference was held, and yelling at each other. O'Toole had accused Morgan of lying about Parker's role in this whole affair. Everyone seemed aghast at that stupidity, which crossed even the most far-left lines.

At that point, Morgan left the room, using some kind of diversionary tactic known only to law enforcement in Montpelier, where it was needed more than in any other place.

Meanwhile, Parker and Carl Johnson found a small dining room that was not in use. Despite a frown from a waiter on his break, they entered the room and hiked up a flight of stairs to a second level.

This was where the bar was located. Parker wondered, as an insurance man would, about the wisdom of placing the bar at the top of a long and curving flight of stairs. Once an insurance man, always. . . . . . .etc., etc., he thought.

They sat in a back corner of this upper level. Johnson looked at Parker with a smile on his face. Parker grinned back. He remembered this man from his last days in the Vermont House.

Parker had spent those final days three years ago in the hospital, and Carl Johnson was one of three reporters to whom he gave the full story of what he had experienced in the previous two months. He also remembered that the pressure was so great on reporters and other news sources that Johnson almost backed out from writing anything about Parker's almost fatal adventure. He decided to go ahead when Parker was recommended by a former Senator who had his total respect.

The ProgDems were furious with Johnson for his articles about what he had learned about Vermont during that same frantic period of time.

Carl was one of the brave ones in that fight, Parker remembered. His job had been at stake and he took on a very chancy assignment without his editor being aware of it. We must have done something right, thought Parker. He's still got his job and I'm still alive.

"Where do we start, Mr. Parker?" Carl asked. "It sounds as if it's a wild adventure, no matter where we begin."

"I guess so," murmured Parker, thinking about the effect this interview would have when, and if, it appeared. "In reality, Carl, everything about these last weeks has been disappointing and frustrating, along with being dangerous. And do you know something, Carl? I was just ahead of a very bad man and his people, or just behind them – I never knew which, most of the time. And I never realized that this danger was close to me – and to others, too. I just seemed to work my way along and damn near got blown up. The things we uncovered will be hard for you to believe, much less appear believable to your own readers."

"I'm ready to write my article, Mr. Parker, or a series, if needed. They'll believe what I write. Your problem is that my circulation won't reach the majority of the citizens of Vermont. And you can bet that the big daily papers either won't print your story or will dilute it so much that nobody will take the time to read it. Another possibility, if I understand who is opposing you, is that they'll twist it so much that *you* will become the 'terrible person' and Naughton, or whatever his real name is, will be made out to be Robin Hood."

Parker smiled. "Can't win for losin', Carl, as they say."

"I'll approach my paper, though, to get their permission to send my article to every daily and weekly outside our readership in the state. We'll see who prints it and who doesn't, and who twists it around if they do print it, and who prints it straight. That'll be fun," he said with satisfaction. "Well, let's get going, sir."

Parker left nothing out. He described the evidence that supported his story, even to an account of his escape, with Jan Evlin, from Naughton's hired killer. He didn't give Mr. Davidson's name, preferring to just describe the man who saved them as "apparently a frustrated enemy of this killer who just appeared out of the woodwork and then just walked away in the night".

He didn't mention Hugo, or Bud Small either, when he described his visit to the Kingdom. But he didn't leave anything else out. As to the fiery end to the three buildings he could not give any information. Probably the kerosene vapors and a lighted cigarette by one or all of the gunmen was the cause, he said.

Johnson kept looking up at Parker as the story progressed, his face carrying a look of incredulity.

"So, that's it, Carl," Parker said, when at last he had finished. "The whole story. What logic will probably tell you is that it's impossible. But it isn't, and wasn't, and the evidence is still piling up."

Johnson sat back, studying the pages of voluminous shorthand notes. Then he looked up at Parker and studied him. "Bill, is this what Vermont, *my* Vermont, has become? You know what I mean. A target? Have we become a repository for the old uneducated socialists and college radicals and their kook agendas?" His face bore a look of huge concern.

"You know, Mr. Parker," Johnson continued, "I look at Vermont today and I see that the ProgDems have won. They have control of our schools, which are failing, our business development, which is languishing, and now they are on the edge of taking over complete control of the money spent on health care, which will place our elderly in jeopardy. What's next, I wonder? There doesn't seem to be much left of importance."

Parker didn't answer.

He just got to his feet. "That's all I've got, Carl. Good luck." He turned to leave when Johnson said, "Do you want to read my article when I get done writing it, and before I submit it?"

Parker shook his head. "You have the facts, Carl. Call me if you need any clarification of something. Use them without any doubt in their truthfulness. But I won't read it. In fact, I'm done with all of it. I'm heading home."

Parker walked across the floor, and down the stairs. When he climbed into his rented pick-up he saw Dieter Paine scuttling across the parking lot toward him. "Bill," he shouted, "give me an exclusive interview and I'll treat you fairly. I can show you that I'm a good guy."

Parker shook his head. When Paine was standing beside his window, Parker said, "You're part of the problem, Paine."

He drove off, figuratively shaking the Montpelier dust from his boots.

69

Carl Johnson was true to his word. He did a beautiful job of organizing his material. He named Parker as his source. His editor delayed running the series for over two weeks, all in a flutter because he couldn't predict what the reaction would be to his paper. Finally, he said, after constant nagging from Johnson, to "run the damn thing".

Carl Johnson called Parker when the series was about to appear. He said that his editor said something like "it's better to be hung for a sheep than a lamb". Parker hadn't heard that expression for forty years. He was surprised when he was told that the editor was 29 years old.

Johnson's article, or his series of articles, caused an uproar in the Northeast Kingdom. They read like a fairy tale that everybody believed. The area of NPF II was besieged by adventuresome visitors. Most of them started walking in to the fire scene, but returned to their vehicles because of the next-to-impossible hike.

Tourists read the articles in the Caledonia Counselor and they dropped by, too. Most of them were also put off by the required walk in the woods.

For those who did hike in, there was nothing much to see, of course, except the blackened ground and charred debris where the three buildings had stood. The visitors took away all of the partially burned mementoes for strange souvenirs.

They even began to find rifle shells on the ground. The stories about them were surprisingly accurate, especially when a sharp-eyed high school student found misshapen lead slugs on the edge of the road where Parker and Small had hidden themselves. The rumors about this began to turn people against the extreme environmentalists. Their organizations began to see their contributions drop sharply.

Members of PRAPPPP arrived and attempted to chase the visitors away. That wasn't wise. They were brushed aside. Then they were pushed aside until welts began to appear. They departed.

Some of them were crying because of the roughness of their treatment.

The state police were called in. Then a young lawyer brought a suit against the state for unlawful exclusion of citizens from land that their tax money had purchased. The Vermont Supreme Court instantly said that the money used to purchase the rights to the property ceased to belong to the citizens when the state used its power to tax them. Therefore, the land belonged to the state and the state could define who could use it. The reasoning used by the Court was unclear to almost everybody except the Mid-Vermont Bugle, the Bennington Beacon, the Brattleboro Opposition, and the Barre North Country-Times Revisionist. The Chittenden Free Progressive was curiously silent on the matter.

None of these "mainstream" papers printed the articles sent to them by Carl Johnson, a fact that didn't surprise Parker, but they did print all the letters against the "Killings in the Kingdom", so named by Dieter Paine in one of his more delusional columns.

The editor of the Mid-Vermont Bugle said, it was reported, when asked why they didn't print letters showing both sides of an issue, that the citizens of Vermont were too busy living their lives to understand the initial letter anyway, so why clutter up their newspaper with something that's forgettable? Parker equated the reasoning of the Mid-Vermont Bugle with that of the Vermont Supreme Court.

Parker was attacked for "snooping on land which was now in the public domain". Parker really couldn't follow that logic, and didn't spend any time trying to do so. He was also accused of "carrying on the killing spree that he started three years before, while in the Statehouse". That caused a flood of anti-Bugle phone calls and letters. The Bugle was surprised that there was any opposition against them still present in Vermont, and stopped using that anti-Parker statement. Their editors would find another, Parker was sure.

What came through, loud and clear, was the proof that all of the papers that refused to print Johnson's articles had a regular stable of letter writers. Whenever a letter was needed to support a ProgDem initiative, or against something or someone that the papers deemed unworthy, a call would go out. Almost instantly, it seemed, a fresh load of letters from the same people would roll in, month after month, and year after year. Not even a funeral or two, after twenty years, seemed to change that roster. Had these people found the elixir of life? Amazing, thought Parker. Nothing seemed to dent that roster of ProgDem letter writers, not even a death or two over the years.

Despite the refusal by these "big time" Vermont papers to print the Parker interview, the Caledonia Counselor saw its subscription and advertising revenue soar. New subscribers appeared from 38 different states. Comments from many people ranged from "this is the most aggressive attempt ever to portray lies into serious news accounts" and "these great news stories you reported are exactly what's going on in my state, too", to "is my state next?"

VTEliteTV and private TV were the most interesting of all to Parker. The privately owned TV news outlet didn't mention Morgan's press conference at all. It was as if it had never happened. Later on it came out that a subtle threat by TETCOV, the Tranquility and Equal Treatment Center of Vermont, against the station's advertisers, had decided the issue.

The station did issue a statement, however, that said that the story of the occurrences in the Northeast Kingdom was supported only by police evidence and not by the compassion of the enlightened members of AVANPA, the Associated Vermont Alliances of Non-Profit Associations. Therefore, the necessary balance in the evidence against Reginald Naughton couldn't be offered by their station. Parker laughed out loud at that one.

Morton Draft of VTEliteTV notoriety was under no such restriction. He reported that the "trumped-up story put out by the Caledonia Counselor" was evidence that the right-wing extremists in Vermont had to be rooted out and exposed for what they were. He went on to say that Reginald Naughton was a "great Vermont advocate" who played an important role in the life of every Vermonter. "His death was unnecessary," howled Draft, "and former Representative Bill Parker has some explaining to do."

Only one news person called Parker. It was a reporter for a weekly in Orange County. Her only question was whether she could print his "inevitable retraction" before anyone else. She seemed completely surprised, and probably offended, when she found that Parker would not be offering a retraction.

Parker wasn't surprised at any of this. The Vermont Prog-Dem Party believed that it was in complete control and could do and say anything it wanted to and its candidates would still be re-elected and re-appointed.

The ProgDems again would campaign on job creation, freedom for parents to select the school of their choice for their children, and the terrible over-burdening regulation by Vermont government, and then do just the opposite when back in the Legislature. These politicians depended on their voters not paying attention – and even when they did pay attention, the ProgDems knew that they would still vote for their candidates.

Vermont was reaping the results of a muddied education of the generations here now and those yet to come. The burden of the influence of the institutions that took in non-taxable funds to support agendas that demanded working men and women pay more taxes every year was a crushing weight to more and more Vermonters.

Parker pitied the teachers who wanted to teach and who expected results from their charges (tough love, I think they call it, he remembered), but who were not supported by their school boards or their union – or even their fellow teachers. He also pitied the parents who still wanted their children to do better than they did, but found that their offspring were not prepared, in a majority of cases, to accomplish even as much.

Maybe sometime, he thought, the ProgDems' failed agenda would be thrown overboard by an aroused electorate. Maybe sometime a person would surface who would run directly against the Vermont media, the radical left, and their agendas, and win. With courageous leadership, maybe Vermont could get out from under the suffocating effects of the ProgDems' style of government – a style that fostered dislike and distrust of anybody who runs a business and creates jobs, a style which demanded higher and higher taxes on their incomes, a style that accepted lower and lower results from their schools, and a style that didn't trust the ordinary citizens to make choices for the benefit of themselves and their families without the "help" of government.

Vermont was not the beckoning country any more.

Addendum

For clarity, the following contains some of the typical non-profits in Vermont that are mentioned in this novel. They represent hundreds of actual non-profits that operate within Vermont's borders. A brief overview of their activities follows the name.

VPIRC - Vermont Peoples Instant Reaction Council (1972) Created by out-of-state entities to stop Vermont's growth as the "Beckoning Country". Extremely anti-job-creation. Frequently joins other groups of the left in opposing legislation containing pro-business incentives. It has national implications because it has groups in 35 states that lobby their legislatures to follow plans tested and initiated in Vermont.

VNRCAUC – Vermont New Relativism Council Against Uncontrolled Commerce (1979) Anti-business, anti-growth, and anti-job creating non-profit. Joins other non-profits where they share interests. Takes in money from out-of-state organizations, such as Socialists for Vermont Progress.Org, and from foreign countries who oppose the United States. Actively supports leftist candidates, providing them money and organizational help during election times, in direct violation of the non-profit laws. It's expert at laundering outside contributions for use in political campaigns of the left.

CPLAG – Citizens Protection League Against Greed (1994).

Organized by groups in California and New York, it has pursued its goal of "eliminating greed in the human spirit". Does special projects for the non-profit organization

SASSY (see below) and, although small in size at this time, its growth will depend on the indoctrination of students in high schools and colleges regarding greed and how to combat it. Dedicated to the elimination of "all interstate business transactions, and allowing only businesses generated, sustained, and maintained by and in the State of Vermont."

TPSCNV - Truth, Prosperity, and Sharing Coalition of Northern Vermont (1982). The largest of the non-profits in Vermont, it is considered the most proficient at directing money coming into the state to support leftist politicians during the months the Legislature is not in session. One of the best recruiters for the ProgDems in Vermont's Chittenden County.

TETCOV – Tranquility and Equal Treatment Center of Vermont (1988). Among the most partisan non-profits of the hard left in Vermont. Constantly recruits and helps fund candidates of the left. Is known to provide the political management of campaigns of the left, which is directly against their charter as a non-profit. Actually sells political campaign literature from its offices opposing all candidates not of the left/liberal/progressive persuasion, including candidates at the national level. Is the most vicious and arrogant of all politically involved non-profits in Vermont.

SASSY – Student Activists for Sympathetic Socialist Youth (2002). A non-profit organization created by a combination of high school and college teachers and professors from around Vermont. Its purpose is to teach all levels of students the elements of a socialist state, and to oppose any school-choice movements. This group works closely with the daily news media of Vermont so that letters and editorials can move the ProgDem agenda along. More information is becoming available regarding this relatively new non-profit.

VTUA – <u>Vermont Teachers United Association (1974).</u> The Vermont school teachers union. Their main purposes are to maintain the number of teachers in spite of decreasing state school populations, increase school spending, promote smaller class sizes as the way to improve test scores, resist testing of school students, and to attack all efforts to achieve school choice. They work closely with SASSY for specialized information.

GAGS – <u>Global Assoc. for Geopolitical Solutions (2001).</u> Established for one purpose: the teaching and eventual imposition of a system of government in America where all elected officials at the national and state levels will have 10 year terms. They promote the system of government embodied in the association known as The Disciples of the New Future. Not much is known about GAGS at this time, except that it works occasionally for the VTUA, SASSY, and CPLAG.

PORK – <u>People's Order of the Religious Keeper (2002).</u> This is a quasi-religious non-profit devoted to the "assimilation of all religious groups that are unable to increase their growth of followers through conventional methods" (according to their brochure in 2002. This brochure vanished from the scene about two months after its publication). One of the main methods to "encourage growth" in the fringe religious community is to teach the small, unconventional, churches that it's acceptable to take over other small churches by requiring their members to join these churches and become church officers. It has direct connections with SASSY.

DRANE – <u>Disciples Recognizing All Needs for Entitlements (1999).</u> This is a non-profit that works directly with VPIRC, CPLAG, and VNRCAUC. It has a persistent lobbying presence in Montpelier. Its primary focus is the creation of expanded and additional programs that will take tax money from Vermont wage-earners and give it to those who believe they are entitled to receive a living wage without having earned it. It has been charged with receiving money from the low-income groups and using it for purposes other than to provide services for their contributors.

PRAPPPP – People's Revolution Against Profits, Production, and Private Property (1979). PRAPPPP is best known for its positions defending any revolutionary group that "hates" America (from their brochure of 1984). It also has, as a long-term goal, the abolition of the institutions of government of America and its economic system. They gained their status as a non-profit in 1979 by stating that their movement is "educational in nature and does not advocate the overthrow of the American government unless a majority of its members vote to do so". Jimmy Carter's people commented that that statement is "inconclusive that overthrow of our government is their aim. And it is a shining beacon of our openness that we accept their application for non-profit status".

CTTVC – The Continuing Tradition Trust for the Victims of Capitalism (1970). This is a complicated organization that uses money from the legislature, along with private contributions, to buy up property rights to land in order to control it. It also buys housing, repairs it, using their own contractors whenever possible, and receives rents from low-income dwellers based on their incomes. It has been reported that incomes of the residents are not checked regularly, thus allowing non-compliant renters to live in housing for which they do not qualify. In addition, the repair costs of the dwellings are more than the rentals will repay, and the taxpayers are forced to pick up the difference.

TPN – The Trust of the Progressive Naturalist (1979). This non-profit is a recruiter for the ProgDems in Vermont. Its main objective is to select candidates who have a total commitment to abolishing businesses that they believe are harming the environment. They became notorious when their lawyers sued a well-known Burlington firm, Index Inc., a large computer programming company, for polluting the "intellectual environment of the globe with programs that are purchased by out-of-state businesses", and "providing work for people who don't view the protection of our environmental space with the same intensity as does TPN." They work in conjunction with SASSY, PRAPPPP, VNRCAUC, and CPLAG. They assist VTEliteTV, with a dedicated lobbying effort in the Statehouse to increase their annual appropriation.